MAXIM JAKUBOWSKI is a London-based novelist and editor. He was born in the UK and educated in France. Following a career in book publishing, he opened the world-famous Murder One bookshop in 1988 and has since combined running it with writing and editing. He is a winner of the Anthony and Karel Awards, a frequent TV and radio broadcaster, crime columnist for the *Guardian* newspaper and Literary Director of London's Crime Scene Festival.

THE MAMMOTH BOOK OF

VINTAGE
WHODUNNITS

Edited by Maxim Jakubowski

CARROLL & GRAF PUBLISHERS
New York

Carroll & Graf Publishers
An imprint of Avalon Publishing Group, Inc.
245 W. 17th Street
11th Floor
New York
NY 10011–5300
www.carrollandgraf.com

AVALON
publishing group incorporated

First Carroll & Graf edition 2006

First published in the UK by Robinson,
an imprint of Constable & Robinson Ltd, 2006

ISBN-13: 978-0-78671-698-2
ISBN-10: 0-7867-1698-3

Printed and bound in the EU

Contents

Acknowledgments

Arnold Bennett, "Murder!" (1926), reprinted from *The Night Visitor and Other Stories* (1931).

Alexander Pushkin, "The Queen of Spades" (1834), reprinted from *An Omnibus of Continental Mysteries*, Part Two.

O. Henry, "A Personal Magnet" (1905), reprinted from *Con Men and Hoboes*.

Bulwer Lytton, "The House and the Brain" (1859), reprinted from *An Omnibus of Continental Mysteries*, Part Two. Thanks to the vigilance of Hugh Lamb, specialist extraordinaire, we understand our version of this story was slightly abridged by American editors in the 1930s to make it less old-fashioned.

Barbey d'Aurevilly, "The Crimson Curtain" (1874), reprinted from *An Omnibus of Continental Mysteries*, Part One.

Edgar Allan Poe, "The Purloined Letter" (1841), reprinted from *The Gift*.

E.W. Hornung, "A Trap to Catch a Cracksman" (1905), reprinted from *Pall Mall Magazine*, July 1905.

Charles Dickens, "Hunted Down" (1859), reprinted from *The New York Ledger*.

Maurice Leblanc, "Edith Swan-Neck" (1913), reprinted from *The Confessions of Arsène Lupin*.

William Hope Hodgson, "The Red Herring" (1917), reprinted from *Captain Gault*.

Mark Twain, "The Stolen White Elephant" (1882), reprinted from *Tom Sawyer Abroad*.

Nick Carter, "Nick Carter, Detective" (1891), reprinted from *Street and Smith's Weekly*.

Alexandre Dumas, "Solange" (1849), reprinted from *An Omnibus of Continental Mysteries*, Part One.

Rudyard Kipling, "The Limitations of Pambé Serang" (1891), reprinted from *Life's Handicap*.

Robert Louis Stevenson, "Markheim" (1886), reprinted from *Selected Writings of Robert Louis Stevenson*.

Ernest Bramah, "The Disappearance of Marie Severe" (1923), reprinted from *The Eyes of Max Carrados*.

Arthur Morrison, "The Lenton Croft Robberies" (1894), reprinted from *Martin Hewitt, Investigator*.

Sir Arthur Conan Doyle, "The Adventures of the Three Students" (1903), reprinted from *The Return of Sherlock Holmes*.

M.P. Shiel, "The Stone of the Edmundsbury Monks" (1895), reprinted from *Prince Zaleski*.

Mrs Belloc Lowndes, "Popeau Investigates" (1926), reprinted from *The World's Best 100 Detective Stories*, Volume One.

E. Charles Vivian, "Locked In" (1926), reprinted from *Fifty Famous Detectives of Fiction*.

J.S. Clouston, "The Millionth Chance" (1920), reprinted from *Carrington's Cases.*

E. Phillips Oppenheim, "The Case of Mr and Mrs Stetson" (1913), reprinted from *Mr Laxworthy's Adventures.*

C. Daly King, "The Episode of *Torment IV*" (1935), reprinted from *The Curious Mr Tarrant.*

Thomas Hardy, "The Three Strangers" (1883), reprinted from *Longman's Magazine.*

Baroness Orczy, "The Dublin Mystery" (1902), reprinted from *The Man in the Corner.*

Wilkie Collins, "The Biter Bit" (1858), reprinted from *Atlantic Monthly.*

Introduction

Welcome to an invigorating walk through the highways and bye-ways of past crime and mystery fiction.

It will no doubt come as a surprise to many casual readers to not only see such eminent names here as Sir Arthur Conan Doyle, Edgar Allan Poe and Wilkie Collins, but also such cornerstones of the literary tradition as Charles Dickens, Arnold Bennett, Mark Twain, Thomas Hardy, Rudyard Kipling and Robert Louis Stevenson, as well as foreign luminaries like Alexandre Dumas and Alexander Pushkin. Mystery writers? Well, yes. The wonderful thing about popular writing mostly at the turn of the twentieth century is that its practitioners saw it as their duty to principally tell stories, whether they were pure derring-do tales of adventures, depiction of life at various levels of society, morality stories about the foibles of human nature or humorous accounts of incidents, class struggle and relationships. And, as a matter of habit, crime and mystery fitted perfectly into these categories (and still does to this day).

In those blessed days, crime writing was therefore not parked into some critically frowned upon ghetto, but was an integral part of people's reading and writers who essayed the field were allowed to practise their craft all over the wide world of writing, whether it be popular or literary. There were no distinctions between genres – would that we had such a healthy situation in today's early twenty-first century.

Of course, many of these famous authors were so successful in their particular areas of expertise that time has now forgotten their occasional forays into the world of mystery, whodunnits and puzzles. Which doesn't make them any less interesting or, for that matter, out of date. There are fiendishly knitted plots and intrigues here to rival any modern writer from Colin Dexter's Morse to Ian Rankin's Inspector Rebus and the classical imagination proves as provocative as today's; there is also a wonderful sense of place and occasion in many of these fascinating stories that brings to life a world and worlds past with uncanny accuracy. You can smell the dark, rainy streets, the smog in the air, the sense of menace in a world where electricity was still uncommon and the electronic grid and the cloak of science that surround us now didn't exist so that amateur sleuths and everyone caught in webs of intrigue truly had to utilize their grey cells and intelligence in their search for the truth. No forensic investigators, no crime scene laboratories, no policemen assisted by cell phones, fast cars and instant forms of communication. This is the ground zero of the whodunnit. And one could easily wax very nostalgic about it in its purity of means and purpose.

In addition, we have a sizzling assortment of sleuths, both dedicated and involuntary, including two of mystery fiction's earliest icons like Sherlock Holmes and the Chevalier Dupin, but also the Old Man in the Corner, created by Baroness Orczy, best remembered today for her Scarlet Pimpernel, Hornung's Raffles, Ernest Bramah's Max Carrados, Prince Zaleski, Nick Carter and Maurice Leblanc's raffish Arsène Lupin. An abundance of elementary investigating and charm indeed.

So, a handful of amazing rediscoveries about the way we were, the way they killed, swindled or stole, the way it was from some of the greatest writers there were.

What more could you ask for? Savour.

Maxim Jakubowski

Murder!

Arnold Bennett

Two men, named respectively Lomax Harder and John Franting, were walking side by side one autumn afternoon, on the Marine Parade of the seaside resort and port of Quangate (English Channel). Both were well dressed and had the air of moderate wealth, and both were about thirty-five years of age. At this point the resemblances between them ceased. Lomax Harder had refined features, an enormous forehead, fair hair, and a delicate, almost apologetic manner. John Franting was low-browed, heavy-chinned, scowling, defiant, indeed what is called a tough customer. Lomax Harder corresponded in appearance with the popular notion of a poet – save that he was carefully barbered. He was in fact a poet, and not unknown in the tiny, trifling, mad world where poetry is a matter of first-rate interest. John Franting corresponded in appearance with the popular notion of a gambler, an amateur boxer, and, in spare time, a deluder of women. Popular notions sometimes fit the truth.

Lomax Harder, somewhat nervously buttoning his overcoat, said in a quiet but firm and insistent tone:

"Haven't you got anything to say?"

John Franting stopped suddenly in front of a shop whose façade bore the sign: GONTLE. GUNSMITH.

"Not in words," answered Franting. "I'm going in here."

And he brusquely entered the small, shabby shop.

Lomax Harder hesitated half a second, and then followed his companion.

The shopman was a middle-aged gentleman wearing a black velvet coat.

"Good afternoon," he greeted Franting, with an expression and in a tone of urbane condescension which seemed to indicate that Franting was a wise as well as fortunate man in that he knew of the excellence of Gontle's and had the wit to come into Gontle's.

For the name of Gontle was favourably and respectfully known wherever triggers are pressed. Not only along the whole length of the Channel Coast, but throughout England, was Gontle's renowned. Sportsmen would travel to Quangate from the far North, and even from London, to buy guns. To say: "I bought it at Gontle's" or "Old Gontle recommended it" was sufficient to silence any dispute concerning the merits of a fire-arm. Experts bowed the head before the unique reputation of Gontle. As for old Gontle, he was extremely and pardonably conceited. His conviction that no other gunsmith in the wide world could compare with him was absolute. He sold guns and rifles with the gesture of a monarch conferring an honour. He never argued, he stated, and the customer who contradicted him was as likely as not to be courteously and icily informed by Gontle of the geographical situation of the shop door. Such shops exist in the English provinces, and nobody knows how they have achieved their renown. They could exist nowhere else.

"'d afternoon," said Franting gruffly, and paused.

"What can I do for you?" asked Mr. Gontle, as if saying: "Now don't be afraid. This shop is tremendous, and I am tremendous; but I shall not eat you."

"I want a revolver," Franting snapped.

"Ah! A revolver!" commented Mr. Gontle, as if saying: "A gun or a rifle, yes! But a revolver – an arm without individuality, manufactured wholesale! . . . However, I suppose I must deign to accommodate you."

"I presume you know something about revolvers?" asked Mr. Gontle, as he began to produce the weapons.

"A little."

"Do you know the Webley Mark III?"

"Can't say that I do."

"Ah! It is the best for all common purposes." And Mr. Gontle's glance said: "Have the goodness not to tell me it isn't."

Franting examined the Webley Mark III.

"You see," said Mr. Gontle, "the point about it is that until the breech is properly closed it cannot be fired. So that it can't blow open and maim or kill the would-be murderer." Mr. Gontle smiled archly at one of his oldest jokes.

"What about suicides?" Franting grimly demanded.

"Ah!"

"You might show me just how to load it," said Franting.

Mr. Gontle, having found ammunition, complied with this reasonable request.

"The barrel's a bit scratched," said Franting.

Mr. Gontle inspected the scratch with pain. He would have denied the scratch, but could not.

"Here's another one," said he, "since you're so particular." He simply had to put customers in their place.

"You might load it," said Franting.

Mr. Gontle loaded the second revolver.

"I'd like to try it," said Franting.

"Certainly," said Mr. Gontle, and led Franting out of the shop by the back, and down to a cellar where revolvers could be experimented with.

Lomax Harder was now alone in the shop. He hesitated a long time and then picked up the revolver rejected by Franting, fingered it, put it down, and picked it up again. The back-door of the shop opened suddenly, and, startled, Harder dropped the revolver into his overcoat pocket: a thoughtless, quite unpremeditated act. He dared not remove the revolver. The revolver was as fast in his pocket as though the pocket had been sewn up.

"And cartridges?" asked Mr. Gontle of Franting.

"Oh," said Franting, "I've only had one shot. Five'll be more than enough for the present. What does it weigh?"

"Let me see. Four-inch barrel? Yes. One pound four ounces."

Franting paid for the revolver, receiving thirteen shillings in change from a five-pound note, and strode out of the shop, weapon in hand. He was gone before Lomax Harder decided upon a course of action.

"And for you, sir?" said Mr. Gontle, addressing the poet.

Harder suddenly comprehended that Mr. Gontle had mistaken him for a separate customer, who had happened to enter the shop a moment after the first one. Harder and Franting had said not a word to one another during the purchase, and Harder well knew that in the most exclusive shops it is the custom utterly to ignore a second customer until the first one has been dealt with.

"I want to see some foils." Harder spoke stammeringly the only words that came into his head.

"Foils!" exclaimed Mr. Gontle, shocked, as if to say: "Is it conceivable that you should imagine that I, Gontle, gunsmith, sell such things as foils?"

After a little talk Harder apologized and departed – a thief.

"I'll call later and pay the fellow," said Harder to his restive conscience. "No. I can't do that. I'll send him some anonymous postal orders."

He crossed the Parade and saw Franting, a small left-handed figure all alone far below on the deserted sands, pointing the revolver. He thought that his ear caught the sound of a discharge, but the distance was too great for him to be sure. He continued to watch, and at length Franting walked westward diagonally across the beach.

"He's going back to the Bellevue," thought Harder, the Bellevue being the hotel from which he had met Franting coming out half an hour earlier. He strolled slowly towards the white hotel. But Franting, who had evidently come up the face of the cliff in the penny lift, was before him. Harder, standing outside, saw Franting seated in the lounge. Then Franting rose and vanished down a long passage at the rear of the lounge. Harder entered the hotel rather guiltily. There was no hall porter at the door, and not a soul in the lounge or in sight of the lounge. Harder went down the long passage.

At the end of the passage Lomax Harder found himself in a billiard room – an apartment built partly of brick and partly of wood on a sort of courtyard behind the main structure of the hotel. The roof, of iron and grimy glass, rose to a point in the middle. On two sides the high walls of the hotel obscured the light. Dusk was already closing in. A small fire burned feebly in the grate. A large radiator under the window was steel-cold, for though summer was finished, winter had not officially begun in the small economically run hotel: so that the room was chilly; nevertheless, in deference to the English passion for fresh air and discomfort, the window was wide open.

Franting, in his overcoat, and an unlit cigarette between his lips, stood lowering with his back to the bit of fire. At sight of Harder he lifted his chin in a dangerous challenge.

"So you're still following me about," he said resentfully to Harder.

"Yes," said the latter, with his curious gentle primness of manner. "I came down here especially to talk to you. I should have said all I had to say earlier, only you happened to be going out of the hotel just as I was coming in. You didn't seem to want to talk in the street; but there's some talking has to be done. I've a few things I must tell you." Harder appeared to be perfectly calm, and he felt perfectly calm. He advanced from the door towards the billiard table.

Franting raised his hand, displaying his square-ended, brutal fingers in the twilight.

"Now listen to me," he said with cold, measured ferocity. "You can't tell me anything I don't know. If there's some talking to be done I'll do it myself, and when I've finished you can get out. I know that my wife has taken a ticket for Copenhagen by the steamer from Harwich, and that she's been seeing to her passport, and packing. And of course I know that you have interests in Copenhagen and spend about half your precious time there. I'm not worrying to connect the two things. All that's got nothing to do with me. Emily has always seen a great deal of you, and I know that the last week or two she's been seeing you more than ever. Not that I mind that. I know that she objects to my treatment of her and my conduct generally. That's all right, but it's a matter that only concerns her and me. I mean that it's no concern of yours, for instance, or anybody else's. If she objects enough she can try and divorce me. I doubt if she'd succeed, but you can never be sure – with these new laws. Anyhow she's my wife till she does divorce me, and so she has the usual duties and responsibilities towards me – even though I was the worst husband in the world. That's how I look at it, in my old-fashioned way. I've just had a letter from her – she knew I was here, and I expect that explains how you knew I was here."

"It does," said Lomax Harder quietly.

Franting pulled a letter out of his inner pocket and unfolded it.

"Yes," he said, glancing at it, and read some sentences aloud: " 'I have absolutely decided to leave you, and I won't hide from you that I know you know who is doing what he can to help me. I can't live with you any longer. You may be very fond of me, as you say, but I find your way of showing your fondness too humiliating and painful. I've said this to you before, and now I'm saying it for the last time.' And so on and so on."

Franting tore the letter in two, dropped one half on the floor, twisted the other half into a spill, turned to the fire, and lit his cigarette.

"That's what I think of her letter," he proceeded, the cigarette between his teeth. "You're helping her, are you? Very well. I don't say you're in love with her, or she with you. I'll make no wild statements. But if you aren't in love with her I wonder why you're taking all this trouble over her. Do you go about the world helping ladies who say they're unhappy just for the pure sake of helping? Never mind. Emily isn't going to leave me. Get that into your head. I shan't let her leave me. She has money and I haven't. I've been living on her, and it would be infernally awkward for me if she left me for good. That's a reason for keeping her, isn't it? But you may believe me or not – it isn't my reason. She's right enough when she says I'm very fond of her. That's reason for keeping her too. But it isn't my reason. My reason is that a wife's a wife, and she can't break her word just because everything isn't lovely in the garden. I've heard it said I'm unmoral. I'm not all unmoral. And I feel particularly strongly about what's called the marriage tie." He drew the revolver from his overcoat pocket, and held it up to view. "You see this thing. You saw me buy it. Now you needn't be afraid. I'm not threatening you; and it's no part of my game to shoot you. I've nothing to do with your goings-on. What I have to do with is the goings-on of my wife. If she deserts me – for you or for anybody or for nobody – I shall follow her, whether it's to Copenhagen or Bangkok or the North Pole, and I shall kill her –

with just this very revolver that you saw me buy. And now you can get out."

Franting replaced the revolver, and began to consume the cigarette with fierce and large puffs.

Lomax Harder looked at the grim, set, brutal, scowling, bitter face, and knew that Franting meant what he had said. Nothing would stop him from carrying out his threat. The fellow was not an argufier; he could not reason; but he had unmistakable grit and would never recoil from the fear of consequences. If Emily left him, Emily was a dead woman; nothing in the end could protect her from the execution of her husband's menace. On the other hand, nothing would persuade her to remain with her husband. She had decided to go, and she would go. And indeed the mere thought of this lady to whom he, Harder, was utterly devoted, staying with her husband and continuing to suffer the tortures and humiliations which she had been suffering for years – this thought revolted him. He could not think it.

He stepped forward along the side of the billiard table, and simultaneously Franting stepped forward to meet him, Lomax Harder snatched the revolver which was in his pocket, aimed, and pulled the trigger.

Franting collapsed, with the upper half of his body somehow balanced on the edge of the billiard table. He was dead. The sound of the report echoed in Harder's ear like the sound of a violin string loudly twanged by a finger. He saw a little reddish hole in Franting's bronzed right temple.

"Well," he thought, "somebody had to die. And it's better him than Emily." He felt that he had performed a righteous act. Also he felt a little sorry for Franting.

Then he was afraid. He was afraid for himself, because he wanted not to die, especially on the scaffold; but also for Emily Franting who would be friendless and helpless without him; he could not bear to think of her alone in the world – the central point of a terrific scandal. He must get away instantly.

Not down the corridor back into the hotel lounge! No! That would be fatal! The window. He glanced at the corpse. It was more odd, curious, than affrighting. He had made the corpse. Strange! He could not unmake it. He had accomplished the irrevocable. Impressive! He saw Franting's cigarette glowing on the linoleum in the deepening dusk, and picked it up and threw it into the fender.

Lace curtains hung across the whole width of the window. He drew one aside, and looked forth. The light was much stronger in the courtyard than within the room. He put his gloves on. He gave a last look at the corpse, straddled the window sill, and was on the brick pavement of the courtyard. He saw that the curtain had fallen back into the perpendicular.

He gazed around. Nobody! Not a light in any window! He saw a green wooden gate, pushed it; it yielded; then a sort of entry-passage . . . In a moment, after two half-turns, he was on the Marine Parade again. He was a fugitive. Should he fly to the right, to the left? Then he had an inspiration. An idea of genius for baffling pursuers. He would go into the hotel by the main entrance. He went slowly and deliberately into the portico, where a middle-aged hall porter was standing in the gloom.

"Good evening, sir."

"Good evening. Have you got any rooms?"

"I think so, sir. The housekeeper is out, but she'll be back in a moment – if you'd like a seat. The manager's away in London."

The hall porter suddenly illuminated the lounge, and Lomax Harder, blinking, entered and sat down.

"I might have a cocktail while I'm waiting," the murderer suggested with a bright and friendly smile. "A Bronx."

"Certainly, sir. The page is off duty. He sees to orders in the lounge, but I'll attend to you myself."

"What a hotel!" thought the murderer, solitary in the chilly lounge, and gave a glance down the long passage. "Is the whole place run by the hall porter? But of course it's the dead season."

Was it conceivable that nobody had heard the sound of the shot?

Harder had a strong impulse to run away. But no! To do so would be highly dangerous. He restrained himself.

"How much?" he asked of the hall porter, who had arrived with surprising quickness, tray in hand and glass on tray.

"A shilling, sir."

The murderer gave him eighteen pence, and drank off the cocktail.

"Thank you very much, sir." The hall porter took the glass.

"See here!" said the murderer. "I'll look in again. I've got one or two little errands to do."

And he went, slowly, into the obscurity of the Marine Parade.

Lomax Harder leant over the left arm of the sea wall of the man-made port of Quangate. Not another soul was there. Night had fallen. The lighthouse at the extremity of the right arm was occulting. The lights – some red, some green, many white – of ships at sea passed in both directions in endless processions. Waves plashed gently against the vast masonry of the wall. The wind, blowing steadily from the northwest, was not cold. Harder, looking about – though he knew he was absolutely alone – took his revolver from his overcoat pocket and stealthily dropped it into the sea. Then he turned round and gazed across the small harbour at the mysterious amphitheatre of the lighted town, and heard public clocks and religious clocks striking the hour.

He was a murderer, but why should he not successfully escape detection? Other murderers had done so. He had all his wits. He was not excited. He was not morbid. His perspective of things was not askew. The hall porter had not seen his first entrance into the hotel, nor his exit after the crime. Nobody had seen them. He had left nothing behind in the billiard room. No finger marks on the window sill. (The putting-on of his gloves was in itself a clear demonstration that he had fully kept his presence of mind.) No footmarks on the hard, dry pavement of the courtyard.

Of course there was the possibility that some person unseen had seen him getting out of the window. Slight: but still a possibility! And there was also the possibility that someone who knew Franting by sight had noted him walking by Franting's side in the streets. If such a person informed the police and gave a description of him, inquiries might be made . . . No! Nothing in it. His appearance offered nothing remarkable to the eye of a casual observer – except his forehead, of which he was rather proud, but which was hidden by his hat.

It was generally believed that criminals always did something silly. But so far he had done nothing silly, and he was convinced that, in regard to the crime, he never would do anything silly. He had none of the desire, supposed to be common among murderers, to revisit the scene of the crime or to look upon the corpse once more. Although he regretted the necessity for his act, he felt no slightest twinge of conscience. Somebody had to die, and surely it was better that a brute should die than the heavenly, enchanting, martyrized creature whom his act had rescued for ever from the brute! He was aware within himself of an ecstasy of devotion to Emily Franting – now a widow and free. She was a unique woman. Strange that a woman of such gifts should have come under the sway of so obvious a scoundrel as Franting. But she was very young at the time, and such freaks of sex had happened before and would happen again; they were a wide-spread phenomenon in the history of the relations of men and women. He would have killed a hundred men if a hundred men had threatened her felicity. His heart was pure; he wanted nothing from Emily in exchange for what he had done in her defence. He was passionate in her defence. When he reflected upon the coarseness and cruelty of the gesture by which Franting had used Emily's letter to light his cigarette, Harder's cheeks grew hot with burning resentment.

A clock struck the quarter. Harder walked quickly to the harbour front, where was a taxi rank, and drove to the station. . . . A sudden apprehension! The crime might have been discovered! Police might already be watching for suspicious-looking travellers! Absurd! Still, the apprehension remained despite its absurdity. The taxi-driver looked at him queerly. No! Imagination! He hesitated on the threshold of the station, then walked boldly in, and showed his return ticket to the ticket-inspector. No sign of a policeman. He got into the Pullman car, where five other passengers were sitting. The train started.

He nearly missed the boat-train at Liverpool Street because according to its custom the Quangate flyer arrived twenty minutes late at Victoria. And at Victoria the foolish part of him, as distinguished from the common-sense part, suffered another spasm of fear. Would detectives, instructed by telegraph, be waiting for the train? No! An absurd idea! The boat-train from Liverpool Street was crowded with travellers, and the platform crowded with senders-off. He gathered from scraps of talk overheard that an international conference was about to take place at Copenhagen. And he had known nothing of it – not seen a word of it in the papers! Excusable, perhaps; graver matters had held his attention.

Useless to look for Emily in the vast bustle of the compartments! She had her through ticket (which she had taken herself in order to avoid possible complications), and she happened to be the only woman in the world who was never late and never in a hurry. She was certain to be in the train. But was she in the train? Something sinister might have come to pass. For instance, a telephone message to the flat that her husband had been found dead with a bullet in his brain.

The swift two-hour journey to Harwich was terrible for Lomax Harder. He remembered that he had left the unburnt part of the letter lying under the billiard table. Forgetful! Silly! One of the silly things that criminals did! And on Parkeston Quay the confusion was enormous. He did not walk, he was swept, onto the great shaking steamer whose dark funnels rose amid wisps of steam into the starry sky. One advantage: detectives would have no chance in that multitudinous scene, unless indeed they held up the ship.

The ship roared a warning, and slid away from the quay, groped down the tortuous channel to the harbour mouth, and was in the North Sea; and England dwindled to naught but a string of lights. He searched every deck from stem to stern, and could not find Emily. She had not caught the train, or, if she had caught the train, she had not boarded the steamer because he had failed to appear. His misery was intense. Everything was going wrong. And on the arrival at Esbjerg would not detectives be lying in wait for the Copenhagen train? . . .

Then he descried her, and she him. She too had been searching. Only chance had kept them apart. Her joy at finding him was ecstatic; tears came into his eyes at sight of it. He was everything to her, absolutely everything. He clasped her right hand in both his hands and gazed at her in the dim, diffused light blended of stars, moon and electricity. No woman was ever like her: mature, innocent, wise, trustful, honest. And the touching beauty of her appealing, sad, happy face, and the pride of her carriage! A unique jewel – snatched from the brutal grasp of that fellow – who had ripped her solemn letter in two

and used it as a spill for his cigarette! She related her movements; and he his. Then she said:

"Well?"

"I didn't go," he answered. "Thought it best not to. I'm
convinced it wouldn't have been any use."

He had not intended to tell her this lie. Yet when it came to
the point, what else could he say? He told one lie instead of
twenty. He was deceiving her, but for her sake. Even if the
worst occurred, she was for ever safe from that brutal grasp.
And he had saved her. As for the conceivable complications of
the future, he refused to front them; he could live in the
marvellous present. He felt suddenly the amazing beauty of
the night at sea, and beneath all his other sensations was the
obscure sensation of a weight at his heart.

"I expect you were right," she angelically acquiesced.

The Superintendent of Police (Quangate was the county town of
the western half of the county), and a detective-sergeant were in
the billiard room of the Bellevue. Both wore mufti. The powerful
green-shaded lamps usual in billiard rooms shone down ruth-
lessly on the green table, and on the reclining body of John
Franting, which had not moved and had not been moved.

A charwoman was just leaving these officers when a stout
gentleman, who had successfully beguiled a policeman guarding
the other end of the long corridor, squeezed past her, greeted
the two officers, and shut the door.

The Superintendent, a thin man, with lips to match, and a
moustache, stared hard at the arrival.

"I am staying with my friend Dr. Furnival," said the arrival
cheerfully. "You telephoned for him, and as he had to go out to
one of those cases in which nature will not wait, I offered to
come in his place. I've met you before, Superintendent, at
Scotland Yard."

"Dr. Austin Bond!" exclaimed the Superintendent.

"He," said the other.

They shook hands, Dr. Bond genially, the Superintendent
half-consequential, half-deferential, as one who had his dignity
to think about; also as one who resented an intrusion, but dared
not show resentment.

The detective-sergeant recoiled at the dazzling name of the great amateur detective, a genius who had solved the famous mysteries of "The Yellow Hat", "The Three Towns", "The Three Feathers", "The Gold Spoon", etc., etc., etc., whose devilish perspicacity had again and again made professional detectives both look and feel foolish, and whose notorious friendship with the loftiest heads of Scotland Yard compelled all police forces to treat him very politely indeed.

"Yes," said Dr. Austin Bond, after detailed examination. "Been shot about ninety minutes, poor fellow! Who found him?"

"That woman who's just gone out. Some servant here. Came in to look after the fire."

"How long since?"

"Oh! About an hour ago."

"Found the bullet? I see it hit the brass on that cue rack there."

The detective-sergeant glanced at the Superintendent, who, however, resolutely remained unastonished.

"Here's the bullet," said the Superintendent.

"Ah!" commented Dr. Austin Bond, glinting through his spectacles at the bullet as it lay in the Superintendent's hand. "Decimal 38, I see. Flattened. It would be."

"Sergeant," said the Superintendent. "You can get help and have the body moved, now Dr. Bond has made his examination. Eh, Doctor?"

"Certainly," answered Dr. Bond, at the fireplace. "He was smoking a cigarette, I see."

"Either he or his murderer."

"You've got a clue?"

"Oh, yes," the Superintendent answered, not without pride. "Look here. Your torch, Sergeant."

The detective-sergeant produced a pocket electric-lamp, and the Superintendent turned to the window sill.

"I've got a stronger one than that," said Dr. Austin Bond, producing another torch.

The Superintendent displayed fingerprints on the window frame, footmarks on the sill, and a few strands of inferior blue cloth. Dr. Austin Bond next produced a magnifying glass, and inspected the evidence at very short range.

"The murderer must have been a tall man – you can judge that from the angle of fire; he wore a blue suit, which he tore slightly on this splintered wood of the window frame; one of his boots had a hole in the middle of the sole, and he'd only three fingers on his left hand. He must have come in by the window and gone out by the window, because the hall porter is sure that nobody except the dead man entered the lounge by any door within an hour of the time when the murder must have been committed." The Superintendent proudly gave many more details, and ended by saying that he had already given instructions to circulate a description.

"Curious," said Dr. Austin Bond, "that a man like John Franting should let anyone enter the room by the window! Especially a shabby-looking man!"

"You knew the deceased personally then?"

"No! But I know he was John Franting."

"How, Doctor?"

"Luck."

"Sergeant," said the Superintendent, piqued. "Tell the constable to fetch the hall porter."

Dr. Austin Bond walked to and fro, peering everywhere, and picked up a piece of paper that had lodged against the step of the platform which ran round two sides of the room for the raising of the spectators' benches. He glanced at the paper casually, and dropped it again.

"My man," the Superintendent addressed the hall porter. "How can you be sure that nobody came in here this afternoon?"

"Because I was in my cubicle all the time, sir."

The hall porter was lying. But he had to think of his own welfare. On the previous day he had been reprimanded for quitting his post against the rule. Taking advantage of the absence of the manager, he had sinned once again, and he lived in fear of dismissal if found out.

"With a full view of the lounge?"

"Yes, sir."

"Might have been in there beforehand," Dr. Austin Bond suggested.

"No," said the Superintendent. "The charwoman came in

twice. Once just before Franting came in. She saw the fire wanted making up and she went for some coal, and then returned later with some coal. But the look of Franting frightened her, and she went back with her coal."

"Yes," said the hall porter. "I saw that."

Another lie.

At a sign from the Superintendent he withdrew.

"I should like to have a word with that charwoman," said Dr. Austin Bond.

The Superintendent hesitated. Why should the great amateur meddle with what did not concern him? Nobody had asked his help. But the Superintendent thought of the amateur's relations with Scotland Yard, and sent for the charwoman.

"Did you clean the window here to-day?" Dr. Austin Bond interrogated her.

"Yes, please, sir."

"Show me your left hand." The slattern obeyed. "How did you lose your little finger?"

"In a mangle accident, sir."

"Just come to the window, will you, and put your hands on it. But take off your left boot first."

The slattern began to weep.

"It's quite all right, my good creature," Dr. Austin Bond reassured her. "Your skirt is torn at the hem, isn't it?"

When the slattern was released from her ordeal and had gone, carrying one boot in her grimy hand, Dr. Austin Bond said genially to the Superintendent:

"Just a fluke. I happened to notice she'd only three fingers on her left hand when she passed me in the corridor. Sorry I've destroyed your evidence. But I felt sure almost from the first that the murderer hadn't either entered or decamped by the window."

"How?"

"Because I think he's still here in the room."

The two police officers gazed about them as if exploring the room for the murderer.

"I think he's there."

Dr. Austin Bond pointed to the corpse.

"And where did he hide the revolver after he'd killed himself?" demanded the thin-lipped Superintendent icily, when he had somewhat recovered his aplomb.

"I'd thought of that, too," said Dr. Austin Bond, beaming. "It is always a very wise course to leave a dead body absolutely untouched until a professional man has seen it. But *looking* at the body can do no harm. You see the left-hand pocket of the overcoat. Notice how it bulges. Something unusual in it. Something that has the shape of a—Just feel inside it, will you?"

The Superintendent, obeying, drew a revolver from the overcoat pocket of the dead man.

"Ah! Yes!" said Dr. Austin Bond. "A Webley Mark III. Quite new. You might take out the ammunition." The Superintendent dismantled the weapon. "Yes, yes! Three chambers empty. Wonder how he used the other two! Now, where's that bullet? You see? He fired. His arm dropped, and the revolver happened to fall into the pocket."

"Fired with his left hand, did he?" asked the Superintendent, foolishly ironic.

"Certainly. A dozen years ago Franting was perhaps the finest amateur lightweight boxer in England. And one reason for it was that he bewildered his opponents by being left-handed. His lefts were much more fatal than his rights. I saw him box several times."

Whereupon Dr. Austin Bond strolled to the step of the platform near the door and picked up the fragment of very thin paper that was lying there.

"This," said he, "must have blown from the hearth to here by the draught from the window when the door was opened. It's part of a letter. You can see the burnt remains of the other part in the corner of the fender. He probably lighted the cigarette with it. Out of bravado! His last bravado! Read this."

The Superintendent read:

". . . repeat that I realize how fond you are of me, but you have killed my affection for you and I shall leave our home to-morrow. This is absolutely final. E."

Dr. Austin Bond, having for the nth time satisfactorily demonstrated in his own unique, rapid way that police officers were a set of numbskulls, bade the Superintendent a most courteous good evening, nodded amicably to the detective-sergeant, and left in triumph.

"I must get some mourning and go back to the flat," said Emily Franting.

She was sitting one morning in the lobby of the Palads Hotel, Copenhagen. Lomax Harder had just called on her with an English newspaper containing an account of the inquest at which the jury had returned a verdict of suicide upon the body of her late husband. Her eyes filled with tears.

"Time will put her right," thought Lomax Harder, tenderly watching her. "I was bound to do what I did. And I can keep a secret for ever."

The Queen of Spades

Alexander Pushkin

I

There was a card party at the rooms of Naroumoff, of the
Horse Guards. The long winter night passed away im-
perceptibly, and it was five o'clock in the morning before the
company sat down to supper. Those who had won ate with a
good appetite; the others sat staring absently at their empty
plates. When the champagne appeared, however, the conversation became more animated, and all took a part in it.

"And how did you fare, Souirin?" asked the host.

"Oh, I lost, as usual. I must confess that I am unlucky. I play
mirandole, I always keep cool, I never allow anything to put me
out, and yet I always lose!"

"And you did not once allow yourself to be tempted to back
the red? Your firmness astonishes me."

"But what do you think of Hermann?" said one of the guests,
pointing to a young engineer. "He has never had a card in his
hand in his life, he has never in his life laid a wager; and yet he
sits here till five o'clock in the morning watching our play."

"Play interests me very much," said Hermann, "but I am not
in the position to sacrifice the necessary in the hope of winning
the superfluous."

"Hermann is a German; he is economical – that is all!" observed Tomsky. "But if there is one person that I cannot understand, it is my grandmother, the Countess Anna Fedorovna!"

"How so?" inquired the guests.

"I cannot understand," continued Tomsky, "how it is that
my grandmother does not punt."

"Then you do not know the reason why?"

"No, really; I haven't the faintest idea. But let me tell you the story. You must know that about sixty years ago, my grandmother went to Paris, where she created quite a sensation. People used to run after her to catch a glimpse of the 'Muscovite Venus.' Richelieu made love to her, and my grandmother maintains that he almost blew out his brains in consequence of her cruelty. At that time ladies used to play at faro. On one occasion at the Court, she lost a very considerable sum to the Duke of Orleans. On returning home, my grandmother removed the patches from her face, took off her hoops, informed my grandfather of her loss at the gaming-table, and ordered him to pay the money. My deceased grandfather, as far as I remember, was a sort of house-steward to my grandmother. He dreaded her like fire; but, on hearing of such a heavy loss, he almost went out of his mind. He calculated the various sums she had lost, and pointed out to her that in six months she had spent half a million of francs; that neither their Moscow nor Saratoff estates were in Paris; and, finally, refused point-blank to pay the debt. My grandmother gave him a box on the ear and slept by herself as a sign of her displeasure. The next day she sent for her husband, hoping that this domestic punishment had produced an effect upon him, but she found him inflexible. For the first time in her life she entered into reasonings and explanations with him, thinking to be able to convince him by pointing out to him that there are debts and debts, and that there is a great difference between a prince and a coachmaker.

"But it was all in vain, my grandfather still remained obdurate. But the matter did not rest there. My grandmother did not know what to do. She had shortly before become acquainted with a very remarkable man. You have heard of Count St. Germain, about whom so many marvelous stories are told. You know that he represented himself as the Wandering Jew, as the discoverer of the elixir of life, of the philosopher's stone, and so forth. Some laughed at him as a charlatan; but Casanova, in his memoirs, says that he was a spy. But be that as it may, St. Germain, in spite of the mystery surrounding him, was a very fascinating person, and was much sought after in the best circles of society. Even to this day my grandmother retains an affec-

tionate recollection of him, and becomes quite angry if anyone
speaks disrespectfully of him. My grandmother knew that St.
Germain had large sums of money at his disposal. She resolved
to have recourse to him, and she wrote a letter to him asking him
to come to her without delay. The queer old man immediately
waited upon her, and found her overwhelmed with grief. She
described to him in the blackest colors the barbarity of her
husband, and ended by declaring that her whole hope depended
upon his friendship and amiability.

"St. Germain reflected.

"'I could advance you the sum you want,' said he, 'but I
know that you would not rest easy until you had paid me back,
and I should not like to bring fresh troubles upon you. But there
is another way of getting out of your difficulty: you can win back
your money.'

"'But, my dear Count,' replied my grandmother, 'I tell you
that I haven't any money left!'

"'Money is not necessary,' replied St. Germain, 'be pleased
to listen to me.'

"Then he revealed to her a secret, for which each of us would
give a good deal."

The young officers listened with increased attention. Tomsky
lit his pipe, puffed away for a moment, and then continued:

"That same evening my grandmother went to Versailles to
the *jeu de la reine*. The Duke of Orleans kept the bank; my
grandmother excused herself in an offhanded manner for not
having yet paid her debt by inventing some little story, and then
began to play against him. She chose three cards and played
them one after the other; all three won *sonika*,★ and my grandmother recovered every farthing that she lost."

"Mere chance!" said one of the guests.

"A tale!" observed Hermann.

"Perhaps they were marked cards!" said a third.

"I do not think so," replied Tomsky, gravely.

"What!" said Naroumoff, "you have a grandmother who
knows how to hit upon three lucky cards in succession, and you
have never yet succeeded in getting the secret of it out of her?"

★ Said of a card when it wins or loses in the quickest possible time.

"That's the deuce of it!" replied Tomsky, "she had four sons, one of whom was my father; all four were determined gamblers, and yet not to one of them did she ever reveal her secret, although it would not have been a bad thing either for them or for me. But this is what I heard from my uncle, Count Ivan Ilitch, and he assured me, on his honor, that it was true. The late Chaplitsky – the same who died in poverty after having squandered millions – once lost, in his youth, about three hundred thousand roubles – to Zoritch, if I remember rightly. He was in despair. My grandmother, who was always very severe upon the extravagance of young men, took pity, however, upon Chaplitsky. She gave him three cards telling him to play them one after the other, at the same time exacting from him a solemn promise that he would never play at cards again as long as he lived. Chaplitsky then went to his victorious opponent, and they began a fresh game. On the first card he staked fifty thousand roubles, and won *sonika*; he doubled the stake, and won again; till at last, by pursuing the same tactics, he won back more than he had lost.

"But it is time to go to bed, it is a quarter to six already." And, indeed, it was already beginning to dawn; the young men emptied their glasses and then took leave of each other.

II

The old Countess A— was seated in her dressing room in front of her looking-glass. Three waiting maids stood around her. One held a small pot of rouge, another a box of hairpins, and the third a tall cap with bright red ribbons. The Countess had no longer the slightest pretensions to beauty, but she still preserved the habits of her youth, dressed in strict accordance with the fashion of seventy years before, and made as long and as careful a toilette as she would have done sixty years previously. Near the window, at an embroidery frame, sat a young lady, her ward.

"Good-morning, grandmamma," said a young officer, entering the room. "*Bonjour*, Mademoiselle Lise. Grandmamma, I want to ask you something."

"What is it, Paul?"

"I want you to let me introduce one of my friends to you, and to allow me to bring him to the ball on Friday."

"Bring him direct to the ball and introduce him to me there. Were you at B—'s yesterday?"

"Yes; everything went off very pleasantly, and dancing was kept up until five o'clock. How charming Eletskaia was!"

"But, my dear, what is there charming about her? Isn't she like her grandmother, the Princess Daria Petrovna? By the way, she must be very old, the Princess Daria Petrovna?"

"How do you mean, old?" cried Tomsky, thoughtlessly, "she died seven years ago."

The young lady raised her head, and made a sign to the young officer. He then remembered that the old Countess was never to be informed of the death of her contemporaries, and he bit his lips. But the old Countess heard the news with the greatest indifference.

"Dead!" said she, "and I did not know it. We were appointed maids of honor at the same time, and when we were presented to the Empress—"

And the Countess for the hundredth time related to her grandson one of her anecdotes.

"Come, Paul," said she, when she had finished her story, "help me to get up. Lizanka,* where is my snuffbox?"

And the Countess with her three maids went behind a screen to finish her toilette. Tomsky was left alone with the young lady.

"Who is the gentleman you wish to introduce to the Countess?" asked Lizaveta Ivanovna in a whisper.

"Naroumoff. Do you know him?"

"No, is he a soldier or a civilian?"

"A soldier."

"Is he in the Engineers?"

"No, in the Cavalry. What made you think that he was in the Engineers?"

The young lady smiled, but made no reply.

"Paul," cried the Countess from behind the screen, "send me some new novel, only pray don't let it be one of the present day style."

* Diminutive of Lizaveta (Elizabeth).

"What do you mean, grandmother?"

"That is, a novel, in which the hero strangles neither his father nor his mother, and in which there are no drowned bodies. I have a great horror of drowned persons."

"There are no such novels nowadays. Would you like a Russian one?"

"Are there any Russian novels? Send me one, my dear, pray send me one!"

"Goodby, grandmother. I am in a hurry . . . Goodby, Lizaveta Ivanovna. What made you think that Naroumoff was in the Engineers?"

And Tomsky left the boudoir.

Lizaveta Ivanovna was left alone. She laid aside her work, and began to look out of the window. A few moments afterwards, at a corner house on the other side of the street, a young officer appeared. A deep flush covered her cheeks; she took up her work again, and bent her head down over the frame. At the same moment the Countess returned, completely dressed.

"Order the carriage, Lizaveta," said she, "we will go out for a drive."

Lizaveta rose from the frame, and began to arrange her work.

"What is the matter with you, my child, are you deaf?" cried the Countess. "Order the carriage to be got ready at once."

"I will do so this moment," replied the young lady, hastening into the anteroom.

A servant entered and gave the Countess some books from Prince Paul Alexandrovitch.

"Tell him that I am much obliged to him," said the Countess. "Lizaveta! Lizaveta! where are you running to?"

"I am going to dress."

"There is plenty of time, my dear. Sit down here. Open the first volume and read to me aloud."

Her companion took the book and read a few lines.

"Louder," said the Countess. "What is the matter with you, my child? Have you lost your voice? Wait—Give me that footstool – a little nearer – that will do!"

Lizaveta read two more pages. The Countess yawned.

"Put the book down," said she, "what a lot of nonsense! Send it back to Prince Paul with my thanks . . . But where is the carriage?"

"The carriage is ready," said Lizaveta, looking out into the street.

"How is it that you are not dressed?" said the Countess. "I must always wait for you. It is intolerable, my dear!"

Liza hastened to her room. She had not been there two minutes before the Countess began to ring with all her might. The three waiting-maids came running in at one door, and the valet at another.

"How is it that you cannot hear me when I ring for you?" said the Countess. "Tell Lizaveta Ivanovna that I am waiting for her."

Lizaveta returned with her hat and cloak on.

"At last you are here!" said the Countess. "But why such an elaborate toilette? Whom do you intend to captivate? What sort of weather is it? It seems rather windy."

"No, your Ladyship, it is very calm," replied the valet.

"You never think of what you are talking about. Open the window. So it is; windy and bitterly cold. Unharness the horses, Lizaveta, we won't go out – there was no need to deck yourself like that."

"What a life is mine!" thought Lizaveta Ivanovna.

And, in truth, Lizaveta Ivanovna was a very unfortunate creature. "The bread of the stranger is bitter," says Dante, "and his staircase hard to climb." But who can know what the bitterness of dependence is so well as the poor companion of an old lady of quality? The Countess A— had by no means a bad heart, but she was capricious, like a woman who had been spoiled by the world, as well as being avaricious and egotistical, like all old people, who have seen their best days, and whose thoughts are with the past, and not the present. She participated in all the vanities of the great world, went to balls, where she sat in a corner, painted and dressed in old-fashioned style, like a deformed but indispensable ornament of the ballroom; all the guests on entering approached her and made a profound bow, as if in accordance with a set ceremony, but after that nobody took any further notice of her. She received the whole town at her house, and observed the strictest etiquette, although she could

no longer recognize the faces of people. Her numerous domestics, growing fat and old in her ante-chamber and servant's hall,
did just as they liked, and vied with each other in robbing the
aged Countess in the most bare-faced manner. Lizaveta Ivanovna was the martyr of the household. She made tea, and was
reproached with using too much sugar; she read novels aloud to
the Countess, and the faults of the author were visited upon her
head; she accompanied the Countess in her walks, and was held
answerable for the weather or the state of the pavement. A
salary was attached to the post, but she very rarely received it,
although she was expected to dress like everybody else, that is to
say, like very few indeed. In society she played the most pitiable
role. Everybody knew her, and nobody paid her any attention.
At balls she danced only when a partner was wanted, and ladies
would only take hold of her arm when it was necessary to lead
her out of the room to attend to their dresses. She was very self-
conscious, and felt her position keenly, and she looked about her
with impatience for a deliverer to come to her rescue; but the
young men, calculating in their giddiness, honored her with but
very little attention, although Lizaveta Ivanovna was a hundred
times prettier than the bare-faced, cold-hearted marriageable
girls around whom they hovered. Many a time did she quietly
slink away from the glittering, but wearisome, drawing-room,
to go and cry in her own poor little room, in which stood a
screen, a chest of drawers, a looking-glass, and a painted bedstead, and where a tallow candle burnt feebly in a copper
candle-stick.

One morning – this was about two days after the evening
party described at the beginning of this story, and a week
previous to the scene at which we have just assisted – Lizaveta
Ivanovna was seated near the window at her embroidery frame,
when, happening to look out into the street, she caught sight of a
young Engineer officer, standing motionless with his eyes fixed
upon her window. She lowered her head, and went on again
with her work. About five minutes afterwards she looked out
again – the young officer was still standing in the same place.
Not being in the habit of coquetting with passing officers, she
did not continue to gaze out into the street, but went on sewing
for a couple of hours, without raising her head. Dinner was

announced. She rose up and began to put her embroidery away, but glancing casually out of the window, she perceived the officer again. This seemed to her very strange. After dinner she went to the window with a certain feeling of uneasiness, but the officer was no longer there – and she thought no more about him.

A couple of days afterwards, just as she was stepping into the carriage with the Countess, she saw him again. He was standing close behind the door, with his face half-concealed by his fur collar, but his dark eyes sparkled beneath his cap. Lizaveta felt alarmed, though she knew not why, and she trembled as she seated herself in the carriage.

On returning home, she hastened to the window – the officer was standing in his accustomed place, with his eyes fixed upon her. She drew back, a prey to curiosity, and agitated by a feeling which was quite new to her.

From that time forward not a day passed without the young officer making his appearance under the window at the custhomary hour, and between him and her there was established a sort of mute acquaintance. Sitting in her place at work, she used to feel his approach, and, raising her head, she would look at him longer and longer each day. The young man seemed to be very grateful to her; she saw with the sharp eye of youth, how a sudden flush covered his pale cheeks each time that their glances met. After about a week she commenced to smile at him. . . .

When Tomsky asked permission of his grandmother, the Countess, to present one of his friends to her, the young girl's heart beat violently. But hearing that Naroumoff was not an Engineer, she regretted that by her thoughtless question, she had betrayed her secret to the volatile Tomsky.

Hermann was the son of a German who had become a naturalized Russian, and from whom he had inherited a small capital. Being firmly convinced of the necessity of preserving his independence, Hermann did not touch his private income, but lived on his pay, without allowing himself the slightest luxury. Moreover, he was reserved and ambitious, and his companions rarely had an opportunity of making merry at the expense of his extreme parsimony. He had strong passions and an ardent imagination, but his firmness of disposition preserved him from the ordinary errors of young men. Thus, though a gamester at heart, he never touched a card, for he considered his position did not allow him – as he said – "to risk the necessary in the hope of winning the superfluous," yet he would sit for nights together at the card table and follow with feverish anxiety the different turns of the game.

The story of the three cards had produced a powerful impression upon his imagination, and all night long he could think of nothing else. "If," he thought to himself the following evening, as he walked along the streets of St. Petersburg, "if the old Countess would but reveal her secret to me! If she would only tell me the names of the three winning cards. Why should I not try my fortune? I must get introduced to her and win her favor – become her lover. . . . But all that will take time, and she is eighty-seven years old. She might be dead in a week, in a couple of days even. But the story itself? Can it really be true? No! Economy, temperance, and industry; those are my three winning cards; by means of them I shall be able to double my capital – increase it sevenfold, and procure for myself ease and independence."

Musing in this manner, he walked on until he found himself in one of the principal streets of St. Petersburg, in front of a house of antiquated architecture. The street was blocked with equipages; carriages one after the other drew up in front of the brilliantly illuminated doorway. At one moment there stepped out onto the pavement the well-shaped little foot of some young beauty, at another the heavy boot of a cavalry officer, and then the silk stockings and shoes of a member of the diplomatic world. Fur and cloaks passed in rapid succession before the gigantic porter at the entrance. Hermann stopped. "Whose house is this?" he asked of the watchman at the corner.

"The Countess A—'s," replied the watchman.

Hermann started. The strange story of the three cards again presented itself to his imagination. He began walking up and down before the house, thinking of its owner and her strange secret. Returning late to his modest lodging, he could not go to sleep for a long time, and when at last he did doze off, he could dream of nothing but cards, green tables, piles of banknotes, and heaps of ducats. He played one card after the other, winning uninterruptedly, and then he gathered up the gold and filled his pockets with the notes. When he woke up late the next morning, he sighed over the loss of his imaginary wealth, and then sallying out into the town, he found himself once more in front of the Countess's residence. Some unknown power seemed to have attracted him thither. He stopped and looked up at the windows. At one of these he saw a head with luxuriant black hair, which was bent down, probably over some book or an embroidery frame. The head was raised. Hermann saw a fresh complexion, and a pair of dark eyes. That moment decided his fate.

III

Lizaveta Ivanovna had scarcely taken off her hat and cloak, when the Countess sent for her, and again ordered her to get the carriage ready. The vehicle drew up before the door, and they prepared to take their seats. Just at the moment when two footmen were assisting the old lady to enter the carriage, Lizaveta saw her Engineer standing close beside the wheel; he grasped her hand; alarm caused her to lose her presence of mind, and the young man disappeared – but not before he had left a letter between her fingers. She concealed it in her glove, and during the whole of the drive she neither saw nor heard anything. It was the custom of the Countess, when out for an airing in her carriage, to be constantly asking such questions as "Who was that person that met us just now? What is the name of this bridge? What is written on that sign-board?" On this occasion, however, Lizaveta returned such vague and absurd answers, that the Countess became angry with her.

"What is the matter with you, my dear?" she exclaimed. "Have you taken leave of your senses, or what is it? Do you not hear me or understand what I say? Heaven be thanked, I am still in my right mind and speak plainly enough!"

Lizaveta Ivanovna did not hear her. On returning home she ran to her room, and drew the letter out of her glove: it was not sealed. Lizaveta read it. The letter contained a declaration of love; it was tender, respectful, and copied word for word from a

German novel. But Lizaveta did not know anything of the German language, and she was quite delighted.

For all that, the letter caused her to feel exceedingly uneasy. For the first time in her life she was entering into secret and confidential relations with a young man. His boldness alarmed her. She reproached herself for her imprudent behavior, and knew not what to do. Should she cease to sit at the window, and, by assuming an appearance of indifference towards him, put a check upon the young officer's desire for further acquaintance with her? Should she send his letter back to him, or should she answer him in a cold and decided manner? There was nobody to whom she could turn in her perplexity, for she had neither female friend nor adviser. At length she resolved to reply to him.

She sat down at her little writing table, took pen and paper, and began to think. Several times she began her letter and then tore it up; the way she had expressed herself seemed to her either too inviting or too cold and decisive. At last she succeeded in writing a few lines with which she felt satisfied.

"I am convinced," she wrote, "that your intentions are honorable, and that you do not wish to offend me by any imprudent behavior, but our acquaintance must not begin in such a manner. I return you your letter, and I hope that I shall never have any cause to complain of this undeserved slight."

The next day, as soon as Hermann made his appearance, Lizaveta rose from her embroidery, went into the drawing-room, opened the ventilator, and threw the letter into the street, trusting that the young officer would have the perception to pick it up.

Hermann hastened forward, picked it up, and then repaired to a confectioner's shop. Breaking the seal of the envelope, he found inside it his own letter and Lizaveta's reply. He had expected this, and he returned home, his mind deeply occupied with his intrigue.

Three days afterwards a bright-eyed young girl from a milliner's establishment brought Lizaveta a letter. Lizaveta opened it with great uneasiness, fearing that it was a demand for money, when, suddenly, she recognized Hermann's handwriting.

"You have made a mistake, my dear," said she. "This letter is not for me."

"Oh, yes, it is for you," replied the girl, smiling very knowingly. "Have the goodness to read it."

Lizaveta glanced at the letter. Hermann requested an interview.

"It cannot be," she cried, alarmed at the audacious request and the manner in which it was made. "This letter is certainly not for me," and she tore it into fragments.

"If the letter was not for you, why have you torn it up?" said the girl. "I should have given it back to the person who sent it."

"Be good enough, my dear," said Lizaveta, disconcerted by this remark, "nor to bring me any more letters in the future, and tell the person who sent you that he ought to be ashamed."

But Hermann was not the man to be thus put off. Every day Lizaveta received from him a letter, sent now in this way, now in that. They were no longer translated from the German. Hermann wrote them under the inspiration of passion, and spoke in his own language, and they bore full testimony to the inflexibility of his desire, and the disordered condition of his uncontrollable imagination. Lizaveta no longer thought of sending them back to him; she became intoxicated with them, and began to reply to them, and little by little her answers became longer and more affectionate. At last she threw out of the window to him the following letter:

"This evening there is going to be a ball at the Embassy. The Countess will be there. We shall remain until two o'clock. You have now an opportunity of seeing me alone. As soon as the Countess is gone, the servants will very probably go out, and there will be nobody left but the Swiss, but he usually goes to sleep in his lodge. Come about half-past eleven. Walk straight upstairs. If you meet anybody in the anteroom, ask if the Countess is at home. You will be told 'No,' in which case there will be nothing left for you to do but to go away again. But it is most probable that you will meet nobody. The maidservants will all be together in one room. On leaving the anteroom, turn to the left, and walk straight on until you reach the Countess's bedroom. In the bedroom, behind a screen, you will find two doors: the one on the right leads to a cabinet, which the

Countess never enters; the one on the left leads to a corridor, at
the end of which is a little winding staircase; this leads to my
room."

Hermann trembled like a tiger as he waited for the appointed
time to arrive. At ten o'clock in the evening he was already in
front of the Countess's house. The weather was terrible; the
wind blew with great violence, the sleety snow fell in large
flakes, the lamps emitted a feeble light, the streets were deserted; from time to time a sledge drawn by a sorry-looking
hack, passed by on the lookout for a belated passenger. Hermann was enveloped in a thick overcoat, and felt neither wind
nor snow.

At last the Countess's carriage drew up. Hermann saw two
footmen carry out in their arms the bent form of the old lady,
wrapped in sable fur, and immediately behind her, clad in a
warm mantle, and with her head ornamented with a wreath of
fresh flowers, followed Lizaveta. The door was closed. The
carriage rolled heavily away through the yielding snow. The
porter shut the street door, the windows became dark.

Hermann began walking up and down near the deserted
house; at length he stopped under a lamp, and glanced at his
watch; it was twenty minutes past eleven. He remained standing
under the lamp, his eyes fixed upon the watch impatiently
waiting for the remaining minutes to pass. At half-past eleven
precisely Hermann ascended the steps of the house and made
his way into the brightly-illuminated vestibule. The porter was
not there. Hermann hastily ascended the staircase, opened the
door of the anteroom, and saw a footman sitting asleep in an
antique chair by the side of a lamp. With a light, firm step
Hermann passed by him. The drawing-room and dining-room
were in darkness, but a feeble reflection penetrated thither from
the lamp in the anteroom.

Hermann reached the Countess's bedroom. Before a shrine,
which was full of old images, a golden lamp was burning. Faded
stuffed chairs and divans with soft cushions stood in melancholy symmetry around the room, the walls of which were hung
with china silk. On one side of the room hung two portraits
painted in Paris by Madame Lebrun. One of these represented a
stout, red-faced man of about forty years of age, in a bright

green uniform, and with a star upon his breast; the other – a beautiful young woman, with an aquiline nose, forehead curls, and a rose in her powdered hair. In the corner stood porcelain shepherds and shepherdesses, dining-room clocks from the workshop of the celebrated Lefroy, bandboxes, roulettes, fans, and the various playthings for the amusement of ladies that were in vogue at the end of the last century, when Montgolfier's balloons and Niesber's magnetism were the rage. Hermann stepped behind the screen. At the back of it stood a little iron bedstead: on the right was the door which led to the cabinet; on the left, the other which led to the corridor. He opened the latter, and saw the little winding staircase which led to the room of the poor companion. But he retraced his steps and entered the dark cabinet.

The time passed slowly. All was still. The clock in the drawing-room struck twelve, the strokes echoed through the room one after the other, and everything was quiet again. Hermann stood leaning against the cold stove. He was calm, his heart beat regularly, like that of a man resolved upon a dangerous but inevitable undertaking. One o'clock in the morning struck; then two, and he heard the distant noise of carriage-wheels. An involuntary agitation took possession of him. The carriage drew near and stopped. He heard the sound of the carriage steps being let down. All was bustle within the house. The servants were running hither and thither, there was a confusion of voices, and the rooms were lit up. Three anti-quated chambermaids entered the bedroom, and they were shortly afterwards followed by the Countess, who, more dead than alive, sank into a Voltaire armchair. Hermann peeped through a chink. Lizaveta Ivanovna passed close by him, and he heard her hurried steps as she hastened up the little spiral staircase. For a moment his heart was assailed by something like a pricking of conscience, but the emotion was only transitory, and his heart became petrified as before.

The Countess began to undress before her looking-glass. Her rose-bedecked cap was taken off, and then her powdered wig was removed from off her white and closely cut hair. Hairpins fell in showers around her. Her yellow satin dress, brocaded with silver, fell down at her swollen feet.

Hermann was a witness of the repugnant mysteries of her toilette; at last the Countess was in her night-cap and dressing-gown, and in this costume, more suitable to her age, she appeared less hideous and deformed.

Like all old people, in general, the Countess suffered from sleeplessness. Having undressed, she seated herself at the window in a Voltaire armchair, and dismissed her maids. The candles were taken away, and once more the room was left with only one lamp burning in it. The Countess sat there looking quite yellow, mumbling with her flaccid lips and swaying to and fro. Her dull eyes expressed complete vacancy of mind, and, looking at her, one would have thought that the rocking of her body was not a voluntary action of her own, but was produced by the action of some concealed galvanic mechanism.

Suddenly the death-like face assumed an inexplicable expression. The lips ceased to tremble, the eyes became animated: before the Countess stood an unknown man.

"Do not be alarmed, for Heaven's sake, do not be alarmed!" said he in a low but distinct voice. "I have no intention of doing you any harm; I have only come to ask a favor of you."

The old woman looked at him in silence, as if she had not heard what he had said. Hermann thought that she was deaf, and, bending down towards her ear, he repeated what he had said. The aged Countess remained silent as before.

"You can insure the happiness of my life," continued Hermann, "and it will cost you nothing. I know that you can name three cards in order—"

Hermann stopped. The Countess appeared now to understand what he wanted; she seemed as if seeking for words to reply.

"It was a joke," she replied at last. "I assure you it was only a joke."

"There is no joking about the matter," replied Hermann, angrily. "Remember Chaplitsky, whom you helped to win."

The Countess became visibly uneasy. Her features expressed strong emotion, but they quickly resumed their former immobility.

"Can you not name me these three winning cards?" continued Hermann.

The Countess remained silent; Hermann continued:

"For whom are you preserving your secret? For your grand-sons? They are rich enough without it, they do not know the worth of money. Your cards would be of no use to a spendthrift. He who cannot preserve his paternal inheritance will die in want, even though he had a demon at his service. I am not a man of that sort. I know the value of money. Your three cards will not be thrown away upon me. Come!"

He paused and tremblingly awaited her reply. The Countess remained silent. Hermann fell upon his knees.

"If your heart has ever known the feeling of love," said he, "if you remember its rapture, if you have ever smiled at the cry of your new-born child, if any human feeling has ever entered into your breast, I entreat you by the feelings of a wife, a lover, a mother, by all that is most sacred in life, not to reject my prayer. Reveal to me your secret. Of what use is it to you? Maybe it is connected with some terrible sin, with the loss of eternal salvation, with some bargain with the devil. Reflect, you are old, you have not long to live – I am ready to take your sins upon my soul. Only reveal to me your secret. Remember that the happiness of a man is in your hands, that not only I, but my children and my grandchildren, will bless your memory and reverence you as a saint."

The old Countess answered not a word.

Hermann rose to his feet.

"You old hag!" he exclaimed, grinding his teeth, "then I will make you answer!" With these words he drew a pistol from his pocket. At the sight of the pistol, the Countess for the second time exhibited strong emotions. She shook her head, and raised her hands as if to protect herself from the shot. Then she fell backwards, and remained motionless.

"Come, an end to this childish nonsense!" said Hermann, taking hold of her hand. "I ask you for the last time: will you tell me the names of your three cards, or will you not?"

The Countess made no reply. Hermann perceived that she was dead!

IV

Lizaveta Ivanovna was sitting in her room, still in her ball dress, lost in deep thought. On returning home, she had hastily dismissed the chambermaid, who very reluctantly came forward to assist her, saying that she would undress herself, and with a trembling heart had gone up to her own room, expecting to find Hermann there, but yet hoping not to find him. At the first glance he was not there, and she thanked her fate for having prevented him from keeping the appointment. She sat down without undressing, and began to call to mind all the circumstances which in a short time had carried her so far. It was not three weeks since the time when she had first seen the young officer from the window – and yet she was already in correspondence with him, and he had succeeded in inducing her to grant him a nocturnal interview. She knew his name only through his having written it at the bottom of some of his letters; she had never spoken to him, had never heard his voice, and had never heard him spoken of until that evening. But, strange to say, that very evening at the ball, Tomsky, being piqued with the young Princess Pauline N—, who, contrary to her usual custom, did not flirt with him, wished to revenge himself by assuming an air of indifference: he therefore engaged Lizaveta Ivanovna, and danced an endless mazurka with her. During the whole of the time he kept teasing her about her partiality for Engineer officers, he assured her that he knew far more than she imagined, and some of his jests were so happily aimed, that Lizaveta thought several times that her secret was known to him.

"From whom have you learned all this?" she asked, smiling.

"From a friend of a person very well known to you," replied Tomsky, "from a very distinguished man."

"And who is this distinguished man?"

"His name is Hermann." Lizaveta made no reply, but her hands and feet lost all sense of feeling.

"This Hermann," continued Tomsky, "is a man of romantic personality. He has the profile of a Napoleon, and the soul of a Mephistopheles. I believe that he has at least three crimes upon his conscience. How pale you have become!"

"I have a headache. But what did this Hermann, or whatever his name is, tell you?"

"Hermann is very dissatisfied with his friend. He says that in his place he would act very differently. I even think that Hermann himself has designs upon you; at least, he listens very attentively to all that his friend has to say about you."

"And where has he seen me?"

"In church, perhaps: or on the parade. God alone knows where. It may have been in your room, while you were asleep, for there is nothing that he—"

Three ladies approaching him with the question: "oubli ou regret?" interrupted the conversation, which had become so tantalizingly interesting to Lizaveta.

The lady chosen by Tomsky was the Princess Pauline herself. She succeeded in effecting a reconciliation with him during the numerous turns of the dance, after which he conducted her to her chair. On returning to his place, Tomsky thought no more either of Hermann or Lizaveta. She longed to renew the interrupted conversation, but the mazurka came to an end, and shortly afterwards the old Countess took her departure.

Tomsky's words were nothing more than the customary small talk of the dance, but they sank deep into the soul of the young dreamer. The portrait, sketched by Tomsky, coincided with the picture she had formed within her own mind, and, thanks to the latest romances, the ordinary countenance of her admirer became invested with attributes capable of alarming her and fascinating her imagination at the same time. She was now sitting with her bare arms crossed, and with her head, still adorned with flowers, sunk upon her uncovered bosom. Suddenly the door opened and Hermann entered. She shuddered.

"Where were you?" she asked in a terrified whisper.

"In the old Countess's bedroom," replied Hermann. "I have just left her. The Countess is dead."

"My God! What do you say?"

"And I am afraid," added Hermann, "that I am the cause of her death."

Lizaveta looked at him, and Tomsky's words found an echo in her soul: "This man has at least three crimes upon his conscience!" Hermann sat down by the window near her, and related all that had happened.

Lizaveta listened to him in terror. So all those passionate letters, those ardent desires, this bold, obstinate pursuit – all this was not love! Money – that was what his soul yearned for! She could not satisfy his desire and make him happy. The poor girl had been nothing but the blind tool of a robber, of the murderer of her aged benefactress! She wept bitter tears of agonized repentance. Hermann gazed at her in silence; his heart, too, was a prey to violent emotion, but neither the tears of the poor girl, nor the wonderful charm of her beauty, enhanced by her grief, could produce any impression upon his hardened soul. He felt no pricking of conscience at the thought of the dead old woman. One thing only grieved him: the irreparable loss of the secret from which he had expected to obtain great wealth.

"You are a monster!" said Lizaveta at last.

"I did not wish for her death," replied Hermann, "my pistol was not loaded." Both remained silent. The day began to dawn. Lizaveta extinguished her candle, a pale light illumined her room. She wiped her tear-stained eyes, and raised them towards Hermann. He was sitting near the window, with his arms crossed, and with a fierce frown upon his forehead. In this attitude he bore a striking resemblance to the portrait of Napoleon. This resemblance struck Lizaveta even.

"How shall I get you out of the house?" said she at last. "I thought of conducting you down the secret staircase."

"I will go alone," he answered.

Lizaveta arose, took from her drawer a key, handed it to Hermann, and gave him the necessary instructions. Hermann pressed her cold, inert hand, kissed her bowed head, and left the room.

He descended the winding staircase, and once more entered the Countess's bedroom. The dead old lady sat as if petrified, her face expressed profound tranquillity. Hermann stopped before her, and gazed long and earnestly at her, as if he wished to convince himself of the terrible reality. At last he entered the cabinet, felt behind the tapestry for the door, and then began to descend the dark staircase, filled with strange emotions. "Down this very staircase," thought he, "perhaps coming from the very same room, and at this very same hour sixty years ago, there may have glided, in an embroidered coat, with his hair dressed *à l'oiseau royal*, and pressing to his heart his three-cornered hat, some young gallant who has long been mouldering in the grave, but the heart of his aged mistress has only to-day ceased to beat."

At the bottom of the staircase Hermann found a door, which he opened with a key, and then traversed a corridor which conducted him into the street.

V

Three days after the fatal night, at nine o'clock in the morning, Hermann repaired to the Convent of—, where the last honors were to be paid to the mortal remains of the old Countess. Although feeling no remorse, he could not altogether stifle the voice of conscience, which said to him: "You are the murderer of the old woman!" In spite of his entertaining very little religious belief, he was exceedingly superstitious; and believing that the dead Countess might exercise an evil influence on his life, he resolved to be present at her obsequies in order to implore her pardon.

The church was full. It was with difficulty that Hermann made his way through the crowd of people. The coffin was placed upon a rich catafalque beneath a velvet baldachin. The deceased Countess lay within it, with her hands crossed upon her breast, with a lace cap upon her head, and dressed in a white satin robe. Around the catafalque stood the members of her household; the servants in black caftans, with armorial ribbons upon their shoulders and candles in their hands; the relatives – children, grandchildren, and great-grandchildren – in deep mourning.

Nobody wept, tears would have been an affectation. The Countess was so old that her death could have surprised nobody, and her relatives had long looked upon her as being out of the world. A famous preacher delivered the funeral sermon. In simple and touching words he described the peaceful passing away of the righteous, who had passed long years in calm preparation for a Christian end. "The angel of death found her," said the orator, "engaged in pious meditation and waiting for the midnight bridegroom."

The service concluded amidst profound silence. The relatives went forward first to take a farewell of the corpse. Then followed the numerous guests, who had come to render the last homage to her who for so many years had been a participator in their frivolous amusements. After these followed the members of the Countess's household. The last of these was an old woman of the same age as the deceased. Two young women led her forward by the hand. She had not strength enough to bow down to the ground – she merely shed a few tears, and kissed the cold hand of her mistress.

Hermann now resolved to approach the coffin. He knelt down upon the cold stones, and remained in that position for some minutes; at last he arose as pale as the deceased Countess herself; he ascended the steps of the catafalque and bent over the corpse. . . . At that moment it seemed to him that the dead woman darted a mocking look at him and winked with one eye. Hermann started back, took a false step, and fell to the ground. Several persons hurried forward and raised him up. At the same moment Lizaveta Ivanovna was borne fainting into the porch of the church. This episode disturbed for some minutes the solemnity of the gloomy ceremony. Among the congregation arose a deep murmur, and a tall, thin chamberlain, a near relative of the deceased, whispered in the ear of an Englishman, who was standing near him, that the young officer was a natural son of the Countess, to which the Englishman coldly replied "Oh!"

During the whole of that day Hermann was strangely excited. Repairing to an out of the way restaurant to dine, he drank a great deal of wine, countrary to his usual custom, in the hope of deadening his inward agitation. But the wine only served to excite his imagination still more. On returning home he threw himself upon his bed without undressing, and fell into a deep sleep.

When he woke up it was already night, and the moon was shining into the room. He looked at his watch: it was a quarter to three. Sleep had left him; he sat down upon his bed, and thought of the funeral of the old Countess.

At that moment somebody in the street looked in at his window and immediately passed on again. Hermann paid no attention to this incident. A few moments afterwards he heard the door of his anteroom open. Hermann thought that it was his orderly, drunk as usual, returning from some nocturnal expedition, but presently he heard footsteps that were unknown to him: somebody was walking softly over the floor in slippers. The door opened, and a woman dressed in white entered the room. Hermann mistook her for his old nurse, and wondered what could bring her there at that hour of the night. But the white woman glided rapidly across the room and stood before him – and Hermann thought he recognized the Countess.

"I have come to you against my wish," she said in a firm voice, "but I have been ordered to grant your request. Three, seven, ace, will win for you if played in succession, but only on these conditions: that you do not play more than one card in twenty-four-hours, and that you never play again during the rest of your life. I forgive you my death, on condition that you marry my companion, Lizaveta Ivanovna."

With these words she turned round very quietly, walked with a shuffling gait towards the door, and disappeared. Hermann heard the street door open and shut, and again he saw someone look in at him through the window.

For a long time Hermann could not recover himself. He then rose up and entered the next room. His orderly was lying asleep upon the floor, and he had much difficulty in waking him. The orderly was drunk as usual, and no information could be obtained from him. The street door was locked. Hermann returned to his room, lit his candle, and wrote down all the details of his vision.

VI

Two fixed ideas can no more exist together in the moral world than two bodies can occupy one and the same physical world. "Three, seven, ace" soon drove out of Hermann's mind the thought of the dead Countess. "Three, seven, ace" were perpetually running through his head, and continually being repeated by his lips. If he saw a young girl, he would say: "How slender she is; quite like the three of hearts." If anybody asked "What is the time?" he would reply: "Five minutes to seven." Every stout man that he saw reminded him of the ace. "Three, seven, ace" haunted him in his sleep, and assumed all possible shapes. The threes bloomed before him in the forms of magnificent flowers, the sevens were represented by Gothic portals, and the aces became transformed into gigantic spiders. One thought alone occupied his whole mind – to make a profitable use of the secret which he had purchased so dearly. He thought of applying for a furlough so as to travel abroad. He wanted to go to Paris and tempt fortune in some gambling houses that abounded there. Chance spared him all this trouble.

There was in Moscow a society of rich gamesters, presided over by the celebrated Chekalinsky, who had passed all his life at the card table, and had amassed millions, accepting bills of exchange for his winnings, and paying his losses in ready money. His long experience secured for him the confidence of his companions, and his open house, his famous cook, and his agreeable and fascinating manners, gained for him the respect of the public. He came to St. Petersburg. The young men of the capital flocked to his rooms, forgetting balls for cards, and preferring the emotions of faro to the seductions of flirting. Naroumoff conducted Hermann to Chekalinsky's residence.

They passed through a suite of rooms, filled with attentive domestics. The place was crowded. Generals and Privy Counsellors were playing at whist, young men were lolling carelessly upon the velvet-covered sofas, eating ices and smoking pipes. In the drawing-room, at the head of a long table, around which were assembled about a score of players, sat the master of the house keeping the bank. He was a man of about sixty years of age, of a very dignified appearance; his head was covered with silvery white hair; his full, florid countenance expressed good-nature, and his eyes twinkled with a perpetual smile. Naroumoff introduced Hermann to him. Chekalinsky shook him by the hand in a friendly manner, requested him not to stand on ceremony, and then went on dealing.

The game occupied some time. On the table lay more than thirty cards. Chekalinsky paused after each throw, in order to give the players time to arrange their cards and note down their losses, listened politely to their requests, and more politely still, straightened the corners of cards that some player's hand had chanced to bend. At last the game was finished. Chekalinsky shuffled the cards, and prepared to deal again.

"Will you allow me to take a card?" said Hermann, stretching out his hand from behind a stout gentleman who was punting.

Chekalinsky smiled and bowed silently, as a sign of acquiescence. Naroumoff laughingly congratulated Hermann on his abjuration of that abstention from cards which he had practised for so long a period, and wished him a lucky beginning.

"Stake!" said Hermann, writing some figures with chalk on the back of his card.

"How much?" asked the banker, contracting the muscles of his eyes, "excuse me, I cannot see quite clearly."

"Forty-seven thousand roubles," replied Hermann. At these words every head in the room turned suddenly round, and all eyes were fixed upon Hermann.

"He has taken leave of his senses!" thought Naroumoff.

"Allow me to inform you," said Chekalinsky, with his eternal smile, "that you are playing very high; nobody here has ever staked more than two hundred and seventy-five roubles at once."

"Very well," replied Hermann, "but do you accept my card or not?"

Chekalinsky bowed in token of consent.

"I only wish to observe," said he, "that although I have the greatest confidence in my friends, I can only play against ready money. For my own part I am quite convinced that your word is sufficient, but for the sake of the order of the game, and to facilitate the reckoning up, I must ask you to put the money on your card."

Hermann drew from his pocket a bank-note, and handed it to Chekalinsky, who, after examining it in a cursory manner, placed it on Hermann's card.

He began to deal. On the right a nine turned up, and on the left a three.

"I have won!" said Hermann, showing his card.

A murmur of astonishment arose among the players. Chekalinsky frowned, but the smile quickly returned to his face. "Do you wish me to settle with you?" he said to Hermann.

"If you please," replied the latter.

Chekalinsky drew from his pocket a number of banknotes and paid at once. Hermann took up his money and left the table. Naroumoff could not recover from his astonishment. Hermann drank a glass of lemonade and returned home.

The next evening he again repaired to Chekalinsky's. The host was dealing. Hermann walked up to the table; the punters immediately made room for him. Chekalinsky greeted him with a gracious bow.

Hermann waited for the next deal, took a card and placed upon it his forty-seven thousand roubles, together with his winnings of the previous evening.

Chekalinsky began to deal. A knave turned up on the right, a seven on the left.

Hermann showed his seven.

There was a general exclamation. Chekalinsky was evidently ill at ease, but he counted out the ninety-four thousand roubles and handed them over to Hermann, who pocketed them in the coolest manner possible, and immediately left the house.

The next evening Hermann appeared again at the table. Everyone was expecting him. The generals and privy counsellors left their whist in order to watch such extraordinary play. The young officers quitted their sofas, and even the servants crowded into the room. All pressed round Hermann. The other players left off punting, impatient to see how it would end. Hermann stood at the table, and prepared to play alone against the pale, but still smiling Chekalinsky. Each opened a pack of cards. Chekalinsky shuffled. Hermann took a card and covered it with a pile of banknotes. It was like a duel. Deep silence reigned around.

Chekalinsky began to deal, his hands trembled. On the right a queen turned up, and on the left an ace.

"Ace has won!" cried Hermann, showing his card.

"Your queen has lost," said Chekalinsky, politely.

Hermann started; instead of an ace, there lay before him the queen of spades! He could not believe his eyes, nor could he understand how he had made such a mistake.

At that moment it seemed to him that the queen of spades smiled ironically, and winked her eye at him. He was struck by her remarkable resemblance. . . .

"The old Countess!" he exclaimed, seized with terror. Chekalinsky gathered up his winnings. For some time Hermann remained perfectly motionless. When at last he left the table, there was a general commotion in the room.

"Splendidly punted!" said the players. Chekalinsky shuffled the cards afresh, and the game went on as usual.

Hermann went out of his mind, and is now confined in room number seventeen of the Oboukhoff Hospital. He never answers any questions, but he constantly mutters with unusual rapidity: "Three, seven, ace! Three, seven, queen!"

Lizaveta Ivanovna has married a very amiable young man, a son of the former steward of the old Countess. He is in the service of the State somewhere, and is in receipt of a good income. Lizaveta is also supporting a poor relative.

Tomsky has been promoted to the rank of captain, and has become the husband of the Princess Pauline.

A Personal Magnet

O. Henry

J eff Peters has been engaged in as many schemes for making money as there are recipes for cooking rice in Charleston, S.C.

Best of all I like to hear him tell of his earlier days when he sold liniments and cough cures on street corners, living hand to mouth, heart to heart with the people, throwing heads or tails with fortune for his last coin.

"I struck Fisher Hill, Arkansaw," said he, "in a buckskin suit, moccasins, long hair and a thirty-carat diamond ring that I got from an actor in Texarkana. I don't know what he ever did with the pocket knife I swapped him for it.

"I was Dr. Waugh-hoo, the celebrated Indian medicine man. I carried only one best bet just then, and that was Resurrection Bitters. It was made of life-giving plants and herbs accidentally discovered by Ta-qua-la, the beautiful wife of the Chief of the Choctaw Nation, while gathering truck to garnish a platter of boiled dog for the annual corn dance.

"Business hadn't been good at the last town, so I only had five dollars. I went to the Fisher Hill druggist and he credited me for half-a-gross of eight-ounce bottles and corks. I had the labels and ingredients in my valise, left over from the last town. Life began to look rosy again after I got to my hotel room with the water running from the tap, and the Resurrection Bitters lining up on the table by the dozen.

"Fake? No, sir. There was two dollars' worth of fluid extract of cinchona and a dime's worth of aniline in that half gross of bitters. I've gone through towns years afterwards and had folks ask for 'em again.

"I hired a wagon that night and commenced selling the bitters on Main Street. Fisher Hill was a low, malarial town; and a compound hypothetical pneumo-cardiac antiscorbutic tonic was just what I diagnosed the crowd as needing. The bitters started off like sweetbreads on toast at a vegetarian dinner. I had sold two dozen at fifty cents apiece when I felt somebody pull my coat tail. I knew what that meant; so I climbed down and sneaked a five-dollar bill into the hand of a man with a German silver star on his lapel.

"'Constable,' says I, 'it's a fine night.'

"'Have you got a city licence,' he asks, 'to sell this illegitimate essence of spooju that you flatter by the name of medicine?'

"'I have not,' says I. 'I didn't know you had a city. If I can find it to-morrow I'll take one out if it's necessary.'

"'I'll have to close you up till you do,' says the constable.

"I quit selling and went back to the hotel. I was talking to the landlord about it.

"'Oh, you won't stand no show in Fisher Hill,' says he. 'Dr. Hoskins, the only doctor here, is a brother-in-law of the Mayor, and they won't allow no fake doctor to practise in town.'

"'I don't practise medicine,' says I. 'I've got a State peddler's licence, and I take out a city one wherever they demand it.'

"I went to the Mayor's office the next morning and they told me he hadn't showed up yet. They didn't know when he'd be down. So Doc Waugh-hoo hunches down again in a hotel chair and lights a jimpson-weed regalia, and waits.

"By and by a young man in a blue necktie slips into the chair next to me and asks the time.

"'Half-past ten,' says I, 'and you are Andy Tucker. I've seen you work. Wasn't it you that put up the Great Cupid Combination package on the Southern States? Let's see, it was a Chilean diamond engagement ring, a wedding ring, a potato masher, a bottle of soothing syrup and Dorothy Vernon – all for fifty cents.'

"Andy was pleased to hear that I remembered him. He was a good street man; and he was more than that – he respected his profession, and he was satisfied with 300 per cent profit. He had plenty of offers to go into the illegitimate drug and garden-seed business; but he was never to be tempted off of the straight path.

"I wanted a partner, so Andy and me agreed to go out together. I told him about the situation in Fisher Hill and how finances was low on account of the local mixture of politics and jalap. Andy had just got in on the train that morning. He was pretty low himself, and was going to canvass the town for a few dollars to build a new battleship by popular subscription at Eureka Springs. So we went out and sat on the porch and talked it over.

"The next morning at eleven o'clock when I was sitting there alone, an Uncle Tom shuffles into the hotel and asked for the doctor to come and see Judge Banks, who, it seems, was the Mayor and a mighty sick man.

" 'I'm no doctor,' says I. 'Why don't you go and get the doctor?'

" 'Boss,' says he, 'Doc Hoskins am done gone twenty miles in de country to see some sick persons. He's de only doctor in de town, and Massa Banks am powerful bad off. He sent me to ask you to please, suh, come.'

" 'As man to man,' says I, 'I'll go and look him over.' So I put a bottle of Resurrection Bitters in my pocket and goes up on the hill to the Mayor's mansion, the finest house in town, with a mansard roof and two cast-iron dogs on the lawn.

"This Mayor Banks was in bed all but his whiskers and feet. He was making internal noises that would have had everybody in San Francisco hiking for the parks. A young man was standing by the bed holding a cup of water.

" 'Doc,' says the Mayor, 'I'm awful sick. I'm about to die. Can't you do nothing for me?'

" 'Mr. Mayor,' says I, 'I'm not a regular preordained disciple of S. Q. Lapius. I never took a course in a medical college,' says I. 'I've just come as a fellow man to see if I could be of assistance.'

" 'I'm deeply obliged,' says he. 'Doc Waugh-hoo, this is my nephew, Mr. Biddle. He has tried to alleviate my distress, but without success. Oh, Lordy! Ow-ow-ow!!' he sings out.

"I nods at Mr. Biddle and sets down by the bed and feels the Mayor's pulse. 'Let me see your liver – your tongue, I mean,' says I. Then I turns up the lids of his eyes and looks close at the pupils of 'em.

" 'How long have you been sick?' I asked.

" 'I was taken down – ow-ouch – last night,' says the Mayor. 'Gimme something for it, Doc, won't you?'

" 'Mr. Fiddle,' says I, 'raise the window shade a bit, will you?'

" 'Biddle,' says the young man. 'Do you feel like you could eat some ham and eggs, Uncle James?'

" 'Mr. Mayor,' says I, after laying my ear to his right shoulder-blade and listening, 'you've got a bad attack of super-inflammation of the right clavicle of the harpsichord!'

" 'Good Lord!' says he, with a groan. 'Can't you rub something on it, or set it or anything?'

"I picks up my hat and starts for the door.

" 'You ain't going, Doc?' says the Mayor with a howl. 'You ain't going away and leave me to die with this – superfluity of the clapboards, are you?'

" 'Common humanity, Dr. Whoa-ha,' says Mr. Biddle, 'ought to prevent your deserting a fellow human in distress.'

" 'Dr. Waugh-hoo, when you get through ploughing,' says I. And then I walks back to the bed and throws back my long hair.

" 'Mr. Mayor,' says I, 'there is only one hope for you. Drugs will do you no good. But there is another power higher yet, although drugs are high enough,' says I.

" 'And what is that?' says he.

" 'Scientific demonstrations,' says I. 'The triumph of mind over sarsaparilla. The belief that there is no pain and sickness except what is produced when we ain't feeling well. Declare yourself in arrears. Demonstrate.'

" 'What is this paraphernalia you speak of, Doc?' asks the Mayor.

" 'I am speaking,' says I, 'of the great doctrine of psychic financiering – of the enlightened school of long-distance, sub-conscientious treatment of fallacies and meningitis – of that wonderful indoor sport known as personal magnetism.'

" 'Can you work it, Doc?' asks the Mayor.

" 'I'm one of the Sole Sanhedrims and Ostensible Hooplas of the Inner Pulpit,' says I. 'The lame walk and the blind rubber whenever I make a pass at 'em. I am a medium, a coloratura hypnotist and a spirituous control. It was only through me at the recent séances at Ann Arbor that the late President of the Vinegar Bitters Company could revisit the earth to communicate with his sister Jane. You see me peddling medicine on the streets,' says I, 'to the poor. I don't practise personal magnetism on them. I do not drag it in the dust,' says I, 'because they haven't got the dust.'

" 'Will you treat my case?' asks the Mayor.

" 'Listen,' says I. 'I've had a good deal of trouble with medical societies everywhere I've been. I don't practise medicine. But, to save your life, I'll give you the psychic treatment if you'll agree as mayor not to push the licence question.'

" 'Of course I will,' says he. 'And now get to work, Doc, for them pains are coming on again.'

" 'My fee will be two hundred and fifty dollars, cure guaranteed in two treatments,' says I.

" 'All right,' says the Mayor. 'I'll pay it. I guess my life's worth that much.'

"I sat down by the bed and looked him straight in the eye.

" 'Now,' says I, 'get your mind off the disease. You ain't sick. You haven't got a heart or a clavicle or a funny bone or brains or anything. You haven't got any pain. Declare error. Now you feel the pain that you didn't have leaving, don't you?'

" 'I do feel some little better, Doc,' says the Mayor, 'darned if I don't. Now state a few lies about my not having this swelling in my left side, and I think I could be propped up and have some sausage and buck-wheat cakes.'

"I made a few passes with my hands.

" 'Now,' says I, 'the inflammation's gone. The right lobe of the perihelion has subsided. You're getting sleepy. You can't hold your eyes open any longer. For the present the disease is checked. Now, you are asleep.'

"The Mayor shut his eyes slowly and began to snore.

" 'You observe, Mr. Tiddle,' says I, 'the wonders of modern science.'

" 'Biddle,' says he. 'When will you give Uncle the rest of the treatment, Dr. Pooh-pooh?'

" 'Waugh-hoo,' says I. 'I'll come back at eleven to-morrow.

When he wakes up give him eight drops of turpentine and three pounds of steak. Good morning.'

"The next morning I went back on time. 'Well, Mr. Biddle,' says I, when he opened the bedroom door, 'and how is Uncle this morning?'

" 'He seems much better,' says the young man.

"The Mayor's colour and pulse was fine. I gave him another treatment, and he said the last of the pain left him.

" 'Now,' says I, 'you'd better stay in bed for a day or two, and you'll be all right. It's a good thing I happened to be in Fisher Hill, Mr. Mayor,' says I, 'for all the remedies in the cornucopia that the regular schools of medicine use couldn't have saved you. And now that error has flew and pain proved a perjurer, let's allude to a cheerfuller subject – say the fee of two hundred and fifty dollars. No cheques, please, I hate to write my name on the back of a cheque almost as bad as I do on the front.'

" 'I've got the cash here,' says the Mayor, pulling a pocket-book from under his pillow.

"He counts out five fifty-dollar notes and holds 'em in his hand.

" 'Bring the receipt,' he says to Biddle.

"I signed the receipt and the Mayor handed me the money. I put it in my inside pocket careful.

" 'Now do your duty, officer,' says the Mayor, grinning much unlike a sick man.

"Mr. Biddle lays his hand on my arm.

" 'You're under arrest, Dr. Waugh-hoo, alias Peters,' says he, 'for practising medicine without authority under the State law.'

" 'Who are you?' I asks.

" 'I'll tell you who he is,' says Mr. Mayor, sitting up in bed. 'He's a detective employed by the State Medical Society. He's been following you over five counties. He came to me yesterday and we fixed up this scheme to catch you. I guess you won't do any more doctoring around these parts, Mr. Fakir. What was it you said I had, Doc,' the Mayor laughs, 'compound – well it wasn't softening of the brain, I guess, anyway.'

" 'A detective,' says I.

" 'Correct,' says Biddle. 'I'll have to turn you over to the Sheriff.'

" 'Let's see you do it,' says I, and I grabs Biddle by the throat and half throws him out the window, but he pulls a gun and sticks it under my chin, and I stand still. Then he puts handcuffs on me, and takes the money out of my pocket.

" 'I witness,' says he, 'that they're the same bills that you and I marked, Judge Banks. I'll turn them over to the Sheriff when we get to his office, and he'll send you a receipt. They'll have to be used as evidence in the case.'

" 'All right, Mr. Biddle,' says the Mayor. 'And now, Doc Waugh-hoo,' he goes on, 'why don't you demonstrate? Can't you pull the cork out of your magnetism with your teeth and hocus-pocus them handcuffs off?'

" 'Come on, officer,' says I, dignified. 'I may as well make the best of it.' And then I turns to old Banks and rattles my chains.

" 'Mr. Mayor,' says I, 'the time will come soon when you'll believe that personal magnetism is a success. And you'll be sure that it succeeded in this case, too.'

"And I guess it did.

"When we got nearly to the gate, I says: 'We might meet somebody now, Andy. I reckon you better take 'em off, and—' Hey? Why, of course it was Andy Tucker. That was his scheme; and that's how we got the capital to go into business together.' "

The House and the Brain

Bulwer Lytton

A friend of mine, who is a man of letters and a philosopher, said to me one day, as if between jest and earnest, "Fancy! since we last met I have discovered a haunted house in the midst of London."

"Really haunted, – and by what? – ghosts?"

"Well, I can't answer that question; all I know is this: six weeks ago my wife and I were in search of a furnished apartment. Passing a quiet street, we saw on the window of one of the houses a bill, 'Apartments, Furnished.' The situation suited us; we entered the house, liked the rooms, engaged them by the week – and left them the third day. No power on earth could have reconciled my wife to stay longer; and I don't wonder at it."

"What did you see?"

"Excuse me; I have no desire to be ridiculed as a superstitious dreamer – nor, on the other hand, could I ask you to accept on my affirmation what you would hold to be incredible without the evidence of your own senses. Let me only say this, it was not so much what we saw or heard (in which you might fairly suppose that we were the dupes of our own excited fancy, or the victims of imposture in others) that drove us away, as it was an indefinable terror which seized both of us whenever we passed by the door of a certain unfurnished room, in which we neither saw nor heard anything. And the strangest marvel of all was, that for once in my life I agreed with my wife, silly woman though she be – and allowed, after the third night, that it was impossible to stay a fourth in that house. Accordingly, on the fourth morning I summoned the woman who kept the house and attended on us, and told her that the rooms did not quite suit us, and we would not stay out our week. She said dryly, 'I know why; you have stayed longer than any other lodger. Few ever stayed a second night; none before you a third. But I take it they have been very kind to you.'

" 'They – who?' I asked, affecting to smile.

" 'Why, they who haunt the house, whoever they are. I don't mind them. I remember them many years ago, when I lived in this house, not as a servant; but I know they will be the death of me some day. I don't care, – I'm old, and must die soon anyhow; and then I shall be with them, and in this house still.' The woman spoke with so dreary a calmness that really it was a sort of awe that prevented my conversing with her further. I paid for my week, and too happy were my wife and I to get off so cheaply."

"You excite my curiosity," said I; "nothing I should like better than to sleep in a haunted house. Pray give me the address of the one which you left so ignominiously."

My friend gave me the address; and when we parted, I walked straight toward the house thus indicated.

It is situated on the north side of Oxford Street, in a dull but respectable thoroughfare. I found the house shut up, – no bill at the window, and no response to my knock. As I was turning away, a beer-boy, collecting pewter pots at the neighboring areas, said to me, "Do you want any one at that house, sir?"

"Yes, I heard it was to be let."

"Let! – why, the woman who kept it is dead, – has been dead these three weeks, and no one can be found to stay there, though Mr. J— offered ever so much. He offered mother, who chars for him, £1 a week just to open and shut the windows, and she would not."

"Would not! – and why?"

"The house is haunted; and the old woman who kept it was found dead in her bed, with her eyes wide open. They say the devil strangled her."

"Pooh! You speak of Mr. J—. Is he the owner of the house?"

"Yes."

"Where does he live?"

"In G— Street, No. –"

"What is he? In any business?"

"No, sir, – nothing particular; a single gentleman."

I gave the potboy the gratuity earned by his liberal information, and proceeded to Mr. J—, in G— Street, which was close by the street that boasted the haunted house. I was lucky enough to find Mr. J— at home – an elderly man with intelligent countenance and prepossessing manners.

I communicated my name and my business frankly. I said I heard the house was considered to be haunted, – that I had a strong desire to examine a house with so equivocal a reputation; that I should be greatly obliged if he would allow me to hire it, though only for a night. I was willing to pay for that privilege whatever he might be inclined to ask. "Sir," said Mr. J—, with great courtesy, "the house is at your service, for as short or as long a time as you please. Rent is out of the question, – the obligation will be on my side should you be able to discover the cause of the strange phenomena which at present deprive it of all value. I cannot let it, for I cannot even get a servant to keep it in order or answer the door. Unluckily the house is haunted, if I may use that expression, not only by night, but by day; though at night the disturbances are of a more unpleasant and sometimes of a more alarming character. The poor old woman who died in it three weeks ago was a pauper whom I took out of a workhouse; for in her childhood she had been known to some of my family, and had once been in such good circumstances that she had rented that house off my uncle. She was a woman of superior education and strong mind, and was the only person I could ever induce to remain in the house. Indeed, since her death, which was sudden, and the coroner's inquest, which gave it a notoriety in the neighborhood, I have so despaired of finding any person to take charge of the house, much more a tenant, that I would willingly let it rent free for a year to anyone who would pay its rates and taxes."

"How long is it since the house acquired this sinister character?"

"That I can scarcely tell you, but very many years since. The old woman I spoke of, said it was haunted when she rented it between thirty and forty years ago. The fact is, that my life has been spent in the East Indies, and in the civil service of the

Company. I returned to England last year, on inheriting the fortune of an uncle, among whose possessions was the house in question. I found it shut up and uninhabited. I was told that it was haunted, that no one would inhabit it. I smiled at what seemed to me so idle a story. I spent some money in repairing it, added to its old-fashioned furniture a few modern articles, advertised it, and obtained a lodger for a year. He was a colonel on half pay. He came in with his family, a son and a daughter, and four or five servants: they all left the house the next day; and, although each of them declared that he had seen something different from that which had scared the others, that something still was equally terrible to all. I really could not in conscience sue, nor even blame, the colonel for breach of agreement. Then I put in the old woman I have spoken of, and she was empowered to let the house in apartments. I never had one lodger who stayed more than three days. I do not tell you their stories – to no two lodgers have there been exactly the same phenomena repeated. It is better that you should judge for yourself, than enter the house with an imagination influenced by previous narratives; only be prepared to see and to hear something or other, and take whatever precautions you yourself please."

"Have you never had a curiosity yourself to pass a night in that house?"

"Yes. I passed not a night, but three hours in broad daylight alone in that house. My curiosity is not satisfied, but it is quenched. I have no desire to renew the experiment. You cannot complain, you see, sir, that I am not sufficiently candid; and unless your interest be exceedingly eager and your nerves unusually strong, I honestly add, that I advise you *not* to pass a night in that house."

"My interest *is* exceedingly keen," said I; "and though only a coward will boast of his nerves in situations wholly unfamiliar to him, yet my nerves have been seasoned in such variety of danger that I have the right to rely on them – even in a haunted house."

Mr. J— said very little more; he took the keys of the house out of his bureau, gave them to me, and thanking him cordially for his frankness, and his urbane concession to my wish, I carried off my prize.

Impatient for the experiment, as soon as I reached home, I summoned my confidential servant – a young man of gay spirits, fearless temper, and as free from superstitious prejudice as anyone I could think of.

"F—," said I, "you remember in Germany how disappointed we were at not finding a ghost in that old castle, which was said to be haunted by a headless apparition? Well, I have heard of a house in London which, I have reason to hope, is decidedly haunted. I mean to sleep there to-night. From what I hear, there is no doubt that something will allow itself to be seen or to be heard – something, perhaps, excessively horrible. Do you think if I take you with me, I may rely on your presence of mind, whatever may happen?"

"Oh, sir, pray trust me," answered F—, grinning with delight.

"Very well; then here are the keys of the house, – this is the address. Go now, – select for me any bedroom you please; and since the house has not been inhabited for weeks, make up a good fire, air the bed well – see, of course, that there are candles as well as fuel. Take with you my revolver and my dagger – so much for my weapons; arm yourself equally well; and if we are not a match for a dozen ghosts, we shall be but a sorry couple of Englishmen."

I was engaged for the rest of the day on business so urgent that I had not leisure to think much on the nocturnal adventure to which I had plighted my honor. I dined alone, and very late, and while dining, read, as is my habit. I selected one of the volumes of Macaulay's Essays. I thought to myself that I would take the book with me; there was so much of healthfulness in the style, and practical life in the subjects, that it would serve as an antidote against the influences of superstitious fancy.

Accordingly, about half-past nine, I put the book into my pocket, and strolled leisurely toward the haunted house. I took with me a favorite dog: an exceedingly sharp, bold, and vigilant bull terrier – a dog fond of prowling about strange, ghostly corners and passages at night in search of rats; a dog of dogs for a ghost.

I reached the house, knocked, and my servant opened with a cheerful smile.

We did not stay long in the drawing-rooms – in fact, they felt so damp and so chilly that I was glad to get to the fire upstairs. We locked the doors of the drawing-rooms – a precaution which, I should observe, we had taken with all the rooms we had searched below. The bedroom my servant had selected for me was the best on the floor – a large one, with two windows fronting the street. The four-posted bed, which took up no inconsiderable space, was opposite to the fire, which burned clear and bright; a door in the wall to the left, between the bed and the window, communicated with the room which my servant appropriated to himself. This last was a small room with a sofa bed, and had no communication with the landing place – no other door but that which conducted to the bedroom I was to occupy. On either side of my fireplace was a cupboard without locks, flush with the wall, and covered with the same dull-brown paper. We examined these cupboards – only hooks to suspend female dresses, nothing else; we sounded the walls – evidently solid, the outer walls of the building. Having finished the survey of these apartments, warmed myself a few moments, and lighted my cigar, I then, still accompanied by F—, went forth to complete my reconnoiter. In the landing place there was another door; it was closed firmly. "Sir," said my servant, in surprise, "I unlocked this door with all the others when I first came; it cannot have got locked from the inside, for—"

Before he had finished his sentence, the door, which neither of us then was touching, opened quietly of itself. We looked at each other a single instant. The same thought seized both – some human agency might be detected here. I rushed in first, my servant followed. A small, blank, dreary room without furniture; a few empty boxes and hampers in a corner; a small window; the shutters closed; not even a fireplace; no other door but that by which we had entered; no carpet on the floor, and the floor seemed very old, uneven, worm-eaten, mended here and there, as was shown by the whiter patches on the wood; but no living being, and no visible place in which a living being could have hidden. As we stood gazing round, the door by which we had entered closed as quietly as it had before opened; we were imprisoned.

For the first time I felt a creep of indefinable horror. Not so my servant. "Why, they don't think to trap us, sir; I could break that trumpery door with a kick of my foot."

"Try first if it will open to your hand," said I, shaking off the vague apprehension that had seized me, "while I unclose the shutters and see what is without."

I unbarred the shutters – the window looked on the little back yard I have before described; there was no ledge without – nothing to break the sheer descent of the wall. No man getting out of that window would have found any footing till he had fallen on the stones below.

F—, meanwhile, was vainly attempting to open the door. He now turned round to me and asked my permission to use force. And I should here state, in justice to the servant, that, far from evincing any superstitious terrors, his nerve, composure, and even gaiety amidst circumstances so extraordinary, compelled my admiration, and made me congratulate myself on having secured a companion in every way fitted to the occasion. I willingly gave him the permission he required. But though he was a remarkably strong man, his force was as idle as his milder efforts; the door did not even shake to his stoutest kick. Breathless and panting, he desisted. I then tried the door myself, equally in vain. As I ceased from the effort, again that creep of horror came over me; but this time it was more cold and stubborn. I felt as if some strange and ghastly exhalation were rising up from the chinks of that rugged floor, and filling the atmosphere with a venomous influence hostile to human life. The door now very slowly and quietly opened as of its own accord. We precipitated ourselves into the landing place. We both saw a large, pale light – as large as the human figure but shapeless and unsubstantial – move before us, and ascend the stairs that led from the landing into the attics. I followed the light, and my servant followed me. It entered, to the right of the landing, a small garret, of which the door stood open. I entered in the same instant. The light then collapsed into a small globule, exceedingly brilliant and vivid, rested a moment on a bed in the corner, quivered, and vanished. We approached the bed and examined it – a half-tester, such as is commonly found in attics devoted to servants. On the drawers that stood near it we perceived an old faded silk kerchief, with the needle still left in a rent half repaired. The kerchief was covered with dust; probably it had belonged to the old woman who had last died in that house, and this might have been her sleeping room. I had sufficient curiosity to open the drawers: there were a few odds and ends of female dress, and two letters tied round with a narrow ribbon of faded yellow. I took the liberty to possess myself of the letters. We found nothing else in the room worth noticing – nor did the light reappear; but we distinctly heard as we turned to go, a pattering footfall on the floor, just before us. We went through the other attics (in all four), the footfall still preceding us. Nothing to be seen – nothing but the footfall heard. I had the letters in my hand; just as I was descending the stairs I distinctly felt my wrist seized, and a faint, soft effort made to draw the letters from my clasp. I only held them the more tightly, and the effort ceased.

We regained the bedchamber appropriated to myself, and I then remarked that my dog had not followed us when we had left it. He was thrusting himself close to the fire, and trembling. I was impatient to examine the letters; and while I read them, my servant opened a little box in which he had deposited the weapons I had ordered him to bring, took them out, placed them on a table close at my bed head, and then occupied himself in soothing the dog, who, however, seemed to heed him very little.

The letters were short – they were dated; the dates exactly thirty-five years ago. They were evidently from a lover to his mistress, or a husband to some young wife. Not only the terms of expression, but a distinct reference to a former voyage, indicated the writer to have been a seafarer. The spelling and handwriting were those of a man imperfectly educated, but still the language itself was forcible. In the expressions of endearment there was a kind of rough, wild love; but here and there were dark unintelligible hints at some secret not of love – some secret that seemed of crime. "We ought to love each other," was one of the sentences I remember, "for how everyone else would execrate us if all was known." Again: "Don't let anyone be in the same room with you at night – you talk in your sleep." And again: "What's done can't be undone; and I tell you there's nothing against us unless the dead could come to life."

Here there was interlined in a better handwriting (a female's), "They do!" At the end of the letter latest in date the same female hand had written these words: "Lost at sea the 4th of June, the same day as—"

I put down the letters, and began to muse over their contents.

Fearing, however, that the train of thought into which I fell might unsteady my nerves, I fully determined to keep my mind in a fit state to cope with whatever of the marvelous the advancing night might bring forth. I roused myself; laid the letters on the table; stirred up the fire, which was still bright and cheering; and opened my volume of Macaulay. I read quietly enough till about half past eleven. I then threw myself dressed upon the bed, and told my servant he might retire to his own room, but must keep himself awake. I bade him leave open the door between the two rooms. Thus alone, I kept two candles burning on the table by my bed head. I placed my watch beside the weapons, and calmly resumed my Macaulay. Opposite to me the fire burned clear; and on the hearth rug, seemingly asleep, lay the dog. In about twenty minutes I felt an exceedingly cold air pass by my cheek, like a sudden draught. I fancied the door to my right, communicating with the landing place, must have got open; but no, it was closed. I then turned my glance to my left, and saw the flame of the candles violently swayed as by a wind. At the same moment the watch beside the revolver softly slid from the table – softly, softly; no visible hand – it was gone. I sprang up, seizing the revolver with the one hand, the dagger with the other; I was not willing that my weapons should share the fate of the watch. Thus armed, I looked round the floor – no sign of the watch. Three slow, loud, distinct knocks were now heard at the bed head; my servant called out, "Is that you, sir?"

"No; be on your guard."

The dog now roused himself and sat on his haunches, his ears moving quickly backward and forward. He kept his eyes fixed on me with a look so strange that he concentered all my attention on himself. Slowly he rose up, all his hair bristling, and stood perfectly rigid, and with the same wild stare. I had no time, however, to examine the dog. Presently my servant emerged from his room; and if ever I saw horror in the human face, it was then. I should not have recognized him had we met in the street, so altered was every lineament. He passed by me quickly, saying, in a whisper that seemed scarcely to come from his lips, "Run, run! it is after me!" He gained the door to the landing, pulled it open, and rushed forth. I followed him into the landing involuntarily, calling him to stop; but without heeding me, he bounded down the stairs, clinging to the balusters, and taking several steps at a time. I heard, where I stood, the street door open – heard it again clap to. I was left alone in the haunted house.

It was but for a moment that I remained undecided whether or not to follow my servant; pride and curiosity alike forbade so dastardly a flight. I reentered my room, closing the door after me, and proceeded cautiously into the interior chamber. I encountered nothing to justify my servant's terror. I again carefully examined the walls, to see if there were any concealed door. I could find me trace of none – not even a seam in the dull-brown paper with which the room was hung. How, then, had the *Thing*, whatever it was, which had so scared him, obtained ingress except through my own chamber?

I returned to my room, shut and locked the door that opened upon the interior one, and stood on the hearth, expectant and prepared. I now perceived that the dog had slunk into an angle of the wall, and was pressing himself close against it, as if literally striving to force his way into it. I approached the animal and spoke to it; the poor brute was evidently beside itself with terror. It showed all its teeth, the slaver dropping from its jaws, and would certainly have bitten me if I had touched it. It did not seem to recognize me. Whoever has seen at the Zoological Gardens a rabbit, fascinated by a serpent, cowering in a corner, may form some idea of the anguish which the dog exhibited. Finding all efforts to soothe the animal in vain, and fearing that his bite might be as venomous in that state as in the madness of hydrophobia, I left him alone, placed my weapons on the table beside the fire, seated myself, and recommenced my Macaulay.

Perhaps, in order not to appear seeking credit for a courage, or rather a coolness, which the reader may conceive I exaggerate, I may be pardoned if I pause to indulge in one or two egotistical remarks.

As I hold presence of mind, or what is called courage, to be precisely proportioned to familiarity with the circumstances that lead to it, so I should say that I had been long sufficiently familiar with all experiments that appertain to the marvelous. I had witnessed many very extraordinary phenomena in various parts of the world – phenomena that would be either totally disbelieved if I stated them, or ascribed to supernatural agencies. Now, my theory is that the supernatural is the impossible, and that what is called supernatural is only a something in the laws of Nature of which we have been hitherto ignorant. Therefore, if a ghost rises before me, I have not the right to say, "So, then, the supernatural is possible;" but rather, "So, then, the apparition of a ghost is, contrary to received opinion, within the laws of Nature – that is, not supernatural."

Now, in all that I had hitherto witnessed, and indeed in all the wonders which the amateurs of mystery in our age record as facts, a material living agency is always required. On the Continent you will find still magicians who assert that they can raise spirits. Assume for the moment that they assert truly, still the living material form of the magician is present; and he is the material agency by which, from some constitutional peculiarities, certain strange phenomena are represented to your natural senses.

Accept, again, as truthful, the tales of spirit manifestation in America – musical or other sounds; writings on paper, produced by no discernible hand; articles of furniture moved without apparent human agency; or the actual sight and touch of hands, to which no bodies seem to belong – still there must be found the *medium*, or living being, with constitutional peculiarities capable of obtaining these signs. In fine, in all such marvels, supposing even that there is no imposture, there must be a human being like ourselves by whom, or through whom, the effects presented to human beings are produced. It is so with the now familiar phenomena of mesmerism or electro-biology; the mind of the person operated on is affected through a material living agent. Nor, supposing it true that a mesmerized patient can respond to the will or passes of a mesmerizer a hundred miles distant, is the response less occasioned by a material being; it may be through a material fluid – call it

Electric, call it Odic, call it what you will – which has the power of traversing space and passing obstacles, that the material effect is communicated from one to the other. Hence, all that I had hitherto witnessed, or expected to witness, in this strange house, I believed to be occasioned through some agency or medium as mortal as myself; and this idea necessarily prevented the awe with which those who regard as supernatural things that are not within the ordinary operations of Nature, might have been impressed by the adventures of that memorable night.

As, then, it was my conjecture that all that was presented, or would be presented to my senses, must originate in some human being gifted by constitution with the power so to present them, and having some motive so to do, I felt an interest in my theory which, in its way, was rather philosophical than superstitious. And I can sincerely say that I was in as tranquil a temper for observation as any practical experimentalist could be in await-ing the effects of some rare, though perhaps perilous, chemical combination. Of course, the more I kept my mind detached from fancy, the more the temper fitted for observation would be obtained; and I therefore riveted eye and thought on the strong daylight sense in the page of my Macaulay.

I now became aware that something interposed between the page and the light – the page was overshadowed. I looked up, and I saw what I shall find it very difficult, perhaps impossible, to describe.

It was a Darkness shaping itself forth from the air in very undefined outline. I cannot say it was of a human form, and yet it had more resemblance to a human form, or rather shadow, than to anything else. As it stood, wholly apart and distinct from the air and the light around it, its dimensions seemed gigantic, the summit nearly touching the ceiling. While I gazed, a feeling of intense cold seized me. An iceberg before me could not more have chilled me; nor could the cold of an iceberg have been more purely physical. I feel convinced that it was not the cold caused by fear. As I continued to gaze, I thought – but this I cannot say with precision – that I distinguished two eyes looking down on me from the height. One moment I fancied that I distinguished them clearly, the next they seemed gone; but still two rays of a pale-blue light frequently shot through the darkness, as from the height on which I half believed, half doubted, that I had encountered the eyes.

I strove to speak – my voice utterly failed me; I could only think to myself, "Is this fear? It is *not* fear!" I strove to rise – in vain; I felt as if weighed down by an irresistible force. Indeed, my impression was that of an immense and overwhelming Power opposed to my volition – that sense of utter inadequacy to cope with a force beyond man's, which one may feel *physically* in a storm at sea, in a conflagration, or when confronting some terrible wild beast, or rather, perhaps, the shark of the ocean, I felt *morally*. Opposed to my will was another will, as far superior to its strength as storm, fire, and shark are superior in material force to the force of man.

And now, as this impression grew on me – now came, at last, horror, horror to a degree that no words can convey. Still I retained pride, if not courage; and in my own mind I said, "This is horror; but it is not fear; unless I fear I cannot be harmed; my reason rejects this thing; it is an illusion – I do not fear." With a violent effort I succeeded at last in stretching out my hand toward the weapon on the table; as I did so, on the arm and shoulder I received a strange shock, and my arm fell to my side powerless. And now, to add to my horror, the light began slowly to wane from the candles – they were not, as it were, extinguished, but their flame seemed very gradually withdrawn; it was the same with the fire – the light was extracted from the fuel; in a few minutes the room was in utter darkness. The dread that came over me, to be thus in the dark with that dark Thing, whose power was so intensely felt, brought a reaction of nerve. In fact, terror had reached that climax, that either my senses must have deserted me, or I must have burst through the spell. I did burst through it. I found voice, though the voice was a shriek. I remember that I broke forth with words like these, "I do not fear, my soul does not fear"; and at the same time I found strength to rise. Still in that profound gloom I rushed to one of the windows; tore aside the curtain; flung open the shutters; my first thought was – *light*. And when I saw the moon high, clear, and calm, I felt a joy that almost compensated for the previous terror. There was the moon, there was also the light from the gas lamps in the deserted slumberous street. I turned to look back into the room; the moon penetrated its shadow very palely and partially – but still there was light. The dark Thing, whatever it might be, was gone – except that I could yet see a dim shadow, which seemed the shadow of that shade, against the opposite wall.

My eye now rested on the table, and from under the table (which was without cloth or cover, – an old mahogany round table) there rose a hand, visible as far as the wrist. It was a hand, seemingly, as much of flesh and blood as my own, but the hand of an aged person, lean, wrinkled, small too – a woman's hand. That hand very softly closed on the two letters that lay on the table; hand and letters both vanished. There then came the same three loud, measured knocks I had heard at the bed head before this extraordinary drama had commenced.

As those sounds slowly ceased, I felt the whole room vibrate sensibly; and at the far end there rose, as from the floor, sparks or globules like bubbles of light, many colored – green, yellow, fire-red, azure. Up and down, to and fro, hither, thither as tiny Will-o'-the-Wisps, the sparks moved, slow or swift, each at its own caprice. A chair (as in the drawing-room below) was now advanced from the wall without apparent agency, and placed at the opposite side of the table. Suddenly, as forth from the chair, there grew a shape – a woman's shape. It was distinct as a shape of life – ghastly as a shape of death. The face was that of youth, with a strange, mournful beauty; the throat and shoulders were bare, the rest of the form in a loose robe of cloudy white. It began sleeking its long, yellow hair, which fell over its shoulders; its eyes were not turned toward me, but to the door; it seemed listening, watching, waiting. The shadow of the shade in the background grew darker; and again I thought I beheld the eyes gleaming out from the summit of the shadow – eyes fixed upon that shape.

As if from the door, though it did not open, there grew out another shape, equally distinct, equally ghastly – a man's shape, a young man's. It was in the dress of the last century, or rather in a likeness of such dress (for both the male shape and the female, though defined, were evidently unsubstantial, impalpable – simulacra, phantasms); and there was something incongruous, grotesque, yet fearful, in the contrast between the elaborate finery, the courtly precision of that old-fashioned garb, with its ruffles and lace and buckles, and the corpselike aspect and ghostlike stillness of the flitting wearer. Just as the male shape approached the female, the dark Shadow started from the wall, all three for a moment wrapped in darkness. When the pale light returned, the two phantoms were as if in the grasp of the Shadow that towered between them; and there was a blood stain on the breast of the female; and the phantom male was leaning on its phantom sword, and blood seemed trickling fast from the ruffles from the lace; and the darkness of the intermediate Shadow swallowed them up – they were gone. And again the bubbles of light shot, and sailed, and undulated, growing thicker and thicker and more wildly confused in their movements.

The closet door to the right of the fireplace now opened, and from the aperture there came the form of an aged woman. In her hand she held letters – the very letters over which I had seen *the* Hand close; and behind her I heard a footstep. She turned round as if to listen, and then she opened the letters and seemed to read; and over her shoulder I saw a livid face, the face as of a man long drowned, – bloated, bleached, seaweed tangled in its dripping hair; and at her feet lay a form as of a corpse; and beside the corpse there cowered a child, a miserable, squalid child, with famine in its cheeks and fear in its eyes. And as I looked in the old woman's face, the wrinkles and lines vanished, and it became a face of youth – hard-eyed, stony, but still youth; and the Shadow darted forth, and darkened over these phantoms as it had darkened over the last.

Nothing now was left but the Shadow, and on that my eyes were intently fixed, till again eyes grew out of the Shadow – malignant, serpent eyes. And the bubbles of light again rose and fell, and in their disordered, irregular, turbulent maze, mingled with the wan moonlight. And now from these globules themselves, as from the shell of an egg, monstrous things burst out; the air grew filled with them: larvæ so bloodless and so hideous that I can in no way describe them except to remind the reader of the swarming life which the solar microscope brings before his eyes in a drop of water – things transparent, supple, agile, chasing each other, devouring each other; forms like naught ever beheld by the naked eye. As the shapes were without symmetry, so their movements were without order. In their very vagrancies there was no sport; they came round me and round, thicker and faster and swifter, swarming over my head, crawling over my right arm, which was outstretched in involuntary command against all evil beings. Sometimes I felt myself touched, but not by them; invisible hands touched me. Once I felt the clutch as of cold, soft fingers at my throat. I was still equally conscious that if I gave way to fear I should be in bodily peril; and I concentered all my faculties in the single focus of resisting stubborn will. And I turned my sight from the Shadow; above all, from those strange serpent eyes – eyes that had now become distinctly visible. For there, though in naught else around me, I was aware that there was a WILL, and a will of intense, creative, working evil, which might crush down my own.

The pale atmosphere in the room began now to redden as if in the air of some near conflagration. The larvæ grew lurid as things that live in fire. Again the room vibrated; again were heard the three measured knocks; and again all things were swallowed up in the darkness of the dark Shadow, as if out of that darkness all had come, into that darkness all returned.

As the gloom receded, the Shadow was wholly gone. Slowly, as it had been withdrawn, the flame grew again into the candles on the table, again into the fuel in the grate. The whole room came once more calmly, healthfully into sight.

The two doors were still closed, the door communicating with the servant's room still locked. In the corner of the wall, into which he had so convulsively niched himself, lay the dog. I called to him – no movement; I approached – the animal was dead: his eyes protruded; his tongue out of his mouth; the froth gathered round his jaws. I took him in my arms; I brought him to the fire. I felt acute grief for the loss of my poor favorite – acute self-reproach; I accused myself of his death; I imagined he had died of fright. But what was my surprise on finding that his neck was actually broken. Had this been done in the dark? Must it not have been by a hand human as mine; must there not have been a human agency all the while in that room? Good cause to suspect it. I cannot tell. I cannot do more than state the fact fairly; the reader may draw his own inference.

Another surprising circumstance – my watch was restored to the table from which it had been so mysteriously withdrawn; but it had stopped at the very moment it was so withdrawn, nor, despite all the skill of the watchmaker, has it ever gone since – that is, it will go in a strange, erratic way for a few hours, and then come to a dead stop; it is worthless.

Nothing more chanced for the rest of the night. Nor, indeed, had I long to wait before the dawn broke. Not till it was broad daylight did I quit the haunted house. Before I did so, I revisited the little blind room in which my servant and myself had been for a time imprisoned. I had a strong impression – for which I could not account – that from that room had originated the mechanism of the phenomena, if I may use the term, which had been experienced in my chamber. And though I entered it now in the clear day, with the sun peering through the filmy window, I still felt, as I stood on its floors, the creep of the horror which I had first there experienced the night before, and which had been so aggravated by what had passed in my own chamber. I could not, indeed, bear to stay more than half a minute within those walls. I descended the stairs, and again I heard the footfall before me; and when I opened the street door, I thought I could distinguish a very low laugh. I gained my own home, expecting to find my runaway servant there; but he had not presented himself, nor did I hear more of him for three days, when I received a letter from him, dated from Liverpool to this effect:—

"Honored Sir, – I humbly entreat your pardon, though I can scarcely hope that you will think that I deserve it, unless – which Heaven forbid! – you saw what I did. I feel that it will be years before I can recover myself; and as to being fit for service, it is out of the question. I am therefore going to my brother-in-law at Melbourne. The ship sails to-morrow. Perhaps the long voyage may set me up. I do nothing now but start and tremble, and fancy it is behind me. I humbly beg you, honored sir, to order my clothes, and whatever wages are due to me, to be sent to my mother's, at Walworth, – John knows her address."

*   *   *

The letter ended with additional apologies, somewhat incoherent, and explanatory details as to effects that had been under the writer's charge.

This flight may perhaps warrant a suspicion that the man wished to go to Australia, and had been somehow or other fraudulently mixed up with the events of the night. I say nothing in refutation of that conjecture; rather, I suggest it as one that would seem to many persons the most probable solution of improbable occurrences. My belief in my own theory remained unshaken. I returned in the evening to the house, to bring away in a hack cab the things I had left there, with my poor dog's body. In this task I was not disturbed, nor did any incident worth note befall me, except that still, on ascending and descending the stairs, I heard the same footfall in advance. On leaving the house, I went to Mr. J——'s. He was at home. I returned him the keys, told him that my curiosity was sufficiently gratified, and was about to relate quickly what had passed, when he stopped me, and said, though with much politeness, that he had no longer any interest in a mystery which none had ever solved.

I determined at least to tell him of the two letters I had read, as well as of the extraordinary manner in which they had disappeared; and I then inquired if he thought they had been addressed to the woman who had died in the house, and if there were anything in her early history which could possibly confirm the dark suspicions to which the letters gave rise. Mr. J—— seemed startled, and, after musing a few moments, answered, "I am but little acquainted with the woman's earlier history, except as I before told you, that her family were known to mine. But you revive some vague reminiscences to her prejudice. I will make inquiries, and inform you of their result. Still, even if we could admit the popular superstition that a person who had been either the perpetrator or the victim of dark crimes in life could revisit, as a restless spirit, the scene in which those crimes had been committed, I should observe that the house was infested by strange sights and sounds before the old woman died – you smile – what would you say?"

"I would say this, that I am convinced, if we could get to the bottom of these mysteries, we should find a living human agency."

"What! you believe it is all an imposture? For what object?"

"Not an imposture in the ordinary sense of the word. If suddenly I were to sink into a deep sleep, from which you could not awake me, but in that sleep could answer questions with an accuracy which I could not pretend to when awake – tell you what money you had in your pocket, nay, describe your very thoughts – it is not necessarily an imposture, any more than it is necessarily supernatural. I should be, unconsciously to myself, under a mesmeric influence, conveyed to me from a distance by a human being who had acquired power over me by previous *rapport*."

"But if a mesmerizer could so affect another living being, can you suppose that a mesmerizer could also affect inanimate objects: move chairs, open and shut doors?"

"Or impress our senses with the belief in such effects – we never having been *en rapport* with the person acting on us? No. What is commonly called mesmerism could not do this; but there may be a power akin to mesmerism, and superior to it – the power that in the old days was called Magic. That such a power may extend to all inanimate objects of matter, I do not say; but if so, it would not be against Nature – it would be only a rare power in Nature which might be given to constitutions with certain peculiarities, and cultivated by practice to an extraordinary degree. That such a power might extend over the dead – that is, over certain thoughts and memories that the dead may still retain – and compel, not that which ought properly to be called the *Soul*, and which is far beyond human reach, but rather a phantom of what has been most earth-stained on earth, to make itself apparent to our senses, is a very ancient though obsolete theory upon which I will hazard no opinion. But I do not conceive the power would be super-natural. Let me illustrate what I mean from an experiment which Paracelsus describes as not difficult, and which the author of the 'Curiosities of Literature' cites as credible: A flower perishes; you burn it. Whatever were the elements of that flower while it lived are gone, dispersed, you know not whither; you can never discover nor re-collect them. But you can, by chemistry, out of the burned dust of that flower, raise a spectrum of the flower, just as it seemed in life. It may be the same with the human being. The soul has as much escaped you as the essence or elements of the flower. Still you may make a spectrum of it. And this phantom, though in the popular superstition it is held to be the soul of the departed, must not be confounded with the true soul; it is but the eidolon of the dead form. Hence, like the best-attested stories of ghosts or spirits, the thing that most strikes us is the absence of what we hold to be soul – that is, of superior emancipated intelligence. These apparitions come for little or no object – they seldom speak when they do come; if they speak, they utter no ideas above those of an ordinary person on earth. American spirit seers have published volumes of communications, in prose and verse, which they assert to be given in the names of the most illustrious dead: Shakespeare, Bacon – Heaven knows whom. Those communications, taking the best, are certainly not a whit of higher order than would be communications from living persons of fair talent and education; they are wondrously inferior to what Bacon, Shakespeare, and Plato said and wrote when on earth. Nor, what is more noticeable, do they ever contain an idea that was not on the earth before. Wonderful, therefore, as such phenomena may be (granting them to be truthful), I see much that philosophy may question, nothing that it is incumbent on philosophy to deny – namely, nothing supernatural. They are but ideas conveyed somehow or other (we have not yet discovered the means) from one mortal brain to another. Whether, in so doing, tables walk of their own accord, or fiendlike shapes appear in a magic circle, or bodiless hands rise and remove material objects, or a Thing of Darkness, such as presented itself to me, freeze our blood, – still am I persuaded that these are but agencies conveyed, as by electric wires, to my own brain from the brain of another. In some constitutions there is a natural chemistry, and those constitutions may produce chemical wonders – in others a natural fluid, call it electricity, and these may produce electric wonders. But the wonders differ from Normal Science in this – they are alike objectless, purposeless, puerile, frivolous. They lead on to no grand results; and therefore the world does not heed, and true sages have not cultivated them. But sure I am, that of all I saw or heard, a man, human as myself, was the remote originator; and I believe unconsciously to himself as to the exact effects produced, for this reason: no two persons, you say, have ever told you that they experienced exactly the same thing. Well, observe, no two persons ever experience exactly the same dream. If this were an ordinary imposture, the machinery would be arranged for results that would but little vary; if it were a supernatural agency permitted by the Almighty, it would surely be for some definite end. These phenomena belong to neither class; my persuasion is, that they originate in some brain now far distant; that that brain had no distinct volition in anything that occurred; that what does occur reflects but its devious, motley, ever-shifting, half-formed thoughts; in short, that it has been but the dreams of such a brain put into action and invested with a semi-substance. That this brain is of immense power, that it can set matter into movement, that it is malignant and destructive, I believe; some material force must have killed my dog; the same force might, for aught I know, have sufficed to kill myself, had I been as subjugated by terror as the dog, – had my intellect or my spirit given me no countervailing resistance in my will."

"It killed your dog – that is fearful! Indeed it is strange that no animal can be induced to stay in that house; not even a cat. Rats and mice are never found in it."

"The instincts of the brute creation detect influences deadly to their existence. Man's reason has a sense less subtle, because it has a resisting power more supreme. But enough; do you comprehend my theory?"

"Yes, though imperfectly – and I accept any crotchet (pardon the word), however odd, rather than embrace at once the notion of ghosts and hobgoblins we imbibed in our nurseries. Still, to my unfortunate house, the evil is the same. What on earth can I do with the house?"

"I will tell you what I would do. I am convinced from my own internal feelings that the small, unfurnished room at right angles to the door of the bedroom which I occupied, forms a starting point or receptacle for the influences which haunt the house; and I strongly advise you to have the walls opened, the floor removed – nay, the whole room pulled down. I observe that it is detached from the body of the house, built over the small backyard, and could be removed without injury to the rest of the building."

"And you think, if I did that—"

"You would cut off the telegraph wires. Try it. I am so persuaded that I am right, that I will pay half the expense if you will allow me to direct the operations."

"Nay, I am well able to afford the cost; for the rest allow me to write to you."

About ten days after I received a letter from Mr. J—, telling me that he had visited the house since I had seen him; that he had found the two letters I had described, replaced in the drawer from which I had taken them; that he had read them with misgivings like my own; that he had instituted a cautious inquiry about the woman to whom I rightly conjectured they had been written. It seemed that thirty-six years ago (a year before the date of the letters) she had married, against the wish of her relations, an American of very suspicious character; in fact, he was generally believed to have been a pirate. She herself was the daughter of very respectable tradespeople, and had served in the capacity of a nursery governess before her marriage. She had a brother, a widower, who was considered wealthy, and who had one child of about six years old. A month after the marriage the body of this brother was found in the Thames, near London Bridge; there seemed some marks of violence about his throat, but they were not deemed sufficient to warrant the inquest in any other verdict than that of "found drowned."

The American and his wife took charge of the little boy, the deceased brother having by his will left his sister the guardian of his only child – and in event of the child's death the sister inherited. The child died about six months afterwards – it was supposed to have been neglected and ill-treated. The neighbors deposed to have heard it shriek at night. The surgeon who had examined it after death said that it was emaciated as if from want of nourishment, and the body was covered with livid bruises. It seemed that one winter night the child had sought to escape; crept out into the back yard; tried to scale the wall; fallen back exhausted; and been found at morning on the stones in a dying state. But though there was some evidence of cruelty, there was none of murder; and the aunt and her husband had sought to palliate cruelty by alleging the exceeding stubbornness and perversity of the child, who was declared to be half-witted. Be that as it may, at the orphan's death the aunt inherited her brother's fortune. Before the first wedded year was out, the American quitted England abruptly, and never returned to it. He obtained a cruising vessel, which was lost in the Atlantic two years afterwards. The widow was left in affluence, but reverses of various kinds had befallen her: a bank broke; an investment failed; she went into a small business and became insolvent; then she entered into service, sinking lower and lower, from housekeeper down to maid-of-all-work – never long retaining a place, though nothing decided against her character was ever alleged. She was considered sober, honest, and peculiarly quiet in her ways; still nothing prospered with her. And so she had dropped into the workhouse, from which Mr. J— had taken her, to be placed in charge of the very house which she had rented as mistress in the first year of her wedded life.

Mr. J— added that he had passed an hour alone in the unfurnished room which I had urged him to destroy, and that his impressions of dread while there were so great, though he had neither heard nor seen anything, that he was eager to have the walls bared and the floors removed as I had suggested. He had engaged persons for the work, and would commence any day I would name.

The day was accordingly fixed. I repaired to the haunted house – we went into the blind, dreary room, took up the skirting, and then the floors. Under the rafters, covered with rubbish, was found a trapdoor, quite large enough to admit a man. It was closely nailed down, with clamps and rivets of iron. On removing these we descended into a room below, the existence of which had never been suspected. In this room there had been a window and a flue, but they had been bricked over, evidently for many years. By the help of candles we examined this place; it still retained some moldering furniture – three chairs, an oak settle, a table – all of the fashion of about eighty years ago. There was a chest of drawers against the wall, in which we found, half rotted away, old-fashioned articles of a man's dress, such as might have been worn eighty or a hundred years ago by a gentleman of some rank; costly steel buckles and buttons, like those yet worn in court dresses, a handsome court sword; in a waistcoat which had once been rich with gold lace, but which was now blackened and foul with damp, we found five guineas, a few silver coins, and an ivory ticket, probably for some place of entertainment long since passed away. But our main discovery was in a kind of iron safe fixed to the wall, the lock of which it cost us much trouble to get picked.

In this safe were three shelves and two small drawers. Ranged on the shelves were several small bottles of crystal, hermetically stopped. They contained colorless, volatile essences, of the nature of which I shall only say that they were not poisons – phosphor and ammonia entered into some of them. There were also some very curious glass tubes, and a small pointed rod of iron, with a large lump of rock crystal, and another of amber – also a loadstone of great power.

In one of the drawers we found a miniature portrait set in gold, and retaining the freshness of its colors most remarkably, considering the length of time it had probably been there. The portrait was that of a man who might be somewhat advanced in middle life, perhaps forty-seven or forty-eight. It was a remarkable face – a most impressive face. If you could fancy some mighty serpent transformed into man, preserving in the human lineaments the old serpent type, you would have a better idea of that countenance than long descriptions can convey: the width and flatness of frontal; the tapering elegance of contour disguising the strength of the deadly jaw; the long, large, terrible eye, glittering and green as the emerald – and withal a certain ruthless calm, as if from the consciousness of an immense power.

Mechanically I turned round the miniature to examine the back of it, and on the back was engraved a pentacle; in the middle of the pentacle a ladder, and the third step of the ladder was formed by the date 1765. Examining still more minutely, I detected a spring; this, on being pressed, opened the back of the miniature as a lid. Withinside the lid were engraved, "Marianna, to thee. Be faithful in life and in death to—." Here follows a name that I will not mention, but it was not unfamiliar

to me. I had heard it spoken of by old men in my childhood as
the name borne by a dazzling charlatan who had made a great
sensation in London for a year or so, and had fled the country
on the charge of a double murder within his own house – that of
his mistress and his rival. I said nothing of this to Mr. J—, to
whom reluctantly I resigned the miniature.

We had found no difficulty in opening the first drawer within
the iron safe; we found great difficulty in opening the second: it
was not locked, but it resisted all efforts, till we inserted in the
chinks the edge of a chisel. When we had thus drawn it forth, we
found a very singular apparatus in the nicest order. Upon a
small, thin book, or rather tablet, was placed a saucer of crystal;
this saucer was filled with a clear liquid – on that liquid floated a
kind of compass, with a needle shifting rapidly round; but
instead of the usual points of a compass were seven strange
characters, not very unlike those used by astrologers to denote
the planets. A peculiar but not strong nor displeasing odor came
from this drawer, which was lined with a wood that we afterwards discovered to be hazel. Whatever the cause of this odor, it
produced a material effect on the nerves. We all felt it, even the
two workmen who were in the room – a creeping, tingling
sensation from the tips of the fingers to the roots of the hair.
Impatient to examine the tablet, I removed the saucer. As I did
so the needle of the compass went round and round with
exceeding swiftness, and I felt a shock that ran through my
whole frame, so that I dropped the saucer on the floor. The
liquid was spilled; the saucer was broken; the compass rolled to
the end of the room, and at that instant the walls shook to and
fro, as if a giant had swayed and rocked them.

The two workmen were so frightened that they ran up the
ladder by which we had descended from the trapdoor; but
seeing that nothing more happened, they were easily induced
to return.

Meanwhile I had opened the tablet: it was bound in plain red
leather, with a silver clasp; it contained but one sheet of thick
vellum, and on that sheet were inscribed, within a double
pentacle, words in old monkish Latin, which are literally to
be translated thus: "On all that it can reach within these walls,
sentient or inanimate, living or dead, as moves the needle, so

works my will! Accursed be the house, and restless be the dwellers therein."

We found no more. Mr. J— burned the tablet and its anathema. He razed to the foundations the part of the building containing the secret room with the chamber over it. He had then the courage to inhabit the house himself for a month, and a quieter, better-conditioned house could not be found in all London. Subsequently he let it to advantage, and his tenant has made no complaints.

The Crimson Curtain

Barbey d'Aurevilly
(Translated by Frances Frenaye)

An inordinate number of years ago I went duck-shooting in the marshlands of Western France, and because there were then no railway lines in that part of the country I traveled in the stagecoach, which I boarded at the crossroads near the Château de Rueil. There was only one other passenger, a remarkable man whom I had met in society and whom, with your leave, I shall call the Vicomte de Brassard. In all probability this disguise will be of little avail, for the few hundred members of the Paris élite will immediately identify his real name.

It was five o'clock in the afternoon and the dying light of the sun lit up a dusty road, bordered on either side by a row of poplars which separated it from the fields beyond. We rode behind three strong horses, whose muscular flanks heaved under every stroke of the postilion's whip. A postilion is somehow symbolical of life, always cracking the whip too much at the start.

The Vicomte de Brassard had left his whip cracking years behind him. But he had the phlegmatic character of an Englishman (having been brought up in England); even if mortally wounded he would not have admitted to a scratch and would have protested, at death's door, that he was very much alive. In everyday life, as in books, we are prone to make fun of a man who has left the inexperience and follies of youth behind him and still lays claim to being young. When such a claim assumes a ridiculous form, there is some reason for our mockery, but when, on the contrary, it nobly reflects the stubborn pride which inspires it, then, although it is apparently pointless, it partakes of the beauty of pointless things. "The Old Guard dies, but it never surrenders" – these were fighting words at Waterloo and they are no less heroic in the face of old age, which has none of the poetry of bayonets to recommend it. For men with a certain soldierly cast of mind, to die rather than surrender is just as important in the struggle to retain their faculties as it is on the field of battle.

The Vicomte de Brassard never surrendered; he is alive to this day and the story of his survival is worth telling. In any case, on the day when he was my stagecoach companion he was what the world (which can be as sharp-tongued as a young woman) called an "old beau." But in the eyes of anyone who does not calculate age in terms of years but recognizes the fact that a man is no older than he feels he was a "beau" pure and simple. The Marquise de V . . ., who was a connoisseur of young men and quite capable of shearing a dozen of them in the way that Delilah sheared Samson, wore in an elegant gold-and-jet bracelet a segment of his red moustache, which owed its bright color not to time but to the devil.

But do not attach to the word "beau," whether old or young, the narrow or frivolous meaning with which common parlance has endowed it. The Vicomte de Brassard was, in body and spirit, aristocratically opulent and deliberate. He was the most magnificent dandy I ever knew, and I witnessed the death of d'Orsay and Beau Brummel's lapse into madness.

A dandy, that is the only way to describe him. Were it not for this he would certainly have been a Marshal of France. In his youth he was one of the most brilliant officers of the last days of the First Empire. I have heard it said by his comrades-at-arms that he possessed the courage of Murat and Marmont together. This quality, combined with coolheadedness, would have won him the highest military rank, if he had not been a dandy. Take the attributes of an ideal officer – discipline and regularity – but mix them with a pinch of dandyism – and what is the result? The officer is blown to bits! If the Vicomte de Brassard did not suffer this fate it was only because, like all dandys, he was lucky. Mazarin would have been happy to have him in his employ, and

so would Mazarin's nieces, although not for the same reason.
He was superbly handsome.

Good looks are especially necessary to a soldier, for they are
the natural accompaniment of youth and French youth is
embodied by the army. Good looks subjugate not only women
but also fickle fortune. And Captain de Brassard had other
advantages as well. He was, I believe, of Norman descent, of the
race of William the Conqueror, and like him he had conquests
to his credit. After the end of the Empire he went over, quite
naturally, to the Bourbons, and during the Hundred Days
remained miraculously faithful to them. When the Bourbons
came back for the second time he was made a Chevalier de
Saint-Louis, at the hand of Charles X (then *Monsieur*). During
the whole of the Restoration he never once mounted guard at
the Tuileries that the Duchesse d'Angoulème did not graciously
hail him as she passed by. The natural graciousness of which
misfortune and sorrow had deprived her reawakened for his
benefit alone. In view of this signal favor the King's minister
was ready to throw all his influence into obtaining his advance-
ment, but with all the good will in the world there was little he
could do for this inveterate dandy, who drew his sword in the
face of his commanding officer when the latter called him to
order in the course of a regimental parade. Under these circumstances it was difficult enough to save him from court
martial.

The Vicomte de Brassard constantly rebelled against discipline, that is, except in time of war, when he lived up to his
officer's role and shirked none of his obligations. Many a time
he risked prolonged arrest by abandoning his quarters and
going off to amuse himself in the nearest town until one of
his soldiers came to advise him that he had best return in time
for some review. For although his superiors did not enjoy
having such a rebel under their command he was adored by
his men and treated them with the utmost consideration. He
demanded only that they be well turned out and show true
military spirit, thereby incarnating the classical type of French
soldier, as *La permission de dix heures* and three or four popular
songs so charmingly depict him. He may have been overly
zealous in behalf of dueling, but it was because this seemed

to him an incomparable way of building up their morale. "I am not a government," he used to say, "and I have no decorations to bestow upon them for this friendly form of combat. But the rewards of which I am the grand-master [he had a considerable private fortune] are gloves, belts and whatever other embellishments the regulations allow them to wear." As a result, the grenadiers of his company were more smartly attired than those of any other regiment of the Guards, who already had a reputation for elegance. He enhanced those characteristics by which the French soldier has always been known: self-satisfaction and coquetry, both of them highly provocative, the former by the manner which it assumes and the latter by the envy it arouses. It is easy to understand why all the other companies of the regiment were jealous of his. Men fought first to get into it and then to avoid being sent away.

Such was the exceptional position which the Vicomte de Brassard enjoyed during the Restoration. Under the Empire every day had offered a chance to display the kind of heroism which makes up for misconduct. But in time of peace he could not hope to be indefinitely forgiven the audacity which would have won him praise on the field of battle. The revolution of 1830 came along just in time to relieve his superiors of the necessity of taking drastic disciplinary measures and to save him from the disgrace with which he was threatened. After suffering a serious wound during the Three Days he refused to pledge allegiance to the new dynasty of Orléans, which he held in utter contempt. The July Revolution, which made them temporarily masters of a country which they were unable to hold under their sway, found him confined to his bed with an injury to the foot which he had acquired while dancing – with the same vigor he would have put into a charge – at the last ball of the Duchesse de Berry, at the first roll of the drum he got up to go join his company, but since the condition of his foot would not allow him to put on his boots he went in silk socks and patent-leather slippers, as if he were going to a ball. Thus accoutred he took command of his grenadiers on the Place de la Bastille, with orders to clear the full length of the boulevard of the same name.

No barricades had yet been erected, and the empty streets wore a sinister and menacing air. The blazing sun was high in the sky, as if threatening to pour down a sheet of fire, a forerunner of the deadly blast which was shortly to break forth from the curtained windows. Captain de Brassard lined up his soldiers on either side of the boulevard, as close as possible to the houses, so that they should be exposed only to the shots from across the way, while he himself, in true dandy style, strode up the middle. He was a perfect target for the thousands of guns, pistols and carbines which were trained upon him, from the Bastille to the Rue de Richelieu, but he remained unscathed in spite of the fact that he threw out his chest, for all the world like a pretty woman. But at the corner of the Rue de Richelieu, just in front of Frascati's, just as he was ordering his men to gather behind him and charge the first of the barricades which obstructed the way, a bullet hit him squarely in the chest, which was conspicuous not only for its breadth but also for the silver braid which swung from one shoulder to the other, and at the same time his arm was broken by a well-aimed stone. All of which did not prevent him from sweeping away the barricade and marching, amid his cheering men, all the way to the Madeleine.

When two ladies who were fleeing in a carriage from the tumultuous city saw an officer of the Guards lying in a pool of blood on one of the stone slabs with which the church, at that time under construction, was still surrounded, they offered to transport him wherever he wished to go. He asked to be taken to the Marshal de Raguse, at the Gros-Caillou, and presented himself to him in these soldierly words: "Marshal, I may not last for more than two hours, but during that time order me to do what you will!" But his calculations were mistaken, for the bullet in the chest did not kill him. When I made his acquaintance, fifteen years later, he claimed that despite the doctor's precise order that he should drink no alcohol until the end of his fever, he owed the preservation of his life to the consumption of a huge quantity of Bordeaux wine.

Of the quantity there can be little doubt, for as a true dandy he was a heavy drinker. He had made for him a special wine glass of Bohemian crystal big enough – God save me! – to hold the contents of a whole bottle, which he was quite capable of downing with a single gulp. He said, when he was in his cups, that he lived his whole life on the same scale, and no doubt this was true. Nowadays, in an age when everything is petty and small, this may not seem an achievement in which to take pride. He was a man of the stamp of Bassompierre and held his liquor as well as he. I have seen him empty his quart glass a dozen times without showing any ill effects. At gatherings of the kind that respectable people term "orgies" he never went beyond the stage of being what he called "a bit high". Because the point of the story that follows hinges upon the understanding of just what kind of a man he was, I must add that he was known to have as many as seven mistresses at a time, the "seven strings of his lyre," he called them, although I cannot approve of this frivolously musical appellation. But what am I to say? If the Vicomte de Brassard had not been the manner of man I have described, my story would be less piquant, and probably I should not think it worth telling.

He was the last person in the world I expected to see when I got into the stagecoach at the crossroads near the Château de Rueil. I had not run into him for some time and I was pleased with the prospect of spending some hours in the company of a man who, although he belonged to our times, was in so many ways alien to them. The Vicomte de Brassard would have been as much at ease in the armor of Francis I as in the trig uniform of the Guards, but neither his build nor his manner resembled those of the most conspicuous young men of our day. The long lasting radiance of this setting sun made the rising crescent moons look pale by comparison. He had the good looks and figure of the Emperor Nicholas but neither his Greek profile nor his idealistic facial expression. His hair and beard were, by some mysterious and miraculous means, still black, and the beard grew high up on his healthy pink cheeks. His convex forehead was white and unwrinkled; the bearskin cap worn by the Guards had thinned his hair and thereby added to its dimensions. His eyes were deep-set but as bright blue and sparkling as sapphires, with a penetrating stare.

We shook hands and fell at once into conversation. Captain de Brassard spoke slowly and in a voice deep enough to be heard over a parade-ground. Perhaps the deliberateness of his speech was due to the fact that he had been brought up in England and the language of this country came most easily to him. But it added flavor to all that he said, especially to the broad jokes which he particularly liked to tell. Captain de Brassard always went "too far," as the Comtesse de F . . . put it, that pretty widow who after her husband's death wore only three colors: black, white and violet. He must have been considered very affable company or else he would have been branded as un-endurable. In the society of the Faubourg Saint-Germain affability covers a multitude of sins.

One of the advantages of conversation in a public conveyance is that when there is nothing more to say it can be broken off without giving offense. In a drawing-room there is no such freedom. Politeness forces a man to go on talking, and his innocent hypocrisy is often punished by the emptiness and boredom of a whole evening during which the greatest fools, even those that are by nature silent, if such there be, make frantic efforts to chatter agreeably. In a public vehicle everyone is, so to speak, in his own home and need not hesitate to relapse into quiet daydreaming. Unfortunately many chance meetings are dull, and in the old days (to which we are already looking back) one might make a dozen trips by coach without running into an interesting companion.

The Vicomte de Brassard made several remarks inspired by the landscape, the incidents of the journey and our common memories of the circumstances under which we had previously met. Then the fall of darkness enveloped us in its silence. In autumn night comes on so fast that it seems to literally drop out of the sky. We pulled our coats around us and rested our heads against the back of the seat, for want of a better pillow. I don't remember whether my companion fell asleep in his corner, but I remained awake in mine. I had covered this route so fre-quently that I paid little attention to the objects outside, which seemed to be flying by in the direction opposite to our own. We passed at intervals through various small towns scattered along this road which the postilions still call "the ribbon," in honor of the band which they formerly wore on their hair. In the pitch blackness these unknown towns took on a strange air, as if we had come to the end of the world. Such sensations no longer have any reason for being and our descendants will never experience them. Now that the railways have built stations on the outskirts of the cities the traveler has no opportunity of examining the streets while he waits for a change of horses. Most of the towns we passed through could afford the luxury of only a very few street-lamps and on the highway there were none. But the country-side received a faint glow from the broad, overhanging sky, while in the sleeping towns the proximity of the houses, the shadows they cast below them and the rarity of the stars glimpsed above the narrow streets added to the atmosphere of mystery. The only human beings to be seen were the stable boys armed with lanterns, who brought fresh horses to the inn doors and whistled or swore as they buckled them into their harness. This sight and the repeated cry of a sleepy traveler: "Postilion, where are we now?" were the only signs of life. Perhaps some dreamer like myself tried to distinguish through the glass the shadowy façades of the houses or let his imagination play over an occasional lighted window, an unusual sight in a provincial town, where the night is made for sleep. The wakefulness of one man, even a sentinel, among his sleeping fellows, has something moving about it. And our ignorance of what is going on behind closed curtains, where a glimmer of light betokens the presence of life and thought, adds the poetry of a dream to that of reality. I, for one, have never looked at a lighted window in a sleeping town, without attempting to guess at the intimate drama behind it. Years later I still recall its melancholy light and when it flashes across my dreams I involuntarily call out:

"What *was* there behind those curtains?"

One of the windows I remember (for a reason which you will understand later) is the town of ***, which we passed through that night. It was three houses beyond the inn where we had stopped to change horses, but I had occasion to observe it for an unusually long time, because one of the coach's wheels was broken and the postilion had to send for a blacksmith to repair it. To wake up a blacksmith in the dead of night and prevail upon him to do such a job, in a town where there is no rival means of transportation and in his absence the travelers would have no choice but to wait over till morning, is no easy matter. In this case, if the fellow happened to be sleeping as soundly as

some of the passengers in the stagecoach, the mere act of
rousing him must have required considerable effort.

From my compartment I could hear the snoring of the
travelers in the main body of the coach behind me. And not
one of the passengers riding outside, who usually jump down at
the slightest provocation in order – like true Frenchmen – to
display the agility with which they can jump up again, had taken
advantage of the delay to give proof of this prowess. To be sure,
the inn was closed and no meals were being served inside; we
had eaten our supper at the previous relay. No sound broke the
silence of the night except for that of a broom with which some
man or woman (it was too dark to make any distinction) was
sweeping the courtyard, whose gate remained open. The slow
motion of the broom made it seem as if this humble instrument
were asleep or wished to be sleeping. The façade of the inn was
dark, and so were those of the adjacent houses, except for the
one which has remained engraved upon my memory. The house
had only one storey, placed high above the street, and the light
in the window glowed rather than shone, mysteriously visible
through the double folds of a crimson curtain.

"Strange," murmured the Vicomte de Brassard, as if he were
talking to himself, "but it looks like the same curtain as before!"

I looked at him, hoping to catch the expression of his face, but
the lamp just below the postilion's box, which lit up not only the
road ahead but also our compartment, had gone out. I had
imagined that he was sleeping, but he was just as awake as I and
equally struck by the mystery of the lighted window. But his
interest had a more precise reason. The tone of voice in which
he made this simple remark was so unfamiliar that I was more
curious than ever to see his face. I struck a match, as if to light
my cigar, and it shed a bluish light through the compartment.
The Vicomte was paler than a dead man, pale as Death.

Why, I wondered? I was puzzled not only by the singularity
of the window but by his extraordinary reaction to it. He was
sanguine by nature and emotion would normally have caused
him to be red in the face; moreover I was sitting so close to him
that I could detect a quiver in the muscles of his thigh. Behind
all this I began to feel sure there must be some story, which with
skill I might be able to extract from him.

"So you too were looking at the window, Captain," I said. "Indeed, you recognize it as one you have seen before." I disguised my curiosity by speaking quite casually and as if I did not really expect a reply.

"That I do," he answered in his usual deep and deliberate voice.

Already he had regained his self-control. Your true dandy scorns any show of emotion; unlike the simple-minded Goethe he regards astonishment as a highly improper state of mind.

"I pass very seldom this way," he went on; "in fact, I do my best to avoid it. But some things are unforgettable. I can think offhand of three: a man's first uniform, his first battle and his first woman. To me there is a fourth, and it happens to be that curtain."

He paused and lowered the glass directly in front of him. Was it in order to look more closely at the window? The postilion had not yet returned with the blacksmith and the fresh horses had not yet been led out of the stable. Those that had brought us thus far stood stock-still in their harness, with their heads hanging down, too tired even to paw the ground to show how impatient they were to be taken to their stalls. The stage-coach looked as if it had been bewitched and brought to a halt in the woodland setting of the Sleeping Beauty story.

"To a man of imagination that window does have something distinctive about it," I ventured.

"I don't know what you see in it," he said, "but I know what it means to me. That was my first lodging as a soldier. I lived there – God help me! – all of thirty-five years ago, behind that curtain, which looks just as it did then, with just the same light inside as when I . . ."

I would not let this train of thought escape him.

"When you sat up late at night, studying tactics, as a young lieutenant?" I put in.

"You flatter me," he said. "I *was* a young lieutenant, to be sure, but I didn't spend my nights studying tactics. If my lamp stayed lit into the wee, small hours, as respectable people would call them, it wasn't in order to pore over the works of Marshal Saxe."

"But perhaps in order to imitate him," I volleyed.

"Not in the way you are thinking," he shot back. "I did that much later. In those days I was a mere shavetail, faultlessly rigged out, but awkward and timid when it came to women, although they refused to believe it, perhaps because of my devil of a face. I failed to reap the reward of my timidity, but then I was only seventeen years old and fresh from the military academy. In those days we finished our training at the age when nowadays they begin. Napoleon was such a man-eater that if he'd lasted any longer than he did he'd have conscripted twelve-year old boys, as raw as the nine-year old girls with whom Eastern sultans people their harems."

"If he goes on about Napoleon and the Eastern sultans," I thought to myself, "we'll never get to the point of the story."

"And yet, Vicomte," I said, "if you have such a vivid memory of that curtain I'll wager it's because there was a woman behind it."

"Sir, you win your wager," he admitted gravely.

"I knew it! If a man of your stamp remembers a small garrison town where he was stationed in his youth, it can only be because he endured some notable siege there or took by storm some beautiful woman. Nothing else could make this window shine out for you in the darkness."

"I endured no siege," he replied, "at least not of the military variety." His manner was grave, but such it was wont to be, even when he was joking. "As for taking a woman, by storm or otherwise, I was, as I said before, quite incapable of it. Upon this occasion *I* was the one to be taken!"

I saluted him, although in the darkness I had no way of knowing whether he noticed my gesture.

"The famous Berg-op-Zoom was taken," I said.

"And seventeen-year-old lieutenants can't usually match the wisdom and continence of an impregnable Berg-op-Zoom!"

"So there was a Madame or Mademoiselle Potiphar," I said gaily.

"Mademoiselle . . ." he said in an almost comically disarming manner.

"A woman like all the rest, Captain! Only in this case Joseph was a soldier, who wouldn't have dreamed of running away . . ."

"He did run away, though," he said coolly, "although only

when it was too late and he was scared out of his wits. His fear helps me to understand the words which I heard with my own ears from the lips of no less a man than Marshal Ney: 'I'd like to see the bastard who's never been afraid!' "

"An event which inspired you with fear must make an interesting story!"

"If it interests you I may as well tell you the whole thing. It was an event that marked my life as deeply as acid biting into steel and cast a shadow over all my subsequent amorous misdemeanors . . . The pursuit of pleasure doesn't always pay." I was surprised by the melancholy of his voice, having always thought of him as a hardened sinner.

He raised the glass which he had opened a few minutes before, either because he did not wish to be heard by anyone outside and failed to realize that there was nobody there, or else because the slow but regular sound of the sweeping broom did not seem to him a fitting accompaniment to his story. I was all attention, sensitive above all to the intonation of his voice, since his face remained invisible in the darkness, and with my eyes fixed on the crimson curtain.

"I was seventeen years old, as I told you, and fresh from the military academy. I was lieutenant in an infantry regiment and as impatient as my fellows to go to Germany and join the Emperor, who was engaged in what later came to be called the 1813 campaign. There was barely time for me to pay a brief visit to my old father, deep in the country, before I reported to my unit, one of two battalions garrisoned in this small town, the other two of the regiment being stationed in even smaller places near by. After such short acquaintance you can hardly imagine what it was like to be condemned to reside here, even temporarily, thirty years ago. The devil himself, who I am convinced has his quarters in the ministry of war, couldn't have thought up a more inauspicious spot for me to begin my army career. Nowhere could there be anything more boring. But because I was so very young and so inebriated with the novelty of wearing a uniform (you do not know this sensation but anyone who has experienced it will testify to its validity) I did not actually suffer from a state of affairs which later on I should have found unendurable. What did the town matter to me, when my uniform, a sartorial masterpiece of Thomassin and Pied, in which I took an inordinate delight, was my real home? Because of the uniform I saw everything through rosy glasses. When the lifelessness of the town was too much for me I put on my full-dress uniform, stiff collar, gold braid and all, and soon my boredom was dispelled. I was like a beautiful woman who dresses up even when she is quite alone and expecting no one to call; my elegance was for my own pleasure. All by myself I enjoyed the cut of the cloth and the gleam of my sword when I went out at four o'clock in the afternoon to stroll on the deserted main street. My chest swelled up with just as much pride as it did some years later, on the boulevard of Ghent where, with a pretty woman on my arm, I heard someone behind me say: "There's a finely turned-out specimen of an officer for you!"

"The town had none of the riches of commerce or industry, only a few half-ruined aristocratic families, who looked askance at the Emperor, because he had not restored the loot taken from them by the blackguards of the Revolution and for this reason made no efforts to entertain his officers with receptions or balls or evening parties. On Sundays, after the noon Mass, a few women exhibited their daughters on the main street, but when the bells rang at two o'clock for Vespers, the street emptied and all the skirts were whisked away. During the Restoration attendance at the noon Mass was made obligatory for all commanding officers, and this created a minimum of stir in otherwise dead garrison towns. Fellows like myself, at an age when women were of passionate concern, had at least this occasion to which to look forward. All of us who were not on guard duty scattered themselves at strategic positions in the nave, preferably behind the pretty women who came there to display their charms, and distracted them, quite successfully, by making audible comments on their figures and dress. Ah, the military Mass, starting-point of many a romance! Young girls left their muffs on the chair when they knelt down beside their mothers and we stuffed notes into them, to which on the following Sunday they brought us a reply.

"But during the Empire there was no such attendance at Mass and we had no means of approaching the well-born pretty girls of the town. They had only the status of dreams, glimpsed behind their veils as they flitted by. For this loss there was no compensation. The brothels, which are not mentioned in polite conversation, were places of horror, and the cafés, where many a man has combatted the enforced idleness and boredom of garrison life were of such low degree that no officer who respected his uniform could frequent them. There were none of the comforts and conveniences which nowadays are spread throughout the land and not a single hotel where we could set up an officers' mess without being bled to death by the exorbitant charges. Most of us had given up any idea of dining together and took our meals with middle-class families which rented out rooms at a high price in order to increase their meager incomes and better the food on their tables.

"I lived myself in such lodgings. One of my friends had taken a room at the *Poste aux Chevaux*, which at that time was a little way down the street behind us, bearing on its facade a faded yellow circle framed by a crimson cloud (perhaps still visible by daylight) and the inscription – 'The Rising Sun'. He found me an apartment near by, yes, the one with that window which, as I see it tonight, still seems to me mine. I let him make the choice because he was my senior in both age and military service and enjoyed piloting a young fellow as inexperienced and heedless as myself. For I had no concern except for the uniform (I stress its importance because your generation, with its peace congresses and its philosophical and humanitarian humbug is on the way to losing sight of it altogether) and for the gunfire of the battle in which I looked forward to losing what I may call my military virginity. I was wrapped up in these two things, especially the second, because we care more for what we have not than for what we have. Like a miser I was in love with the future. I understood the fanatical piety of people who live in this transitory life as if it were a dangerous bivouac which they must quit on the morrow. A soldier is quite the opposite of a monk and yet this was the attitude I took toward my garrison existence.

"Except at meals, which I took with my landlords, and at daily drills and maneuver, I spent most of my time in my own room, lying on a dark blue leather sofa, which was as refreshing to the touch as a cold bath after exercise. I got up from this only to practice fencing and play cards with my friend, Louis de Meung, who lived across the way and was less lazy than myself simply because he had picked up a mistress in the town, who served, as he said, to kill time. What I knew about women did not inspire me to follow his example. My knowledge was confined to that which the cadets of Saint-Cyr acquire on days when they have leave. Besides, some temperaments are slow to awaken. Did you ever know Saint-Rémy, the most dissipated man of a city famous for its dissipation, who was called the 'Minotaur,' not on account of his cuckold's horns (he eventually killed his wife's lover) but on account of the number of young girls he had devoured?"

"Yes, I knew him," I replied, "but when he was an old man, sinking deeper into vice with every succeeding year. Lord, yes, I knew the 'incorrigible' Saint Rémy, as Brantôme would have called him!"

"Quite so; he was a character out of Brantôme. Well, at twenty-seven years of age Saint-Rémy had touched neither wine nor women! He'd have told you so himself. At twenty-seven years of age he was as innocent as a newborn baby. He no longer had a wet-nurse, but he never drank anything except milk and water."

"He certainly made up for that lost time!"

"So did I, and faster than he did. My youthful continence didn't last very long after I left my first post. Even then I wasn't as complete a virgin as the young Saint-Rémy, but I did live pretty much as a Knight of Malta. As a matter of fact I am one, by birth, did you know that? I might have inherited the rank of one of my uncles if the Revolution hadn't swept the order away. Even after it was abolished I was vain enough to wear its ribbon!

"As for my landlords, they were as middle-class as could be. There were only two of them – man and wife – no longer young and actually quite well-mannered. They showed me a kind of politeness seldom to be found nowadays, especially among their class, which is like the lingering perfume of times gone by. I was not at an observant or analytical age and took too little interest in them to dig into their past. Indeed I had nothing at all to do with them except during the noon and evening meals which I ate at their table. Their conversation was concerned with the people of the town, of whom the husband spoke with a certain light-hearted malice and the wife more discreetly but with almost equal pleasure. I seem to remember hearing him say that he had traveled in his youth on some business or other and that he found her waiting to marry him when he came home. They were good, gentle people; she spent her time knitting him socks and he scraped old tunes of Viotti on a violin, in an attic over my room. Perhaps they had once been more prosperous than they were then and reduced circumstances obliged them to take a boarder. But this fact was not evident in any other way. Their house had all the comforts of a bygone age: sweet-smelling linen, heavy silver and furniture so permanent that they wouldn't have dreamed of replacing it. The table was good and I had permission to leave it as soon as I had 'wiped my beard,' as the old servant, Olive, put it, in terms very flattering to my scrawny moustache.

"I was there six months without ever hearing my hosts refer to the existence of any other member of the family. Then one day, when I came down to dinner, I saw a young woman in one corner of the dining-room, hanging her hat on a rack, as casually as if she had just come in from a stroll. As she stood on tiptoe, reaching up for the rack, she displayed a waist as slender as that of a ballet dancer, encased in a green silk bodice with a green fringe which fell over a white skirt, so tight about the hips as to set off their contour. When she heard me come in she turned around, with her arms in mid-air, twisting her neck in such a way that I glimpsed her face. Then she went on with what she was doing, just as if I were not there. She made sure that the ribbons of her hat were not rumpled, with an almost imperti-nently deliberate motion, for she knew perfectly well that I was waiting to greet her. Finally she honored me with a glance out of two black eyes to which the curls on her forehead gave a cold expression. I could not imagine who she might be, for no guest ever came to dinner and yet this seemed to be her intention since four places were set at the table. I was even more astonished when I discovered her identity. For just at that moment my hosts came into the room and introduced her as their daughter who had just come home from school to live with them.

"Their daughter! Nothing in the world could have been more

unexpected. Not that a pretty girl can't be born to the most unlikely parents. I have known many such a one and so, no doubt, have you. Physiologically speaking, the very ugliest people can have the handsomest children. But between this couple and their offspring there was an abyss, almost of race. But, to repeat a pedantic word proper to your generation rather than to mine, it was from a physiological point of view that she was remarkable. For such a young girl she had a strangely impassive air. Without it, one would have said: 'There's a pretty girl!' and left it at that, just the way one does with the pretty girls one notices on the street and never thinks of again. But this impassive air which set her apart not only from her parents but also from the common passions of the rest of humanity made it impossible to take one's eyes off her. Velasquez' portrait, *The Infanta with a Spaniel*, if you know it, might give you some idea of her expression. She did not look at people proudly or disdainfully, which would have made them feel that they did, at least, exist, since she took the trouble to scorn them. No, she seemed simply to say: 'For me you are not there.'

"On that day of our first meeting and on many others to follow I asked myself a question to which I never found a reply. How could such a lovely girl be the child of this stuttering, heavy-set man in a yellowish-green frock coat and white waistcoat, with a face as red as his wife's jam and a huge mole sticking over the edge of his muslin collar? His looks didn't bother me so much, since he was of the same sex as my own, but those of his wife were even more inappropriate and puzzling, in relation to the daughter. Mademoiselle Albertine, or Alberte (the becoming nickname by which her parents addressed her) was like an archduchess whom some caprice of fate had sent from above to this middle-class couple with neither of whom she had any real connection. At our first meal together and at the others that followed she behaved like a well brought-up, unaffected, reserved girl, who knew how to express herself but said no more than she had to say. Of course, no matter how brilliant she might have been these family dinners gave her no occasion to display it. Her parents toned down their conversation and no longer regaled me with local gossip; we spoke, quite literally, of nothing more exciting than the weather. I was soon bored with the girl's impassive air, since she had nothing more to offer. If I had met her among people of my own station, then I might have been stimulated to satisfy my curiosity about her. But the circumstance of our meeting forbade me to embark upon even the most innocent flirtation. My status as a boarder in her parents' house was a delicate one and the least misstep would have upset it. She was neither so near nor so far as to provoke my interest and I quickly became indifferent to her.

"This attitude remained unaltered on both sides; we never spoke except in terms of rigid politeness. To me she was no more than a fleeting apparition, and to her I seemed even less. At the table, which was the only place we met, she looked more often at the sugar-bowl or the carafe of wine than at my person. The occasional well-turned but insignificant phrase that dropped from her lips gave no clue to her character. I might have gone on indefinitely without seeking to penetrate her misleadingly haughty and impassive air, had I not been aroused by an event as startling as a bolt of lightning in a calm summer sky.

"One evening, about a month after her arrival, she sat down beside me, instead of between her parents, at the dinner table, a fact which at the moment I failed so much as to notice. But just as I was spreading my napkin on my lap – how can I describe my utter astonishment? – I felt a hand firmly grasp mine under the table. I thought I must be dreaming . . . Actually, I thought nothing at all, but was overcome by such incredible boldness. At her touch my blood rushed by precipitate attraction from my heart into my hand and then, as if driven by a pump, back into my heart. My ears rang and my eyes saw double; I felt that I must have turned deadly pale and might dissolve and faint away in this almost boyishly powerful embrace.

"In a very young man pleasure is attended by fear. I attempted to withdraw my hand but, as if aware of the sensation she had imparted to me she closed hers all the more firmly upon it, overriding not only my physical resistance but also my will. This was thirty-five years ago, and you can easily believe that a woman's hand has lost its ability to enthrall me, but I recall as vividly as if it were yesterday the passionate tyranny of her clasp. I trembled all over, fearful lest her parents might become

aware of the incredible source of my emotion. I was ashamed to
fall short of the daring which enabled her to coolheadedly cover
up her aberration, and bit my lip until it bled in an effort to
regain self-control. At the same time I gazed at her other hand,
which was calmly turning the switch of a light which had just
been put on the table. Was this the companion of the hand
which, through mine, was sending rays of fire through my
whole body? In the light of the lamp, which fell directly upon it,
it was slightly heavy, but with long, shapely fingers, and it
turned the switch with languorous ease and grace.

"But we could not remain this way indefinitely; we needed
our hands to eat our dinner. She relaxed her grasp, but simultaneously she placed her foot, with equally calm yet despotic
passion, upon mine and left it there for the whole length of our
all-too-short sojourn at the table. It gave me the same sensation
as that of an overly hot bath, to which one gradually accustoms
oneself to the point where it is so pleasant that it seems as if the
damned souls in hell might eventually be as happy there as fish
in water.

"You can imagine how lightly I dined that night and how
little I joined in the innocuous conversation of my placid hosts,
who had no idea of the drama being played out under the table.
They saw nothing, but they might very well have seen, and I
was worried more on their behalf than on hers and mine, for I
had all the candor and quickly moved pity of seventeen. Fran-
tically I wondered: Is she mad? Or merely shameless? Looking
at her out of the corner of my eye I marvelled at how, if she were
mad, she had maintained the dignity of a princess at court, with
her face as untroubled as if her foot had not committed such
unimaginable follies. To tell the truth, I marvelled more at her
self-containment than at her effrontery. I had read my share of
frivolous books in which women are treated with slight regard
and I had attended a military academy. Theoretically, at least, I
was the smug Lovelace, the model of every handsome fellow
who has kissed his mother's chambermaid behind the stairs. But
what had just happened threw me off balance. Nothing I had
heard or read portrayed so vividly women's natural ability to lie
and to mask even the most violent emotions. After all, she was
only eighteen years old, if she was that, and she had come from a

boarding-school which must have been carefully chosen by her virtuous mother. Her lack of embarrassment and indeed of shame, the coolness with which she had run so considerable a risk, both of them totally unforeseen, appeared for what they quite clearly were in my mind, even amid the tumult of my feelings.

"But neither then nor later did I pause to philosophize. The girl's terrifying precocity inspired me with no insincere horror. Neither at my age nor at one more advanced does a man judge a woman to be depraved simply because she throws herself at him. He is inclined to find it quite natural and if he says to himself: 'Poor girl!' it is with a feeling of modesty rather than commiseration. Besides, in spite of the fact that I was timid, I had no wish to pass for a fool. Is not this the classical French excuse for sinning without remorse? I knew, of course, that what she felt for me was not love, for love is neither so aggressive nor so shameless. And I had no illusion about the nature of my own feeling, either. But love or no love, I wanted to enjoy it. I got up from the table in a resolute frame of mind. Alberte's hand, which I had not so much as noticed before it seized mine, had left me desirous of holding her whole body in the same close embrace.

"I rushed upstairs like a madman and then, after cooling myself off with a few minutes of reflection, wondered what steps I should take to enter into an 'affair,' as they call it in the provinces, with such a diabolically provocative girl. I knew – as well as I could know without ever having given the matter any thought – that she never left her mother's side, but shared her needle work in the alcove at one end of the combined living- and dining-room, that no other girls came to see her and that she rarely went out except to Sunday Mass and Vespers, with her parents. It was not a very encouraging picture. I began to be sorry that I had not established a closer relationship with the two old people, having treated them cordially enough but with the distracted politeness one observes toward persons of secondary interest. At this point, however, I could not very well alter my behavior without arousing the very suspicions which I wanted to lull.

"The only occasion I had for speaking secretly to Mademoi-

selle Alberte was when I was going up or downstairs, but the
staircase was a place where we might easily be seen or heard. In
such a small and well regulated house my only recourse was to
write, and since her hand had been bold enough to seek mine
under the table I felt that it would find no difficulty in taking a
letter. My missive was just what the circumstances required:
the imperious and intoxicated plea of a man who has had one
draught of happiness and asks for another. I could not deliver it
until dinner-time of the following day; the time seemed inter-
minably long, but at last it went by. The inflammatory hand,
whose touch I had not ceased to feel for the past twenty-four
hours, sought mine in just the same way as before, perceived the
paper and promptly appropriated it. I had not foreseen that,
with the same impassive, Infanta-like air, she would convey it at
once to her bosom, masking the gesture with the pretense of
straightening her lace collar. She did it so quickly and naturally
that her mother, who was busy ladling out the soup, saw
nothing and her father, who was always humming when he
was not playing his violin, perceived nothing but a reflection of
the fire."

"No deceived man ever sees any more, Captain," I interrupted. The story seemed to me to be taking a conventionally
amorous turn; little did I know how it was to develop. "Just a
few days ago, at the Opera," I went on, "a woman of the same
type as your Mademoiselle Alberte was sitting in the box next to
mine. She was no more than eighteen years old, but I swear I
have never seen a greater model of decorum. She sat as motionless as a statue through the performance, turning neither to
right nor left, although I later realized that she must have eyes
in her beautiful, bare shoulders. For all the time there was
sitting behind me, in my box, a young man who seemed as
indifferent as she to everything except what was going on the
stage. He made none of those grimaces with which, in a public
place, men convey what might be called a telegraphic declaration of love to a woman. But when the opera was over and the
boxes began to empty, amid general confusion, I heard the
woman say to her husband in a conjugally imperious manner:
'Henri, pick up my hood!' Then, over his bent back she
stretched out her arm and took a note from the young man,

as casually as if it were a fan or a bouquet handed her by her husband. Meanwhile her husband, poor fellow, straightened himself up, holding her crimson hood (no more crimson than his face), which at the risk of apoplexy he had picked up from under her chair. This sight made such an impression on me that I went away thinking that instead of giving the hood to his wife he might better have thrown it over his own head in order to hide the cuckold's horns which were about to sprout from it!"

"That's a good story," said the Vicomte coolly, as if under other circumstances he might have enjoyed it better, "but let me finish mine. Since she was the kind of a girl she was I did not worry about the fate of my letter. 'No matter how tightly she clings to her mother's apron-strings,' I said to myself, 'she'll manage to read it and give me a reply.' I was counting on a continuous exchange of correspondence, by the same channels, and fully expected an answer to my letter when I entered the dining-room the next evening. For a moment I thought that my eyes had deceived me when I saw that the table settings had been rearranged and Mademoiselle Alberte was sitting back where she belonged, between her father and mother. What had been going on behind my back that might account for this change? Did the father and mother have any suspicions? Mademoiselle Alberte was sitting directly opposite me and I stared insistently at her. There were a hundred questions in my eyes, but hers were as blank and indifferent as ever and seemed to look straight through me. Nothing could be more aggravating than that long, cool gaze, which seemed to be directed at an inanimate object. I was boiling over with anxiety, curiosity and a host of other conflicting feelings, and this girl, with her nerves of steel, seemed afraid to give me an imperceptible sign to the effect that we were accomplices in the same mystery, call it love or whatever you will!

"Was this the same woman that had so skillfully deployed her hand and foot under the table, that had stuffed my letter of the day before into her bosom, as naturally as if it were a handkerchief? After all these feats, why should she be afraid to shoot me a glance? But I received nothing. The dinner went by without this look which I awaited so eagerly and tried in vain to kindle. 'She must have thought of some other means to give me a reply,' I said to myself as I left the table and went up to my room. I could not believe that after such an advance she could beat a retreat or admit that she should be fearful and cautious when it came to satisfying her fancies – and she surely had taken a fancy to me.

" 'If her parents do not suspect,' I reflected, 'and sheer chance determined the change of seating, then tomorrow I shall find myself once more sitting beside her.' But this was not the case, either the next day or those that followed. Mademoiselle Alberte continued to wear the same impenetrable expression and speak in the same detached way of the commonplace things that were the subjects of conversation at this middle-class table. I continued, of course, to study her face. She looked superlatively unmoved when I was beside myself with anger and obliged at the same time to conceal it. This indifference made her seem even more than a table's-breadth away from me, and finally I became so exasperated that I did not hesitate to compromise her, to pierce her icy eyes with the enflamed and threatening stare of mine. Was it wile or coquetry that she was practicing upon me? Was it another form of caprice, opposite to the first, or simple stupidity? 'If one knew the right moment!' Ninon used to say. Had the moment to which Ninon referred passed away? I was still waiting for something – a sign, a whispered word amid the shuffling of chairs drawn back from the table, and when it did not come I fell into the wildest and most absurd suppositions. I began to think that on account of all the obstacles with which we were surrounded in the house she would send me a letter by post, that she would be clever enough, when she went out with her mother, to slip it into the box. With this idea in mind I was devoured by impatience twice a day, during the hour before the postman passed by. A dozen times during that hour I said to old Olive: 'Is there no letter for me?' to which she imperturbably replied: 'No, none.'

"Finally my exasperation passed all bounds, and disappointment turned into hatred. In my bitterness I attributed Alberte's behavior to the most contemptible motives, for hatred feeds on contempt. 'The cowardly little slut,' I said to myself; 'she's afraid to write me a letter!' As you can see, I stooped to the most abusive language. I insulted her in my imagination, and thought that even my insults were too good for her. I tried not to think about her at all and spoke of her in true soldierly lingo to my friend, Louis de Meung. Exasperation had downed any feeling of chivalry and I told him the whole story. He twisted the ends of his long, blonde moustache and said quite forthrightly (the 27th regiment was anything but squeamish): 'Do as I do! You must fight fire with fire. Take a little shopgirl for a mistress, and put this one out of your mind.'

"But I did not follow his advice; I was too far gone for that. If I could have been sure that she would hear about my taking a mistress, I might have taken one, just to spite her. But how was she to hear? If I had brought a woman to my room, as Louis did to the *Poste aux Chevaux*, my landlords would immediately have asked me to move away. And I did not wish to give up even the possibility of touching the hand or the foot of Alberte, in spite of the fact that she seemed to have permanently embraced the role of *Mademoiselle Impassible*."

'*Mademoiselle Impossible*, that's what I call her,' said Louis teasingly.

"A month went by, and in spite of my efforts to match her coldness and indifference I was constantly on the alert, a condition which I cannot bear, even when I am hunting. I was on the alert when I came into the dining-room, hoping to find her alone, as I had on the day of her arrival. On the alert during dinner, when I scrutinized her face first from one side and then from the other, meeting always the same calm look, which neither sought nor avoided mine. On the alert after dinner, when the ladies retired to their needlework in the alcove and I lingered on, to see if *she* would drop a thimble or a pair of scissors, anything that I might pick up, as an excuse to touch her hand, which was by now my obsession. On the alert in my room, where I listened for the light tread of the foot that had so willfully pressed mine, and on the stairs, where one day to my embarrassment, Olive caught me hopefully watching. On the alert at my window, the one you see before you, where I posted myself to see her go out with her mother and stayed – to no purpose – until their return. When she went out, draped in a girlish red-and-white striped shawl, with black and yellow flowers printed on it, she never once turned her insolently proud body, and when she came back, still at her mother's side, she never raised her head, or even her eyes, to the window where I was standing. Such was the miserable routine to which she had condemned me. Of course, all women demand that we wait upon them, but surely not to this point of enslavement. Even now my masculine vanity rebels against it.

"No longer did my uniform have the power to delight me. After the day's drill or parade I hurried home, but not to read the mémoires or novels which had formerly given me pleasure. I did not touch my foils or go to see Louis de Meung. And I had not the soothing resource of tobacco, which is a commonplace to the young men of today. In the 27th Regiment there was no smoking, except among the common soldiers, when they played cards on a drumhead in the guardroom. I was utterly idle, eating my heart out (if it was my heart); even the cool touch of the sofa had no power to calm me, and I paced up and down the six square feet of my room like a lion-cub in his cage, catching the scent of raw meat outside.

"This, then, was the way I spent my days, and also my nights. I went to bed late and slept little, obsessed as I was by the thought of Alberte, who had fired the blood in my veins and then run away, like an incendiary who does not even turn his head to look at the conflagration he has kindled behind him. I drew the curtain, in just the way you see it drawn tonight," – here the Vicomte ran his hand over the glass in front of him, in order to clear it of vapor—"so that my inquisitive provincial neighbors should not see inside. The large, high-ceilinged room was decorated in Empire style, with a parquet floor of Hungarian design and cherry-wood furniture with bronze fittings. There were bronze sphinxes on the bedposts and bronze lion's claws on the legs, bronze lion's heads on the bureau and desk drawers, with copper rings hanging from the mouths, which served to pull them open. A square table of a cherry-wood rosier than the rest, with a grey, copper-rimmed marble top, stood opposite the bed, against the wall between the window and the dressing-room door. Across from the fireplace there was the blue leather sofa which I have already described. A triangular cupboard was set into each of the four dark corners, and one of these was surmounted by a mysteriously contrasting white bust of Niobe, which seemed utterly out of place in this middle-class environment, no less incongruous, however, than the daughter of the house. The panelled walls, painted a cream color, were bare of paintings or engravings of any kind. On them I had hung my arms, suspended from gilded copper hooks. When I first rented this great barn of a room, as Louis de Meung most unpoetically called it, I installed in the center a big round table, which I littered with my books and military papers. This was the desk at which I occasionally wrote.

"Now one evening, or rather late at night, I had rolled the sofa over to this table and sat there drawing by the light of the lamp, not in order to distract myself from my woe, but rather to plunge into it more deeply, for I was drawing the head of Alberte, by whom I was as possessed as truly if she were the devil. Then, as now, two stagecoaches, faring in opposite directions, passed through the street below and stopped at the *Poste aux Chevaux* to change horses, the first at quarter to one and the second at half past two in the morning. But at this hour all was silent. I could have heard a fly, but if there was one in the room it must have been glued to the window or hiding in the folds of the crimson, silk curtain, which I had loosed from its hook so that it hung, stiff and immobile, before the window. The only sounds were those of my pencil and eraser. I was drawing the head of Alberte, God knows with how tender a hand and with what passion. Suddenly, without any warning turn of the knob, the door opened halfway, with a creak due to unoiled hinges. I raised my eyes, thinking that I must have left it incompletely closed and it had opened of its own accord, provoking a noise which might have startled anyone that was still awake and roused anyone sleeping from his slumber. I got up to go shut it, but before I could cross the room, it swung wide open, repeating the same creaking sound, and I saw Alberte, who for all her prudence had not been able to prevent it from giving her away.

"Believers speak of being blinded by visions, but no vision could have made my heart first stand still and then pound wildly as did the sight of Alberte, terror-stricken by the sound of the opening door, which she knew must be repeated when she closed it. Remember that I was only seventeen! Seeing that

her terror was contagious she made an abrupt gesture to prevent
me from crying out, which otherwise I should surely have done,
and shut the door, with extreme rapidity, hoping thus to
prevent a repetition of the sound, but only causing it to recur
even more shrilly than before. Then she leaned her ear against
it, to make sure that another sound, still more terrifying, did not
follow. Imagining that I saw her sway, I rushed forward and
within a second she was in my arms."

"She was a quick worker, your Alberte!" I put in.

"You may think," he went on, heedless of my remarks, "that
she was driven into my arms by fear, believing herself pursued
or in danger of pursuit, or that, having committed an irretrie-
vable folly, she had lost her head and surrendered to the demon
who they say would reign supreme over every woman's heart
were there not two other forces – cowardice and shame – to
oppose him. But you would be grievously mistaken, for she
knew no such commonplace fear. Actually, it was she that took
me into her arms rather than I that took her into mine. Her first
impulse was to lean her head against my breast, but she soon
raised it and stared at me out of wide-open eyes to make sure
that I myself, and no other, was in her embrace. She was paler
than I had ever seen her, but her regal expression was as firm
and immobile as that of a face on a coin. Only on her slightly
swollen lips there was a trace of delirium, which did not bespeak
satisfied or soon-to-be satisfied passion. This was so disturbing
that in order to cut it off from my view I hurriedly imprinted on
her lips the kiss of triumphant desire. Her mouth half opened,
but her deep, black eyes, whose lashes were brushing mine, did
not close, and in them I read the same madness. As she stood
transfixed by my burning kiss, with my lips penetrating hers
and my breath sucking hers in, I carried her clinging body over
to the blue sofa, for the past month my bed of pain, whose
leather now crackled under her bare back. She had come, half-
undressed, out of her bed, crossing her parents' room on the
way, with her hands stretched gropingly before her so that she
should not bump into some piece of furniture and awaken
them."

"No soldier in the trenches could show more bravery than
that," I said. "She was a worthy mistress to a fighting man!"

"My mistress she was, from that very first night," said the Vicomte. "She was as violent as I, and I was violent enough, I assure you. But there was another side to the medal. Even at the height of our transports we could not forget the precariousness of the situation into which she had led us. In the midst of our mutual happiness she seemed to be stupefied by the magnitude of the act which she had so stubbornly and audaciously brought to a conclusion. This did not surprise me, for I was equally stupefied myself. A terrible anxiety, which I took pains to conceal, gnawed at my heart while she pressed it to hers. Through her sighs and kisses, through the terrifying silence of the confidently sleeping house I listened for some sign of her mother's awakening, of her father's footsteps on the floor. Over her shoulder I stared at the door, from which, for fear of making a noise, she had not removed the key and wondered if it would open again and reveal the Medusa-like heads of the two old people whom we were so shamelessly deceiving, come to protest against the outrage to decency and the laws of hospitality which I had committed against them. Even the voluptuous crackling of the sofa, which had been the trumpet call of love, filled me with alarm. And her heart seemed to echo the pounding of mine. It was intoxicating and disintoxicating at the same time, but the general effect was one of fear. Eventually this sensation faded away. By dint of repetition this incredibly bold act lost its terror, and living in constant peril I became hardened to it.

"After the danger of this experience, which presaged further danger to come, Alberte decided that she would come to my room every other night. I could not go to hers, because it could be reached only by crossing that of her parents. She followed this program faithfully, but never without the same troubled feelings as the first time. Unlike myself she did not become callous. And invariably, even lying beside me, she remained silent for, as you have already realized, she was a woman of few words. As time went by, and impunity lent me increasing courage, I talked to her, the way any man talks to his mistress, of what had passed between us and even of the strange coldness which had followed upon her audacity; I besieged her with the insatiable 'why's' of love, which is, in the last analysis, a form of curiosity. But her only answer was to embrace me; her melancholy lips were prodigal of nothing but kisses. Some women say: 'I am ruining myself for you,' others: 'You may despise me,' and both these phrases are expressions of the fatality of love. But she never said a word. It was a strange phenomenon, and she was an even stranger person. I began to think of her as a marble slab, with a devouring fire beneath it. Eventually, I imagined, the slab would be cracked by the heat, but such was not the case and it never gave way. With the passage of time she was no more relaxed, no more loquacious. To use an ecclessiastical expression, she remained just as 'difficult to confess' as she had been at the start. I could get nothing out of her, except an occasional monosyllable. Her lips, which I adored all the more for the cold and indifferent expression they wore during the day, dropped no more than a few murmurs, and these shed no light upon her character. She remained more of a sphinx than any of those which decorated the furniture of my Empire room."

"But, Captain," I expostulated, "all these things must have added up to some conclusion. You are a strong-willed man and there are no sphinxes in real life; they exist only in fable. Eventually you must have found out what she had in her noodle."

"A conclusion? Yes, there was a conclusion." The Vicomte lowered the glass of our compartment again, as if his powerful lungs were gasping for air and he needed more oxygen to finish his story. "No, I never found out what was in her 'noodle.' Our relationship, our affair, or whatever you choose to call it, gave me sensations which I have never experienced since, not even with women whom I loved far more than I did Alberte, if it is indeed possible to speak of 'love' between us. For I never really knew what it was, in all of the six months that it lasted. All I knew was a happiness quite incredible for my age, the kind of happiness that thrives on concealment. I understood the mysterious joy of conspiracy, which is sufficient unto itself, even if it attains no fulfillment.

"At the dinner table Alberte was still the Infanta that had made the original impression upon me. Her classical forehead, under the stiff blue-black curls that came down to her eyebrows, was as smooth and imperturbable as ever and no blush on her cheeks betrayed the guilt of the night before. I tried to match her calm, but a dozen times I should have given myself away to an acute observer. Within I took a deep, sensual pride in the knowledge that her superb indifference belonged to me, that for my sake she sank to the depths of passion, if passion can sink so low. I delighted in the fact that no one else on the face of the earth knew, not even Louis de Meung, to whom I had said nothing of my success. He must have guessed it, because he was abnormally discreet and never asked me a question. I had returned to my old footing of intimacy with him, to the promenades on the main street, in dress or undress uniform, to the fencing bouts, the card games and the punch which we drank together. The assurance that a pretty girl in the throes of passion would come to my room at night did much to simplify my everyday existence."

"Alberte's parents must have slept like the Seven Sleepers," I said jokingly, in order not to show how very much I was absorbed by his story. Only an attitude of mockery can win the respect of a dandy.

"You don't think I'm making it all up, do you?" he asked. "I'm no novelist. Sometimes, of course, Alberte did not show up. There were nights when the door hinges, which were now well oiled, failed to open. This meant that her mother had called out in her sleep or her father had seen her groping her way across the room. But Alberte always had the presence of mind to furnish some explanation. She claimed to have an upset stomach and to be going after some medicine. If she had not lit the lamp it was because she did not wish to arouse them."

"Such presence of mind isn't as rare as you seem to think, Captain," I interrupted, for the sake of argument. "Your Alberte was no more resourceful than the young girl who received her lover every night in the room where her grandmother was sleeping. He came through the window, and since they had no blue leather sofa they lay down, quite simply, on the floor. Doubtless you've heard the story. One night the girl was so happy that she gave an unusually loud sigh. From her curtained bed the grandmother called out: 'What's the matter, my girl?' The girl nearly fainted away in her lover's arms, but she managed to answer: "I'm looking for a needle that fell on the floor and the ribs of my corset stuck into my side when I bent over."

"Yes, I've heard it," said the Vicomte, not in the least convinced that this heroine was any more ingenious than Alberte. "The girl in question was a Guise, if I remember correctly, and she lived up to her royal name. But you forgot to say that after that night she never opened the window to her lover again, whereas Alberte exposed herself repeatedly to the same danger. I was only a young lieutenant and mathematics was not my strong point, but the laws of probability demanded that one day – or one night – there should be a reckoning and some sort of violent conclusion to the story."

"You mean the conclusion that acquainted you for the first time with fear?" I said, remembering his previous words.

"Exactly," he said, with a gravity which was in strong contrast to my affectation of cynical lightheartedness. "You have seen for yourself that, from the moment when she first took my hand under the table to the night when she appeared like a ghost at my door, Alberte did not spare me violent emotion. She had caused me more than once to shudder, but I was like a man with bullets whistling around his head, who may tremble for his life, yet still goes on living. But now things took a different turn. I came to know real fear, not for Alberte but for myself, the kind of fear that makes a man's heart as pale as his face and causes whole regiments to flee in panic. Since then I have seen a whole division of cavalry, known for its heroism, abandon its horses and crawl madly on the ground, taking its colonel and all the rest of its officers with it. But at this time I was still a novice and what I learned was inconceivable to me.

"It happened one night . . . In the life we were leading that was inevitable. It was in the course of a long, calm winter night – for all our nights were calm and happy. We slept unconcerned on a charge of gunpowder, or suspended on the edge of a sword-blade, such as the Turks imagine bridges the path to hell. Alberte had come earlier than usual to my room in order to remain with me longer. My first attention was always for her feet, no longer encased in green or blue slippers, but bare, in order that they should make no sound, and cold from contact with the tiled floor of the long passageway between her parents' room and mine. For my sake she came out of a cosy bed and down this icy corridor, exposing herself to a fatal chill, and it was natural that I should seek to warm her. I was adept at kissing her feet, but on this night my lips were powerless to restore their rosy color.

"Alberte was more silently passionate than ever. Her embrace was so eloquent that even although I continued to pour intoxicated words into her ears I no longer demanded a verbal reply. I understood the language of her caresses. But all of a sudden this communication was shut off. Her arms relaxed their grasp and I thought she must have fainted away, as she often did at the height of her passion, although heretofore she had always clung closely to me. You and I are men and there is no no need for prudery between us. I had experienced Alberte's orgasm, without abbreviating my caresses when it came upon her. And so I remained just as I was, waiting for her to come back to herself. I was quite sure that she would recover her senses under the impact of mine, that when lightning struck her for the second time it would resuscitate her. But my expectation was deluded. I lay there, as close as one human being can be to another, waiting for the moment when her sparkling, black, velvety eyes would open and her teeth, which used to clench so tightly as to almost chip the enamel when I kissed her neck or shoulder, would part and release her first breath. But neither eyes nor teeth moved, and the iciness of her feet seemed to mount to her lips, which were pressed to mine. At the touch of this horrible chill, I drew back and stared down at her; I tore myself from the grasp of her arms, of which one fell limply across her body and the other over the side of the sofa. Fearfully, but with complete presence of mind, I laid my hand on her heart. There was no beat, either there or in her pulses or in the arteries of her neck. Death had invaded her whole body and congealed it.

"I knew that she was dead, and yet I could not believe it. The human mind can close itself against the most overwhelming evidence. Alberte was dead. For what reason? I was not a doctor, and I had no way of knowing. Although I clearly realized that there was nothing I could do, I proceeded to do it. In my total lack of medicaments or other recources, I emptied my bottle of toilet water on her forehead and slapped her hands, at the risk of giving the alarm which we had so often avoided. I had heard one of my uncles, a squadron leader of the 4th Dragoons, tell how he had revived a friend from a fit of apoplexy by bleeding him with the sort of lancet that is used on horses. There were plenty of weapons in the room, and I pricked one of Alberte's beautiful arms with a dagger. But only a few drops of blood came out, and they were coagulated. Neither kisses, nor bites nor suction had any effect upon her. Hardly aware of what I was doing I finally stretched myself out on her body, the method of resuscitation following said to have been employed by ancient magicians. I did not really hope to revive her, but I acted on this supposition. As I lay there an idea shot through my clouded mind – and I was afraid.

"The extent of my fear defies description. Alberte had died in my room, and her death told the whole story. What was I to do? What could become of me? The cold hand of fear made my hair stand on end and my backbone turn to jelly. I struggled in vain against this shameful sensation, telling myself to brace up and act like a man and a soldier. I buried my head in my hands, and as my reason slowly returned I tried to examine my desperate situation, to sort out the wild thoughts that whirled about in my brain. Every one of them ran up against the same obstacle, the body of Alberte, unable to return to her bed, and certain to be discovered by her mother 'in the officer's room,' dead and dishonored. The idea of this woman, whose daughter I had defiled and perhaps killed, was even more painful to me than that of Alberte. Nothing could wipe out the death, but was there no way of concealing the disgrace? All my thoughts focussed on this question. The more I considered it, the more unanswerable it became. At moments I suffered from the terrifying hallucination that the corpse filled the whole room and could not be carried through the door. If only her parents' room had not stood in the way of hers I could, at grave risk, have carried it back to her bed. But with her body in my arms, how could I hope to retrace the path she had so imprudently followed, through a room I had never seen, where two old people were fitfully sleeping?

And yet, in my distraught state of mind, I was so tormented by the prospect of the body's inevitable discovery on the morrow that the idea of carrying it back struck me as the only possible way to save the girl's reputation and to spare me her parents' reproaches . . . Can you believe it? I myself find it quite incredible . . . I found the strength to hoist Alberte's body onto my shoulders. What a horrible burden, heavier than that borne by the damned in Dante's Hell! To know what I went through you would have to have carried, as I did, this bundle of flesh which only an hour before had made my blood boil with desire and now appalled me.

"With this charge on my shoulders I opened the door, and barefoot as she had been, in order to muffle any sound, I started down the corridor leading to her parents' room, swaying at every step and pausing at frequent intervals to listen to the surrounding silence, which I could not hear for the pounding of my heart. Nothing stirred, and I went on, step after step. But when I reached the fateful door, which she had left half-open in view of her return, and heard the old people's regular breathing, my courage abandoned me altogether. I did not dare cross the dark threshold, but drew back and almost ran to my own room. I laid the body on the sofa, knelt down beside it and hammered my brain with the same questions as before: What was I to do? What would become of me?

"In my confusion I conceived the idea of throwing the body of this beautiful girl, for six months my mistress, out the window. Think ill of me, if you will! I pulled back the crimson curtain, opened the window and looked down into the street, whose paving was barely visible in the darkness. 'They'll think she committed suicide,' I said to myself reassuringly, and started once more to pick up the body. But suddenly a ray of common sense broke across my folly. 'When they find the body, from what place will they suppose she fell?' I was overcome by the impracticability of my plan. I shut the window, causing its hinges to creak, and drew the curtain, trembling with fright at every sound. Wherever I might try to rid myself of the body – out the window, in the hall or on the stairs – it was no use. An autopsy would tell the whole story, and no matter what a doctor or a coroner tried to conceal, a mother's intuitive eye would detect it.

"I was so thoroughly demoralized (to use a word coined by
Napoleon, whose full meaning I grasped much later in life) that
as I looked up at the weapons gleaming on the wall I thought for
a minute of taking a pistol and putting an end to it all. But – why
not admit it? – I was only seventeen years old, and I loved not
only life but also my military vocation. I was ambitious, and
waiting eagerly to take part in my first battle. In the regiment
we made fun of the pitiful figure of Werther, a literary hero of
the time. The quickly dismissed thought of my gun led to
another, which promised a much more reasonable form of
salvation. What if I were to go to my colonel. Was he not,
under the circumstances, my spiritual father? I dressed myself
as hurriedly as if there had been a surprise attack and a call to
arms, strapping my pistols to my belt as a precautionary
measure. With youthful fervor I kissed for the last time the
lips of Alberte – hardly more mute now than they had been for
the entire six months of our passion – and tiptoed down the
stairs, anxious to leave this house of death behind me. After
what seemed like an hour I managed to turn the big key in the
lock of the downstairs door and, like a thief, to close it after me,
I ran, as if in fear for my life, to the colonel's door and banged
upon it as loudly as if the enemy were about to bear away the
regimental colors. Brushing aside the orderly who tried to block
my way I went straight to his bed, and when my cries finally
awakened him I poured my whole story, at breakneck speed,
into his ears and implored him to save me.

"The colonel was a real man, and understood at once the
gravity of my dilemma. He took pity on me as 'the youngest of
his children,' and indeed there must have been something
pitiful about me. With the most typical of French oaths he
abjured me to leave town without delay, promising that he
would take the matter into his own hands after my departure. I
was to board the stagecoach which was due in just six minutes to
change horses at the *Poste aux Chevaux* and go to another town,
where he would send further orders. He supplied me with
money, which I had forgotten to bring along, pressed his grey
moustache to my cheeks and sent me packing. Ten minutes later
I climbed into the only remaining outside seat of the stage,
which followed the same route as we are following tonight. You

can imagine with what troubled feelings I looked up at the room where I had left the dead Alberte – with the light shining behind the curtain just as it is now – as the horses galloped by . . .''

The Vicomte de Brassard came to a pause, and there was a tremor in his voice which restrained me from any further levity.

"And then?" I asked after a short silence.

"And then . . . nothing. I was tormented by the total absence of news. Following the colonel's instructions I waited impatiently for a letter which should tell me what had happened. But the colonel was not given to writing, except with the point of his sword on the enemy's face, and a month later I received not a letter, but orders to join, within the space of twenty-four hours, another regiment, the 35th, which was about to go into battle. The events of my first military campaign, the battles I fought and the women with whom I slept, prevented me from communicating with the colonel and distracted me from my memory of Alberte, although without effacing it from my mind, for it was embedded deep within me, like a bullet which defies extrication. I kept thinking that one day or another I should run into the colonel and hear the sequel of the story. But he was killed, while leading his regiment, at Leipzig, and Louis de Meung died a month before him.

"It's rather a contemptible story, but the truth is that a strong-minded man can forget anything; perhaps that's the secret of his strength. Eventually I lost even my curiosity. With the passing of the years I could perfectly well have come back, without being recognized, to this town and have enquired of the local people what version had come down to them of my tragic adventure. Certainly no sensitivity to public opinion deterred me, for I've never cared a fig for that. It must have been something akin to my original fear . . .''

This was the end of the grim story, so unlike any I should have expected to hear from the lips of a dandy. I realized that the dashing Vicomte de Brassard, with his taste for women and Bordeaux wine, had depths within him which I had never suspected, and saw the meaning of his reference to the shadow that had been cast over all his amorous misdemeanors.

"Look!" he said, suddenly grasping my arm. "Look at the curtain!"

For the slender form of a woman had just passed, in silhouette, across it.

"The ghost of Alberte!" the captain exclaimed. "Fate is bent on making sport of me tonight."

Now the curtain was no more than an unbroken, crimson square. The blacksmith had finished his work on the wheel and the fresh horses were champing at the bit and pawing the ground. The postilion, with an astrakhan cap pulled down over his ears and the list of passengers between his teeth, climbed to his seat, picked up the reins and shouted in a clear, commanding voice:

"Get on with you!"

We drove on, leaving behind us the mysterious window with its crimson curtain, which still haunts my dreams.

The Purloined Letter

Edgar Allan Poe

At Paris, just after dark one gusty evening in the autumn of 18—, I was enjoying the twofold luxury of meditation and meerschaum in company with my friend, C. Auguste Dupin, in his little back library, or book-closet, *au troisième*, No. 33 Rue Dunot, Faubourg St. Germain. For one hour at least we had maintained a profound silence: while each, to any casual observer, might have seemed intently and exclusively occupied with the curling eddies of smoke that oppressed the atmosphere of the chamber. For myself, however, I was mentally discussing certain topics which had formed matter for conversation between us at an earlier period of the evening; I mean the affair of the Rue Morgue and the mystery attending the murder of Marie Roget. I looked upon it, therefore, as something of a coincidence when the door of our apartment was thrown open and admitted our old acquaintance, Monsieur G—, the Prefect of the Parisian police.

We gave him a hearty welcome: for there was nearly half as much of the entertaining as of the contemptible about the man, and we had not seen him for several years. We had been sitting in the dark, and Dupin now arose for the purpose of lighting a lamp, but sat down again, without doing so, upon G—'s saying that he had called to consult us, or rather to ask the opinion of my friend, about some official business which had occasioned a great deal of trouble.

"If it is any point requiring reflection," observed Dupin, as he forebore to enkindle the wick, "we shall examine it to better purpose in the dark."

"That is another of your odd notions," said the Prefect, who had the fashion of calling everything "odd" that was beyond his comprehension, and thus lived amid an absolute legion of "oddities."

"Very true," said Dupin, as he supplied his visitor with a pipe and rolled toward him a comfortable chair.

"And what is the difficulty now?" I asked. "Nothing more in the assassination way, I hope?"

"Oh, no; nothing of that nature. The fact is, the business is *very* simple indeed, and I make no doubt that we can manage it sufficiently well ourselves; but then I thought Dupin would like to hear the details of it, because it is so excessively *odd*."

"Simple and odd?" said Dupin.

"Why, yes; and not exactly that either. The fact is, we have all been a good deal puzzled because the affair is so simple, and yet baffles us altogether."

"Perhaps it is the very simplicity of the thing which puts you at fault," said my friend.

"What nonsense you *do* talk!" replied the Prefect, laughing heartily.

"Perhaps the mystery is a little *too* plain," said Dupin.

"Oh, good heavens! who ever heard of such an idea?"

"A little *too* self-evident."

"Ha! ha! ha!–ha! ha! ha! – ho! ho! ho!" roared our visitor, profoundly amused. "Oh, Dupin, you will be the death of me yet."

"And what, after all, *is* the matter on hand?" I asked.

"Why, I will tell you," replied the Prefect, as he gave a long steady and contemplative, puff and settled himself in his chair – "I will tell you in a few words; but, before I begin, let me caution you that this is an affair demanding the greatest secrecy, and that I should most probably lose the position I now hold were it known that I confided it to anyone at all."

"Proceed," said I.

"Or not," said Dupin.

"Well, then; I have received personal information, from a very high quarter, that a certain document of the last importance has been purloined from the royal apartments. The individual who purloined it is known – this beyond a doubt;

he was seen to take it. It is known, also, that it still remains in his possession."

"How is this known?" asked Dupin.

"It is clearly inferred," replied the Prefect, "from the nature of the document and from the non-appearance of certain re-sults, which would at once arise from its passing out of the robber's possession, that is to say, from his employing it as he must design in the end to employ it."

"Be a little more explicit," I said.

"Well, I may venture so far as to say that the paper gives its holder a certain power in a certain quarter where such power is immensely valuable." The Prefect was fond of the cant of diplomacy.

"Still I do not quite understand," said Dupin.

"No? Well; the disclosure of the document to a third person, who shall be nameless, would bring in question the honor of a personage of most exalted station; and this fact gives the holder of the document an ascendancy over the illustrious personage whose honor and peace are so jeopardized."

"But this ascendancy," I interposed, "would depend upon the robber's knowledge of the loser's knowledge of the robber. Who would dare—"

"The thief," said G—, "is the Minister D—, who dares all things, those unbecoming as well as those becoming a man. The method of the theft was not less ingenious than bold. The document in question – a letter, to be frank – had been received by the personage robbed while alone in the royal boudoir. During its perusal she was suddenly interrupted by the entrance of the other exalted personage from whom especially it was her wish to conceal it. After a hurried and vain endeavor to thrust it in a drawer, she was forced to place it, open as it was, upon a table. The address however, was uppermost, and the content thus unexposed the letter escaped notice. At this juncture enters the Minister D—. His lynx eye immediately perceives the paper, recognizes the handwriting of the address, observes the confusion of the personage addressed, and fathoms her secret. After some business transactions, hurried through in his ordinary manner, he produces a letter somewhat similar to the one in question, opens it, pretends to read it, and then places it in close juxtaposition to the other. Again he converses for some fifteen minutes upon the public affairs. At length, in taking leave, he takes also from the table the letter to which he had no claim. Its rightful owner saw, but, of course, dared not call attention to the fact, in the presence of the third personage, who stood at her elbow. The Minister decamped, leaving his own letter, one of no importance, upon the table."

"Here, then," said Dupin to me, "you have precisely what you demand to make the ascendancy complete, the robber's knowledge of the loser's knowledge of the robber."

"Yes," replied the Prefect; "and the power thus attained has, for some months past, been wielded, for political purposes, to a very dangerous extent. The personage robbed is more thoroughly convinced every day of the necessity of reclaiming her letter. But this, of course, cannot be done openly. In fine, driven to despair, she has committed the matter to me."

"Than whom," said Dupin, amid a perfect whirlwind of smoke, "no more sagacious agent could, I suppose, be desired or even imagined."

"You flatter me," replied the Prefect; "but it is possible that some such opinion may have been entertained."

"It is clear," said I, "as you observe, that the letter is still in the possession of the Minister; since it is his possession, and not any employment of the letter, which bestows the power. With the employment the power departs."

"True," said G—; "and upon this conviction I proceeded. My first care was to make thorough search of the Minister's hotel; and here my chief embarrassment lay in the necessity of searching without his knowledge. Beyond all things, I have been warned of the danger which would result from giving him reason to suspect our design."

"But," said I, "you are quite *au fait* in these investigations. The Parisian police have done this thing often before."

"Oh, yes; and for this reason I did not despair. The habits of the Minister gave me, too, a great advantage. He is frequently absent from home all night. His servants are by no means numerous. They sleep at a distance from their master's apartment, and, being chiefly Neapolitans are readily made drunk. I have keys as you know with which I can open any chamber of cabinet in Paris. For three months a night has not passed, during the greater part of which I have not been engaged, personally, in ransacking the D— Hotel. My honor is interested, and, to mention a great secret, the reward is enormous. So I did not abandon the search until I had become fully satisfied that the thief is a more astute man than myself. I fancy that I have investigated every nook and corner of the premises in which it is possible that the paper can be concealed."

"But is it not possible," I suggested, "that although the letter may be in possession of the Minister, as it unquestionably is, he may have concealed it elsewhere than upon his own premises?"

"This is barely possible," said Dupin. "The present peculiar condition of affairs at court, and especially of those intrigues in which D— is known to be involved, would render the instant availability of the document, its susceptibility of being produced at a moment's notice, a point of nearly equal importance with its possession."

"Its susceptibility of being produced?" said I.

"That is to say, of being *destroyed*," said Dupin.

"True," I observed; "the paper is clearly, then, upon the premises. As for its being upon the person of the minister, we may consider that as out of the question."

"Entirely," said the Prefect. "He has been twice waylaid, as if by footpads, and his person rigidly searched under my own inspection."

"You might have spared yourself this trouble," said Dupin. "D—, I presume, is not altogether a fool, and, if not, must have anticipated these waylayings, as a matter of course."

"Not *altogether* a fool," said G—, "but then he is a poet, which I take to be one remove from a fool."

"True," said Dupin, after a long and thoughtful whiff from his meerschaum, "although I have been guilty of certain doggerel myself."

"Suppose you detail," said I, "the particulars of your search."

"Why, the fact is, we took our time, and we searched *everywhere*. I have had long experience in these affairs. I took the entire building, room by room; devoting the nights of a whole week to each. We examined, first, the furniture of each apartment. We opened every possible drawer; and I presume you know that, to a properly trained police-agent, such a thing as a *secret* drawer is impossible. Any man is a dolt who permits a 'secret' drawer to escape him in a search of this kind. The thing is *so* plain. There is a certain amount of bulk, of space, to be accounted for in every cabinet. Then we have accurate rules. The fiftieth part of a line could not escape us. After the cabinets we took the chairs. The cushions we probed with the fine long needles you have seen me employ. From the tables we removed the tops."

"Why so?"

"Sometimes the top of a table or other similarly arranged piece of furniture is removed by the person wishing to conceal an article; then the leg is excavated, the article deposited within the cavity, and the top replaced. The bottoms and tops of bedposts are employed in the same way."

"But could not the cavity be detected by sounding?" I asked.

"By no means, if, when the article is deposited, a sufficient wadding of cotton be placed around it. Besides, in our case, we were obliged to proceed without noise."

"But you could not have removed, you could not have taken to pieces *all* articles of furniture in which it would have been possible to make a deposit in the manner you mention. A letter may be compressed into a thin spiral roll, not differing much in shape or bulk from a large knitting-needle, and in this form it might be inserted into the rung of a chair, for example. You did not take to pieces all the chairs?"

"Certainly not, but we did better: we examined the rungs of every chair in the hotel, and, indeed, the jointings of every description of furniture, by the aid of a most powerful microscope. Had there been any traces of recent disturbance we should not have failed to detect it instantly. A single gram of gimlet-dust, for example, would have been as obvious as an apple. Any disorder in the gluing, any unusual gaping in the joints, would have sufficed to insure detection."

"I presume you looked to the mirrors, between the boards and the plates, and you probed the beds and the bedclothes, as well as the curtains and carpets."

"That of course; and when we had absolutely completed

every particle of the furniture in this way, then we examined the house itself. We divided its entire surface into compartments, which we numbered, so that none might be missed; then we scrutinized each individual square inch throughout the premises, including the two houses immediately adjoining, with the microscope, as before."

"The two houses adjoining!" I exclaimed, "you must have had a great deal of trouble."

"We had; but the reward offered is prodigious."

"You included the *grounds* about the houses?"

"All the grounds are paved with brick. They gave us comparatively little trouble. We examined the moss between the bricks and found it undisturbed."

"You looked among D—'s papers, of course, and into the books of the library?"

"Certainly; we opened every package and parcel; we not only opened every book, but we turned over every leaf in each volume, not contenting ourselves with a mere shake, according to the fashion of some of our police officers. We also measured the thickness of every book-cover with the most accurate measurement, and applied to each the most jealous scrutiny of the microscope. Had any of the bindings been recently meddled with, it would have been utterly impossible that the fact should have escaped observation. Some five or six volumes, just from the hands of the binder, we carefully probed, longitudinally, with the needles."

"You explored the floors beneath the carpets?"

"Beyond doubt. We removed every carpet and examined the boards with the microscope."

"And the paper on the walls?"

"Yes."

"You looked into the cellars?"

"We did."

"Then," I said, "you have been making a miscalculation, and the letter is *not* upon the premises."

"I fear you are right there," said the Prefect. "And now, Dupin, what would you advise me to do?"

"To make a thorough search of the premises."

"That is absolutely needless," replied G—. "I am not

more sure that I breathe than I am that the letter is not at the hotel."

"I have no better advice to give you," said Dupin. "You have, of course, a description of the letter?"

"Oh, yes!" and here the Prefect, producing a memorandum-book, proceeded to read aloud a minute account of the internal, and especially of the external, appearance of the missing document. Soon after finishing the perusal of this description he took his departure, more entirely depressed in spirits than I had ever known the good gentleman before.

In about a month afterward he paid us another visit, and found us occupied very nearly as before. He took a pipe and a chair and entered into some ordinary conversation. At length I said:

"Well, but, G——, what of the purloined letter? I presume you have at last made up your mind that there is no overreaching the Minister?"

"Confound him! say I – yes; I made the re-examination, however, as Dupin suggested, but it was all labor lost, as I knew it would be."

"How much was the reward offered, did you say?" asked Dupin.

"Why, a very great deal, a *very* liberal reward; I don't like to say how much, precisely; but one thing I *will* say – that I wouldn't mind giving my individual check for fifty thousand francs to anyone who could obtain me that letter. The fact is, it is becoming of more and more importance every day; and the reward has been lately doubled. If it were trebled, however, I could do no more than I have done."

"Why, yes," said Dupin, drawlingly, between the whiffs of his meerschaum, "I really – think, G——, you have not exerted yourself – to the utmost in this matter. You might – do a little more, I think, eh?"

"How? in what way?"

"Why – puff, puff – you might – puff, puff – employ counsel in the matter eh? – puff, puff, puff. Do you remember the story of Abernethy?"

"No; hang Abernethy!"

"To be sure, hang him and welcome. But, once upon a time, a

certain rich miser conceived the design of sponging upon this Abernethy for a medical opinion. Getting up, for this purpose, an ordinary conversation in a private company, he insinuated his case to the physician as that of an imaginary individual.

" 'We will suppose,' said the miser, 'that his symptoms are such and such; now, Doctor, what would *you* have directed him to take?' "

" 'Take,' said Abernethy, 'why, take advice, to be sure.' "

"But," said the Prefect, a little discomposed, "I am *perfectly* willing to take advice and to pay for it. I would *really* give fifty thousand francs to anyone who would aid me in the matter."

"In that case," replied Dupin, opening a drawer and producing a checkbook, "you may as well fill me up a check for that amount mentioned. When you have signed it I will hand you the letter."

I was astounded. The Prefect appeared absolutely thunder-stricken. For some minutes he remained speechless and motionless, looking incredulously at my friend with open mouth, and eyes that seemed starting from their sockets; then, apparently recovering himself in some measure, he seized a pen, and after several pauses and vacant stares finally filled up and signed a check for fifty thousand francs and handed it across the table to Dupin. The latter examined it carefully and deposited it in his pocketbook; then, unlocking an escritoire, took thence a letter and gave it to the Prefect. This functionary grasped it in a perfect agony of joy, opened it with a trembling hand, cast a rapid glance at its contents, and then, scrambling and struggling to the door, rushed at length unceremoniously from the room and from the house without having uttered a syllable since Dupin had requested him to fill up the check.

When he had gone, my friend entered into some explanation.

"The Parisian police," he said, "are exceedingly able in their way. They are persevering, ingenious, cunning, and thoroughly versed in the knowledge which their duties seem chiefly to demand. Thus, when G— detailed to us his mode of searching the premises at the Hotel D—, I felt entire confidence in his having made a satisfactory examination, so far as his labors extended."

" 'So far as his labors extended?' " said I.

"Yes," said Dupin. "The measures adopted were not only the best of their kind, but carried out to absolute perfection. Had the letter been deposited within the range of their search, these fellows would, beyond a question, have found it."

I merely laughed, but he seemed quite serious in all that he said.

"The measures, then," he continued, "were good in their kind and well executed; their defect lay in their being inapplicable to the case and to the man. A certain set of highly ingenious resources are, with the Prefect, a sort of Procrustean bed, to which he forcibly adapts his designs. But he perpetually errs by being too deep or too shallow for the matter in hand; and many a schoolboy is a better reasoner than he. I knew one about eight years of age, whose success at guessing in the game of 'even and odd' attracted universal admiration. This game is simple, and is played with marbles. One player holds in his hand a number of these toys and demands of another whether that number is even or odd. If the guess is right, the guesser wins one; if wrong, he loses one. The boy to whom I allude won all the marbles of the school. Of course he had some principle of guessing, and this lay in mere observation and admeasurement of the astuteness of his opponents. For example, an arrant simpleton is his opponent, and, holding up his closed hand, asks, 'Are they even or odd?' Our schoolboy replies, 'Odd,' and loses; but upon the second trial he wins, for he then says to himself: 'The simpleton had them even upon the first trial, and his amount of cunning is just sufficient to make him have them odd upon the second; I will therefore guess odd'; he guesses odd and wins. Now, with a simpleton a degree above the first, he would have reasoned thus: 'This fellow finds that in the first instance I guessed odd, and in the second he will propose to himself, upon the first impulse, a simple variation from even to odd, as did the first simpleton; but then a second thought will suggest that this is too simple a variation, and finally he will decide upon putting it even as before. I will therefore guess even'; – he guesses even and wins. Now this mode of reasoning in the schoolboy, whom his fellows termed 'lucky,' – what, in its last analysis, is it?"

"It is merely," I said, "an identification of the reasoner's intellect with that of his opponent."

"It is," said Dupin; "and upon inquiring of the boy by what means he effected the thorough identification in which his success consisted, I received answer as follows: 'When I wish to find out how wise, or how stupid, or how good, or how wicked is anyone, or what are his thoughts at the moment, I fashion the expression of my face, as accurately as possible, in accordance with the expression of his and then wait to see what thoughts or sentiments arise in my mind or heart, as if to match or correspond with the expression.' This response of the school-boy lies at the bottom of all the spurious profundity which has been attributed to Rochefoucauld, to La Bruyère, to Machiavelli, and to Campanella."

"And the identification," I said, "of the reasoner's intellect with that of his opponent depends, if I understand you aright, upon the accuracy with which the opponent's intellect is ad-measured."

"For its practical value it depends upon this," replied Dupin; "and the Prefect and his cohort fail so frequently, first, by default of this identification, and, secondly, by ill-admeasurement, or rather through non-admeasurement, of the intellect with which they are engaged. They consider only their *own* ideas of ingenuity; and, in searching for anything hidden, advert only to the modes in which *they* would have hidden it. They are right in this much, that their own ingenuity is a faithful representative of that of *the mass;* but when the cunning of the individual felon is diverse in character from their own, the felon foils them, of course. This always happens when it is above their own, and very usually when it is below. They have no variation of principle in their investigations; at best, when urged by some unusual emergency, by some extraordinary reward, they extend or exaggerate their old modes of practice without touching their principles. What, for example, in this case of D—, has been done to vary the principle of action? What is all this boring, and probing, and sounding, and scrutinizing with the microscope, and dividing the surface of the building into registered square inches; what is it all but an exaggeration of the application of the one principle or set of principles of search, which are based upon the one set of notions regarding human ingenuity, to which the Prefect, in the long routine of his duty, has been accustomed? Do you not see he has taken it for granted that *all* men proceed to conceal a letter, not exactly in a gimlet-hole bored in a chair-leg, but, at least, in *some* out-of-the-way hole or corner suggested by the same tenor of thought which would urge a man to secrete a letter in a gimlet-hole bored in a chair-leg? And do you not see, also, that such *recherchés* nooks for concealment are adapted only for ordinary occasions, and would be adopted only by ordinary intellects; for, in all cases of concealment, a disposal of it in this *recherché* manner, is, in the very first instance, presumable and presumed; and thus its discovery depends, not at all upon the acumen, but altogether upon the mere care, patience, and determination of the seekers; and where the case is of importance, or, what amounts to the same thing in the policial eyes, when the reward is of magnitude, the qualities in question have *never* been known to fail. You will now understand what I meant in suggesting that had the purloined letter been hidden anywhere within the limits of the Prefect's examination – in other words, had the principle of its concealment been comprehended within the principles of the Prefect – its discovery would have been a matter altogether beyond question. This functionary, however, has been thoroughly mystified; and the remote source of his defeat lies in the supposition that the Minister is a fool, because he has acquired renown as a poet. All fools are poets: this the Prefect *feels*; and he is merely guilty of a *non distributio medii* in thence inferring that all poets are fools."

"But is this really the poet?" I asked. "There are two brothers, I know and both have attained reputation in letters. The Minister, I believe, has written learnedly on the Differential Calculus. He is a mathematician and no poet."

"You are mistaken; I know him well; he is both. As poet *and* mathematician, he would reason well; as mere mathematician, he could not have reasoned at all, and thus would have been at the mercy of the Prefect."

"You surprise me," I said, "by these opinions, which have been contradicted by the voice of the world. You do not mean to set at naught the well-digested idea of centuries? The mathematical reason has long been regarded as *the* reason *par excellence*."

" '*Il y a à parier,*' " replied Dupin, quoting from Chamfort, " '*que toute idee publique, toute convention reçue, est une sottise, car elle a convenu au plus grand nombre.*' The mathematicians, I grant you, have done their best to promulgate the popular error to which you allude, and which is none the less an error for its promulgation as truth. With an art worthy a better cause, for example, they have insinuated the term 'analysis' into application to algebra. The French are the originators of this particular deception; but if a term is of any importance, if words derive any value from applicability, then 'analysis' conveys 'algebra' about as much, as in Latin, '*ambitus*' implies 'ambition,' '*religio*' 'religion,' or '*homines honesti*' a set of *honorable* men."

"You have a quarrel on hand, I see," said I, "with some of the algebraists of Paris: but proceed."

"I dispute the availability, and thus the value, of that reason which is cultivated in any especial form other than the abstractly logical. I dispute, in particular, the reason educed by mathematical study. The mathematics are the science of form and quantity; mathematical reasoning is merely logic applied to observation upon form and quantity. The great error lies in supposing that even the truths of what is called *pure* algebra are abstract or general truths. And this error is so egregious that I am confounded at the universality with which it has been received. Mathematical axioms are *not* axioms of general truth. What is true of relation, of form and quantity, is often grossly false in regard to morals, for example. In this latter science it is very usually *un*true that the aggregated parts are equal to the whole. In chemistry, also, the axiom fails. In the consideration of motive it fails; for two motives, each of a given value, have not, necessarily, a value, when united, equal to the sum of their values apart. There are numerous other mathematical truths which are only truths within the limits of relation. But the mathematician argues from his *finite truths*, through habit, as if they were of an absolutely general applicability, as the world indeed imagines them to be. Bryant, in his very learned *Mythology*, mentions an analogous source of error when he says that 'although the pagan fables are not believed, yet we forget ourselves continually and make inferences from them as existing realities.' With the algebraists, however, who are pagans

themselves, the 'pagan fables' *are* believed, and the inferences
are made, not so much through lapse of memory as through an
unaccountable addling of the brains. In short, I never yet
encountered the mere mathematician who could be trusted
out of equal roots, or one who did not clandestinely hold it
as a point of his faith that $x^2 + px$ was absolutely and un-
conditionally equal to q. Say to one of these gentlemen, by way
of experiment, if you please, that you believe occasions may
occur where $x^2 + px$ is *not* altogether equal to q, and, having
made him understand what you mean, get out of his reach as
speedily as convenient, for, beyond doubt, he will endeavor to
knock you down.

"I mean to say," continued Dupin, while I merely laughed at
his last observations, "that if the Minister had been no more
than a mathematician, the Prefect would have been under no
necessity of giving me this check. I knew him, however, as both
mathematician and poet, and my measures were adapted to his
capacity with reference to the circumstances by which he was
surrounded. I knew him as a courtier, too, and as a bold
intrigant. Such a man, I considered, could not fail to be aware
of the ordinary policial modes of action. He could not have
failed to anticipate – and events have proved that he did not fail
to anticipate – the waylayings to which he was subjected. He
must have foreseen, I reflected, the secret investigations of his
premises. His frequent absences from home at night, which
were hailed by the Prefect as certain aids to his success, I
regarded only as ruses to afford opportunity for thorough
search to the police, and thus the sooner to impress them with
the conviction, to which G—, in fact, did finally arrive – the
conviction that the letter was not upon the premises. I felt, also,
that the whole train of thought, which I was at some pains in
detailing to you just now, concerning the invariable principle of
political action in searches for articles concealed – I felt that this
whole train of thought would necessarily pass through the mind
of the Minister. It would imperatively lead him to despise all
the ordinary nooks of concealment. *He* could not, I reflected, be
so weak as not to see that the most intricate and remote recess of
his hotel would be as open as his commonest closers to the eyes
to the probes, to the gunlets, and to the microscopes of the

Prefect. I saw, in fine, that he would be driven, as a matter of course, to simplicity, if not deliberately induced to it as a matter of choice. You will remember, perhaps, how desperately the Prefect laughed when I suggested, upon our first interview, that it was just possible this mystery troubled him on account of its being so very self-evident."

"Yes," said I, "I remember his merriment well. I really thought he would have fallen into convulsions."

"The material world," continued Dupin, "abounds with very strict analogies to the immaterial and thus some color of truths has been given to the rhetorical dogma that metaphor, or simile, may be made to strengthen an argument as well as to embellish a description. The principle of the *vis inertiæ*, for example, seems to be identical in physics and metaphysics. It is not more true in the former, that a large body is with more difficulty set in motion than a smaller one, and that its subsequent momentum is commensurate with this difficulty, than it is, in the latter, that intellects of the vaster capacity, while more forcible, more constant, and more eventful in their movements than those of inferior grade, are yet the less readily moved, and more embarrassed, and full of hesitation in the first few steps of their progress. Again: have you ever noticed which of the street signs, over the shop doors, are the most attractive of attention?"

"I have never given the matter a thought," I said.

"There is a game of puzzles," he resumed, "which is played upon a map. One party playing requires another to find a given word, the name of town, river, state, or empire – any word, in short, upon the motley and perplexed surface of the chart. A novice in the game generally seeks to embarrass his opponents by giving them the most minutely lettered names; but the adept selects such words as stretch, in large characters, from one end of the chart to the other. These, like the over-largely lettered signs and placards of the street, escape observation by dint of being excessively obvious; and here the physical oversight is precisely analagous with the moral inapprehension by which the intellect suffers to pass unnoticed those considerations which are too obtrusively and too palpably self-evident. But this is a point, it appears, somewhat above or beneath the understanding of the Prefect. He never once thought it probable, or possible, that the Minister had deposited the letter immediately beneath the nose of the whole world, by way of best preventing any portion of that world from perceiving it.

"But the more I reflected upon the daring, dashing and discriminating ingenuity of D—, upon the fact that the document must always have been at hand, if he intended to use it to good purpose; and upon the decisive evidence, obtained by the Prefect, that it was not hidden within the limits of that dignitary's ordinary search, the more satisfied I became that, to conceal this letter, the Minister had resorted to the comprehensive and sagacious expedient of not attempting to conceal it at all.

"Full of these ideas, I prepared myself with a pair of green spectacles, and called one fine morning, quite by accident, at the ministerial hotel. I found D— at home, yawning, lounging, and dawdling, as usual, and pretending to be in the last extremity of *ennui*. He is, perhaps, the most really energetic human being now alive; but that is only when nobody sees him.

"To be even with him, I complained of my weak eyes and lamented the necessity of the spectacles under cover of which I cautiously and thoroughly surveyed the whole apartment, while seemingly intent only upon the conversation of my host.

"I paid especial attention to a large writing-table near which he sat, and upon which lay confusedly some miscellaneous letters and other papers, with one or two musical instruments and a few books. Here, however, after a long and very deliberate scrutiny, I saw nothing to excite particular suspicion.

"At length my eyes, in going the circuit of the room, fell upon a trumpery filigree card-rack of pasteboard that hung dangling by a dirty blue ribbon from a little brass knob just beneath the middle of the mantelpiece. In this rack, which had three or four compartments, were five or six visiting-cards and a solitary letter. This last was much soiled and crumpled. It was torn nearly in two, across the middle, as if a design, in the first instance, to tear it entirely up as worthless had been altered, or stayed, in the second. It had a large black seal, bearing the D— cipher *very* conspicuously, and was addressed, in a diminutive female hand, to D—, the Minister, himself. It was thrust carelessly, and even, as it seemed, contemptuously, into one of the uppermost divisions of the rack.

"No sooner had I glanced at this letter than I concluded it to be that of which I was in search. To be sure, it was, to all appearance, radically different from the one of which the Prefect had read us so minute a description. Here the seal was large and black, with the D— cipher, there it was small and red, with the ducal arms of the S— family. Here, the address, to the Minister, was diminutive and feminine; there the superscription, to a certain royal personage, was markedly bold and decided; the size alone formed a point of correspondence. But then, the radicalness of these differences, which was excessive: the dirt; the soiled and torn condition of the paper, so inconsistent with the *true* methodical habits of D—, and so suggestive of a design to delude the beholder into an idea of the worthlessness of the document – these things, together with the hyperobtrusive situation of this document, full in the view of every visitor, and thus exactly in accordance with the conclusions to which I had previously arrived; these things, I say, were strongly corroborative of suspicion, in one who came with the intention to suspect.

"I protracted my visit as long as possible, and, while I maintained a most animated discussion with the Minister upon a topic which I knew well had never failed to interest and excite him, I kept my attention really riveted upon the letter. In this examination, I committed to memory its external appearance and arrangement in the rack; and also fell, at length, upon a discovery which set at rest whatever trivial doubt I might have entertained. In scrutinizing the edges of the paper, I observed them to be more chafed than seemed necessary. They presented the broken appearance which is manifested when a stiff paper, having been once folded and pressed with a folder, is refolded in a reversed direction, in the same creases or edges which had formed the original fold. This discovery was sufficient. It was clear to me that the letter had been turned, as a glove, inside out, redirected and resealed. I bade the Minister good morning, and took my departure at once, leaving a gold snuff-box upon the table.

"The next morning I called for the snuff-box, when we

resumed, quite eagerly, the conversation of the preceding day. While thus engaged, however, a loud report, as if of a pistol, was heard immediately beneath the windows of the hotel, and was succeeded by a series of fearful screams, and the shoutings of a terrified mob. D— rushed to a casement, threw it open, and looked out. In the meantime I stepped to the card-rack, took the letter, put it in my pocket, and replaced it by a facsimile (so far as regards externals) which I had carefully prepared at my lodgings, imitating the D— cipher very readily by means of a seal formed of bread.

"The disturbance in the street had been occasioned by the frantic behavior of a man with a musket. He had fired it among a crowd of women and children. It proved, however, to have been without a ball, and the fellow was suffered to go his way as a lunatic or a drunkard. When he had gone D—came from the window, whither I had followed him immediately upon securing the object in view. Soon afterward I bade him farewell. The pretended lunatic was a man in my own pay."

"But what purpose had you," I asked, "in replacing the letter by a facsimile? Would it not have been better, at the first visit, to have seized it openly and departed?"

"D—," replied Dupin, "is a desperate man, and a man of nerve. His hotel, too, is not without attendants devoted to his interests. Had I made the wild attempt you suggest, I might never have left the ministerial presence alive. The good people of Paris might have heard of me no more. But I had an object apart from these considerations. You know my political prepossessions. In this matter, I act as a partisan of the lady concerned. For eighteen months the Minister has had her in his power. She has now him in hers, since, being unaware that the letter is not in his possession, he will proceed with his exactions as if it was. Thus will he inevitably commit himself, at once, to his political destruction. His downfall, too, will not be more precipitate than awkward. It is all very well to talk about the *facilis descensus Averni*; but in all kinds of climbing, as Catalani said of singing, it is far more easy to get up than to come down. In the present instance I have no sympathy, at least no pity, for him who descends. He is that *monstrum horrendum*, an unprincipled man of genius. I confess, however, that I should like very well to know the precise character of his thoughts, when, being defied by her whom the Prefect terms 'a certain personage,' he is reduced to opening the letter which I left for him in the card-rack."

"How? Did you put anything particular in it?"

"Why, it did not seem altogether right to leave the interior blank; that would have been insulting. D—, at Vienna once, did me an evil turn, which I told him, quite good-humoredly, that I should remember. So, as I knew he would feel some curiosity in regard to the identity of the person who had outwitted him, I thought it a pity not to give him a clue. He is well acquainted with my MSS., and I just copied into the middle of the blank sheets the words

> " '— *Un dessein si funeste,*
> *S'il n'est digne d'Atrée, est digne de Thyeste.*'

They are to be found in Crébillon's *Atrée*."

A Trap to Catch
a Cracksman

E.W. Hornung

I was just putting out my light when the telephone rang a
furious tocsin in the next room. I flounced out of bed more
asleep than awake; in another minute I should have been past
ringing up. It was one o'clock in the morning, and I had been
dining with Swigger Morrison at his club.

"Hulloa!"

"That you, Bunny?"

"Yes – are you Raffles?"

"What's left of me! Bunny, I want you – quick."

And even over the wire his voice was faint with anxiety and
apprehension.

"What on earth has happened?"

"Don't ask! You never know—"

"I'll come at once. Are you there, Raffles?"

"What's that?"

"Are you there, man?"

"Ye – e – es."

"At the Albany?"

"No, no, at Maguire's."

"You never said so. And where's Maguire?"

"In Halfmoon Street."

"I know that. Is he there now?"

"No – not come in yet – and I'm caught."

"Caught!"

"In that trap he bragged about. It serves me right. I didn't
believe in it. But I'm caught at last . . . caught . . . at last!"

"When he told us he set it every night! Oh, Raffles, what sort of a trap is it? What shall I do? What shall I bring?"

But his voice had grown fainter and wearier with every answer, and now there was no answer at all. Again and again I asked Raffles if he was there; the only sound to reach me in reply was the low metallic hum of the live wire between his ear and mine. And then, as I sat gazing distractedly at my four safe walls, with the receiver still pressed to my head, there came a single groan, followed by the dull and dreadful crash of a human body falling in a heap.

In utter panic I rushed back into my bedroom, and flung myself into the crumpled shirt and evening clothes that lay where I had cast them off. But I knew no more what I was doing than what to do next. I afterwards found that I had taken out a fresh tie, and tied it rather better than usual; but I can remember thinking of nothing but Raffles in some diabolical man-trap, and of a grinning monster stealing in to strike him senseless with one murderous blow. I must have looked in the glass to array myself as I did; but the mind's eye was the seeing eye, and it was filled with this frightful vision of the notorious pugilist known to fame and infamy as Barney Maguire.

It was only the week before that Raffles and I had been introduced to him at the Imperial Boxing Club. Heavyweight champion of the United States, the fellow was still drunk with his sanguinary triumphs on that side, and clamouring for fresh conquests on ours. But his reputation had crossed the Atlantic before Maguire himself; the grandiose hotels had closed their doors to him; and he had already taken and sumptuously furnished the house in Halfmoon Street which does not re-let to this day. Raffles had made friends with the magnificent brute, while I took timid stock of his diamond studs, his jewelled watch-chain, his eighteen-carat bangle, and his six-inch lower jaw. I had shuddered to see Raffles admiring the gewgaws in his turn, in his own brazen fashion, with that air of the cool connoisseur which had its double meaning for me. I for my part would as lief have looked a tiger in the teeth. And when we finally went home with Maguire to see his other trophies, it seemed to me like entering the tiger's lair. But an astounding lair it proved, fitted throughout by one eminent firm, and ringing to the rafters with the last word on fantastic furniture.

The trophies were a still greater surprise. They opened my eyes to the rosier aspect of the noble art, as presently practised on the right side of the Atlantic. Among other offerings, we were permitted to handle the jewelled belt presented to the pugilist by the State of Nevada, a gold brick from the citizens of Sacramento, and a model of himself in solid silver from the Fisticuff Club in New York. I still remember waiting with bated breath for Raffles to ask Maguire if he were not afraid of burglars, and Maguire replying that he had a trap to catch the cleverest cracksman alive, but flatly refusing to tell us what it was. I could not at the moment conceive a more terrible trap than the heavyweight himself behind a curtain. Yet it was easy to see that Raffles had accepted the braggart's boast as a challenge. Nor did he deny it later when I taxed him with his mad resolve; he merely refused to allow me to implicate myself in its execution. Well, there was a spice of savage satisfaction in the thought that Raffles had been obliged to turn to me in the end. And, but for the dreadful thud which I had heard over the telephone, I might have extracted some genuine comfort from the unerring sagacity with which he had chosen his night.

Within the last twenty-four hours Barney Maguire had fought his first great battle on British soil. Obviously, he would no longer be the man that he had been in the strict training before the fight; never, as I gathered, was such a ruffian more off his guard, or less capable of protecting himself and his possessions, than in these first hours of relaxation and inevitable debauchery for which Raffles had waited with characteristic foresight. Nor was the terrible Barney likely to be the more abstemious for signal punishment sustained in a far from bloodless victory. Then what could be the meaning of that sickening and most suggestive thud? Could it be the champion himself who had received the *coup de grâce* in his cups? Raffles was the very man to administer it – but he had not talked like that man through the telephone.

And yet – and yet – what else could have happened? I must have asked myself the question between each and all of the

above reflections, made partly as I dressed and partly in the
hansom on the way to Halfmoon Street. It was as yet the only
question in my mind. You must know what your emergency is
before you can decide how to cope with it; and to this day I
sometimes tremble to think of the rashly direct method by
which I set about obtaining the requisite information. I drove
every yard of the way to the pugilist's very door. You will
remember that I had been dining with Swigger Morrison at his
club.

Yet at the last I had a rough idea of what I meant to say when
the door was opened. It seemed almost probable that the tragic
end of our talk over the telephone had been caused by the
sudden arrival and as sudden violence of Barney Maguire. In
that case I was resolved to tell him that Raffles and I had made a
bet about his burglar trap, and that I had come to see who had
won. I might or might not confess that Raffles had rung me out
of bed to this end. If, however, I was wrong about Maguire, and
he had not come home at all, then my action would depend upon
the menial who answered my reckless ring. But it should result
in the rescue of Raffles by hook or crook.

I had the more time to come to some decision, since I rang
and rang in vain. The hall, indeed, was in darkness; but when I
peeped through the letter-box I could see a faint beam of light
from the back room. That was the room in which Maguire kept
his trophies and set his trap. All was quiet in the house: could
they have hauled the intruder to Vine Street in the short twenty
minutes which it had taken me to dress and to drive to the spot?
That was an awful thought; but even as I hoped against hope,
and rang once more, speculation and suspense were cut short in
the last fashion to be foreseen.

A brougham was coming sedately down the street from
Piccadilly; to my horror, it stopped behind me as I peered,
once more through the letter-box, and out tumbled the dishevelled prizefighter and two companions. I was nicely caught in
my turn. There was a lamp-post right opposite the door, and I
can still see the three of them regarding me in its light. The
pugilist had been at least a fine figure of a bully and a braggart
when I saw him before his fight; now he had a black eye and a
bloated lip, hat on the back of his head, and made-up tie under

one ear. His companions were his sallow little Yankee secretary, whose name I really forget, but whom I had met with Maguire at the Boxing Club, and a very grand person in a second skin of shimmering sequins.

I can neither forget nor report the terms in which Barney Maguire asked me who I was and what I was doing there. Thanks, however, to Swigger Morrison's hospitality, I readily reminded him of our former meeting, and of more that I only recalled as the words were in my mouth.

"You'll remember Raffles," said I, "if you don't remember me. You showed us your trophies the other night, and asked us both to look you up at any hour of any day or night after the fight."

I was going on to add that I had expected to find Raffles there before me, to settle a wager that we had made about the man-trap. But the indiscretion was interrupted by Maguire himself, whose dreadful fist became a hand that gripped mine with brute fervour, while with the other he clouted me on the back.

"You don't say!" he cried. "I took you for some darned crook, but now I remember you perfectly. If you hadn't 've spoke up slick I'd have bu'st your face in, sonny. I would, sure! Come right in, and have a drink to show there's – Jee-hosha-phat!"

The secretary had turned the latch-key in the door, only to be hauled back by the collar as the door stood open, and the light from the inner room was seen streaming upon the banisters at the foot of the narrow stairs.

"A light in my den," said Maguire in a mighty whisper, "and the blamed door open, though the key's in my pocket and we left it locked! Talk about crooks, eh? Holy smoke, how I hope we've landed one alive! You ladies and gentlemen, lay round where you are, while I see."

And the hulking figure advanced on tiptoe, like a performing elephant, until just at the open door, when for a second we saw his left revolving like a piston and his head thrown back at its fighting angle. But in another second his fists were hands again, and Maguire was rubbing them together as he stood shaking with laughter in the light of the open door.

"Walk up!" he cried, as he beckoned to us three. "Walk up

and see one o' their blamed British crooks laid as low as the blamed carpet, and nailed as tight!"

Imagine my feelings on the mat! The sallow secretary went first; the party in the sequins glittered at his heels; and for one base moment I was on the brink of bolting through the street door. It had never been shut behind us. I shut it myself in the end. Yet it was small credit to me that I actually remained on the same side of the door as Raffles.

"Reel home-grown, low-down, unwashed Whitechapel!" I had heard Maguire remark within. "Blamed if our Bowery boys ain't cock-angels to scum like this. Ah, you biter, I wouldn't soil my knuckles on your ugly face; but if I had my thick boots on I'd dance the soul out of your carcase for two cents!"

After this it required less courage to join the others in the inner room; and for some moments even I failed to identify the truly repulsive object about which I found them grouped. There was no false hair upon the face, but it was as black as any sweep's. The clothes, on the other hand, were new to me, though older and more pestiferous in themselves than most worn by Raffles for professional purposes. And at first, as I say, I was far from sure whether it was Raffles at all; but I remembered the crash that cut short our talk over the telephone; and his inanimate heap of rags was lying directly underneath a wall instrument, with the receiver dangling over him.

"Think you know him?" asked the sallow secretary, as I stooped and peered with my heart in my boots.

"Good Lord, no! I only wanted to see if he was dead," I explained, having satisfied myself that it was really Raffles, and that Raffles was really insensible. "But what on earth has happened?" I asked in my turn.

"That's what I want to know," whined the party in sequins, who had contributed various ejaculations unworthy of report, and finally subsided behind an ostentatious fan.

"I should judge," observed the secretary, "that it's for Mr. Maguire to say, or not to say, just as he darn' pleases."

But the celebrated Barney stood upon a Persian hearth-rug, beaming upon us all in a triumph too delicious for immediate translation into words. The room was furnished as a study, and most artistically furnished, if you consider outlandish shapes in fumed oak artistic. There was nothing of the traditional prize-fighter about Barney Maguire, except his vocabulary and his lower jaw. I had seen over his house already, and it was fitted and decorated throughout by a high-art firm which exhibits just such a room as that which was the scene of our tragedietta. The person in the sequins lay glistening like a landed salmon in a quaint chair of enormous nails and tapestry compact. The secretary leaned against an escritoire with huge hinges of beaten metal. The pugilist's own background presented an elaborate scheme of oak and tiles, with inglenooks green from the joiner, and a china cupboard with leaded panes behind his bullet head. And his bloodshot eyes rolled with rich delight from the decanter and glasses on the octagonal table to another decanter in the quaintest and craftiest of revolving spirit tables.

"Isn't it bully?" asked the prizefighter, smiling on us each in turn, with his black and bloodshot eyes and his bloated lip. "To think that I've only to invent a trap to catch a crook, for a blamed crook to walk right into it! You, Mr. Man—" and he nodded his great head at me – "You'll recollect me telling you that I'd gotten one when you come in that night with the other sport? Say, pity he's not with you now; he was a good boy, and I liked him a lot; but I'm liable to tell you now, or else bu'st. See that decanter on the table?"

"I was just looking at it," said the person in sequins. "You don't know what a turn I've had, or you'd offer me a little something."

"You shall have a little something in a minute," rejoined Maguire. "But if you take a little anything out of that decanter, you'll collapse like our friend upon the floor."

"Good heavens!" I cried out, with involuntary indignation, as his fell scheme broke upon me in a clap.

"Yes, sir!" said Maguire, fixing me with his bloodshot orbs. "My trap for crooks and cracksmen is a bottle of hocussed whisky, and I guess that's it on the table, with the silver label around its neck. Now look at this other decanter, without any label at all; but for that they're the dead spit of each other. I'll put them side by side, so you can see. It isn't only the decanters, but the liquor looks the same in both, and tastes so you wouldn't know the difference till you woke up in your tracks. I got the poison from a blamed Indian away West, and it's rather ticklish stuff. So I keep the label around the trap bottle, and only leave it out nights. That's the idea, and that's all there is to it," added Maguire, putting the labelled decanter back in the stand. "But I figure it's enough for ninety-nine crooks out of a hundred, and nineteen out of twenty'll have their liquor before they go to work."

"I wouldn't figure on that," observed the secretary, with a downward glance as though at the prostrate Raffles. "Have you looked to see if the trophies are all safe?"

"Not yet," said Maguire, with a glance at the pseudo-antique cabinet in which he kept them.

"Then you can save yourself the trouble," rejoined the secretary, as he dived under the octagonal table, and came up with a small black bag that I knew at a glance. It was the one that Raffles had used for heavy plunder ever since I had known him.

The bag was so heavy now that the secretary used both hands to lift it up on the table. In another moment he had taken out the jewelled belt presented to Maguire by the State of Nevada, the solid silver statuette of himself, and the gold brick from the citizens of Sacramento.

Either the sight of his treasures, so nearly lost, or the feeling that the thief had dared to tamper with them after all, suddenly infuriated Maguire to such an extent that he had bestowed a couple of brutal kicks upon the senseless form of Raffles before the secretary and I could interfere.

"Play light, Mr. Maguire!" cried the sallow secretary. "The man's drugged, as well as down."

"He'll be lucky if he ever gets up, blight and blister him!"

"I should judge it about time to telephone for the police."

"Not till I've done with him. Wait till he comes to! I guess I'll punch his face into a jam pudding! He shall wash down his teeth with his blood before the coppers come in for what's left!"

"You make me feel quite ill," complained the grand lady in the chair. "I wish you'd give me a little something, and not be more vulgar than you can 'elp."

"Help yourself," said Maguire, ungallantly, "and don't talk through your hat. Say, what's the matter with the phone?"

The secretary had picked up the dangling receiver.

"It looks to me," said he, "as though the crook had rung up somebody before he went off."

I turned and assisted the grand lady to the refreshment that she craved.

"Like his cheek!" Maguire thundered. "But who in blazes should *he* ring up?"

"It'll all come out," said the secretary. "They'll tell us at the central, and we shall find out fast enough."

"It don't matter now," said Maguire. "Let's have a drink and then rouse the devil up."

But now I was shaking in my shoes. I saw quite clearly what this meant. Even if I rescued Raffles for the time being, the police would promptly ascertain that it was I who had been rung up by the burglar, and the fact of my not having said a word about it would be directly damning to me, if in the end it did not incriminate us both. It made me quite faint to feel that we might escape the Scylla of our present peril and yet split on the Charybdis of circumstantial evidence. Yet I could see no middle course of conceivable safety, if I held my tongue another moment. So I spoke up desperately, with the rash resolution which was the novel feature of my whole conduct on this occasion. But any sheep would be resolute and rash after dining with Swigger Morrison at his club.

"I wonder if he rang *me* up!" I exclaimed as if inspired.

"You, sonny?" echoed Maguire, decanter in hand. "What in hell could he know about you?"

"Or what could you know about him?" amended the secretary, fixing me with eyes like drills.

"Nothing," I admitted, regretting my temerity with all my heart. "But someone did ring me up about an hour ago. I thought it was Raffles. I told you I expected to find him here, if you remember."

"But I don't see what that's got to do with the crook," pursued the secretary, with his relentless eyes boring deeper and deeper into mine.

"No more do I," was my miserable reply. But there was a certain comfort in his words, and some simultaneous promise in the quantity of spirit which Maguire splashed into his glass.

"Were you cut off sudden?" asked the secretary, reaching for the decanter, as the three of us sat round the octagonal table.

"So suddenly," I replied, "that I never knew who it was who rang me up. No, thank you – not any for me."

"What!" cried Maguire, raising a depressed head suddenly. "You won't have a drink in my house? Take care, young man. That's not being a good boy!"

"But I've been dining out," I expostulated, "and had my whack. I really have."

Barney Maguire smote the table with terrific fist.

"Say, sonny, I like you a lot," said he. "But I shan't like you any if you're not a good boy!"

"Very well, very well," I said hurriedly. "One finger, if I must."

And the secretary helped me to not more than two.

"Why should it have been your friend Raffles?" he inquired, returning remorselessly to the charge, while Maguire roared "Drink up!" and then drooped once more.

"I was half asleep," I answered, "and he was the first person who occurred to me. And we had made a bet . . ."

The glass was at my lips, but I was able to set it down untouched. Maguire's huge jaw had dropped upon his spreading shirt front, and beyond him I saw the person in sequins fast asleep in the artistic armchair.

"What bet?" asked a voice with a sudden start in it. The secretary was blinking as he drained his glass.

"About the very thing we've just had explained to us," said I, watching my man intently as I spoke. "I made sure it was a man-trap. Raffles thought it must be something else. We had a tremendous argument about it. Raffles said it wasn't a man-trap. I said it was. We had a bet about it in the end. I put my money on the man-trap. Raffles put his upon the other thing. And Raffles was right – it wasn't a man-trap. But it's every bit as good – every little bit – and the whole boiling of you are caught in it except me!"

I sank my voice with the past sentence, but I might just as well have raised it instead. I had said the same thing over and over again to see whether the wilful tautology would cause the secretary to open his eyes. It seemed to have had the very opposite effect. His head fell forward on the table, with never a quiver at the blow, never a twitch when I pillowed it upon one of his own sprawling arms. And there sat Maguire bolt upright, but for the jowl upon his shirt-front, while the sequins twinkled in a regular rise and fall upon the reclining form of the lady in the fanciful chair. All three were sound asleep, by what accident or by whose design I did not pause to inquire; it was enough to ascertain the fact beyond all chance of error.

I turned my attention to Raffles last of all. There was the other side of the medal. Raffles was still sleeping as sound as the enemy – or so I feared at first. I shook him gently: he made no sign. I introduced vigour into the process: he muttered incoherently. I caught and twisted an unresisting wrist – and at that he yelped profanely. But it was many and many an anxious moment before his blinking eyes knew mine.

"Bunny!" he yawned, and nothing more until his position came back to him. "So you came to me," he went on, in a tone that thrilled me with its affectionate appreciation, "as I knew you would! Have they turned up yet? They will any minute, you know; there's not one to lose."

"No, they won't, old man!" I whispered. And he sat up and saw the comatose trio for himself.

Raffles seemed less amazed at the result than I had been as a puzzled witness of the process; on the other hand, I had never seen anything quite so exultant as the smile that broke through his blackened countenance like a light. It was all obviously no great surprise, and no puzzle at all, to Raffles.

"How much did they have, Bunny?" were his first whispered words.

"Maguire a good three fingers, and the others at least two."

"Then we needn't lower our voices, and we needn't walk on our toes. Eheu! I dreamed somebody was kicking me in the ribs, and I believe it must have been true."

He had risen with a hand to his side and a wry look on his sweep's face.

"You can guess which of them it was," said I. "The beast is jolly well served!"

And I shook my fist in the paralytic face of the most brutal bruiser of his time.

"He is safe till the forenoon, unless they bring a doctor to him," said Raffles. "I don't suppose we could rouse him now if we tried. How much of the fearsome stuff do you suppose I took? About a tablespoonful! I guessed what it was, and couldn't resist making sure; the minute I was satisfied, I changed the label and the position of the two decanters, little thinking I should stay to see the fun; but in another minute I could hardly keep my eyes open. I realized then that I was poisoned with some subtle drug. If I left the house at all in that state, I must leave the spoil behind, or be found drunk in the gutter with my head on the swag itself. In any case I should have been picked up and run in, and that might have led to anything."

"So you rang me up!"

"It was my last brilliant inspiration – a sort of flash in the brain pan before the end – and I remember very little about it. I was more asleep than awake at the time."

"You sounded like it, Raffles, now that one has the clue."

"I can't remember a word I said, or what was the end of it, Bunny."

"You fell in a heap before you came to the end."

"You didn't hear that through the telephone?"

"As though we had been in the same room; only I thought it was Maguire who had stolen a march on you and knocked you out."

I had never seen Raffles more interested and impressed; but at this point his smile altered, his eyes softened, and his dear old hand sought mine.

"You thought that, and yet you came like a shot to do battle for my body with Barney Maguire! Jack the Giant Killer wasn't in it with you, Bunny!"

"It was no credit to me – it was rather the other thing," said I, remembering my rashness and my luck, and confessing both in a breath. "You know old Swigger Morrison?" I added in final explanation. "I had been dining with him at his club!"

Raffles shook his long old head. And the kindly light in his eyes was still my infinite reward.

"I don't care," said he, "how deeply you had been dining: *in vino veritas*, Bunny, and your pluck would always out! I have never doubted it, and I never shall. In fact, I rely on nothing else to get us out of this mess."

My face must have fallen, as my heart sank at these words. I had said to myself that we were out of the mess already – that we had merely to make a clean escape from the house – now the easiest thing in the world. But as I looked at Raffles, and as Raffles looked at me, on the threshold of the room where the three sleepers slept on without sound or movement, I grasped the real problem that lay before us. It was twofold; and the funny thing was that I had seen both horns of the dilemma for myself, before Raffles came to his senses. But with Raffles in his right mind, I had ceased to apply my own, or to carry my share of our common burden another inch. It had been an unconscious withdrawal on my part, an instinctive tribute to my leader; but I was sufficiently ashamed of it as we stood and faced the problem in each other's eyes.

"If we simply cleared out," continued Raffles, "you would be incriminated in the first place as my accomplice, and once they had you they would have a compass with the needle pointing straight to me. They mustn't have either of us, Bunny, or they will get us both. And for my part they may as well!"

I echoed a sentiment that was generosity itself in Raffles, but in my case a mere truism.

"It's easy enough for me," he went on. "I am a common house-breaker, and I escape. They don't know me from Noah. But they do know you; and how do you come to let me escape? What has happened to you, Bunny? That's the crux. What could have happened after they all dropped off?" And for a minute Raffles frowned and smiled like a sensation novelist working out a plot; then the light broke, and transfigured him through his burnt cork. "I've got it, Bunny!" he exclaimed. "You took some of the stuff yourself, though of course not nearly so much as they did."

"Splendid!" I cried. "They really were pressing it upon me at the end, and I did say it must be very little."

"You dozed off in your turn, but you were naturally the first to come to yourself. I had flown; so had the gold brick, the jewelled belt, and the silver statuette. You tried to rouse the others. You couldn't succeed; nor would you if you did try. So what did you do? What's the only really innocent thing you could do in the circumstances?"

"Go for the police," I suggested dubiously, little relishing the prospect.

"There's a telephone installed for the purpose," said Raffles. "I should ring them up, if I were you. Try not to look blue about it, Bunny. They're quite the nicest fellows in the world, and what you have to tell them is a mere microbe to the camels I've made them swallow without a grain of salt. It's really the most convincing story one could conceive; but unfortunately there's another point which will take more explaining away."

And even Raffles looked grave enough as I nodded.

"You mean that they'll find out you rang me up?"

"They may," said Raffles. "I see that I managed to replace the receiver all right. But still – they may."

"I'm afraid they will," said I, uncomfortably. "I'm very much afraid I gave something of the kind away. You see, you had *not* replaced the receiver; it was dangling over you where you lay. This very question came up, and the brutes themselves seemed so quick to see its possibilities that I thought it best to take the bull by the horns and own that I had been rung up by somebody. To be absolutely honest, I even went so far as to say I thought it was Raffles!"

"You didn't, Bunny!"

"What could I say? I was obliged to think of somebody, and I saw they were not going to recognize you. So I put up a yarn about a wager we had made about this very trap of Maguire's. You see, Raffles, I've never properly told you how I got in, and there's no time now; but the first thing I had said was that I half expected to find you here before me. That was in case they spotted you at once. But it made all that part about the telephone fit in rather well."

"I should think it did, Bunny," murmured Raffles, in a tone that added sensibly to my reward. "I couldn't have done better myself, and you will forgive my saying that you have never in your life done half so well. But the bother of it is that there's still so much to do, and to hit upon, and so precious little time for thought as well as action."

I took out my watch and showed it to Raffles without a word.

It was three o'clock in the morning, and the latter end of March. In little more than an hour there would be dim daylight in the streets. Raffles roused himself from a reverie with sudden decision.

"There's only one thing for it, Bunny," said he. "We must trust each other and divide the labour. You ring up the police, and leave the rest to me."

"You haven't hit upon any reason for the sort of burglar they think you were ringing up the kind of man they know I am?"

"Not yet, Bunny, but I shall. It may not be wanted for a day or so, and after all it isn't for you to give the explanation. It would be highly suspicious if you did."

"So it would," I agreed.

"Then will you trust me to hit on something – if possible before morning – in any case by the time it's wanted? I won't fail you, Bunny."

That settled it. I gripped his hand without another word, and remained on guard over the three sleepers while Raffles stole upstairs. I have since learned that there were servants at the top of the house, and in the basement a man, who actually heard some of our proceedings! But he was mercifully too accustomed to nocturnal orgies, and of a far more uproarious character, to appear unless summoned to the scene. I believe he heard Raffles leave. But no secret was made of his exit: he let himself out, and told me afterwards that the first person he encountered in the street was the constable on the beat. Raffles wished him good morning, as well he might; for he had been upstairs to wash his face and hands; and in the prizefighter's great hat and fur coat he might have marched round Scotland Yard itself, in spite of his having the gold brick from Sacramento in one pocket, the silver statuette of Maguire in the other, and round his waist the jewelled belt presented to that worthy by the State of Nevada.

My immediate part was a little hard after the excitement of those small hours. I will only say that we had agreed that it would be wisest for me to lie like a log among the rest for half an hour, before staggering to my feet and rousing house and police; and that in that half-hour Barney Maguire crashed to the floor, without waking either himself or his companions, though not without bringing my beating heart into the very roof of my mouth.

It was daybreak when I gave the alarm with bell and telephone. In a few minutes we had the house congested with dishevelled domestics, irascible doctors, and arbitrary minions of the law. If I told my story once, I told it a dozen times, and all on an empty stomach. But it was certainly a most plausible and consistent tale, even without that confirmation which none of the other victims was as yet sufficiently recovered to supply. And in the end I was permitted to retire from the scene until required to give further information, or to identify the prisoner whom the good police confidently expected to make before the day was out.

I drove straight to the flat. The porter flew to help me out of my hansom. His face alarmed me more than any I had left in Halfmoon Street. It alone might have spelled my ruin.

"Your flat's been entered in the night, sir," he cried. "The thieves have taken everything they could lay hands on."

"Thieves in my flat!" I ejaculated aghast. There were one or two incriminating possessions up there, as well as at the Albany.

"The door's been forced with a jimmy," said the porter. "It was the milkman who found it out. There's a constable up there now."

A constable poking about in my flat of all others! I rushed upstairs without waiting for the lift. The invader was moistening his pencil between laborious notes in a fat pocketbook; he had penetrated no farther than the forced door. I dashed past him in a fever. I kept *my* trophies in a wardrobe drawer specially fitted with a Bramah lock. The lock was broken – the drawer void.

"Something valuable, sir?" inquired the intrusive constable at my heels.

"Yes, indeed – some old family silver," I answered. It was quite true. But the family was not mine.

And not till then did the truth flash across my mind. Nothing else of value had been taken. But there was a meaningless litter in all the rooms. I turned to the porter, who had followed me up from the street; it was his wife who looked after the flat.

"Get rid of this idiot as quick as you can," I whispered. "I'm going straight to Scotland Yard myself. Let your wife tidy the place while I'm gone, and have the lock mended before she leaves. I'm going as I am, this minute!"

And go I did, in the first hansom I could find – but not straight to Scotland Yard. I stopped the cab in Piccadilly on the way.

Old Raffles opened his own door to me. I cannot remember finding him fresher, more immaculate, more delightful to behold in every way. Could I paint a picture of Raffles with something other than my pen, it would be as I saw him that bright March morning, at his open door in the Albany, a trim, slim figure in matutinal grey, cool and gay and breezy as incarnate spring.

"What on earth did you do it for?" I asked within.

"It was the only solution," he answered, handing me the cigarettes. "I saw it the moment I got outside."

"I don't see it yet."

"Why should a burglar call an innocent gentleman away from home?"

"That's what we couldn't make out."

"I tell you I got it directly I had left you. He called you away in order to burgle you too, of course!"

And Raffles stood smiling upon me in all his incomparable radiance and audacity.

"But why me?" I asked. "Why on earth should he burgle *me?*"

"My dear Bunny, we must leave something to the imagination of the police. But we will assist them to a fact or two in due season. It was the dead of night when Maguire first took us to his house; it was at the Imperial Boxing Club we met him; and you meet queer fish at the Imperial Boxing Club. You may remember that he telephoned to his man to prepare supper for us, and that you and he discussed telephones and treasure as we marched through the midnight streets. He was certainly bucking about his trophies, and for the sake of the argument you will be good enough to admit that you probably bucked about yours. What happens? You are overheard; you are followed; you are worked into the same scheme, and robbed on the same night."

"And you really think this will meet the case?"

"I am quite certain of it, Bunny, so far as it rests with us to meet the case at all."

"Then give me another cigarette, my dear fellow, and let me push on to Scotland Yard."

Raffles held up both hands in admiring horror.

"Scotland Yard!"

"To give a false description of what you took from that drawer in my wardrobe."

"A false description! Bunny, you have no more to learn from me. Time was when I wouldn't have let you go there without me to retrieve a lost umbrella – let alone a lost cause!"

And for once I was not sorry for Raffles to have the last unworthy word, as he stood once more at his outer door and gaily waved me down the stairs.

Hunted Down

Charles Dickens

The partition which separated my own office from our general outer office in the City was of thick plate glass. I could see through it what passed in the outer office, without hearing a word. I had it put up in place of a wall that had been there for years – ever since the house was built. It is no matter whether I did or did not make the change in order that I might derive my first impression of strangers, who came to us on business, from their faces alone, without being influenced by anything they said. Enough to mention that I turned my glass partition to that account, and that a Life Assurance Office is at all times exposed to be practised upon by the most crafty and cruel of the human race.

It was through my glass partition that I first saw the gentleman whose story I am going to tell.

He had come in without my observing it, and had put his hat and umbrella on the broad counter, and was bending over it to take some papers from one of the clerks. He was about forty or so, dark, exceedingly well dressed in black – being in mourning – and the hand he extended with a polite air had a particularly well-fitting black kid glove upon it. His hair, which was elaborately brushed and oiled, was parted straight up the middle; and he presented this parting to the clerk, exactly (to my thinking) as if he had said, in so many words: "You must take me, if you please, my friend, just as I show myself. Come straight up here, follow the gravel path, keep off the grass, I allow no trespassing."

I conceived a very great aversion to that man the moment I thus saw him.

He had asked for some of our printed forms, and the clerk was giving them to him and explaining them. An obliged and agreeable smile was on his face, and his eyes met those of the clerk with a sprightly look. (I have known a vast quantity of nonsense talked about bad men not looking you in the face. Don't trust that conventional idea. Dishonesty will stare honesty out of countenance, any day in the week, if there is anything to be got by it.)

I saw, in the corner of his eyelash, that he became aware of my looking at him. Immediately he turned the parting in his hair toward the glass partition, as if he said to me with a sweet smile, "Straight up here, if you please. Off the grass!"

In a few moments he had put on his hat and taken up his umbrella, and was gone.

I beckoned the clerk into my room, and asked, "Who was that?"

He had the gentleman's card in his hand. "Mr. Julius Slinkton, Middle Temple."

"A barrister, Mr. Adams?"

"I think not, sir."

"I should have thought him a clergyman, but for his having no Reverend here," said I.

"Probably, from his appearance," Mr. Adams replied, "he is reading for orders."

I should mention that he wore a dainty white cravat, and dainty linen altogether.

"What did he want, Mr. Adams?"

"Merely a form of proposal, sir, and form of reference."

"Recommended here? Did he say?"

"Yes, he said he was recommended here by a friend of yours. He noticed you, but said that as he had not the pleasure of your personal acquaintance he would not trouble you."

"Did he know my name?"

"Oh, yes, sir! He said, 'There *is* Mr. Sampson, I see!'"

"A well-spoken gentleman, apparently?"

"Remarkably so, sir."

"Insinuating manners, apparently?"

"Very much so, indeed, sir."

"Hah!" said I. "I want nothing at present, Mr. Adams."

Within a fortnight of that day I went to dine with a friend of mine, a merchant, a man of taste, who buys pictures and books, and the first man I saw among the company was Mr. Julius Slinkton. There he was, standing before the fire, with good large eyes and an open expression of face; but still (I thought) requiring everybody to come at him by the prepared way he offered, and by no other.

I noticed him ask my friend to introduce him to Mr. Sampson, and my friend did so. Mr. Slinkton was very happy to see me. Not too happy; there was no overdoing of the matter; happy in a thoroughly well-bred, perfectly unmeaning way.

"I thought you had met," our host observed.

"No," said Mr. Slinkton. "I did look in at Mr. Sampson's office, on your recommendation; but I really did not feel justified in troubling Mr. Sampson himself, on a point in the everyday routine of a clerk."

I said I should have been glad to show him any attention on our friend's introduction.

"I am sure of that," said he, "and am much obliged. At another time, perhaps, I may be less delicate. Only, however, if I have real business; for I know, Mr. Sampson, how precious business time is, and what a vast number of impertinent people there are in the world."

I acknowledged his consideration with a slight bow. "You were thinking," said I, "of effecting a policy on your life."

"Oh dear no! I am afraid I am not so prudent as you pay me the compliment of supposing me to be, Mr. Sampson. I merely inquired for a friend. But you know what friends are in such matters. Nothing may ever come of it. I have the greatest reluctance to trouble men of business with inquiries for friends, knowing the probabilities to be a thousand to one that the friends will never follow them up. People are so fickle, so selfish, so inconsiderate. Don't you, in your business, find them so every day?"

I was going to give a qualified answer; but he turned his smooth, white parting on me with its "Straight up here, if you please!" and I answered, "Yes."

"I hear, Mr. Sampson," he resumed presently, for our friend had a new cook, and dinner was not so punctual as usual, "that your profession has recently suffered a great loss."

"In money?" said I.

"No, in talent and vigor."

Not at once following out his allusion, I considered for a moment.

"*Has* it sustained a loss of that kind?" said I. "I was not aware of it."

"Understand me, Mr. Sampson. I don't imagine that you have retired. It is not so bad as that. But Mr. Meltham—"

"Oh, to be sure!" said I. "Yes! Mr. Meltham, the young actuary of the 'Inestimable.'"

"Just so," he returned in a consoling way.

"He is a great loss. He was at once the most profound, the most original, and the most energetic man I have ever known connected with Life Assurance."

I spoke strongly; for I had a high esteem and admiration for Meltham; and my gentleman had indefinitely conveyed to me some suspicion that he wanted to sneer at him. He recalled me to my guard by presenting that trim pathway up his head, with its infernal "Not on the grass, if you please – the gravel."

"You knew him, Mr. Slinkton?"

"Only by reputation. To have known him as an acquaintance or as a friend, is an honor I should have sought if he had remained in society, though I might never have had the good fortune to attain it, being a man of far inferior mark. He was scarcely above thirty, I suppose?"

"About thirty."

"Ah!" he sighed in his former consoling way. "What creatures we are! To break up, Mr. Sampson, and become incapable of business at that time of life! – Any reason assigned for the melancholy fact?"

("Humph!" thought I, as I looked at him. "But I won't go up the track, and I will go on the grass.")

"What reason have you heard assigned, Mr. Slinkton?" I asked, point-blank.

"Most likely a false one. You know what Rumor is, Mr. Sampson. I never repeat what I hear; it is the only way of paring the nails and shaving the head of Rumor. But when *you* ask me what reason I have heard assigned for Mr. Meltham's passing away from among men, it is another thing. I am not gratifying idle gossip then. I was told, Mr. Sampson, that Mr. Meltham had relinquished all his avocations and all his prospects, because he was, in fact, broken-hearted. A disappointed attachment, I heard – though it hardly seems probable, in the case of a man so distinguished and so attractive."

"Attractions and distinctions are no armor against death," said I.

"Oh, she died? Pray pardon me. I did not hear that. That, indeed, makes it very, very sad. Poor Mr. Meltham! Ah, dear me! Lamentable, lamentable!"

I still thought his pity was not quite genuine, and I still suspected an unaccountable sneer under all this, until he said, as we were parted, like the other knots of talkers, by the announcement of dinner:

"Mr. Sampson, you are surprised to see me so moved on behalf of a man whom I have never known. I am not so disinterested as you may suppose. I have suffered, and recently too, from death myself. I have lost one of two charming nieces, who were my constant companions. She died young – barely three-and-twenty; and even her remaining sister is far from strong. The world is a grave!"

He said this with deep feeling, and I felt reproached for the coldness of my manner. Coldness and distrust had been engendered in me, I knew, by my bad experiences; they were not natural to me; and I often thought how much I had lost in life, losing trustfulness, and how little I had gained, gaining hard caution. This state of mind being habitual to me, I troubled myself more about this conversation than I might have troubled myself about a greater matter. I listened to his talk at dinner, and observed how readily other men responded to it, and with what a graceful instinct he adapted his subjects to the knowledge and habits of those he talked with. As, in talking with me, he had easily started the subject I might be supposed to understand best, and to be the most interested in, so, in talking with others, he guided himself by the same rule. The company was of a varied character; but he was not at fault, that I could discover, with any member of it. He knew just as much of each man's pursuit as made him agreeable to that man in reference to it, and just as little as made it natural in him to seek modestly for information when the theme was broached.

As he talked and talked – but really not too much, for the rest of us seemed to force it upon him – I became quite angry with myself. I took his face to pieces in my mind, like a watch, and examined it in detail. I could not say much against any of his features separately; I could say even less against them when they were put together. "Then is it not monstrous," I asked myself, "that because a man happens to part his hair straight up the middle of his head, I should permit myself to suspect, and even to detest him?"

(I may stop to remark that this was no proof of my sense. An observer of men who finds himself steadily repelled by some apparently trifling thing in a stranger is right to give it great weight. It may be the clue to the whole mystery. A hair or two will show where a lion is hidden. A very little key will open a very heavy door.)

I took my part in the conversation with him after a time, and we got on remarkably well. In the drawing room I asked the host how long he had known Mr. Slinkton. He answered, not many months; he had met him at the house of a celebrated painter then present, who had known him well when he was traveling with his nieces in Italy for their health. His plans in life being broken by the death of one of them, he was reading with the intention of going back to college as a matter of form, taking his degree, and going into orders. I could not but argue with myself that here was the true explanation of his interest in poor Meltham, and that I had been almost brutal in my distrust on that simple head.

On the very next day but one I was sitting behind my glass partition, as before, when he came into the outer office, as before. The moment I saw him again without hearing him, I hated him worse than ever.

It was only for a moment that I had this opportunity; for he waved his tight-fitting black glove the instant I looked at him, and came straight in.

"Mr. Sampson, good day! I presume, you see, upon your kind permission to intrude upon you. I don't keep my word in being justified by business, for my business here – if I may so abuse the word – is of the slightest nature."

I asked, was it anything I could assist him in?

"I thank you, no. I merely called to inquire outside whether my dilatory friend had been so false to himself as to be practical and sensible. But, of course, he has done nothing. I gave him your papers with my own hand, and he was hot upon the intention, but of course he has done nothing. Apart from the general human disinclination to do anything that ought to be done, I dare say there is a specialty about assuring one's life. You find it like will-making. People are so superstitious, and take it for granted they will die soon afterwards."

"Up here, if you please; straight up here, Mr. Sampson. Neither to the right nor to the left." I almost fancied I could hear him breathe the words as he sat smiling at me, with that intolerable parting exactly opposite the bridge of my nose.

"There is such a feeling sometimes, no doubt," I replied; "but I don't think it obtains to any great extent."

"Well," said he, with a shrug and a smile, "I wish some good angel would influence my friend in the right direction. I rashly promised his mother and sister in Norfolk to see it done, and he promised them that he would do it. But I suppose he never will."

He spoke for a minute or two on indifferent topics, and went away.

I had scarcely unlocked the drawers of my writing table next morning, when he reappeared. I noticed that he came straight to the door in the glass partition, and did not pause a single moment outside.

"Can you spare me two minutes, my dear Mr. Sampson?"

"By all means."

"Much obliged," laying his hat and umbrella on the table; "I came early, not to interrupt you. The fact is, I am taken by surprise in reference to this proposal my friend has made."

"Has he made one?" said I.

"Ye-es," he answered, deliberately looking at me; and then a bright idea seemed to strike him – "or he only tells me he has. Perhaps that may be a new way of evading the matter. By Jupiter, I never thought of that!"

Mr. Adams was opening the morning's letters in the outer office. "What is the name, Mr. Slinkton?" I asked.

"Beckwith."

I looked out at the door and requested Mr. Adams, if there were a proposal in that name, to bring it in. He had already laid it out of his hand on the counter. It was easily selected from the rest, and he gave it me. Alfred Beckwith. Proposal to effect a policy with us for two thousand pounds. Dated yesterday.

"From the Middle Temple, I see, Mr. Slinkton."

"Yes. He lives on the same staircase with me; his door is opposite. I never thought he would make me his reference though."

"It seems natural enough that he should."

"Quite so, Mr. Sampson; but I never thought of it. Let me see." He took the printed paper from his pocket. "How am I to answer all these questions?"

"According to the truth, of course," said I.

"Oh, of course!" he answered, looking up from the paper with a smile; "I meant they were so many. But you do right to be particular. It stands to reason that you must be particular. Will you allow me to use your pen and ink?"

"Certainly."

"And your desk?"

"Certainly."

He had been hovering about between his hat and his umbrella for a place to write on. He now sat down in my chair, at my blotting-paper and inkstand, with the long walk up his head in accurate perspective before me, as I stood with my back to the fire.

Before answering each question he ran over it aloud, and discussed it. How long had he known Mr. Alfred Beckwith? That he had to calculate by years upon his fingers. What were his habits? No difficulty about them; temperate in the last degree, and took a little too much exercise, if anything. All the answers were satisfactory. When he had written them all, he looked them over, and finally signed them in a very pretty hand. He supposed he had now done with the business. I told him he was not likely to be troubled any further. Should he leave the papers there? If he pleased. Much obliged. Good morning.

I had had one other visitor before him; not at the office, but at my own house. That visitor had come to my bedside when it was not yet daylight, and had been seen by no one else but my faithful confidential servant.

A second reference paper (for we required always two) was sent down into Norfolk, and was duly received back by post. This, likewise, was satisfactorily answered in every respect. Our forms were all complied with; we accepted the proposal, and the premium for one year was paid.

For six or seven months I saw no more of Mr. Slinkton. He called once at my house, but I was not at home; and he once asked me to dine with him in the Temple, but I was engaged. His friend's assurance was effected in March. Late in September or early in October I was down at Scarborough for a breath of sea air, where I met him on the beach. It was a hot evening; he came toward me with his hat in his hand; and there was the walk I had felt so strongly disinclined to take in perfect order again, exactly in front of the bridge of my nose.

He was not alone, but had a young lady on his arm.

She was dressed in mourning, and I looked at her with great interest. She had the appearance of being extremely delicate, and her face was remarkably pale and melancholy; but she was very pretty. He introduced her as his niece, Miss Niner.

"Are you strolling, Mr. Sampson? Is it possible you can be idle?" It *was* possible, and I *was* strolling.

"Shall we stroll together?"

"With pleasure."

The young lady walked between us, and we walked on the cool sea sand, in the direction of Filey.

"There have been wheels here," said Mr. Slinkton. "And now I look again, the wheels of a hand-carriage! Margaret, my love, your shadow without doubt!"

"Miss Niner's shadow?" I repeated, looking down at it on the sand.

"Not that one," Mr. Slinkton returned, laughing. "Margaret, my dear, tell Mr. Sampson."

"Indeed," said the young lady, turning to me, "there is nothing to tell – except that I constantly see the same invalid old gentleman at all times, wherever I go. I have mentioned it to my uncle, and he calls the gentleman my shadow."

"Does he live in Scarborough?" I asked.

"He is staying here."

"Do you live in Scarborough?"

"No, I am staying here. My uncle has placed me with a family here, for my health."

"And your shadow?" said I, smiling.

"My shadow," she answered, smiling too, "is – like myself – not very robust, I fear; for I lose my shadow sometimes, as my shadow loses me at other times. We both seem liable to confinement to the house. I have not seen my shadow for days and days; but it does oddly happen, occasionally, that wherever I go, for many days together, this gentleman goes. We have come together in the most unfrequented nooks on this shore."

"Is this he?" said I, pointing before us.

The wheels had swept down to the water's edge, and described a great loop on the sand in turning. Bringing the loop back towards us, and spinning it out as it came, was a hand-carriage, drawn by a man.

"Yes," said Miss Niner, "this really is my shadow, uncle."

As the carriage approached us and we approached the carriage, I saw within it an old man, whose head was sunk on his breast, and who was enveloped in a variety of wrappers. He was drawn by a very quiet but very keen-looking man, with iron-gray hair, who was slightly lame. They had passed us, when the carriage stopped, and the old gentleman within, putting out his arm, called to me by my name. I went back, and was absent from Mr. Slinkton and his niece for about five minutes.

When I rejoined them, Mr. Slinkton was the first to speak. Indeed, he said to me in a raised voice before I came up with him:

"It is well you have not been longer, or my niece might have died of curiosity to know who her shadow is, Mr. Sampson."

"An old East India Director," said I. "An intimate friend of our friend's, at whose house I first had the pleasure of meeting you. A certain Major Banks. You have heard of him?"

"Never."

"Very rich, Miss Niner; but very old, and very crippled. An

amiable man, sensible – much interested in you. He has just been expatiating on the affection that he has observed to exist between you and your uncle."

Mr. Slinkton was holding his hat again, and he passed his hand up the straight walk, as if he himself went up it serenely, after me.

"Mr. Sampson," he said, tenderly pressing his niece's arm in his, "our affection was always a strong one, for we have had but few near ties. We have still fewer now. We have associations to bring us together, that are not of this world, Margaret."

"Dear uncle!" murmured the young lady, and turned her face aside to hide her tears.

"My niece and I have such remembrances and regrets in common, Mr. Sampson," he feelingly pursued, "that it would be strange indeed if the relations between us were cold or indifferent. If I remember a conversation we once had together, you will understand the reference I make. Cheer up, dear Margaret. Don't droop, don't droop. My Margaret! I cannot bear to see you droop!"

The poor young lady was very much affected, but controlled herself. His feelings, too, were very acute. In a word, he found himself under such great need of a restorative, that he presently went away, to take a bath of sea water, leaving the young lady and me sitting by a point of rock, and probably presuming – but that you will say was a pardonable indulgence in a luxury – that she would praise him with all her heart.

She did, poor thing! With all her confiding heart, she praised him to me, for his care of her dead sister, and for his untiring devotion in her last illness. The sister had wasted away very slowly, and wild and terrible fantasies had come over her toward the end, but he had never been impatient with her, or at a loss; had always been gentle, watchful, and self-possessed. The sister had known him, as she had known him, to be the best of men, the kindest of men, and yet a man of such admirable strength of character, as to be a very tower for the support of their weak natures while their poor lives endured.

"I shall leave him, Mr. Sampson, very soon," said the young lady; "I know my life is drawing to an end; and when I am gone,

I hope he will marry and be happy. I am sure he has lived single so long, only for my sake, and for my poor, poor sister's."

The little hand-carriage had made another great loop on the damp sand, and was coming back again, gradually spinning out a slim figure eight, half a mile long.

"Young lady," said I, looking around, laying my hand upon her arm, and speaking in a low voice, "time presses. You hear the gentle murmur of that sea?"

She looked at me with the utmost wonder and alarm, saying, "Yes!"

"And you know what a voice is in it when the storm comes?" "Yes!"

"You see how quiet and peaceful it lies before us, and you know what an awful sight of power without pity it might be, this very night!"

"Yes!"

"But if you had never heard or seen it, or heard of it in its cruelty, could you believe that it beats every inanimate thing in its way to pieces, without mercy, and destroys life without remorse?"

"You terrify me, sir, by these questions!"

"To save you, young lady, to save you! For God's sake, collect your strength and collect your firmness! If you were here alone. and hemmed in by the rising tide on the flow to fifty feet above your head, you could not be in greater danger than the danger you are now to be saved from."

The figure on the sand was spun out, and straggled off into a crooked little jerk that ended at the cliff very near us.

"As I am, before Heaven and the Judge of all mankind, your friend, and your dead sister's friend, I solemnly entreat you, Miss Niner, without one moment's loss of time, to come to this gentleman with me!"

If the little carriage had been less near to us, I doubt if I could have got her away; but it was so near that we were there before she had recovered the hurry of being urged from the rock. I did not remain there with her two minutes. Certainly within five, I had the inexpressible satisfaction of seeing her – from the point we had sat on, and to which I had returned – half supported and half carried up some rude steps notched in the cliff, by the figure of an active man. With that figure beside her, I knew she was safe anywhere.

I sat alone on the rock, awaiting Mr. Slinkton's return. The twilight was deepening and the shadows were heavy, when he came round the point, with his hat hanging at his buttonhole, smoothing his wet hair with one of his hands, and picking out the old path with the other and a pocket-comb.

"My niece not here, Mr. Sampson?" he said, looking about.

"Miss Niner seemed to feel a chill in the air after the sun was down, and has gone home."

He looked surprised, as though she were not accustomed to do anything without him.

"I persuaded Miss Niner," I explained.

"Ah!" said he. "She is easily persuaded – for her good. Thank you, Mr. Sampson; she is better within doors. The bathing place was farther than I thought, to say the truth."

"Miss Niner is very delicate," I observed.

He shook his head and drew a deep sigh. "Very, very, very. You may recollect my saying so. The time that has since intervened has not strengthened her. The gloomy shadow that fell upon her sister so early in life seems, in my anxious eyes, to gather over her, ever darker, ever darker. Dear Margaret, dear Margaret! But we must hope."

The hand-carriage was spinning away before us at a most indecorous pace for an invalid vehicle, and was making most irregular curves upon the sand. Mr. Slinkton, noticing it, said:

"If I may judge from appearances, your friend will be upset, Mr. Sampson."

"It looks probable, certainly," said I.

"The servants must be drunk."

"The servants of old gentlemen will get drunk sometimes," said I.

"The major draws very light, Mr. Sampson."

"The major does draw light," said I.

By this time the carriage, much to my relief, was lost in the darkness. We walked on for a little, side by side over the sand, in silence. After a short while he said, in a voice still affected by the emotion that his niece's state of health had awakened in him,

"Do you stay here long, Mr. Sampson?"

"Why, no. I am going away tonight."

"So soon? But business always holds you in request. Men like Mr. Sampson are too important to others, to be spared to their own need of relaxation and enjoyment."

"I don't know about that," said I. "However, I am going back. To London."

"I shall be there too, soon after you."

I knew that as well as he did. But I did not tell him so. Any more than I told him what defensive weapon my right hand rested on in my pocket, as I walked by his side. Any more than I told him why I did not walk on the sea side of him with the night closing in.

We left the beach, and our ways diverged. We exchanged good night, and had parted indeed, when he said, returning,

"Mr. Sampson, *may* I ask? Poor Meltham whom we spoke of – dead yet?"

"Not when I last heard of him; but too broken a man to live long, and hopelessly lost to his old calling."

"Dear, dear, dear!" said he, with great feeling. "Sad, sad, sad! The world is a grave!" And so went his way.

It was not his fault if the world were not a grave; but I did not call that observation after him, any more than I had mentioned those other things just now enumerated. He went his way, and I went mine with all expedition. This happened, as I have said, either at the end of September or beginning of October. The next time I saw him, and the last, was late in November.

I had a very particular engagement to breakfast in the Temple. It was a bitter northeasterly morning, and the sleet and slush lay inches deep in the streets. I could get no conveyance, and was soon wet to the knees; but I should have been true to that appointment, though I had to wade to it up to my neck in the same impediments.

The appointment took me to some chambers in the Temple. They were at the top of a lonely corner house overlooking the river. The name, MR. ALFRED BECKWITH, was painted on the outer door. On the door opposite, on the same landing, the name MR. JULIUS SLINKTON. The doors of both sets of chambers stood open, so that anything said aloud in one set could be heard in the other.

I had never been in those chambers before. They were dismal, close, unwholesome, and oppressive; the furniture, originally good, and not yet old, was faded and dirty – the rooms were in great disorder; there was a strong prevailing smell of opium, brandy, and tobacco; the grate and fire irons were splashed all over with unsightly blotches of rust; and on a sofa by the fire, in the room where breakfast had been prepared, lay the host, Mr. Beckwith, a man with all the appearances of the worst kind of drunkard, very far advanced upon his shameful way to death.

"Slinkton is not come yet," said this creature, staggering up when I went in; "I'll call him – Halloa! Julius Caesar! Come and drink!" As he hoarsely roared this out, he beat the poker and tongs together in a mad way, as if that were his usual manner of summoning his associate.

The voice of Mr. Slinkton was heard through the clatter from the opposite side of the staircase, and he came in. He had not expected the pleasure of meeting me. I have seen several artful men brought to a stand, but I never saw a man so aghast as he was when his eyes rested on mine.

"Julius Caesar," cried Beckwith, staggering between us, "Mist' Sampson! Mist' Sampson, Julius Caesar! Julius, Mist' Sampson, is the friend of my soul. Julius keeps me plied with liquor, morning, noon, and night. Julius is a real benefactor. Julius threw the tea and coffee out of window when I used to have any. Julius empties all the water jugs of their contents, and fills 'em with spirits. Julius winds me up and keeps me going – Boil the brandy, Julius!"

There was a rusty and furred saucepan in the ashes – the ashes looked like the accumulation of weeks – and Beckwith, rolling and staggering between us as if he were going to plunge headlong into the fire, got the saucepan out, and tried to force it into Slinkton's hand.

"Boil the brandy, Julius Caesar! Come! Do your usual office. Boil the brandy!"

He became so fierce in his gesticulations with the saucepan, that I expected to see him lay open Slinkton's head with it. I therefore put out my hand to check him. He reeled back to the sofa, and sat there panting, shaking, and red-eyed, in his rags of dressing gown, looking at us both. I noticed then that there was nothing to drink on the table but brandy, and nothing to eat but salted herrings, and a hot, sickly, highly-peppered stew.

"At all events, Mr. Sampson," said Slinkton, offering me the smooth gravel path for the last time, "I thank you for interfering between me and this unfortunate man's violence. However you came here, Mr. Sampson, or with whatever motive you came here, at least I thank you for that."

Without gratifying his desire to know how I came there, I said, quietly, "How is your niece, Mr. Slinkton?"

He looked hard at me, and I looked hard at him.

"I am sorry to say, Mr. Sampson, that my niece has proved treacherous and ungrateful to her best friend. She left me without a word of notice or explanation. She was misled, no doubt, by some designing rascal. Perhaps you may have heard of it."

"I did hear that she was misled by a designing rascal. In fact, I have proof of it."

"Are you sure of that?" said he.

"Quite."

"Boil the brandy," muttered Beckwith. "Company to breakfast, Julius Caesar. Do your usual office – provide the usual breakfast, dinner, tea, and supper. Boil the brandy!"

The eyes of Slinkton looked from him to me, and he said, after a moment's consideration,

"Mr. Sampson, you are a man of the world, and so am I. I will be plain with you."

"And I tell you you will not," said I. "I know all about you. *You* plain with any one? Nonsense, nonsense!"

"I plainly tell you, Mr. Sampson," he went on, with a manner almost composed, "that I understand your object. You want to save your funds, and escape from your liabilities; these are old tricks of trade with you Office-gentlemen. But you will not do it, sir; you will not succeed. You have not an easy adversary to play against, when you play against me. We shall have to inquire, in due time, when and how Mr. Beckwith fell into his present habits. With that remark, sir, I put this poor creature, and his incoherent wanderings of speech, aside, and wish you a good morning and a better case next time."

While he was saying this, Beckwith had filled a half-pint glass with brandy. At this moment, he threw the brandy at his face, and threw the glass after it. Slinkton put his hands up, half blinded with the spirit, and cut with the glass across the forehead. At the sound of the breakage, a fourth person came into the room, closed the door, and stood at it; he was a very quiet but very keen-looking man, with iron-gray hair, and slightly lame.

Slinkton pulled out his handkerchief, assuaged the pain in his smarting eyes, and dabbled the blood on his forehead. He was a long time about it, and I saw that in the doing of it, a tremendous change came over him, occasioned by the change in Beckwith – who ceased to pant and tremble, sat upright, and never took his eyes off him. I never in my life saw a face in which abhorrence and determination were so forcibly painted as in Beckwith's then.

"Look at me, you villain," said Beckwith, "and see me as I really am. I took these rooms, to make them a trap for you. I came into them as a drunkard, to bait the trap for you. You fell into the trap, and you will never leave it alive. On the morning when you last went to Mr. Sampson's office, I had seen him first. Your plot has been known to both of us, all along, and you have been counter-plotted all along. What? Having been cajoled into putting that prize of two thousand pounds in your power, I was to be done to death with brandy, and, brandy not proving quick enough, with something quicker? Have I never seen you, when you thought my senses gone, pouring from your little bottle into my glass? Why, you Murderer and Forger, alone here with you in the dead of night, as I have so often been, I have had my hand upon the trigger of a pistol, twenty times, to blow your brains out!"

This sudden starting up of the thing that he had supposed to be his imbecile victim into a determined man, with a settled resolution to hunt him down and be the death of him, mercilessly expressed from head to foot, was, in the first shock, too much for him. Without any figure of speech, he staggered under it. But there is no greater mistake than to suppose that a man who is a calculating criminal, is, in any phase of his guilt, otherwise than true to himself, and perfectly consistent with his whole character. Such a man commits murder, and murder is the natural culmination of his course; such a man has to outface murder, and will do it with hardihood and effrontery. It is a sort of fashion to express surprise that any notorious criminal, having such crime upon his conscience, can so brave it out. Do you think that if he had it on his conscience at all, or had a conscience to have it upon, he would ever have committed the crime?

Perfectly consistent with himself, as I believe all such monsters to be, this Slinkton recovered himself, and showed a defiance that was sufficiently cold and quiet. He was white, he was haggard, he was changed; but only as a sharper who had played for a great stake and had been outwitted.

"Listen to me, you villain," said Beckwith, "and let every word you hear me say be a stab in your wicked heart. When I took these rooms, to throw myself in your way and lead you on to the scheme that I knew my appearance and supposed character and habits would suggest to such a devil, how did I know that? Because you were no stranger to me. I knew you well. And I knew you to be the cruel wretch who, for so much money, had killed one innocent girl while she trusted him implicitly, and who was by inches killing another."

Slinkton took out a snuff-box, took a pinch of snuff, and laughed.

"But see here," said Beckwith, never looking away, never raising his voice, never relaxing his face, never unclenching his hand. "See what a dull wolf you have been, after all! The infatuated drunkard who never drank a fiftieth part of the liquor you plied him with, but poured it away, here, there, everywhere – almost before your eyes; who brought over the fellow you set to watch him and to ply him, by outbidding you in his bribe, before he had been at his work three days – with whom you have observed no caution, yet who was so bent on ridding the earth of you as a wild beast, that he should have defeated you if you had been ever so prudent – that drunkard whom you have, many a time, left on the floor of this room, and who has even let you go out of it, alive and undeceived, when you have turned him over with your foot – has, almost as often, on the same night, within an hour, within a few minutes, watched you awake, had his hand at your pillow when you were asleep, turned over your papers, taken samples from your bottles and packets of powder, changed their contents, rifled every secret of your life!"

He had had another pinch of snuff in his hand, but had gradually let it drop from between his fingers to the floor; where he now smoothed it out with his foot, looking down at it the while.

"That drunkard," said Beckwith, "who had free access to your rooms at all times, that he might drink the strong drinks that you left in his way and be the sooner ended, holding no more terms with you than he would hold with a tiger, has had his master key for all your locks, his test for all your poisons, his clue to your cipher-writing. He can tell you, as well as you can tell him, how long it took to complete that deed, what doses there were, what intervals, what signs of gradual decay upon mind and body; what distempered fancies were produced, what observable changes, what physical pain. He can tell you, as well as you can tell him, that all this was recorded day by day, as a lesson of experience for future service. He can tell you, better than you can tell him, where that journal is now."

Slinkton stopped the action of his foot, and looked at Beckwith.

"No," said the latter, as if answering a question from him. "Not in the drawer of the writing desk that opens with a spring; it is not there, and it never will be there again."

"Then you are a thief!" said Slinkton.

Without any change whatever in the inflexible purpose, which it was quite terrific even to me to contemplate, and from the power of which I had always felt convinced it was impossible for this wretch to escape, Beckwith returned.

"I am your niece's shadow, too."

With an imprecation Slinkton put his hand to his head, tore out some hair, and flung it to the ground. It was the end of the smooth walk; he destroyed it in the action, and it will soon be seen that his use for it was past.

Beckwith went on: "Whenever you left here, I left here. Although I understood that you found it necessary to pause in the completion of that purpose, to avert suspicion, still I watched you close, with the poor confiding girl. When I had the diary, and could read it word by word – it was only about the night before your last visit to Scarborough – you remember the night? you slept with a small flat vial tied to your wrist – I sent to Mr. Sampson, who was kept out of view. This is Mr. Sampson's trusty servant standing by the door. We three saved your niece among us."

Slinkton looked at us all, took an uncertain step or two from the place where he stood, returned to it, and glanced about him in a very curious way – as one of the meaner reptiles might, looking for a hole to hide in. I noticed at the same time, that a singular change took place in the figure of the man – as if it collapsed within his clothes, and they consequently became ill-shapen and ill-fitting.

"You shall know," said Beckwith, "for I hope the knowledge will be bitter and terrible to you, why you have been pursued by one man, and why, when the whole interest that Mr. Sampson represents would have expended any money in hunting you down, you have been tracked to death at a single individual's charge. I hear you have had the name of Meltham on your lips sometimes?"

I saw, in addition to those other changes, a sudden stoppage come upon his breathing.

"When you sent the sweet girl whom you murdered (you know with what artfully made-out surroundings and probabilities you sent her) to Meltham's office, before taking her abroad to originate the transaction that doomed her to the grave, it fell to Meltham's lot to see her and to speak with her. It did not fall to his lot to save her, though I know he would freely give his own life to have done it. He admired her – I would say he loved her deeply, if I thought it possible that you could understand the word. When she was sacrificed, he was thoroughly assured of your guilt. Having lost her, he had but one object left in life, and that was to avenge her and destroy you.

"That man Meltham," Beckwith steadily pursued, "was as absolutely certain that you could never elude him in this world, if he devoted himself to your destruction with his utmost fidelity and earnestness, and if he divided the sacred duty with no other duty in life, as he was certain that in achieving it he would be a poor instrument in the hands of Providence, and would do well before Heaven in striking you out from among living men. I am that man, and I thank God I have done my work!"

If Slinkton had been running for his life from swift-footed savages, a dozen miles, he could not have shown more emphatic signs of being oppressed at heart and laboring for breath, than he showed now, when he looked at the pursuer who had so relentlessly hunted him down.

"You never saw me under my right name before; you see me under my right name now. You shall see me once again in the body, when you are tried for your life. You shall see me once again in the spirit, when the cord is round your neck, and the crowd are crying against you!"

When Meltham had spoken these last words, the miscreant suddenly turned away his face, and seemed to strike his mouth with his open hand. At the same instant, the room was filled with a new and powerful odor, and, almost at the same instant, he broke into a crooked run, leap, start – I have no name for the spasm – and fell, with a dull weight that shook the heavy old doors and windows.

That was the fitting end of him.

When we saw that he was dead, we drew away from the room, and Meltham, giving me his hand, said, wearily, "I have no more work on earth, my friend. But I shall see her again elsewhere."

It was in vain that I tried to rally him. He might have saved her, he said; he had not saved her, and he reproached himself; he had lost her, and he was brokenhearted.

"The purpose that sustained me is over, Sampson, and there is nothing now to hold me to life. I am not fit for life; I am weak and spiritless; I have no hope and no object."

In truth, I could hardly have believed that the broken man who then spoke to me was the man who had so strongly and so differently impressed me when his purpose was before him. I used such entreaties with him as I could; but he still said, and always said, in a patient, undemonstrative way – nothing could avail him – he was brokenhearted.

He died early in the next spring. He was buried by the side of the poor young lady for whom he had cherished those tender and unhappy regrets; and he left all he had to her sister. She lived to be a happy wife and mother; she married my sister's son, who succeeded poor Meltham; she is living now, and her children ride about the garden on my walking stick when I go to see her.

Edith Swan-Neck

Maurice Leblanc

" **A** rsène Lupin, what's your real opinion of Inspector Ganimard?"

"A very high one, my dear fellow."

"A very high one? Then why do you never miss a chance of turning him into ridicule?"

"It's a bad habit; and I'm sorry for it. But what can I say? It's the way of the world. Here's a decent detective chap, here's a whole pack of decent men, who stand for law and order, who protect us against the apaches, who risk their lives for honest people like you and me; and we have nothing to give them in return but flouts and gibes. It's preposterous!"

"Bravo, Lupin! You're talking like a respectable tax-payer!"

"What else am I? I may have peculiar views about other people's property; but I assure you that it's very different when my own's at stake. By Jove, it doesn't do to lay hands on what belongs to me! Then I'm out for blood! Aha! It's *my* pocket, *my* money, *my* watch . . . hands off! I have the soul of a conservative, my dear fellow, the instincts of a retired tradesman and a due respect for every sort of tradition and authority. And that is why Ganimard inspires me with no little gratitude and esteem."

"But not much admiration?"

"Plenty of admiration, too. Over and above the dauntless courage which comes natural to all those gentry at the Criminal Investigation Department, Ganimard possesses very sterling qualities: decision, insight, judgement. I have watched him at work. He's somebody, when all's said. Do you know the Edith Swan-Neck story, as it was called?"

"I know as much as everybody knows."

"That means that you don't know it at all. Well, that job was, I dare say, the one which I thought out most cleverly, with the utmost care and the utmost precaution, the one which I shrouded in the greatest darkness and mystery, the one which it took the biggest generalship to carry through. It was a regular game of chess, played according to strict scientific and mathematical rules. And yet Ganimard ended by unravelling the knot. Thanks to him, they know the truth today on the Quai des Orfèvres. And it is a truth quite out of the common, I assure you."

"May I hope to hear it?"

"Certainly . . . one of these days . . . when I have time . . . But the Brunelli is dancing at the Opera to-night; and, if she were not to see me in my stall . . .!"

I do not meet Lupin often. He confesses with difficulty, when it suits him. It was only gradually, by snatches, by odds and ends of confidences, that I was able to obtain the different incidents and to piece the story together in all its details.

The main features are well known and I will merely mention the facts.

Three years ago, when the train from Brest arrived at Rennes, the door of one of the luggage vans was found smashed in. This van had been booked by Colonel Sparmiento, a rich Brazilian, who was travelling with his wife in the same train. It contained a complete set of tapestry hangings. The case in which one of these was packed had been broken open and the tapestry had disappeared.

Colonel Sparmiento started proceedings against the railway company, claiming heavy damages, not only for the stolen tapestry, but also for the loss in value which the whole collection suffered in consequence of the theft.

The police instituted inquiries. The company offered a large reward. A fortnight later, a letter which had come undone in the post was opened by the authorities and revealed the fact that the theft had been carried out under the direction of Arsène Lupin and that a package was to leave next day for the United States. That same evening, the tapestry was discovered in a trunk deposited in the cloakroom at the Gare Saint-Lazare.

The scheme, therefore, had miscarried. Lupin felt the disappointment so much that he vented his ill-humour in a communication to Colonel Sparmiento, ending with the following words, which were clear enough for anybody:

It was very considerate of me to take only one. Next time, I shall take the twelve. *Verbum sap.*

A.L.

Colonel Sparmiento had been living for some months in a house standing at the end of a small garden at the corner of the Rue de la Faisanderie and the Rue Dufresnoy. He was a rather thick-set, broad-shouldered man, with black hair and a swarthy skin, always well and quietly dressed. He was married to an extremely pretty but delicate Englishwoman, who was much upset by the business of the tapestries. From the first she implored her husband to sell them for what they would fetch. The Colonel had much too forcible and dogged a nature to yield to what he had every right to describe as a woman's fancies. He sold nothing, but he redoubled his precautions and adopted every measure that was likely to make an attempt at burglary impossible.

To begin with, so that he might confine his watch to the garden front, he walled up all the windows on the ground floor and the first floor overlooking the Rue Dufresnoy. Next, he enlisted the services of a firm which made a speciality of protecting private houses against robberies. Every window of the gallery in which the tapestries were hung was fitted with invisible burglar alarms, the position of which was known to none but himself. These, at the least touch, switched on all the electric lights and set a whole system of bells and gongs ringing.

In addition to this, the insurance companies to which he applied refused to grant policies to any considerable amount unless he consented to let three men, supplied by the companies and paid by himself, occupy the ground floor of his house every night. They selected for the purpose three ex-detectives, tried and trustworthy men, all of whom hated Lupin like poison. As for the servants, the Colonel had known them for years and was ready to vouch for them.

After taking these steps and organizing the defence of the house as though it were a fortress, the Colonel gave a great house-warming, a sort of private view, to which he invited the members of both his clubs, as well as a certain number of ladies, journalists, art patrons and critics.

They felt, as they passed through the garden gate, much as if they were walking into a prison. The three private detectives, posted at the foot of the stairs, asked for each visitor's invitation card and eyed him up and down suspiciously, making him feel as though they were going to search his pockets or take his fingerprints.

The Colonel, who received his guests on the first floor, made laughing apologies and seemed delighted at the opportunity of explaining the arrangements which he had invented to secure the safety of his hangings. His wife stood by him, looking charmingly young and pretty, fair-haired, pale and sinuous, with a sad and gentle expression, the expression of resignation often worn by those who are threatened by fate.

When all the guests had come, the garden gates and the hall doors were closed. Then everybody filed into the middle gallery, which was reached through two steel doors, while its windows, with their huge shutters, were protected by iron bars. This was where the twelve tapestries were kept.

They were matchless works of art and, taking their inspiration from the famous Bayeux Tapestry, attributed to Queen Matilda, they represented the story of the Norman Conquest. They had been ordered in the fourteenth century by the descendant of a man-at-arms in William the Conqueror's train; were executed by Jehan Gosset, a famous Arras weaver; and were discovered, five hundred years later, in an old Breton manor house. On hearing of this, the Colonel had struck a bargain for fifty thousand francs. They were worth ten times the money.

But the finest of the twelve hangings composing the set, the most uncommon because the subject had not been treated by Queen Matilda, was the one which Arsène Lupin had stolen and which had been so fortunately recovered. It portrayed Edith Swan-Neck on the battlefield of Hastings, seeking among the dead for the body of her sweetheart Harold, last of the Saxon kings.

The guests were lost in enthusiasm over this tapestry, over the unsophisticated beauty of the design, over the faded colours, over the life-like grouping of the figures and the pitiful sadness of the scene. Poor Edith Swan-Neck stood drooping like an overweighted lily. Her white gown revealed the lines of her languid figure. Her long, tapering hands were outstretched in a gesture of terror and entreaty. And nothing could be more mournful than her profile, over which flickered the most dejected and despairing of smiles.

"A harrowing smile," remarked one of the critics, to whom the others listened with deference. "A very charming smile, besides; and it reminds me, Colonel, of the smile of Mme. Sparmiento."

And seeing that the observation seemed to meet with approval, he enlarged upon his idea:

"There are other points of resemblance that struck me at once, such as the very graceful curve of the neck, and the delicacy of the hands . . . and also something about the figure, about the general attitude . . ."

"What you say is so true," said the Colonel, "that I confess that it was this likeness that decided me to buy the hangings. And there was another reason, which was that, by a really curious chance, my wife's name happens to be Edith. I have called her Edith Swan-Neck ever since." And the Colonel added, with a laugh, "I hope that the coincidence will stop at this and that my dear Edith will never have to go in search of her true love's body, like her prototype."

He laughed as he uttered these words, but his laugh met with no echo; and we find the same impression of awkward silence in all the accounts of the evening that appeared during the next few days. The people standing near him did not know what to say. One of them tried to jest:

"Your name isn't Harold, Colonel?"

"No, thank you," he declared, with continued merriment. "No, that's not my name; nor am I in the least like the Saxon king."

All have since agreed that at that moment, as the Colonel finished speaking, the first alarm rang from the windows – the right or the middle window: opinions differ on this point – rang short and shrill on a single note. The peal of the alarm bell was

followed by an exclamation of terror uttered by Mme. Sparmiento, who caught hold of her husband's arm. He cried:

"What's the matter? What does this mean?"

The guests stood motionless, with their eyes staring at the
windows. The Colonel repeated:

"What does it mean? I don't understand. No-one but myself
knows where that bell is fixed. . . ."

And, at that moment – here again the evidence is unanimous –
at that moment came sudden, absolute darkness, followed
immediately by the maddening din of all the bells and all the
gongs, from top to bottom of the house, in every room and at
every window.

For a few seconds, a stupid disorder, an insane terror,
reigned. The women screamed. The men banged with their
fists on the closed doors. They hustled and fought. People fell to
the floor and were trampled underfoot. It was like a panic-
stricken crowd, scared by threatening flames or by a bursting
shell. And, above the uproar, rose the Colonel's voice, shouting:

"Silence! . . . Don't move! . . . It's all right! . . . The switch is
over there, in the corner. . . . Wait a bit. . . . Here!"

He had pushed his way through his guests and reached a
corner of the gallery; and, all at once, the electric light blazed up
again, while the pandemonium of bells stopped.

Then, in the sudden light, a strange sight met the eyes. Two
ladies had fainted. Mme. Sparmiento, hanging to her husband's
arm, with her knees dragging on the floor, and livid in the face,
appeared half-dead. The men, pale, with their neckties awry,
looked as if they had all been in the wars.

"The tapestries are there!" cried someone.

There was a great surprise, as though the disappearance of
those hangings ought to have been the natural result and the
only plausible explanation of the incident. But nothing had been
moved. A few valuable pictures, hanging on the walls, were
there still. And, though the same din had reverberated all over
the house, though all the rooms had been thrown into darkness,
the detectives had seen no-one entering or trying to enter.

"Besides," said the Colonel, "it's only the windows of the
gallery that have alarms. Nobody but myself understands how
they work; and I had not set them yet."

People laughed loudly at the way in which they had been frightened, but they laughed without conviction and in a more or less shamefaced fashion, for each of them was keenly alive to the absurdity of his conduct. And they had but one thought – to get out of that house where, say what you would, the atmosphere was one of agonizing anxiety.

Two journalists stayed behind, however; and the Colonel joined them, after attending to Edith and handing her over to her maids. The three of them, together with the detectives, made a search that did not lead to the discovery of anything of the least interest. Then the Colonel sent for some champagne; and the result was that it was not until a late hour – to be exact, a quarter to three in the morning – that the journalists took their leave, the Colonel retired to his quarters, and the detectives withdrew to the room which had been set aside for them on the ground floor.

They took the watch by turns, a watch consisting, in the first place, in keeping awake and, next, in looking round the garden and visiting the gallery at intervals.

These orders were scrupulously carried out, except between five and seven in the morning, when sleep gained the mastery and the men ceased to go their rounds. But it was broad daylight out of doors. Besides, if there had been the least sound of bells, would they not have waked up?

Nevertheless, when one of them, at twenty minutes past seven, opened the door of the gallery and flung back the shutters, he saw that the twelve tapestries were gone.

This man and the others were blamed afterward for not giving the alarm at once and for starting their own investigations before informing the Colonel and telephoning to the local commissary. Yet this very excusable delay can hardly be said to have hampered the action of the police. In any case, the Colonel was not told until half-past eight. He was dressed and ready to go out. The news did not seem to upset him beyond measure, or, at least, he managed to control his emotion. But the effort must have been too much for him, for he suddenly dropped into a chair and, for some moments, gave way to a regular fit of despair and anguish, most painful to behold in a man of his resolute appearance.

Recovering and mastering himself, he went to the gallery, stared at the bare walls and then sat down at a table and hastily scribbled a letter, which he put into an envelope and sealed.

"There," he said. "I'm in a hurry. . . . I have an important engagement. . . . Here is a letter for the Commissary of Police." And, seeing the detectives' eyes upon him, he added, "I am giving the Commissary my views . . . telling him of a suspicion that occurs to me. . . . He must follow it up. . . . I will do what I can. . . ."

He left the house at a run, with excited gestures which the detectives were subsequently to remember.

A few minutes later, the Commissary of Police arrived. He was handed the letter, which contained the following words:

I am at the end of my tether. The theft of those tapestries completes the crash which I have been trying to conceal for the past year. I bought them as a speculation and was hoping to get a million francs for them, thanks to the fuss that was made about them. As it was, an American offered me six hundred thousand. It meant my salvation. This means utter destruction.

I hope that my dear wife will forgive the sorrow which I am bringing upon her. Her name will be on my lips at the last moment.

Mme. Sparmiento was informed. She remained aghast with horror, while inquiries were instituted and attempts made to trace the Colonel's movements.

Late in the afternoon, a telephone message came from Ville d'Avray. A gang of railway-men had found a man's body lying at the entrance to a tunnel after a train had passed. The body was hideously mutilated; the face had lost all resemblance to anything human. There were no papers in the pockets. But the description answered to that of the Colonel.

Mme. Sparmiento arrived at Ville d'Avray, by motor-car, at seven o'clock in the evening. She was taken to a room at the railway station. When the sheet that covered it was removed, Edith – Edith Swan-Neck – recognized her husband's body.

★   ★   ★

In these circumstances, Lupin did not receive his usual good notices in the press:

> Let him look to himself [jeered one feature writer, summing up the general opinion]. It would not take many exploits of this kind for him to forfeit the popularity which has not been grudged him hitherto. We have no use for Lupin, except when his rogueries are perpetrated at the expense of shady company promoters, foreign adventurers, German barons, banks and financial companies. And, above all, no murders! A burglar we can put up with; but a murderer, no! If he is not directly guilty, he is at least responsible for this death. There is blood upon his hands; the arms on his escutcheon are stained gules.

The public anger and disgust were increased by the pity which Edith's pale face aroused. The guests of the night before gave their version of what had happened, omitting none of the impressive details; and a legend formed straightway around the fair-haired Englishwoman, a legend that assumed a really tragic character, owing to the popular story of the swan-necked heroine.

And yet the public could not withhold its admiration of the extraordinary skill with which the theft had been effected. The police explained it, after a fashion. The detectives had noticed from the first and subsequently stated that one of the three windows of the gallery was wide open. There could be no doubt that Lupin and his confederates had entered through this window. It seemed a very plausible suggestion. Still, in that case, how were they able, first, to climb the garden railings, in coming and going, without being seen; second, to cross the garden and put up a ladder on the flower border, without leaving the least trace behind; third, to open the shutters and the window, without starting the bells and switching on the lights in the house?

The police accused the three detectives of complicity. The magistrate in charge of the case examined them at length, made minute inquiries into their private lives and stated formally that they were above all suspicion. As for the tapestries, there seemed to be no hope that they would be recovered.

It was at this moment that Chief Inspector Ganimard returned from India, where he had been hunting for Lupin on the strength of a number of most convincing proofs supplied by former confederates of Lupin himself. Feeling that he had once more been tricked by his everlasting adversary, fully believing that Lupin had dispatched him on this wild-goose chase so as to be rid of him during the business of the tapestries, he asked for a fortnight's leave of absence, called on Mme. Sparmiento, and promised to avenge her husband.

Edith had reached the point at which not even the thought of vengeance relieves the sufferer's pain. She had dismissed the three detectives on the day of the funeral and engaged just one man and an old cook-housekeeper to take the place of the large staff of servants the sight of whom reminded her too cruelly of the past. Not caring what happened, she kept her room and left Ganimard free to act as he pleased.

He took up his quarters on the ground floor and at once instituted a series of the most minute investigations. He started the inquiry afresh, questioned the people in the neighbourhood, studied the distribution of the rooms and set each of the burglar alarms going thirty and forty times over.

At the end of the fortnight he asked for an extension of leave. The Chief of the Detective Service, who was at that time M. Dudouis, came to see him and found him perched on the top of a ladder, in the gallery. That day, the Chief Inspector admitted that all his searches had proved useless.

Two days later, however, M. Dudouis called again and discovered Ganimard in a very thoughtful frame of mind. A bundle of newspapers lay spread in front of him. At last, in reply to his superior's urgent questions, the Chief Inspector muttered:

"I know nothing, Chief, absolutely nothing; but there's a confounded notion worrying me . . . Only it seems so absurd. . . . And then it doesn't explain things . . . On the contrary, it confuses them rather . . ."

"Then . . .?"

"Then I implore you, Chief, to have a little patience . . . to let me go my own way. But if I telephone to you, some day or other, suddenly, you must jump into a taxi, without losing a minute. It will mean that I have discovered the secret."

Forty-eight hours passed. Then, one morning, M. Dudouis received a telegram:

GOING TO LILLE.

GANIMARD.

"What the dickens can he want to go to Lille for?" wondered the Chief Detective.

The day passed without news, followed by another day. But M. Dudouis had every confidence in Ganimard. He knew his man, knew that the old detective was not one of those people who excite themselves for nothing. When Ganimard "got a move on him," it meant that he had sound reasons for doing so.

As a matter of fact, on the evening of that second day, M. Dudouis was called to the telephone.

"Is that you, Chief?"

"Is it Ganimard speaking?"

Cautious men both, they began by making sure of each other's identity. As soon as his mind was eased on this point, Ganimard continued, hurriedly:

"Ten men, Chief, at once. And please come yourself."

"Where are you?"

"In the house, on the ground floor. But I will wait for you just inside the garden gate."

"I'll come at once. In a taxi, of course?"

"Yes, Chief. Stop the taxi fifty yards from the house. I'll let you in when you whistle."

Things took place as Ganimard had arranged. Shortly after midnight, when all the lights were out on the upper floors, he slipped into the street and went to meet M. Dudouis. There was a hurried consultation. The officers distributed themselves as Ganimard ordered. Then the Chief and the Chief Inspector walked back together, noiselessly crossed the garden and closeted themselves with every precaution.

"Well, what's it all about?" asked M. Dudouis. "What does all this mean? Upon my word, we look like a pair of conspirators!"

But Ganimard was not laughing. His Chief had never seen

him in such a state of perturbation, nor heard him speak in a voice denoting such excitement.

"Any news, Ganimard?"

"Yes, Chief, and . . . this time . . .! But I can hardly believe it myself. . . . And yet I'm not mistaken: I know the real truth. . . . It may be as unlikely as you please, but it is the truth, the whole truth and nothing but the truth."

He wiped away the drops of perspiration that trickled down his forehead, and, after a further question from M. Dudouis, pulled himself together, swallowed a glass of water and began:

"Lupin has often got the better of me . . ."

"Look here, Ganimard," said M. Dudouis, interrupting him. "Why can't you come straight to the point? Tell me, in two words, what's happened."

"No, Chief," retorted the Chief Inspector, "it is essential that you should know the different stages which I have passed through. Excuse me, but I consider it indispensable." And he repeated: "I was saying, Chief, that Lupin has often got the better of me and led me many a dance. But, in this contest in which I have always come out worst . . . so far . . . I have at least gained experience of his manner of play and learnt to know his tactics. Now, in the matter of the tapestries, it occurred to me almost from the start to set myself two problems. In the first place, Lupin, who never makes a move without knowing what he is after, was obviously aware that Colonel Sparmiento had come to the end of his money and that the loss of the tapestries might drive him to suicide. Nevertheless, Lupin, who hates the very thought of bloodshed, stole the tapestries."

"There was the inducement," said M. Dudouis, "of the five or six hundred thousand francs which they are worth."

"No, Chief, I tell you once more, whatever the occasion might be, Lupin would not take life, nor be the cause of another person's death, not for anything in this world, not for millions and millions. That's the first point. In the second place, what was the object of all that disturbance, in the evening, during the house-warming party? Obviously, don't you think, to surround the business with an atmosphere of anxiety and terror, in the shortest possible time, and also to divert suspicion from the

truth, which, otherwise, might easily have been suspected? . . .
You seem not to understand, Chief."

"Upon my word, I do not!"

"As a matter of fact," said Ganimard, "as a matter of fact, it is
not particularly plain. And I myself, when I put the problem
before my mind in those same words, did not understand it very
clearly. . . . And yet I felt that I was on the right track. . . . Yes,
there was no doubt that Lupin wanted to divert suspicion . . . to
divert it *to* himself, Lupin, mark you . . . so that the real person
who was working the business might remain unknown."

"A confederate," suggested M. Dudouis. "A confederate,
moving among the visitors, who set the alarms going . . . and
who managed to hide in the house after the party had broken
up."

"You're getting warm, Chief, you're getting warm! It is
certain that the tapestries, as they cannot have been stolen
by anyone making his way surreptitiously into the house, were
stolen by somebody who remained in the house; and it is equally
certain that, by taking the list of the people invited and inquiring into the antecedents of each of them, one might . . ."

"Well?"

"Well, Chief, there's a 'but,' namely, that the three detectives
had this list in their hands when the guests arrived and that they
still had it when the guests left. Now sixty-three came in and
sixty-three went away. So you see . . ."

"Then do you suppose a servant? . . ."

"No."

"The detectives?"

"No."

"But, still . . . but, still," said the Chief, impatiently, "if the
robbery was committed from the inside. . . ."

"That is beyond dispute," declared the Inspector, whose
excitement seemed to be nearing fever point. "There is no
question about it. All my investigations led to the same certainty. And my conviction gradually became so positive that I
ended, one day, by drawing up this startling axiom: in theory
and in fact, the robbery can only have been committed with the
assistance of an accomplice staying in the house. Whereas there
was no accomplice!"

"That's absurd," said Dudouis.

"Quite absurd," said Ganimard. "But, at the very moment when I uttered that absurd sentence, the truth flashed upon me."

"Eh?"

"Oh, a very dim, very incomplete, but still sufficient truth! With that clue to guide me, I was bound to find the way. Do you follow me, Chief?"

M. Dudouis sat silent. The same phenomenon that had taken place in Ganimard's mind was evidently taking place in his. He muttered:

"If it's not one of the guests, nor the servants, nor the private detectives, then there's no-one left. . . ."

"Yes, Chief, there's one left. . . ."

M. Dudouis started as though he had received a shock; and, in a voice that betrayed his excitement:

"But, look here, that's preposterous."

"Why?"

"Come, think for yourself!"

"Go on, Chief: say what's in your mind."

"Nonsense! What do you mean?"

"Go on, Chief."

"It's impossible! How can Sparmiento have been Lupin's accomplice?"

Ganimard gave a little chuckle.

"Exactly, Arsène Lupin's accomplice! . . . That explains everything. During the night, while the three detectives were downstairs watching, or sleeping rather, for Colonel Sparmiento had given them champagne to drink and perhaps doctored it beforehand, the said Colonel took down the hangings and passed them out through the window of his bedroom. The room is on the second floor and looks out on another street, which was not watched, because the lower windows are walled up."

M. Dudouis reflected and then shrugged his shoulders:

"It's preposterous!" he repeated.

"Why?"

"Why? Because, if the Colonel had been Arsène Lupin's accomplice, he would not have committed suicide after achieving his success."

"Who says that he committed suicide?"

"Why, he was found dead on the line!"

"I told you, there is no such thing as death with Lupin."

"Still this was genuine enough. Besides, Mme. Sparmiento identified the body."

"I thought you would say that, Chief. The argument worried me too. There was I, all of a sudden, with three people in front of me instead of one: first, Arsène Lupin, cracksman; second, Colonel Sparmiento, his accomplice; third, a dead man. Spare us! It was too much of a good thing!"

Ganimard took a bundle of newspapers, untied it and handed one of them to M. Dudouis:

"You remember, Chief, last time you were here, I was looking through the papers . . . I wanted to see if something had not happened, at that period, that might bear upon the case and confirm my supposition. Please read this paragraph."

M. Dudouis took the paper and read aloud:

"Our Lille correspondent informs us that a curious incident has occurred in that town. A corpse has disappeared from the local morgue – the corpse of an unknown man who threw himself under the wheels of a tramcar on the day before. No-one is able to suggest a reason for this disappearance."

M. Dudouis sat thinking and then asked:

"So . . . you believe . . .?"

"I have just come from Lille," replied Ganimard, "and my inquiries leave not a doubt in my mind. The corpse was removed the same night on which Colonel Sparmiento gave his house-warming. It was taken straight to Ville d'Avray by motor-car; and the car remained near the railway-line until the evening."

"Near the tunnel, therefore," said M. Dudouis.

"Next to it, Chief."

"So that the body which was found is merely that body, dressed in Colonel Sparmiento's clothes."

"Precisely, Chief."

"Then Colonel Sparmiento is not dead?"

"No more dead than you or I, Chief."

"But then why all these complications? Why the theft of one tapestry, followed by its recovery, followed by the theft of the twelve? Why that house-warming? Why that disturbance? Why everything? Your story won't hold water, Ganimard!"

"Only because you, Chief, like myself, have stopped half-way; because, strange as this story already sounds, we must go still farther, very much farther, in the direction of the improbable and the astounding. And why not, after all? Remember that we are dealing with Arsène Lupin. With him, is it not always just the improbable and the astounding that we must look for? Must we not always go straight for the maddest suppositions? And, when I say the maddest, I am using the wrong word. On the contrary, the whole thing is wonderfully logical and so simple that a child could understand it. Confederates only betray you. Why employ confederates, when it is so easy and so natural to act for yourself, by yourself, with your own hands and by the means within your own reach?"

"What are you saying? . . . What are you saying? . . . What are you saying?" cried M. Dudouis, in a sort of sing-song voice and a tone of bewilderment that increased with each separate question.

Ganimard gave a fresh chuckle.

"Takes your breath away, Chief, doesn't it? So it did mine on the day when you came to see me here and when the notion was beginning to grow upon me. I was flabbergasted with aston-ishment. And yet I've had experience with my customer. I know what he's capable of. . . . But this, no, this was really a bit too stiff!"

"It's impossible! It's impossible!" said M. Dudouis, in a low voice.

"On the contrary, Chief, it's quite possible and quite logical. It's the threefold incarnation of one and the same individual. A schoolboy would solve the problem in a minute, by a simple process of elimination. Take away the dead man: there remain Sparmiento and Lupin. Take away Sparmiento . . ."

"There remains Lupin," muttered M. Dudouis.

"Yes, Chief, Lupin simply, Lupin in five letters and two syllables, Lupin taken out of his Brazilian skin, Lupin revived

from the dead, Lupin translated for the past six months into
Colonel Sparmiento, travelling in Brittany, hearing of the
discovery of the twelve tapestries, buying them, planning the
theft of the best of them, so as to draw attention to himself,
Lupin, and divert it from himself, Sparmiento. Next, he brings
about, in full view of the gaping public, a noisy contest between
Lupin and Sparmiento or Sparmiento and Lupin, plots and
gives the house-warming party, terrifies his guests and, when
everything is ready, arranges for Lupin to steal Sparmiento's
tapestries and for Sparmiento, Lupin's victim, to disappear
from sight and die unsuspected, unsuspectable, regretted by his
friends, pitied by the public and leaving behind him, to pocket
the profits of the swindle . . ."

Ganimard stopped, looked the Chief in the eyes and, in a
voice that emphasized the importance of his words, concluded:

"Leaving behind him a disconsolate widow."

"Mme. Sparmiento! You really believe . . .?"

"Hang it all!" said the Chief Inspector. "People don't work
up a whole business of this sort without seeing something ahead
of them . . . solid profits."

"But the profits, it seems to me, lie in the sale of the tapestries
which Lupin will effect in America or elsewhere."

"First of all, yes. But Colonel Sparmiento could effect that
sale just as well. And even better. So there's something more."

"Something more?"

"Come, Chief, you're forgetting that Colonel Sparmiento has
been the victim of an important robbery and that, though he
may be dead, at least his widow remains. So it's his widow who
will get the money."

"What money?"

"What money? Why, the money due to her! The insurance
money, of course!"

M. Dudouis was staggered. The whole business suddenly
became clear to him, with its real meaning. He muttered:

"That's true! . . . That's true! . . . The Colonel had insured
his tapestries . . ."

"Rather! And for no trifle either."

"For how much?"

"Eight hundred thousand francs."

"Eight hundred thousand?"

"Just so. In five different companies."

"And has Mme. Sparmiento had the money?"

"She got a hundred and fifty thousand francs yesterday and two hundred thousand to-day – while I was away. The remaining payments are to be made in the course of this week."

"But this is terrible! You ought to have . . ."

"What, Chief? To begin with, they took advantage of my absence to settle up accounts with two of the companies. I only heard about it on my return when I ran up against an insurance manager whom I happen to know and took the opportunity of drawing him out."

The Chief Detective was silent for some time, not knowing what to say. Then he mumbled:

"What a fellow, though!"

Ganimard nodded his head:

"Yes, Chief – a blackguard, I can't help saying, a devil of a clever fellow. For his plan to succeed, he had to manage in such a way that, for four or five weeks, no-one could express or even conceive the least suspicion of the part played by Colonel Sparmiento. All the indignation and all the inquiries had to be concentrated upon Lupin alone. In the last resort, people had to find themselves faced simply with a mournful, pitiful, penniless widow, poor Edith Swan-Neck, a beautiful and legendary vision, a creature so pathetic that the gentlemen of the insurance companies were almost glad to place something in her hands to relieve her poverty and her grief. That's what was planned and that's what happened."

The two men were close together and did not take their eyes from each other's faces.

The Chief asked:

"Who is that woman?"

"Sonia Kritchnoff."

"Sonia Kritchnoff?"

"Yes, the Russian girl whom I arrested last year at the time of the theft of the coronet, and whom Lupin helped to escape."

"Are you sure?"

"Absolutely. I was put off the scent, like everybody else, by Lupin's machinations, and had paid no particular attention to her. But, when I knew the part which she was playing, I remembered. She is certainly Sonia, metamorphosed into an English-woman; Sonia, the most innocent-looking and the trickiest of actresses; Sonia, who would not hesitate to face death for love of Lupin."

"A good capture, Ganimard," said M. Dudouis, approvingly.

"I've something better still for you, Chief!"

"Really? What?"

"Lupin's old foster mother."

"Victoire?"

"She has been here since Mme. Sparmiento began playing the widow; she's the cook."

"Oho!" said M. Dudouis. "My congratulations, Ganimard!"

"I've something for you, Chief, that's even better than that!"

M. Dudouis gave a start. The Inspector's hand clutched his and was shaking with excitement.

"What do you mean, Ganimard?"

"Do you think, Chief, that I would have brought you here, at this late hour, if I had had nothing more attractive to offer you than Sonia and Victoire? Pah! They'd have kept!"

"You mean to say . . .?" whispered M. Dudouis, at last, understanding the Chief Inspector's agitation.

"You've guessed it, Chief!"

"Is *he* here?"

"He's here."

"In hiding?"

"Not a bit of it. Simply in disguise. He's the man-servant."

This time, M. Dudouis did not utter a word nor make a gesture. Lupin's audacity confounded him.

Ganimard chuckled.

"It's no longer a threefold, but a fourfold incarnation. Edith Swan-Neck might have blundered. The master's presence was necessary; and he had the cheek to return. For three weeks, he has been beside me during my inquiry, calmly following the progress made."

"Did you recognize him?"

"One doesn't recognize him. He has a knack of making up his face and altering the proportions of his body so as to prevent anyone from knowing him. Besides, I was miles from suspecting. . . . But, this evening, as I was watching Sonia in the shadow of the stairs, I heard Victoire speak to the man-servant and call him 'Dearie.' A light flashed in upon me. 'Dearie!' That was what she always used to call him. And I knew where I was."

M. Dudouis seemed flustered, in his turn, by the presence of the enemy, so often pursued and always so intangible:

"We've got him this time," he said, between his teeth. "We've got him and he can't escape us."

"No, Chief, he can't: neither he nor the two women."

"Where are they?"

"Sonia and Victoire are on the second floor; Lupin is on the third."

M. Dudouis suddenly became anxious:

"Why, it was through the windows of one of those floors that the tapestries were passed when they disappeared!"

"That's so, Chief."

"In that case, Lupin can get away too. The windows look out on the Rue Dufresnoy."

"Of course they do, Chief; but I have taken my precautions. The moment you arrived, I sent four of our men to keep watch under the windows in the Rue Dufresnoy. They have strict instructions to shoot, if anyone appears at the windows and looks like coming down. Blank cartridges for the first shot, ball-cartridges for the next."

"Good, Ganimard! You have thought of everything. We'll wait here; and, immediately after sunrise . . ."

"Wait, Chief? Stand on ceremony with that rascal? Bother about rules and regulations, legal hours and all that rot? And suppose he's not quite so polite to us and gives us the slip meanwhile? Suppose he plays us one of his Lupin tricks? No, no, we must have no nonsense! We've got him: let's collar him – and without delay!"

And Ganimard, all aquiver with indignant impatience, went out, walked across the garden and presently returned with half a dozen men:

"It's all right, Chief. I've told them in the Rue Dufresnoy to get their revolvers out and aim at the windows. Come along."

These alarums and excursions had not been effected without

a certain amount of noise, which was bound to be heard by the inhabitants of the house. M. Dudouis felt that his hand was forced. He made up his mind to act:

"Come on, then," he said.

The thing did not take long. The eight of them, Browning pistols in hand, went up the stairs without overmuch caution, eager to surprise Lupin before he had time to organize his defences.

"Open the door!" roared Ganimard, rushing at the door of Mme. Sparmiento's bedroom.

A policeman smashed it in with his shoulder.

There was no-one in the room; and no-one in Victoire's bedroom either.

"They're all upstairs!" shouted Ganimard. "They've gone up to Lupin in his attic. Be careful now!"

All eight ran up the third flight of stairs. To his great astonishment, Ganimard found the door of the attic open and the attic empty. And the other rooms were empty too.

"Blast them!" he cursed. "What's become of them?"

But the Chief called him. M. Dudouis, who had gone down again to the second floor, noticed that one of the windows was not latched, but just pushed to.

"There," he said to Ganimard, "that's the road they took – the road of the tapestries. I warned you – the Rue Dufresnoy. . . ."

"But our men would have fired on them," protested Ganimard, grinding his teeth with rage. "The street's guarded."

"They must have gone before the street was guarded."

"All three of them were in their rooms when I rang you up, Chief!"

"They must have gone while you were waiting for me in the garden."

"But why? Why? There was no reason why they should go to-day rather than to-morrow, or the next day, or next week, for that matter, when they had pocketed all the insurance money!"

Yes, there was a reason; and Ganimard knew it when he saw a letter on the table addressed to himself. He opened it and read it. The letter was worded in the style of the testimonials which are handed to people in service when they have given satisfaction:

I, the undersigned, Arsène Lupin, gentleman burglar, ex-colonel, ex-man-of-all-work, ex-corpse, hereby certify that the person of the name of Ganimard gave proof of the most remarkable qualities during his stay in this house. He was exemplary in his behaviour, thoroughly devoted and attentive; and, unaided by the least clue, he foiled a part of my plans and saved the insurance companies four hundred and fifty thousand francs. I congratulate him; and I am quite willing to overlook his blunder in not anticipating that the downstair telephone communicates with the telephone in Sonia Kritchnoff's bedroom and that, when telephoning to Mr. Chief Detective, he was at the same time telephoning to me to clear out as fast as I could. It was a pardonable slip, which must not be allowed to dim the glamour of his services.

Having said this, I beg him to accept the homage of my admiration.

ARSÈNE LUPIN.

The Red Herring

William Hope Hodgson

S.S *Calypso*,
August 10.

W e docked this morning, and the customs gave us the very
devil of a turnout; but they found nothing.

"We shall get you, one of these days, Captain Gault," the
head of the searchers told me. "We've gone through you pretty
carefully; but I'm not satisfied. We've had information that I
could swear was sound; but where you've hidden the stuff I'll
confess stumps me."

"Don't be so infernally ready to give the dog the bad name,
and then add insult to injury by trying to hang him," I said.
"You know you've never caught me yet trying to shove stuff
through."

The head searcher laughed.

"Don't rub it in, Captain," he said. "That's just it! Take the
last little flutter of yours, with the pigeons, and the way you
made money both ways, both on the hens and on the diamonds;
and all the rest of your devil's tricks. You've got the nerve! You
ought to be able to retire by now."

"I'm afraid I'm neither so fortunate nor so clever as you seem
to think, Mr. Anderson," I told him: "You had no right to kill
my hens, and I made your man apologize for his abominable
suggestion about the pigeons!"

"You did so, Cap'n," he said. "But we'll get you yet. And I'll
eat my hat if you get a thing through the gates this time, even if
we've missed finding it now. We're bound to get you at last.
Good morning, Captain."

"Good morning, Mr. Anderson," I said. And he went ashore.

There you have the position. I've got six thousand pounds' worth of pearls in a remarkable little hiding place of my own aboard; and somehow word has been passed to the Customs, and it's going to make the getting of them ashore a deuced difficult thing, that will take some planning. All my old methods they're up to. Besides, I never try the same plan twice, if I can help it: for it is altogether too risky.

And a lot of them are not half so practicable as they appear at first. That carrier-pigeon idea, for instance, was both good and bad; but Mr. Brown and I lost nearly a thousand pounds' worth of stones through it; for there's a class of oaf with a gun who would shoot his own mother-in-law, if she passed him on wings. Perhaps he'd not be really to blame in such circumstances; but he is certainly to blame when he looses off at a "carrier." Any shooting man should be able to recognize them from the common or garden variety. But I fancy the afore-mentioned oaf does the recognizing cheerfully, and shoots promptly. Some of these gentlemen must have made a haul! That was why we never loosed off the pigeons before reaching port. We never meant to trust all that value in the air, except as a last resort.

Anyway, Mr. Anderson and his lot have got it in for me; and I shall have a job to get the stuff safely into the right hands by the twentieth, which is the date we sail.

August 11.

I have hit on what I believe is rather a smart notion, and I began to develop it today.

When I went up to the dock gates this morning, with my bag, I was met by a very courteous and superior person of the Customs Department, who invited me to step into his office. Here, I was again invited into quite a snug little cubicle, and there two searchers made a very thorough examination of me (very thorough indeed!), also of my bag; but, as you may imagine, there was nothing dutiable within a hundred yards of me – that is, nothing of mine.

At the conclusion of the search, after the superior and affable personage had departed, pleasingly apologetic, I was left to acquire clothing and mental equilibrium in almost equal quantities; for I can tell you I was a bit wrathy. And then – perhaps it was just because my mental pot was so a-boil – up simmered *the* idea; and I began straight away on the afore-mentioned developing.

By the time that I had completed my dressing, I had learned not only that the names of the two official searchers were Wentock and Ewiss, but also the numbers of their respective families, and other pleasing details. I dispensed tact and bonhomie with liberality, and eventually suggested an adjournment to the place across the road, for a drink.

But my two new (very new) friends shook their heads at this. The "boss" might see them. It would not do. I nodded a complete comprehension. Would they be off duty tonight? They would, at six-thirty prompt.

"Meet me at the corner at seven o'clock," I said. "I've nothing to do and no one to talk to. We'll make an evening of it."

They smiled cheerfully and expansively, and agreed – well, as only such people do agree!

August 18.

The dinner came off, and was in every way a success, both from their point and my point of view. And I think I may say the same of the two dinners that followed on the fifteenth and the seventeenth. That was yesterday.

It is now the evening of the eighteenth, and I'm jotting down what happened, in due order.

It was last night, at our third little dinner together (which for a change I had aboard), that we got really friendly over some of my liqueur whisky. And I saw the chance had come to ask them straight out if they were open to make a fiver each.

The two men looked at each other for a few moments, without speaking.

"Well, sir, it all depends," said Wentock, the older of the two.

"On what?" I asked.

"We've our place to think of," he said. "It's no use asking us to risk anything, if that's what you mean, sir."

"There's no risk at all," I told him. "At least, I mean the risk is so infinitesimal as hardly to count at all. What I want you to do is simply this. Tonight, if you agree, I'll hand you over this bag I've got here with me. Take it down to the gates tomorrow, and put it somewhere handy in the office. When I come off from the ship, to come ashore through the gates, I shall be carrying another bag, exactly the same as this in every single detail. You see, I've got two of them, made exactly alike.

"Well, I shall be stopped, as usual, at the gates, and taken into the office, and I and my bag will be pretty well turned inside out again; which I can tell you I'm getting sick of, only your people have got it in for me, pretty savage."

The two searchers grinned at this.

"I ain't surprised, Cap'n," said Wentock, "with a reputation like yours. Why, they say as you could retire this minute, with the brass you've made, running in stuff without our smelling out the way you do it."

"Don't be so infernally flattering," I told him. "You mustn't believe half you hear. And I don't want you to get imagining I do this kind of thing regularly. It's just a few trifling trinkets I want to pass in, as a favour to a friend. Not a habit of mine; but just once in a way."

Both of the men burst into roars of laughter. They evidently considered this a great joke.

"Well," I said, "let me tell you just what I want you to do.

"When I go into the office, one of you always takes my bag from me. Well, I simply want you to substitute for it the one I shall give you tonight, and which, of course, you can search then as hard as you like, before the boss. Then, when he goes out hand me back the unsearched one, and I shall just clear off with it, and the trick is done. No risk for you at all. You've simply to take this bag I have here, with a few shore clothes in it, up to the office tomorrow. When I appear, and am searched, you substitute this Number 1 bag for Number 2 which I shall bring in; and you search this Number 1 as fiercely as you like before the boss. Then, when I am let out, you hand me Number 2, and I go. As for Number 1 I'll make you a present of it, as a little souvenir. Now, say 'yes,' and I'll hand you the fivers now."

Wentock said "yes" promptly for the two of them, and I pulled out my pocket book, and handed each a five-pound note.

"No," said Wentock quickly. "Gold, if you please, Cap'n. Them things is too easy traced."

I laughed, and passed him across ten sovereigns, and took back my notes.

"You're a smart man, Wentock," I said.

"Have to be, sir, in our business," he replied, grinning in his cheerfully unscrupulous fashion.

August 19. a.m.

I sail tomorrow; so if I don't manage to get the stuff through today, I shall be in a hole; for I promised it faithfully for not later than the twentieth.

Later. p.m.

When I took my bag down to the gates today to go out, it can be easily imagined that I felt a bit of tension. Six thousand pounds is a lot of risk, apart from the possibility of serious trouble if one is nailed.

However, it had to be done; so I went up to the gates, trying to look as cheerful as usual, and made my accustomed protest against searching, to the genial and diplomatic officer who met me, and invited me to my expected séance in the cubicle.

As I was entering the doorway of the outer office, a messenger boy came up to me, and touched his cap.

"Are you Cap'n Gault, sir?" he asked me.

"I am," I said.

"I just been down to the ship, sir," he explained. "They said you was just off through the gates, and I might catch you if I hurried. I'm to deliver this letter to you, sir, and to tell you there ain't no answer. Good morning, sir."

"Good morning," I said, and tipped him a quarter. Then, as I entered the office with my polite official, I opened the letter.

What I found therein could hardly be supposed to decrease my feelings of tension. The note was printed, crudely, so as to disguise the handwriting. It ran exactly thus:

CAPTAIN GAULT,
s.s. *Calypso*.
Sir

Be advised, and do not attempt to smuggle your stuff through the Customs. You will be sold if you do, and someone who cannot help a friendly feeling for you would regret not to have given you this chance to draw back. Pay the duty, even if you lose money. The Authorities know far more than you can think. They know absolutely that you bought the "material" you wish to smuggle through, and they know the price you paid, which was £5997. That is a lot of money to risk losing, apart from fines and imprisonment. So be warned and pay the duty in the ordinary way. I can do no more for you than this.

A WELLWISHER.

Now, that was what might really be called a nerve-racker to read, and just after I had entered the very place that the warning begged me to avoid, at least in what I might call a "smuggling capacity." I could not possibly back out now; for suspicion would be inevitable; also my plans were all arranged.

I went straight on into the place, looking more comfortable than I felt. I took a quick look round the inner office, and saw the end of a bag, half hidden, under a table. That, at any rate, looked as if Ewiss and Wentock meant to be faithful and carry out the substitution, as arranged. If they had given me away, it might be supposed that the bag I had given them would be now in the hands of their superior officers.

I looked at the problem every way. And all the time, as I puzzled, I kept asking myself not only who *wrote* that warning; but who, of all the people I knew, had the necessary *knowledge of detail* that it showed.

Ewiss and Wentock rose from their desks as I entered the private room, and Wentock came forward and took my bag from me, while Ewiss beckoned me towards the cubicle.

The search they made of me was not drastic; but even had it been I should not have minded, in the circumstances. What I was thinking about, all the time, was the bags, and whether the two searchers meant to be faithful to their part of our bargain.

One thing, at first, I placed as an argument in their favour. It was that the unemotional courtesy of the head official was quite unimpaired; and I could not imagine that even he would be able to remain so absolutely and almost statuesquely calm if my two presumed confederates had given me away to him, and told him that a big capture was on the carpet (it was really linoleum, and cold to the feet).

There was, however, something disturbing in the attitude of Ewiss. The man seemed almost hangdoggish, in the way he avoided meeting my eye. But I could not say this of Wentock; for that cheerful person was completely his own glad and (as I always felt) unscrupulous self.

While I was dressing, my bag was banged down onto the table, and I knew the instant it was thrown open that Wentock and Ewiss had sold me; for they had not carried out the substitution of the Number 1 bag for the Number 2 which I had just brought in; but had frankly and brutally ignored our whole arrangement, and opened Number 1 – the bag I had bargained with them should not be opened.

As he flung the bag open, Wentock looked up at me and grinned broadly. He considered it evidently a splendid effort of smartness; but it was a faint comfort to my belief in the good-ness of human nature that Ewiss looked down at the table and seemed decidedly uncomfortable.

I felt so fierce that I could have given them away, in turn, to their superior for accepting bribes; for it was quite plain now that they had said nothing to him about the plan I had proposed to them to substitute one bag for the other. I could see their way of looking at the whole business. They were not readily brib-able; but if people were foolish enough to offer them a bribe it was accepted – as a *present*; and so much the worse for the person who offered it, and so much the better for the officer presented with this kind of – shall I say "honorarium"! I think anyone must admit I had cause to feel bitter.

I did not, of course, think really of giving them away; for there might have been a charge made of bribery and corruption; whilst they, as I was pretty sure, would say nothing, lest they be mulcted of the "presents" I had made them; and also, possibly, have a reprimand for meddling with my proposition in any way at all.

The search Wentock gave that bag was a revelation of drastic thoroughness. I remonstrated once, and said I would put in a claim for a new bag; for Wentock, as he went further and further, and found nothing, seemed almost inclined to rip the bag to pieces, so sure was he that he "had me safe."

At last, he had to give it up, and pronounced it free of all dutiable stuff, which of course it was; for, as I told him later, I had considered the chances of their proving treacherous, and had carefully omitted on this occasion to put anything dutiable into the bag. I told them that it must be regarded as a kind of trial trip, to test their intentions.

This was as soon as the Boss had left the cubicle; and then I cut loose on the two of them.

"For a couple of treacherous, grunting human hogs, you two are something to talk about!" I told them. "You take my money with one hand, and try to do me in with the other. Suppose you hand out that cash I gave you!"

Wentock laughed outright at this, as if it were a particularly nutty kind of joke; but I was glad to see that Ewiss looked more uncomfortable than ever.

"Our perquisites, Cap'n," said Wentock. "We're often asked out to a bit of dinner, and we get people who are mighty anxious to hand us nice little cash presents, ad lib., as you might say, every once in a while. And we don't say 'no,' do we, Ewiss? Seeing we're both married men, with families to bring up, and remembering, Cap'n, how affectionate you've asked after the youngsters, you might remember us again, Cap'n, when you've any odd cash as you don't want burning holes in your pocket. Likewise we both admired them dinners you stood us uptown. You can do it again, Cap'n, any time you like, and keep on doing it. We're always open. If you can stand it, we can. Now, how would tonight suit you? We're both free and—"

"Go to blazes!" I said, "and stay there. You're a pair of treacherous animals, like all your kind, and you might have ruined me, if I hadn't been careful. Give me my bags, and be damned to you! They say never trust a policeman, even if he's your own brother. He'll lock you up the first chance he gets for the sake of promotion. And I guess you're the same kind of cheap stuff."

And with that I picked up my bags and walked out, Wentock holding the door for me. But Ewiss was looking as thoroughly miserable and ashamed as a man need look.

"How would tonight suit you, sir?" called Wentock after me as I passed through the gates.

"Go to the devil!" I said. "And get him to shut your infernal mouth with a red-hot brick."

And with that I boarded a streetcar and went rather thoughtfully uptown.

> August 19. Later still.

As it chances, I have invited the men to dinner again – both of them; for I'm not the kind of man who likes taking a fall too quietly.

This is what I wrote, addressing it to Wentock at the office:

DEAR MR. WENTOCK,

I have been thinking things over a bit, and have come to the conclusion that everything was not said at our last meeting that might have been said. I bear no malice at all for the somewhat pungent wit you handed out to me. I guess I was in the position that invited a few jabs.

I have been thinking that perhaps there is still a way to arrange this affair a little more to my liking, and I can assure you and your friend that you will be the gainers, and without having your strict feelings for high honesty and fairness out-raged.

Will you both meet me at our little restaurant tonight at the usual time, and I will go thoroughly into the matter; for as I start off tomorrow, it is imperative to me to carry through my plan before I sail.

Remember, I bear no malice at all. Look upon this as an entirely businesslike and reasonable friendly little invite.

Yours sincerely,
G. GAULT.

I sent this by messenger, and tonight I shall be at the restaurant.

> August 20.

They both came to time. Wentock as cheerful and unscrupulous as ever. Ewiss, looking awkward, and as if he would rather have stopped away.

"Now," I said as we sat down, "pleasure first and business afterwards." And I reached for the hock.

"One moment, sir," said Ewiss, suddenly, and pushed forward a small roll of paper, which I took from him, feeling a little puzzled.

It contained dollar notes to the approximate value of five pounds. I looked across at Ewiss with sudden gladness and respect in my heart, for I understood. But what I said was:

"What are these, Mr. Ewiss?"

"It's your brass, Cap'n," he said. "I've thought a deal lately, an' I reckon I can't hold onto it. I'm not grumbling at Mr. Wentock's way of looking at it. Lots of our men look at it that way; but even if you'd no right to try to bribe me, that doesn't say as I'm right to take your brass, an' mean to sell you all the time. If I'm above the job you wanted me to do, I feel I ought to be above taking the brass for it, too. So take it back, sir; an' after that I shall enjoy my dinner with you as well as anyone."

I looked across at Wentock.

"And you?" I asked.

"Well," he said, grinning in his cheerful fashion, "I don't see it that way, Cap'n. Ewiss, here, always was a bit funny on that point. Sometimes I've screwed him up to our general way of looking at it; but, in the main, he's not built on those lines, and I don't grumble at him any more than he don't grumble at me. I look at it this way. You, or any man as insults me by tryin' to buy me, has got to pay for it."

"Good man, Wentock," I said. "It takes a deal of different opinions to oil the different kinds of consciences. I've a brand of my own, and you've a brand of your own, and Mr. Ewiss, there, has his. Anyway, you're welcome to the cash, Mr. Wentock. As for you, Mr. Ewiss, I see you can't take yours; so I'll have it back, and I apologize to you. I think your way is the soundest of the three of us. Now, forgetting all this, let's drop the serious for a time, and we'll have our dinner."

It was over the wine that I explained to Wentock the things I had to explain. Ewiss was out of it, though he listened quietly, with the deepest interest, and a flash of a smile now and again that showed he had a sense of humour.

"You see, Wentock," I said, "I never meant to bribe either of you, but only to make you *think* that I did. No man in his senses would risk £6000 – to be exact £5997—" I glanced at Ewiss and smiled; for I had guessed who was my "wellwisher" – "on a piffly little bribe like a couple of fivers. If I had seriously meant to buy you, I should have offered something nearer your price, say fifty or a hundred pounds. As it was, I wanted merely, by means of my trifling bribes, to make you think I was going to run the stuff through in the way I explained so carefully. In other words, I wished to focus your entire suspicions upon Number 2 bag, thereby insuring that the Number 1 bag, which I left in your hands, should receive only the most casual attention; for you would, naturally, taking my plan at its face value, think only of the second bag, which I assured you I did not want searched. Moreover, it would seem self-evident to you that the Number 1 bag, which I handed entirely over to your care, would never have anything dutiable in it; for, had you acted up to your agreement, there was no apparent reason for supposing that I would ever even handle it again. To insure your subconsciously realizing this, I even told you you could keep it, once it had served me in the matter of the substitution.

"Of course, had you been faithful to our arrangement and substituted the Number 1 bag, to be searched, for the Number 2 bag, which I brought with me, I might have been in a hole. You see, the handle of the Number 1 bag contained the particular, shall we say, trinkets you were anxious to lay hands on.

"But then, I knew, both from the smallness of my bribe and from my reading of your faces, and from the ways of customs officials in general, that you would go for the big 'cop' you felt sure you were wise to. It might have meant promotion – oh, and quite a number of desirable things, from your point of view.

"After all, Wentock, even you," I said quietly and pleasantly, "will now agree that honesty's the best policy!

"And that concludes all I have to say, practically. I planned it all out, even to the burst of anger and the snatching up of both my bags and walking off in that quite superb indignation, on discovery of your treachery. I did it well, didn't I? – while you were so pleasingly and wittily inviting yourself to this final little dinner, which I had, even then, planned, like all the rest of it.

"As I said in my note, you would be the gainers for coming tonight. That is so; for you are the richer for a dinner and an explanation, and Mr. Ewiss for an apology. That is all."

The Stolen White Elephant

Mark Twain

The following curious history was related to me by a chance railway acquaintance. He was a gentleman more than seventy years of age, and his thoroughly good and gentle face and earnest and sincere manner imprinted the unmistakable stamp of truth upon every statement which fell from his lips. He said:

You know in what reverence the royal white elephant of Siam is held by the people of that country. You know it is sacred to kings, only kings may possess it, and that it is indeed in a measure even superior to kings, since it receives not merely honor but worship. Very well; five years ago, when the troubles concerning the frontier line arose between Great Britain and Siam, it was presently manifest that Siam had been in the wrong. Therefore every reparation was quickly made, and the British representative stated that he was satisfied and the past should be forgotten. This greatly relieved the king of Siam, and partly as a token of gratitude, but partly also, perhaps, to wipe out any little remaining vestige of unpleasantness which England might feel toward him, he wished to send the queen a present – the sole sure way of propitiating an enemy, according to Oriental ideas. This present ought not only to be a royal one, but transcendently royal. Wherefore, what offering could be so meet as that of a white elephant? My position in the Indian civil service was such that I was deemed peculiarly worthy of the honor of conveying the present to her majesty. A ship was fitted out for me and my servants and the officers and attendants of the elephant and in due time I arrived in New York harbor and placed my royal charge in admirable quarters in Jersey City. It was necessary to remain a while in order to recruit the animal's health before resuming the voyage.

All went well during a fortnight – then my calamities began. The white elephant was stolen! I was called up at dead of night and informed of this fearful misfortune. For some moments I was beside myself with terror and anxiety; I was helpless. Then I grew calmer and collected my faculties. I soon saw my course – for indeed there was but the one course for an intelligent man to pursue. Late as it was, I flew to New York and got a policeman to conduct me to the headquarters of the detective force. Fortunately I arrived in time, though the chief of the force, the celebrated Inspector Blunt, was just on the point of leaving for his home. He was a man of middle size and compact frame, and when he was thinking deeply he had a way of knitting his brows and tapping his forehead reflectively with his finger, which impressed you at once with the conviction that you stood in the presence of a person of no common order. The very sight of him gave me confidence and made me hopeful. I stated my errand. It did not flurry him in the least; it had no more visible effect upon his iron self-possession than if I had told him somebody had stolen my dog. He motioned me to a seat, and said calmly:

"Allow me to think a moment, please."

So saying, he sat down at his office table and leaned his head upon his hand. Several clerks were at work at the other end of the room; the scratching of their pens was all the sound I heard during the next six or seven minutes. Meantime the inspector sat there, buried in thought. Finally he raised his head, and there was that in the firm lines of his face which showed me that his brain had done its work and his plan was made. Said he – and his voice was low and impressive:

"This is no ordinary case. Every step must be warily taken; each step must be made sure before the next is ventured. And secrecy must be observed – secrecy profound and absolute. Speak to no one about the matter, not even the reporters. I will take care of *them;* I will see that they get only what it may suit my ends to let them know." He touched a bell; a youth appeared. "Alaric, tell the reporters to remain for the present." The boy retired. "Now let us proceed to business – and systematically. Nothing can be accomplished in this trade of mine without strict and minute method."

He took a pen and some paper. "Now – name of the elephant?"

"Hassan Ben Ali Ben Selim Abdallah Mohammed Moisé Alhammal Jamsetjejeebhoy Dhuleep Sultan Ebu Bhudpoor."

"Very well. Given name?"

"Jumbo."

"Very well. Place of birth?"

"The capital city of Siam."

"Parents living?"

"No – dead."

"Had they any other issue besides this one?"

"None. He was an only child."

"Very well. These matters are sufficient under that head. Now please describe the elephant and leave out no particular, however insignificant – that is, insignificant from *your* point of view. To men in my profession there *are* no insignificant particulars; they do not exist."

I described – he wrote. When I was done, he said:

"Now listen. If I have made any mistakes, correct me."

He read as follows:

"Height, nineteen feet; length from apex of forehead to insertion of tail, twenty-six feet; length of trunk, sixteen feet; length of tail, six feet; total length, including trunk and tail, forty-eight feet; length of tusks, nine and a half feet; ears in keeping with these dimensions; footprint resembles the mark left when one upends a barrel in the snow; color of the elephant, a dull white; has a hole the size of a plate in each ear for the insertion of jewelry, and possesses the habit in a remarkable degree of squirting water upon spectators and of maltreating with his trunk not only such persons as he is acquainted with, but even entire strangers; limps slightly with his right hind leg, and has a small scar in his left armpit caused by a former boil; had on, when stolen, a castle containing seats for fifteen persons, and a gold-cloth saddle-blanket the size of an ordinary carpet."

There were no mistakes. The inspector touched the bell, handed the description to Alaric, and said:

"Have fifty thousand copies of this printed at once and mailed to every detective office and pawnbroker's shop on the continent." Alaric retired. "There – so far, so good. Next, I must have a photograph of the property."

I gave him one. He examined it critically, and said:

"It must do, since we can do no better; but he has his trunk curled up and tucked into his mouth. That is unfortunate, and is calculated to mislead, for of course he does not usually have it in that position." He touched his bell.

"Alaric, have fifty thousand copies of this photograph made, the first thing in the morning, and mail them with the descriptive circulars."

Alaric retired to execute his orders. The inspector said:

"It will be necessary to offer a reward, of course. Now as to the amount?"

"What sum would you suggest?"

"To *begin* with, I should say – well, twenty-five thousand dollars. It is an intricate and difficult business; there are a thousand avenues of escape and opportunities of concealment. These thieves have friends and pals everywhere—"

"Bless me, do you know who they are?"

The wary face, practiced in concealing the thoughts and feelings within, gave me no token, nor yet the replying words, so quietly uttered:

"Never mind about that. I may, and I may not. We generally gather a pretty shrewd inkling of who our man is by the manner of his work and the size of the game he goes after. We are not dealing with a pickpocket or a hall thief, now, make up your mind to that. This property was not 'lifted' by a novice. But, as I was saying, considering the amount of travel which will have to be done, and the diligence with which the thieves will cover up their traces as they move along, twenty-five thousand may be too small a sum to offer, yet I think it worth while to start with that."

So we determined upon that figure, as a beginning. Then this man, whom nothing escaped which could by any possibility be made to serve as a clue, said:

"There are cases in detective history to show that criminals have been detected through peculiarities in their appetites. Now, what does this elephant eat, and how much?"

"Well, as to *what* he eats, he will eat *anything*. He will eat a man, he will eat a Bible, he will eat anything *between* a man and a Bible."

"Good, very good indeed, but too general. Details are necessary – details are the only valuable things in our trade. Very well – as to men. At one meal – or, if you prefer, during one day – how many men will he eat, if fresh?"

"He would not care whether they were fresh or not; at a single meal he would eat five ordinary men."

"Very good; five men: we will put that down. What nationalities would he prefer?"

"He is indifferent about nationalities. He prefers acquaintances, but is not prejudiced against strangers."

"Very good. Now, as to Bibles. How many Bibles would he eat at a meal?"

"He would eat an entire edition."

"It is hardly succinct enough. Do you mean the ordinary octavo, or the family illustrated?"

"I think he would be indifferent to illustrations; that is, I think he would not value illustrations above simple letterpress."

"No, you do not get my idea. I refer to bulk. The ordinary octavo Bible weighs about two pounds and a half, while the great quarto with the illustrations weighs ten or twelve. How many Doré Bibles would he eat at a meal?"

"If you knew this elephant, you could not ask. He would take what they had."

"Well, put it in dollars and cents, then. We must get at it somehow. The Doré costs a hundred dollars a copy, Russia leather, beveled."

"He would require about fifty thousand dollars' worth – say an edition of five hundred copies."

"Now that is more exact. I will put that down. Very well; he likes men and Bibles; so far, so good. What else will he eat? I want particulars."

"He will leave Bibles to eat bricks, he will leave bricks to eat bottles, he will leave bottles to eat clothing, he will leave clothing to eat cats, he will leave cats to eat oysters, he will leave oysters to eat ham, he will leave ham to eat sugar, he will leave sugar to eat pie, he will leave pie to eat potatoes, he will leave potatoes to eat bran, he will leave bran to eat hay, he will leave hay to eat oats, he will leave oats to eat rice, for he was mainly raised on it. There is nothing whatever that he will not eat but European butter, and he would eat that if he could taste it."

"Very good. General quantity at a meal – say about—"

"Well, anywhere from a quarter to half a ton."

"And he drinks—"

"Everything that is fluid. Milk, water, whiskey, molasses, castor oil, camphene, carbolic acid – it is no use to go into particulars; whatever fluid occurs to you set it down. He will drink anything that is fluid, except European coffee."

"Very good. As to quantity?"

"Put it down five to fifteen barrels – his thirst varies; his other appetites do not."

"These things are unusual. They ought to furnish quite good clues toward tracing him."

He touched the bell.

"Alaric, summon Captain Burns."

Burns appeared. Inspector Blunt unfolded the whole matter to him, detail by detail. Then he said in the clear, decisive tones of a man whose plans are clearly defined in his head, and who is accustomed to command – "Captain Burns, detail Detectives Jones, Davis, Halsey, Bates, and Hackett to shadow the elephant."

"Yes, sir."

"Detail Detectives Moses, Dakin, Murphy, Rogers, Tupper, Higgins, and Bartholomew to shadow the thieves."

"Yes, sir."

"Place a strong guard – a guard of thirty picked men, with a relief of thirty – over the place from whence the elephant was stolen, to keep strict watch there night and day, and allow none to approach – except reporters – without written authority from me."

"Yes, sir."

"Place detectives in plainclothes in the railway, steamship, and ferry depots, and upon all roadways leading out of Jersey City, with orders to search all suspicious persons."

"Yes, sir."

"Furnish all these men with photograph and accompanying description of the elephant, and instruct them to search all trains and outgoing ferry boats and other vessels."

"Yes, sir."

"If the elephant should be found, let him be seized, and the information forwarded to me by telegraph."

"Yes, sir."

"Let me be informed at once if any clues should be found – footprints of the animal, or anything of that kind."

"Yes, sir."

"Get an order commanding the harbor police to patrol the frontages vigilantly."

"Yes, sir."

"Dispatch detectives in plainclothes over all the railways, north as far as Canada, west as far as Ohio, south as far as Washington."

"Yes, sir."

"Place experts in all the telegraph offices to listen to all messages; and let them require that all cipher dispatches be interpreted to them."

"Yes, sir."

"Let all these things be done with the utmost secrecy – mind, the most impenetrable secrecy."

"Yes, sir."

"Report to me promptly at the usual hour."

"Yes, sir."

"Go!"

"Yes, sir."

He was gone.

Inspector Blunt was silent and thoughtful a moment, while the fire in his eye cooled down and faded out. Then he turned to me and said in a placid voice:

"I am not given to boasting, it is not my habit; but – we shall find the elephant."

I shook him warmly by the hand and thanked him; and I *felt* my thanks, too. The more I had seen of the man the more I liked him and the more I admired him and marveled over the mysterious wonders of his profession. Then we parted for the night, and I went home with a far happier heart than I had carried with me to his office.

Next morning it was all in the newspapers, in the minutest detail. It even had additions – consisting of Detective This, Detective That, and Detective The Other's "theory" as to how the robbery was done, who the robbers were, and whither they had flown with their booty. There were eleven of these theories, and they covered all the possibilities; and this single fact shows what independent thinkers detectives are. No two theories were alike, or even much resembled each other, save in one striking particular, and in that one all the eleven theories were absolutely agreed. That was, that although the rear of my building was torn out and the only door remained locked, the elephant had not been removed through the rent, but by some other (undiscovered) outlet. All agreed that the robbers had made that rent only to mislead the detectives. That never would have occurred to me or to any other layman, perhaps, but it had not deceived the detectives for a moment. Thus, what I had supposed was the only thing that had no mystery about it was in fact the very thing I had gone furthest astray in. The eleven theories all named the supposed robbers, but no two named the same robbers; the total number of suspected persons was thirty-seven. The various newspaper accounts all closed with the most important opinion of all – that of Chief Inspector Blunt. A portion of this statement read as follows:

> The chief knows who the two principals are, namely, "Brick" Duffy and "Red" McFadden. Ten days before the robbery was achieved he was already aware that it was to be attempted, and had quietly proceeded to shadow these two noted villains; but unfortunately on the night in question their track was lost, and before it could be found again the bird was flown – that is, the elephant.
>
> Duffy and McFadden are the boldest scoundrels in the profession; the chief has reasons for believing that they are the men who stole the stove out of the detective head-quarters on a bitter night last winter – in consequence of

which the chief and every detective present were in the hands of the physicians before morning, some with frozen feet, others with frozen fingers, ears, and other members.

When I read the first half of that I was more astonished than ever at the wonderful sagacity of this strange man. He not only saw everything in the present with a clear eye, but even the future could not be hidden from him. I was soon at his office, and said I could not help wishing he had had those men arrested, and so prevented the trouble and loss; but his reply was simple and unanswerable:

"It is not our province to prevent crime, but to punish it. We cannot punish it until it is committed."

I remarked that the secrecy with which we had begun had been marred by the newspapers; not only all our facts but all our plans and purposes had been revealed; even all the suspected persons had been named; these would doubtless disguise themselves now, or go into hiding.

"Let them. They will find that when I am ready for them my hand will descend upon them, in their secret places, as unerringly as the hand of fate. As to the newspapers, we *must* keep in with them. Fame, reputation, constant public mention – these are the detective's bread and butter. He must publish his facts, else he will be supposed to have none; he must publish his theory, for nothing is so strange or striking as a detective's theory, or brings him so much wondering respect; we must publish our plans, for these the journals insist upon having, and we could not deny them without offending. We must constantly show the public what we are doing, or they will believe we are doing nothing. It is much pleasanter to have a newspaper say, 'Inspector Blunt's ingenious and extraordinary theory is as follows,' than to have it say some harsh thing, or worse still, some sarcastic one."

"I see the force of what you say. But I noticed that in one part of your remarks in the papers this morning you refused to reveal your opinion upon a certain minor point."

"Yes, we always do that; it has a good effect. Besides, I had not formed any opinion on that point, anyway."

I deposited a considerable sum of money with the inspector,

to meet current expenses, and sat down to wait for news. We were expecting the telegrams to begin to arrive at any moment now. Meantime I reread the newspapers and also our descriptive circular, and observed that our twenty-five-thousand-dollar reward seemed to be offered only to detectives. I said I thought it ought to be offered to anybody who would catch the elephant. The inspector said:

"It is the detectives who will find the elephant, hence the reward will go to the right place. If other people found the animal, it would only be by watching the detectives and taking advantage of clues and indications stolen from them, and that would entitle the detectives to the reward, after all. The proper office of a reward is to stimulate the men who deliver up their time and their trained sagacities to this sort of work, and not to confer benefits upon chance citizens who stumble upon a capture without having earned the benefits by their own merits and labors."

This was reasonable enough, certainly. Now the telegraphic machine in the corner began to click, and the following dispatch was the result.

> Flower Station, N.Y., 7:30 a.m.
> Have got a clue. Found a succession of deep tracks across a farm near here. Followed them two miles east without result; think elephant went west. Shall now shadow him in that direction.
>
> Darley, Detective

"Darley's one of the best men on the force," said the inspector. "We shall hear from him again before long."

Telegram number two came:

> Barker's, N.J., 7:40 a.m.
> Just arrived. Glass factory broken open here during night, and eight hundred bottles taken. Only water in large quantity near here is five miles distant. Shall strike for there. Elephant will be thirsty. Bottles were empty.
>
> Baker, Detective

"That promises well, too," said the inspector. "I told you the creature's appetites would not be bad clues."

Telegram number three:

> Taylorville, L.I., 8:15 a.m.
> A haystack near here disappeared during night. Probably eaten. Have got a clue, and am off.
>
> Hubbard, Detective

"How he does move around!" said the inspector. "I knew we had a difficult job on hand, but we shall catch him yet."

> Flower Station, N.Y., 9 a.m.
> Shadowed the tracks three miles westward. Large, deep, and ragged. Have just met a farmer who says they are not elephant tracks. Says they are holes where he dug up saplings for shade-trees when ground was frozen last winter. Give me orders how to proceed.
>
> Darley, Detective

"Aha! a confederate of the thieves! The thing grows warm," said the inspector.

He dictated the following telegram to Darley:

> Arrest the man and force him to name his pals. Continue to follow the tracks – to the Pacific, if necessary.
>
> Chief Blunt

Next telegram:

> Coney Point, Pa., 8:45 a.m.
> Gas office broken open here during night and three months' unpaid gas bills taken. Have got a clue and am away.
>
> Murphy, Detective

"Heavens!" said the inspector; "would he eat gas bills?"

"Through ignorance, yes; but they cannot support life. At least, unassisted."

Now came this exciting telegram:

Ironville, N.Y., 9:30 a.m.

Just arrived. This village in consternation. Elephant passed through here at five this morning. Some say he went east, some say west, some north, some south – but all say they did not wait to notice particularly. He killed a horse; have secured a piece of it for a clue. Killed it with his trunk; from style of blow, think he struck it left-handed. From position in which horse lies, think elephant traveled northward along line of Berkley railway. Has four and a half hours' start, but I move on his track at once.

Hawes, Detective

I uttered exclamations of joy. The inspector was as self-contained as a graven image. He calmly touched his bell.

"Alaric, send Captain Burns here."

Burns appeared.

"How many men are ready for instant orders?"

"Ninety-six, sir."

"Send them north at once. Let them concentrate along the line of the Berkley road north of Ironville."

"Yes, sir."

"Let them conduct their movements with the utmost secrecy. As fast as others are at liberty, hold them for orders."

"Yes, sir."

"Go!"

"Yes, sir."

Presently came another telegram:

Sage Corners, N.Y., 10:30

Just arrived. Elephant passed through here at 8:15. All escaped from the town but a policeman. Apparently elephant did not strike at policeman, but at the lamp-post. Got both. I have secured a portion of the policeman as clue.

Stumm, Detective

"So the elephant has turned westward," said the inspector. "However, he will not escape, for my men are scattered all over that region."

The next telegram said:

> Glover's, 11:15
>
> Just arrived. Village deserted, except sick and aged. Elephant passed through three-quarters of an hour ago. The anti-temperance mass meeting was in session; he put his trunk in at a window and washed it out with water from cistern. Some swallowed it – since dead; several drowned. Detectives Cross and O'Shaughnessy were passing through town, but going south – so missed elephant. Whole region for many miles around in terror – people flying from their homes. Wherever they turn they meet elephant, and many are killed.
>
> Brant, Detective

I could have shed tears, this havoc so distressed me. But the inspector only said—

"You see – we are closing in on him. He feels our presence; he has turned eastward again."

Yet further troublous news was in store for us. The telegraph brought this:

> Hoganport, 12:19
>
> Just arrived. Elephant passed through half an hour ago, creating wildest fright and excitement. Elephant raged around streets; two plumbers going by, killed one – other escaped. Regret general.
>
> O'Flaherty, Detective

"Now he is right in the midst of my men," said the inspector. "Nothing can save him."

A succession of telegrams came from detectives who were scattered through New Jersey and Pennsylvania, and who were following clues consisting of ravaged barns, factories, and Sunday school libraries, with high hopes – hopes amounting to certainties, indeed. The inspector said: "I wish I could communicate with them and order them north, but that is impossible. A detective only visits a telegraph office to send his report; then he is

off again, and you don't know where to put your hand
on him."

Now came this dispatch:

> Bridgeport, Ct., 12:15
>
> Barnum offers rate of $4000 a year for exclusive privi-
> lege of using elephant as traveling advertising medium
> from now till detectives find him. Wants to paste circus
> posters on him. Desires immediate answer.
>
> Boggs, Detective

"That is perfectly absurd!" I exclaimed.

"Of course it is," said the inspector. "Evidently Mr. Barnum,
who thinks he is so sharp, does not know me – but I know him."

Then he dictated this answer to the dispatch:

> Mr. Barnum's offer declined. Make it $7,000 or nothing.
>
> Chief Blunt

"There. We shall not have to wait long for an answer. Mr.
Barnum is not at home; he is in the telegraph office – it is his
way when he has business on hand. Inside of three—"

> Done – P. T. Barnum

So interrupted the clicking telegraphic instrument. Before I
could make a comment upon this extraordinary episode, the
following dispatch carried my thoughts into another and very
distressing channel:

> Bolivia, N.Y., 12:50
>
> Elephant arrived here from the south and passed
> through toward the forest at 11:50, dispersing a funeral
> on the way, and diminishing the mourners by two. Citi-
> zens fired some small cannonballs into him, and then fled.
> Detective Burke and I arrived ten minutes later, from the
> north, but mistook some excavations for footprints, and so
> lost a good deal of time; but at last we struck the right trail
> and followed it to the woods. We then got down on our

hands and knees and continued to keep a sharp eye on the
track, and so shadowed it into the brush. Burke was in
advance. Unfortunately the animal had stopped to rest;
therefore, Burke having his head down, intent upon the
track, butted up against the elephant's hind legs before he
was aware of his vicinity. Burke instantly rose to his feet,
seized the tail, and exclaimed joyfully, "I claim the re—"
but got no further, for a single blow of the huge trunk laid
the brave fellow's fragments low in death. I fled rearward,
and the elephant turned and shadowed me to the edge of
the wood, making tremendous speed, and I should inevitably have been lost, but that the remains of the funeral
providentially intervened again and diverted his attention.
I have just learned that nothing of that funeral is now left;
but this is no loss, for there is an abundance of material for
another. Meantime, the elephant has disappeared again.

                                    Mulrooney, Detective

We heard no news except from the diligent and confident
detectives scattered about New Jersey, Pennsylvania, Delaware,
and Virginia – who were all following fresh and encouraging
clues – until shortly after 2 p.m., when this telegram came:

                                    Baxter Center, 2:15
Elephant been here, plastered over with circus bills, and
broke up a revival, striking down and damaging many who
were on the point of entering upon a better life. Citizens
penned him up, and established a guard. When Detective
Brown and I arrived, some time after, we entered enclosure
and proceeded to identify elephant by photograph and
description. All marks tallied exactly except one, which
we could not see – the boil scar under armpit. To make sure,
Brown crept under to look, and was immediately brained –
that is, head crushed and destroyed, though nothing issued
from debris. All fled; so did elephant, striking right and left
with much effect. Has escaped, but left bold blood track
from cannon wounds. Rediscovery certain. He broke south-
ward, through a dense forest.

                                    Brent, Detective

That was the last telegram. At nightfall a fog shut down which was so dense that objects but three feet away could not be discerned. This lasted all night. The ferry boats and even the omnibuses had to stop running.

Next morning the papers were as full of detective theories as before; they had all our tragic facts in detail also, and a great many more which they had received from their telegraphic correspondents. Column after column was occupied, a third of its way down, with glaring headlines, which it made my heart sick to read. Their general tone was like this:

THE WHITE ELEPHANT AT LARGE! HE MOVES UPON HIS FATAL MARCH! WHOLE VILLAGES DESERTED BY THEIR FRIGHT-STRICKEN OCCUPANTS! PALE TERROR GOES BEFORE HIM, DEATH AND DEVASTATION FOLLOW AFTER! AFTER THESE, THE DETECTIVES. BARNS DESTROYED, FACTORIES GUTTED, HARVESTS DEVOURED, PUBLIC ASSEMBLAGES DISPERSED, AC-COMPANIED BY SCENES OF CARNAGE IMPOSSIBLE TO DESCRIBE! THEORIES OF THIRTY-FOUR OF THE MOST DISTINGUISHED DETECTIVES ON THE FORCE! THEORY OF CHIEF BLUNT!

"There!" said Inspector Blunt, almost betrayed into excitement, "this is magnificent! This is the greatest windfall that any detective organization ever had. The fame of it will travel to the ends of the earth, and endure to the end of time, and my name with it."

But there was no joy for me. I felt as if I had committed all those red crimes, and that the elephant was only my irresponsible agent. And how the list had grown! In one place he had "interfered with an election and killed five repeaters." He had followed this act with the destruction of two poor fellows, named O'Donohue and McFlannigan, who had "found a refuge in the home of the oppressed of all lands only the day before, and were in the act of exercising for the first time the noble right of American citizens at the polls, when stricken down by the relentless hand of the Scourge of Siam." In another, he had "found a crazy sensation-preacher preparing his next season's heroic attacks on the dance, the theater, and other things which can't strike back, and had stepped on him." And in still another place he had "killed a lightning-rod agent." And so the list went on, growing redder and redder, and more and more heart-breaking. Sixty persons had been killed, and two hundred and forty wounded. All the accounts bore just testimony to the activity and devotion of the detectives, and all closed with the remark that "three hundred thousand citizens and four detectives saw the dread creature, and two of the latter he destroyed."

I dreaded to hear the telegraphic instrument begin to click again. By and by the messages began to pour in, but I was happily disappointed in their nature. It was soon apparent that all trace of the elephant was lost. The fog had enabled him to search out a good hiding place unobserved. Telegrams from the most absurdly distant points reported that a dim vast mass had been glimpsed there through the fog at such and such an hour, and was "undoubtedly the elephant." This dim vast mass had been glimpsed in New Haven, in New Jersey, in Pennsylvania, in interior New York, in Brooklyn, and even in the city of New York itself! But in all cases the dim vast mass had vanished quickly and left no trace. Every detective of the large force scattered over this huge extent of country sent his hourly report, and each and every one of them had a clue, and was shadowing something, and was hot upon the heels of it.

But the day passed without other result.

The next day the same.

The next just the same.

The newspaper reports began to grow monotonous with facts that amounted to nothing, clues which led to nothing, and theories which had nearly exhausted the elements which surprise and delight and dazzle.

By advice of the inspector I doubled the reward.

Four more dull days followed. Then came a bitter blow to the poor, hard-working detectives – the journalists declined to print their theories, and coldly said, "Give us a rest."

Two weeks after the elephant's disappearance I raised the reward to seventy-five thousand dollars by the inspector's advice. It was a great sum, but I felt that I would rather sacrifice my whole private fortune than lose my credit with my government. Now that the detectives were in adversity, the newspapers turned upon them, and began to fling the most stinging sarcasms at them. This gave the minstrels an idea, and they dressed themselves as detectives and hunted the elephant on the stage in the most extravagant way. The caricaturists made pictures of detectives scanning the country with spy-glasses, while the elephant, at their back, stole apples out of their pockets. And they made all sorts of ridiculous pictures of the detective badge – you have seen that badge printed in gold on the back of detective novels, no doubt – it is a wide-staring eye, with the legend, WE NEVER SLEEP. When detectives called for a drink, the would-be facetious barkeeper resurrected an obsolete form of expression and said, "Will you have an eye-opener?" All the air was thick with sarcasms.

But there was one man who moved calm, untouched, un-affected, through it all. It was that heart of oak, the chief inspector. His brave eye never drooped, his serene confidence never wavered. He always said:

"Let them rail on; he laughs best who laughs last."

My admiration for the man grew into a species of worship. I was at his side always. His office had become an unpleasant place to me, and now became daily more and more so. Yet if he could endure it I meant to do so also; at least, as long as I could. So I came regularly, and stayed – the only outsider who seemed to be capable of it. Everybody wondered how I could; and often it seemed to me that I must desert, but at such times I looked into that calm and apparently unconscious face, and held my ground.

About three weeks after the elephant's disappearance I was about to say, one morning, that I should *have* to strike my colors and retire, when the great detective arrested the thought by proposing one more superb and masterly move.

This was to compromise with the robbers. The fertility of this man's invention exceeded anything I have ever seen, and I have had a wide intercourse with the world's finest minds. He said he was confident he could compromise for one hundred thousand dollars and recover the elephant. I said I believed I could scrape the amount together, but what would become of the poor detectives who had worked so faithfully? He said:

"In compromises they always get half."

This removed my only objection. So the inspector wrote two notes, in this form:

> Dear Madam,
> Your husband can make a large sum of money (and be entirely protected from the law) by making an immediate appointment with me.
>
> > Chief Blunt

He sent one of these by his confidential messenger to the "reputed wife" of Brick Duffy, and the other to the reputed wife of Red McFadden.

Within the hour these offensive answers came:

> Ye owld fool:
> brick McDuffys bin ded 2 yere.
>
> > Bridget Mahoney

> Chief Bat,
> Red McFadden is hung and in heving 18 month. Any Ass but a detective knose that.
>
> > Mary O'Hooligan

"I had long suspected these facts," said the inspector; "this testimony proves the accuracy of my instinct."

The moment one resource failed him he was ready with another. He immediately wrote an advertisement for the morning papers, and I kept a copy of it:

> A. – xwblv. 242 N. Tjnd – fz328wmlg. Ozpo, –; 2m! ogw. Mum.

He said that if the thief was alive this would bring him to the usual rendezvous. He further explained that the usual rendezvous was a place where all business affairs between detectives and criminals were conducted. This meeting would take place at twelve the next night.

We could do nothing till then, and I lost no time in getting out of the office, and was grateful indeed for the privilege.

At eleven the next night I brought one hundred thousand dollars in banknotes and put them into the chief's hands, and shortly afterward he took his leave, with the brave old undimmed confidence in his eye. An almost intolerable hour dragged to a close; then I heard his welcome tread, and rose gasping and tottered to meet him. How his fine eyes flamed with triumph! He said:

"We've compromised! The jokers will sing a different tune tomorrow! Follow me!"

He took a lighted candle and strode down into the vast vaulted basement where sixty detectives always slept, and where a score were now playing cards to while the time. I followed close after him. He walked swiftly down to the dim remote end of the place, and just as I succumbed to the pangs of suffocation and was swooning away he stumbled and fell over the outlying members of a mighty object, and I heard him exclaim as he went down:

"Our noble profession is vindicated. Here is your elephant!"

I was carried to the office above and restored with carbolic acid. The whole detective force swarmed in, and such another season of triumphant rejoicing ensued as I had never witnessed before. The reporters were called, baskets of champagne were opened, toasts were drunk, the handshakings and congratulations were continuous and enthusiastic. Naturally the chief was the hero of the hour, and his happiness was so complete and had been so patiently and worthily and bravely won that it made me happy to see it, though I stood there a homeless beggar, my priceless charge dead, and my position in my country's service lost to me through what would always seem my fatally careless execution of a great trust. Many an eloquent eye testified its deep admiration for the chief, and many a detective's voice murmured, "Look at him – just the king of the profession – only give him a clue, it's all he wants, and there ain't anything hid that he can't find." The dividing of the fifty thousand dollars made great pleasure; when it was finished the chief made a little speech while he put his share in his pocket, in which he said, "Enjoy it, boys, for you've earned it; and more than that you've earned for the detective profession undying fame."

A telegram arrived, which read:

Monroe, Mich., 10 p.m.

First time I've stuck a telegraph office in over three weeks. Have followed those footprints, horseback, through the woods, a thousand miles to here, and they get stronger and bigger and fresher every day. Don't worry – inside of another week I'll have the elephant. This is dead sure.

Darley, Detective

The chief ordered three cheers for "Darley, one of the finest minds on the force," and then commanded that he be telegraphed to come home and receive his share of the reward.

So ended that marvelous episode of the stolen elephant. The newspapers were pleasant with praises once more, the next day, with one contemptible exception. This sheet said, "Great is the detective! He may be a little slow in finding a little thing like a mislaid elephant – he may hunt him all day and sleep with his rotting carcass all night for three weeks, but he will find him at last – if he can get the man who mislaid him to show him the place!"

Poor Hassan was lost to me forever. The cannon shots had wounded him fatally, he had crept to that unfriendly place in the fog, and there, surrounded by his enemies and in constant danger of detection, he had wasted away with hunger and suffering till death gave him peace.

The compromise cost me one hundred thousand dollars; my detective expenses were forty-two thousand dollars more; I never applied for a place again under my government; I am a ruined man and a wanderer in the earth – but my admiration for that man, whom I believe to be the greatest detective the world has ever produced, remains undimmed to this day, and will so remain unto the end.

Nick Carter, Detective

Nick Carter

The Murder in Forty-Seventh Street

T he city of New York was electrified one evening by the news that one of its greatest favorites had been foully murdered.

Eugenie La Verde had been found dead in her room, and the murderer had not left a single clew, however slight, by which he could be traced.

Mademoiselle La Verde had been before the public for two seasons as a *danseuse*, and by her remarkable beauty and modesty, as well as by the unparalleled grace with which she executed her inimitable steps, she had won her way to the hearts of all.

On the evening preceding her death she had danced as usual, winning round after round of applause, and a deluge of flowers.

Immediately after the performance she had been driven to her home in Forty-seventh street, accompanied only by her maid, who had been with her for many years, and who scarcely ever left her presence.

The maid had attended her as usual that night: had remained with her until she had disrobed, and then, at her mistress' request, had given her a book, and retired.

Eugenie had bade her servant good-night as usual, adding the injunction that she did not wish to be disturbed before ten o'clock on the following morning.

At ten o'clock precisely on the morning of the succeeding day, the maid, whose name was Delia Dent, had gone to her mistress' room to assist her in dressing, and upon entering had been so horrified by the sight that met her gaze that she had swooned away then and there.

Eugene La Verde was lying upon her bed, clad in the soft wrapper which the maid had helped her to don before leaving her on the preceding night.

Her face was distorted and swollen almost beyond recognition, and in spots was highly discolored, where the blood had coagulated beneath the skin. Her mouth was open, and her eyes were wide and staring, even yet filled with an expression of the horror through which she had passed just before her death. Her delicate hands, pretty enough for an artist's model, were clenched until the finger-nails had sunk into the tender flesh and drawn blood. The figure bore every evidence of a wild and terrific struggle to escape from the grasp in which she had been seized, while the dull blue mark around her throat told only too plainly how her death had been accomplished.

The bed bore every evidence of a wild and terrific struggle. The coverings were tumbled in great confusion, one pillow had fallen upon the floor, and the book which the murdered girl had been engaged in reading when the grip of the assassin had seized her, was torn and crumpled.

Eugenie was dead, and everything in the room bore mute evidence that she had died horribly, and that she had struggled desperately to free herself from the attack of her slayer.

In searching for evidence of the presence of the murderer, not a clew of any kind could be found.

How he had gained access to the room where the *danseuse* was reading, or how he had left it after consummating the horrible deed, were mysteries which the keenest detectives failed to fathom.

Theories were as plenty as mosquitoes in June, but there was positively no proof in support of any of them, and one by one they fell to the ground and were abandoned as useless or absurd.

As a last resort, Delia Dent, the maid, fell under the ban of suspicion. But only for a time. The most stupid of investigators could not long believe her guilty of a crime so heinous, while, moreover, it was certain that she was not possessed of the necessary physical strength to accomplish the deed.

Neither had she the will power, for beyond her love for her dead mistress, the woman was weak and yielding in her nature.

Delia Dent did not long survive her mistress.

The terrible shock caused by the discovery of Eugenie's dead body was more than her frail strength could bear. She was prostrated nervously, and after growing steadily worse for a period of four weeks, she died at the hospital where she had been taken.

One theory, which for a time found many supporters, was that Delia Dent had been in league with the murderer; had admitted him to the house, and had allowed him quietly to depart after the deed was done.

But that theory was also abandoned, as being even more absurd than the others that had been advanced. Delia was conscious to the last, during her sickness, at the hospital, and just before her death she devised all her savings – a sum amounting to nearly ten thousand dollars – to her lawyer, in trust for the person who should succeed in bringing the murderer of Eugenie La Verde to justice.

The house in Forty-seventh street, where Eugenie had been killed, was, at the time, occupied solely by herself and the maid Delia, and the basement was never used by them at all. Once a month the man who examined the gas-meter came to attend to his duty, and upon such occasions he passed through the basement hall on his way to the cellar. But when his work was done, Delia always locked and chained the door which communicated between the basement and the parlor floor, and it was never again disturbed until the same necessity arose during the following month.

Eugenie never dined at home, and her maid never left her. Her breakfast, which consisted only of coffee and a roll, was always prepared by the maid over an alcoholic lamp in the room where Eugenie slept.

After the discovery of the crime, a careful examination was made of every window and door in the house which communicated by any possibility with the outside world.

All were found securely locked, and every door was provided with the additional security afforded by a chair. Even the scuttle had an intricate padlock.

Nothing had been molested.

Window-fastenings, door-locks, chain-bolts, scuttle and sky-light were alike undisturbed.

From the circumstances of the case as they were discovered after the commission of the crime, it was absolutely impossible for the murderer to have gained access to the house without leaving some evidence of the fact. Again, supposing the assassin to have been already concealed therein, it was equally impossible that he could have gotten out without furnishing some clew.

Delia Dent, as has been said, had fainted when she discovered the dead body of her young mistress. Upon reviving, she had staggered to a messenger call in the hall-way, having barely strength to ring for the police. Then, still half-fainting, she had managed to reach the foot of the stairs, but had not yet unchained the front door when her call was answered. She believed that she fainted twice, or that she was in a state of semi-consciousness during the interval that elapsed between the discovery of the crime and the arrival of the police.

The more thorough the investigation, the deeper grew the mystery.

Old and tried detectives were put upon the case. At first they looked wise and assured everybody of the speedy apprehension of the fiend who had committed the deed. Then they became puzzled, and finally utterly confounded. The bravest of them at last confessed that they were no nearer the truth than at the beginning, and one of them, the shrewdest of all, boldly stated that the only way in which the assassin would ever be discovered would be by his voluntary confession, which was not likely to ensue.

Thus matters drifted on until the public mind found other things to think of. The papers at first devoted pages to the event; then a few columns. In a week, one column sufficed. Finally the reports dwindled down to a single comment, and then to nothing, and the mysterious murder was practically relegated to history and forgotten.

There was one, however, who had not forgotten it, and that one was the Inspector in Chief, at Police Headquarters.

Every resource at his command had been exhausted. His best men had taken the case in hand and failed. He had personally given all the time he could spare from his other duties to the murder of Eugenie La Verde, and was yet as greatly mystified as ever. There was no palpable or reasonable solution to the problem.

Her jewels, of great value, were found untouched upon the dressing-case. A roll of bills amounting to several hundred dollars was in the top drawer, where it had evidently been carelessly thrown by the murdered girl that very night.

The murderer had doubtless approached stealthily, giving her no warning. He had seized her in his vise-like grip, choked her to death, and left her as stealthily as he had come. Her body was undefiled by bruises, contusions, or other marks, showing that he had given his attention solely to the work of killing. It was even evident that he had not sought to put a stop to her struggles by the exercise of physical violence, other than that of choking his victim.

The marks upon her throat were peculiar and very striking.

Some of the detectives thought that the assassin had used both hands simultaneously; others believed that he had made use of a rope, holding one end in either hand and winding it twice around her neck.

There was one fact which seemed to upset every theory that was advanced. The door between the room and the hall-way was closed, although not locked.

The bed on which Eugenie was murdered was so situated that it would have been absolutely impossible for anyone to enter the room without being seen by her. The gas was brilliantly lighted, and was so found in the morning after the crime. Delia Dent had never known her mistress to fall asleep while reading, or to neglect to extinguish the gas when ready to compose herself for the night.

Was there a third person in the house, whose presence was known to her alone?

Preposterous! Delia could not have failed to be aware of such a fact, and the person could not have left the house without being discovered, or leaving traces of his manner of exit.

Nothing had ever been whispered against the character of

Eugenie La Verde, and the coroner's inquest proved that she had been worthy of her reputation for modesty and purity.

The crime was a month old when, one evening shortly after dark, Inspector Byrnes went quietly up the steps of Nick Carter's residence.

Everybody believed that the chief had given the matter up, and he was perfectly willing that the public should have that opinion.

In the meantime, he had decided that there was one man in New York who might be able to solve the mystery.

Hence, his quiet call upon Nick Carter.

The Interview

Nick Carter was at home when the inspector called, and he received him as he would have received no other man in the whole city of New York; in his own proper person. One of the cardinal points of Nick's faith in himself was that by keeping himself entirely unknown to everybody his various disguises were rendered absolutely impenetrable.

"I am glad to see you, inspector," was his greeting to the chief. "Sit down, help yourself to a cigar and we will talk it all over, for I suppose you are here on business."

"You are right, Nick."

"You never come unless there is something of importance on hand. What is it to-night?"

"The Eugenie La Verde affair."

"Why, I thought that was given up."

"So it is – by everybody except myself."

"Ah! By the way, I see that—"

"That Delia Dent is dead? Yes."

"Do you take any stock in her knowing aught of the murder, inspector?"

"None whatever. She was as innocent as you, or I."

"My opinion, although of course I know nothing about the case."

"Have you a theory, Nick?"

"No, I avoid theories as I do the typhus or the smallpox. They are dangerous and very 'catching.'"

"Exactly, Still one thinks."

"Yes – unfortunately."

"Nick, I want you to take this matter in hand and sift it to the bottom."

"Easier said than done, inspector."

"I believe that you can do it."

"It is a very blind case."

"Everybody else has failed. Will you try it, Nick? There is a murderer somewhere, and he must be found if it takes years to do it. Will you try it?"

"Yes."

"Thank you. I feared that you would refuse, and yet—"

"I may want a favor sometime, eh?"

"Precisely."

"When am I to begin, and what are your instructions?"

"Begin when you choose, and follow your own bent independently of everybody. I have only one order to give."

"What is that?"

"That no one but ourselves must know that you are on the case."

"I should have made that point a condition of my taking it, inspector."

"You are familiar with the details of the case, I suppose?"

"Yes, sufficiently to begin, unless you have some particular pointer to give me."

"No, there are no pointers in the case."

"Humph! Did Eugenie have any relatives living?"

"Yes; a mother."

"She left some property, did she not?"

"Yes, her mother inherits. I have not learned very much regarding her connections."

"What becomes of the house? Did she own it?"

"Yes. It is at present locked and deserted."

"Ah – and you have the key?"

"Certainly."

"Will you give it to me."

"Yes. I have it with me. Here it is."

"Good. While I am at work upon the case, inspector, will you see that the house remains undisturbed?"

"I will."

"Did the newspapers recount everything concerning the murder correctly?"

"Oh, yes. There was so little to say regarding the surroundings, that I am sure they covered the ground."

"You looked for trap-doors, sliding panels, movable casings, and all such things, I suppose?"

"Certainly, We looked very thoroughly."

"And found nothing?"

"Nothing."

"Still, it will do no harm for me to have a try."

"Certainly not."

"I have found such things in houses where I least expected them before now. It may be that I will find something of the kind there."

"It may be."

"But you do not think so?"

"No, frankly, I do not."

"And yet, how else could the murderer have entered and left the house?"

"My dear Nick, I have asked myself that question at least ten thousand times."

"And found no answer?"

"None."

"Well, I'm inclined to the belief that I will find something of the kind there."

"I hope you will."

"The case stands this way. A girl was murdered. To have been murdered it seems probable that a stranger gained access to her room."

"Yes."

"And yet the condition in which the house was found was such that it is apparently impossible that any one did enter or leave the house after Delia Dent left her mistress that night."

"Precisely."

"Therefore it must have been by some means or method of which you are ignorant."

"Of course."

"How then, if not by a secret door, sliding panel, or some like contrivance?"

"That is the question. How, then?"

"Well, that is then the first thing I am going to look for."

"And the next?"

"Will depend upon my success with the first. Is that all, inspector?"

"Nearly. You will find the house exactly as I found it when I first went there to investigate; and now, good-night, Nick," continued the inspector, rising, and taking a large envelope from his pocket.

"This," he said, "contains the entire case from first to last, and you may read it over at your convenience. Nothing is omitted, and yet very little is said that is worth reading."

"It is that Eugenie La Verde was choked to death, and that the murderer escaped and left not the slightest clew as to his identity or his haunts."

"Exactly. And now you must find him."

"I will try."

"If anybody can succeed, you can and will."

"Thanks; I will try."

"Good-night."

"Good-night."

The door closed, and the great director of detectives was gone.

The First Clew

On the following morning Nick went at once to Eugenie La Verde's house in Forty-seventh street, disguised as a plumber.

The room which she had formerly occupied was nearly in the same condition in which it had been found on the morning after the murder, and a careful search offered no immediate suggestion to the detective.

From the sleeping room, he passed to the parlor floor, where he inspected all of the window-catches and appliances, casings, and panels.

Again without result.

Presently, he approached the stairs which led from the parlor floor to that below.

The door of communication was at the foot of the stairs, and was both locked and chained on the inner, or parlor-floor side.

There was nothing faulty about either the lock, chain, or door. They were evidently perfect, and he turned his attention to the stairs.

Stair-ways are convenient arrangements through which to construct a secret passage-way, and Nick never neglected them.

Suddenly he made a discovery. The third step from the bottom was not secure in its place.

For more than two hours he continued the search, but without further result.

It was nearly dark when Nick was reminded of the fact that he was hungry, and he quietly left the house in search of a convenient restaurant.

Two blocks away he found a beer saloon, which advertised meals at all hours.

Having entered and ordered what he wanted, he was presently engaged in eating it, when two swarthy, ill-conditioned fellows entered the saloon and seated themselves at the second table from him.

The very first words uttered by the men caused him to listen attentively:

"Captain, Inspector Byrnes made a call last night."

"Where?" asked the one addressed as captain.

"Upon that devil of a detective. I don't care to mention his name here."

"Ah; the one whom Sindahr calls 'the little giant'?"

"Exactly."

"Well, what of it?"

"It may be that he has set him upon us."

"Bah! No. There are no reasons for that. The inspector does not even know that we exist."

"He knows most things."

"Yes, but nothing of us. Still it may be well to – did you watch for the 'the little giant'?"

"Yes."

"Has he gone out?"

"One never can tell, but I think not. I left there an hour ago, and Tony has taken my place. I could swear that he had not left the house when I came away."

Nick smiled.

"Come, John," said the captain. "We have been here long enough and we have other work to do. It is dark now. Come."

They rose quickly and left the place, and upon the instant Nick decided to shadow them.

Shadowing

Nick did not rush from the saloon as soon as the two men left, but sauntered carelessly to the bar, paid for what he had eaten and drank, and then went slowly out.

As he had suspected, they were not far away. They were standing upon the curbstone apparently engaged in earnest conversation, but in reality waiting to see if they would be followed.

The fact that they were so cautious, gave added zest to the chase.

Nick sauntered carelessly past them, to the avenue which was only about two hundred feet farther on.

A hall-way door between two stores stood conveniently ajar on the opposite side, and he entered it with the air of one who lived there.

Pausing in the dark hall-way, he began a rapid change in his disguise, and presently he looked like an old man in poor circumstances who worked hard all day, and took an airing and a glass or two of toddy in the evening.

Five or ten minutes passed, and then the two men suddenly separated, the one called John going away rapidly in the opposite direction, and the captain jumped upon a car that was passing at that moment.

He took his stand upon the rear platform with his back toward the car, as though he thought that he might be followed.

A car was coming up the avenue. It had to pass between Nick and the car that the captain had boarded.

For a moment, Nick would be screened from view from the platform of the down-town car.

He utilized that moment to the best advantage.

He leaped nimbly into the street and succeeded in getting two doors away before the cars had passed each other.

When they had passed, he was standing idly before the door of a "gin-mill" leisurely picking his teeth, as though he had just come out.

Presently he walked down the street, rather rapidly, to be sure, but not fast enough to excite the suspicion that he was following anybody.

Soon a second car overtook him, and he got upon the front platform.

The two cars were less than a block apart, and the detective could see his man easily.

At Fourteenth street the captain turned and abruptly entered the car on which he was riding and passed out upon the front platform.

Here the spasmodic flashing of a match presently denoted that he was lighting a cigar.

Then, with a quick run, Nick left his car and overtook the one in which the captain was a passenger, and going inside, seated himself at the forward end.

"This is more comfortable," he thought. "It is much less work to watch him from here."

Block after block was passed, but the captain showed no sign of leaving the car, nor did he, until it reached the end of the route at the Astor House.

Then he stepped off and boarded a south-bound Broadway car, upon which he remained until it reached South Ferry.

There the captain took the Hamilton Ferry boat, landed in Brooklyn, and started away down the street along the water-front.

Nick followed for a mile or more, when suddenly the captain turned and went out upon a pier.

"He will stop and look around when he gets out there," thought Nick, "so I will wait here."

He dodged into a deep shadow close to the water's edge, just where a boat was tied by a rope to a cleat upon the dock.

"The very thing!" thought Nick.

In an instant he had untied the rope and seized one of the

oars; the next, he was sculling the little craft rapidly and silently along in the shadow of the pier.

Suddenly the man whom he was following, paused. Then turning he came to the edge of the pier and looked over, full at Nick.

Trapped

"Hey, there!" said the captain, in a voice loud enough for Nick to hear, and yet with considerable caution.

Nick ceased sculling, but did not reply.

"Do you want to earn a dollar or two?" was the first question.

"Sure!" was Nick's laconic reply.

"Take me aboard, then."

"What fur?"

"I want to go down the bay a little way."

"Ye've struck the wrong party, boss. I ain't on that kind of a lay."

"I'll make it five."

"How fur d'ye wanter go?"

"About half a mile."

"What fur?"

"That's my business. Come, will you take me or won't you? I can't stand here arguing all night."

"Cops after you, boss?"

The man shrugged his shoulders and turned away.

"I'll take ye ef it ain't too fur," called Nick. "Climb in."

The captain returned. The boat was drawn up close to the dock, and with a quick spring the stranger alighted upon one of the midship seats.

"Now make haste," he ordered.

"Which way, boss?"

"Down."

"How fur?"

"Go until I tell you to stop."

Nick obeyed.

The tide was with them and was running like a mill-race, so that they made quick time, and a mile was passed over in silence.

Then Nick stopped rowing.

"Say, boss," he remarked, "you said half a mile, an' we've already came over a mile. Is the place much furder?"

"Only a little way. Row on."

"Well, I want my five dollars afore I go any furder."

"You do, eh? Well, look at this."

He was pointing a six-shooter directly at Nick's heart.

"I'm a-lookin'," said Nick, coolly, "but that ain't no five dollars."

"Will you row on?"

"No, not till I gits me pay."

"Curse you, do as I tell you or I'll put a hole in you big enough to see through."

Nick calmly drew the oars into the boat.

"Look ahere," he said, "wot d'ye take me fur, anyhow, boss? D'ye think that I'm a rabbit that I'm afraid o' that pop-gun o' yourn? Not much! Don't ye s'pose I know ye das-sent use it out here at this time o' night? It's too early for killin', boss. I've done a job 'r two of that kind myself, an' I'm posted. Fork over, an' I'll row ye where ye wanter go, but I'm blowed ef I will ef ye don't, see?"

The passenger growled out something which sounded very much like a curse, but he drew a gold piece from his pocket and flung it to Nick.

"Now go ahead," he muttered, "for I'm losing time."

"Nobody's fault but yer own," was Nick's reply, and then he seized the oars and the boat shot ahead again.

"Easy, there, easy," said the passenger, suddenly. "Do you see that sloop yonder?"

"I do."

"Put me aboard of her."

"Keyreckt, boss. I've had my eye on her before."

"You have, eh? Why?"

"That's my bizness, see? To have my eye on such things."

"Ah! a river pirate, eh?"

"Me? Oh, no! I'm a harbor-broker. Here you are. Ketch hold of the rail. So."

The passenger climbed aboard of the sloop, while Nick allowed his boat to remain just where it was.

"Well, what are you waiting for?" asked the captain.

"Fur you. Don't ye want me to take ye back?"

"No. I do not."

"Nor come after ye?"

"No."

"What are ye goin' ter do? Swim ashore?"

"Perhaps."

"Well, good-night, boss. Be keerful of the pop-gun: it may go off sometime."

"It will be very apt to if you don't become scarce around here pretty soon."

Nick laughed lightly and pushed his boat away from the sloop. Then he picked up his oars and rowed away in the darkness.

"I wonder what he would say if he knew that it was Nick Carter who rowed him down the river to-night?" thought the young detective.

Not very far away from where the sloop was anchored was another craft of less pretentious build, although considerably larger.

It was a schooner, and Nick pointed his boat's prow directly at it.

The outlines were just visible, for the night was growing steadily darker.

Huge clouds were rolling up from the eastward, and the detective noticed with satisfaction that here another half-hour the night would be literally black.

He reached the schooner, passed it, and then ceased rowing, allowing his boat to drift slowly back until he was thoroughly concealed behind the black hull.

Then an entire half-hour he sat there and waited.

Darker and darker grew the night.

The darkness became so intense that he could not see his hand before his eyes, and great drops of rain began to spatter upon him.

"A perfect night for this sort of work," he mused, as he pushed his boat free from the schooner's side, "and unless I am greatly mistaken, I can make fast to that sloop without being seen or heard. I'm going to try, anyhow."

The tide was still running very strong, and it was hardly necessary for him to do more than steer in order to reach the desired spot.

Not a thing could be seen. It seemed as though the whole world had suddenly gone out of existence, having naught but blackness behind.

Presently he drew in his oar and went to the bow.

He was not a moment too soon.

Knowing instinctively, rather than seeing, that he was about to collide with the hull of the sloop, he put out his right hand, and was thus enabled to prevent the shock and noise of a collision. Certain discovery would have followed, and his plans would have failed.

Thus far he had made not a sound.

Nick climbed aboard, and crept softly toward the companion-way, pausing every second step to listen, but hearing nothing.

He went over the entire deck, and finally descended to the cabin, moving with the same stealthy caution.

Nick had almost decided that he had been outwitted, and that the sloop was deserted, when suddenly, without any warning whatever, he received a violent blow on the head and sank senseless to the deck.

"Did you lay him out, John?" asked the cool tone of the man whom we know as captain.

"As stiff as a door, cap."

"Good. Close the hatch so that no light can get out, and we'll have a look at him."

"Better chuck him into the river now," said John, gruffly. "I hit him hard enough to break a dozen heads."

"No. Do as I say. Time enough to throw him overboard when we know he's dead."

The hatchway was closed and a light procured.

The captain bent over the senseless form of Nick Carter and closely examined his face.

"Boys," he said, presently, "this fellow is made up. He is a fly cop, as I more than half suspected, and he must die."

Tony, the Strangler

An ominous silence followed the captain's discovery, which was presently broken by the voice of John, who growled:

"Shall I stick him now?"

"No – no; wait. Haste never does any good. Besides, I want to question him before he takes his bath."

Some brandy was poured into Nick's mouth, and he presently opened his eyes, and looked around him.

He saw that five men were in the cabin with him, and realized instantly that he was in the hands of a gang who would not hesitate at murder, and by the expression of their faces he judged that they meant to mete out small mercy for him.

That he was right, the sequel proved.

The captain stood nearest him, and Nick noticed that his face was hard and cruel.

He also noticed another thing with a great amount of satisfaction.

The men were so confident of the strength of superior numbers, and the meekness consequent upon the force of the blow that their victim had received, that they had not thought it worth their while to bind him.

It did not occur to them that one man could get away from five, particularly when they surrounded him in a little cabin like that of the sloop.

"Who are you?" asked the captain, coldly.

"Jest what I was wonderin'," replied Nick. "I feel sorter dazed with the hit on my head."

"Answer me!"

The voice was cold and stern, and the demand was emphasized by the exhibition of a glittering knife held menacingly before the detective's eyes.

"I'm a river-broker," said Nick, coolly.

"Let me remind you that we are not now on the open river, young man, and that this thing makes no noise. You were plucky enough when you knew that I would not shoot, but I promise you that I will cut if you trifle with us now. Answer me; who are you?"

"I'm Flood-tide-Billy. Ever heard of me?"

"That's too thin, my friend. We all know Billy."

"Do, eh. All right. Then what did ye ask me fur?"

"Your name?"

"Well, ye got it, didn't ye?"

"Not the right one."

"Mebby you know more about it than I do."

"Why did you return to this sloop?"

"Why do I go to any sloop, or schooner, or any other craft? say!"

"Come – come! you can't play that game on us. We're 'onto' you, my man. River pirates don't go around with wigs and false mustaches."

"Don't, eh?"

"You're a fly cop."

"Am, eh?"

"And we want to know your lay."

"Do, eh?"

"Yes, we do, eh! We're not out here to-night for pleasure."

"Neither was I."

"For what, then?"

"Profit."

Nick had been gaining both time and strength during the short conference, as well as studying the faces and comparative strength of the men around him.

He had made up his mind to make a bold dash for liberty, relying upon his wonderful strength and agility to accomplish it.

He was still flat upon the deck, but to him that fact made little difference, for his muscles were so active that he could leap to his feet from such a position as quickly as from a chair.

The captain quietly took out his watch.

"I will give you one minute in which to decide whether you will make a clean breast of the whole thing, or die," he said. "Draw your knives, boys, and when I drop this handkerchief, you may make short work of the cop."

Five knives glittered in as many hands upon the instant.

"Fifteen seconds," said the captain.

Nick's eyes roamed from face to face, seeking that which belonged to the man whom he wanted to attack first.

"Thirty seconds."

Still Nick remained quiet, while the ruffians seemed to grow eager for the instant to arrive when they could fall upon him and hack him to pieces.

"Forty-five seconds."

Nothing could be heard but the ticking of the watch which the captain held in his hand.

"Fifty seconds."

Then Nick acted.

Like a flash of lightning he was upon his feet.

His fist shot out like a cannon-ball, and John, who was a little in advance of the others, fell back like a stricken bullock.

With cries resembling the roar of wild beasts, the others then threw themselves forward with uplifted knives and murderous hearts.

But again Nick was too much for them.

His foot flew up and knocked the knife from the foremost man's hand. His fist followed and the fellow was hurled backward against his companion, utterly confusing them for an instant.

Nick quickly followed up the advantage thus gained.

He bounded forward and seized in an iron grasp the man whom he had just struck.

Then, raising him from the floor as though he were a babe, the detective hurled him bodily, straight at the now advancing men.

The human missile flew true to its aim, and three of the ruffians went down as though laid low by the sweep of a scythe.

The fourth was the captain.

He leaped toward Nick, doubly infuriated by the fact that he was now thoroughly satisfied that it was none other than Nick Carter, the "little giant," who was before him.

But Nick met him half way.

With a lightning-like movement he seized the hand which held the knife.

Then, exerting all of his great strength, he bent the captain's wrist quickly backward.

There was a snap like the breaking of a pipe-stem, and a yell of pain from the captain.

Nick's left arm shot out and his fist landed with terrific force squarely on the fellow's nose.

Now was the detective's time, if ever.

He turned, and with one bound reached the hatchway.

It was closed and fastened, but again his strength proved too great for ordinary opposition.

In an instant he tore the hatch open and leaped out into the darkness, followed by the report of two revolvers and the ringing of a couple of bullets in his ears.

But he was unhurt.

The night was as black as Erebus as he bounded forward and crouched behind a small boat that was overturned upon the sloop's deck.

The men rushed upon the deck in their eager haste to capture him.

One of them had been thoughtful enough to seize a bull's-eye lantern which was already lighted, and with it he searched the water around the sloop as far as the rays would reach.

Of course he could see nothing of Nick.

"Let's search the deck," said one of them. "Mebby he didn't go overboard."

"Bah! d'ye think he'd stay here? Not much!"

"He's a terror, ain't he?"

"Lightnin's nothin' to that feller."

"Who is he?"

"Look here, Tony, there's only one man in New York who could do what he did, an' that's the young devil they call Nick Carter."

"Ah! the 'little giant.' "

"That's him, an' he's got to be done up."

The man called Tony chuckled audibly.

"A job for me, eh, Morgan?" he said; and Nick was conscious of a shiver when he heard the exultation in the man's voice.

"Yes – you an' yer string."

"I am never without it, Morgan. The time I spent in India wasn't lost, and there is nothing like the string for making a corpse. Do you remember Red Mike?"

"B-i-r-r-r!" said Morgan. "You give me the horrors, Tony. I kin stand knifin' a man, or puttin' a chunk o' cold lead into him, but when it comes to windin' that cord o' yourn 'round a feller's throat, and a-makin' his tongue an' his eye-balls stick out like fingers, I ain't in it."

A low laugh was Tony's reply, and then the men began a search of the deck.

But they had no idea that Nick remained aboard of the sloop, and not expecting to find their man, the search was only a half-hearted one, so that the detective had no difficulty in keeping out of their way by dodging around the boat.

The light thrown by a bull's-eye lantern reaches only the point at which it is directed, and renders the surrounding darkness much greater by contrast.

This fact was a great advantage to Nick, and he did not fail to make the most of it.

When he had first heard the word string mentioned in connection with killing he had become greatly interested in the conversation, and from the subsequent remarks made by the men it became evident that Tony was a strangler.

His reference to India as the place where he had learned the art of using his peculiar yet terrible weapon was full of meaning.

Everybody knows of that strange, wild sect. They are as stealthy as a cat, as determined as Fate, and as deadly as a cobra.

Eugenie La Verde was strangled to death. Could it be possible that there was any connection between her murder and this gang of men who made a sloop in New York Bay their place of rendezvous?

Had Nick stumbled upon a clew to the crime in Forty-seventh street, where he least expected it?

At all events he resolved to have a good look at the man Tony, and to learn more concerning the purposes of these five men.

The Strangler's Threat

After satisfying themselves that the detective had made good his escape, the three men, Tony, Morgan and their companion, who was known among them as Crofty, returned to the cabin of the sloop.

Nick followed them closely, and reached the hatchway in time to hear all that was said.

"Well?" demanded the captain when the three men returned from the deck.

"Skipped," replied Morgan, laconically.

"How?"

"Flew away, I guess. There was not a sign of him."

"See!" and the captain held up his right arm, the wrist of which Nick had broken in the struggle. "My wrist is broken. He must pay for it. Do you know who it was, Tony?"

"Morgan told me."

"What did he say?"

"The little giant."

"Right. He could have been none other. I have heard of him often, but have never seen him before. Tony, he must die."

"At my hands?"

"Yes."

"When?"

"At once. The sooner, the better."

"To-morrow, then."

"Bah! If you get him foul within a week, I will give you a thousand dollars."

"Done, cap. He's a dead man. My string never failed me yet. More than one has gone down beneath it, and oh, how I love to see them gasp for breath."

"How is the wind?" asked the captain, curtly.

"None at all," replied Morgan. "The rain has knocked it all out. We could not reach the nest to-night if we tried."

"Then let us go ashore. Sindahr will be there. Come."

Nick waited to hear no more, but went hastily to his boat and untied the painter.

As he drifted away, he heard the low murmur of voices as the men came upon deck from the cabin of the sloop.

Soon there came a gentle splash in the water, and he knew that they had put the boat over the side – the very one behind which he had hidden, when they were searching for him so eagerly.

That they had some rendezvous on shore near that point, Nick felt certain, and he resolved to follow them at all risks.

Standing in the stern of his own boat with a single oar, he could force her through the water as silently as a shadow, while he conjectured that they would row, and that he could thus follow the sound of their oars in the water.

He was right.

They were soon in the boat and rowing rapidly away, while Nick followed them, sculling as fast as they rowed. A long pier stretched far out into the bay, near by, and they made directly for it.

The noise made by their oars in the water ceased, and Nick paused, knowing that they had gone beneath the pier.

Presently he sculled cautiously forward.

His boat touched the pier, and drawing in his oar, he used his hands upon the planking, to force his boat ahead.

When far beneath the pier, he stopped and listened again.

The silence of death and the blackness of the Styx reigned supreme.

Cautiously Nick drew his little dark-lantern from his pocket, pressed the spring and opened the slide.

A ray of light shot out over the water.

The empty boat employed by the men in coming from the sloop was immediately before him, but the men had disappeared.

The boat was fastened to a cross-beam of the pier, just where a crib was sunk into the water.

It was not likely that they had jumped into the river, and therefore it followed that there must be a way of passing through the crib, or of reaching the dock from that point.

Nick pulled his boat forward.

He searched the crib and was examining it intently, when something, he knew not what, caused him to turn his head suddenly.

The act saved his life.

There was a flash and a loud report, and a bullet whizzed past his ear.

Like a shot he turned and leaped toward the point from whence the flash had proceeded, for in that one instant he had seen the dark form of a man.

He reached him and seized him in his iron grasp, but even as he did so, the man who had fired the shot was endeavoring to escape.

They grappled just as he was balanced on the gunwale of the boat, and the next instant they were in the river and floating away with the tide.

The struggle was short, for one man was no match for Nick.

As soon as they came to the surface. Nick twisted himself free from his opponent's grasp, and struck him a violent blow in the face with his fist.

He would not have been rendered senseless more quickly if struck with a hammer, and Nick quietly swam to the nearest wharf with his prisoner.

Having reached it, he pulled the fellow upon the planks, and then with all the expertness of a pickpocket, searched him.

He found nothing of interest to him, and so left the man upon the dock, to revive as best he could, or to stay there senseless until found. Nick, who was an extremely expert swimmer, again plunged boldly into the water.

He headed straight for the pier where he had left his boat, and reached it without accident. Then he set out at once for the pier where the boat had been procured, realizing that the men were too much on their guard for him to learn more that night.

Once landed, he hurried to the ferry, crossed to New York, and took the elevated road.

His destination was the house in Forty-seventh street.

"It is my belief that these men know something about the death of Eugenie La Verde," he thought, "and that Tony knows more of the particulars than the others.

"For the sake of the argument, I will premise that Tony went to the house on the night of the murder, and that he strangled the girl with his cord.

"What was the motive for the crime, if he committed it?

"What did these men expect to gain by murdering a *danseuse?* Not money or jewels, certainly, for they left both, to a considerable amount, on the bureau.

"How did they enter the house from the street, and how leave it?

"In what way is this captain, who is evidently an American, to be benefited by Eugenie's death?

"Those fellows are on their guard, now. They know that I am after them and they will be more than ordinarily cautious, unless Tony succeeds in getting his deadly string around my neck!"

He was soon again in the house in Forty-seventh street, where the beautiful Eugenie La Verde had met her sudden and mysterious fate.

When he entered, he went straight to Eugenie's room.

As he stood upon the threshold, he thought he heard a rustling noise not unlike that made by the dress of a woman as she passed across a floor.

He paused suddenly and listened.

The noise came again.

Quickly he brought forth his little lantern, and touched the button, throwing a gleam of light into the apartment.

From point to point he turned the ray of light, himself remaining standing in the door-way.

The room was empty.

A moment's search satisfied him on that point, but he was equally sure that he had heard something.

What?

Had a person been there when he stepped over the threshold? and if so, by what means had that person left the room?

The noises that he had heard could not have been made by a rat, or a mouse.

If the room had been tenanted by a human being who wished to escape observation, why had that person not gone while he was yet in the lower hall, instead of waiting until he stood upon the very threshold of the room?

Perhaps the occupant of the apartment was sleeping when he entered, and did not rouse until the last moment.

Wonderingly, Nick approached the bed, for he had a peculiar feeling that it was not a human being that had been in the room when he entered, and yet his reason told him that it was.

Suddenly, having lighted the gas and turned toward the bed, he started.

Before him was the proof that somebody or something had been there since he had left the place.

He remembered perfectly how the pillows had been placed when he was there before, and now they were differently located. One of them was near the foot of the bed and the other was on the floor.

Both were crushed, as though they had been used.

A Fight with a "Shadow"

Nick did not know, until some time afterward, how near he had been to death at the moment when he crossed the threshold of Eugenie La Verde's room that night.

Nevertheless strange thoughts suggested themselves to his mind as he prosecuted his search through the place, and examined the pillows.

He was conscious, too, of a peculiar odor that he did not recognize, and which made his nerves tingle with an odd sensation that he could not explain.

The pillow on the floor looked as though somebody had pounded it out of all shape, as one will do at times in order to lie more comfortably. But the bed gave no signs of recent occupancy.

Had a man or a woman been there and lain upon the bed, some marked evidence of the fact would have been left. However, there was none.

It had been Nick's intention to take a hasty survey of the house and then go home and rest until the following day.

Now, however, he hesitated.

Presently he went slowly down the stairs, opened and closed the front door, and instead of going out, returned silently to the foot of the stairs and stood, listening.

For an hour he remained perfectly motionless, but not a sound came to him to reveal the presence of anyone, and at last, satisfied that he would gain nothing by waiting longer that night, he noiselessly left the house and started homeward.

As Nick drew near to his own residence, a slight motion made by a dark shadow on the opposite side of the street attracted his attention.

"Somebody watching for me," was his mental comment. "I wonder if it is Tony, with his string? If so, he has made good time, and his presence here so quickly may account for the noise

I heard in the house in Forty-seventh street. In case it is the strangler, I'll give him a little sport before dawn."

He went directly up the steps of his own house and entered.

People knew well enough the house where Nick lived, but nobody knew that he also owned the house directly back of it, fronting upon the other street.

He had purchased it some time before, and had so arranged that he could enter or leave his own house by the other one without fear of being seen or shadowed.

Just now, however, his purpose was to let Tony know that he was Nick Carter.

Hastening to his room, he hurriedly removed his wet clothes, placed a few necessary things in his pockets, and again went out.

Turning down the street, he soon became convinced that Tony was following him, and then he set out in earnest.

Hurrying over to Third avenue, he ran up the steps and caught a down train, just as it was moving out of the station.

The purpose in that was to compel Tony to run also, for Nick's real idea in "having some fun" with the strangler was only to get a good view of his face.

True, he had seen him in the cabin of the sloop, at the time of the row. But he had also seen them all, and he had no idea which one was Tony.

Nick saw his "shadow" running, and watched him as, disregarding the rules of the road, he leaped upon the platform of the train after it was in motion, in spite of the efforts of the guard to thrust him back.

The detective walked back through the cars until he came to the one in which Tony was quietly seated.

There was a seat directly opposite the strangler, and Nick took it, while, without any effort to conceal his purpose, he carefully studied the man's face.

When the train reached Houston street, Nick rose and left the car.

Tony did likewise.

Nick passed down the stairs and boarded an up-town surface car.

Tony did the same.

"Cheeky!" muttered Nick. "I wonder if he thinks I'm a fool? Well, I'm tired of this, and I'll shake him and go home."

He remained on the car until he reached Fourteenth street, when he got down and went westward as far as the Morton House.

He turned the corner of Broadway and Fourteenth street about two hundred feet in advance of Tony.

The distance was not much, but it was enough.

As soon as he turned, Nick began making a rapid change.

He had not gone twenty feet before his appearance was entirely altered.

From a young man he was changed to a very old one. A light mustache had given place to a set of snow-white whiskers patterned à la Greeley. The derby hat that he had worn had disappeared – for it was of the "crush" kind – and in its place was a broad-brimmed felt. The jaunty cane that he had carried was taken apart and thrust into a pocket. A pair of spectacles adorned his nose, and he walked with the hesitation of one who has long suffered the tortures of rheumatism.

The entire change had not occupied more than one minute of actual time, and as soon as it was completed Nick wheeled abruptly and retraced his steps.

He turned the corner and went on toward Third avenue.

He met Tony and passed him, smiling when he saw that the strangler had quickened his steps.

He could have touched the fellow as he passed, and he felt a strong inclination to do so with no very gentle hand.

However, he did not, and in another moment Tony had turned the corner and disappeared.

"I guess I am done with him for to-night," thought Nick, "and now I'll go home and go to bed."

He reached Third avenue, boarded a car, rode to his corner and got down.

Then he paused, while an amused smile stole over his features.

Tony was standing on the corner as though awaiting his arrival.

"That fellow is smarter than I thought," muttered Nick. "Has he penetrated my disguise, or is he only waiting here in the hope that I will show up in the old shape?"

Again he passed Tony, but the fellow did not look at him.

Walking on down the street, he presently took a small mirror from his pocket and held it up before him.

The glass reflected the form of Tony skulking along rapidly behind, and gaining with every step.

"The scoundrel is going to try his game on to-night," muttered Nick. "I hope he may succeed if I don't give him a dose that he'll remember many a day."

Tony drew nearer and nearer.

Nick still held the mirror so that he could see the skulking, snake-like figure of the would-be murderer.

He could see something of eagerness in the man's gait, as though he thirsted for blood, and could ill-restrain his passion for murder when the moment drew near for its accomplishment.

Nearer and yet nearer.

They had reached a place along the block where the darkness was greater than in the portion that they had already traversed.

Suddenly Tony darted forward, moving like a cat.

At the same instant Nick turned.

He stooped and jumped aside in the selfsame second.

Just in time.

There was an angry swish through the air, made by the cord of the strangler as he attempted to wind it around Nick's throat.

With a quick bound, Nick was at Tony's side.

He seized him and was about to hurl him to the pavement when the fellow seemed to slip from his grasp like an eel.

Again the swish of the cord, and again Nick dodged just in time to avoid the strange but deadly weapon.

The detective knew that, strong as he was, if the cord once touched his neck, nothing could save him.

Once more he leaped toward Tony. Again he seized him, and this time the fellow did not slip away as before.

He could not play the same trick twice upon Nick Carter.

But even as the detective seized the man, he heard a loud hiss, and a noxious odor filled the air.

It was the suffocating smell of the cobra. Like a flash Nick realized that the man was a snake-charmer and that his pets would protect him.

He loosened his hold and leaped back out of danger.

Then his fist shot out, striking the strangler squarely between the eyes.

A Scoundrel's Scheme

It is needless to say that Tony, the strangler, went down beneath the fist of Nick Carter as though he had been shot.

Neither did he attempt to rise, for the force of the blow had rendered him as senseless as a dead man.

Nick drew nearer and regarded him earnestly, but an angry hiss warned him not to go too close, and at the same instant, two bead-like eyes, glowing like sparks of fire, swayed to and fro above the strangler's heart.

The deadly cobra was there, and with a serpent's wisdom, it knew that its master had been hurt.

With a shudder Nick turned away, knowing that Tony would presently revive, and that the snake would not leave him.

Fearing, however, that some person might come along who would attempt to rouse the senseless form of Tony and so get bitten by the cobra, he stepped into a door-way near at hand and waited.

No one came, fortunately, and presently Tony began to show signs of returning consciousness.

After a little he sat up and rubbed his head in a dazed sort of way, as though he wondered where he was and how he got there.

Recollection returned very suddenly when it did come, for he leaped quickly to his feet and started away at a rapid pace.

Nick followed, changing his disguise again as he went.

The opportunity was too good a one to be lost.

Evidently Tony had no use for cars, for he continued to walk until he had covered the whole distance from Forty-seventh street to East Houston.

Down that he went to Goerck street, where he suddenly darted into the hall-way of a high and dirty tenement house of the very worst description.

Nick was not far behind him.

The strangler mounted to the topmost floor of the house and Nick kept close behind, moving silently as a shadow.

He reached the door through which Tony had passed, almost as soon as it was closed, and his ear was instantly at the keyhole.

"Well!" he heard the gruff voice of John demand, "did you do it?"

"No."

"Why not?"

"Let that be your answer!" and Tony pointed to the contusion between his eyes.

John laughed audibly.

"Ye found one feller that yer string didn't fit, didn't ye?" he jeered.

"It will fit you," was the meaning reply, and it evidently had its effect upon John, for he jeered no more.

"I went out to strangle the detective to-night," continued Tony, "because the captain wished him out of the way. Now I will pursue him until he is dead, because he struck me – because he defeated me."

"Mebby he'll be so fly that ye can't git the string onto him at all."

"Then there is another way, even surer."

"How?"

"Look!"

A loud hiss told Nick that Tony had taken the cobra from his breast.

"Ugh!" grunted John. "I hate that thing! What d'ye bring it here for anyway?"

"The cobra is always with me. We are never apart."

"Ugh! whew! Say Tony, I've had snakes afore now, but I'm blamed if I'd want 'em always. I don't like 'em."

"They were not of this kind."

"No, most of mine were green, an' some of 'em had seven heads. Say, put that thing away, or I'll have 'em again; it makes me shake all over."

"You're a fool, John!"

"Why? 'Cos I don't like snakes? Mebby so, but that's a matter of opinion. Now that that pretty little pet o' yourn is outer sight, tell me how you'd use it to 'do up' the fly cop if the string didn't work."

"I would not use this one, but others like it."

"Ye've got more, hey?"

"I have many. What would be easier than to turn them loose in the detective's house?"

"By thunder! that's a great idea!"

"A bite from the cobra means certain death."

"But, I say!"

"Well?"

"Others would be bitten too, wouldn't they? The whole family, hey?"

"What matter?"

"Oh, nothin'; jest curious, that's all."

"So that the detective dies, I do not care how many go with him. And he shall die!"

"Shake, Tony."

The two men sealed the compact of death by clasping hands.

"When are ye goin' ter do it?" continued John.

"I shall try the string once more. If it fails me again, then the snakes."

"Can ye git in the house?"

"Have you ever seen a house that I could not enter?"

"No."

"I have but to open the front door, remove the cover from my basket and toss the whole thing inside. The jar and the sudden awakening will make the cobras angry. They will crawl out and scatter over the house. If they find a bed, they will enter it. If a person is there, so much the better, for it will be warmer. When the person moves, against whom they are coiled, the cobra will be angry again, for they have bad tempers. The person may turn over in his sleep and so roll upon the cobra: if so, he will be bitten. He may waken and attempt to leave the bed; if so, the cobra will do its work before he can get out of reach. He may wake suddenly and find a swaying head, a darting tongue, and two bright eyes within a foot of his face. He will scream with horror and attempt to escape. The scream and the attempt will be fatal. His only chance of safety would be in keeping perfectly still and closing his eyes, but what man would have strength enough to do it? Would you?"

"No, I'm cussed if I would."

"Next time you have the 'snakes,' try it, John."

"I have, Tony, and then, instead of one, I would have four thousand. But say."

"What!"

"There won't be anything left alive in the house but snakes, when morning comes."

"No – nothing."

"B-i-r-r! I think I'd rather be hung."

"You will probably have your wish, unless you get familiar with my cobras."

"Which I'll take care not to do. No offense, Tony, but it strikes me that you're a snakey lot. Even the girl Eug—"

"Stop! How many times must I tell you never to mention that name to me?"

Tony's voice was intense with anger. He paused a second and then continued:

"John, I swear if you speak that name again, in my presence, or allude to the manner of her death, I will set my cobra upon you by throwing him in your face. Remember, for I mean what I say."

"I'm sorry, Tony. I forgot."

"See that you do not forget again. You may rest assured that Sindahr will not. Bah! pass that bottle unless you want it all."

There were a few moments of silence, and then John's voice asked:

"When are you going to the 'nest'?"

"Time enough for that when the detective, Nick Carter, is dead."

"Sure!"

"We can do nothing with that fellow constantly about our heels."

"He's a baby terror, he is."

"Ay, he has the strength of three men."

"Of three? A dozen would be nearer the mark. He's quicker'n a flash, an' ain't afraid o' nothin'."

"He is doomed."

"Well, I'd rather be John Crispy than Nick Carter jest now. Where'd you meet him to-night?"

"At his house. He went in and came out again."

"S'pose he hadn't come out again?"

"I should have gone in."

"And strangled him in bed, eh?"

"Precisely."

"That's yer favorite way, ain't it?"

"I like it best."

"When are ye goin' to try the trick on again, Tony?"

"The first time that I think he has gone to sleep in his own bed. Let him do that once, after to-night, and he will never waken. I will strangle him so quickly and so silently that a person in the same bed will not know what has happened until in his struggles he awakens somebody."

There were short snatches of conversation after that, but in a few moments the two scoundrels threw themselves upon their beds and went soundly to sleep.

Then Nick turned away, well satisfied to go home.

But his heart was filled with dread for his Ethel.

Of himself he did not think, but the recollection of Tony's threat, and the vivid description he had given of the consequences to be expected from the presence of cobras in the house, made Nick realize more than ever before, something of the danger to which he was constantly exposing himself.

"Ah, well; forewarned is forearmed," he murmured, "and I do not believe that Fate meant me or my beloved wife for a victim of Tony, the strangler. Tony will be after me early to-morrow, and I must be ready for him."

And he was.

Solving Problems

On the following day Nick went again to the house in Forty-seventh street in order to continue his researches, for he realized that a very necessary part of the evidence he had to furnish in the case, was an explanation of the murderer's method of entering and leaving the house.

He found everything just as he had left it on the previous night.

Whoever had been in the room when he crossed the threshold, had evidently deemed it unwise to return.

The detective went at once to the cellar, and began an

exhaustive search for the secret passage-way, but after an hour vainly spent, he again sought the stair-way which had puzzled him.

The greater discoveries are made by accident, and so it happened in this case.

He had arranged a box on which to stand while examining the underside of the stairs, but in putting it in place, he had not fixed it securely, and accordingly, just as he was becoming interested in his task, the box toppled from its place.

Nick lost his balance and would have fallen had he not thrown up his hands to save himself; as he did so, he grasped a two-by-four inch timber which looked as though it had been placed there for additional support to the stairs.

The timber was not stationary, however. It came loose in his hand, but with sufficient difficulty to save him from falling.

Leaping down, he rearranged the box and again mounted it.

The necessity for searching was, however, ended.

The removal of the stick of wood disclosed an ordinary staple and hook which fastened the movable stairs in place.

He removed the hook, and the stairs worked just as he had expected them to.

A person could go from the cellar to the parlor floor without having to pass through a door.

The discovery was one which filled Nick with pleasure, and there only remained now to find an equally easy way into the street.

But hour after hour passed, and found him still searching.

At last he turned away, noticing, as he did so, that one of the stays which supported the floor above, was out of place.

It did not occur to him that he could straighten it, and yet he put out his hand and gave it a sharp pull.

What was his surprise to find it was loose at the top.

As he pulled there was resistance enough to satisfy him that the support acted as a lever, while behind him he heard a slight grating noise as of something moving on small iron wheels.

Turning, he flashed his light along the wall, but saw nothing.

Nevertheless he pulled the lever away over, and then placed a weight upon it to hold it down while he searched for the aperture of which he felt certain it was the instrument.

"Ah!"

He paused with the glad exclamation on his lips.

Before him, close to the wall, was an opening in the cellar-floor.

One of the stones, with which the floor was paved, had settled down nearly five feet, leaving an opening quite large enough to admit him, and when he flashed his light along the underground gallery that he saw, he discovered that it led toward the street, and was, without doubt, the secret entrance for which he had been searching.

Nick took the precaution to put more weight upon the lever before descending into the forbidding opening that it had revealed.

Then with his dark lantern in hand, he entered.

The passage-way was not high enough for him to stand upright, and was only sufficiently wide to accommodate his body.

It led him about twenty feet, diagonally in the direction of the street, and then abruptly ended.

He looked up.

Over his head were the stone steps which led to the front door of the house.

"More stair-way doors," he muttered. "This will not be so well concealed."

Nor was it.

There was an ordinary bolt such as are used for fastening doors, which he easily moved, noticing, as he did so, that the bolt was so arranged that it could be worked from the outside.

That is, a portion of the next toe piece had been chipped off, leaving a space through which a small steel rod could be thrust, to move the fastening.

First, he tried to push the stone up, but in vain.

Then he endeavored to pull it down toward him, but it refused to move.

There was but one way left and that was to slide it away lengthwise.

The effort met with instant success.

The stone slid along easily, offering little or no resistance, and thus afforded an opening sufficiently large for an ordinary-sized man to squeeze through.

A means by which a murderer could have entered and left the house when Eugenie La Verde was choked to death was now found.

That portion of the case was no longer a mystery.

It was still daylight in the street, and Nick hastily closed the aperture, having studied out how he could open it from the outside if necessary.

He returned to the cellar and removed the weights that he had placed upon the lever.

It remained down, as, indeed, he had expected it would.

Then once more to the secret passage-way.

There, he raised the stone and put it in place.

On the underside was a handle.

He grasped that, pulled upon it, and the stone came down in his grasp.

The secret was now entirely his.

He could go either way through the hidden passage without any trouble.

The mystery was a mystery no longer.

"I have only to satisfy myself, now, that Tony is the murderer, and then the whole story is in my possession. But I must find a motive," he thought. "Why did those men want Eugenie La Verde out of the way? There is another mystery still, to solve."

The flat stone which covered the opening in the cellar-floor, was worked by the lever, by means of a long steel rod and two cog-wheels.

It was a clever mechanical device, and whoever planned it must have had a strong incentive.

"There is nothing more to do here now," he thought. "I will go home."

He had been at home about an hour when he rose and went to the window, whistling softly to himself, and lost in thought.

Suddenly he started.

Darkness was just settling over the city, and half concealed in the door-way of a vacant house opposite was Tony, the strangler.

"I had forgotten all about him," mused Nick. "It won't do to let that fellow run at large. I think I will arrest him, cobra and all, and take him down to headquarters. If he gets a chance, he'll fill the house with snakes, and I don't want that, particularly in my absence."

Nick remained at the window several moments, lost in thought.

Suddenly he smiled. A good idea had occurred to him.

He went to the telephone and called up Inspector Byrnes.

"I am going to bring you a man whom I want you to hold for me till called for," he said, as soon as they were in communication.

"All right," replied the officer. "What do you know about him?"

"I know he is a murderer although perhaps not *the* murderer."

"He will do to keep, anyhow."

"Rather. Say!"

"Hello."

"This fellow is a snake-charmer, and in order to take him in, I have got to kill a cobra which he carries around with him. Will you have two men on the corner of Mott and Bleecker for me, in an hour?"

"Yes. How will they know you?"

"Easily. They will see me knock my man down first. Then they will see a cobra stick its head out of the fellow's coat after which, if they look sharp, they will see me shoot the cobra."

"Good; but don't kill the man instead of the cobra."

"I guess not."

"How are you going to get him there?"

"He's outside now, waiting for me."

"Waiting for you to take him in?"

"Yes. He's in the shadow business. He's made a contract to strangle me to death with a cord, and is on my trail now."

"Ah! Well, fetch him in: I'd like to have a look at him."

"All right. Good-by."

"Good-by."

Nick hung up the ear-piece and hastily made a few changes in his appearance.

Then he started out to lead Tony to the Central Office of the police, where he proposed to keep him out of mischief by locking him up in a cell.

"Now, my gentle Tony, come along," murmured Nick, as he ran down the steps. "I can't keep on with this case and feel easy about matters at home unless I put you where you will be out of mischief, and since you are kind enough to follow me, I'll show you the way."

In order to make it perfectly easy for the strangler to keep track of him, Nick avoided the elevated road, and took a surface car.

Bleecker street and the Bowery were duly reached by Nick with Tony a close second.

There the detective dismounted from the car and walked leisurely westward, purposely going slowly so that the strangler could gain upon him without the appearance of haste.

Tony came near. There were many people on Bleecker street at that hour, and in order to be sure of not losing sight of his prey, the strangler was obliged to keep quite close.

When the corner of Mott street was reached, they were not more than ten feet apart.

Nick kept steadily on until he reached the curbstone.

Then he turned suddenly and in an instant was face to face with the man who was seeking an opportunity to strangle him.

Tony was evidently startled and puzzled by the maneuver, but Nick did not leave him long in doubt.

The detective's fist shot out, propelled by all the force of which he was master.

There was no withstanding such a blow.

Tony fell as though he had been shot; his head struck the pavement first, and he was instantly deprived of consciousness.

Ere a single moment had passed the thing happened which Nick had expected.

The hooded and hideous head of the cobra was raised menacingly over the senseless man's breast, where it swayed to and fro like the pendulum of a clock.

Several who had gathered around at the first sign of a disturbance, started back in horror when they saw the snake.

Nick waved them all back and then he drew his revolver.

"Stop!" cried somebody in the crowd: "you will kill the man."

But Nick Carter knew his own skill too well to fear such a result. He stooped low down, so that the bullet, after penetrating the snake's head, could not hit Tony.

One quick glance satisfied him that there was no danger to others.

Suddenly there was a flash and a loud report.

The snake, pierced through the head, writhed and twisted until it was free from Tony's clothing.

The moment it was upon the pavement it was pounced upon by men and boys, who pounded it with clubs and paving stones until it would have been a hard matter to have recognized its original shape.

While the rabble were still annihilating the reptile, two men approached Nick and announced themselves at his service.

"Pick up that fellow and bring him along," said Nick, pointing to Tony.

The men hesitated.

They thought that perhaps there might be more snakes hidden away in his clothing.

A few words reassured them, and Tony was presently securely locked in a cell at Police Headquarters, while Nick was closeted with the inspector.

But he did not remain long, and only gave the chief a brief outline of all that he had accomplished.

"You are a wonderful fellow, Nick," said the chief admiringly, "and that was a remarkable shot with no light but the flaring torch of a peanut stand. What next?"

"I don't know. Good-night. Keep my man securely for me, for I shall want him again. I'll drop in to-morrow and talk with him, if I have time."

Nick left hurriedly, and was quickly on his way to Goerck street.

He felt confident that he would find John there, and he wanted to use him.

When near his destination, he stepped into a hall-way for a few moments, and when he emerged, it was in the character of a

Negro, whose face was as black as the night which surrounded him.

He was just in time, for the captain and Morgan soon came out of their Goerck street rendezvous and went off together toward Houston street.

Nick followed at a safe distance.

The two men boarded a green car which took them to the foot of West Forty-second street.

There they took the Weehawken ferry, and Nick did likewise.

He felt that he was on his way to the "nest" at last.

At Weehawken, the captain and Morgan went directly to a little stable in a deserted quarter and presently were seated together in an open buggy behind a powerful horse.

How was Nick to follow them without being seen?

It was a hard question to answer, and he began to think that he would lose them after all, when he heard the captain tell Morgan to hold the horse while he went across the street for some cigars.

Morgan went to the horse's head, and the captain started away.

Now, if ever, was Nick's time.

He crept cautiously forward in the darkness until he reached the off-hind wheel of the buggy.

A man of less strength than Nick Carter's, could not have accomplished what he did then.

He seized the nut which held the wheel upon the axle, and without the aid of a wrench he unscrewed it and put it in his pocket.

Then, as silently as a shadow, he shrank back again out of sight.

The next moment the captain reappeared, and he and Morgan leaped into the buggy together.

They drove away rapidly, and Nick, running swiftly, followed them, knowing that they would not go far before the wheel would run off, and throw them into the road.

However, the wheel did better than might have been expected, for they drove nearly a mile before the accident occurred.

Nick was glad of an opportunity to rest, for the pace had been very rapid.

Fortunately for the men in the buggy, they had just slowed down a little to give their horse a chance to breathe, when the axle dropped.

Morgan fell into the road, and cursed loudly at the bruises he received, but the captain escaped uninjured, by leaping out on the other side.

Then they examined the wheel, and quickly found what was the matter.

"Well, we haven't much farther to go," said the captain.

After considerable maneuvering they managed to fasten the wheel so that by driving very slowly they kept it in place, while Nick was enabled to follow them without any difficulty whatever.

They traveled in that way for an hour or more, and then turned off from the main road into a lane. A quarter of a mile along the lane brought them to a commodious house which stood all alone at the edge of a wood, and looked as though it were uninhabited.

"The 'nest,'" thought Nick. "The next few hours ought to tell me a good deal, and they must."

The two men drove behind the house to an old barn where they cared for the horse, Nick never for a moment losing sight of them.

At last they entered the house, and as soon as it was safe to do so without unnecessary danger of immediate discovery, Nick followed.

Two Murders in One Night

Nick found himself in total darkness, but that was quickly dispelled by touching the button of his little bull's-eye lantern and throwing a brilliant stream of light across the room.

Before him was a door, and he passed through it into a wide hall-way.

He could not hear a sound until he reached the lower floor.

Then the low murmur of voices came to him.

He followed the direction of the sound until he came to a door which evidently opened into the room where the men were sitting.

The gruff voice of Morgan was easily recognized, and now and then the even tones of the captain penetrated the door.

There was another voice too, not loud enough to be distinguishable, but Nick decided that it belonged to Sindahr.

He could not catch a word of what they were saying, and he looked about him for a way to get nearer.

Farther down the hall was another door which led into the room adjoining the one where the men were talking, and he crept along the hall and passed through it.

At once the voices became plainer.

Flashing his light around Nick saw that he was in what had once been a dining-room, and also that there were cupboards against the partition which separated it from the room where the men were talking.

If it so happened that those cupboards opened through the partition, which was probable, it would be an easy matter for him to hear all that was being said.

Exerting all his caution, and moving as silently as a shadow, Nick carefully opened one of the cupboard doors.

The cupboards not only connected the two rooms, but the doors on the opposite side of the partition were made of glass and he could plainly see all that was taking place as well as hear every word that was uttered.

The group that he saw was a strange one.

There were the captain, Morgan, Sindahr, and an aged Negress who was listening intently to all that was said.

They were all seated around a dining-table upon which were a bottle, some glasses, and a box of cigars.

"No," the captain was saying; "there is no danger of his coming here to-night. I wish there was. He will never escape me again, I swear."

"He's a devil!" ventured Morgan.

"Devil or not, if I ever have another opportunity such as I once had, he shall die. I will not wait to make terms with him."

"How do you know that he is onto this place?" asked Morgan.

"I do not know it, but I fear it. If he is, we will all be captured like so many rats in a trap."

"Sure!"

"At all events it is safer to leave."

"This is a hard place to get to."

"Yes, and it would be an easy matter to shadow any of us for the greater part of the distance. The house in Forty-seventh street is the safest place for us now."

Nick became more interested.

"Isn't that house watched?"

"Bah, no."

"I should think it would be."

"They gave up looking for the murderer long ago, and the house is as deserted as the grave."

Morgan chuckled.

"Fancy a detective smart enough to run that crime down," he said.

Then both men laughed.

"I think it's funnier to fancy him getting his handcuffs on to the murderer."

The thought evidently struck them as very funny, for they laughed uproariously.

"I'd like to see him try it," said Morgan when his mirth had subsided, "particularly that fellow Nick Carter."

"Yes, I think we'd be well rid of him. His fists and his strength would not count for so much—. I say, where do you suppose Tony was to-night?"

"I don't know. Perhaps Carter downed him and took him in."

"Cobra and all?"

"That would make it difficult. Still, that fellow can do anything."

"No, cap, there's one thing he can't do."

"What's that?"

"Capture the murderer of Eugenie La Verde."

"He may."

"Why, I thought you settled his hash."

"No, Tony didn't want me to, and I let him have his way."

"He's a queer fish."

"Rather. He takes food there every week!"

"The devil! Feeding the murderer of his own sister!"

"Exactly!"

"Say, cap!"

"What?"

"I think you'll have to count me out on living in that house."

"Nonsense!"

"I mean it. I've no relish for the place, since we would not be alone."

The captain laughed.

"You are afraid of Eugenie's slayer, eh?"

"Frankly, I am."

"Well, I don't know that I blame you, Morgan. Yet there is no danger."

To say that Nick was interested in the conversation that he had heard would be a feeble expression of his sensations.

He had learned many surprising things almost in one breath.

First, neither Tony, nor Morgan, nor Sindahr, was the murderer of Eugenie La Verde, although they all seemed to know who was.

Second, the murderer was in hiding in the very house where the crime had been committed.

Third, Tony was Eugenie La Verde's brother, and he was not only protecting the murderer of his sister, but carrying food to him from time to time.

Nick realized that he had not yet seen the real murderer, although he had once stood within a few feet of him in the dark, when he crossed the threshold of Eugenie La Verde's room and heard the rustle made by someone escaping from the place.

"If he is as dangerous as Morgan's fear of him would imply, why in the world didn't he try to choke me just as he did Eugenie?" muttered the detective.

The captain abruptly changed the subject.

He looked at his watch.

"Come," he said, "it is nearly midnight, and we must go."

The Negress left the room to obey an order from the captain, and so left the three villains alone together.

"Morgan," said the captain, "you had better go first and Sindahr and I will follow with the other horse. Drive right on to the ferry boat and thence to the house in Forty-seventh street. Go slowly after you get to New York, so that Sindahr and I can get to the house first."

"Sindahr not going," said the Arabian, calmly.

"What!" cried the captain.

"Sindahr will not go there."

"You will have to, my friend."

"Sindahr never enter that house while he is alive."

"So you refuse to obey me?"

"Sindahr has spoken."

"Curse you! take that."

Like a flash the captain drew a revolver and discharged it almost in the Arabian's face.

The man sank back dead without a single groan.

"Shove him under the table; I was tired of him, anyhow," said the captain, coolly, replacing his revolver in his pocket, "and between you and me, Morgan, I am getting tired of Tony also."

"Let him kill the detective and then we can give him away. It will save the trouble of killing him," said Morgan.

"So that we get rid of him, I don't care how it's done."

"What shall we do with this body?"

"Let it lie there under the table and rot. We leave this house to-night, forever."

"Now, a word about other matters before Sal returns. Is everything ready for our scheme?"

"Everything."

"When do we spring it?"

"This is Wednesday. The time is fixed for Friday at midnight."

"And we get—"

"One hundred thousand."

"Good! One more question."

"Well?"

"Why need we share that with John and Tony?"

"Because John and Tony are alive."

"Exactly; but if they were dead?"

"I suppose it would be all ours."

"Would that please you, Phil?"

"I won't ask any questions if they don't show up for their share."

"Good! here comes Sal."

The next moment Sal entered the room.

Morgan presently, at a sign from the captain, rose, and left the house.

"Don't go until I come out," said the captain, and then he was alone with the Negress.

"Well, Sal," he said, "we won't require your services any longer, and I'll pay you now."

"Yes, sah."

"How much do I owe you?"

"Twenty-fo' dollars, sah."

"No more? Why, that is cheap. Come here and get it."

The Negress went around the table toward the captain unsuspiciously. Even Nick had no idea what was coming.

"Here is your pay!" exclaimed the villain, when Sal was close enough, and at the same instant he plunged a knife into her heart.

She uttered one loud gasp, and sank back lifeless.

Captain Philip had committed two deliberate murders in one night.

Bringing Threads Together

It would have been an easy matter for Nick to have captured the two men then and there, but from his standpoint it was not good judgment to do so.

Eugenie La Verde's murderer was still unknown, and these men would be very valuable, at large, in helping him to solve the mystery.

They were going directly to the house in Forty-seventh street, and he could arrest them there at any time, when he had used them all he cared to.

As soon as the Negress expired, the captain walked calmly from the room, leaving the corpses of his two victims there without an atom of remorse.

Nick followed, not by leaving the house the way he had entered it, but by going directly in the path of Captain Philip.

Morgan had the horse and buggy nearly ready, and his companion helped him to finish the task.

"Climb in," said the captain.

"What are you going to do with the other horse since we don't need him?"

"Leave him. He is worthless, anyway."

"But he will starve."

"Let him."

"At least set him loose."

"Bah! Chicken! Climb in, I tell you. I have no time for trifles."

Morgan obeyed, and Nick shuddered at the wanton cruelty of the two men.

Nevertheless they had unwittingly done him a service, for he was now provided with a means of returning to the city without walking.

He had no thought of following them, for he knew where to find them when he wanted them.

In the meantime he had something else to do.

After waiting long enough to give them a good start, he brought the other horse out of the stable.

There was an old harness in the barn, which he adjusted after some trouble.

In his pocket was the missing nut for the open buggy, and he was soon bowling along the road at a rapid pace.

He did not stop at Weehawken, but continued on to Hoboken.

There he gave the horse in charge of a liveryman with instructions to keep it until called for, and hurried to New York.

He went straight to the house of Inspector Byrnes.

"Inspector," he said, when the chief had admitted him, "there were two murders committed to-night by the men I have been pursuing. They are also the ones who know all about the killing of Eugenie La Verde! The bodies of their victims are now lying where they left them in a house not far from the palisades."

"You're a marvel, Nick. Tell me where the house is and I'll wire the Jersey police."

Nick did so, but added:

"Don't make the case too hot till I say the word. Tell Chief Murphy, in Jersey, that you know who the murderer is, and that you will hand him over before the week is out. In the meantime I don't want to scare my man."

"Good!"

"Two more things."

"Well?"

"Will you go with me in person to arrest the murderer of Eugenie La Verde?"

"I will; when?"

"To-morrow night. Come to my house at eight."

"I'll be there. Now the other thing."

"An order from you to let me see the prisoner I took to headquarters. I want to talk with him."

"Now?"

"Yes."

The order was quickly filled out, and Nick lost no time in reaching headquarters in Mulberry street.

He was shown at once to Tony's cell.

"Do you know me, Tony?" he asked.

"No. I don't know niggers."

"Don't, eh? Well, I know you, and I want to ask you some questions."

"Ask 'em."

"Why do you feed your sister's murderer?"

"To keep him alive."

"I should think you would rather kill him."

"Bah! Why? I would rather strangle the man who killed my pet cobra."

"You would, eh? What would you do if I brought you face to face with that man?"

"Anything you ask."

"Let me see you feed the murderer of your sister Engenie, and I will do it."

"How do you know she was my sister?"

"Never mind. I do know it."

"He must be fed soon, or he will starve, or else leave the house."

"Will to-morrow night do?"

"Yes, but he will be cross."

"Are you afraid of him?"

"I? No, He dare not hurt me."

"Very well. To-morrow night I will take you there, and I

promise you that you shall be brought face to face with the man who shot your cobra."

"With my hands free?"

"Yes."

"Who are you?"

"Does that matter, if I keep my word?"

"No."

"Good-by then till to-morrow night."

Promptly at eight o'clock on the following night Inspector Byrnes was at the house of Nick Carter.

In a few words Nick related the entire story of his adventures from first to last.

Then, while the chief waited, Nick hurried to headquarters and got Tony.

The strangler was kept securely handcuffed on the street, but Nick, who had again assumed the guise of the Negro, assured him that he would be set free when once the house in Forty-seventh street was reached.

When the house was reached, Nick, much to Tony's astonishment, entered by the secret passage-way under the steps.

He had asked Tony what food he should provide for the murderer, and the strangler had assured him that he had some concealed in the house.

So they entered.

Leaving the others in the cellar, Nick went silently upstairs and found that the captain was there alone. He was sitting calmly in the back parlor, reading a paper, as unconcerned as though he owned the house.

Nick made a slight noise to attract his attention, and the captain looked up quickly.

Then, pistol in hand, he rose and went toward the hallway, where Nick was waiting in the dark for him.

As soon as the captain was in reach, Nick seized him.

He had no time to use his weapon, and in a twinkling he was thrown upon his back upon the floor, and handcuffed, and anklets were locked around his ankles.

"There, Captain Philip, that settles your hash, I think," said Nick, pleasantly.

The captain did not say a word. He did not even curse. He was calm, and evidently trying to think of a plan of escape.

When Nick returned to the cellar a surprise awaited him, for he found that Inspector Byrnes had captured Morgan in almost the same manner.

He had heard him coming through the secret passage-way, and had nabbed him before he knew what had happened.

The two men were securely fastened together in the back parlor.

"Now, Tony," said Nick, "we will feed the murderer. Come."

"Don't let him see you," said Tony.

"No. We will keep out of sight."

"Take off these bracelets."

Nick removed them and Tony led the way upstairs.

"Where is the food?" asked Nick.

"In the same room: hidden away."

"Ah! Well, go ahead."

Tony led the way to the door of Eugenie's room.

There, he paused and listened.

Presently he opened the door, passed in quickly and lighted the gas.

Eugenie's Murderer Finds Another Victim

Tony stood in the center of the room and clapped his hands loudly together.

Instantly a big picture which hung upon the wall trembled violently.

Suddenly the head of a serpent issued from behind the picture, and swayed back and forth.

Tony began to chant, and the serpent drew nearer, until Nick and the inspector saw a python over twelve feet in length swing itself to the bureau and thence to the floor.

They drew back, keeping well out of sight, while Nick held his trusty revolver in readiness.

Tony began to sway his head, chanting all the time, and keeping his place in the center of the room, while the python glided nearer and nearer.

Presently it reared its head until its glaring eyes were but a few inches from those of Tony.

Then it rested its head upon him and gliding on and on wound its hideous body round and round the strangler.

Then Tony turned and went toward another picture which he moved aside, revealing a grated aperture.

He opened that, thrust in his arm, and drew forth a rabbit which dropped upon the floor.

There it hopped around aimlessly for a moment, and then, discovering the open door, darted through it and disappeared.

Tony attempted to intercept it, but he had not taken a step before he uttered a cry of pain, and stopped.

The python, angered by the escape of the rabbit, was tightening its coils around the body of the strangler.

In vain Tony chanted. In vain he used every trick known to his profession. The snake would not be charmed.

Tighter and tighter grew the coils, while the python's head swayed malignantly before the face of its victim.

Suddenly Tony fell to the floor, and the serpent seemed to change its hold.

Its coils seemed to glide up and encircle the neck of the strangler.

Nick had meanwhile been watching for a chance to use his revolver.

The chance came when the python next raised its head.

The bullet sped true to its aim, and the python's head was pierced by the lead.

Nick and the inspector leaped forward.

They seized and raised him up.

He was senseless, but not dead.

"He cannot live," said Nick. "Let us revive him if we can. His ribs are broken, and he is bleeding internally. It was terrible."

Tony at last opened his eyes.

The story he told was disjointed, but in substance it was as follows:

He belonged to a family of snake-charmers, of which he and his sister Eugenie were the most expert.

Long ago he and Eugenie had quarreled because of his dishonest ways. She would have no more to do with him.

At Captain Phil's request, he had persuaded her to take the house in Forty-seventh street, which had long been a resort for certain criminals, who had managed to keep it so unsuspected by the police.

The secret passages were old. He did not know who had made them or where they were constructed.

Eugenie had given all the serpents to Tony except the python, of which she was very fond.

Even her maid, Delia Dent, had been unaware of the python's presence, and knew nothing of Eugenie's passion for snakes.

Tony had come to the house on the night of his sister's death, accompanied by John and Sindahr, to demand money.

He had reached the door of his sister's room just as the python had glided from its hiding place in the wall behind the picture.

His presence had seemed to anger the reptile, which had wound itself around its mistress' neck and hissed loudly.

He saw that it was choking Eugenie, and rushed forward to save her.

Then the python would have attacked him, but, realizing it, he turned and fled, leaving her there to her fate.

He had told John and Sindahr all that he had seen, and had learned for the first time that Sindahr had been charmed by a serpent when a child, and could not go near one without falling under the peculiar magnetic spell which they exert. He had a horror of the house because of the presence of the python.

Later Tony had returned and fed the reptile. Why, he did not know, except that he loved serpents.

He told them where his cobras were concealed, and the inspector took good care to have them exterminated.

Tony died from his injuries before he had quite completed his story, and the true nativity of Eugenie La Verde was never known.

But her murderer was found and he was a serpent.

A visit to Goerck street revealed the fact that Morgan had made good his threat, and killed John, for he was found with a dirk in his heart, and evidence was adduced to prove that Morgan put it there.

Both he and Captain Philip subsequently paid the penalty of their crimes, the latter being given up to the tender mercies of Jersey justice.

The schooner and the retreat under the pier in South Brooklyn were both searched. The former was sold and the latter was filled with stones.

The murder of Eugenie La Verde was a mystery no longer, and the murderer, a serpent, died by a bullet from Nick Carter's revolver.

Solange

Dr. Ledru's Story of the Reign of Terror

Alexandre Dumas

L eaving l'Abbaye, I walked straight across the Place Turenne to the Rue Tournon, where I had lodgings, when I
heard a woman scream for help.

It could not be an assault to commit robbery, for it was hardly
ten o'clock in the evening. I ran to the corner of the place
whence the sounds proceeded, and by the light of the moon, just
then breaking through the clouds, I beheld a woman in the
midst of a patrol of sans-culottes.

The lady observed me at the same instant, and seeing, by the
character of my dress, that I did not belong to the common
order of people, she ran toward me, exclaiming:

"There is M. Albert! He knows me! He will tell you that I am
the daughter of Mme. Ledieu, the laundress."

With these words the poor creature, pale and trembling with
excitement, seized my arm and clung to me as a shipwrecked
sailor to a spar.

"No matter whether you are the daughter of Mme. Ledieu or
someone else, as you have no pass, you must go with us to the
guard-house."

The young girl pressed my arm. I perceived in this pressure
the expression of her great distress of mind. I understood it.

"So it is you, my poor Solange?" I said. "What are you doing
here?"

"There, messieurs!" she exclaimed in tones of deep anxiety;
"do you believe me now?"

"You might at least say 'citizens'!"

"Ah, sergeant, do not blame me for speaking that way," said the pretty young girl; "my mother has many customers among the great people; and taught me to be polite. That's how I acquired this bad habit – the habit of the aristocrats; and, you know, sergeant, it's so hard to shake off old habits!"

This answer, delivered in trembling accents, concealed a delicate irony that was lost on all save me. I asked myself, who is this young woman? The mystery seemed complete. This alone was clear, she was not the daughter of a laundress.

"How did I come here, Citizen Albert?" she asked. "Well, I will tell you. I went to deliver some washing. The lady was not at home, and so I waited; for in these hard times every one needs what little money is coming to him. In that way it grew dark, and so I fell among these gentlemen – beg pardon, I would say citizens. They asked for my pass. As I did not have it with me, they were going to take me to the guard-house. I cried out in terror, which brought you to the scene; and as luck would have it, you are a friend. I said to myself, as M. Albert knows my name to be Solange Ledieu, he will vouch for me; and that you will, will you not, M. Albert?"

"Certainly, I will vouch for you."

"Very well," said the leader of the patrol; "and who, pray, will vouch for you, my friend?"

"Danton! Do you know him? Is he a good patriot?"

"Oh, if Danton will vouch for you, I have nothing to say."

"Well, there is a session of the Cordeliers to-day. Let us go to the Cordeliers."

The club of the Cordeliers met at the old Cordelier monastery in the Rue l'Observance. We arrived there after scarce a minute's walk. At the door I tore a page from my note-book, wrote a few words upon it with a lead pencil, gave it to the sergeant, and requested him to hand it to Danton, while I waited outside with the men.

The sergeant entered the clubhouse and returned with Danton.

"What!" said he to me; "they have arrested you, my friend? You, the friend of Camilles – you, one of the most loyal republicans? Citizens," he continued, addressing the sergeant, "I vouch for him. Is that sufficient?"

"You vouch for him. Do you also vouch for her?" asked the stubborn sergeant.

"For her? To whom do you refer?"

"This girl."

"For everything; for everybody who may be in his company. Does that satisfy you?"

"Yes," said the man; "especially since I have had the privilege of seeing you."

With a cheer for Danton, the patrol marched away. I was about to thank Danton, when his name was called repeatedly within.

"Pardon me, my friend," he said; "you hear? There is my hand; I must leave you – the left. I gave my right to the sergeant. Who knows, the good patriot may have scrofula?

"I'm coming!" he exclaimed, addressing those within in his mighty voice with which he could pacify or arouse the masses. He hastened into the house.

I remained standing at the door, alone with my unknown.

"And now, my lady," I said, "whither would you have me escort you? I am at your disposal."

"Why, to Mme. Ledieu," she said with a laugh. "I told you she was my mother."

"And where does Mme. Ledieu reside?"

"Rue Ferou, 24."

"Then, let us proceed to Rue Ferou, 24."

On the way neither of us spoke a word. But by the light of the moon, enthroned in serene glory in the sky, I was able to observe her at my leisure. She was a charming girl of twenty or twenty-two – brunette, with large blue eyes, more expressive of intelligence than melancholy – a finely chiseled nose, mocking lips, teeth of pearl, hands like a queen's, and feet like a child's: and all these, in spite of her costume of a laundress, betokened an aristocratic air that had aroused the sergeant's suspicions not without justice.

Arrived at the door of the house, we looked at each other a moment in silence.

"Well, my dear M. Albert, what do you wish?" my fair unknown asked with a smile.

"I was about to say, my dear Mlle. Solange, that it was hardly worth while to meet if we are to part so soon."

"Oh, I beg ten thousand pardons! I find it was well worth the while; for if I had not met you, I should have been dragged to the guard-house, and there it would have been discovered that I am not the daughter of Mme. Ledieu – in fact, it would have developed that I am an aristocrat, and in all likelihood they would have cut off my head."

"You admit, then, that you are an aristocrat? At least you might tell me your name."

"Solange."

"I know very well that this name, which I gave you on the inspiration of the moment, is not your right name."

"No matter; I like it, and I am going to keep it – at least for you."

"Why should you keep it for me, if we are not to meet again?"

"I did not say that. I only said that if we should meet again it will not be necessary for you to know my name any more than that I should know yours. To me you will be known as Albert, and to you I shall always be Solange."

"So be it, then; but I say, Solange," I began.

"I am listening, Albert," she replied.

"You are an aristocrat – that you admit."

"If I did not admit it, you would surmise it, and so my admission would be divested of half its merit."

"And you were pursued because you were suspected of being an aristocrat?"

"I fear so."

"And you are hiding to escape persecution?"

"In the Rue Ferou, No. 24, with Mme. Ledieu, whose husband was my father's coachman. You see, I have no secret from you."

"And your father?"

"I shall make no concealment, my dear Albert, of anything that relates to me. But my father's secrets are not my own. My father is in hiding, hoping to make his escape. That is all I can tell you."

"And what are you going to do?"

"Go with my father, if that be possible. If not, allow him to depart without me until the opportunity offers itself to me to join him."

"Were you coming from your father when the guard arrested you to-night?"

"Yes."

"Listen, dearest Solange."

"I am all attention."

"You observed all that took place to-night?"

"Yes. I saw that you had powerful influence."

"I regret my power is not very great. However, I have friends."

"I made the acquaintance of one of them."

"And you know he is not one of the least powerful men of the times."

"Do you intend to enlist his influence to enable my father to escape?"

"No, I reserve him for you."

"But my father?"

"I have other ways of helping your father."

"Other ways?" exclaimed Solange, seizing my hands and studying me with an anxious expression.

"If I serve your father, will you then sometimes think kindly of me?"

"Oh, I shall all my life hold you in grateful remembrance!"

She uttered these words with an enchanting expression of devotion. Then she looked at me beseechingly and said:

"But will that satisfy you?"

"Yes," I said.

"Ah, I was not mistaken. You are kind, generous. I thank you for my father and myself. Even if you should fail, I shall be grateful for what you have already done!"

"When shall we meet again, Solange?"

"When do you think it necessary to see me again?"

"To-morrow, when I hope to have good news for you."

"Well, then, to-morrow."

"Where?"

"Here."

"Here in the street?"

"Well, mon Dieu!" she exclaimed. "You see, it is the safest place. For thirty minutes, while we have been talking here, not a soul has passed."

"Why may I not go to you, or you come to me?"

"Because it would compromise the good people if you should come to me, and you would incur serious risk if I should go to you."

"Oh, I would give you the pass of one of my relatives."

"And send your relative to the guillotine if I should be accidentally arrested!"

"True. I will bring you a pass made out in the name of Solange."

"Charming! You observe Solange is my real name."

"And the hour?"

"The same at which we met to-night – ten o'clock, if you please."

"All right; ten o'clock. And how shall we meet?"

"That is very simple. Be at the door at five minutes of ten, and at ten I will come down."

"Then, at ten to-morrow, dear Solange."

"To-morrow at ten, dear Albert."

I wanted to kiss her hand; she offered me her brow.

The next day I was in the street at half-past nine. At a quarter of ten Solange opened the door. We were both ahead of time.

With one leap I was by her side.

"I see you have good news," she said.

"Excellent! First, here is a pass for you."

"First my father!"

She repelled my hand.

"Your father is saved, if he wishes."

"Wishes, you say? What is required of him?"

"He must trust me."

"That is assured."

"Have you seen him?"

"Yes."

"You have discussed the situation with him?"

"It was unavoidable. Heaven will help us."

"Did you tell your father all?"

"I told him you had saved my life yesterday, and that you would perhaps save his to-morrow."

"To-morrow! Yes, quite right; to-morrow I shall save his life, if it is his will."

"How? What? Speak! Speak! If that were possible, how fortunately all things have come to pass!"

"However—" I began hesitatingly.

"Well?"

"It will be impossible for you to accompany him."

"I told you I was resolute."

"I am quite confident, however, that I shall be able later to procure a passport for you."

"First tell me about my father; my own distress is less important."

"Well, I told you I had friends, did I not?"

"Yes."

"To-day I sought out one of them."

"Proceed."

"A man whose name is familiar to you; whose name is a guarantee of courage and honour."

"And this man is?"

"Marceau."

"General Marceau?"

"Yes."

"True, he will keep a promise."

"Well, he has promised."

"Mon Dieu! How happy you make me! What has he promised? Tell me all."

"He has promised to help us."

"In what manner?"

"In a very simple manner. Kléber has just had him promoted to the command of the western army. He departs to-morrow night."

"To-morrow night! We shall have no time to make the smallest preparation."

"There are no preparations to make."

"I do not understand."

"He will take your father with him."

"My father?"

"Yes, as his secretary. Arrived in the Vendée, your father will pledge his word to the general to undertake nothing against France. From there he will escape to Brittany, and from Brittany to England. When he arrives in London, he will inform you; I shall obtain a passport for you, and you will join him in London."

"To-morrow," exclaimed Solange; "my father departs to-morrow!"

"There is no time to waste."

"My father has not been informed."

"Inform him."

"To-night?"

"To-night?"

"But how, at this hour?"

"You have a pass and my arm."

"True. My pass."

I gave it to her. She thrust it into her bosom.

"Now, your arm."

I gave her my arm, and we walked away. When we arrived at the Place Turenne – that is, the spot where we had met the night before – she said: "Await me here."

I bowed and waited.

She disappeared around the corner of what was formerly the Hôtel Malignon. After a lapse of fifteen minutes she returned.

"Come," she said, "my father wishes to receive and thank you."

She took my arm and led me up to the Rue St. Guillaume, opposite the Hôtel Mortemart. Arrived here, she took a bunch of keys from her pocket, opened a small, concealed door, took me by the hand, conducted me up two flights of steps, and knocked in a peculiar manner.

A man of forty-eight or fifty years opened the door. He was dressed as a working-man and appeared to be a bookbinder. But at the first utterance that burst from his lips, the evidence of the seigneur was unmistakable.

"Monsieur," he said, "Providence has sent you to us. I regard you an emissary of fate. Is it true that you can save me, or, what is more, that you wish to save me?"

I admitted him completely to my confidence. I informed him that Marceau would take him as his secretary, and would exact no promise other than that he would not take up arms against France.

"I cheerfully promise it now, and will repeat it to him."

"I thank you in his name as well as in my own."

"But when does Marceau depart?"

"To-morrow."

"Shall I go to him to-night?"

"Whenever you please; he expects you."

Father and daughter looked at each other.

"I think it would be wise to go this very night," said Solange.

"I am ready; but if I should be arrested, seeing that I have no permit?"

"Here is mine."

"But you?"

"Oh, I am known."

"Where does Marceau reside?"

"Rue de l'Université, 40, with his sister, Mlle. Dégraviers-Marceau."

"Will you accompany me?"

"I shall follow you at a distance, to accompany mademoiselle home when you are gone."

"How will Marceau know that I am the man of whom you spoke to him?"

"You will hand him this tri-coloured cockade; that is the sign of identification."

"And how shall I reward my liberator?"

"By allowing him to save your daughter also."

"Very well."

He put on his hat and extinguished the lights, and we descended by the gleam of the moon which penetrated the stairwindows.

At the foot of the steps he took his daughter's arm, and by way of the Rue des Saints Pères we reached Rue de l'Université. I followed them at a distance of ten paces. We arrived at No. 40 without having met anyone. I rejoined them there.

"That is a good omen," I said; "do you wish me to go up with you?"

"No. Do not compromise yourself any further. Await my daughter here."

I bowed.

"And now, once more, thanks and farewell," he said, giving me his hand. "Language has no words to express my gratitude.

I pray that heaven may some day grant me the opportunity of giving fuller expression to my feelings."

I answered him with a pressure of the hand.

He entered the house. Solange followed him; but she, too, pressed my hand before she entered.

In ten minutes the door was reopened.

"Well?" I asked.

"Your friend," she said, "is worthy of his name; he is as kind and considerate as yourself. He knows that it will contribute to my happiness to remain with my father until the moment of departure. His sister has ordered a bed placed in her room. To-morrow at three o'clock my father will be out of danger. To-morrow evening at ten I shall expect you in the Rue Ferou, if the gratitude of a daughter who owes her father's life to you is worth the trouble."

"Oh, be sure I shall come. Did your father charge you with any message for me?"

"He thanks you for your pass, which he returns to you, and begs you to join me to him as soon as possible."

"Whenever it may be your desire to go," I said, with a strange sensation at my heart.

"At least, I must know where I am to join him," she said. "Ah, you are not yet rid of me!"

I seized her hand and pressed it against my heart, but she offered me her brow, as on the previous evening, and said: "Until to-morrow."

I kissed her on the brow; but now I no longer strained her head against my breast, but her heaving bosom, her throbbing heart.

I went home in a state of delirious ecstasy such as I had never experienced. Was it the consciousness of a generous action, or was it love for this adorable creature? I know not whether I slept or woke. I only know that all the harmonies of nature were singing within me; that the night seemed endless, and the day eternal; I know that though I wished to speed the time, I did not wish to lose a moment of the days still to come.

The next day I was in the Rue Ferou at nine o'clock. At half-past nine Solange made her appearance.

She approached me and threw her arms around my neck.

"Saved!" she said; "my father is saved! And this I owe you. Oh, how I love you!"

Two weeks later Solange received a letter announcing her father's safe arrival in England.

The next day I brought her a passport.

When Solange received it she burst into tears.

"You do not love me!" she exclaimed.

"I love you better than my life," I replied; "but I pledged your father my word, and I must keep it."

"Then, I will break mine," she said. "Yes, Albert; if you have the heart to let me go, I have not the courage to leave you."

Alas, she remained!

Three months had passed since that night on which we talked of her escape, and in all that time not a word of parting had passed her lips.

Solange had taken lodgings in the Rue Turenne. I had rented them in her name. I knew no other, while she always addressed me as Albert. I had found her a place as teacher in a young ladies' seminary solely to withdraw her from the espionage of the revolutionary police, which had become more scrutinizing than ever.

Sundays we passed together in the small dwelling, from the bedroom of which we could see the spot where we had first met. We exchanged letters daily, she writing to me under the name of Solange, and I to her under that of Albert.

Those three months were the happiest of my life.

In the meantime I was making some interesting experiments suggested by one of the guillotiniers. I had obtained permission to make certain scientific tests with the bodies and heads of those who perished on the scaffold. Sad to say, available subjects were not wanting. Not a day passed but thirty or forty persons were guillotined, and blood flowed so copiously on the Place de la Révolution that it became necessary to dig a trench three feet deep around the scaffolding. This trench was covered with deals. One of them loosened under the feet of an eight-year-old lad, who fell into the abominable pit and was drowned.

For self-evident reasons I said nothing to Solange of the studies that occupied my attention during the day. In the beginning my occupation had inspired me with pity and loathing, but as time wore on I said: "These studies are for the good of humanity," for I hoped to convince the lawmakers of the wisdom of abolishing capital punishment.

The Cemetery of Clamart had been assigned to me, and all the heads and trunks of the victims of the executioner had been placed at my disposal. A small chapel in one corner of the cemetery had been converted into a kind of laboratory for my benefit. You know, when the queens were driven from the palaces, God was banished from the churches.

Every day at six the horrible procession filed in. The bodies were heaped together in a wagon, the heads in a sack. I chose some bodies and heads in a haphazard fashion, while the remainder were thrown into a common grave.

In the midst of this occupation with the dead, my love for Solange increased from day to day; while the poor child reciprocated my affection with the whole power of her pure soul.

Often I had thought of making her my wife; often we had mutually pictured to ourselves the happiness of such a union. But in order to become my wife, it would be necessary for Solange to reveal her name; and this name, which was that of an emigrant, an aristocrat, meant death.

Her father had repeatedly urged her by letter to hasten her departure, but she had informed him of our engagement. She had requested his consent, and he had given it, so that all had gone well to this extent.

The trial and execution of the queen, Marie Antoinette, had plunged me, too, into deepest sadness. Solange was all tears, and we could not rid ourselves of a strange feeling of despondency, a presentiment of approaching danger, that compressed our hearts. In vain I tried to whisper courage to Solange. Weeping, she reclined in my arms, and I could not comfort her, because my own words lacked the ring of confidence.

We passed the night together as usual, but the night was even more depressing than the day. I recall now that a dog, locked up in a room below us, howled till two o'clock in the morning. The next day we were told that the dog's master had gone away with the key in his pocket, had been arrested on the way, tried at three, and executed at four.

The time had come for us to part. Solange's duties at the

school began at nine o'clock in the morning. Her school was in the vicinity of the Botanic Gardens. I hesitated long to let her go; she, too, was loath to part from me. But it must be. Solange was prone to be an object of unpleasant inquiries.

I called a conveyance and accompanied her as far as the Rue des Fosses-Saint-Bernard, where I got out and left her to pursue her way alone. All the way we lay mutely wrapped in each other's arms, mingling tears with our kisses.

After leaving the carriage, I stood as if rooted to the ground. I heard Solange call me, but I dared not go to her, because her face, moist with tears, and her hysterical manner were calculated to attract attention.

Utterly wretched, I returned home, passing the entire day in writing to Solange. In the evening I sent her an entire volume of love-pledges.

My letter had hardly gone to the post when I received one from her.

She had been sharply reprimanded for coming late; had been subjected to a severe cross-examination, and threatened with forfeiture of her next holiday. But she vowed to join me even at the cost of her place. I thought I should go mad at the prospect of being parted from her a whole week. I was more depressed because a letter which had arrived from her father appeared to have been tampered with.

I passed a wretched night and a still more miserable day.

The next day the weather was appalling. Nature seemed to be dissolving in a cold, ceaseless rain – a rain like that which announces the approach of winter. All the way to the laboratory my ears were tortured with the cries announcing the names of the condemned, a large number of men, women, and children. The bloody harvest was over-rich. I should not lack subjects for my investigations that day.

The day ended early. At four o'clock I arrived at Clamart; it was almost night.

The view of the cemetery, with its large, new-made graves; the sparse, leafless trees that swayed in the wind, was desolate, almost appalling.

A large, open pit yawned before me. It was to receive today's harvest from the Place de la Révolution. An exceedingly large number of victims was expected, for the pit was deeper than usual.

Mechanically I approached the grave. In the bottom the water had gathered in a pool and my feet slipped; I came within an inch of falling in. My hair stood on end. The rain had drenched me to the skin. I shuddered and hastened into the laboratory.

It was, as I have said, an abandoned chapel.

I struck a light and deposited the candle on the operating-table on which lay scattered a miscellaneous assortment of the strange instruments I employed. I sat down and fell into a reverie.

As I sat thus, absorbed in gloomy meditation, wind and rain without redoubled in fury. The rain-drops dashed against the window-panes, the storm swept with melancholy moaning through the branches of the trees. Anon there mingled with the violence of the elements the sound of wheels.

It was the executioner's red hearse with its ghastly freight from the Place de la Révolution.

The door of the little chapel was pushed ajar, and two men, drenched with rain, entered, carrying a sack between them.

"There, M. Ledru," said the guillotinier; "there is what your heart longs for! Be in no hurry this night! We'll leave you to enjoy their society alone. Orders are not to cover them up till to-morrow, and so they'll not take cold."

With a horrible laugh, the two executioners deposited the sack in a corner, near the former altar, right in front of me. Thereupon they sauntered out, leaving open the door, which swung furiously on its hinges till my candle flashed and flared in the fierce draft.

I heard them unharness the horse, lock the cemetery, and go away.

I was strangely impelled to go with them, but an indefinable power fettered me in my place. I could not repress a shudder. I had no fear; but the violence of the storm, the splashing of the rain, the whistling sounds of the atmosphere, which made my candle tremble – all this filled me with a vague terror that began at the roots of my hair and communicated itself to every part of my body.

Suddenly I fancied I heard a voice! A voice at once soft and plaintive; a voice within the chapel, pronouncing the name of "Albert!"

I bolted out of my chair, frozen with horror.

The voice seemed to proceed from the sack!

I touched myself to make sure that I was awake; then I walked toward the sack with my arms extended before me, but stark and staring with horror. I thrust my hand into it. Then it seemed to me as if two lips, still warm, pressed a kiss upon my fingers!

I had reached that stage of boundless terror where the excess of fear turns into the audacity of despair. I seized the head and, collapsing in my chair, placed it in front of me.

Then I gave vent to a fearful scream. This head, with its lips still warm, with eyes half closed, was the head of Solange!

I thought I should go mad.

Three times I called:

"Solange! Solange! Solange!"

At the third time she opened her eyes and looked at me. Tears trickled down her cheeks; then a moist blow darted from her eyes, as if the soul were passing, and the eyes closed, never to open again.

I sprang to my feet a raving maniac. I wanted to fly; I knocked against the table; it fell. The candle was extinguished; the head rolled upon the floor, and I fell prostrate, as if a terrible fever had stricken me down – an icy shudder convulsed me, and, with a deep sigh, I swooned.

The following morning at six the gravediggers found me, cold as the flagstones on which I lay.

Solange, betrayed by her father's letter, had been arrested the same day, condemned, and executed.

The head that had called me, the eyes that had looked at me, were the head, the eyes of Solange!

The Limitations
of Pambé Serang

Rudyard Kipling

I f you consider the circumstances of the case, it was the only thing that he could do. But Pambé Serang has been hanged by the neck till he is dead, and Nurkeed is dead also.

Three years ago, when the Elsass-Lothringen steamer *Saarbruck* was coaling at Aden and the weather was very hot indeed, Nurkeed, the big fat Zanzibar stoker who fed the second right furnace thirty feet down in the hold, got leave to go ashore. He departed a "Seedee boy," as they call the stokers; he returned the full-blooded Sultan of Zanzibar – His Highness Sayyid Burgash, with a bottle in each hand. Then he sat on the forehatch grating, eating salt fish and onions, and singing the songs of a far country. The food belonged to Pambé, the Serang or head man of the lascar sailors. He had just cooked it for himself, turned to borrow some salt, and when he came back Nurkeed's dirty black fingers were spading into the rice.

A serang is a person of importance, far above a stoker, though the stoker draws better pay. He sets the chorus of "Hya! Hulla! Hee-ah! Heh!" when the captain's gig is pulled up to the davits; he heaves the lead too; and sometimes, when all the ship is lazy, he puts on his whitest muslin and a big red sash, and plays with the passengers' children on the quarter-deck. Then the passengers give him money, and he saves it all up for an orgy at Bombay or Calcutta, or Pulu Penang.

"Ho! you fat black barrel, you're eating my food!" said Pambé, in the Other Lingua Franca that begins where the Levant tongue stops, and runs from Port Said eastward till east is west, and the sealing-brigs of the Kurile Islands gossip with the strayed Hakodate junks.

"Son of Eblis, monkey-face, dried shark's liver, pig-man, I am the Sultan Sayyid Burgash, and the commander of all this ship. Take away your garbage," and Nurkeed thrust the empty pewter rice-plate into Pambé's hand.

Pambé beat it into a basin over Nurkeed's woolly head. Nurkeed drew his sheath knife and stabbed Pambé in the leg. Pambé drew *his* sheath knife; but Nurkeed dropped down into the darkness of the hold and spat through the grating at Pambé, who was staining the clean foredeck with his blood.

Only the white moon saw these things; for the officers were looking after the coaling, and the passengers were tossing in their close cabins. "All right," said Pambé – and went forward to tie up his leg – "we will settle the account later on."

He was a Malay born in India: married once in Burma, where his wife had a cigar shop on the Shwe Dagon road; once in Singapore, to a Chinese girl; and once in Madras, to a Mahometan woman who sold fowls. The English sailor cannot, owing to postal and telegraph facilities, marry as profusely as he used to do; but native sailors can, being uninfluenced by the barbarous inventions of the Western savage. Pambé was a good husband when he happened to remember the existence of a wife; but he was also a very good Malay; and it is not wise to offend a Malay, because he does not forget anything. Moreover, in Pambé's case blood had been drawn and food spoiled.

Next morning Nurkeed rose with a blank mind. He was no longer Sultan of Zanzibar, but a very hot stoker. So he went on deck and opened his jacket to the morning breeze, till a sheath knife came like a flying-fish and stuck into the woodwork of the cook's galley half an inch from his right armpit. He ran down below before his time, trying to remember what he could have said to the owner of the weapon. At noon, when all the ship's lascars were feeding, Nurkeed advanced into their midst, and, being a placid man with a large regard for his own skin, he opened negotiations, saying, "Men of the ship, last night I was drunk, and this morning I know that I behaved unseemly to someone or another of you. Who was that man, that I may meet him face to face and say that I was drunk?"

Pambé measured the distance to Nurkeed's naked breast. If he sprang at him he might be tripped up, and a blind blow at the chest sometimes only means a gash on the breastbone. Ribs are difficult to thrust between unless the subject be asleep. So he said nothing; nor did the other lascars. Their faces immediately dropped all expression, as is the custom of the Oriental when there is killing on the carpet or any chance of trouble. Nurkeed looked long at the white eyeballs. He was only an African, and could not read characters. A big sigh – almost a groan – broke from him, and he went back to the furnaces. The lascars took up the conversation where he had interrupted it. They talked of the best methods of cooking rice.

Nurkeed suffered considerably from lack of fresh air during the run to Bombay. He only came on deck to breathe when all the world was about; and even then a heavy block once dropped from a derrick within a foot of his head, and an apparently firm-lashed grating on which he set his foot began to turn over with the intention of dropping him on the cased cargo fifteen feet below; and one insupportable night the sheath knife dropped from the fo'c's'le, and this time it drew blood. So Nurkeed made complaint; and, when the *Saarbruck* reached Bombay, fled and buried himself among eight hundred thousand people, and did not sign articles till the ship had been a month gone from the port. Pambé waited too; but his Bombay wife grew clamorous, and he was forced to sign in the *Spicheren* to Hong Kong, because he realized that all play and no work gives Jack a ragged shirt. In the foggy China seas he thought a great deal of Nurkeed, and, when Elsass-Lothringen steamers lay in port with the *Spicheren*, inquired after him and found he had gone to England via the Cape, on the *Gravelotte*. Pambé came to England on the *Worth*. The *Spicheren* met her by the Nore Light. Nurkeed was going out with the *Spicheren* to the Calicut coast.

"Want to find a friend, my trap-mouthed coal-scuttle?" said a gentleman in the mercantile service. "Nothing easier. Wait at the Nyanza Docks till he comes. Everyone comes to the Nyanza Docks, Wait, you poor heathen." The gentleman spoke truth. There are three great doors in the world where, if you stand long enough, you shall meet anyone you wish. The head of the

Suez Canal is one, but there Death comes also; Charing Cross Station is the second – for inland work; and the Nyanza Docks is the third. At each of these places are men and women looking eternally for those who will surely come. So Pambé waited at the docks. Time was no object to him; and the wives could wait, as he did from day to day, week to week, and month to month, by the Blue Diamond funnels, the Red Dot smokestacks, the Yellow Streaks, and the nameless dingy gypsies of the sea that loaded and unloaded, jostled, whistled, and roared in the everlasting fog. When money failed, a kind gentleman told Pambé to become a Christian; and Pambé became one with great speed, getting his religious teachings between ship and ship's arrival, and six or seven shillings a week for distributing tracts to mariners. What the faith was Pambé did not in the least care; but he knew if he said "Native Ki-lis-ti-an, Sar" to men with long black coats he might get a few coppers; and the tracts were vendible at a little public-house that sold shag by the "dottel," which is even smaller weight than the "half-screw," which is less than the half-ounce, and a most profitable retail trade.

But after eight months Pambé fell sick with pneumonia, contracted from long standing still in slush; and much against his will he was forced to lie down in his two-and-sixpenny room raging against Fate.

The kind gentleman sat by his bedside, and grieved to find that Pambé talked in strange tongues, instead of listening to good books, and almost seemed to become a benighted heathen again – till one day he was roused from semi-stupor by a voice in the street by the dock-head. "My friend – he," whispered Pambé. "Call now – call Nurkeed. Quick! God has sent him!"

"He wanted one of his own race," said the kind gentleman; and, going out, he called "Nurkeed!" at the top of his voice. A colored man in a rasping white shirt and brand-new slops, a shining hat, and a breastpin, turned round. Many voyages had taught Nurkeed how to spend his money and made him a citizen of the world.

"Hi! Yes!" said he, when the situation was explained. "Command him – when I was in the *Saarbruck*. Ole Pambé, good ole Pambé. Dam lascar. Show him up, Sar," and he followed into the room. One glance told the stoker what the kind gentleman had overlooked. Pambé was desperately poor. Nurkeed drove his hands deep into his pockets, then advanced with clenched fists on the sick, shouting, "Hya, Pambé. Hya! Hee-ah! Hulla! Heh! Takilo! Takilo! Make fast aft, Pambé. You know, Pambé. You know me. Dekho, jee! Look! Dam big fat lazy lascar!"

Pambé beckoned with his left hand. His right was under his pillow. Nurkeed removed his gorgeous hat and stooped over Pambé till he could catch a faint whisper. "How beautiful!" said the kind gentleman. "How these Orientals love like children!"

"Spit him out," said Nurkeed, leaning over Pambé yet more closely.

"Touching the matter of that fish and onions—" said Pambé – and sent the knife home under the edge of the rib-bone upwards and forwards.

There was a thick sick cough, and the body of the African slid slowly from the bed, his clutching hands letting fall a shower of silver pieces that ran across the room.

"Now I can die!" said Pambé.

But he did not die. He was nursed back to life with all the skill that money could buy, for the Law wanted him; and in the end he grew sufficiently healthy to be hanged in due and proper form.

Pambé did not care particularly; but it was a sad blow to the kind gentleman.

Markheim

Robert Louis Stevenson

"Yes," said the dealer, "our windfalls are of various kinds. Some customers are ignorant, and then I touch a dividend of my superior knowledge. Some are dishonest," and here he held up the candle, so that the light fell strongly on his visitor, "and in that case," he continued, "I profit by my virtue."

Markheim had but just entered from the daylight streets, and his eyes had not yet grown familiar with the mingled shine and darkness in the shop. At these pointed words, and before the near presence of the flame, he blinked painfully and looked aside.

The dealer chuckled. "You come to me on Christmas Day," he resumed, "when you know that I am alone in my house, put up my shutters, and make a point of refusing business. Well, you will have to pay for that; you will have to pay for my loss of time, when I should be balancing my books; you will have to pay, besides, for a kind of manner that I remark in you today very strongly. I am the essence of discretion, and ask no awkward questions; but when a customer cannot look me in the eye, he has to pay for it." The dealer once more chuckled; and then, changing to his usual business voice, though still with a note of irony, "You can give, as usual, a clear account of how you came into the possession of the object?" he continued. "Still your uncle's cabinet? A remarkable collector, sir!"

And the little, pale, round-shouldered dealer stood almost on tiptoe, looking over the top of his gold spectacles, and nodding his head with every mark of disbelief. Markheim returned his gaze with one of infinite pity, and a touch of horror.

"This time," said he, "you are in error. I have not come to sell, but to buy. I have no curios to dispose of; my uncle's cabinet is bare to the wainscot; even were it still intact, I have done well on the Stock Exchange, and should more likely add to it than otherwise, and my errand today is simplicity itself. I seek a Christmas present for a lady," he continued, waxing more fluent as he struck into the speech he had prepared; "and certainly I owe you every excuse for thus disturbing you upon so small a matter. But the thing was neglected yesterday; I must produce my little compliment at dinner; and, as you very well know, a rich marriage is not a thing to be neglected."

There followed a pause, during which the dealer seemed to weigh this statement incredulously. The ticking of many clocks among the curious lumber of the shop, and the faint rushing of the cabs in a near thoroughfare, filled up the interval of silence.

"Well, sir," said the dealer, "be it so. You are an old customer after all; and if, as you say, you have the chance of a good marriage, far be it from me to be an obstacle. Here is a nice thing for a lady now," he went on, "this hand glass – fifteenth century, warranted; comes from a good collection, too; but I reserve the name, in the interests of my customer, who was just like yourself, my dear sir, the nephew and sole heir of a remarkable collector."

The dealer, while he thus ran on in his dry and biting voice, had stooped to take the object from its place; and, as he had done so, a shock had passed through Markheim, a start both of hand and foot, a sudden leap of many tumultuous passions to the face. It passed as swiftly as it came, and left no trace beyond a certain trembling of the hand that now received the glass.

"A glass," he said hoarsely, and then paused, and repeated it more clearly. "A glass? For Christmas? Surely not?"

"And why not?" cried the dealer. "Why not a glass?"

Markheim was looking upon him with an indefinable expression. "You ask me why not?" he said. "Why, look here – look in it – look at yourself! Do you like to see it? No! nor I – nor any man."

The little man had jumped back when Markheim had so suddenly confronted him with the mirror; but now, perceiving there was nothing worse on hand, he chuckled. "Your future lady, sir, must be pretty hard favored," said he.

"I ask you," said Markheim, "for a Christmas present, and you give me this – this damned reminder of years and sins and follies – this hand-conscience! Did you mean it? Had you a thought in your mind? Tell me. It will be better for you if you do. Come, tell me about yourself. I hazard a guess now, that you are in secret a very charitable man?"

The dealer looked closely at his companion. It was very odd, Markheim did not appear to be laughing; there was something in his face like an eager sparkle of hope, but nothing of mirth.

"What are you driving at?" the dealer asked.

"Not charitable?" returned the other, gloomily. "Not charitable; not pious; not scrupulous; unloving, unbeloved; a hand to get money, a safe to keep it. Is that all? Dear God, man, is that all?"

"I will tell you what it is," began the dealer, with some sharpness, and then broke off again into a chuckle. "But I see this is a love match of yours, and you have been drinking the lady's health."

"Ah!" cried Markheim, with a strange curiosity. "Ah, have you been in love? Tell me about that."

"I," cried the dealer. "I in love! I never had the time, nor have I the time today for all this nonsense. Will you take the glass?"

"Where is the hurry?" returned Markheim. "It is very pleasant to stand here talking; and life is so short and insecure that I would not hurry away from any pleasure – no, not even from so mild a one as this. We should rather cling, cling to what little we can get, like a man at a cliff's edge. Every second is a cliff, if you think upon it – a cliff a mile high – high enough, if we fall, to dash us out of every feature of humanity. Hence it is best to talk pleasantly. Let us talk of each other; why should we wear this mask? Let us be confidential. Who knows, we might become friends?"

"I have just one word to say to you," said the dealer. "Either make your purchase, or walk out of my shop."

"True, true," said Markheim. "Enough fooling. To business. Show me something else."

The dealer stooped once more, this time to replace the glass upon the shelf, his thin blond hair falling over his eyes as he did so. Markheim moved a little nearer, with one hand in the pocket of his greatcoat; he drew himself up and filled his lungs; at the same time different emotions were depicted together on his face – terror, horror and resolve, fascination and a physical repulsion; and through a haggard lift of his upper lip, his teeth looked out.

"This, perhaps, may suit," observed the dealer; and then, as he began to re-arise, Markheim bounded from behind upon his victim. The long, skewerlike dagger flashed and fell. The dealer struggled like a hen, striking his temple on the shelf, and then tumbled on the floor in a heap.

Time had some score of small voices in that shop, some stately and slow as was becoming to their great age; others garrulous and hurried. All these told out the seconds in an intricate chorus of tickings. Then the passage of a lad's feet, heavily running on the pavement, broke in upon these smaller voices and startled Markheim into the consciousness of his surroundings. He looked about him awfully. The candle stood on the counter, its flame solemnly wagging in a draught; and by that inconsiderable movement; the whole room was filled with noiseless bustle and kept heaving like a sea: the tall shadows nodding, the gross blots of darkness swelling and dwindling as with respiration, the faces of the portraits and the china gods changing and wavering like images in water. The inner door stood ajar, and peered into that leaguer of shadows with a long slit of daylight like a pointing finger.

From these fear-stricken rovings, Markheim's eyes returned to the body of his victim, where it lay both humped and sprawling, incredibly small and strangely meaner than in life. In these poor, miserly clothes, in that ungainly attitude, the dealer lay like so much sawdust. Markheim had feared to see it, and, lo! it was nothing. And yet, as he gazed, this bundle of old clothes and pool of blood began to find eloquent voices. There it must lie; there was none to work the cunning hinges or direct the miracle of locomotion – there it must lie till it was found. Found! ay, and then? Then would this dead flesh lift up a cry that would ring over England, and fill the world with the echoes of pursuit. Ay, dead or not, this was still the enemy. "Time was that when the brains were out," he thought; and the first word struck into his mind. Time, now that the deed was accomplished – time, which had closed for the victim, had become momentous for him.

The thought was yet in his mind, when, first one and then another, with every variety of pace and voice – one deep as the bell from a cathedral turret, another ringing on its treble notes the prelude of a waltz – the clocks began to strike the hour of three in the afternoon.

The sudden outbreak of so many tongues in that dumb chamber staggered him. He began to bestir himself, going to and fro with the candle, beleaguered by moving shadows, and startled to the soul by chance reflections. In many rich mirrors, some of home designs, some from Venice or Amsterdam, he saw his face repeated and repeated, as it were an army of spies; his own eyes met and detected him; and the sound of his own steps, lightly as they fell, vexed the surrounding quiet. And still as he continued to fill his pockets, his mind accused him with a sickening iteration, of the thousand faults of his design. He should have chosen a more quiet hour; he should have prepared an alibi; he should not have used a knife; he should have been more cautious, and only bound and gagged the dealer, and not killed him; he should have been more bold, and killed the servant also; he should have done all things otherwise; poignant regrets, weary, incessant toiling of the mind to change what was unchangeable, to plan what was now useless, to be the architect of the irrevocable past. Meanwhile, and behind all this activity, brute terrors, like the scurrying of rats in a deserted attic, filled the more remote chambers of his brain with riot; the hand of the constable would fall heavy on his shoulder, and his nerves would jerk like a hooked fish; or he beheld, in galloping defile, the dock, the prison, the gallows and the black coffin.

Terror of the people in the street sat down before his mind like a besieging army. It was impossible, he thought, but that some rumor of the struggle must have reached their ears and set on edge their curiosity; and now, in all the neighboring houses, he divined them sitting motionless and with uplifted ear – solitary people, condemned to spend Christmas dwelling alone on memories of the past, and now startlingly recalled from that tender exercise; happy family parties, struck into silence round the table, the mother still with raised finger: every degree and age and humor, but all, by their own hearts, prying and hearkening and weaving the rope that was to hang him. Sometimes it seemed to him he could not move too softly; the clink of the tall Bohemian goblets rang out loudly like a bell; and alarmed by the bigness of the ticking, he was tempted to stop the clocks. And then, again, with a swift transition of his terrors, the very silence of the place appeared a source of peril, and a thing to strike and freeze the passer-by; and he would step more boldly, and bustle aloud among the contents of the shop, and imitate, with elaborate bravado, the movements of a busy man at ease in his own house.

But he was now so pulled about by different alarms that, while one portion of his mind was still alert and cunning, another trembled on the brink of lunacy. One hallucination in particular took a strong hold on his credulity. The neighbor hearkening with white face beside his window, the passer-by arrested by a horrible surmise on the pavement – these could at worst suspect, they could not know; through the brick walls and shuttered windows only sounds could penetrate. But here, within the house, was he alone? He knew he was; he had watched the servant set forth sweethearting, in her poor best, "out for the day" written in every ribbon and smile. Yes, he was alone, of course; and yet, in the bulk of empty house above him, he could surely hear a stir of delicate footing – he was surely conscious, inexplicably conscious of some presence. Ay, surely; to every room and corner of the house his imagination followed it; and now it was a faceless thing, and yet had eyes to see with; and again it was a shadow of himself; and yet again beheld the image of the dead dealer, reinspired with cunning and hatred.

At times, with a strong effort, he would glance at the open door which still seemed to repel his eyes. The house was tall, the skylight small and dirty, the day blind with fog; and the light that filtered down to the ground story was exceedingly faint, and showed dimly on the threshold of the shop. And yet, in that strip of doubtful brightness, did there not hang, wavering, a shadow?

Suddenly, from the street outside, a very jovial gentleman began to beat with a staff on the shopdoor, accompanying his

blows with shouts and railleries in which the dealer was continually called upon by name. Markheim, smitten into ice,
glanced at the dead man. But no! he lay quite still; he was fled
away far beyond earshot of these blows and shoutings; he was
sunk beneath seas of silence; and his name, which would once
have caught his notice above the howling of a storm, had
become an empty sound. And presently the jovial gentleman
desisted from his knocking and departed.

Here was a broad hint to hurry what remained to be done, to
get forth from this accusing neighborhood, to plunge into a bath
of London multitudes, and to reach, on the other side of day,
that haven of safety and apparent innocence – his bed. One
visitor had come: at any moment another might follow and be
more obstinate. To have done the deed, and yet not to reap the
profit, would be too abhorrent a failure. The money, that was
now Markheim's concern; and as a means to that, the keys.

He glanced over his shoulder at the open door, where the
shadow was still lingering and shivering; and with no conscious
repugnance of the mind, yet with a tremor of the belly, he drew
near the body of his victim. The human character had quite
departed. Like a suit half stuffed with bran, the limbs lay
scattered, the trunk doubled, on the floor; and yet the thing
repelled him. Although so dingy and inconsiderable to the eye,
he feared it might have more significance to the touch. He took
the body by the shoulders, and turned it on its back. It was
strangely light and supple, and the limbs, as if they had been
broken, fell into the oddest postures. The face was robbed of all
expression; but it was as pale as wax, and shockingly smeared
with blood about one temple. That was, for Markheim, the one
displeasing circumstance. It carried him back, upon the instant,
to a certain fair day in a fishers' village; a gray day, a piping
wind, a crowd upon the street, the blare of brasses, the booming
of drums, the nasal voice of a ballad singer; and a boy going to
and fro, buried over head in the crowd and divided between
interest and fear, until, coming out upon the chief place of
concourse, he beheld a booth and a great screen with pictures,
dismally designed, garishly colored: Brownrigg with her ap-
prentice; the Mannings with their murdered guest; Weare in the
death-grip of Thurtell; and a score besides of famous crimes.

The thing was as clear as an illusion; he was once again that little boy; he was looking once again, and with the same sense of physical revolt, at these vile pictures; he was still stunned by the thumping of the drums. A bar of that day's music returned upon his memory; and at that, for the first time, a qualm came over him, a breath of nausea, a sudden weakness of the joints, which he must instantly resist and conquer.

He judged it more prudent to confront than to flee from these considerations, looking the more hardily in the dead face, bending his mind to realize the nature and greatness of his crime. So little a while ago, that face had moved with every change of sentiment, that pale mouth had spoken, that body had been all on fire with governable energies; and now, and by his act, that piece of life had been arrested, as the horologist, with interjected finger, arrests the beating of the clock. So he reasoned in vain; he could rise to no more remorseful consciousness; the same heart which had shuddered before the painted effigies of crime, looked on its reality unmoved. At best, he felt a gleam of pity for one who had been endowed in vain with all those faculties that can make the world a garden of enchantment, one who had never lived and who was now dead. But of penitence, no, not a tremor.

With that, shaking himself clear of these considerations, he found the keys and advanced towards the open door of the shop. Outside, it had begun to rain smartly; and the sound of the shower upon the roof had banished silence. Like some dripping cavern, the chambers of the house were haunted by an incessant echoing, which filled the ear and mingled with the ticking of the clocks. And, as Markheim approached the door, he seemed to hear, in answer to his own cautious tread, the steps of another foot withdrawing up the stair. The shadow still palpitated loosely on the threshold. He threw a ton's weight of resolve upon his muscles, and drew back the door.

The faint, foggy daylight glimmered dimly on the bare floor and stairs; on the bright suit of armor posted, halbert in hand, upon the landing; and on the dark wood carvings, and framed pictures that hung against the yellow panels of the wainscot. So loud was the beating of the rain through all the house that, in Markheim's ears, it began to be distinguished into many different sounds. Footsteps and sighs, the tread of regiments marching in the distance, the clink of money in the counting, and the creaking of doors held stealthily ajar, appeared to mingle with the patter of the drops upon the cupola and the gushing of the water in the pipes. The sense that he was not alone grew upon him to the verge of madness. On every side he was haunted and begirt by presences. He heard them moving in the upper chambers; from the shop, he heard the dead man getting to his legs; and as he began with a great effort to mount the stairs, feet fled quietly before him and followed stealthily behind. If he were but deaf, he thought, how tranquilly he would possess his soul! And then again, and hearkening with ever fresh attention, he blessed himself for that unresting sense which held the outposts and stood a trusty sentinel upon his life. His head turned continually on his neck; his eyes, which seemed starting from their orbits, scouted on every side, and on every side were half rewarded as with the tail of something nameless vanishing. The four-and-twenty steps to the first floor were four-and-twenty agonies.

On that first storey the doors stood ajar, three of them like three ambushes, shaking his nerves like the throats of cannon. He could never again, he felt, be sufficiently immured and fortified from men's observing eyes; he longed to be home, girt in by walls, buried among bedclothes, and invisible to all but God. And at that thought he wondered a little, recollecting tales of other murderers and the fear they were said to entertain of heavenly avengers. It was not so, at least, with him. He feared the laws of nature, lest, in their callous and immutable procedure, they should preserve some damning evidence of his crime. He feared tenfold more, with a slavish, superstitious terror, some scission in the continuity of man's experience, some willful illegality of nature. He played a game of skill, depending on the rules, calculating consequence from cause; and what if nature, as the defeated tyrant overthrew the chessboard, should break the mold of their succession? The like had befallen Napoleon (so writers said) when the winter changed the time of its appearance. The like might befall Markheim; the solid walls might become transparent and reveal his doings like those of bees in a glass hive; the stout planks might yield under his foot like quicksands and detain him in their clutch; ay, and there were soberer accidents that might destroy him: if, for instance, the house should fall and imprison him beside the body of his victim; or the house next door should fly on fire, and the firemen invade him from all sides. These things he feared; and, in a sense, these things might be called the hands of God reached forth against sin. But about God himself he was at ease; his act was doubtless exceptional, but so were his excuses, which God knew; it was there, and not among men, that he felt sure of justice.

When he had got safe into the drawing room, and shut the door behind him, he was aware of a respite from alarms. The room was quite dismantled, uncarpeted besides, and strewn with packing cases and incongruous furniture; several great pier glasses, in which he beheld himself at various angles, like an actor on a stage; many pictures, framed and unframed, standing, with their faces to the wall; a fine Sheraton sideboard, a cabinet of marquetry, and a great old bed, with tapestry hangings. The windows opened to the floor; but by great good fortune the lower part of the shutters had been closed, and this concealed him from the neighbors. Here, then, Markheim drew in a packing case before the cabinet, and began to search among the keys. It was a long business, for there were many; and it was irksome besides; for, after all, there might be nothing in the cabinet, and time was on the wing. But the closeness of the occupation sobered him. With the tail of his eye he saw the door – even glanced at it from time to time directly, like a besieged commander pleased to verify the good estate of his defenses. But in truth he was at peace. The rain falling in the street sounded natural and pleasant. Presently, on the other side, the notes of a piano were wakened to the music of a hymn, and the voices of many children took up the air and words. How stately, how comfortable was the melody! How fresh the youthful voices! Markheim gave ear to it, smilingly, as he sorted out the keys; and his mind was thronged with answerable ideas and images; church-going children and the pealing of the high organ; children afield, bathers by the brookside, ramblers on the brambly common, kite-fliers in the windy and cloud-navigated sky; and then, at another cadence of the hymn, back again to church, and the somnolence of summer Sundays, and the high genteel voice of the parson (which he smiled a little to recall) and the painted Jacobean tombs, and the dim lettering of the Ten Commandments in the chancel.

And as he sat thus, at once busy and absent, he was startled to his feet. A flash of ice, a flash of fire, a bursting gush of blood, went over him, and then he stood transfixed and thrilling. A step mounted the stair slowly and steadily, and presently a hand was laid upon the knob, and the lock clicked, and the door opened.

Fear held Markheim in a vice. What to expect he knew not, whether the dead man walking, or the official ministers of human justice, or some chance witness blindly stumbling in to consign him to the gallows. But when a face was thrust into the aperture, glanced round the room, looked at him, nodded and smiled as if in friendly recognition, and then withdrew again, and the door closed behind it, his fear broke loose from his control in a hoarse cry. At the sound of this the visitant returned.

"Did you call me?" he asked, pleasantly, and with that he entered the room and closed the door behind him.

Markheim stood and gazed at him with all his eyes. Perhaps there was a film upon his sight, but the outlines of the newcomer seemed to change and waver like those of the idols in the wavering candlelight of the shop; and at times he thought he knew him; and at times he thought he bore a likeness to himself; and always, like a lump of living terror, there lay in his bosom the conviction that this thing was not of the earth and not of God.

And yet the creature had a strange air of the commonplace, as he stood looking on Markheim with a smile; and when he added: "You are looking for the money, I believe?" it was in the tones of everyday politeness.

Markheim made no answer.

"I should warn you," resumed the other, "that the maid has left her sweetheart earlier than usual and will soon be here. If Mr. Markheim be found in this house, I need not describe to him the consequences."

"You know me?" cried the murderer.

The visitor smiled. "You have long been a favorite of mine," he said; "and I have long observed and often sought to help you."

"What are you?" cried Markheim: "the devil?"

"What I may be," returned the other, "cannot affect the service I propose to render you."

"It can," cried Markheim; "it does! Be helped by you? No, never; not by you! You do not know me yet; thank God, you do not know me!"

"I know you," replied the visitant, with a sort of kind severity or rather firmness. "I know you to the soul."

"Know me!" cried Markheim. "Who can do so? My life is but a travesty and slander on myself. I have lived to belie my nature. All men do; all men are better than this disguise that grows about and stifles them. You see each dragged away by life, like one whom bravos have seized and muffled in a cloak. If they had their own control – if you could see their faces, they would be altogether different, they would shine out for heroes and saints! I am worse than most; my self is more overlaid; my excuse is known to me and God. But, had I the time, I could disclose myself."

"To me?" inquired the visitant.

"To you before all," returned the murderer. "I supposed you were intelligent. I thought – since you exist – you would prove a reader of the heart. And yet you would propose to judge me by my acts! Think of it; my acts! I was born and I have lived in a land of giants; giants have dragged me by the wrists since I was born out of my mother – the giants of circumstance. And you would judge me by my acts! But can you not look within? Can you not understand that evil is hateful to me? Can you not see within me the clear writing of conscience, never blurred by any willful sophistry, although too often disregarded? Can you not read me for a thing that surely must be common as humanity – the unwilling sinner?"

"All this is very feelingly expressed," was the reply, "but it regards me not. These points of consistency are beyond my province, and I care not in the least by what compulsion you may have been dragged away, so as you are but carried in the right direction. But time flies; the servant delays, looking in the faces of the crowd and at the pictures on the boardings, but still she keeps moving nearer; and remember, it is as if the gallows itself was striding towards you through the Christmas streets! Shall I help you; I, who know all? Shall I tell you where to find the money?"

"For what price?" asked Markheim.

"I offer you the service for a Christmas gift," returned the other.

Markheim could not refrain from smiling with a kind of bitter triumph. "No," said he, "I will take nothing at your hands; if I were dying of thirst, and it was your hand that put the pitcher to my lips, I should find the courage to refuse. It may be credulous, but I will do nothing to commit myself to evil."

"I have no objection to a deathbed repentance," observed the visitant.

"Because you disbelieve their efficacy!" Markheim cried.

"I do not say so," returned the other; "but I look on these things from a different side, and when the life is done my interest falls. The man has lived to serve me, to spread black looks under color of religion, or to sow tares in the wheatfield, as you do, in a course of weak compliance with desire. Now that he draws so near to his deliverance, he can add but one act of service – to repent, to die, smiling, and thus to build up in confidence and hope the more timorous of my surviving followers. I am not so hard a master. Try me. Accept my help. Please yourself in life as you have done hitherto; please yourself more amply, spread your elbows at the board; and when the night begins to fall and the curtains to be drawn, I tell you, for your greater comfort, that you will find it even easy to compound your quarrel with your conscience, and to make a truckling peace with God. I came but now from such a deathbed, and the room was full of sincere mourners, listening to the man's last words: and when I looked into that face, which had been set as a flint against mercy, I found it smiling with hope."

"And do you, then, suppose me such a creature?" asked Markheim. "Do you think I have no more generous aspirations than to sin, and sin, and sin, and, at last, sneak into heaven? My heart rises at the thought. Is this, then, your experience of mankind? Or is it because you find me with red hands that you presume such baseness? And is this crime of murder indeed so impious as to dry up the very springs of good?"

"Murder is to me no special category," replied the other. "All sins are murder, even as all life is war. I behold your race, like starving mariners on a raft, plucking crusts out of the hands of famine and feeding on each other's lives. I follow sins beyond the moment of their acting; I find in all that the last consequence is death; and to my eyes, the pretty maid who thwarts her mother with such taking graces on a question of a ball, drips no less visibly with human gore than such a murderer as yourself. Do I say that I follow sins? I follow virtues also; they differ not by the thickness of a nail, they are both scythes for the reaping angel of Death. Evil, for which I live, consists not in action but in character. The bad man is dear to me; not the bad act, whose fruits, if we could follow them far enough down the hurtling cataract of the ages, might yet be found more blessed than those of the rarest virtues. And it is not because you have killed a dealer, but because you are Markheim that I offered to forward your escape."

"I will lay my heart open to you," answered Markheim. "This crime on which you find me is my last. On my way to it I have learned many lessons; itself is a lesson, a momentous lesson. Hitherto I have been driven with revolt to what I would not; I was a bond-slave to poverty, driven and scourged. There are robust virtues that can stand in these temptations; mine was not so: I had a thirst for pleasure. But today, and out of this deed, I pluck both warning and riches – both the power and a fresh resolve to be myself. I become in all things a free actor in the world; I begin to see myself all changed, these hands the agents of good, this heart at peace. Something comes over me out of the past; something of what I have dreamed on Sabbath evenings to the sound of the church organ, of what I forecast when I shed tears over noble books, or talked, an innocent child, with my mother. There lies my life; I have wandered a few years, but now I see once more my city of destination."

"You are to use this money on the Stock Exchange, I think?" remarked the visitor; "and there, if I mistake not, you have already lost some thousands?"

"Ah," said Markheim, "but this time I have a sure thing."

"This time, again, you will lose," replied the visitor quietly.

"Ah, but I keep back the half!" cried Markheim.

"That also you will lose," said the other.

The sweat started upon Markheim's brow. "Well, then, what matter?" he exclaimed. "Say it be lost, say I am plunged again in poverty, shall one part of me, and that the worst, continue until the end to override the better? Evil and good run strong in me, hauling me both ways. I do not love the one thing, I love all. I can conceive great deeds, renunciations, martyrdoms; and though I be fallen to such a crime as murder, pity is no stranger to my thoughts. I pity the poor; who knows their trials better than myself? I pity and help them; I prize love, I love honest laughter; there is no good thing nor true thing on earth but I love it from my heart. And are my vices only to direct my life, and my virtues to lie without effect, like some passive lumber of the mind? Not so; good, also, is a spring of acts."

But the visitant raised his finger. "For six-and-thirty years that you have been in this world," said he, "through many changes of fortune and varieties of humor, I have watched you steadily fall. Fifteen years ago you would have started at a theft. Three years back you would have blanched at the name of murder. Is there any crime, is there any cruelty or meanness, from which you still recoil – five years from now I shall detect you in the fact! Downward, downward, lies your way; nor can anything but death avail to stop you."

"It is true," Markheim said huskily, "I have in some degree complied with evil. But it is so with all: the very saints, in the mere exercise of living, grow less dainty, and take on the tone of their surroundings."

"I will propound to you one simple question," said the other; "and as you answer, I shall read to you your moral horoscope. You have grown in many things more lax; possibly you do right to be so; and at any account, it is the same with all men. But granting that, are you in any one particular, however trifling, more difficult to please with your own conduct, or do you go in all things with a looser rein?"

"In any one?" repeated Markheim, with an anguish of consideration. "No," he added, with despair, "in none! I have gone down in all."

"Then," said the visitor, "content yourself with what you are, for you will never change; and the words of your part on this stage are irrevocably written."

Markheim stood for a long while silent, and indeed it was the visitor who first broke the silence. "That being so," he said, "shall I show you the money?"

"And grace?" cried Markheim.

"Have you not tried it?" returned the other. "Two or three years ago, did I not see you on the platform of revival meetings, and was not your voice the loudest in the hymn?"

"It is true," said Markheim, "and I see clearly what remains for me by way of duty. I thank you for these lessons from my soul; my eyes are opened, and I behold myself at last for what I am."

At this moment, the sharp note of the doorbell rang through the house; and the visitant, as though this were some concerted signal for which he had been waiting, changed at once in his demeanor.

"The maid!" he cried. "She has returned, as I forewarned you, and there is now before you one more difficult passage. Her master, you must say, is ill; you must let her in, with an assured but rather serious countenance – no smiles, no over-acting, and I promise you success! Once the girl is within, and the door closed, the same dexterity that has already rid you of the dealer will relieve you of this last danger in your path. Thenceforward you have the whole evening – the whole night, if needful – to ransack the treasures of the house and to make good your safety. This is help that comes to you with the mask of danger. Up!" he cried. "Up, friend; your life hangs trembling in the scales: up, and act!"

Markheim steadily regarded his counsellor. "If I be con-demned to evil acts," he said, "there is still one door of freedom open – I can cease from action. If my life be an ill thing, I can lay it down. Though I be, as you say truly, at the beck of every small temptation, I can yet, by one decisive gesture, place myself beyond the reach of all. My love of good is damned to barrenness; it may, and let it be! But I have still my hatred of evil; and from that, to your galling disappointment, you shall see that I can draw both energy and courage."

The features of the visitor began to undergo a wonderful and lovely change: they brightened and softened with a tender triumph; and, even as they brightened, faded and dislimned. But Markheim did not pause to watch or understand the transformation. He opened the door and went downstairs very slowly, thinking to himself. His past went soberly before him; he beheld it as it was, ugly and strenuous like a dream, random as chance-medley – a scene of defeat. Life, as he thus reviewed it, tempted him no longer; but on the further side he perceived a quiet haven for his bark. He paused in the passage, and looked into the shop, where the candle still burned by the dead body. It was strangely silent. Thoughts of the dealer swarmed into his mind, as he stood gazing. And then the bell once more broke out into impatient clamor.

He confronted the maid upon the threshold with something like a smile.

"You had better go for the police," said he: "I have killed your master."

The Disappearance of
Marie Severe

Ernest Bramah

"I wonder if you might happen to be interested in this case of Marie Severe, Mr. Carrados?"

If Carrados's eyes had been in the habit of expressing emotion they would doubtless have twinkled as Inspector Beedel thus casually introduced the subject of the Swanstead-on-Thames schoolgirl whose inexplicable disappearance two weeks earlier had filled column upon column of every newspaper with excited speculation until the sheer impossibility of keeping the sensation going without a shred of actual fact had relegated Marie Severe to the obscurity of an occasional paragraph.

"If you are concerned with it, I am sure that I shall be interested, Inspector," said the blind man encouragingly. "It is still being followed, then?"

"Why, yes, sir, I have it in hand, but as for following it – well, 'following' is perhaps scarcely the word now."

"Ah," commented Carrados. "There was very little to follow, I remember."

"I don't think that I've ever known a case of the kind with less, sir. For all the trace she left, the girl might have melted out of existence, and from that day to this, with the exception of that printed communication received by the mother – you remember that, Mr. Carrados? – there hasn't been a clue worth wasting so much as shoe leather on."

"You have had plenty of hints all the same, I suppose?"

Inspector Beedel threw out a gesture of mild despair. It

conveyed the patient exasperation of the conscientious and long-suffering man.

"I should say that the case 'took on' remarkably, Mr. Carrados. I doubt if there has been a more popular sensation of its kind for years. Mind you, I'm all in favour of publicity in the circumstances; the photographs and description *may* bring important facts to light, but sometimes it's a bit trying for those who have to do the work at our end. 'Seen in Northampton,' 'seen in Ealing,' 'heard of in West Croydon,' 'girl answering to the description observed in the waiting-room at Charing Cross,' 'suspicious-looking man with likely girl noticed about the Victoria Dock, Hull,' 'seen and spoken to near Chorley, Lancs,' 'caught sight of apparently struggling in a luxurious motor car on the Portsmouth Road,' 'believed to have visited a Watford picture palace' – they've all been gone into as carefully as though we believed that each one was the real thing at last."

"And you haven't, eh?"

The inspector looked round. He knew well enough that they were alone in the study at The Turrets, but the action had become something of a mannerism with him.

"I don't mind admitting to *you*, sir, that I've never had my other opinion than that the father of the little girl went down that day and got her away. Where she is now, and whether dead or alive, I can't pretend to say, but that he's at the bottom of it I'm firmly convinced. And what's more," he added with slow significance, "I *hope* so."

"Why in particular?" inquired the other.

Beedel felt in his breast-pocket, took out a formidable wallet, and from among its multitudinous contents selected a cabinet photograph sheathed in its protecting envelope of glazed transparent paper.

"If you could make out anything of what this portrait shows, you'd understand better what I mean, Mr. Carrados," he replied delicately.

Carrados shook his head but nevertheless held out his hand for the photograph.

"No good, I'm afraid," he confessed, before he took it. "A print of this sort is one of the few things that afford no graduation to the sense of touch. No, no" – as he passed his finger-tips over the paper – "a gelatino-chloride surface of mathematical uniformity, Inspector, and nothing more. Now had it been the negative—"

"I am sure that that could be procured if you wished to have it, Mr. Carrados. Anyway, I dare say that you've seen in some of the papers what this young girl is like. She is ten years old and big – or at least tall – for her age. This picture is the last taken – some time this year – and I am told that it is just like her."

"How should you describe it, Inspector?"

"I am not much good at that sort of thing," said the large man with a shy awkwardness, "but it makes as sweet a picture as ever I've seen. She is very straight-set, and yet with a sort of gracefulness such as a young wild animal might have. It's a full-faced position and she is looking straight out at you with an expression that is partly serious and partly amused, and as noble and gracious with it all as a young princess might be. I have children of my own, Mr. Carrados, and, of course, I think they're very nice and pretty, but this – this is quite a different thing. Her hair is curly without being in separate curls, and the description calls it black. Eyes dark brown with straight eyebrows, complexion a sort of glowing brown, small regular teeth. Of course we have a full description of what she was wearing and so forth."

"Yes, yes," assented Carrados idly. "The Van Brown Studio, photographers, eh? These people are quite well off, then?"

"Oh, yes; very nice house and good position – Mrs. Severe, that is to say. You will remember that she obtained a divorce from her husband four or five years ago. I've turned up the particulars and it wasn't what you'd call a bad case as things go, but the lady seemed determined, and in the end Severe didn't defend. She had five or six hundred a year of her own, but he had nothing beyond his salary, and he threw his position up then, and ever since he has been going steadily down. He's almost on the last rung now and picks up his living casual."

"What's the case against him?"

"Well, it scarcely amounts to a case as yet because there is no evidence of his being seen with the child, nor is there anything to connect him with her after the disappearance. Still, it is a working hypothesis. If it was the act of a tramp or a maniac, experience goes to show that we should have found her, dead or alive, by now. Mrs. Severe is all for it being her husband. Of course, the decree gave her the custody of Marie. Severe asked to be allowed to see her occasionally, and at first a servant took the child to have tea with him once a month. That was at his rooms. Then he asked to be met in one of the parks or at a gallery. He hadn't got so much as a room then, you see, sir. At last the servant reported that he had grown so shabby as to shame her that the child should be seen with him, though she did say that he was always sober and very kind to Marie, bringing her a little toy or something even when he didn't seem to have sixpence for himself. After that the visits were stopped altogether. Then about a month ago these two, husband and wife, met accidentally in the street. Severe said that he hoped to be doing a bit better soon, and asked for the visits to be continued. How it would have gone I cannot say, but Mrs. Severe happened to have a friend with her, an American lady called Miss Julp, who seems to be living with her now, and this middle-aged female – she's a hard sister, that Cornelia Julp, I should say – pushed her way into the conversation and gave her views on his conduct until Severe must have had some trouble with his hands. Finally Mrs. Severe had an unfortunate impulse to end the discussion by giving her husband a bank-note. She says she got the most awful look she ever saw on any face. Then Severe very deliberately tore up the note, dropped the pieces down a gutter grid that they were standing near, dusted his fingers on his handkerchief, raised his hat and walked away without another word. That was the last she saw of him, but she professes to have been afraid of something happening ever since."

"Then something happens, and so, of course, it must be Severe?" suggested Carrados.

"It does look a bit like that so far, I must admit, sir," assented the inspector. "Still, Mrs. Severe's opinions aren't quite all. Severe's account of his movements on the afternoon in question – say between twelve-thirty and four in particular – are not satisfactory. Latterly he has been occupying a miserable room off Red Lion Street. He went out at twelve and returned about five – that he doesn't deny. Says he spent the time walking about the streets and in the Holborn news-room, but can mention no one who saw him during those five hours. On the other hand, a porter at Swanstead station identifies him as a passenger who alighted there from the 1.17 that afternoon."

"From a newspaper likeness?"

"In the first instance, Mr. Carrados. Afterwards in person."

"Did they speak, or is it merely visual?"

"Only from what he saw of him."

"Struck, I suppose, by the remarkable fact that the passenger wore a hat and a tie – as shown in the picture; or inspired to notice him closely by something indescribably suggestive in the passenger's way of giving up his ticket? It may be all right, Beedel, I admit, but I heartily distrust the weight of importance that these casual identifications are being given on vital points nowadays. Are you satisfied with this yourself?"

"Only as corroborative, sir. Until we find the girl or some trace of her we're bound to make casts in the hope of picking up a line. Well, then there's the letter Mrs. Severe received."

"Have you that with you?"

The inspector took up the wallet that he had not yet returned to his pocket and selected another enclosure.

"It's a very unusual form," he commented as he handed the envelope to Mr. Carrados and waited for his opinion.

The blind man passed his finger-tips across the paper and at once understood the point of singularity. The lines were printed, but not in consecutive form, every letter being on a little separate square of paper. It was evident that they had been cut out from some other sheet and then pasted on the envelope to form the address.

"London, E.C., 5.30 p.m., 15th May," read Carrados from the postmark.

"The day of the kidnapping. There is a train from Swanstead arriving at Lambeth Bridge at 4.47," remarked Beedel.

"What was your porter doing when that left?"

"He was off duty, sir."

Carrados took out the enclosure and read it off as he had already done the envelope, but with a more deliberative touch, for the print was smaller. The type and the paper were suggestive of a newspaper origin. In most cases whole words had been found available.

"Do not be alarmed," ran the patchwork message. "The girl is in good hands. Only risk lies in pressing search. Wait and she will return uninjured."

"You have identified the newspaper?"

"Yes; it is all cut from *The Times* of May 13th. The printing on the back of the words fixes it absolutely. Premeditated, Mr. Carrados."

"The whole incident points to that. The date of the newspaper means little, but the deliberate selection of words, the careful way they have been cut out and aligned, taken in conjunction with the time the child disappeared and the time that this was posted – yes, I think you may assume premeditation, Inspector."

"Stationery of the commonest description; immediate return to London, and the method of a man who used this print because he feared that under any disguise his handwriting might be recognized."

Carrados nodded.

"Severe cannot hope to retain the child, of course," he remarked casually. "What motive do you infer?"

"Mrs. Severe is convinced that it is to distress her, out of revenge."

"And this letter is to reassure her?"

The inspector bit his lip as he smiled at the quiet thrust.

"It might also be to influence her towards suspending her search," he suggested.

"At all events I dare say that it has reassured her?"

"In a certain way, yes, it has. It has enabled us to establish that the act is not one of casual lust or vagabondage. There is an alternative that we naturally did not suggest to her."

"And that is?"

"Another Thelby Wood case, Mr. Carrados. The maniacal infatuation of someone who would be the last to be suspected. Some man of good position, a friend and neighbour possibly, who sees this beautiful young creature – the school friend of his own daughters or sitting before him in church it may be – and becomes the slave of his diseased imagination until he is prepared to risk everything for that one overpowering object. A primitive man for the time, one may say, or, even worse, a satyr or a gorilla."

"I wonder," observed Carrados thoughtfully, "if you also have ever felt that you would like to drop it and become a monk, Inspector. Or a stylite on a pole."

Beedel laughed softly and then rubbed his chin in the same contemplative spirit.

"I think I know what you mean, sir," he admitted. "It's a black page. But," he added with wholesome philosophy, "after all, it *is* only a page in a longish book. And if I was in a monastery there'd be one or two more things done that I've helped to keep undone."

"Including the cracking of my head, Inspector? Very true. We must take the world as we find it and ourselves as we are. And I wish that I could agree with you about Severe. It would be a more endurable outlook: spite and revenge are at least decent human motives. Unfortunately, the only hint I can offer is a negative one." He indicated printed cuttings on the sheet that Beedel had submitted to him. "This photo-mountant costs about sixpence a pot, but you can buy a bottle of gum for a penny."

"Well, sir," said Beedel, "I did think of having that examined, but I waited for you to see the letter as it stood. After all, it didn't strike me as a point one could put much reliance on."

"Quite right," assented Mr. Carrados, "there is nothing personal or definite in it. It may suggest a photographer, amateur or professional, but it would be preposterous to assume so much from this alone. Severe, even, may have – there are hundreds of chances. I should disregard it for the moment."

"There is nothing more to be got from the letter?"

"There may be, but it is rather elusive at present. What has been done with it?"

"I received it from Mrs. Severe and it has been in my possession ever since."

"You haven't submitted it to a chemist for any purpose?"

"No, sir. I gave a copy of the wording to some newspaper gentlemen, but no one but myself has handled it."

"Very good. Now if you care to leave it with me for a few days—"

Inspector Beedel expressed his immediate willingness and would have added his tribute or obligation for Mr. Carrados's service, but the blind man cut him short.

"Don't rely on anything, Inspector," he warned him. "I am afraid that this resolves itself into a game of chance. Just one touch of luck may give us a winning point, or it may go the other way. In any case there is no reason why I should not motor round by Swanstead one of these days when I am out. If anything fresh turns up before you hear from me you had better telephone me. Now exactly where did this happen?"

The actual facts surrounding the disappearance of Marie Severe constituted the real mystery of the case. Arling Avenue, Swanstead, was one of those leisurely suburban roads where it is impossible to imagine anything happening hurriedly from the delivery of an occasional telegram to the activity of the local builder. Houses, detached houses, each surrounded by its rood or more of garden, had been built here and there along its length at one time or another, but even the most modern one had now become matured, and the vacant plots between them had reverted from the condition of "eligible sites" into very passable fields of buttercups and daisies again, so that Arling Avenue remained a pleasant and exclusive thoroughfare. One side of the road was entirely unbuilt on and afforded the prospect of a level meadow where hay was made and real animals grazed in due season. The inhabitants of Arling Avenue never failed to point out to visitors this evidence of undeniable rurality. It even figured in the prospectus of Homewood, the Arling Avenue day school for girls and little boys which the Misses Chibwell had carried on with equal success and inconspicuousness until the Severe affair suddenly brought them into the glare of a terrifying publicity.

Mrs. Severe's house, The Hollies, was the first in the road, as the road was generally regarded – that is to say, from the direction of the station. Beedel picked up a loose sheet of paper and scored it heavily with a plan of the neighbourhood as he explained the position with some minuteness. Next to The Hollies came Arling Lodge. After Arling Lodge there was one of the vacant plots of ground before the next house was reached, but between the Lodge and the vacant plot was a broad grassy opening, unfenced towards the road, and here the inspector's pencil underlined the deepest significance, culminating in an ominous x about the centre of the space. Originally the opening had doubtless marked the projection of another road, but the scheme had come to nothing. Occasionally a little band of exploring children with the fictitious optimism of youth pecked among its rank and tangled growth in the affectation of hoping to find blackberries there; once in a while a passing chair-mender or travelling tinker regarded it favourably for the scene of his midday siesta, but its only legitimate use seemed to be that of affording access to the side door of Arling Lodge garden. The inspector pencilled in the garden door as an afterthought, with the parenthesis that it was seldom used and always kept locked. Then he followed out the Avenue as far as the school, indicating all the houses and other features. The whole distance traversed did not exceed two hundred yards.

A few minutes before two o'clock on the afternoon of her disappearance, Marie Severe set out as usual for Miss Chibwell's school. Since the incident of the unfortunate encounter with her former husband Mrs. Severe had considered it necessary to exercise a peculiar vigilance over her only child. Thenceforward Marie never went out alone; never, with the exception of the short walk to school and back, that is to say, for in that quiet straight road, in the full light of day, it was ridiculous to imagine that anything could happen. It was ridiculous, but all the same the vaguely uneasy woman generally walked to the garden gate with the little girl and watched her until the diminished figure passed, with a last gay wave of hand or satchel, out of her sight into the school-yard.

"That's how it would have been on this occasion," narrated Beedel, "only just as they got to the garden gate a tradesman whom Mrs. Severe wanted to speak with drove up and passed in by the back way. The lady looked along the avenue, and as it happened at that moment Miss Chibwell was standing in the road by her gate. No one else was in sight, so it isn't to be wondered at that Mrs. Severe went back to the house immediately without another thought.

"That was the last that has been seen of Marie. As a matter of fact, Miss Chibwell turned back into her garden almost as soon as Mrs. Severe did. When the child did not appear for the afternoon school the mistress thought nothing of it. She is a little short-sighted and although she had seen the two at their gate she concluded that they were going out together somewhere. Consequently it was not until four o'clock, when Marie did not return home, that the alarm was raised."

Continuous narration was not congenial to Inspector Beedel's mental attitude. He made frequent pauses as though to invite cross-examination. Sometimes Carrados ignored the opening, at others he found it more convenient to comply.

"The inference is that someone was waiting in this space just beyond Arling Lodge?" he now contributed.

"I think it is reasonable to assume that, sir. Premeditated, we both admit. Doubtless a favourable opportunity was being looked for and there it was. At all events there" – he tapped the x as the paper lay beneath Carrados's hand – "there is the very last tract that we can rely on."

"The scent, you mean?"

"Yes, Mr. Carrados. We got one of our dogs down the next morning and put him on the trail. We gave him the scent of a boot, and from the gate he brought us without a pause to where I have marked this x. There the line ended. There can be no doubt that from that point the girl had been picked up and carried. That is a very remarkable thing. It could scarcely have been done openly past the houses. The fences on all sides are of such a nature that it is incredible for any man to have got an unwilling or insensible burden of that sort over without at least laying it down in the process. If our dog is to be trusted, it wasn't laid down. Some sort of a vehicle remains. We find no recent wheel-marks and no one seems to have seen anything that would answer about at that time."

"You are determined to mystify me, Inspector," smiled Carrados.

"I'm that way myself, sir," said the detective.

"And I know you too well to ask if you have done this and that—"

"I've done everything," admitted Beedel modestly.

"Is this x spot commanded by any of the houses? Here is Arling Lodge—"

"There is one window overlooking, but now the trees are too much out for anything to be seen. Besides, it's only a passage window. Dr. Ellerslie took me up there himself to settle the point."

"Ellerslie – Dr. Ellerslie?"

"The gentleman who lives there. At least he doesn't live altogether there, as I understand that he has it for a week-end place. Boating, I believe, sir. His regular practice is in town."

"Harley Street? Prescott Ellerslie, do you know?"

"That is the same, Mr. Carrados."

"Oh, a very well-known man. He has a great reputation as an operator for peritonitis. Nothing less than fifty guineas a time, Inspector." Perhaps the fee did not greatly impress Mr. Carrados, but he doubtless judged that it would interest Inspector Beedel. "And this house on the other side – Lyncote?"

"A retired Indian army colonel lives there – Colonel Doige."

"I mean as regards overlooking the spot."

"No; it is quite cut off from there. It cannot be seen."

Carrados's interpreting finger stopped lightly over a detail of the plan that it was again exploring. The inspector's pencil had now added a line of dots leading from The Hollies gate to the x.

"The line the dog took," Beedel explained, following the other's movement. "You notice that the girl turned sharply out of the avenue into this opening at right angles."

"I was just considering that."

"Something took her attention suddenly or someone called her there – I wonder what, Mr. Carrados."

"I wonder," echoed the blind man, raising the anonymous letter to his face again.

Mr. Carrados frequently professed to find inspiration in the surroundings of light and brilliance to which his physical sense was dead, but when he wished to go about his work with everyone else at a notable disadvantage he not unnaturally chose the dark. It was therefore night when in accordance with his promise to Beedel, he motored round by Swanstead, or, more exactly, it was morning, for the clock in the square ivied tower of the parish church struck two as the car switchbacked over the humped bridge from Middlesex into Surrey.

"This will do, Harris; wait here," he said a little later. He knew that there were trees above and wide open spaces on both sides. The station lay just beyond, and from the station to Arling Avenue was a negligible step. Even at that hour Arling Avenue might have been awake to the intrusion of an alien car of rather noticeable proportions.

The adaptable Harris picked out Mr. Carrados's most substantial rug and went to sleep, to dream of a wayside cycle shop and tea-rooms where he could devote himself to pedigree Wyandottes. With Parkinson at his elbow Carrados walked slowly on to Arling Avenue. What was lacking on Beedel's plan Parkinson's eyes supplied; on a subtler plane, in the moist, warm night, full of quiet sounds and earthly odours, other details were filled in like the work of a lightning cartoonist before the blind man's understanding.

They walked the length of the avenue once and then returned to the grassy opening where the last trace of Marie Severe had evaporated.

"I will stay here. You walk on back to the highroad and wait for me. I may be some time. If I want you, you will hear the whistle."

"Very good, sir." Parkinson knew of old that there were times when his master would have no human eye upon him as he went about his work, and with a magnificent stolidity the man had not a particle of curiosity. It did not even occur to him to wonder. But for nearly half an hour the more inquiring creatures of the night looked down or up, according to their natures – to observe the strange attitudes and quiet persistence of the disturber of the solitude as he crossed and recrossed their little domain, studied its boundaries, and explored every corner of its miniature thickets. A single petal picked up near the locked door to the garden of Arling Lodge seemed a small return for such perseverance, but it is to be presumed that the patient search had not been in vain, for it was immediately after the discovery that Carrados left the opening, and with the cool effrontery that marked his methods he opened the front gate of Dr. Ellerslie's garden and made his way with slow but unerring insight along the boundary wall.

"A blind man," he had once replied to Mr. Carlyle's nervous remonstrance, "a blind man carries on his face a sufficient excuse for every indiscretion."

It was nearly three o'clock when, by the light of the street lamp at the corner of the avenue and the highroad, Parkinson saw his master approaching. But to the patient and excellent servitor's disappointment Carrados at that moment turned back and retraced his steps in the same leisurely manner. As a matter of fact, a new consideration had occurred to the blind man and he continued to pace up and down the footpath as he considered it.

"Oh, sir!"

He stopped at once, but betraying no surprise, without the start which few can restrain when addressed suddenly in the dark. It was always dark to him, but was it ever sudden? Was he indeed ignorant of the obscure figure that had appeared at the gate during his perambulation?

"I have seen you walking up and down at this hour and I wondered – I wondered whether you had any news."

"Who are you?" he asked.

"I am Mrs. Severe. My little girl Marie disappeared from here two weeks ago. You must surely know about it, everybody does."

"Yes, I know," he admitted. "Inspector Beedel told me."

"Oh, Inspector Beedel!" There was obvious disappointment in her voice. "He is very kind and promises – but nothing comes of it, and the days go on, the days go on," she repeated tragically.

"Ida! Ida!" Someone was calling from one of the upper windows, but Carrados was speaking also, and Mrs. Severe merely waved her hand back towards the house without responding.

"Your little girl was very fond of flowers?"

"Oh, yes, indeed." The pleasant recollection dwarfed the poor lady's present sense of calamity and for a moment she was quite bright. "She loved them. She would bury her face in a bunch of flowers and drink their scent. She almost lived in the garden. They were more to her than toys or dolls, I am sure. But how do you know?"

"I only guessed."

"Ida! Ida!" The rather insistent, nasally querulous voice was raised again, and this time Mrs. Severe replied.

"Yes, dear, immediately," she called back, still lingering, however, to discover whether she had anything to hope from this outlandish visitant.

"Had Marie been ill recently?" Carrados detained her with the question.

"Ill! Oh, no." The reply was instant and emphatic. It was almost – if one could credit a mother's pride in her child's health being carried to such a length – it was almost resentful.

"Nothing that required the services of a doctor?"

"Marie never requires the services of a doctor." The tone, distant and constrained, made it clear that Mrs. Severe had given up any expectations in this quarter. "My child, I am glad to say, does not know what illness means," she added deliberately.

"Ida! Oh, here you are." The very unromantically accoutred form of a keen-visaged, middle-aged female, padding heavily in bedroom slippers along the garden walk, gave its quietus to the situation. "What a scare you gave me, dearie. Why, whoever—"

"Good night," said Mrs. Severe, turning from the gate.

Carrados raised his hat and resumed his interrupted stroll. He had not sought the interview and he made no effort to prolong it, for there was little to be got from that source.

"A strange flare of maternal pride," he remarked in his usual detached fashion as he rejoined Parkinson.

About five o'clock on the same day – five o'clock in the afternoon, let it be understood – Inspector Beedel was called to the telephone.

"Oh, nothing fresh so far, Mr. Carrados," he reported when he identified his caller. "I shan't forget to let you know whenever there is.

"But I think that possibly there is," replied Mr. Carrados. "Or at least there might be if you went down to Arling Lodge and insisted on seeing the child who slept there last night."

"Arling Lodge? Dr. Ellerslie's? You don't mean to say, sir—"

"That is for you to satisfy yourself. Dr. Ellerslie is a widower with no children. Marie Severe was drugged by phronolal on some flowers which she was given. Phronolal is a new anæsthetic which is practically unknown outside medical circles. She was carried into the garden of Arling Lodge and into the house. The bunch of flowers was thrown down temporarily inside the wall, probably while the door was relocked. The girl's hair caught on a raspberry cane six yards from the back door along the path leading there. Ellerslie had previously sent away the two people who look after the place – a housekeeper and her husband who sees to the garden. That letter, by the way, was associable with phronolal. Now you have all that I know, Inspector, and I hope to goodness that I am clear of it."

"But, good heavens, Mr. Carrados, this is really terrible!" protested Beedel, moved to emotion in spite of his rich experience of questionable humanity. "A man in his position! Is he a maniac?"

"I don't know. To tell you frankly, Inspector, I haven't gone an inch further than I was compelled to go in order to be sure. Make use of the information as you like, but I don't want to have anything more to do with the case. It isn't a pleasant thing to have pulled down a man like Ellerslie – a callous, exacting machine in the operating-room, one hears, but a man who was doing fine work – saving useful lives every day. I'm sick of it, Beedel, that's all."

"I understand, sir. Still, there's the other side, isn't there, after all? Of course I'll keep your name out of it as you wish, but I shall be given a good deal of credit that I oughtn't to accept. If you don't do anything for a few weeks the papers are always more complimentary when you do do it."

"I'm afraid that you will have to put up with that," replied Carrados dryly.

There was an acquiescent laugh from the other end and a reference to the speaker's indebtedness. Then: "Well, I'll get the necessary authority and go down at once, sir."

"Yes. Good-bye," said Carrados. He hung up the receiver with the only satisfaction that he had experienced since he had fixed on Ellerslie – satisfaction to have done with it. The thing was unpalatable enough in itself, and to add another element of distaste, through one or two circumstances that had come his way in the past, he had an actual regard for the surgeon whom some called brutal, but who was universally admitted to be splendidly efficient. It would have been a much more congenial business to the blind man to clear him than to implicate. He betook himself to a tray of Sicilian coins of the autonomous period to get the taste out of his mouth and swore that he would not read a word of any stage of the proceedings.

"A Mr. Severe wishes to see you, sir."

So it happened that about an hour after he had definitely shelved his interest in the case Max Carrados was again drawn into its complications. Had Severe been merely a well-to-do suppliant, perhaps . . . but the blind man had enough of the vagabond spirit to ensure his sympathy towards one whom he knew, on the contrary, to be extremely ill-to-do. In a flash of imagination he saw the out-cast walking from Red Lion Street to Richmond, and, denied admission, from Richmond back to Red Lion Street again, because he hadn't sixpence to squander, the man who always bought a little toy.

"It is nearly seven, isn't it. Parkinson? Mr. Severe will stay and dine with me," were almost the first words the visitor heard.

"Very well, sir."

"I? Dine?" interposed Severe quickly. "No, no. I really—"

"If you will be so good as to keep me company," said Carrados with suave determination. Parkinson retired, knowing that the thing was settled. "I am quite alone, Mr. Severe, and my selfishness takes that form. If a man calls on me about breakfast-time he must stay to breakfast, at lunch-time to lunch, and so on."

"Your friends, doubtless," suggested Severe with latent bitterness.

"Well, I am inclined to describe anyone who will lighten my darkness for an hour as a friend. You would yourself in the circumstances, you know." And then, quite unconsciously, under this treatment the years of degradation suddenly slipped from Severe and he found himself accepting the invitation in the conventional phrases and talking to his host just as though they were two men of the same world in the old times. Guessing what had brought him, and knowing that it mattered little or nothing then, Carrados kept his guest clear of the subject of the disappearance until they were alone again after dinner. Then, to be denied no longer, Severe tackled it with a blunt inquiry:

"Scotland Yard has been consulting you about Marie, Mr. Carrados?"

"Surely that is not in the papers?"

"I don't know," replied Severe, "but they aren't my authority. Among the people I have mostly to do with many shrewd bits of information circulate that never get into the Press. Sometimes they are mere bead-work, of course, but quite often they have ground. Just at present I am something of a celebrity in my usual haunts – I am 'Jones' in town, by the way, but my identity has come out – and everything to do with the notorious Severe affair comes round to me. I hear that Inspector Beedel, who has the case in hand, has just been to see you. Your co-operation is inferred."

"And if so?" queried Carrados.

"If so," continued his visitor, "I have a word to say. Beedel got it into his thick, unimaginative skull that I must be the kidnapper because, on the orthodox 'motive' lines, he couldn't fix on anyone else. As a matter of fact, Mr. Carrados, I have rather too much affection for my little daughter to have taken her out of a comfortable home. My unfortunate wife may have her faults – I don't mind admitting that she has – serious faults and a great many of them, but she would at least give Marie decent surroundings. When I heard of the child's disappearance – it was in the early evening papers the next morning – I was distracted. I dreaded every edition to see a placard announcing that the body had been found and to read the usual horrible details of insane or bestial outrage. I searched my pockets and found a shilling and a few coppers. Without any clear idea of what I expected to do, I tore off to the station and spent my money on a third single to Swanstead."

"Oh," interposed Carrados, "the 1.17 arrival?"

Severe laughed contemptuously.

"The station porter, you mean?" he said. "Yes; that bright youth merely predated his experience by twenty-four hours when he saw that there was bunce in it a few days later. Oh, I dare say he really thought it then. As for me, before I had got to Swanstead I had realized my mistake. What could I do in any case? Nothing that the least efficient local bobby could not do much better. Least of all did I wish to meet Ida – Mrs. Severe. No, I walked out of the station, turned to the right instead of the left and padded back to town."

"And you have come now, a fortnight or more after, to tell me this, Mr. Severe?"

"Well, I have come to have small hopes of Beedel. At first I didn't care two straws what they thought, expecting every hour to hear the worst. But that may not have happened. Two weeks have passed without anything being found, so that the child may be alive somewhere. If you are taking it up there is a chance – provided only that you don't let them obsess you with the idea that *I* have had anything to do with it."

"I don't imagine that you have had anything to do with it, Mr. Severe, and I believe that Marie is still alive."

"Thank God for that," said Severe with sudden intensity. "I am very, very glad to hear you express that opinion, Mr. Carrados. I don't suppose that I shall see much of the girl as time goes on or that she will be taught to regard the Fifth Commandment very seriously. All the same, the relief of hearing that makes me your debtor for ever. . . . Anxious as I am, I will be content with that. I won't worry you for your clues or your ideas . . . but I will tell you one thing. It may amuse you. *My* notion, a few days ago, of what might have happened—"

"Yes?" encouraged his host.

"It shows you the wild ideas one gets in such circumstances. My former wife is, if I may be permitted to say so, the most amiable and devoted creature in the world. Subject to that, I will readily concede that a more self-opinionated, credulous, dogmatically wrong-headed and crank-ridden woman does not exist. There isn't a silly fad that she hasn't taken up – and what's more tragic, absolutely believed in for the time – from ozonized milk to rhythmic yawning. Some time ago she was swept into Christian Science. An atrocious harpy called Julp – a professional 'healer' – fastened on her and has dominated her ever since. Well, fantastic as it seems now, I was actually prepared to believe that Marie had been ill and under their really sincere but grotesque 'healing' had died. Then to hide the failure of their creed or because they got panic-stricken—"

Then Carrados interrupted, an incivility he rarely committed.

"Yes, yes, I see," he said quickly. "But your daughter never is ill?"

"Never ill? Marie? Oh, isn't she! In the past six months I've—"

"But Mrs. Severe deliberately said – her words – that Marie 'does not know what illness means.'"

"That's their jargon. They hold that illness does not exist and so it has no meaning. But I should describe Marie as a delicate child on the whole – bilious attacks and so on."

"Christian Scientists . . . gastric trouble . . . Prescott Ellerslie? Good heavens! This comes of half doing a thing," muttered Carrados.

"Nothing wrong, I hope?" ventured the visitor.

"Wait." Severe wondered what the deuce turn the business was taking, but there being no incentive to do anything else, he waited. Coffee, rather more fragrant than that purveyed at the nocturnal stall, and fat Egyptian cigarettes of a subtle aroma somehow failed nevertheless to make the time pass quickly. Yet five minutes would have covered Carrados's absence.

"Nothing wrong, but an unfortunate oversight," he remarked when he returned. "I was too late to catch Beedel, so we must try to mend matters at the other end if we can. I shall have to ask you to go with me. I have ordered the car and I can tell you how we stand on the way."

"I shall be glad if you can make any use of me," said Severe.

"I hope that I may. And as for anything being wrong," added Carrados with deliberation, "so far as Marie is concerned I think we may find that the one thing necessary for her future welfare has been achieved."

"That's all I ask," said Severe.

"But it isn't all that I ask," retorted the blind man almost sharply.

This time there was nothing clandestine about the visit to Arling Avenue. On the contrary, the pace they kept up made it necessary that the horn should give pretty continuous notice of their presence. If it was a race, however, they had the satisfaction of being successful: the manner – more suggestive of the trained nurse than the domestic servant – of the maid who came to the door of Arling Lodge made it clear to Carrados, apart from any other indication, that the catastrophe of Beedel's arrival had not yet been launched. When the young person at the door began conscientiously, but with obvious inexperience, to prevaricate with the truth, the caller merely accepted her statements and wrote a few words on his card.

"When Dr. Ellerslie does return, will you please give him this at once," he said. "I will wait."

It is to be inferred that the great specialist's return had been providentially timed, for Carrados was scarcely seated when Prescott Ellerslie hurried into the room with the visiting-card in his hand.

"Mr. Carrados?" he postulated. "Will you please explain this rather unusually worded request for an interview?"

"Certainly I will," replied Carrados. "The wording is prompted by the necessity of compelling your immediate attention. The interview is the outcome of my desire to be of use to you."

"Thank you," said Ellerslie with non-committal courtesy. "And the occasion?"

"The occasion is the impending visit of Inspector Beedel from Scotland Yard, not, this time, to look out of your landing window, but to demand the surrender of the missing Marie Severe and, if you deny any knowledge of her, armed with authority to search your house."

"Oh," replied the doctor with astonishing composure. "And if the situation develops on the lines which you have so pointedly indicated, how do you propose to help me?"

"That depends a little on your explanation of the circumstances."

"Surely between Mr. Carrados and Scotland Yard there is nothing that remains to be explained!"

"Mr. Carrados can only speak for himself," replied the blind man with unmoved good humour. "And in his case there are several things to be explained. There is probably not a great deal of time before the inspector's arrival, but there may be enough if you are disposed—"

"Very well," acquiesced Ellerslie. "You are quite right in

assuming Marie Severe to be in this house. I had her brought here . . . out of revenge, to redress an old and very grievous injury. Perhaps you had guessed that?"

"Not in those terms," said Carrados mildly.

"Yet so it was. Ten years ago a very sweet and precious little child, my only daughter, was wantonly done to death by an ignorant and credulous woman who had charge of her, in the tenets of her faith. It is called Christian Science. The opportunity was put before me and to-day I stand convicted of having outraged every social and legal form by snatching Marie Severe from just that same fate."

Carrados nodded gravely.

"Yes," he assented. "That is the thing I missed."

"I used to see her on her way to school, whenever I was here," went on the doctor wistfully, "and soon I came to watch for her and to know the times at which she ought to pass. She was of all living creatures the gayest and the most vivid, glowing and vibrant with the compelling joy of life, a little being of wonderful grace, delicacy and charm. She had, I found when I came to know her somewhat, that distinction of manner which one is prone to associate unreasonably only with the children of the great and wealthy – a young nobility. In much she reminded me constantly of my own lost child; in other ways she attracted me by her diversity. Such, Mr. Carrados, was the nature of my interest in Marie Severe.

"I don't know the Severes and I have never even spoken to the mother. I believe that she has lived here only about a year, and in any case I have no concern in the social life of Swanstead. But a few months ago my worthy old housekeeper struck up an acquaintance with one of Mrs. Severe's servants, a staid, middle-aged person who had gone into the family as Marie's nurse. The friendship begun down our respective gardens – they adjoin – developed to the stage of these two dames taking tea occasionally with one another. My Mrs. Glass is a garrulous old woman. Hitherto my difficulty had often been to keep her quiet. Now I let her talk and deftly steered the conversation. I learned that my neighbours were Christian Scientists and had a so-called 'healer' living with them. The information struck me with a sudden dread.

" 'I suppose they are never ill, then?' I inquired carelessly.

"Mrs. Severe had not been ill since she had embraced Christian Science, and Miss Julp was described, in a phrase obviously of her own importing, as being 'all selvage.' The servants were allowed to see a doctor if they wished, although they were strongly pressed to have done with such 'trickery' in dispelling a mere 'illusion.'

" 'And isn't there a child?' I asked.

"Marie, it appeared, had from time to time suffered from the 'illusion' that she had not felt well – had suffered pain. Under Miss Julp's spiritual treatment the 'hallucination' had been dispelled. Mrs. Glass had laughed, looked very knowing and then given her friend away in her appreciation of the joke. The faithful nurse had accepted the situation, and as soon as her mistress's back was turned, had doctored Marie according to her own simple notions. Under this double influence the child had always picked up again, but the two women had ominously speculated what would happen if, she fell 'really ill.' I led her on to details of the sickness – their symptoms, frequency and so on. It was a congenial topic between the motherly old creature and the nurse and I could not have had a better medium. I learned a good deal from her chatter. It did not reassure me.

"From that time, without allowing my interest to appear, I sought better opportunities to see the child. I inspired Mrs. Glass to suggest to the nurse that Miss Marie might come and explore the garden here – it is a large and tangled place, such as an adventuring child would love to roam in, and this one, as I found, was passionately fond of flowers and growing things and birds and little animals. I got a pair of tame squirrels and turned them loose here. You can guess her enchantment when she discovered them. I went out with nuts for her to give them and we were friends at once. All the time I was examining her without her knowledge. I don't suppose it ever occurred to her that I might be a doctor. The result practically confirmed the growing suspicion that everything I had heard pointed to. And the tragic irony of the situation was that it had been appendicitis that my child – *my* child – had perished from!"

"Oh, so this was appendicitis, then?"

"Yes. It was appendicitis of that insidious and misleading

type to which children are particularly liable. These apparently negligible turns at intervals of weeks were really inflammation of the appendix and the condition was inevitably passing into one of general suppurative peritonitis. Very soon there would come another 'illusion' according to the mother and Miss Julp, another 'bilious turn' according to the nurse, similar to those already experienced, but apparently more obstinate. The Christian Scientists would argue with it, Hannah would surreptitiously dose it. This time, however, it would hang on. Still there would be no really very alarming symptoms to wring the natural affection of the mother, nothing severe enough to drive the nurse into mutiny. The pulse running at about a hundred and forty would be the last thing they would notice."

"And then?" Ellerslie was pacing the room in savage indignation, but Carrados had Beedel's impending visit continually before him.

"Then she would be dead. Quite suddenly and unceremoniously this fair young life, which in ten minutes I could render immune from this danger for all the future, would go clean out – extinguished to demonstrate that appendicitis does not exist and that Mind is All in All. If my diagnosis was correct there could be no appeal, no shockful realization of the true position to give the mother a chance. It would be inevitable, but it would be quite unlooked for.

"What was I to do, should you say, Mr. Carrados, in this emergency? I had dealt with these fanatics before and I knew that if I took so unusual a course as to go to Mrs. Severe I should at the best be met by polite incredulity and a text from Mrs. Mary Baker Eddy's immortal work. And by doing that I should have made any other line of action risky, if not impossible. You, I believe, are a humane man. What was I to do?"

"What you did do," said his visitor, "was about the most dangerous thing that a doctor could be mixed up in."

"Oh, no," replied Ellerslie, "he does a much more dangerous thing whenever he operates on a septiferous subject, whenever he enters a fever-stricken house. To career and reputation, you would say; but, believe me, Mr. Carrados, life is quite as important as livelihood, and every doctor does that sort of thing every day. Well, like many very ordinary men whom you may meet, I am something of a maniac and something of a mystic. Incredible as it will doubtless seem to the world tomorrow, I found that, at the risk of my professional career, at the risk, possibly, of a criminal conviction, the greatest thing that I should ever do would be to save this one exquisite young life. Elsewhere other men just as good could take my place, but here it was I and I alone."

"Well, you did it?" prompted Carrados. "I must remind you that the time presses and I want to know the facts."

"Yes, I did it. I won't delay with the precautions I had taken in securing the child or with the scheme that I had worked out for returning her. I believe that I had a very good chance of coming through undiscovered, and I infer that I have to thank you that I did not. Marie has not the slightest idea where she is, and when I go into the room I am sufficiently disguised. She thinks that she has had an accident."

"Of course you must have had assistance?"

"I have had the devoted help of an assistant and two nurses, but the whole responsibility is mine. I managed to send off Mrs. Glass and her husband for a holiday so as to keep them out of it. That was after I had decided upon the operation. To justify what I was about to do there had to be no mistake about the necessity. I contrived a final test.

"Less than three weeks ago I saw Hannah and the little girl come to the house one afternoon. Shortly afterward Mrs. Glass knocked at my door. Could she ask Hannah to tea and, as Mrs. Severe and her friend were staying out until late, might Miss Marie also stay? There was, as she knew, no need for her to ask me, but my housekeeper is primitive in her ideas of duty. Of course I readily assented, but I suggested that Marie should have tea with me; and so it was arranged.

"Before tea she amused herself about the garden. I told her to gather me a bunch of flowers and when she came in with them I noticed that she had scratched her arm with a thorn, I hurried through the meal, for I had then determined what to do. When we had finished, without ringing the bell, I gave her a chair in front of the fire and sat down opposite her. There was a true story about a clever goose that I had promised her.

" 'But you are going to sleep, Marie,' I said, looking at her fixedly. 'It is the heat of the fire.'

" 'I think I must be,' she admitted drowsily. 'Oh, how silly. I can scarcely keep my eyes open.'

" 'You are going to sleep,' I repeated. 'You are very, very tired.' I raised my hand and moved it slowly before her face. 'You can hardly see my hand now. Your eyes are closed. When I stop speaking you will be asleep.' I dropped my hand and she was fast asleep.

"I had made my arrangements and had everything ready. From her arm, where the puncture of the needle was masked by the scratch, I secured a few drops of blood. Then I applied a simple styptic to the place and verified by a more leisurely examination some of the symptoms I had already looked for. When I woke her, a few minutes later, she had no inkling of what had passed.

" 'Why,' I was saying as she awakened, 'I don't believe that you have heard a word about old Solomon.'

"I applied the various laboratory tests to the blood which I had obtained without delay. The result, taken in conjunction with the other symptoms, was conclusive. I was resolved upon my course from that moment. The operation itself was simple and completely successful. The condition demonstrated the pressing necessity for what I did. Marie Severe will probably outlive her mother now – especially if the lady remains faithful to Christian Science. As for the sequel . . . I am sorry, but I don't regret."

"A surprise, eh, Inspector?"

Inspector Beedel, accompanied by Mrs. Severe and – if the comparative degree may be used to indicate her relative importance – even more accompanied by Miss Julp, had arrived at Arling Lodge and been given immediate admission. It was Carrados who thus greeted him.

Beedel looked at his friend and then at Dr. Ellerslie. With unconscious habit he even noticed the proportions of the room, the position of the door and window, and the chief articles of furniture. His mind moved rather slowly, but always logically, and in cases where "sound intelligence" sufficed he was rarely unsuccessful. He had brought Mrs. Severe to identify Marie, whom he had never seen, and his men remained outside within whistle-call in case of any emergency. He now saw that he might have to shift his ground and he at once proceeded cautiously.

"Well, sir," he admitted, "I did not expect to see you here."

"Nor did I anticipate coming. Mrs. Severe" – he bowed to her – "I think that we have already met informally. Your friend, Miss Julp, unless I am mistaken? It is a good thing that we are all here."

"That is my name, sir," struck in the recalcitrant Cornelia, "but I am not aware—"

"At the gate early – very early – this morning, Miss Julp, I recognize your step. But accept my assurance, my dear lady" – for Miss Julp had given a start of maidenly confusion at the recollection – "that although I heard, I did *not* see you. Well, Inspector, I have since found that I misled you. The mistake was mine – a fundamental error. You were right. Mrs. Severe was right. Dr. Ellerslie is unassailably right. I speak for him because it was I who fastened an unsupportable motive on his actions. Marie Severe is in this house, but she was received here by Dr. Ellerslie in his professional capacity and strictly in the relation of doctor and patient. . . . Mr. Severe has at length admitted that he alone is to blame. You see, you were right after all."

"Arthur! Oh!" exclaimed Mrs. Severe, deeply moved.

"But why," demanded the other lady hostilely, "why should the man want her here?"

"Mr. Severe was apprehensive on account of his daughter's health," replied Carrados gravely. "His story is that, fearing something serious, he submitted her to this eminent specialist, who found a dangerous – a critical – condition that could only be removed by immediate operation. Dr. Ellerslie has saved your daughter's life, Mrs. Severe."

"Fiddlesticks!" shouted Miss Julp excitedly. "It's an outrage – a criminal outrage. An operation! There was no danger – there couldn't be with *me* at hand. You've done it this time, *Doctor* Ellerslie. My gosh, but this will be a case!"

Mrs. Severe sank into a chair, pale and trembling.

"I can scarcely believe it," she managed to say. "It is a crime.

Dr. Ellerslie – no doctor had the right. Mr. Severe has no authority whatever. The Court gave me sole control of Marie."

"Excuse me," put in Carrados with the blandness of perfect self-control and cognisance of his point, "excuse me, but have you ever informed Dr. Ellerslie of that ruling?"

"No," admitted Mrs. Severe with faint surprise. "No. Why should I?"

"Quite so. Why should you? But have you any knowledge that Dr. Ellerslie is acquainted with the details of your unhappy domestic differences?"

"I do not know at all. What do these things matter?"

"Only this: Why should Dr. Ellerslie question the authority of a parent who brings his child? It shows at least that he is the one who is concerned about her welfare. For all Dr. Ellerslie knew, you might be the unauthorized one, Mrs. Severe. A doctor can scarcely be expected to withhold a critical operation while he investigates the family affairs of his patients."

"But all this time – this dreadful suspense. He must have known."

Carrados shrugged his shoulders and seemed to glance across the room to where their host had so far stood immovable.

"I did know, Mrs. Severe. I could not help knowing. But I knew something else, and to a doctor the interests of his patient must overrule every ordinary consideration. Should the occasion arise, I shall be prepared at any time to justify my silence."

"Oh, the occasion will arise and pretty sharp, don't you fear," chimed in the irrepressible Miss Julp. "There's a sight more in this business, Ida, than we've got at yet. A mighty cute idea putting up Severe now. I never did believe that he was in it. He's a piece too mean-spirited to have the nerve. And where is Arthur Severe now? Gone, of course; quit the country and at someone else's expense."

"Not at all," said Carrados very obligingly. "Since you ask, Miss Julp" – he raised his voice – "Mr. Severe—"

The door opened and Severe strolled into the room with great sang-froid. He bowed distantly to his wife and nodded familiarly to the police official.

"Well, Inspector," he remarked. "you've cornered me at last, you see."

"I'm not so sure of that," retorted Beedel shortly.

"Oh, come now; you are too modest. My unconvincing alibi that you broke down. The printed letter so conclusively from my hand. And Grigson – your irrefutable, steadfast witness from the station here, Inspector. There's no getting round Grigson now, you know."

Beedel rubbed his chin helpfully but made no answer. Things seemed to have reached a momentary impasse.

"Perhaps we may at least all sit down," suggested Ellerslie, to break the silence. "There are rather a lot of us, but I think the chairs will go round."

"If I wasn't just dead tired I would sooner drop than sit down in the house of a man calling himself a doctor," declared Miss Julp. Then she sat down rather heavily. Sharp on the action came a piercing yell, a deep-wrung "Yag!" of pain and alarm, and the lady was seen bounding to her feet, to turn and look suspiciously at the place she had just vacated.

"It was a needle, Cornelia," said Mrs. Severe, who sat next to her. "See, here it is."

"Dear me, how unfortunate," exclaimed Ellerslie, following the action; "one of my surgical needles. I do hope that it has been properly sterilized since the last operation."

"What's that?" demanded Miss Julp sharply.

"Well," explained the doctor slowly, "I mean that there is such a thing as blood-poisoning. At least," he amended, "for me there is such a thing as blood-poisoning. For you, fortunately, it does not exist. Any more than pain does," he added thoughtfully.

"Do you mean," demanded Miss Julp with slow precision, "that through your carelessness, your criminal carelessness, I run any risk of blood-poisoning?"

"Cornelia!" exclaimed Mrs. Severe in pale incredulity.

"Of course not," retorted the surgeon. "How can you if such a thing does not exist?"

"I don't care whether it exists or not—"

"Cornelia" repeated her faithful disciple in horror.

"Be quiet, Ida. This is my business. It isn't like an ordinary illness. I've always had a horror of blood-poisoning. I have nightmares about it. My father died of it. He had to have glass tubes put in his veins, and the night he died— Oh, I tell you I can't stand the thought of it. There's nothing else I believe in, but blood-poisoning—" She shuddered. "I tell you, doctor," she declared with a sudden descent to the practical, "if I get laid up from this you'll have to stand the racket, and pretty considerable damages as well."

"But at the worst this is a very simple matter," protested Ellerslie. "If you will let me dress the place—"

Miss Julp went as red as a swarthy complexioned lady of forty-five could be expected to go.

"How can I let you dress the place?" she snapped. "It is—"

"Oh, Cornelia, Cornelia!" exclaimed Mrs. Severe reproachfully, through her disillusioned tears, "would you really be so false to the great principles which you have taught me?"

"I have a trained nurse here," suggested the doctor. "She would do it as well as I could."

"Are you really going?" demanded Mrs. Severe, for there was no doubt that Miss Julp was going, and going with alacrity.

"I don't abate one iota of my principles, Ida," she remarked. "But one has to discriminate. There are natural illnesses and there are unnatural illnesses. We say with truth that there can be no death, but no one will deny that Christian Scientists do, as a matter of fact, in the ordinary sense, die. Perhaps this is rather beyond you yet, dear, but I hope that some day you will see it in the light of its deeper mystery."

"Do you?" replied Mrs. Severe with cold disdain. "At present I only see that there is one law of indulgence for yourself and another for your dupes."

"After all," interposed Ellerslie, "this embarrassing discussion need never have arisen. I now see that the offending implement is only one of Mrs. Glass's darning-needles. How careless of her! You need have no fear, Miss Julp."

"Oh, you coward!" exclaimed Miss Julp breathlessly. "You coward! I won't stay here a moment longer. I will go home."

"I won't detain you," said Mrs. Severe as Cornelia passed her. "Your home is in Chicago, I believe? Ann will help you to pack."

Carrados rose and touched Beedel on the arm.

"You and I are not wanted here, Inspector," he whispered.

"The bottom's dropped out of the case," and they slipped away together.

Mrs. Severe looked across the room towards her late husband, hesitated and then slowly walked up to him.

"There is a great deal here that I do not understand," she said, "but is not this so, that you were willing to go to prison to shield this man who has been good to Marie?"

Severe flushed a little. Then he dropped his deliberate reply.

"I am willing to go to hell for this man for his goodness to Marie," he said curtly.

"Oh!" exclaimed Mrs. Severe with a little cry. "I wish – You never said that you would go to hell for me!"

The outcast stared. Then a curious look, a twisted smile of tenderness and half-mocking humour crossed his features.

"My dear," he responded gravely, "perhaps not. But I often thought it!"

Dr. Ellerslie, who had followed out the last two of his departing guests, looked in at the door.

"Marie is awake, I hear," he said. "Will you go up now, Mrs. Severe?"

With a shy smile the lady held out her hand towards the shabby man.

"You must go with me, Arthur," she stipulated.

The Lenton Croft Robberies

Arthur Morrison

Those who retain any memory of the great law cases of fifteen or twenty years back will remember, at least, the title of that extraordinary will case, "Bartley v. Bartley and others," which occupied the Probate Court for some weeks on end, and caused an amount of public interest rarely accorded to any but the cases considered in the other division of the same court. The case itself was noted for the large quantity of remarkable and unusual evidence presented by the plaintiff's side – evidence that took the other party completely by surprise, and overthrew their case like a house of cards. The affair will, perhaps, be more readily recalled as the occasion of the sudden rise to eminence in their profession of Messrs. Crellan, Hunt & Crellan, solicitors for the plaintiff – a result due entirely to the wonderful ability shown in this case of building up, apparently out of nothing, a smashing weight of irresistible evidence. That the firm has since maintained – indeed, enhanced – the position it then won for itself need scarcely be said here; its name is familiar to everybody. But there are not many of the outside public who know that the credit of the whole performance was primarily due to a young clerk in the employ of Messrs. Crellan who had been given charge of the seemingly desperate task of collecting evidence in the case.

This Mr. Martin Hewitt had, however, full credit and reward for his exploit from his firm and from their client, and more than one other firm of lawyers engaged in contentious work made good offers to entice Hewitt to change his employers. Instead of this, however, he determined to work independently for the future, having conceived the idea of making a regular business of doing, on behalf of such clients as might retain him, similar work to that he had just done with such conspicuous success for Messrs. Crellan, Hunt & Crellan. This was the beginning of the private detective business of Martin Hewitt, and his action at that time has been completely justified by the brilliant professional successes he has since achieved.

His business has always been conducted in the most private manner, and he has always declined the help of professional assistants, preferring to carry out himself such of the many investigations offered him as he could manage. He has always maintained that he has never lost by this policy, since the chance of his refusing a case begets competition for his services, and his fees rise by a natural process. At the same time, no man could know better how to employ casual assistance at the right time.

Some curiosity has been expressed as to Mr. Martin Hewitt's system, and, as he himself always consistently maintains that he has no system beyond a judicious use of ordinary faculties, I intend setting forth in detail a few of the more interesting of his cases in order that the public may judge for itself if I am right in estimating Mr. Hewitt's "ordinary faculties" as faculties very extraordinary indeed. He is not a man who has made many friendships (this, probably, for professional reasons), notwithstanding his genial and companionable manners. I myself first made his acquaintance as a result of an accident resulting in a fire at the old house in which Hewitt's office was situated, and in an upper floor of which I occupied bachelor chambers. I was able to help in saving a quantity of extremely important papers relating to his business, and, while repairs were being made, allowed him to lock them in an old wall-safe in one of my rooms which the fire had scarcely damaged.

The acquaintance thus begun has lasted many years, and has become a rather close friendship. I have even accompanied Hewitt on some of his expeditions, and, in a humble way, helped him. Such of the cases, however, as I personally saw nothing of I have put into narrative form from the particulars given me.

"I consider you, Brett," he said, addressing me, "the most remarkable journalist alive. Not because you're particularly clever, you know, because, between ourselves, I hope you'll admit you're not; but because you have known something of me and my doings for some years, and have never yet been guilty of giving away any of my little business secrets you may have become acquainted with. I'm afraid you're not so enterprising a journalist as some, Brett. But now, since you ask, you shall write something – if you think it worth while."

This he said, as he said most things, with a cheery, chaffing good-nature that would have been, perhaps, surprising to a stranger who thought of him only as a grim and mysterious discoverer of secrets and crimes. Indeed, the man had always as little of the aspect of the conventional detective as may be imagined. Nobody could appear more cordial or less observant in manner, although there was to be seen a certain sharpness of the eye – which might, after all, only be the twinkle of good-humor.

I *did* think it worth while to write something of Martin Hewitt's investigations, and a description of one of his adventures follows.

At the head of the first flight of a dingy staircase leading up from an ever-open portal in a street by the Strand stood a door, the dusty ground-glass upper panel of which carried in its center the single word "Hewitt," while at its right-hand lower corner, in smaller letters, "Clerk's Office" appeared. On a morning when the clerks in the ground-floor offices had barely hung up their hats, a short, well-dressed young man, wearing spectacles, hastening to open the dusty door, ran into the arms of another man who suddenly issued from it.

"I beg pardon," the first said. "Is this Hewitt's Detective Agency Office?"

"Yes, I believe you will find it so," the other replied. He was a stoutish, clean-shaven man, of middle height, and of a cheerful, round countenance. "You'd better speak to the clerk."

In the little outer office the visitor was met by a sharp lad with inky fingers, who presented him with a pen and a printed slip. The printed slip having been filled with the visitor's name and present business, and conveyed through an inner door, the lad reappeared with an invitation to the private office. There, behind a writing-table, sat the stoutish man himself, who had only just advised an appeal to the clerk.

"Good-morning, Mr. Lloyd – Mr. Vernon Lloyd," he said affably, looking again at the slip. "You'll excuse my care to start even with my visitors – I must, you know. You come from Sir James Norris, I see."

"Yes; I am his secretary. I have only to ask you to go straight to Lenton Croft at once, if you can, on very important business. Sir James would have wired, but had not your precise address. Can you go by the next train? Eleven-thirty is the first available from Paddington."

"Quite possibly. Do you know anything of the business?"

"It is a case of a robbery in the house, or, rather, I fancy, of several robberies. Jewelry has been stolen from rooms occupied by visitors to the Croft. The first case occurred some months ago – nearly a year ago, in fact. Last night there was another. But I think you had better get the details on the spot. Sir James has told me to telegraph if you are coming, so that he may meet you himself at the station; and I must hurry, as his drive to the station will be rather a long one. Then I take it you will go, Mr. Hewitt? Twyford is the station."

"Yes, I shall come, and by the 11:30. Are you going by that train yourself?"

"No, I have several things to attend to now I am in town. Good-morning; I shall wire at once."

Mr. Martin Hewitt locked the drawer of his table and sent his clerk for a cab.

At Twyford Station Sir James Norris was waiting with a dog-cart. Sir James was a tall, florid man of fifty or thereabout, known away from home as something of a county historian, and nearer his own parts as a great supporter of the hunt, and a gentleman much troubled with poachers. As soon as he and Hewitt had found one another the baronet hurried the detective into his dog-cart. "We've something over seven miles to drive," he said, "and I can tell you all about this wretched business as we go. That is why I came for you myself, and alone."

Hewitt nodded.

"I have sent for you, as Lloyd probably told you, because of a robbery at my place last evening. It appears, as far as I can guess, to be one of three by the same hand, or by the same gang. Late yesterday afternoon—"

"Pardon me, Sir James," Hewitt interrupted, "but I think I must ask you to begin at the first robbery and tell me the whole tale in proper order. It makes things clearer, and sets them in their proper shape."

"Very well! Eleven months ago, or thereabout, I had rather a large party of visitors, and among them Colonel Heath and Mrs. Heath – the lady being a relative of my own late wife. Colonel Heath has not been long retired, you know – used to be political resident in an Indian native state. Mrs. Heath had rather a good stock of jewelry of one sort and another, about the most valuable piece being a bracelet set with a particularly fine pearl – quite an exceptional pearl, in fact – that had been one of a heap of presents from the maharajah of his state when Heath left India.

"It was a very noticeable bracelet, the gold setting being a mere feather-weight piece of native filigree work – almost too fragile to trust on the wrist – and the pearl being, as I have said, of a size and quality not often seen. Well, Heath and his wife arrived late one evening, and after lunch the following day, most of the men being off by themselves – shooting, I think – my daughter, my sister (who is very often down here), and Mrs. Heath took it into their heads to go walking – fern-hunting, and so on. My sister was rather long dressing, and, while they waited, my daughter went into Mrs. Heath's room, where Mrs. Heath turned over all her treasures to show her, as women do, you know. When my sister was at last ready, they came straight away, leaving the things littering about the room rather than stay longer to pack them up. The bracelet, with other things, was on the dressing-table then."

"One moment. As to the door?"

"They locked it. As they came away my daughter suggested turning the key, as we had one or two new servants about."

"And the window?"

"That they left open, as I was going to tell you. Well, they went on their walk and came back, with Lloyd (whom they had met somewhere) carrying their ferns for them. It was dusk and almost dinner-time. Mrs. Heath went straight to her room, and – the bracelet was gone."

"Was the room disturbed?"

"Not a bit. Everything was precisely where it had been left, except the bracelet. The door hadn't been tampered with, but of course the window was open, as I have told you."

"You called the police, of course?"

"Yes, and had a man from Scotland Yard down in the morning. He seemed a pretty smart fellow, and the first thing he noticed on the dressing-table, within an inch or two of where the bracelet had been, was a match, which had been lit and thrown down. Now nobody about the house had had occasion to use a match in that room that day, and, if they had, certainly wouldn't have thrown it on the cover of the dressing-table. So that, presuming the thief to have used that match, the robbery must have been committed when the room was getting dark – immediately before Mrs. Heath returned, in fact. The thief had evidently struck the match, passed it hurriedly over the various trinkets lying about, and taken the most valuable."

"Nothing else was even moved?"

"Nothing at all. Then the thief must have escaped by the window, although it was not quite clear how. The walking party approached the house with a full view of the window, but saw nothing, although the robbery must have been actually taking place a moment or two before they turned up.

"There was no water-pipe within any practicable distance of the window, but a ladder usually kept in the stable-yard was found lying along the edge of the lawn. The gardener explained, however, that he had put the ladder there after using it himself early in the afternoon."

"Of course it might easily have been used again after that and put back."

"Just what the Scotland Yard man said. He was pretty sharp, too, on the gardener, but very soon decided that he knew nothing of it. No stranger had been seen in the neighborhood, nor had passed the lodge gates. Besides, as the detective said, it scarcely seemed the work of a stranger. A stranger could scarcely have known enough to go straight to the room where a lady – only arrived the day before – had left a valuable jewel, and away again without being seen. So all the people about the house were suspected in turn. The servants offered, in a body, to have their boxes searched, and this was done; everything was turned over, from the butler's to the new kitchen-maid's. I don't know that I should have had this carried quite so far if I had been the loser myself, but it was my guest, and I was in such a horrible position. Well, there's little more to be said about that, unfortunately. Nothing came of it all, and the thing's as great a mystery now as ever. I believed the Scotland Yard man got as far as suspecting *me* before he gave it up altogether, but give it up he did in the end. I think that's all I know about the first robbery. Is it clear?"

"Oh, yes; I shall probably want to ask a few questions when I have seen the place, but they can wait. What next?"

"Well," Sir James pursued, "the next was a very trumpery affair, that I should have forgotten all about, probably, if it hadn't been for one circumstance. Even now I hardly think it could have been the work of the same hand. Four months or thereabout after Mrs. Heath's disaster – in February of this year, in fact – Mrs. Armitage, a young widow, who had been a school-fellow of my daughter's, stayed with us for a week or so. The girls don't trouble about the London season, you know, and I have no town house, so they were glad to have their old friend here for a little in the dull time. Mrs. Armitage is a very active young lady, and was scarcely in the house half-an-hour before she arranged a drive in a pony-cart with Eva – my daughter – to look up old people in the village that she used to know before she was married. So they set off in the afternoon, and made such a round of it that they were late for dinner. Mrs. Armitage had a small plain gold brooch – not at all valuable, you know; two or three pounds, I suppose – which she used to pin up a cloak or anything of that sort. Before she went out she stuck this in the pin-cushion on her dressing-table, and left a ring – rather a good one, I believe – lying close by."

"This," asked Hewitt, "was not in the room that Mrs. Heath had occupied, I take it?"

"No; this was in another part of the building. Well, the brooch went – taken, evidently, by some one in a deuce of a hurry, for, when Mrs. Armitage got back to her room, there was the pin-cushion with a little tear in it, where the brooch had been simply snatched off. But the curious thing was that the ring – worth a dozen of the brooch – was left where it had been put. Mrs. Armitage didn't remember whether or not she had locked the door herself, although she found it locked when she returned; but my niece, who was indoors all the time, went and tried it once – because she remembered that a gas-fitter was at work on the landing near by – and found it safely locked. The gas-fitter, whom we didn't know at the time, but who since seems to be quite an honest fellow, was ready to swear that nobody but my niece had been to the door while he was in sight of it – which was almost all the time. As to the window, the sash-line had broken that very morning, and Mrs. Armitage had propped open the bottom half about eight or ten inches with a brush; and, when she returned, that brush, sash, and all were exactly as she had left them. Now I scarcely need tell *you* what an awkward job it must have been for anybody to get noiselessly in at that unsupported window; and how unlikely he would have been to replace it, with the brush, exactly as he found it."

"Just so. I suppose the brooch was really gone? I mean, there was no chance of Mrs. Armitage having mislaid it?"

"Oh, none at all! There was a most careful search."

"Then, as to getting in at the window, would it have been easy?"

"Well, yes," Sir James replied; "yes, perhaps it would. It is a first-floor window, and it looks over the roof and skylight of the billiard-room. I built the billiard-room myself – built it out from a smoking-room just at this corner. It would be easy enough to get at the window from the billiard-room roof. But, then," he added, "that couldn't have been the way. Somebody or other was in the billiard-room the whole time, and nobody could have got over the roof (which is nearly all skylight) without being seen and heard. I was there myself for an hour or two, taking a little practise."

"Well, was anything done?"

"Strict enquiry was made among the servants, of course, but nothing came of it. It was such a small matter that Mrs. Armitage wouldn't hear of my calling in the police or anything of that sort, although I felt pretty certain that there must be a dishonest servant about somewhere. A servant might take a plain brooch, you know, who would feel afraid of a valuable ring, the loss of which would be made a greater matter of."

"Well, yes, perhaps so, in the case of an inexperienced thief, who also would be likely to snatch up whatever she took in a hurry. But I'm doubtful. What made you connect these two robberies together?"

"Nothing whatever – for some months. They seemed quite of a different sort. But scarcely more than a month ago I met Mrs. Armitage at Brighton, and we talked, among other things, of the previous robbery – that of Mrs. Heath's bracelet. I described the circumstances pretty minutely, and, when I mentioned the match found on the table, she said: 'How strange! Why, *my* thief left a match on the dressing-table when he took my poor little brooch!'"

Hewitt nodded. "Yes," he said. "A spent match, of course?"

"Yes, of course, a spent match. She noticed it lying close by the pin-cushion, but threw it away without mentioning the circumstance. Still, it seemed rather curious to me that a match should be lit and dropped, in each case, on the dressing-cover an inch from where the article was taken. I mentioned it to Lloyd when I got back, and he agreed that it seemed significant."

"Scarcely," said Hewitt, shaking his head. "Scarcely, so far, to be called significant, although worth following up. Everybody uses matches in the dark, you know."

"Well, at any rate, the coincidence appealed to me so far that it struck me it might be worth while to describe the brooch to the police in order that they could trace it if it had been pawned. They had tried that, of course, over the bracelet without any result, but I fancied the shot might be worth making, and might possibly lead us on the track of the more serious robbery."

"Quite so. It was the right thing to do. Well?"

"Well, they found it. A woman had pawned it in London – at a shop in Chelsea. But that was sometime before, and the pawnbroker had clean forgotten all about the woman's appearance. The name and address she gave were false. So that was the end of that business."

"Had any of your servants left you between the time the brooch was lost and the date of the pawn ticket?"

"No."

"Were all your servants at home on the day the brooch was pawned?"

"Oh, yes! I made that enquiry myself."

"Very good! What next?"

"Yesterday – and this is what made me send for you. My late wife's sister came here last Tuesday, and we gave her the room from which Mrs. Heath lost her bracelet. She had with her a very old-fashioned brooch, containing a miniature of her father, and set in front with three very fine brilliants and a few smaller stones. Here we are, though, at the Croft. I'll tell you the rest indoors."

Hewitt laid his hand on the baronet's arm. "Don't pull up, Sir James," he said. "Drive a little further. I should like to have a general idea of the whole case before we go in."

"Very good!" Sir James Norris straightened the horse's head again and went on. "Late yesterday afternoon, as my sister-in-law was changing her dress, she left her room for a moment to speak to my daughter in her room, almost adjoining. She was gone no more than three minutes, or five at most, but on her return the brooch, which had been left on the table, had gone. Now the window was shut fast, and had not been tampered with. Of course the door was open, but so was my daughter's, and anybody walking near must have been heard. But the strangest circumstance, and one that almost makes me wonder whether I have been awake to-day or not, was that there lay *a used match* on the very spot, as nearly as possible, where the brooch had been – and it was broad daylight!"

Hewitt rubbed his nose and looked thoughtfully before him. "Um – curious, certainly," he said. "Anything else?"

"Nothing more than you shall see for yourself. I have had the room locked and watched till you could examine it. My sister-in-law had heard of your name, and suggested that you should be called in; so, of course, I did exactly as she wanted. That she should have lost that brooch, of all things, in my house is most unfortunate; you see, there was some small difference about the thing between my late wife and her sister when their mother died and left it. It's almost worse than the Heaths' bracelet business, and altogether I'm not pleased with things, I can assure you. See what a position it is for me! Here are three ladies, in the space of one year, robbed one after another in this mysterious fashion in my house, and I can't find the thief! It's horrible! People will be afraid to come near the place. And I can do nothing!"

"Ah, well, we'll see. Perhaps we had better turn back now. By-the-bye, were you thinking of having any alterations or additions made to your house?"

"No. What makes you ask?"

"I think you might at least consider the question of painting and decorating, Sir James – or, say, putting up another coach-house, or something. Because I should like to be (to the servants) the architect – or the builder, if you please – come to look around. You haven't told any of them about this business?"

"Not a word. Nobody knows but my relatives and Lloyd. I took every precaution myself, at once. As to your little disguise, be the architect by all means, and do as you please. If you can only find this thief and put an end to this horrible state of affairs, you'll do me the greatest service I've ever asked for – and as to your fee, I'll gladly make it whatever is usual, and three hundred in addition."

Martin Hewitt bowed. "You're very generous, Sir James, and you may be sure I'll do what I can. As a professional man, of course, a good fee always stimulates my interest, although this case of yours certainly seems interesting enough by itself."

"Most extraordinary! Don't you think so? Here are three persons, all ladies, all in my house, two even in the same room, each successively robbed of a piece of jewelry, each from a dressing-table, and a used match left behind in every case. All in the most difficult – one would say impossible – circumstances for a thief, and yet there is no clue!"

"Well, we won't say that just yet, Sir James; we must see. And we must guard against any undue predisposition to consider the robberies in a lump. Here we are at the lodge gate again. Is that your gardener – the man who left the ladder by the lawn on the first occasion you spoke of?" Mr. Hewitt nodded in the direction of a man who was clipping a box border.

"Yes; will you ask him anything?"

"No, no; at any rate, not now. Remember the building

alterations. I think, if there is no objection, I will look first at the room that the lady – Mrs.—'' Hewitt looked up enquiringly.

"My sister-in-law? Mrs. Cazenove. Oh, yes! you shall come to her room at once.''

"Thank you. And I think Mrs Cazenove had better be there.''

They alighted, and a boy from the lodge led the horse and dog-cart away.

Mrs. Cazenove was a thin and faded, but quick and energetic, lady of middle age. She bent her head very slightly on learning Martin Hewitt's name, and said: "I must thank you, Mr. Hewitt, for your very prompt attention. I need scarcely say that any help you can afford in tracing the thief who has my property – whoever it may be – will make me most grateful. My room is quite ready for you to examine.''

The room was on the second floor – the top floor at that part of the building. Some slight confusion of small articles of dress was observable in parts of the room.

"This, I take it,'' enquired Hewitt, "is exactly as it was at the time the brooch was missed?''

"Precisely,'' Mrs. Cazenove answered. "I have used another room, and put myself to some other inconveniences, to avoid any disturbance.''

Hewitt stood before the dressing-table. "Then this is the used match,'' he observed, "exactly where it was found?''

"Yes.''

"Where was the brooch?''

"I should say almost on the very same spot. Certainly no more than a very few inches away.''

Hewitt examined the match closely. "It is burned very little,'' he remarked. "It would appear to have gone out at once. Could you hear it struck?''

"I heard nothing whatever; absolutely nothing.''

"If you will step into Miss Norris's room now for a moment,'' Hewitt suggested, "we will try an experiment. Tell me if you hear matches struck, and how many. Where is the match-stand?''

The match-stand proved to be empty, but matches were found in Miss Norris's room, and the test was made. Each striking could be heard distinctly, even with one of the doors pushed to.

"Both your own door and Miss Norris's were open, I understand; the window shut and fastened inside as it is now, and nothing but the brooch was disturbed?"

"Yes, that was so."

"Thank you, Mrs. Cazenove. I don't think I need trouble you further just at present. I think, Sir James," Hewitt added, turning to the baronet, who was standing by the door – "I think we will see the other room and take a walk outside the house, if you please. I suppose, by-the-bye, that there is no getting at the matches left behind on the first and second occasions?"

"No," Sir James answered. "Certainly not here. The Scotland Yard man may have kept his."

The room that Mrs. Armitage had occupied presented no peculiar feature. A few feet below the window the roof of the billiard-room was visible, consisting largely of skylight. Hewitt glanced casually about the walls, ascertained that the furniture and hangings had not been materially changed since the second robbery, and expressed his desire to see the windows from the outside. Before leaving the room, however, he wished to know the names of any persons who were known to have been about the house on the occasions of all three robberies.

"Just carry your mind back, Sir James," he said. "Begin with yourself, for instance. Where were you at these times?"

"When Mrs. Heath lost her bracelet, I was in Tagley Wood all the afternoon. When Mrs. Armitage was robbed, I believe I was somewhere about the place most of the time she was out. Yesterday I was down at the farm." Sir James's face broadened. "I don't know whether you call those suspicious movements," he added, and laughed.

"Not at all; I only asked you so that, remembering your own movements, you might the better recall those of the rest of the household. Was anybody, to your knowledge – *anybody*, mind – in the house on all three occasions?"

"Well, you know, it's quite impossible to answer for all the servants. You'll only get that by direct questioning – I can't possibly remember things of that sort. As to the family and visitors – why, you don't suspect any of them, do you?"

"I don't suspect a soul, Sir James," Hewitt answered, beaming genially, "not a soul. You see, I *can't* suspect people till I know something about where they were. It's quite possible there will be independent evidence enough as it is, but you must help me if you can. The visitors, now. Was there any visitor here each time – or even on the first and last occasions only?"

"No, not one. And my own sister, perhaps you will be pleased to know, was only there at the time of the first robbery."

"Just so! And your daughter, as I have gathered, was clearly absent from the spot each time – indeed, was in company with the party robbed. Your niece, now?"

"Why, hang it all, Mr. Hewitt, I can't talk of my niece as a suspected criminal! The poor girl's under my protection, and I really can't allow—"

Hewitt raised his hand and shook his head deprecatingly.

"My dear sir, haven't I said that I don't suspect a soul? *Do* let me know how the people were distributed, as nearly as possible. Let me see. It was your niece, I think, who found that Mrs. Armitage's door was locked – this door, in fact – on the day she lost her brooch?"

"Yes, it was."

"Just so – at the time when Mrs. Armitage herself had forgotten whether she locked it or not. And yesterday – was she out then?"

"No, I think not. Indeed, she goes out very little – her health is usually bad. She was indoors, too, at the time of the Heath robbery, since you ask. But come, now, I don't like this. It's ridiculous to suppose that *she* knows anything of it."

"I don't suppose it, as I have said. I am only asking for information. That is all your resident family, I take it, and you know nothing of anybody else's movements – except, perhaps, Mr. Lloyd's?"

"Lloyd? Well, you know yourself that he was out with the ladies when the first robbery took place. As to the others, I don't remember. Yesterday he was probably in his room, writing. I think that acquits *him*, eh?" Sir James looked quizzically into the broad face of the affable detective, who smiled and replied:

"Oh, of course nobody can be in two places at once, else what would become of the *alibi* as an institution? But, as I have said, I am only setting my facts in order. Now, you see, we get down to the servants – unless some stranger is the party wanted. Shall we go outside now?"

Lenton Croft was a large, desultory sort of house, nowhere more than three floors high, and mostly only two. It had been added to bit by bit, till it zig-zagged about its site, as Sir James Norris expressed it, "like a game of dominoes." Hewitt scrutinized its external features carefully as they strolled round, and stopped some little while before the windows of the two bedrooms he had just seen from the inside. Presently they approached the stables and coach-house, where a groom was washing the wheels of the dog-cart.

"Do you mind my smoking?" Hewitt asked Sir James. "Perhaps you will take a cigar yourself – they are not so bad, I think. I will ask your man for a light."

Sir James felt for his own match-box, but Hewitt had gone, and was lighting his cigar with a match from a box handed him by the groom. A smart little terrier was trotting about by the coach-house, and Hewitt stopped to rub its head. Then he made some observation about the dog which enlisted the groom's interest, and was soon absorbed in a chat with the man. Sir James, waiting a little way off, tapped the stones rather impatiently with his foot, and presently moved away.

For full a quarter of an hour Hewitt chatted with the groom, and, when at last he came away and overtook Sir James, that gentleman was about reentering the house.

"I beg your pardon, Sir James," Hewitt said, "for leaving you in that unceremonious fashion to talk to your groom, but a dog, Sir James – a good dog – will draw me anywhere."

"Oh!" replied Sir James shortly.

"There is one other thing," Hewitt went on, disregarding the other's curtness, "that I should like to know: There are two windows directly below that of the room occupied yesterday by Mrs. Cazenove – one on each floor. What rooms do they light?"

"That on the ground floor is the morning-room; the other is Mr. Lloyd's – my secretary. A sort of study or sitting-room."

"Now you will see at once, Sir James," Hewitt pursued, with an affable determination to win the baronet back to good-humor – "you will see at once that, if a ladder had been used in Mrs.

Heath's case, anybody looking from either of these rooms would have seen it."

"Of course! The Scotland Yard man questioned everybody as to that, but nobody seemed to have been in either of the rooms when the thing occurred; at any rate, nobody saw anything."

"Still, I think I should like to look out of those windows myself; it will, at least, give me an idea of what *was* in view and what was not, if anybody had been there."

Sir James Norris led the way to the morning-room. As they reached the door a young lady, carrying a book and walking very languidly, came out. Hewitt stepped aside to let her pass, and afterward said interrogatively: "Miss Norris, your daughter, Sir John?"

"No, my niece. Do you want to ask her anything? Dora, my dear," Sir James added, following her in the corridor, "this is Mr. Hewitt, who is investigating these wretched robberies for me. I think he would like to hear if you remember anything happening at any of the three times."

The lady bowed slightly, and said in a plaintive drawl: "I, uncle? Really, I don't remember anything; nothing at all."

"You found Mrs. Armitage's door locked, I believe," asked Hewitt, "when you tried it, on the afternoon when she lost her brooch?"

"Oh, yes; I believe it was locked. Yes, it was."

"Had the key been left in?"

"The key? Oh, no! I think not; no."

"Do you remember anything out of the common happening – anything whatever, no matter how trivial – on the day Mrs. Heath lost her bracelet?"

"No, really, I don't. I can't remember at all."

"Nor yesterday?"

"No, nothing. I don't remember anything."

"Thank you," said Hewitt hastily; "thank you. Now the morning-room, Sir James."

In the morning-room Hewitt stayed but a few seconds, doing little more than casually glance out of the windows. In the room above he took a little longer time. It was a comfortable room, but with rather effeminate indications about its contents. Little pieces of draped silk-work hung about the furniture, and Japanese silk fans decorated the mantel-piece. Near the window was a cage containing a gray parrot, and the writing-table was decorated with two vases of flowers.

"Lloyd makes himself pretty comfortable, eh?" Sir James observed. "But it isn't likely anybody would be here while he was out, at the time that bracelet went."

"No," replied Hewitt meditatively. "No, I suppose not."

He stared thoughtfully out of the window, and then, still deep in thought, rattled at the wires of the cage with a quill tooth-pick and played a moment with the parrot. Then, looking up at the window again, he said: "That is Mr. Lloyd, isn't it, coming back in a fly?"

"Yes, I think so. Is there anything else you would care to see here?"

"No, thank you," Hewitt replied; "I don't think there is."

They went down to the smoking-room, and Sir James went away to speak to his secretary. When he returned, Hewitt said quietly: "I think, Sir James – I *think* that I shall be able to give you your thief presently."

"What! Have you a clue? Who do you think? I began to believe you were hopelessly stumped."

"Well, yes. I have rather a good clue, although I can't tell you much about it just yet. But it is so good a clue that I should like to know now whether you are determined to prosecute when you have the criminal?"

"Why, bless me, of course," Sir James replied with surprise. "It doesn't rest with me, you know – the property belongs to my friends. And even if *they* were disposed to let the thing slide, I shouldn't allow it – I couldn't, after they had been robbed in my house."

"Of course, of course! Then, if I can, I should like to send a message to Twyford by somebody perfectly trustworthy – not a servant. Could anybody go?"

"Well, there's Lloyd, although he's only just back from his journey. But, if it's important, he'll go."

"It is important. The fact is we must have a policeman or two here this evening, and I'd like Mr. Lloyd to fetch them without telling anybody else."

Sir James rang, and, in response to his message, Mr. Lloyd appeared. While Sir James gave his secretary his instructions, Hewitt strolled to the door of the smoking-room, and intercepted the latter as he came out.

"I'm sorry to give you this trouble, Mr. Lloyd," he said, "but I must stay here myself for a little, and somebody who can be trusted must go. Will you just bring back a police-constable with you? or rather two – two would be better. That is all that is wanted. You won't let the servants know, will you? Of course there will be a female searcher at the Twyford police-station? Ah – of course. Well, you needn't bring her, you know. That sort of thing is done at the station." And, chatting thus confidentially, Martin Hewitt saw him off.

When Hewitt returned to the smoking-room, Sir James said suddenly: "Why, bless my soul, Mr. Hewitt, we haven't fed you! I'm awfully sorry. We came in rather late for lunch, you know, and this business has bothered me so I clean forgot everything else. There's no dinner till seven, so you'd better let me give you something now. I'm really sorry. Come along."

"Thank you, Sir James," Hewitt replied; "I won't take much. A few biscuits, perhaps, or something of that sort. And, by-the-bye, if you don't mind, I rather think I should like to take it alone. The fact is I want to go over this case thoroughly by myself. Can you put me in a room?"

"Any room you like. Where will you go? The dining-room's rather large, but there's my study, that's pretty snug, or—"

"Perhaps I can go into Mr. Lloyd's room for half-an-hour or so; I don't think he'll mind, and it's pretty comfortable."

"Certainly, if you'd like. I'll tell them to send you whatever they've got."

"Thank you very much. Perhaps they'll also send me a lump of sugar and a walnut; it's – it's just a little fad of mine."

"A – what? A lump of sugar and a walnut?" Sir James stopped for a moment, with his hand on the bellrope. "Oh, certainly, if you'd like it; certainly," he added, and stared after this detective of curious tastes as he left the room.

When the vehicle bringing back the secretary and the policemen drew up on the drive, Martin Hewitt left the room on the first floor and proceeded downstairs. On the landing he met Sir

James Norris and Mrs. Cazenove, who stared with astonishment on perceiving that the detective carried in his hand the parrot-cage.

"I think our business is about brought to a head now," Hewitt remarked on the stairs. "Here are the police-officers from Twyford." The men were standing in the hall with Mr. Lloyd, who, catching sight of the cage in Hewitt's hand, paled suddenly.

"This is the person who will be charged, I think," Hewitt pursued, addressing the officers, and indicating Lloyd with his finger.

"What, Lloyd?" gasped Sir James, aghast. "No – not Lloyd – nonsense!"

"He doesn't seem to think it nonsense himself, does he?" Hewitt placidly observed. Lloyd had sunk on a chair, and, gray of face, was staring blindly at the man he had run against at the office door that morning. His lips moved in spasms, but there was no sound. The wilted flower fell from his button-hole to the floor, but he did not move.

"This is his accomplice," Hewitt went on, placing the parrot and cage on the hall table, "though I doubt whether there will be any use in charging *him*. Eh, Polly?"

The parrot put his head aside and chuckled. "Hullo, Polly!" it quietly gurgled. "Come along!"

Sir James Norris was hopelessly bewildered. "Lloyd – Lloyd," he said, under his breath, "Lloyd – and that!"

"This was his little messenger, his useful Mercury," Hewitt explained, tapping the cage complacently; "in fact, the actual lifter. Hold him up!"

The last remark referred to the wretched Lloyd, who had fallen forward with something between a sob and a loud sigh. The policemen took him by the arms and propped him in his chair.

"System?" said Hewitt, with a shrug of the shoulders, an hour or two after in Sir James's study. "I can't say I have a system. I call it nothing but common-sense and a sharp pair of eyes. Nobody using these could help taking the right road in this case. I began at the match, just as the Scotland Yard man did, but I had the advantage of taking a line through three cases. To begin with, it was plain that that match, being left there in daylight, in Mrs. Cazenove's room, could not have been used to light the table-top, in the full glare of the window; therefore it had been used for some other purpose – *what* purpose I could not, at the moment, guess. Habitual thieves, you know, often have curious superstitions, and some will never take anything without leaving something behind – a pebble or a piece of coal, or something like that – in the premises they have been robbing. It seemed at first extremely likely that this was a case of that kind. The match had clearly been *brought in* – because, when I asked for matches, there were none in the stand, not even an empty box, and the room had not been disturbed. Also the match probably had not been struck there, nothing having been heard, although, of course, a mistake in this matter was just possible. This match, then, it was fair to assume, had been lit somewhere else and blown out immediately – I remarked at the time that it was very little burned. Plainly it could not have been treated thus for nothing, and the only possible object would have been to prevent it igniting accidentally. Following on this, it became obvious that the match was used, for whatever purpose, not *as* a match, but merely as a convenient splinter of wood.

"So far so good. But on examining the match very closely I observed, as you can see for yourself, certain rather sharp indentations in the wood. They are very small, you see, and scarcely visible, except upon narrow inspection; but there they are, and their positions are regular. See – there are two on each side, each opposite the corresponding mark of the other pair. The match, in fact, would seem to have been gripped in some fairly sharp instrument, holding it at two points above and two below – an instrument, holding as it may at once strike you, not unlike the beak of a bird.

"Now here was an idea. What living creature but a bird could possibly have entered Mrs. Heath's window without a ladder – supposing no ladder to have been used – or could have got into Mrs. Armitage's window without lifting the sash higher than the eight or ten inches it was already open? Plainly, nothing. Further, it is significant that only *one* article was stolen at a time, although others were about. A human being could have carried any reasonable number, but a bird could only take one at a time. But why should a bird carry a match in its beak? Certainly it must have been trained to do that for a purpose, and a little consideration made that purpose pretty clear. A noisy, chattering bird would probably betray itself at once. Therefore it must be trained to keep quiet both while going for and coming away with its plunder. What readier or more probably effectual way then, while teaching it to carry without dropping, to teach it also to keep quiet while carrying? The one thing would practically cover the other.

"I thought at once, of course, of a jackdaw or a magpie – these birds' thievish reputations made the guess natural. But the marks on the match were much too wide apart to have been made by the beak of either. I conjectured, therefore, that it must be a raven. So that, when we arrived near the coach-house, I seized the opportunity of a little chat with your groom on the subject of dogs and pets in general, and ascertained that there was no tame raven in the place. I also, incidentally, by getting a light from the coach-house box of matches, ascertained that the match found was of the sort generally used about the establishment – the large, thick, red-topped English match. But I further found that Mr. Lloyd had a parrot which was a most intelligent pet, and had been trained into comparative quietness – for a parrot. Also, I learned that more than once the groom had met Mr. Lloyd carrying his parrot under his coat, it having, as its owner explained, learned the trick of opening its cage-door and escaping.

"I said nothing, of course, to you of all this, because I had as yet nothing but a train of argument and no results. I got to Lloyd's rooms as soon as possible. My chief object in going there was achieved when I played with the parrot, and induced it to bite a quill tooth-pick.

"When you left me in the smoking-room, I compared the quill and the match very carefully, and found that the marks corresponded exactly. After this I felt very little doubt indeed. The fact of Lloyd having met the ladies walking before dark on the day of the first robbery proved nothing, because, since it was clear that the match had *not* been used to procure a light, the robbery might as easily have taken place in daylight as not –

must have so taken place, in fact, if my conjectures were right. That they were right I felt no doubt. There could be no other explanation.

"When Mrs. Heath left her window open and her door shut, anybody climbing upon the open sash of Lloyd's high window could have put the bird upon the sill above. The match placed in the bird's beak for the purpose I have indicated, and struck first, in case by accident it should ignite by rubbing against something and startle the bird – this match would, of course, be dropped just where the object to be removed was taken up; as you know, in every case the match was found almost upon the spot where the missing article had been left – scarcely a likely triple coincidence had the match been used by a human thief. This would have been done as soon after the ladies had left as possible, and there would then have been plenty of time for Lloyd to hurry out and meet them before dark – especially plenty of time to meet them *coming back*, as they must have been, since they were carrying their ferns. The match was an article well chosen for its purpose, as being a not altogether unlikely thing to find on a dressing-table, and, if noticed, likely to lead to the wrong conclusions adopted by the official detective.

"In Mrs. Armitage's case the taking of an inferior brooch and the leaving of a more valuable ring pointed clearly either to the operator being a fool or unable to distinguish values, and certainly, from other indications, the thief seemed no fool. The door was locked, and the gas-fitter, so to speak, on guard, and the window was only eight or ten inches open and propped with a brush. A human thief entering the window would have disturbed this arrangement, and would scarcely risk discovery by attempting to replace it, especially a thief in so great a hurry as to snatch the brooch up without unfastening the pin. The bird could pass through the opening as it was and *would have* to tear the pin cushion to pull the brooch off, probably holding the cushion down with its claw the while.

"Now in yesterday's case we had an alteration of conditions. The window was shut and fastened, but the door was open – but only left for a few minutes, during which time no sound was heard either of coming or going. Was it not possible, then, that the thief was *already* in the room, in hiding, while Mrs. Cazenove was there, and seized its first opportunity on her temporary absence? The room is full of draperies, hangings, and what-not, allowing of plenty of concealment for a bird and a bird could leave the place noiselessly and quickly. That the whole scheme was strange mattered not at all. Robberies presenting such unaccountable features must have been effected by strange means of one sort or another. There was no improbability – consider how many hundreds of examples of infinitely higher degrees of bird-training are exhibited in the London streets every week for coppers.

"So that, on the whole, I felt pretty sure of my ground. But before taking any definite steps. I resolved to see if Polly could not be persuaded to exhibit his accomplishments to an indulgent stranger. For that purpose I contrived to send Lloyd away again and have a quiet hour alone with his bird. A piece of sugar, as everybody knows, is a good parrot bribe; but a walnut, split in half, is a better – especially if the bird be used to it; so I got you to furnish me with both. Polly was shy at first, but I generally get along very well with pets, and a little perseverance soon led to a complete private performance for my benefit. Polly would take the match, mute as wax, jump on the table, pick up the brightest thing he could see, in a great hurry, leave the match behind and scuttle away round the room; but at first wouldn't give up the plunder to *me*. It was enough. I also took the liberty, as you know, of a general look round, and discovered that little collection of Brummagem rings and trinkets that you have just seen – used in Polly's education, no doubt. When we sent Lloyd away, it struck me that he might as well be usefully employed as not, so I got him to fetch the police, deluding him a little, I fear, by talking about the servants and a female searcher. There will be no trouble about evidence; he'll confess: of that I'm sure. I know the sort of man. But I doubt if you'll get Mrs. Cazenove's brooch back. You see, he has been to London to-day, and by this time the swag is probably broken up."

Sir James listened to Hewitt's explanation with many expressions of assent and some of surprise. When it was over, he smoked a few whiffs and then said: "But Mrs. Armitage's brooch was pawned, and by a woman."

"Exactly. I expect our friend Lloyd was rather disgusted at his small luck – probably gave the brooch to some female connection in London, and she realized on it. Such persons don't always trouble to give a correct address."

The two smoked in silence for a few minutes, and then Hewitt continued: "I don't expect our friend has had an easy job altogether with that bird. His successes at most have only been three, and I suspect he had many failures and not a few anxious moments that we know nothing of. I should judge as much merely from what the groom told me of frequently meeting Lloyd with his parrot. But the plan was not a bad one – not at all. Even if the bird had been caught in the act, it would only have been 'That mischievous parrot!' you see. And his master would only have been looking for him."

The Adventure of
the Three Students

Sir Arthur Conan Doyle

I t was in the year '95 that a combination of events, into which I need not enter, caused Mr. Sherlock Holmes and myself to spend some weeks in one of our great University towns, and it was during this time that the small but instructive adventure which I am about to relate befell us. It will be obvious that any details which would help the reader to exactly identify the college or the criminal would be injudicious and offensive. So painful a scandal may well be allowed to die out. With due discretion the incident itself may, however, be described, since it serves to illustrate some of those qualities for which my friend was remarkable. I will endeavour in my statement to avoid such terms as would serve to limit the events to any particular place, or give a clue as to the people concerned.

We were residing at the time in furnished lodgings close to a library where Sherlock Holmes was pursuing some laborious researches in Early English charters – researches which led to results so striking that they may be the subject of one of my future narratives. Here it was that one evening we received a visit from an acquaintance, Mr. Hilton Soames, tutor and lecturer at the College of St. Luke's. Mr. Soames was a tall, spare man, of a nervous and excitable temperament. I had always known him to be restless in his manner, but on this particular occasion he was in such a state of uncontrollable agitation that it was clear something very unusual had occurred.

"I trust Mr. Holmes, that you can spare me a few hours of your valuable time. We have had a very painful incident at St.

Luke's, and really, but for the happy chance of your being in the town, I should have been at a loss what to do."

"I am very busy just now, and I desire no distractions," my friend answered. "I should much prefer that you called in the aid of the police."

"No, no, my dear sir; such a course is utterly impossible. When once the law is evoked it cannot be stayed again, and this is just one of those cases where, for the credit of the college, it is most essential to avoid scandal. Your discretion is as well known as your powers, and you are the one man in the world who can help me. I beg you, Mr. Holmes, to do what you can."

Mr friend's temper had not improved since he had been deprived of the congenial surroundings of Baker Street. Without his scrapbooks, his chemicals, and his homely untidiness, he was an uncomfortable man. He shrugged his shoulders in ungracious acquiescence, while our visitor in hurried words and with much excitable gesticulation poured forth his story.

"I must explain to you, Mr. Holmes, that to-morrow is the first day of the examination for the Fortescue Scholarship. I am one of the examiners. My subject is Greek, and the first of the papers consists of a large passage of Greek translation which the candidate has not seen. This passage is printed on the examination paper, and it would naturally be an immense advantage if the candidate could prepare it in advance. For this reason great care is taken to keep the paper secret.

"To-day about three o'clock the proofs of this paper arrived from the printers. The exercise consists of half a chapter of Thucydides. I had to read it over carefully, as the text must be absolutely correct. At four-thirty my task was not yet completed. I had, however, promised to take tea in a friend's rooms, so I left the proof upon my desk. I was absent rather more than an hour. You are aware, Mr. Holmes, that our college doors are double – a green baize one within and a heavy oak one without. As I approached my outer door I was amazed to see a key in it. For an instant I imagined that I had left my own there, but on feeling in my pocket I found that it was all right. The only duplicate which existed, so far as I knew, was that which belonged to my servant, Bannister, a man who has looked after my room for ten years, and whose honesty is absolutely above suspicion. I found that the key was indeed his, that he had entered my room to know if I wanted tea, and that he had very carelessly left the key in the door when he came out. His visit to my room must have been within a very few minutes of my leaving it. His forgetfulness about the key would have mattered little upon any other occasion, but on this one day it has produced the most deplorable consequences.

"The moment I looked at my table I was aware that some one had rummaged among my papers. The proof was in three long slips. I had left them all together. Now I found that one of them was lying on the floor, one was on the side table near the window, and the third was where I had left it."

Holmes stirred for the first time.

"The first page on the floor, the second in the window, and the third where you left it," said he.

"Exactly, Mr. Holmes. You amaze me. How could you possibly know that?"

"Pray continue your very interesting statement."

"For an instant I imagined that Bannister had taken the unpardonable liberty of examining my papers. He denied it, however, with the utmost earnestness, and I am convinced that he was speaking the truth. The alternative was that someone passing had observed the key in the door, had known that I was out, and had entered to look at the papers. A large sum of money is at stake, for the scholarship is a very valuable one, and an unscrupulous man might very well run a risk in order to gain advantage over his fellows.

"Bannister was very much upset by the incident. He had nearly fainted when we found that the papers had undoubtedly been tampered with. I gave him a little brandy, and left him collapsed in a chair while I made a most careful examination of the room. I soon saw that the intruder had left other traces of his presence besides the rumpled papers. On the table in the window were several shreds from a pencil which had been sharpened. A broken tip of lead was lying there also. Evidently the rascal had copied the paper in a great hurry, had broken his pencil, and had been compelled to put a fresh point to it."

"Excellent!" said Holmes, who was recovering his good

humour as his attention became more engrossed by the case. "Fortune has been your friend."

"This was not all. I have a new writing-table with a fine surface of red leather. I am prepared to swear, and so is Bannister, that it was smooth and unstained. Now I found a clean cut in it about three inches long – not a mere scratch, but a positive cut. Not only this, but on the table I found a small ball of black dough, or clay, with specks of something which looks like sawdust in it. I am convinced that these marks were left by the man who rifled the papers. There were no footmarks and no other evidence as to his identity. I was at my wits' end, when suddenly the happy thought occurred to me that you were in the town, and I came straight round to put the matter into your hands. Do help me, Mr. Holmes! You see my dilemma. Either I must find the man, or else the examination must be postponed until fresh papers are prepared, and since this cannot be done without explanation, there will ensue a hideous scandal, which will throw a cloud not only on the college but on the University. Above all things, I desire to settle the matter quietly and discreetly."

"I shall be happy to look into it and to give you such advice as I can," said Holmes, rising and putting on his overcoat. "This case is not entirely devoid of interest. Had any one visited you in your room after the papers came to you?"

"Yes; young Daulat Ras, an Indian student who lives on the same stair, came in to ask me some particulars about the examination."

"For which he was entered?"

"Yes."

"And the papers were on your table?"

"To the best of my belief they were rolled up."

"But might be recognised as proofs?"

"Possibly."

"No one else in your room?"

"No."

"Did anyone know that these proofs would be there?"

"No one save the printer."

"Did this man Bannister know?"

"No, certainly not. No one knew."

"Where is Bannister now?"

"He was very ill, poor fellow! I left him collapsed in the chair. I was in such a hurry to come to you."

"You left your door open?"

"I locked the papers up first."

"Then it amounts to this, Mr. Soames, that unless the Indian student recognised the roll as being proofs, the man who tampered with them came upon them accidentally without knowing that they were there."

"So it seems to me."

Holmes gave an enigmatic smile.

"Well," said he, "let us go round. Not one of your cases, Watson – mental, not physical. All right; come if you want to. Now, Mr. Soames – at your disposal!"

The sitting-room of our client opened by a long, low, latticed window on to the ancient lichen-tinted court of the old college. A Gothic arched door led to a worn stone staircase. On the ground floor was the tutor's room. Above were three students, one on each storey. It was already twilight when we reached the scene of our problem. Holmes halted and looked earnestly at the window. Then he approached it, and, standing on tiptoe, with his neck craned, he looked into the room.

"He must have entered through the door. There is no opening except the one pane," said our learned guide.

"Dear me!" said Holmes, and he smiled in a singular way as he glanced at our companion. "Well, if there is nothing to be learned here we had best go inside."

The lecturer unlocked the outer door and ushered us into his room. We stood at the entrance while Holmes made an examination of the carpet.

"I am afraid there are no signs here," said he. "One could hardly hope for any upon so dry a day. Your servant seems to have quite recovered. You left him in a chair, you say; which chair?"

"By the window there."

"I see. Near this little table. You can come in now. I have finished with the carpet. Let us take the little table first. Of course, what has happened is very clear. The man entered and took the papers, sheet by sheet, from the central table. He carried them over to the window table, because from there he could see if you came across the courtyard, and so could effect an escape."

"As a matter of fact, he could not," said Soames, "for I entered by the side door."

"Ah, that's good! Well, anyhow, that was in my mind. Let me see the three strips. No finger impressions – no! Well, he carried over this one first and he copied it. How long would it take him to do that, using every possible contraction? A quarter of an hour, not less. Then he tossed it down and seized the next. He was in the midst of that when your return caused him to make a very hurried retreat – *very* hurried, since he had not time to replace the papers which would tell you that he had been there. You were not aware of any hurrying feet on the stair as you entered the outer door?"

"No, I can't say I was."

"Well, he wrote so furiously that he broke his pencil and had, as you observe, to sharpen it again. This is of interest, Watson. The pencil was not an ordinary one. It was about the usual size with a soft lead; the outer colour was dark blue, the maker's name was printed in silver lettering, and the piece remaining is only about an inch and a half long. Look for such a pencil, Mr. Soames, and you have got your man. When I add that he possesses a large and very blunt knife, you have an additional aid."

Mr. Soames was somewhat overwhelmed by this flood of information. "I can follow the other points," said he, "but really in this matter of the length—"

Holmes held out a small chip with the letters NN and a space of clear wood after them.

"You see?"

"No, I fear that even now—"

"Watson, I have always done you an injustice. There are others. What could this NN be? It is at the end of a word. You are aware that Johann Faber is the most common maker's name. Is it not clear that there is just as much of the pencil left as usually follows the Johann?" He held the small table sideways to the electric light. "I was hoping that if the paper on which he wrote was thin some trace of it might come through upon this polished surface. No, I see nothing. I don't think there is anything more to be learned here. Now for the central table. This small pellet is, I presume, the black, doughy mass you spoke of. Roughly pyramidal in shape and hollowed out, I perceive. As you say, there appear to be grains of sawdust in it. Dear me, this is very interesting. And the cut – a positive tear, I see. It began with a thin scratch and ended in a jagged hole. I am much indebted to you for directing my attention to this case, Mr. Soames. Where does that door lead to?"

"To my bedroom."

"Have you been in it since your adventure?"

"No; I came straight away for you."

"I should like to have a glance round. What a charming, old-fashioned room! Perhaps you will kindly wait a minute until I have examined the floor. No, I see nothing. What about this curtain? You hang your clothes behind it. If any one were forced to conceal himself in this room he must do it there, since the bed is too low and the wardrobe too shallow. No one there, I suppose?"

As Holmes drew the curtain I was aware, from some little rigidity and alertness of his attitude, that he was prepared for an emergency. As a matter of fact the drawn curtain disclosed nothing but three or four suits of clothes hanging from a line of pegs. Holmes turned away, and stooped suddenly to the floor.

"Halloa! What's this?" said he.

It was a small pyramid of black, putty-like stuff, exactly like the one upon the table of the study. Holmes held it out on his open palm in the glare of the electric light.

"Your visitor seems to have left traces in your bedroom as well as in your sitting-room, Mr. Soames."

"What could he have wanted there?"

"I think it is clear enough. You came back by an unexpected way, and so he had no warning until you were at the very door. What could he do? He caught up everything which would betray him, and he rushed into your bedroom to conceal himself."

"Good gracious, Mr. Holmes, do you mean to tell me that all the time I was talking to Bannister in this room we had the man prisoner if we had only known it?"

"So I read it."

"Surely there is another alternative, Mr. Holmes? I don't know whether you observed my bedroom window."

"Lattice-paned, lead framework, three separate windows, one swinging on hinges and large enough to admit a man."

"Exactly. And it looks out on an angle of the courtyard so as to be partly invisible. The man might have effected his entrance there, left traces as he passed through the bedroom, and, finally, finding the door open, have escaped that way."

Holmes shook his head impatiently.

"Let us be practical," said he. "I understand you to say that there are three students who use this stair and are in the habit of passing your door?"

"Yes, there are."

"And they are all in for this examination?"

"Yes."

"Have you any reason to suspect any one of them more than the others?"

Soames hesitated.

"It is a very delicate question," said he. "One hardly likes to throw suspicion where there are no proofs."

"Let us hear the suspicions. I will look after the proofs."

"I will tell you, then, in a few words, the character of the three men who inhabit these rooms. The lower of the three is Gilchrist, a fine scholar and athlete; plays in the Rugby team and the cricket team for the college, and got his Blue for the hurdles and the long jump. He is a fine manly fellow. His father was the notorious Sir Jabez Gilchrist, who ruined himself on the Turf. My scholar has been left very poor, but he is hard-working and industrious. He will do well.

"The second floor is inhabited by Daulat Ras, the Indian. He is a quiet, inscrutable fellow, as most of those Indians are. He is well up in his work, though his Greek is his weak subject. He is steady and methodical.

"The top floor belongs to Miles McLaren. He is a brilliant fellow when he chooses to work – one of the brightest intellects of the University; but he is wayward, dissipated, and unprincipled. He was nearly expelled over a card scandal in his first year. He has been idling all this term, and he must look forward with dread to the examination."

"Then it is he whom you suspect?"

"I dare not go so far as that. But of the three he is perhaps the least unlikely."

"Exactly. Now, Mr. Soames, let us have a look at your servant, Bannister."

He was a little, white-faced, clean-shaven, grizzly-haired fellow of fifty. He was still suffering from this sudden disturbance of the quiet routine of his life. His plump face was twitching with his nervousness, and his fingers could not keep still.

"We are investigating this unhappy business, Bannister," said his master.

"Yes, sir."

"I understand," said Holmes, "that you left your key in the door?"

"Yes, sir."

"Was it not very extraordinary that you should do this on the very day when there were these papers inside?"

"It was most unfortunate, sir. But I have occasionally done the same thing at other times."

"When did you enter the room?"

"It was about half-past four. That is Mr. Soames's tea-time."

"How long did you stay?"

"When I saw that he was absent I withdrew at once."

"Did you look at these papers on the table?"

"No, sir; certainly not."

"How came you to leave the key in the door?"

"I had the tea-tray in my hand. I thought I would come back for the key. Then I forgot."

"Has the outer door a spring lock?"

"No, sir."

"Then it was open all the time?"

"Yes, sir."

"Any one in the room could get out?"

"Yes, sir."

"When Mr. Soames returned and called for you, you were very much disturbed?"

"Yes, sir. Such a thing has never happened during the many years that I have been here. I nearly fainted, sir."

"So I understand. Where were you when you began to feel bad?"

"Where was I, sir? Why, here, near the door."

"That is singular, because you sat down in that chair over yonder near the corner. Why did you pass these other chairs?"

"I really don't know, sir. It didn't matter to me where I sat."

"I really don't think he knew much about it, Mr. Holmes. He was looking very bad – quite ghastly."

"You stayed here when your master left?"

"Only for a minute or so. Then I locked the door and went to my room."

"Whom do you suspect?"

"Oh, I would not venture to say, sir. I don't believe there is any gentleman in this University who is capable of profiting by such an action. No, sir, I'll not believe it."

"Thank you; that will do," said Holmes. "Oh, one more word. You have not mentioned to any of the three gentlemen whom you attend that anything is amiss?"

"No, sir; not a word."

"You haven't seen any of them?"

"No, sir."

"Very good. Now, Mr. Soames, we will take a walk in the quadrangle, if you please."

Three yellow squares of light shone above us in the gathering gloom.

"Your three birds are all in their nests," said Holmes, looking up. "Halloa! What's that? One of them seems restless enough."

It was the Indian, whose dark silhouette appeared suddenly upon the blind. He was pacing swiftly up and down his room.

"I should like to have a peep at each of them," said Holmes. "Is it possible?"

"No difficulty in the world," Soames answered. "This set of rooms is quite the oldest in the college, and it is not unusual for visitors to go over them. Come along, and I will personally conduct you."

"No names, please!" said Holmes, as we knocked at Gilchrist's door. A tall, flaxen-haired, slim young fellow opened it, and made us welcome when he understood our errand. There were some really curious pieces of mediæval domestic architecture within. Holmes was so charmed with one of them that he insisted on drawing it on his notebook, broke his pencil, had to borrow one from our host, and finally borrowed a knife to sharpen his own. The same curious accident happened to him in the rooms of the Indian – a silent little hook-nosed fellow, who eyed us askance and was obviously glad when Holmes's architectural studies had come to an end. I could not see that in either case Holmes had come upon the clue for which he was searching. Only at the third did our visit prove abortive. The outer door would not open to our knock, and nothing more substantial than a torrent of bad language came from behind it. "I don't care who you are. You can go to blazes!" roared the angry voice. "To-morrow's the exam, and I won't be drawn by any one."

"A rude fellow," said our guide, flushing with anger as we withdrew down the stair. "Of course, he did not realise that it was I who was knocking, but none the less his conduct was very uncourteous, and, indeed, under the circumstances, rather suspicious."

Holmes's response was a curious one.

"Can you tell me his exact height?" he asked.

"Really, Mr. Holmes, I cannot undertake to say. He is taller than the Indian, not so tall as Gilchrist. I suppose five foot six would be about it."

"That is very important," said Holmes. "And now, Mr. Soames, I wish you good-night."

Our guide cried aloud in his astonishment and dismay. "Good gracious, Mr. Holmes, you are surely not going to leave me in this abrupt fashion! You don't seem to realise the position. Tomorrow is the examination. I must take some definite action to-night. I cannot allow the examination to be held if one of the papers has been tampered with. The situation must be faced."

"You must leave it as it is. I shall drop round early to-morrow morning and chat the matter over. It is possible that I may be in a position then to indicate some course of action. Meanwhile you change nothing – nothing at all."

"Very good, Mr. Holmes."

"You can be perfectly easy in your mind. We shall certainly find some way out of your difficulties. I will take the black clay with me, also the pencil cuttings. Good-bye."

When we were out in the darkness of the quadrangle we again looked up at the windows. The Indian still paced his room. The others were invisible.

"Well, Watson, what do you think of it?" Holmes asked as we came out into the main street. "Quite a little parlour game – sort of three-card trick, is it not? There are your three men. It must be one of them. You take your choice. Which is yours?"

"The foul-mouthed fellow at the top. He is the one with the worst record. And yet that Indian was a sly fellow also. Why should he be pacing his room all the time?"

"There is nothing in that. Many men do it when they are trying to learn anything by heart."

"He looked at us in a queer way."

"So would you if a flock of strangers came in on you when you were preparing for an examination next day, and every moment was of value. No, I see nothing in that. Pencils, too, and knives – all was satisfactory. But that fellow *does* puzzle me."

"Who?"

"Why, Bannister, the servant. What's his game in the matter?"

"He impressed me as being a perfectly honest man."

"So he did me. That's the puzzling part. Why should a perfectly honest man – well, here's a large stationer's. We shall begin our researches here."

There were only four stationers of any consequence in the town, and at each Holmes produced his pencil chips and bid high for a duplicate. All were agreed that one could be ordered, but that it was not a usual size of pencil, and that it was seldom kept in stock. My friend did not appear to be depressed by his failure, but shrugged his shoulders in half-humorous resignation.

"No good, my dear Watson. This, the best and only final clue, has run to nothing. But, indeed, I have little doubt that we can build up a sufficient case without it. By Jove! my dear fellow, it is nearly nine, and the landlady babbled of green peas at seven-thirty. What with your eternal tobacco, Watson, and your irregularity at meals, I expect that you will get notice to quit, and that I shall share your downfall – not, however, before we have solved the problem of the nervous tutor, the careless servant, and the three enterprising students."

Holmes made no further allusion to the matter that day, though he sat lost in thought for a long time after our belated dinner. At eight in the morning he came into my room just as I finished my toilet.

"Well, Watson," said he, "it is time we went down to St. Luke's. Can you do without breakfast?"

"Certainly."

"Soames will be in a dreadful fidget until we are able to tell him something positive."

"Have you anything positive to tell him?"

"I think so."

"You have formed a conclusion?"

"Yes, my dear Watson; I have solved the mystery."

"But what fresh evidence could you have got?"

"Aha! It is not for nothing that I have turned myself out of bed at the untimely hour of six. I have put in two hours' hard work and covered at least five miles, with something to show for it. Look at that!"

He held out his hand. On the palm were three little pyramids of black, doughy clay.

"Why, Holmes, you had only two yesterday!"

"And one more this morning. It is a fair argument, that wherever No. 3 came from is also the source of Nos. 1 and 2. Eh, Watson? Well, come along and put friend Soames out of his pain."

The unfortunate tutor was certainly in a state of pitiable agitation when we found him in his chambers. In a few hours the examinations would commence, and he was still in the dilemma between making the facts public and allowing the culprit to compete for the valuable scholarship. He could hardly stand still, so great was his mental agitation, and he ran towards Holmes with two eager hands outstretched.

"Thank Heaven that you have come! I feared that you had given it up in despair. What am I to do? Shall the examination proceed?"

"Yes; let it proceed, by all means."

"But this rascal—?"

"He shall not compete."

"You know him?"

"I think so. If this matter is not to become public we must give ourselves certain powers, and resolve ourselves into a small private court-martial. You there, if you please, Soames! Watson, you here! I'll take the arm-chair in the middle. I think that we are now sufficiently imposing to strike terror into a guilty breast. Kindly ring the bell!"

Bannister entered, and shrank back in evident surprise and fear at our judicial appearance.

"You will kindly close the door," said Holmes. "Now, Bannister, will you please tell us the truth about yesterday's incident?"

The man turned white to the roots of his hair.

"I have told you everything, sir."

"Nothing to add?"

"Nothing at all, sir."

"Well, then, I must make some suggestions to you. When you sat down on that chair yesterday, did you do so in order to conceal some object which would have shown who had been in the room?"

Bannister's face was ghastly.

"No, sir; certainly not."

"It is only a suggestion," said Holmes suavely. "I frankly admit that I am unable to prove it. But it seems probable enough, since the moment that Mr. Soames's back was turned you released the man who was hiding in that bedroom."

Bannister licked his dry lips.

"There was no man, sir."

"Ah, that's a pity, Bannister. Up to now you may have spoken the truth, but now I know that you have lied."

The man's face set in sullen defiance.

"There was no man, sir,"

"Come, come, Bannister."

"No, sir; there was no one."

"In that case you can give us no further information. Would you please remain in the room? Stand over there near the bedroom door. Now, Soames, I am going to ask you to have the great kindness to go up to the room of young Gilchrist, and to ask him to step down into yours."

An instant later the tutor returned, bringing with him the student. He was a fine figure of a man, tall, lithe, and agile, with a springy step and a pleasant, open face. His troubled blue eyes glanced at each of us, and finally rested with an expression of blank dismay upon Bannister in the farther corner.

"Just close the door," said Holmes. "Now, Mr. Gilchrist, we are all quite alone here, and no one need ever know one word of what passes between us. We can be perfectly frank with each other. We want to know, Mr. Gilchrist, how you, an honourable man, ever came to commit such an action as that of yesterday?"

The unfortunate young man staggered back, and cast a look full of horror and reproach at Bannister.

"No, no, Mr. Gilchrist, sir; I never said a word – never one word!" cried the servant.

"No, but you have now," said Holmes. "Now, sir, you must see that after Bannister's words your position is hopeless, and that your only chance lies in a frank confession."

For a moment Gilchrist, with upraised hand, tried to control his writhing features. The next he had thrown himself on his knees beside the table, and, burying his face in his hands, he burst into a storm of passionate sobbing.

"Come, come," said Holmes kindly; "it is human to err, and at least no one can accuse you of being a callous criminal. Perhaps it would be easier for you if I were to tell Mr. Soames what occurred, and you can check me where I am wrong. Shall I do so? Well, well, don't trouble to answer. Listen, and see that I do you no injustice.

"From the moment Mr. Soames, that you said to me that no one, not even Bannister, could have told that the papers were in your room, the case began to take a definite shape in my mind. The printer one could, of course, dismiss. He could examine the papers in his own office. The Indian I also thought nothing of. If the proofs were in a roll he could not possibly know what they were. On the other hand, it seemed an unthinkable coincidence that a man should dare to enter the room, and that by chance on that very day the papers were on the table. I dismissed that. The man who entered knew that the papers were there. How did he know?

"When I approached your room I examined the window. You amused me by supposing that I was contemplating the possibility of someone having in broad daylight, under the eyes of all these opposite rooms, forced himself through it. Such an idea was absurd. I was measuring how tall a man would need to be in order to see as he passed what papers were on the central table. I am six feet high, and I could do it with an effort. No one less than that would have a chance. Already, you see, I had reason to think that if one of your three students was a man of unusual height he was the most worth watching of the three.

"I entered, and I took you into my confidence as to the suggestions of the side table. Of the centre table I could make nothing, until in your description of Gilchrist you mentioned that he was a long-distance jumper. Then the whole thing came to me in an instant, and I only needed certain corroborative proofs, which I speedily obtained.

"What happened was this. This young fellow had employed his afternoon at the athletic grounds, where he had been practising the jump. He returned carrying his jumping shoes, which are provided, as you are aware, with several spikes. As he passed your window he saw, by means of his great height, these proofs upon your table, and conjectured what they were. No harm would have been done had it not been that as he passed your door he perceived the key which had been left by the carelessness of your servant. A sudden impulse came over him to enter and see if they were indeed the proofs. It was not a dangerous exploit, for he could always pretend that he had simply looked in to ask a question.

"Well, when he saw that they were indeed the proofs, it was then that he yielded to temptation. He put his shoes on the table. What was it you put on that chair near the window?"

"Gloves," said the young man.

Holmes looked triumphantly at Bannister.

"He put his gloves on the chair, and he took the proofs, sheet by sheet, to copy them. He thought the tutor must return by the main gate, and that he would see him. As we know, he came back by the side gate. Suddenly he heard him at the very door. There was no possible escape. He forgot his gloves, but he caught up his shoes and darted into the bedroom. You observe that the scratch on that table is slight at one side, but deepens in the direction of the bedroom door. That in itself is enough to show us that the shoes had been drawn in that direction, and that the culprit had taken refuge there. The earth round the spike had been left on the table, and a second sample was loosened and fell in the bedroom. I may add that I walked out to the athletic grounds this morning, saw that tenacious black clay is used in the jumping pit, and carried away a specimen of it, together with some of the fine tan or sawdust which is strewn over it to prevent the athlete from slipping. Have I told the truth, Mr. Gilchrist?"

The student had drawn himself erect.

"Yes, sir, it is true," said he.

"Good heavens, have you nothing to add?" cried Soames.

"Yes, sir, I have, but the shock of this disgraceful exposure has bewildered me. I have a letter here, Mr. Soames, which I wrote to you early this morning in the middle of a restless night. It was before I knew that my sin had found me out. Here it is, sir. You will see that I have said, 'I have determined not to go in for the examination. I have been offered a commission in the Rhodesian Police, and I am going out to South Africa at once.'"

"I am indeed pleased to hear that you did not intend to profit by your unfair advantage," said Soames. "But why did you change your purpose?"

Gilchrist pointed to Bannister.

"There is the man who sent me in the right path," said he.

"Come now, Bannister," said Holmes. "It will be clear to you from what I have said that only you could have let this young man out, since you were left in the room and must have locked the door when you went out. As to his escaping by that window, it was incredible. Can you not clear up the last point in this mystery, and tell us the reason for your action?"

"It was simple enough, sir, if you only had known; but with all your cleverness it was impossible that you could know. Time was, sir, when I was butler to old Sir Jabez Gilchrist, this young gentleman's father. When he was ruined I came to the college as servant, but I never forgot my old employer because he was down in the world. I watched his son all I could for the sake of the old days. Well, sir, when I came into this room yesterday when the alarm was given, the first thing I saw was Mr. Gilchrist's tan gloves a-lying in that chair. I knew those gloves well, and I understood their message. If Mr. Soames saw them the game was up. I flopped down into that chair, and nothing would budge me until Mr. Soames he went for you. Then out came my poor young master, whom I had dandled on my knee, and confessed it all to me. Wasn't it natural, sir, that I should save him, and wasn't it natural also that I should try to speak to him as his dead father would have done, and make him understand that he could not profit by such a deed? Could you blame me, sir?"

"No, indeed!" said Holmes heartily, springing to his feet. "Well, Soames, I think we have cleared your little problem up, and our breakfast awaits us at home. Come, Watson! As to you, sir, I trust that a bright future awaits you in Rhodesia. For once you have fallen low. Let us see in the future how high you can rise."

The Stone of the
Edmundsbury Monks

M.P. Shiel

"**R**ussia," said Prince Zaleski to me one day, when I happened to be on a visit to him in his darksome sanctuary – "Russia may be regarded as land surrounded by ocean; that is to say, she is an island. In the same way, it is sheer gross irrelevancy to speak of *Britain* as an island, unless indeed the word be understood as a mere *modus loquendi* arising out of a rather poor geographical pleasantry. Britain, in reality, is a small continent. Near her – a little to the south-east – is situated the large island of Europe. Thus, the enlightened French traveller passing to these shores should commune within himself: 'I now cross to the Mainland'; and retracing his steps: 'I now return to the fragment rent by wrack and earthshock from the Mother-country.' And this I say not in the way of paradox, but as the expression of a sober truth. I have in my mind merely the relative depth and extent – the *non-insularity*, in fact – of the impressions made by the several nations on the world. But this island of Europe has herself an island of her own: the name of it, Russia. She, of all lands, is the *terra incognita*, the unknown land; till quite lately she was more – she was the undiscovered, the unsuspected land. She *has* a literature, you know, and a history, and a language, and a purpose – but of all this the world has hardly so much as heard. Indeed, she, and not any Antarctic Sea whatever, is the real Ultima Thule of modern times, the true Island of Mystery."

I reproduce these remarks of Zaleski here, not so much on account of the splendid tribute to my country contained in them, as because it ever seemed to me – and especially in connection with the incident I am about to recall – that in this respect at least he was a genuine son of Russia; if she is the Land, so truly was he the Man, of Mystery. I who knew him best alone knew that it was impossible to know him. He was a being little of the present: with one arm he embraced the whole past; the fingers of the other heaved on the vibrant pulse of the future. He seemed to me – I say it deliberately and with forethought – to possess the unparalleled power not merely of disentangling in retrospect, but of unravelling in prospect, and I have known him to relate *coming* events with unimaginable minuteness of precision. He was nothing if not superlative: his diatribes, now culminating in a very *extravangaza* of hyperbole – now sailing with loose wing through the downy, witched, Dutch cloud-heaps of some quaintest tramontane Nephelococcugia of thought – now laying down law of the Medes for the actual world of to-day – had oft-times the strange effect of bringing back to my mind the very singular old-epic epithet, ηνεμσεν – *airy* – as applied to human thought. The mere grip of his memory was not simply extraordinary, it had in it a token, a hint, of the strange, the pythic – nay, the sibylline. And as his reflecting intellect, moreover, had all the lightness of foot of a chamois kid, unless you could contrive to follow each dazzlingly swift successive step, by the sum of which he attained his Alp-heights, he inevitably left on you the astounding, the confounding impression of mental omnipresence.

I had brought with me a certain document, a massive book bound in iron and leather, the diary of one Sir Jocelin Saul. This I had abstracted from a gentleman of my acquaintance, the head of a firm of inquiry agents in London, into whose hand, only the day before, it had come. A distant neighbour of Sir Jocelin, hearing by chance of his extremity, had invoked the assistance of this firm; but the aged baronet, being in a state of the utmost feebleness, terror, and indeed hysterical incoherence, had been able to utter no word in explanation of his condition or wishes, and, in silent abandonment, had merely handed the book to the agent.

A day or two after I had reached the desolate old mansion which the prince occupied, knowing that he might sometimes be induced to take an absorbing interest in questions that had proved themselves too profound, or too intricate, for ordinary solution, I asked him if he was willing to hear the details read out from the diary, and on his assenting, I proceeded to do so.

The brief narrative had reference to a very large and very valuable oval gem enclosed in the substance of a golden chalice, which chalice, in the monastery of St. Edmundsbury, had once lain centuries long within the Loculus, or inmost coffin, wherein reposed the body of St. Edmund. By pressing a hidden pivot, the cup (which was composed of two equal parts, connected by minute hinges) sprang open, and in a hollow space at the bottom was disclosed the gem. Sir Jocelin Saul, I may say, was lineally connected with – though, of course, not descendant from – that same Jocelin of Brakelonda, a brother of the Edmundsbury convent, who wrote the now so celebrated *Jocelini Chronica*: and the chalice had fallen into the possession of the family, seemingly at some time prior to the suppression of the monastery about 1537. On it was inscribed in old English characters of unknown date the words:

Shulde this Ston stalen bee,
Or shuld it chaunges dre,
The Houss of Sawl and hys Hed anoon shal de.

The stone itself was an intaglio, and had engraved on its surface the figure of a mythological animal, together with some nearly obliterated letters, of which the only ones remaining legible were those forming the word "Has." As a sure precaution against the loss of the gem, another cup had been made and engraved in an exactly similar manner, inside of which, to complete the delusion, another stone of the same size and cut, but of comparatively valueless material, had been placed.

Sir Jocelin Saul, a man of intense nervosity, lived his life alone in a remote old manor-house in Suffolk, his only companion being a person of Eastern origin, named Ul-Jabal. The baronet had consumed his vitality in the life-long attempt to sound the too fervid Maelstrom of Oriental research, and his mind had perhaps caught from his studies a tinge of their morbidness, their esotericism, their insanity. He had for some years past been engaged in the task of writing a stupendous work on Pre-Zoroastrian Theogonies, in which, it is to be supposed, Ul-Jabal acted somewhat in the capacity of secretary. But I will give *verbatim* the extracts from his diary:

"*June* 11. – This is my birthday. Seventy years ago exactly I slid from the belly of the great Dark into this Light and Life. My God! My God! it is briefer than the rage of an hour, fleeter than a midday trance. Ul-Jabal greeted me warmly – seemed to have been looking forward to it – and pointed out that seventy is of the fateful numbers, its only factors being seven, five, and two: the last denoting the duality of Birth and Death; five, Isolation; seven, Infinity. I informed him that this was also my father's birthday; and *his* father's; and repeated the oft-told tale of how the latter, just seventy years ago to-day, walking at twilight by the churchyard-wall, saw the figure of *himself* sitting on a gravestone, and died five weeks later riving with the pangs of hell. Whereat the sceptic showed his two huge rows of teeth.

"What is his peculiar interest in the Edmundsbury chalice? On each successive birthday when the cup has been produced, he has asked me to show him the stone. Without any well-defined reason I have always declined, but to-day I yielded. He gazed long into its sky-blue depth, and then asked if I had no idea what the inscription 'Has' meant. I informed him that it was one of the lost secrets of the world.

"*June* 15. – Some new element has entered into our existence here. Something threatens me. I hear the echo of a menace against my sanity and my life. It is as if the garment which enwraps me has grown too hot, too heavy for me. A notable drowsiness has settled on my brain – a drowsiness in which thought, though slow, is a thousandfold more fiery-vivid than ever. Oh, fair goddess of Reason, desert not me, thy chosen child!

"*June* 18.– Ul-Jabal? – that man is *the very Devil incarnate!*

"*June* 19. – So much for my bounty, all my munificence, to this poisonous worm. I picked him up on the heights of the Mountain of Lebanon, a cultured savage among cultured savages, and brought him here to be a prince of thought by my side. What though his plundered wealth – the debt I owe him – has saved me from a sort of ruin? Have not *I* instructed him in the sweet secret of Reason?

"I lay back on my bed in the lonely morning watches, my soul heavy as with the distilled essence of opiates, and in vivid vision knew that he had entered my apartment. In the twilight gloom his glittering rows of shark's teeth seemed impacted on my eyeball – I saw *them*, and nothing else. I was not aware when he vanished from the room. But at daybreak I crawled on hands and knees to the cabinet containing the chalice. The viperous murderer! He has stolen my gem, well knowing that with it he has stolen my life. The stone is gone – gone, my precious gem. A weakness overtook me, and I lay for many dreamless hours naked on the marble floor.

"Does the fool think to hide ought from my eyes? Can he imagine that I shall not recover my precious gem, my stone of Saul?

"*June* 20.– Ah, Ul-Jabal – my brave, my noble Son of the Prophet of God! He has replaced the stone! He would not slay an aged man. The yellow ray of his eye, it is but the gleam of the great thinker, not – not – the gleam of the assassin. Again, as I lay in semi-somnolence, I saw him enter my room, this time more distinctly. He went up to the cabinet. Shaking the chalice in the dawning, some hours after he had left, I heard with delight the rattle of the stone. I might have known he would replace it; I should not have doubted his clemency to a poor man like me. But the strange being! – he has taken the *other* stone from the *other* cup – a thing of little value to any man! Is Ul-Jabal mad or I?

"*June* 21.– Merciful Lord in Heaven! he has *not* replaced it – not *it* – but another instead of it. To-day I actually opened the chalice, and saw. He has put a stone there, the same in size, in cut, in engraving, but different in colour, in quality, in value – a stone I have never seen before. How has he obtained it – whence? I must brace myself to probe, to watch; I must turn myself into an eye to search this devil's-bosom. My life, this subtle, cunning Reason of mine, hangs in the balance.

"*June* 22. – Just now he offered me a cup of wine. I almost dashed it to the ground before him. But he looked steadfastly into my eye. I flinched: and drank – drank.

"Years ago, when, as I remember, we were at Balbec, I saw him one day make an almost tasteless preparation out of pure black nicotine, which in mere wanton lust he afterwards gave to some of the dwellers by the Caspian to drink. But the fiend would surely never dream of giving to me that browse of hell – to me an aged man, and a thinker, a seer.

"*June* 23. – The mysterious, the unfathomable Ul-Jabal! Once again, as I lay in heavy trance at midnight, has he invaded, calm and noiseless as a spirit, the sanctity of my chamber. Serene on the swaying air, which, radiant with soft beams of vermil and violet light, rocked me into variant visions of heaven, I reclined and regarded him unmoved. The man has replaced the valueless stone in the modern-made chalice, and has now stolen the false stone from the other, which *he himself* put there! In patience will I possess this my soul, and watch what shall betide. My eyes shall know no slumber!

"*June* 24. – No more – no more shall I drink wine from the hand of Ul-Jabal. My knees totter beneath the weight of my lean body. Daggers of lambent fever race through my brain incessant. Some fibrillary twitchings at the right angle of the mouth have also arrested my attention.

"*June* 25. – He has dared at open midday to enter my room. I watched him from an angle of the stairs pass along the corridor and open my door. But for the terrifying, death-boding thump, thump of my heart, I should have faced the traitor then, and told him that I knew all his treachery. Did I say that I had strange fibrillary twitchings at the right angle of my mouth, and a brain on fire? I have ceased to write my book – the more the pity for the world, not for me.

"*June* 26. – Marvellous to tell, the traitor, Ul-Jabal, has now placed *another* stone in the Edmundsbury chalice – also identical in nearly every respect with the original gem. This, then, was the object of his entry into my room yesterday. So that he has first stolen the real stone and replaced it by another; then he has stolen this other and replaced it by yet another; he has beside stolen the valueless stone from the modern chalice, and then replaced it. Surely a man gone rabid, a man gone dancing, foaming, raving mad!

"*June* 28. – I have now set myself to the task of recovering my jewel. It is here, and I shall find it. Life against life – and which is the best life, mine or this accursed Ishmaelite's? If need be, I will do murder – I, with this withered hand – so that I get back the heritage which is mine.

"To-day, when I thought he was wandering in the park, I stole into his room, locking the door on the inside. I trembled exceedingly, knowing that his eyes are in every place. I ransacked the chamber, dived among his clothes, but found no stone. One singular thing in a drawer I saw: a long, white beard, and a wig of long and snow-white hair. As I passed out of the chamber, to, he stood face to face with me at the door in the passage. My heart gave one bound, and then seemed wholly to cease its travail. Oh, I must be sick unto death, weaker than a bruised reed! When I woke from my swoon he was supporting me in his arms. 'Now,' he said, grinning down at me, 'now you have at last delivered all into my hands.' He left me, and I saw him go into his room and lock the door upon himself. What is it I have delivered into the madman's hands?

"*July* 1. – Life against life – and his, the young, the stalwart, rather than mine, the mouldering, the sere. I love life. Not *yet* am I ready to weigh anchor, and reeve halliard, and turn my prow over the watery paths of the wine-brown Deeps. Oh no. Not yet. Let *him* die. Many and many are the days in which I shall yet see the light, walk, think. I am averse to end the number of my years: there is even a feeling in me at times that this worn body shall never, never taste of death. The chalice predicts indeed that I and my house shall end when the stone is lost – a mere fiction *at first*, an idler's dream *then*, but now – now – that the prophecy has stood so long a part of the reality of things, and a fact among facts – no longer fiction, but Adamant, stern as the very word of God. Do I not feel hourly since it has gone how the surges of life ebb, ebb ever lower in my heart? Nay, nay, but there is hope. I have here beside me an Arab blade of subtle Damascene steel, insinuous to pierce and to hew, with which in a street of Bethlehem I saw a Syrian's head cleft open –

a gallant stroke! The edges of this I have made bright and white for a nuptial of blood.

"*July* 2. – I spent the whole of the last night in searching every nook and crack of the house, using a powerful magnifying lens. At times I thought Ul-Jabal was watching me, and would pounce out and murder me. Convulsive tremors shook my frame like earthquake. Ah me, I fear I am all too frail for this work. Yet dear is the love of life.

"*July* 7. – The last days I have passed in carefully searching the grounds, with the lens as before. Ul-Jabal constantly found pretexts for following me, and I am confident that every step I took was known to him. No sign anywhere of the grass having been disturbed. Yet my lands are wide, and I cannot be sure. The burden of this mighty task is greater than I can bear. I am weaker than a bruised reed. Shall I not slay my enemy, and make an end?

"*July* 8.– Ul-Jabal has been in my chamber again! I watched him through a crack in the panelling. His form was hidden by the bed, but I could see his hand reflected in the great mirror opposite the door. First, I cannot guess why, he moved to a point in front of the mirror the chair in which I sometimes sit. He then went to the box in which lie my few garments – and opened it. Ah, I have the stone – safe – safe! He fears my cunning, ancient eyes, and has hidden it in the one place where I would be least likely to seek it – *in my own trunk!* And yet I dread, most intensely I dread, to look.

"*July* 9. – The stone, alas, is not there! At the last moment he must have changed his purpose. Could his wondrous sensitiveness of intuition have made him feel that my eyes were looking in on him?

"*July* 10. – In the dead of night I knew that a stealthy foot had gone past my door. I rose and threw a mantle round me; I put on my head my cap of fur; I took the tempered blade in my hands; then crept out into the dark, and followed. Ul-Jabal carried a small lantern which revealed him to me. My feet were bare, but he wore felted slippers, which to my unfailing ear were not utterly noiseless. He descended the stairs to the bottom of the house, while I crouched behind him in the deepest gloom of the corners and walls. At the bottom he walked into the pantry:

there stopped, and turned the lantern full in the direction of the spot where I stood; but so agilely did I slide behind a pillar, that he could not have seen me. In the pantry he lifted the trap-door, and descended still further into the vaults beneath the house. Ah, the vaults – the long, the tortuous, the darksome vaults – how had I forgotten them? Still I followed, rent by seismic shocks of terror. I had not forgotten the weapon: could I creep near enough, I felt that I might plunge it into the marrow of his back. He opened the iron door of the first vault and passed in. If I could lock him in? – but he held the key. On and on he wound his way, holding the lantern near the ground, his head bent down. The thought came to me *then*, that, had I but the courage, one swift sweep, and all were over. I crept closer, closer. Suddenly he turned round, and made a quick step in my direction. I saw his eyes, the murderous grin of his jaw. I know not if he saw me – thought forsook me. The weapon fell with clatter and clangor from my grasp, and in panic fright I fled with extended arms and the headlong swiftness of a stripling, through the black labyrinths of the caverns, through the vacant corridors of the house, till I reached my chamber, the door of which I had time to fasten on myself before I dropped, gasping, panting for very life, on the floor.

"*July* 11. – I had not the courage to see Ul-Jabal to-day. I have remained locked in my chamber all the time without food or water. My tongue cleaves to the roof of my mouth.

"*July* 12. – I took heart and crept downstairs. I met him in the study. He smiled on me, and I on him, as if nothing had happened between us. Oh, our old friendship, how it has turned into bitterest hate! I had taken the false stone from the Edmundsbury chalice and put it in the pocket of my brown gown, with the bold intention of showing it to him, and asking him if he knew aught of it. But when I faced him, my courage failed again. We drank together and ate together as in the old days of love.

"*July* 13. – I cannot think that I have not again imbibed some soporiferous drug. A great heaviness of sleep weighed on my brain till late in the day. When I woke my thoughts were in wild distraction, and a most peculiar condition of my skin held me fixed before the mirror. It is dry as parchment, and brown as the leaves of autumn.

"*July* 14. – Ul-Jabal is gone! And I am left a lonely, a desolate old man! He said, though I swore it was false, that I had grown to mistrust him! That I was hiding something from him! That he could live with me no more! No more, he said, should I see his face! The debt I owe him he would forgive. He has taken one small parcel with him – and is gone!

"*July* 15. – Gone! gone! In mazeful dream I wander with uncovered head far and wide over my domain, seeking I know not what. The stone he has with him – the precious stone of Saul. I feel the life-surge ebbing, ebbing in my heart."

Here the manuscript abruptly ended.

Prince Zaleski had listened as I read aloud, lying back on his Moorish couch and breathing slowly from his lips a heavy reddish vapour, which he imbibed from a very small, carved, bismuth pipette. His face, as far as I could see in the green-grey crepuscular atmosphere of the apartment, was expressionless. But when I had finished he turned fully round on me, and said:

"You perceive, I hope, the sinister meaning of all this?"

"*Has* it a meaning?"

Zaleski smiled.

"Can you doubt it? In the shape of a cloud, the pitch of a thrush's note, the *nuance* of a sea-shell you would find, had you only insight *enough*, inductive and deductive cunning *enough*, not only a meaning, but, I am convinced, a quite endless significance. Undoubtedly, in a human document of this kind, there is a meaning; and I may say at once that this meaning is entirely transparent to me. Pity only that you did not read the diary to me before."

"Why?"

"Because we might, between us, have prevented a crime, and saved a life. The last entry in the diary was made on the 15th of July. What day is this?"

"This is the 20th."

"Then I would wager a thousand to one that we are too late. There is still, however, the one chance left. The time is now seven o'clock: seven of the evening, I think, not of the morning; the houses of business in London are therefore closed. But why not send my man, Ham, with a letter by train to the private address of the person from whom you obtained the diary, telling him to hasten immediately to Sir Jocelin Saul, and on no consideration to leave his side for a moment? Ham would reach this person before midnight, and understanding that the matter was one of life and death, he would assuredly do your bidding."

As I was writing the note suggested by Zaleski, I turned and asked him:

"From whom shall I say that the danger is to be expected – from the Indian?"

"From Ul-Jabal, yes; but by no means Indian – Persian."

Profoundly impressed by this knowledge of detail derived from sources which had brought me no intelligence, I handed the note to the negro, telling him how to proceed, and instructing him before starting from the station to search all the procurable papers of the last few days, and to return in case he found in any of them a notice of the death of Sir Jocelin Saul. Then I resumed my seat by the side of Zaleski.

"As I have told you," he said, "I am fully convinced that our messenger has gone on a bootless errand. I believe you will find that what has really occurred is this: either yesterday, or the day before, Sir Jocelin was found by his servant – I imagine he had a servant, though no mention is made of any – lying on the marble floor of his chamber, dead. Near him, probably by his side, will be found a gem – an oval stone, white in colour – the same in fact which Ul-Jabal last placed in the Edmundsbury chalice. There will be no marks of violence – no trace of poison – the death will be found to be a perfectly natural one. Yet, in this case, a particularly wicked murder has been committed. There are, I assure you, to my positive knowledge forty-three – and in one island in the South Seas, forty-four – different methods of doing murder, any one of which would be entirely beyond the scope of the introspective agencies at the ordinary disposal of society.

"But let us bend our minds to the details of this matter. Let us ask first, *who* is this Ul-Jabal? I have said that he is a Persian, and of this there is abundant evidence in the narrative other than his mere name. Fragmentary as the document is, and not intended by the writer to afford the information, there

is yet evidence of the religion of this man, of the particular
sect of that religion to which he belonged, of his peculiar
shade of colour, of the object of his stay at the manor-house of
Saul, of the special tribe amongst whom he formerly lived.
'What,' he asks, when his greedy eyes first light on the long-
desired gem, 'what is the meaning of the inscription "Has"' –
the meaning which *he* so well knew. 'One of the lost secrets of
the world,' replies the baronet. But I can hardly understand a
learned Orientalist speaking in that way about what appears to
me a very patent circumstance: it is clear that he never
earnestly applied himself to the solution of the riddle, or else
– what is more likely, in spite of his rather high-flown estimate
of his own 'Reason' – that his mind, and the mind of his
ancestors, never was able to go farther back in time than the
Edmundsbury Monks. But *they* did not make the stone, nor
did they dig it from the depths of the earth in Suflolk – they
got it from someone, and it is not difficult to say with certainty
from whom. The stone, then, might have been engraved by
that someone, or by the someone from whom *he* received it,
and so on back into the dimnesses of time. And consider the
character of the engraving – it consists of *a mythological
animal*, and some words, of which the letters 'Has' only are
distinguishable. But the animal, at least, is pure Persian. The
Persians, you know, were not only quite worthy competitors
with the Hebrews, the Egyptians, and later on the Greeks, for
excellence in the glyptic art, but this fact is remarkable, that in
much the same way that the figure of the *scarabœus* on an
intaglio or cameo is a pretty infallible indication of an Egyptian hand, so is that of a priest or a grotesque animal a sure
indication of a Persian. We may say, then, from that evidence
alone – though there is more – that this gem was certainly
Persian. And having reached that point, the mystery of 'Has'
vanishes: for we at once jump at the conclusion that that too is
Persian. But Persian, you say, written in English characters?
Yes, and it was precisely this fact that made its meaning one of
what the baronet childishly calls 'the lost secrets of the world':
for every successive inquirer, believing it part of an English
phrase, was thus hopelessly led astray in his investigation.
'Has' is, in fact, part of the word 'Hasn-us-Sabah,' and the

mere circumstance that some of it has been obliterated, while
the figure of the mystic animal remains intact, shows that it
was executed by one of a nation less skilled in the art of
graving in precious stones than the Persians – by a rude,
mediæval Englishman, in short, – the modern revival of the art
owing its origin, of course, to the Medici of a later age. And of
this Englishman – who either graved the stone himself, or got
some one else to do it for him – do we know nothing? We
know, at least, that he was certainly a fighter, probably a
Norman baron, that on his arm he bore the cross of red, that
he trod the sacred soil of Palestine. Perhaps, to prove this, I
need hardly remind you who Hasn-us-Sabah was. It is enough
if I say that he was greatly mixed up in the affairs of the
Crusaders, lending his irresistible arms now to this side, now
to that. He was the chief of the heterodox Mohammedan sect
of the Assassins (this word, I believe, is actually derived from
his name); imagined himself to be an incarnation of the Deity,
and from his inaccessible rock-fortress of Alamut in the
Elburz exercised a sinister influence on the intricate politics
of the day. The Red Cross Knights called him Shaikh-ul-Jabal
– the Old Man of the Mountains, that very nickname con-
necting him infallibly with the Ul-Jabal of our own times.
Now three well-known facts occur to me in connection with
this stone of the House of Saul: the first, that Saladin met in
battle, and defeated, *and plundered*, in a certain place, on a
certain day, this Hasn-us-Sabah, or one of his successors
bearing the same name; the second, that about this time there
was a cordial *rapprochement* between Saladin and Richard the
Lion, and between the Infidels and the Christians generally,
during which a free interchange of gems, then regarded as of
deep mystic importance, took place – remember 'The Talis-
man,' and the 'Lee Penny'; the third, that soon after the
fighters of Richard, and then himself, returned to England,
the loculus or coffin of St. Edmund (as we are informed by the
Jocelini Chronica) was *opened by the Abbot* at midnight, and the
body of the martyr exposed. On such occasions it was customary to place gems and relics in the coffin, when it was
again closed up. Now, the chalice with the stone was taken
from this loculus; and is it possible not to believe that some

knight, to whom it had been presented by one of Saladin's men, had in turn presented it to the monastery, first scratching uncouthly on its surface the name of Hasn to mark its semi-sacred origin, or perhaps bidding the monks to do so? But the Assassins, now called, I think, 'al Hasani' or 'Ismaili' – 'that accursed *Ishmaelite*,' the baronet exclaims in one place – still live, are still a flourishing sect impelled by fervid religious fanaticisms. And where think you is their chief place of settlement? Where, but on the heights of that same 'Lebanon' on which Sir Jocelin 'picked up' his too doubtful scribe and literary helper?

"It now becomes evident that Ul-Jabal was one of the sect of the Assassins, and that the object of his sojourn at the manor-house, of his financial help to the baronet, of his whole journey perhaps to England, was the recovery of the sacred gem which once glittered on the breast of the founder of his sect. In dread of spoiling all by over-rashness, he waits, perhaps for years, till he makes sure that the stone is the right one by seeing it with his own eyes, and learns the secret of the spring by which the chalice is opened. He then proceeds to steal it. So far all is clear enough. Now, this too is conceivable, that, intending to commit the theft, he had beforehand provided himself with another stone similar in size and shape – these being well known to him – to the other, in order to substitute it for the real stone, and so, for a time at least, escape detection. It is presumable that the chalice was not often *opened* by the baronet, and this would therefore have been a perfectly rational device on the part of Ul-Jabal. But assuming this to be his mode of thinking, how ludicrously absurd appears all the trouble he took to *engrave* the false stone in an exactly similar manner to the other. *That* could not help him in producing the deception, for that he did not contemplate the stone being *seen*, but only *heard* in the cup, is proved by the fact that he selected a stone of a different *colour*. This colour, as I shall afterwards show you, was that of a pale, brown-spotted stone. But we are met with something more extraordinary still when we come to the last stone, the white one – I shall prove that it was white – which Ul-Jabal placed in the cup. Is it possible that he had provided *two* substitutes, and that he had engraved these *two*, without object, in the same minutely careful manner? Your mind refuses to conceive it; and *having* done this declines, in addition, to believe that he had prepared even one substitute; and I am fully in accord with you in this conclusion.

"We may say then that Ul-Jabal had not *prepared* any substitute; and it may be added that it was a thing altogether beyond the limits of the probable that he could *by chance* have possessed two old gems exactly similar in every detail down to the very half-obliterated letters of the word 'Hasn-us-Sabah.' I have now shown, you perceive, that he did not make them purposely, and that he did not possess them accidentally. Nor were they the baronet's, for we have his declaration that he had never seen them before. Whence then did the Persian obtain them? That point will immediately emerge into clearness, when we have sounded his motive for replacing the one false stone by the other, and, above all, for taking away the valueless stone, and then replacing it. And in order to lead you up to the comprehension of this motive, I begin by making the bold assertion that Ul-Jabal had not in his possession the real St. Edmundsbury stone at all.

"You are surprised; for you argue that if we are to take the baronet's evidence at all, we must take it in this particular also, and he positively asserts that he saw the Persian take the stone. It is true that there are indubitable signs of insanity in the document, but it is the insanity of a diseased mind manifesting itself by fantastic exaggeration of sentiment, rather than of a mind confiding to itself its own delusions as to matters of fact. There is therefore nothing so certain as that Ul-Jabal did steal the gem; but these two things are equally evident: that by some means or other it very soon passed out of his possession, and that when it had so passed, he, for his part, believed it to be in the possession of the baronet. 'Now,' he cries in triumph, one day as he catches Sir Jocelin in his room – '*now* you have delivered all into my hands.' 'All' what, Sir Jocelin wonders. 'All,' of course, meant the stone. He believes that the baronet has done precisely what the baronet afterwards believes that *he* has done – hidden away the stone in the most secret of all places, in his own apartment, to wit. The Persian, sure now at last of victory, accordingly hastens into his chamber, and 'locks the door,' in order, by an easy search, to secure his prize. When, moreover, the baronet is examining the house at night with his lens, he believes that Ul-Jabal is spying on his movements; when he extends his operations to the park, the other finds pretexts to be near him. Ul-Jabal dogs his footsteps like a shadow. But supposing he had really had the jewel, and had deposited it in a place of perfect safety – such as, with or without lenses, the extensive grounds of the manor-house would certainly have afforded – his more reasonable role would have been that of unconscious *nonchalance*, rather than of agonised interest. But, in fact, he supposed the owner of the stone to be himself seeking a secure hiding-place for it, and is resolved at all costs on knowing the secret. And again in the vaults beneath the house Sir Jocelin reports that Ul-Jabal 'holds the lantern near the ground, with his head bent down': can anything be better descriptive of the attitude of *search*? Yet each is so sure that the other possesses the gem, that neither is able to suspect that both are seekers.

"But, after all, there is far better evidence of the non-possession of the stone by the Persian than all this – and that is the murder of the baronet, for I can almost promise you that our messenger will return in a few minutes. Now, it seems to me that Ul-Jabal was not really murderous, averse rather to murder; thus the baronet is often in his power, swoons in his arms, lies under the influence of narcotics in semi-sleep while the Persian is in his room, and yet no injury is done him. Still, when the clear necessity to murder – the clear means of gaining the stone – presents itself to Ul-Jabal, he does not hesitate a moment – indeed, he has already made elaborate preparations for that very necessity. And when was it that this necessity presented itself? It was when the baronet put the false stone in the pocket of a loose gown for the purpose of confronting the Persian with it. But what kind of pocket? I think you will agree with me, that male garments, admitting of the designation 'gown,' have usually only outer pockets – large, square pockets, simply sewed on to the outside of the robe. But a stone of that size *must* have made such a pocket bulge outwards. Ul-Jabal must have noticed it. Never before has he been perfectly sure that the baronet carried the long-

desired gem about on his body; but now at last he knows
beyond all doubt. To obtain it, there are several courses open
to him: he may rush there and then on the weak old man and
tear the stone from him; he may ply him with narcotics, and
extract it from the pocket during sleep. But in these there is a
small chance of failure; there is a certainty of near or ultimate
detection, pursuit – and this is a land of Law, swift and fairly
sure. No, the old man must die: only thus – thus surely, and
thus secretly – can the outraged dignity of Hasn-us-Sabah be
appeased. On the very next day he leaves the house – no more
shall the mistrustful baronet, who is 'hiding something from
him,' see his face. He carries with him a small parcel. Let me
tell you what was in that parcel: it contained the baronet's fur
cap, one of his 'brown gowns,' and a snow-white beard and
wig. Of the cap we can be sure; for from the fact that, on
leaving his room at midnight to follow the Persian through the
house, he put it on his head, I gather that he wore it habitually
during all his waking hours; yet after Ul-Jabal has left him he
wanders *far and wide* 'with uncovered head.' Can you not
picture the distracted old man seeking ever and anon with
absent mind for his long-accustomed head-gear, and seeking
in vain? Of the gown, too, we may be equally certain: for it
was the procuring of this that led Ul-Jabal to the baronet's
trunk; we now know that he did not go there to *hide* the stone,
for he had it not to hide; nor to *seek* it, for he would be unable
to believe the baronet childish enough to deposit it in so
obvious a place. As for the wig and beard, they had been
previously seen in his room. But before he leaves the house
Ul-Jabal has one more work to do: once more the two eat and
drink together as in 'the old days of love'; once more the
baronet is drunken with a deep sleep, and when he wakes, his
skin is 'brown as the leaves of autumn.' That is the evidence of
which I spake in the beginning as giving us a hint of the exact
shade of the Oriental's colour – it was the yellowish-brown of
a sered leaf. And now that the face of the baronet has been
smeared with this indelible pigment, all is ready for the
tragedy, and Ul-Jabal departs. He will return, but not immediately, for he will at least give the eyes of his victim time
to grow accustomed to the change of colour in his face; nor

will he tarry long, for there is no telling whether, or whither, the stone may not disappear from that outer pocket. I therefore surmise that the tragedy took place a day or two ago. I remembered the feebleness of the old man, his highly neurotic condition; I thought of those 'fibrillary twitchings,' indicating the onset of a well-known nervous disorder sure to end in sudden death; I recalled his belief that on account of the loss of the stone, in which he felt his life bound up, the chariot of death was urgent on his footsteps; I bore in mind his memory of his grandfather dying in agony just seventy years ago after seeing his own wraith by the churchyard-wall; I knew that such a man could not be struck by the sudden, the terrific shock of seeing *himself* sitting in the chair before the mirror (the chair, you remember, had been *placed* there by Ul-Jabal) without dropping down stone dead on the spot. I was thus able to predict the manner and place of the baronet's death – if he *be* dead. Beside him, I said, would probably be found a white stone. For Ul-Jabal, his ghastly impersonation ended, would hurry to the pocket, snatch out the stone, and finding it not the stone he sought, would in all likelihood dash it down, fly away from the corpse as if from plague, and, I hope, straightway go and – hang himself."

It was at this point that the black mask of Ham framed itself between the python-skin tapestries of the doorway. I tore from him the paper, now two days old, which he held in his hand, and under the heading, "Sudden death of a Baronet," read a nearly exact account of the facts which Zaleski had been detailing to me.

"I can see by your face that I was not altogether at fault," he said, with one of his musical laughs; "but there still remains for us to discover whence Ul-Jabal obtained his two substitutes, his motive for exchanging one for the other, and for stealing the valueless gem; but, above all, we must find where the real stone was all the time that these two men so sedulously sought it, and where it now is. Now, let us turn our attention to this stone, and ask, first, what light does the inscription on the cup throw on its nature? The inscription assures us that if 'this stone be stolen,' or if it 'chaunges dre,' the House of Saul and its head 'anoon' (i.e. anon, at once) shall die. 'Dre,' I may remind you, is an old

English word, used, I think, by Burns, identical with the Saxon '*dreogan*,' meaning to 'suffer.' So that the writer at least contemplated that the stone might 'suffer changes.' But what kind of changes – external or internal? External change – change of environment – is already provided for when he says, 'shulde this Ston stalen bee'; 'chaunges,' therefore, in *his* mind, meant internal changes. But is such a thing possible for any precious stone, and for this one in particular? As to that, we might answer when we know the name of this one. It nowhere appears in the manuscript, and yet it is immediately discoverable. For it was a 'sky-blue' stone; a sky-blue, sacred stone; a sky-blue, sacred, Persian stone. That at once gives us its name – it was a *turquoise*. But can the turquoise, to the certain knowledge of a mediaeval writer, 'chaunges dre'? Let us turn for light to old Anselm de Boot: that is he in pig-skin on the shelf behind the bronze Hera."

I handed the volume to Zaleski. He pointed to a passage which read as follows:

"Assuredly the turquoise doth possess a soul more intelligent than that of man. But we cannot be wholly sure of the presence of Angels in precious stones. I do rather opine that the evil spirit doth take up his abode therein, transforming himself into an angel of light, to the end that we put our trust not in God, but in the precious stone; and thus, perhaps, doth he deceive our spirits by the turquoise: for the turquoise is of two sorts: those which keep their colour, and those which lose it."*

"You thus see," resumed Zaleski, "that the turquoise was believed to have the property of changing its colour – a change which was universally supposed to indicate the fading away and

---

* "Assurément la turquoise a une ame plus intelligente que l'ame de l'homme. Mais nous ne pouvons rien establir de certain touchant la presence des Anges dans les pierres precieuses. Mon jugement seroit plustot que le mauvais esprit, qui se transforme en Ange de lumiere se loge dans les pierres precieuses, à fin que l'on ne recoure pas à Dieu, mais que l'on repose sa creance dans la pierre precieuse; ainsi, peut-être, il deçoit nos esprits par la turquoise: car la turquoise est de deux sortes, les unes qui conservent leur couleur et les autres qui la perdent." – *Anselm de Boot*, Book II.

death of its owner. The good De Boot, alas, believed this to be a property of too many other stones beside, like the Hebrews in respect of their urim and thummim; but in the case of the turquoise, at least, it is a well-authenticated natural phenomenon, and I have myself seen such a specimen. In some cases the change is a gradual process; in others it may occur suddenly within an hour, especially when the gem, long kept in the dark, is exposed to brilliant sunshine. I should say, however, that in this metamorphosis there is always an intermediate stage: the stone first changes from blue to a pale colour spotted with brown, and, lastly, to a pure white. Thus, Ul-Jabal having stolen the stone, finds that it is of the wrong colour, and soon after replaces it; he supposes that in the darkness he has selected the wrong chalice, and so takes the valueless stone from the other. This, too, he replaces, and, infinitely puzzled, makes yet another hopeless trial of the Edmundsbury chalice, and, again baffled, again replaces it, concluding now that the baronet has suspected his designs, and substituted a false stone for the real one. But *after* this last replacement, the stone assumes its final hue of white, and thus the baronet is led to think that two stones have been substituted by Ul-Jabal for his own invaluable gem. All this while the gem was lying serenely in its place in the chalice. And thus it came to pass that in the Manor-house of Saul there arose a somewhat considerable Ado about Nothing."

For a moment Zaleski paused; then, turning round and laying his hand on the brown forehead of the mummy by his side, he said:

"My friend here could tell you, an' he would, a fine tale of the immensely important part which jewels in all ages have played in human history, human religions, institutions, ideas. He flourished some five centuries before the Messiah, was a Memphian priest of Amsu, and, as the hieroglyphics on his coffin assure me, a prime favourite with one Queen Amyntas. Beneath these mouldering swaddlings of the grave a great ruby still cherishes its blood-guilty secret on the forefinger of his right hand. Most curious is it to reflect how in *all* lands, and at *all* times, precious minerals have been endowed by men with mystic virtues. The Persians, for instance, believed that spinelle and the garnet were harbingers of joy. Have you read the ancient Bishop of Rennes on the subject? Really, I almost think there must be some truth in all this. The instinct of universal man is rarely far at fault. Already you have a semi-comic 'gold-cure' for alcoholism, and you have heard of the geophagism of certain African tribes. What if the scientist of the future be destined to discover that the diamond, and it alone, is a specific for cholera, that powdered rubellite cures fever, and the chrysoberyl gout? It would be in exact conformity with what I have hitherto observed of a general trend towards a certain inborn perverseness and whimsicality in Nature."

Note. – As some proof of the fineness of intuition evidenced by Zaleski, as distinct from his more conspicuous powers of reasoning, I may here state that some years after the occurrence of the tragedy I have recorded above, the skeleton of a man was discovered in the vaults of the Manor-house of Saul. I have not the least doubt that it was the skeleton of Ul-Jabal. The teeth were very prominent. A rotten rope was found loosely knotted round the vertebræ of his neck.

Popeau Intervenes

Mrs Belloc Lowndes

Prologue

"This is dear, delightful Paris! Paris, which I love; Paris, where I have always been so happy with Bob. It's foolish of me to feel depressed. I've nothing to be depressed about—"

Such were the voiceless thoughts which filled the mind of Lady Waverton as she walked down one of the platforms of the vast grey Gare du Nord on a hot, airless, July night. She formed one of a party of three; the other two being her husband, Lord Waverton, and a beautiful Russian emigrée, Countess Filenska, with whom they had become friends. It was the lovely Russian who had persuaded the Wavertons to take a little jaunt to Paris "on the cheap," that is without maids and valet. The Countess had drawn a delightful picture of an old hostelry on the left bank of the Seine called the Hotel Paragon, where they would find pleasant quiet rooms.

Perhaps the journey had tired the charming, over-refined woman her friends called Gracie Waverton. Yet this morning she had looked as well and happy as she ever did look, for she was not strong, and for some time past she had felt that she and her husband, whom in her gentle, reserved way, she loved deeply, were drifting apart. Like all very rich men, Lord Waverton had a dozen ways of killing time in which his wife could play no part. Still, according to modern ideas, they were a happy couple.

It did not take long for the autobus to glide across Paris at this time of the night, and when they turned into the quiet *cul de sac*, across the end of which rose the superb eighteenth-century mansion which had been the town palace of one of Marie Antoinette's platonic adorers, Monsieur le Duc de Paragon, Lady Waverton lost her vague feeling of despondency. There was something so cheery, as well as truly welcoming, about Monsieur and Madame Bonchamp, mine host and his wife; and she was enchanted with the high ceilinged, panelled rooms, which had been reserved for their party, and which overlooked a spacious leafy garden.

As Lady Waverton and her Russian friend kissed each other good-night, the Englishwoman exclaimed, "You didn't say a word too much, Olga. This is a delightful place!"

I

"Robert? This is *too* exquisite! You are the most generous man in the world!"

Olga Filenska was gazing, with greedy eyes, at an open blue velvet-lined jewel-case containing a superb emerald pendant.

"I'm glad you like it, darling—"

Lord Waverton seized the white hand, and made its owner put what it held on a table near which they both stood. Then he clasped her in his arms, and their lips met and clung together.

The secret lovers were standing in the centre of the large, barely-furnished *salon*, which belonged to the private suite of rooms which had been reserved for the party; and they felt secure from sudden surprise by a high screen which masked the door giving into the corridor.

At last, releasing her, he moodily exclaimed, "Why did you make me bring my wife to Paris? It spoils everything, and makes me feel, too, such a cad!"

"Remember my reputation, Robert. It is all I have left of my vanished treasures."

He caught her to him again, and once more kissed her long and thirstily.

"My God, how I love you!" he said in a strangled whisper. "There's nothing, nothing, *nothing* I wouldn't do, to have you for ever as my own!"

"Is that really true?" she asked with a searching look.

"Haven't I offered to give up everything, and make a bolt? It's you who refuse to do the straight thing."

"Your wife," he murmured, in a low bitter tone, "would never divorce you. She thinks divorce wicked."

"If I'm willing to give up my country, and everything I care for – for love of you, why shouldn't you do as much for me?"

To that she made no answer, only sighed, and looked at him appealingly.

What would each of them have felt had it suddenly been revealed that their every word had been overheard, and each passionate gesture of love witnessed, by an invisible listener and watcher? Yet such was the strange, and the almost incredible, fact. Hercules Popeau, but lately retired on a pension from the Criminal Investigation Branch of the Préfecture de Police, had long made the Hotel Paragon his home, and his comfortable study lay to the right of the stately octagon *salon* which terminated Lord and Lady Waverton's suite of rooms.

Popeau had lived in the splendid seventeenth-century house for quite a long time, before he had discovered – with annoyance rather than satisfaction – that just behind the arm-chair in which he usually sat, and cleverly concealed in the wainscoting, was a slanting sliding panel which enabled him both to hear and see everything that went on in the next room. This sinister "Judas," as it was well called, dated from the days of Louis the Fifteenth, when a diseased inquisitiveness was the outstanding peculiarity of both the great and the humble; even the King would spend his leisure in reading copies of the love letters intercepted in the post, of those of his faithful subjects who were known to him.

Hercules Popeau had been closely connected with the British army during the Great War, and he remembered that Lord Waverton, then little more than a boy, had performed an act of signal valour at Beaumont Hamel. That fact had so far interested him in the three tourists, as to have caused him to watch the party while they had sat at dinner in their private sitting-room the evening following their arrival in Paris. The famous secret agent was very human and he had taken a liking to fragile-looking Lady Waverton, and a dislike to her lovely Russian friend. The scene he was now witnessing confirmed his first judgment of the Countess Filenska.

"I wish Gracie were not here!" exclaimed Lord Waverton.

"She is – how do you call it? – too much thinking of herself to think of us," was the confident answer of Lady Waverton's false friend.

There came a look of discomfort and shame over the man's face. "You women are such damn good actresses! Then you think Gracie is really ill this morning?"

" 'Ill' is a big word. Still, she is willing to see a doctor. It is fortunate that I know a very good Paris physician. He will be here very soon; but she wants us to start for Versailles now, before he comes."

"All right! I'll go and get ready."

When she believed herself to be absolutely alone, Countess Filenska walked across to the long mirror between the two windows and stood there, looking at herself in the bright light with a close dispassionate scrutiny.

Hercules Popeau, as he gazed at her through his hidden "Judas," told himself that though in his time he had been brought in contact with many beautiful women, rarely had he seen so exquisite a creature as was Olga Filenska. While very dark, she had no touch of swarthiness, and her oval face had the luminosity of a white camellia petal. She had had the courage to remain unshingled, and the Frenchman, faithful to far away memories of youth, visioned the glorious mantle her tightly coiled hair must form when unbound. Her figure, at once slender and rounded, was completely revealed, as is the fashion to-day, by a plain black dress.

Was she really Russian? Hercules Popeau shook his head. That southern type of beauty is unmistakable. He had known a Georgian princess who might have been the twin sister of the woman he saw before him now.

The hidden watcher's lifelong business had been to guess the innermost thoughts of men and women. But he felt he had no clue as to what was making this dark lady smile, as she was doing now in so inscrutable a way, at herself.

At last she turned round and left the room, and at once her unseen admirer, and, yes, judge, closed the tiny slit in the panelled wall.

What a curious, romantic, and yes, sinister page, he had just turned in the great Book of Life! A page of a not uncommon story; that of a beautiful, unscrupulous woman, playing the part of serpent in a modern Garden of Eden.

It was clear that Lord Waverton was infatuated with this lovely creature, but there had been no touch of genuine passion in her seductive voice, or even in her apparently eager response to his ardour.

Hercules Popeau had a copy of the latest *Who's Who?* on his writing table, and he opened the section containing the letter W.

The entry he sought for, began: "Waverton, Robert Hichfield, of Hichfield, York. Second Baron."

And then there came back to him the knowledge that this man's father had been one of the greatest of Victorian millionaires. No wonder he had been able to present the woman he loved in secret with that magnificent jewel!

There came the sounds of a motor drawing up under the huge *porte-cochère* of the Hotel Paragon; and, rising, the Frenchman went quickly over to the open window on his right.

Yes, there was a big car, the best money could hire, with his lordship standing by the bonnet. Waverton looked the ideal "Milord" of French fancy, for he was a tall, broad man, with fair hair having in it a touch of red.

Just now he was obviously impatient and ill at ease. But he had not long to wait, for in a very few moments Countess Filenska stepped out of the great house into the courtyard. Even in her plain motor bonnet she looked entrancingly lovely.

Popeau took a step backwards from his window, as there floated upwards the voices of the two people whose secret he now shared.

"Did you see Gracie?" asked Lord Waverton abruptly.

"Yes, and she was so sweet and kind! She begs us not to hurry back; and she is quite looking forward to the visit of my old friend, Dr. Scorpion."

Scorpion? A curious name – not a happy name – for a medical man. Hercules Popeau remembered that he had once known a doctor of that name.

"Are you ready, Olga?"

"Quite ready, *mon ami*," and she smiled up into his face.

A moment later they were side by side, and Lord Waverton took the wheel.

As the motor rolled out on to the boulevard, the Frenchman went back to his desk, and, taking up the speaking-tube, he whistled down it.

"Madame Bonchamp? I have something important to say to you." He heard the quick answer: "At your service always, Monsieur."

"Listen to me!"

"I am listening."

"A doctor is coming to see Lady Waverton this morning. *Before* he sees Miladi, show him yourself into my bedroom."

There came a surprised, "Do you feel ill, Monsieur?"

"I am not very well; and I have reason to think this doctor is an old friend of mine. *But I do not wish him to know that he is not being shown straight into the bedroom of his English lady patient.* Have I made myself clear?"

He heard her eager word of assent. Madame Bonchamp was as sharp as a needle, and she had once had reason to be profoundly grateful to Hercules Popeau. He knew he could trust her absolutely; sometimes he called her, by way of a joke, "Madame Discretion."

II

Hercules Popeau always did everything in what he called to himself an artistic – an Englishman would have said a thorough – way. Before getting into bed, he entirely undressed, and then drew together the curtains of his bedroom window. Thus anyone coming into the room from the corridor would feel as if in complete darkness, while to one whose eyes were already accustomed to the dim light, everything would be perfectly clear.

The time went by slowly, and he had already been in bed half an hour, when at last the door of the room opened, and he heard Madame Bonchamp exclaim: "*Entrez, Monsieur le Docteur!*" And then his heart gave a leap, for the slight elderly individual who had just been shown into the darkened room, was undoubtedly the man he had known twenty years ago.

Quickly the ex-secret agent told himself that as the doctor had been about thirty years of age when he had got into the very serious trouble which had brought him into touch with the then Chief of the French Criminal Investigation Department, he must now be fifty.

With a sardonic look on his powerful face Hercules Popeau watched his visitor grope his way forward into the darkened room.

"Miladi," he said at last, in an ill-assured tone, "I will ask your permission to draw the curtains a little? Otherwise, I cannot see you." He put his hat on a chair as he spoke, and then he went towards the nearest window, and pulled apart the curtains.

Letting in a stream of light, he turned towards the bed. When he saw that it was a man, and not a woman who was sitting up there, he gave a slight gasp of astonishment.

"It is a long time since we have met, is it not, my good Doctor Scorpion?"

For a moment Popeau thought that the man who stood stock still, staring at him as if petrified, was about to fall down in a faint. And a feeling of regret, almost of shame, came over him – for he was a kindly man – at having played the other such a trick.

But the visitor made a great effort to regain his composure, and at last with a certain show of valour, he exclaimed: "I have been shown into the wrong room. I came here to see an English lady, who is ill."

"That is so," said Popeau quietly. "But I, too, feel ill, and hearing that you had been called to this hotel, I thought I would like to see you first, and ask your advice. I confess I rather hoped you were the Dr. Scorpion I had once known."

To the unfortunate man who stood in the middle of the large room there was a terrible edge of irony in the voice that uttered those quiet words.

"Of course, I know, that is in the old days, you were more accustomed to diagnose the condition of an ailing woman than that of a man," went on the ex-police chief pitilessly.

And then he changed his tone. "Come, come!" he exclaimed. "I have no right to go back to the past. Draw a chair close up to my bed, and tell me how you have got on all these years?"

With obvious reluctance the doctor complied with this almost command. "I have now been in very respectable practice for some time," he said in a low voice.

He waited a moment, then he added bitterly: "Can you wonder that seeing you gave me a moment of great discomfort and pain, reminding me, as this meeting must do, of certain errors of my youth of which I have repented."

"I am glad to hear you have repented," said Popeau heartily.

In a clearer, calmer tone, Scorpion went on: "I made a good marriage; I have a sweet wife, and two excellent children."

"Good! Good!"

Hercules Popeau's manner altered. He felt convinced that this man's account of himself was substantially true. And yet? And yet a doubt remained.

"Are you always called in to the clients of this hotel?" he asked suddenly.

The other hesitated, and the ex-police chief again felt a touch of misgiving.

"No, I am not the regular medical attendant of the Hotel Paragon," answered Scorpion at last. "But I've been here before, and oddly enough," he concluded jauntily, "to see another foreign lady."

"Then who sent for you now, to-day?"

Again the doctor did not answer at once; but when he did speak it was to say, with a forced smile: "A lady whom I attended for a quinsy, the last time she was in this hotel. It is to see a friend of hers that I am here."

The doctor's statement fitted in with what he, Hercules Popeau, knew to be true. Yet something – a kind of sixth sense which sometimes came to his aid – made Popeau tell his visitor a lie of which he was ashamed.

"Although I know seeing me again must have revived sore memories, I am glad to have seen you, Scorpion, and to have heard that the past is dead. Now tell me if I can safely go off tonight to Niort, where I am to spend the rest of this hot summer?"

The doctor at once assumed a professional manner. He peered into his new patient's throat, he felt his new patient's pulse, and at last he said gravely: "Yes, you can leave Paris to-night, though it might be more prudent to stay till to-morrow morning."

"Now that you have reassured me, I shall go to-night."

Then Dr. Scorpion asked, almost in spite of himself, a question: "Are you still connected with the police, Monsieur Popeau?"

"No, I took my pension at the end of the war, and I am now a rolling stone, for I have not the good fortune, like you, to be married to a woman I love. Also, alas! I am not a father." He waited a moment. "And now for what the British call a good hand-shake."

He held out his hand, and then felt a sensation of violent recoil, for it was as if the hand he held was a dead hand. Though to-day was a very hot day, that hand was icy cold – an infallible sign of shock.

The ex-member of the dreaded Sûreté felt a touch of sharp remorse. He had nothing in him of the feline human being who likes to play with a man or a woman as a cat plays with a mouse.

As soon as he had dressed himself Hercules Popeau spoke down his speaking-tube. "Has the doctor left?" he asked casually.

"Yes, some minutes ago."

He went down to the office, and drew a bow at a venture: "You knew Dr. Scorpion before, eh?"

Madame Bonchamp said in a singular tone: "The Countess Filenska and that little doctor have been great friends for a long time. Beauty sometimes likes Ugly, and Ugly always likes Beauty."

Popeau had meant to go upstairs again, but after that casual word or two, instead of going upstairs, he walked out of the hotel.

Sauntering along, he crossed a bridge, and came at last to the big building, the very name of which fills every Parisian's heart with awe.

Now there is a small, almost hidden, door in the Préfecture of Police which is only used by the various heads of departments. It was through this door that Popeau went up to his former quarters, being warmly greeted on the way by various ex-colleagues with whom he had been popular.

Soon he was in the familiar room where are kept the secret *dossiers*, or records which play so important a part in the lives of certain people, and very soon there was laid before him an envelope with the name of *Victor Alger Scorpion* inscribed on it. Glancing over the big sheet of copy paper he saw at once the entry concerning the serious affair in which Scorpion had been concerned some twenty years before. And then came *General Remarks*:

> Victor Alger Scorpion has made a great effort to become respectable. He is living a quiet, moral life with his wife and two children, and to the latter he is passionately devoted. But it is more than suspected that now and again he will take a serious risk in order to make a big sum of money to add to his meagre savings. *Such risks are always associated with—*

Then followed three capital letters with whose meaning Hercules Popeau was acquainted, though he had never been directly in touch with that side of the police force which concerns itself specially with morals.

He read on:

> Just after the end of the war, Scorpion was concerned with the mysterious death of a young Spanish lady. But though he was under grave suspicion, it was impossible actually to prove anything against him; also the fact that he had done even more than his duty as a surgeon in the war, benefited him in the circumstances. He was, however, warned that he would be kept under observation. Since then there has been nothing to report.

III

Lord and Lady Waverton and their friend had arrived on a Saturday night, and Dr. Scorpion's first visit to the hotel had been paid on the Monday morning. As the days went on, Lady Waverton, while still keeping to her room, became convalescent, though the doctor recommended that her ladyship should go on being careful till she was to leave Paris, on the following Saturday.

Hercules Popeau, who had constituted himself a voluntary prisoner, cursed himself for a suspicious fool. Cynically he told himself that though marital infidelity is extremely common, murder is comparatively rare.

On the Friday morning Madame Bonchamp herself brought up his *petit déjeuner*. She looked anxious and worried. "Miladi is worse," she said abruptly. "I have already telephoned for the doctor. The Countess Filenska is greatly distressed! I must hurry, now, as I have to serve an English breakfast for two in the next room at once."

A few minutes later Popeau, peeping through the slanting "Judas," sat watching Lord Waverton and his beautiful companion. After having exchanged a long passionate embrace, they sat down, but the excellent omelette provided by Madame Bonchamp remained untasted for a while.

"I don't see why you should be going to England to-day!" exclaimed Lord Waverton.

She said firmly: "It is imperative that I should see the picture dealer who will start for Russia to-morrow."

"Well then, if you must go" – he had the grace to look ashamed – "I don't see why I shouldn't go, too, darling? Gracie hates to have me about when she's ill, and I can't help thinking that the sensible thing to do would be to get a trained nurse over from England. I've only got to telephone to my mother to have a nurse here by to-morrow morning."

The Countess looked violently disturbed. "I know Gracie would not like that!" she exclaimed.

She was pouring some black coffee into her cup, and Popeau saw that the lovely hand shook. "You cannot do better than leave Gracie in my French doctor's hands," she went on. "I was seriously ill here last year, and he was wonderful!"

There came a knock at the door, and the man to whom his ex-patient had just given such a good character, came into the sitting-room.

Dr. Scorpion was pale, but composed: "I am indeed sorry," he began, "to hear that my patient is worse—"

The Countess cut him short, almost rudely. "Let us go to

her," she cried, and together they left the room. But in a few moments she came back, alone.

"Gracie is much better," she observed. "She will probably be able to go home Friday."

She put her hand caressingly through Lord Waverton's arm. "I will go over to England to-day at four o'clock, and I will be back here by to-morrow night. What do you say to *that* for devotion?"

Her lover's face cleared. "Does that mean—"

"—that I'm a foolish woman? That I do not like being away from you even for quite a little while? Yes, it does mean that!"

She submitted – the unseen watcher thought with a touch of impatience – to his ardent caresses.

Suddenly the door behind the screen opened. The two sprang apart, and, as the doctor edged his way in again, Lord Waverton left the room.

"What have you come back to tell me?" said the Countess sharply.

Scorpion looked at her fixedly. "Is it true that Madame la Comtesse is going away to England to-day?"

"I am returning to Paris at once," she said evasively.

"I have thought matters over, and I refuse to go on with the treatment before payment, or part payment, is made," he said firmly.

"Come! Don't be unreasonable!" she exclaimed.

He answered at once, in a fierce, surly tone: "I refuse to risk my head unless it is made worth my while. I did not think it possible that you meant to leave me to face a terrible danger alone."

"I tell you that I am coming back to-morrow night! Also it is absolutely true that I have no money – as yet."

"Surely the Milord would give you some money? Cannot you invent something which requires at once an advance of say—" he hesitated, then slowly uttered the words, "fifty thousand francs."

Popeau expected to hear a cry of protest, but the beautiful woman who now stood close to the ugly, clever-looking little doctor, opened her handbag and said coldly: "I have something here which is worth a great deal more than fifty thousand francs," and she handed him the jewel-case which contained the emerald pendant.

Scorpion opened the case. "Is the stone real?" he asked suspiciously.

"Fool!" she said angrily, "walk into the first jeweller's shop you pass by, offer it for sale, and see."

He was looking at the gorgeous stone with glistening, avid eyes. Slowly he shut the jewel-case and put it in his pocket. "I know where I can dispose of it, should it become necessary that I should do so."

"Then you will keep your promise?"

There was a long pause. Then the doctor produced a loose-leaved prescription block.

"I will fulfil my promise," he said firmly, "if you will write on this sheet of paper what I dictate."

He handed her a fountain pen:

> "My dear friend and doctor: I beg you to accept the jewel I am sending you, a square-cut emerald, which is my own property to dispose of, in consideration of the great care and kindness you showed me when I was so extremely ill last year. – Your ever grateful, Olga Filenska."

She hesitated for what seemed both to the invisible watcher, and to her accomplice, a long time. But at last she wrote out the words he again dictated, and he put the piece of paper in the pocket where already reposed the small jewel-case.

"*C'est entendu*," he exclaimed, and turned towards the door.

A moment later Hercules Popeau took off his telephone receiver. "Invent a pretext to keep the doctor till I come down!" he exclaimed.

Then, taking out of a drawer a large sheet of notepaper headed *Préfecture de Police, Paris*, he wrote on it:

Madame la Comtesse,

    You are in grave danger. The man you are employing to rid you of your rival is affiliated to the French Police. He has revealed your plot. An affidavit sworn by him will reach Scotland Yard in the course of to-morrow. A copy of the sworn statement of Dr. Scorpion will also be laid before Lord Waverton, who will be summoned to appear as a witness at the extradition proceedings. An admirer of your beauty thinks it kind to warn you that you will be well advised to break your journey to-day, and proceed to some other destination than England. The value of the jewel which I enclose is eight hundred pounds sterling. Lord Waverton paid for it close on two thousand pounds.

He put this letter in a drawer, and then went down to the hall of the hotel.

Dr. Scorpion was chatting to Madame Bonchamp, and looked startled and disturbed when he saw Hercules Popeau coming to wards him.

"I found Niort dull, so I came back to Paris," said the latter genially. "How is your patient, my good Scorpion?"

"Going on fairly," said the other hesitatingly. "Though not well enough to leave the hotel this week, as she had hoped to do. Well! Now I must be off—"

"I have a further word to say to you, Scorpion."

Popeau's voice had become cold and very grave. "Come upstairs to my rooms."

Scorpion stumbled up the staircase of the grand old house, too frightened, now, to know what he was doing, or where he was going.

When they reached the corridor, the other man took hold of his shoulder, and pushed him through into his study. Then he locked the door, and turning, faced his abject visitor.

"The first thing I ask you to do is to put on the table the emerald which has just been given you as the price of blood."

"The emerald?"

Scorpion was shaking, now, as if he had the ague. "What do you mean?" he faltered, "I know nothing of any emerald."

"Come – come! Don't be a fool."

A look of rage came over the livid face. "Does that woman dare to call me a thief?" he exclaimed. "See what she herself wrote when she gave me this jewel!"

With a shaking hand he drew a folded sheet of paper from his pocket.

"I want that, too, of course."

Scorpion sank down on to a chair. He asked himself seriously if Hercules Popeau was in league with the Devil?

The ex-police chief came and stood over him. "Listen carefully to what I am going to say. It is important."

The wretched man looked up, his eyes full of terror, while Popeau went on, tonelessly.

"Once more I am going to allow you to escape the fate which is your due. Last time it was for the sake of your mother. This time it will be for the sake of two women – your good wife, and the unfortunate lady whom you, or perhaps I ought to say, your temptress and accomplice, had doomed to a hideous death by poison."

Scorpion stared at Hercules Popeau. His face had gone the colour of chalk.

"Get up!"

The unhappy man stood up on his trembling legs.

"Just now you dictated a letter to your accomplice, and I now dictate to you the following confession."

He placed a piece of notepaper on his writing-table, and forced the other man to go and sit down in his own arm-chair. Then, slowly, he dictated the following!

"I, Victor Scorpion, confess to having entered into a conspiracy with a woman I know under the name of the Countess Filenska, to bring about the death of Lady Waverton on—"

Popeau stopped his dictation and looked fixedly at Scorpion.

"What day was she to die?" he asked.

Scorpion stared woefully at his tormentor. He did not, he felt he could not, answer.

"Must I repeat my question?"

In a whimpering voice he said: "I did not mean that she should die."

"What was the exact proposal made to you?"

Twice the man moistened his lips, then at last he answered:

"Five hundred pounds sterling within a fortnight of – of the accident, and ten thousand pounds sterling within six months of the Countess's marriage to Lord Waverton."

"To your mind I suppose the emerald represented the five hundred pounds?"

"She was going away," murmured Scorpion. "I might not have got anything, the more so that I did not mean the poor Miladi to die."

"On what day did the Countess expect her victim to die?"

Popeau had to bend down to hear the two words. "Next Friday."

"I see. Write down the following:

"I was to receive five hundred pounds sterling on the day of her death, and within six months of the Countess's marriage to Lord Waverton ten thousand pounds sterling, whatever the rate of exchange might be at the time. (Signed) Victor Alger Scorpion."

"Do allow me to put down that I did not intend to carry out this infamous plan?" asked the unhappy wretch pleadingly.

Popeau hesitated a moment. "No," he said firmly, "I will not allow you to do that. But this I will promise. Within a few hours from now, you yourself shall do what you wish with that piece of paper."

"And the emerald?" said Scorpion in a faltering voice.

"The emerald," said Popeau thoughtfully, "will be returned to its owner. I regret that necessity almost as much as you do. But it is to your interest, Scorpion, as to that of others concerned, that the Countess Filenska should have enough to live on till she has found another lover."

"Perhaps you are right," muttered Scorpion sadly.

"Of course I am right! And now," went on Popeau, "you can make yourself at home in these two rooms for a while, and you can have the use of my bathroom also, should you care to take a bath."

He smiled genially. "You may telephone home to your wife, saying you will not be home till late."

"Can I trust you?" asked his prisoner. "Remember that I am

a father. It was for the sake of my dear children that I placed myself in this dangerous position!"

"I have never yet betrayed any human being," said Hercules Popeau seriously. "I am not likely to begin by you, who are such an old—" he hesitated, and then he said "acquaintance."

Epilogue

The beautiful cosmopolitan woman, who had made so many warm friends in English society, had just settled herself comfortably in a first-class compartment of the Paris-Calais express. She was quite alone, for in July there are few travellers to England. So she was rather taken aback when a big man, dressed in a pale grey alpaca suit, suddenly thrust his body and head through the aperture leading into the corridor.

"Have I the honour of speaking to Countess Filenska?" he asked.

She hesitated a moment. Then she saw that he held in his hand a bulky envelope, and involuntarily she smiled. From dear foolish Waverton, of course! A *billet doux*, accompanied no doubt by some delightful gift. So, "I am the Countess Filenska," she answered.

"I have been told to give you this little parcel, Madame la Comtesse. I am glad I had the good fortune to arrive before your train started."

The Frenchman had a cultivated voice, and a good manner. No doubt he was a jeweller. She was pleased, being the kind of woman she was, that there need be no question of a gratuity.

"I thank you, monsieur," she said graciously.

He lifted his hat, and went off. She thought, but she may have been mistaken, that she heard a chuckle in the corridor.

The train started; slowly the traveller broke the seal of the big envelope. Yes! As she had half expected, there was a jewel-case wrapped up in a piece of notepaper. Eagerly she opened the case, and then came mingled disappointment and surprise, for it only contained the emerald which she had given that morning to Scorpion.

With a feeling of sudden apprehension she quickly unfolded the piece of notepaper and then, slowly, with eyes dilated with terror, she read the terrible words written there. The warning sent her, maybe, from some old ex-lover, from the Préfecture de Police.

Could she leap now, out of the train? No, it was now gathering speed, and she could not afford to risk an accident.

Feverishly she counted over her money. Yes, she had enough, amply enough to break her journey at Calais, and go on to—?

After a moment's deep thought she uttered aloud the word "*Berlin.*"

Late that same afternoon Madame Bonchamp opened the door of Hercules Popeau's study. "Milord Waverton," she murmured nervously, and the Englishman walked into the room.

He looked uncomfortable, even a little suspicious. He had not been able to understand exactly what was wanted of him, only that a Frenchman, whose name he did not know, desired his presence – at once.

He felt anxious. Was his wife worse, and was the man who had asked to see him so urgently a specialist called in by the Countess's French doctor?

"I have a painful, as well as a serious, communication to make to your lordship," began Hercules Popeau in slow, deliberate tones. He spoke with a strong French accent, but otherwise his English was perfect.

"I belong to the French branch of what in England is called the Criminal Investigation Department, and a most sinister fact has just been brought to our notice."

He looked fixedly – it was a long, searching glance – into the other man's bewildered face. And then he felt a thrill of genuine relief. His instinct had been right! Lord Waverton, so much was clear, was quite unconscious of the horrible plot which had had for object that of ridding him of his wife.

"The fact brought to our notice," went on Popeau quietly, "does not concern your lordship; it concerns Lady Waverton."

"My wife? Impossible!"

Lord Waverton drew himself up to his full height. He looked angry, as well as incredulous.

"Lady Waverton," went on the other, "possesses a terrible enemy."

"I assure you," said Lord Waverton coldly, "that the French police have made some absurd mistake. My wife is the best of women, kindness itself to all those with whom she comes in contact. *I* may have enemies; she has none."

"Lady Waverton has an enemy," said Popeau positively. "And what is more, that enemy intended to compass her death, and indeed nearly succeeded in doing so."

The Englishman stared at the Frenchman. He felt as if he was confronting a lunatic.

"This enemy of Lady Waverton's laid her plans – for it is a woman – very cleverly," said Popeau gravely. "She discovered in this city of Paris a man who will do anything for money. That man is a doctor, and for what appeared to him a sufficient consideration, he undertook to poison her ladyship."

He waited a moment, then added in an almost casual tone, "Lady Waverton's death was to have occurred next Friday."

"What!" exclaimed Lord Waverton, in a horror-stricken voice, "do you mean that the little French doctor who has been attending my wife is—"

"—a would-be murderer? Yes," said Hercules Popeau stolidly. "Dr. Scorpion had undertaken to bring about what would have appeared to everybody here, in the Hotel Paragon, a natural death."

Lord Waverton covered his face with his hands. Yet even now no suspicion of the woman who had been behind Scorpion had reached his brain. He was trying to remember the name of a French maid his wife had had for a short time soon after their marriage, and who had been dismissed without a character.

"Most fortunately for you, Lord Waverton, this infamous fellow-countryman of mine had already had trouble with the police. So he grew suddenly afraid, and made a full confession of the hideous plot. He brought with him a written proof, as well *as a valuable emerald*, which was part of the price his infamous temptress was willing to pay the man she intended should be the actual murderer."

The speaker turned away, for he desired to spare the unhappy man, whose sudden quick, deep breathing, showed the awful effect those last words had had on him.

"The rest of the blood money – ten thousand pounds sterling

– was to be paid when Scorpion's temptress became the second wife of a wealthy English peer."

Lord Waverton gave a strangled cry.

"I should now like to show you the proof of the story I have told you. I take it you do not desire to see the emerald?"

The other shook his head violently.

"That is as well," said Popeau calmly, "for it is once more in the possession of the woman who calls herself the Countess Filenska."

He took out of his pocket the two documents, the deed of gift written out by the Countess, and the confession signed by Scorpion himself.

"I will ask you to read these through," he said, "and then I must beg you to put a firm restraint upon yourself. I have kept the man here so that he may confirm the fact that the whole of this statement is in his handwriting."

Popeau waited till Lord Waverton had read Scorpion's confession. Then he opened the door of his bedroom.

"Come here for a moment," he called out in a quick, business-like tone. "I have done with that paper I asked you to sign, and I am ready to give you it back the moment you have informed this gentleman that you wrote it."

Scorpion sidled into the room.

"Now then," said Popeau sharply, "say in English, 'I, Scorpion, swear that all I wrote down here is true, and that this is my signature.'"

The man repeated the words in a faltering voice.

Popeau handed him back the confession.

"Take this piece of paper," he observed, "down into the courtyard; there set a light to it, and watch it burn; then go home and thank the good God, and your good wife, that you have not begun the long road which leads to the Devil's Island."

After Scorpion had left the room, Hercules Popeau turned to the Englishman. "I trust," he said, "that your lordship will not think it impertinent if I ask you to listen to me for yet another two or three minutes?"

Lord Waverton bent his head. His face had gone grey under its tan.

"I am old enough to be your father, and this I would say to

you, and I trust that you will take it in good part. There was a time when a man in your position was guarded by high invisible barriers from many terrible dangers. Those barriers, Milord, are no longer there, and—"

There came a knock at the door. A telegram was handed to Lord Waverton. He tore open the envelope.

> An unexpected chance has come my way of getting back to Russia, and of recovering some of my lost property. Good-bye, dear friends. Thank you both for your goodness to an unhappy woman. Dear love to Gracie.

As Lord Waverton handed the two slips of paper to his new friend, Hercules Popeau looked much relieved.

"All you have to do," he exclaimed, "is to show Miladi this telegram, and then to give her – how do you say it in English? – a good kiss on her sweet face!"

Locked In

E. Charles Vivian

I

"Twenty-three years ago," said Superintendent Wadden, "his father committed suicide. I remember, because it was the year after I married. And now – well, a family habit, by the look of it."

"Perhaps." Seated beside his chief in the big police saloon, Inspector Head made the rejoinder sound entirely non-committal.

"Whaddye mean, man – perhaps?" Wadden snapped, accompanying the query with the glare of his fierce eyes: having been turned out at eight in the morning to investigate the reported suicide, he was a trifle short of temper. But Head, gazing at the road ahead, wisely ignored both the stare and the question.

"It's the next gateway on the right, Jeffries," he said to the driver of the car, "and stop a full 20 yards short of the front door. Don't drive up to it."

Laurels, backed by old cedars, hid the house as Jeffries turned the saloon into the drive. Two hundred yards or less revealed a tiled Elizabethan roof with spiralling chimneys, and such of the frontage as a gorgeous-leaved virginia creeper let appear showed century-mellowed in tint. To the left of the big main doorway two diamond-paned casement windows showed; over and between them was a single first-floor window of similar type and against it a ladder was reared. And, Head noted as he got out from the car, no fewer than four of the diamond panes of this first-floor window were broken, and their leaden framing bent aside, as if to admit a hand from without.

"Wait, Jeffries – I don't think we shall need you," Wadden said as he got out from the saloon. "What about Wells, Head?"

"You'd better come along, sergeant," Head said to the fourth occupant of the car. "Bring your outfit, in case we need it."

Thereupon Sergeant Wells followed his two superiors towards the entrance, bearing the black leather case in which reposed a fingerprint-detecting outfit and a camera. Before Head, leading the way, could pull the big, old-fashioned bell handle beside the doorpost, the door itself swung open, and a stout, fair-haired man frowned out at him before glancing at Wadden and the sergeant.

"If you're Press," he snapped, "you can get out. I'll give you two policemen particulars for the inquest. It's purely formal."

Wadden gave him a glare from his fierce eyes. "Oh, is it?" he snapped back. "That's Inspector Head you're speaking to, and he'll take charge of the formalities. What's your name?"

"Keller," the other man said, far more meekly. "Percival Keller. Mr. Garnham is my half-brother – was, that is, till he shot himself."

"Then, for a start, we'll see the body," Wadden announced. "Was it you who telephoned us to come out here?"

"No," Keller answered, standing back for them to enter. "That was Kennett, Mr. Garnham's man. But I told him to telephone."

He gave Head another unregarded, resentful look, as if he were incensed at a mere police inspector masquerading in a well-cut lounge suit instead of appearing in uniform. But Head was surveying the magnificently carved staircase that went diagonally across the back of the big square entrance hall, giving access to a gallery that ran along the sides and back of the apartment at first-floor level.

"A fine piece of woodwork," he observed, with apparent irrelevance to their task.

"Yes," Keller said, ingratiatingly. "One of the Garnhams brought it over from Italy in the eighteenth century and put it up here. It came from a villa of Alexander Borgia's – his arms are repeated on the newels. Three of the doors on the gallery belong with it."

"And now, the body," Head suggested.

"I'll take you up," Keller answered. "Mere formality, of

course. We had to break the outside window to get into the room – he'd locked himself in and left the key in the lock."

The three followed him up the staircase and along the left side gallery to a door that appeared as a museum piece – Cellini or Michael Angelo himself might have proportioned it and designed its ornament. Keller reached out for the handle, but Head spoke before he touched it.

"Who else has turned that handle this morning?" he asked.

"Kennett, and Mrs. Garnham," Keller answered, readily but with visible irritation. "Why? I tell you he'd locked himself in."

"And the keyhole?" Head queried blandly. "I see none."

Keller pressed a wooden shield, bearing similar designs to those on the staircase newels, and set quite a foot back from the edge of the door. It slid aside, revealing a keyhole a good two inches in length.

"I see," Head remarked. "Now we can go in."

Again Keller led, and they followed. Halfway between the door and the window which Head had seen as broken from outside the house, lay the body of a delicately featured, scholarly looking man of early middle age, and by it an overturned chair that had stood at a flat topped writing-desk so angled from the window that the light would fall over the left shoulder of one seated at the kneehole. Behind the right ear of the prostrate figure was a neat round hole, from which a very little blood had oozed to trickle down to the back of the dead man's neck and there congeal. A small, nickel-plated revolver gleamed ominously from the carpet, and, kneeling, Head took it up by inserting a pencil in the barrel, handing it to Wells, who took hold of the pencil and so avoided touching the weapon itself.

"Has anyone handled that thing, do you know?" Head inquired.

Keller shook his head. "Nobody," he answered. "Old Joe, the gardener, got in through the window and unlocked the door for us, and I warned him and Kennett and Mrs. Garnham too, not to touch anything. And the doctor didn't touch it either, I know."

"What doctor?" Wadden put in abruptly.

"Why, his own doctor. Tyrrell, his name is."

"And where is Dr. Tyrrell?" Wadden persisted.

"I told him he needn't stay – he had an urgent confinement case," Keller explained. "He saw all he wanted to see for the inquest."

"Oh, did he?" Wadden snapped. "Well, I'll get Bennett, our own surgeon, out to make a proper examination. You appear to have taken a good deal on yourself, Mr. Keller. What's your jumping-off point, Head?"

"I'll begin on this man Joe," Head answered. "He was first into the room, it seems. Then I can decide whom to take next. Dust that revolver for any fingerprints, Wells—"

"You won't find any," Keller broke in. "He's lying on his right hand, but it's all bandaged up – he scalded it badly two days ago."

"See what you can find, Wells," Head insisted quietly.

"But – to what purpose?" Keller demanded irritably. "I tell you, he locked himself in before he shot himself. Examine the window and then the door – see for yourself that he must have been absolutely alone in here. You're only making the tragedy worse for Mrs. Garnham with all this fuss – this useless fuss!"

"And now" Head remarked, even more quietly, "perhaps you will be so good as to find this man Joe for me, Mr. Keller. Would you mind?"

II

Down in the big entrance hall, while Wells busied himself over the revolver with his fingerprinting outfit, Keller escorted in from the back premises an oldish man, grey-haired and grey-bearded, and himself drew forward a chair as if to become a member of the party.

"We shall not need you, Mr. Keller," Head told him. "Thanks for the trouble you have taken, though."

Without replying, Keller went out. Then Joe, the gardener, owned to having been employed here for over forty years, rising from third gardener to headship, and also confessed to the fitting surname of Plant.

"And you discovered Mr. Garnham's body?" Head asked him.

"Saw it through the window, sir," Joe answered. "It'd be about seven o'clock this mornin' or a little past seven."

"And how did you happen to be up a ladder outside that window at that time?" Head inquired.

"Well, sir, about leavin' off time last night, the master – Mr. Garnham, that is – come to me as I was lockin' up my things in the barn, and said if I didn't cut back the creeper round that window he'd soon need a light in the room at midday. He told me to make it my first job to-day, but I'd hardly started when I saw him wi' the hole in his skull and the pistol alongside him—"

"Wait a bit," Head interrupted. "When you put up that ladder, were there any footprints in the geranium bed under the windows?"

Joe shook his head decidedly. "There was not, sir, and there's none now, either. I put down boards to prevent either footprints or ladder marks. But if you mean did anyone climb in or out of that window, sir, I can tell you it was impossible. I had to break four panes to shoot back the bolts from the outside, and if anyone had got in and closed it from the inside, they'd be still in the room, because the door was locked with the key on the inside."

"Unless Mr. Garnham let them out, Joe," Wadden interposed.

"Yes, sir, but since both the window and door were fastened inside the room like that, Mr. Garnham must have been alone when he shot himself," Joe insisted, respectfully but firmly.

"You'd think so, wouldn't you?" Wadden half-soliloquised. "Carry on with what you did, though."

"I got down the ladder, and went, in at the back of the house," Joe continued. "Cook and Gladys – that's the house-maid – were in the kitchen, and I got Gladys to fetch Kennett, and then told him. He said get in by the window, because you'd have to ruin the door to force it, and unlock the door from the inside. While I was doin' that, he rung for Dr. Tyrrell and the police, which was you gentlemen, I take it."

"Did Mr. Keller have anything to do with ringing for the doctor and for us?" Head asked after a thoughtful pause.

"No, sir. He hadn't come down, then. Kennett went to the telephone here," Joe pointed at the instrument, "while I went out at the front door to break the window and get into the room."

There was thus one – possibly unimportant – error in Keller's account of his own actions, Head reflected.

"And Mrs. Garnham – where was she?" he asked.

"I dunno, sir. Not up, I think. Gladys told me before you got here that Mr. Keller broke the news to her. I haven't seen her to-day."

"Married – how long?" Head asked next.

"It'll be – September, they were married – yes, three years next month. But I don't see—" He broke off, doubtfully.

"Happily married, of course," Head persisted.

Joe Plant shook his head. "All the years I've been here, sir, I've never gossiped about the family and their affairs," he said.

"Quite right of you," Head approved. "This Mr. Keller, though. Do you count him as one of the family?"

"No, I don't." There was sudden heat in the reply. "A double-dyed waster, everlastin'ly spongin' on the master, who was always far too good-natured. His mother was a widow, and he was a kid of five when the master's father married her, and even then he was a little devil. They say he spent every penny she left him, and that was a considerable lot, an' for the last two years he's been no more'n the mistletoe, with the master as the oak. A parasite, an' no more."

"Umm-m! This man Kennett, now?"

"Quite a good chap, sir. He was batman to the master in the war, and been here ever since he was demobbed. Him and I get on well."

"His duties being what?"

"Oh, a bit of secretarying, an' kept the two cars in order, an' looked after the master's clothes. An' he's the only one the master let have the run of that room – the one where the body is – to clean it. The master kept all his books an' papers in there, you see, sir."

"This is an old house, Joe," Wadden put in abruptly, "and old houses are queer, sometimes. Apart from the window and the door, is there any way into that room that you've heard about in your 40 years here?"

"No, sir," Joe answered with unhesitating sincerity. "You mean—"

"Nothing," Head interrupted him. "What other servants are there?"

"There's cook, and Gladys I spoke of, an' Rose – she's the parlourmaid. An' Mrs. Higgs comes over from Todlington three days a week to do rough work – sort of charring."

"Well, I think that's all we want you to tell us, for the present, Joe. Now send Gladys along to us here, and – do you know the general run of the house, though?"

"Every inch of it, sir."

"Well, when she comes along, I want you to take Sergeant Wells round and show him every room and explain what it's used for. That's all, thanks – we have to do these things, you know."

He signed to Wells as the gardener went out.

"The bedrooms, Wells – take each one as we handle the occupants, especially Keller's. I'm not happy about this at all. That pistol?"

"Old-fashioned hammerless Smith and Wesson, Mr. Head, .32 bore. Only one shot fired. No print of any kind on it anywhere."

Head took it from him and inspected it. "That muzzle looks very clean for a fired pistol," he observed.

"I get you, sir," Wells answered.

Head slipped the pistol into his pocket as Gladys entered the room.

III

Standing side by side, Wadden and Head watched while Bennett, the police surgeon, conducted his examination of the body, and Tyrrell the practitioner who had attended Garnham in life and so perfunctorily assumed his death as that of a suicide, also watched, having been summoned back to the house by Wadden. Eventually Bennett stood up.

"Instantaneous," he said. "At some time between eleven last night and one this morning. Quite instantaneous – hardly any blood."

"The perfect story-book situation," Wadden observed pensively. "Dead man on his own carpet, revolver beside him. Would he have fallen like that and dragged the chair over, though?"

"Hard to say," Bennett answered. "Reflex muscular action after death is impossible to predicate."

"And he was certainly locked in the room," Wadden observed again. "We have done enough questioning and inspecting to be pretty certain there are no secret passages or anything of that sort. No chimney, because no fireplace. Therefore, Head, if anyone else shot him, he got up and locked the door after dying instantaneously and letting the other man out, and then came back and lay down again."

"See Euclid on the point," Head said thoughtfully. "But – doctor, take another careful look at that hole behind his ear and then come down and out with me. Out into the garden."

He left the room and went downstairs, while Wadden merely went to the window of the room to watch. By the time Bennett got out into the garden Head had arranged a stuffed and mounted antelope head, which he had taken from the entrance-hall, on a sundial.

"Now, watch, doctor," he bade. "This" – he took the revolver from his pocket – "is what killed Garnham. See this – the hair is about the same length as Garnham's behind his ear. Now" – he placed the pistol against the stuffed neck and pulled the trigger – "come and examine the hole," he invited, after the faint curl of smoke following on the explosion had drifted away. "For a good quarter of an inch round the hole, the hair is badly burned, as you see."

"Yes, I see," Bennett agreed, beginning to understand.

"Now, again. Watch this," Head bade.

With the pistol muzzle a good foot distant from the head, he fired again. Again Bennett examined the hole.

"Diffused scorching," Head pointed out, "and some shrivelled hairs where grains of only partially burned powder struck. A patchy burn, in fact. Now just one more, at about eighteen inches."

With the surgeon watching very intently now, he fired again, and, even with the longer interval between the muzzle of the pistol and the skin, there were traces of burning round the bullet hole.

"Garnham was fair-haired," he remarked, "and there isn't a trace of burning round the bullet hole in his head. You showed us his right hand, and it's a pretty bad scald. Now – I'll hold this pistol only a foot from my own head, which would burn the hair if I pulled the trigger – and now tell me where the muzzle is pointing."

"Ah, you can't see it of course," Bennett answered. "The bullet would graze the top of your skull – perhaps. It wouldn't go in behind your ear. And the muzzle isn't nine inches away, let alone a foot."

"Try it yourself, if you like," Head offered.

"Not I! There's another live cartridge in that pistol, isn't there? But I see your point. With that scalded and bandaged hand of his Garnham couldn't have—"

"And, therefore, who did?" Head questioned, after waiting vainly for the end of the remark. "Also, what is the third way out of that room?"

"There isn't one," Bennett said. "I saw you and the supe examine the room. Hallo! Barton! Now who told him Garnham was dead?"

For, passing the police saloon, a car drew up before the entrance to the house, and from it descended Lucas Barton, the principal Westingborough solicitor, with two obvious clerks. Head reached the open doorway in time to face the pompous, elderly man of law.

"Ah! Good morning, inspector," Barton said frostily. "May I ask what has happened to bring *you* here?" The accent on the pronoun was definitely satiric. "A broken window, I see. Burglary, perhaps?"

"May I ask what brings you here?" Head retorted.

"I'm afraid not." Barton smiled. "My business is with Mr. Garnham. Excuse me, please."

He reached past Head for the bell-pull.

"Don't ring," Head said. "Garnham is lying dead inside there."

"He's *what*?" And Barton's hand dropped. "Nonsense, man."

"Why is it nonsense?" Head inquired curiously.

"Well – I mean – are you sure? He rang me at my home last night and asked me to be here at eleven this morning, with a – well, to be here at eleven. And it is eleven, now."

The booming gong of a clock inside the entrance hall confirmed his assertion. "But—" he added, as he took out his watch and looked at it – "he's not dead, surely? Can't be."

Head held up the pistol. "By this," he said. "But you, Mr. Barton, would only fetch two clerks out here for one purpose that I can think of. Because of this –" again he indicated the pistol – "I think it may be of some help in my inquiries if you tell me just *why* Mr. Garnham asked you to call here – with two men capable of witnessing his signature, at eleven this morning."

And, after only a momentary hesitation, Barton told.

IV

"The wife, or the half-brother," Wadden surmised.

"Or the confidential manservant – or even old Joe Plant," Head added for him. "And until we can find out how the one who pulled that trigger got out of this room, applying for a warrant would be merely asking for trouble. Imploring, in fact. Now how?"

He looked round the spacious room. Garnham's body had been removed: the overturned chair lay as they had first seen it, except that it bore signs of having been subjected to examination for fingerprints. Wadden's gaze, too, roved round the apartment.

"The window," he said, "is quite out of the question."

"And the walls," Head added.

"Likewise floor and ceiling, as viewed and measured by me from below and above," Wadden completed. "Maybe you'd like to verify—"

But Head moved over to the entrance. "Remains a door, a very beautifully carved door, that once hung in a villa belonging to Alexander Borgia, I understand. And Alexander was a man of ideas."

"Wasn't he the pope of that family?" Wadden asked.

"He was a rip," Head answered gravely. "A brainy rip, too."

He swung the heavy door wide open, and began a close scrutiny of its outer side, now exposed to the light from the window in the room. Within the top part of the heavy framing were two panels carved in low relief, with all the intricacy of detail of Italian renaissance work, to represent hunting scenes. Beneath these were a pair of plain panels, mellowed almost to blackness by age and polishing, and each a little more than a foot square, and then the lower third of the door was occupied by one very large panel, carved as were the two at the top, and representing Cupid leading a garlanded faun toward – presumably – Psyche, a youthful and nude female figure with outstretched arms.

"It's a lovely piece of work," Head observed.

He passed his hand over the projecting points of the two top panels, touching one after another and then, with extended fingers, trying them in pairs, but without result. Then he sat down on the floor, and taking the door by its edge, moved it back and forth to get a reflection of midday light from the window on first one and then the other of the two smooth panels.

"Yes," he said at last, "it's worth a puff from Wells' blower. Please, chief – while I go on looking for the key."

Wadden bellowed for the sergeant, who answered from where he waited in the entrance hall, and then appeared.

"Test both these smooth panels for prints," Head bade. "Don't mind me – I'm looking for something else."

He went on feeling, rather than looking, over the big carved panel beneath the smooth ones. Presently, with his fingers on Cupid's face, he emitted a little, inarticulate sound, but then shook his head and sat back, watching while Wells' blower revealed two sets of four prints each. They were almost perfect impressions of the top phalanges of the fingers of a pair of hands, and had been made by placing the fingers on the panel with the tips pointing upward.

"Photograph 'em, Wells," Head bade unemotionally.

"But what a blasted fool, to leave a set like that!" Wadden exclaimed, and blew with disgust at such folly.

"An open and shut case of suicide, chief, remember," Head reminded him. "And I'd say there was probably no chance to wipe these off – the sound of the shot might have disturbed someone, or the one who fired it might have been scared of being seen – outside the door, remember. But I want that key – I can't do a thing till I get it."

"What key?" Wadden asked.

But Head did not reply. He sat on the carpet, gazing pensively at the beautiful carving of the lower panel while Wells, kneeling, focused the camera and took shots of the fingerprints.

"Cupid is traditionally blind," he remarked eventually.

"Which is why the lady ain't worried about her wardrobe, probably," Wadden suggested. "It's a bit – well, frank, as a work of art."

"I wonder – let's try blinding her too," Head said.

Swinging the door back to its limit to permit of pressure on its surface, he placed the thumb and middle finger of his right hand on the Cupid's eyes, and a finger and thumb of the left hand over those of Psyche. At this sudden pressure on all four points, the panel that Wells had photographed slid smoothly downward, leaving an oblong hole in the door under the lock. Head reached through and turned the big, highly ornamented key, which was still in the lock from the inside of the door, once or twice.

"Well, I'm damned!" said Superintendent Wadden.

Head stood up. "We won't try to close the panel again now," he observed. "I rather think you have to lift it most of the way and then slide it by pressing your finger-tips against it."

"What made you think of it?" Wadden asked.

"Well, we'd eliminated everything but the door, and the dead man didn't lock it, since he didn't shoot himself. Take this door off its hinges, Wells – you and Jeffries. It will be exhibit number three, I think, if we make the revolver number one."

"Then what's number two, you secretive devil?" Wadden demanded.

"A lady's handkerchief, retrieved from a bag of soiled linen by Wells while I was questioning its owner," Head answered imperturbably. "She used it to wipe all the fingerprints off the revolver before putting it down, and either didn't notice or didn't care about the ring of black fouling from the pistol muzzle that came off on to the handkerchief – stuff easily identifiable as a nitro powder residue."

"But – you've got to show a motive, man," Wadden protested.

"Of course, you didn't hear what Barton had to tell me,"

Head recollected aloud. "Garnham rang him last night and told him to get here at eleven this morning to consult about an action for divorce, naming this man Keller as co-respondent in the case. Also, and much worse, Barton was to draw up a new will, in which the lady was not mentioned. Knowing the secret of the door, she made her gamble – and if she'd held that pistol a foot closer to her husband's head, she might have won."

"But – Keller—" Wadden began, half protestingly.

"It's her handkerchief, and they are her fingerprints on that panel – eh, Wells?" He turned to the sergeant.

"As nearly as I could see, they correspond to the ones I found on Mrs. Garnham's hair brush and Thand mirror handles," Wells answered.

"Therefore—" Head pressed a bell push – "I think we might have the lady in and – Oh, Gladys, I think your name is – tell Mrs. Garnham I should be glad if she'd see me in here, please."

He waited with his back to the door, covering from sight the hole from which the secret panel had slid away.

The Millionth Chance

J.S. Clouston

"Surprises?" said Carrington. "By Jingo, I should think I do get some! Fellows like Sherlock Holmes may always have known what was going to happen, but certainly I don't. I remember one case—" He paused, and a reminiscent smile stole over his face as he lit a fresh cigarette.

"Anything you can tell?" asked one of us.

"Ye-es," he drawled. "I don't really see why I shouldn't, provided I don't give you the right names."

We settled ourselves down in our chairs, and he began.

"It was quite early on in the war, when the scare about spies and aliens in our midst and so on was at its height. I had just started my secret service work and was busy over some case or other up at the head office when Livermere walked into the room.

"'I wish you'd come along and help me to interview a lady,' he said.

"'What's it about?' I asked.

"'Her name is Mrs. Schultze,' said he. 'You remember the case of Herman Schultze, the fellow we were going to intern, only he gave us the slip? Well, this is his wife.'

"'German too?'

"'English as they make 'em. Above suspicion one would say, if she hadn't been married to this fellow. But as it is, one never knows. They've got a country place in Norfolk, a little too near the coast to let us run any risks. Now she has discovered she is being watched – someone hasn't been exactly tactful I fancy – and she has come up full of righteous indignation. If we suspect her of anything, then let us out with it and give her a fair trial; if we don't, then why watch her house? That's the line she's taking.'

"'And what do you want me to do?'

"'Hear her talk, ask her a few questions, and see what you think of her. You call yourself a judge of character, don't you?'

"'It was a risky remark if I did make it!' I replied. 'That's to say, if you mean to put any money on my tips. They don't always come off. However, let me see the lady and I'll give you my impressions for what they are worth.'

"He took me into his room, and I must frankly confess that for a moment my breath was fairly taken away. Livermere had left me deliberately unprepared for what was coming, and I'd naturally enough fancied I should see an average British matron. Instead, I saw one of the most bewitching creatures I have ever come across in a considerable experience. Slender, dark, piquante, breeding to the tips of her fingers, gowns made in Paris, voice that would have stirred a door-mat – that was the lady I found in Livermere's room. He introduced us, and I bowed as gracefully as nature has permitted me, and smiled within the same limitations. She seemed a trifle surprised at seeing such a peaceful and amiable apparition. Then she drew herself up and became the traduced patriot again – and a more charming and animated patriot I never want to meet. In fact, I was quite near enough being bowled over by this one.

"'I have been telling Captain Livermere,' she said, and her voice had a curious subtle thrill in it, 'that I am either a traitor to my country or I am not. If you think I am, then place your spies openly in my house – read my letters – question my servants frankly – arrest me if anything is suspicious, and try me! If you don't think I am, then leave me alone to do the work I'm trying to do for my country!'

"'What work is that?' I ventured to ask, very politely indeed, I assure you.

"'I have offered my house as a hospital. If the Government will take it, I am willing to scrub my own floors so long as I may work in it! Just now I am helping in another hospital.'

"'Nursing?'

"'I wish I could! At present I am driving my car for them. It's a hospital for wounded officers.'

"Livermere shot a quick glance at me. Of course I knew what was in his mind. A beautiful woman like that could extract a good deal of information from wounded officers in the course of a drive. However, we neither of us dropped the least hint of what we were thinking.

"'And what do you complain of, Mrs. Schultze?' I inquired.

"'I complain of my house being watched surreptitiously, servants being questioned, and letters being tampered with!'

"'But isn't that what you have just been inviting us to do?' said Livermere.

"'I ask you to do it openly and thoroughly – so that you can really *see* whether I am capable of being what you suspect! You are finding out nothing like this – because there is nothing to find out! And yet you keep on suspecting.'

"Livermere is a first-class fellow, but I could see he was only irritating the lady to no purpose, so I tipped him a wink and he left us alone together. I don't mind confessing that I didn't hurry the interview, and by the end of it I was quite smitten – as I often am, though luckily always temporarily so far. As for the lady, I really think she thought me rather a nice sort of fellow. In fact, since I wanted to produce a good impression both for business reasons and because I couldn't help it, and since one gets a little practice in my job in producing the kind of impression one wants, I may even say that she very possibly thought I was a bit carried away by her charms.

"After we had parted on very amicable terms I had a little talk with Livermere.

"'Well, what do you think of her?' said he.

"'Either she's no traitress or else a spy in a million.'

"'So that it's a million to one on her being straight?'

"When it was put to me like that I hesitated for a moment, and then took the plunge.

"'Yes,' I said, 'I think I'd be willing to let it go at that.'

"'And otherwise very charming?' he smiled.

"'Quite delightful. A woman with a temperament, mind you; capable of a devilish lot if the temperament ran away with her. One could tell that by something in the quality of her voice alone. What's Schultze like, by the way?'

"'Stout prosperous party of the commercial type; quite a bit older than she is. He's rolling in money and she hadn't a sou. Hence the marriage, I believe.'

" 'Doesn't sound likely to have roused the temperament to the pitch of betraying her country,' I said. 'I think you can risk it, Livermere.'

"Well, three or four weeks passed and I heard nothing more of the matter. And then one day Livermere called me into his room. I could see that something was worrying him pretty seriously.

" 'You remember the fair Mrs. Schultze?' he began.

" 'I remember the dark Mrs. Schultze,' I said.

" 'You were right,' said he, though hardly in the tone in which one usually makes that remark.

" 'About her being straight?'

" 'No, about taking your tips.'

"I looked as calmly superior as possible, and merely asked—

" 'In what way can I assist you this time, Livermere?'

" 'We'll come to that in a moment,' said he. 'In the first place here are the facts. I acted on your judgment and stopped doing anything that could annoy her. Of course we kept a general eye on the place, but there was no more regular watching. In a little while rumours began to go about. They came from one of her servants first of all in the form of a ghost story.'

" 'A ghost story!' I exclaimed.

" 'First of all – odd sounds in her house and so on. Then a glimpse of a figure was seen in a passage where nobody had any business to be; seen by a fairly reliable witness too. And then came an even more specific tale of mysterious sounds and movements. Finally, I have got hold of a very full and particular description of the house, with a number of plans, from an architect who was employed by Schultze a few years ago to make some alterations, and I find it's an old rambling Tudor place, with secret stairs and passages and priests' hiding-holes, and the Lord knows what all.'

" 'And you want me—?' I began.

" 'To take the thing up,' said he in his crisp way.

"There seemed to be but four explanations: spooks, rats, men, or lies. Not being a spookest myself, I eliminated that alternative. A very little careful inquiry showed that though there might be exaggeration, the stories were founded on fact of some sort. Sifting the evidence as thoroughly as it could be sifted, rats wouldn't account for everything. Therefore men alone remained. I studied the plans of the house to see how the secret stairs, etcetera, ran, and I found they were not in the servants' quarters. Their part of the house in fact was comparatively modern. I also inquired into the servants' characters, and found they were under a regular dragon of a housekeeper – a model of all the virtues, especially the more aggressive ones. The very idea of anything improper going on under this elderly virgin's eye made the villagers smile.

" 'She has made a fool of me!' I said to myself; and yet I was loth to believe it. In fact, I still declined to believe it until I could find evidence of one thing.

"And here came the most mysterious part of the business. If this lady were harbouring spies, they would have to get in and out, or what good would they be doing? And the one bit of evidence lacking was evidence of any suspicious character entering that house, leaving it, lingering in its neighbourhood, or in fact of being within fifty miles of it. I was having the place watched day and night. My watchers included two or three fellows in corduroys cleaning ditches and clipping hedges, an elderly-looking botanical enthusiast, in short, a really excellent mixed bag of disguises, and first-rate men at their job too; for I tell you I was now on my mettle. Best of all, they included the austere housekeeper, who turned out to have lost two nephews at Mons, and to be as down on Huns as on lapses from virtue. She had a natural suspicion of beautiful women, and had been quietly keeping her eye on her mistress all along.

"And yet something was still going on in that house beyond the shadow of a doubt.

"And then a certain bit of information came to my ears. I made inquiries in quite another direction – in the neighbourhood of the port of Hull this time, and, by Jingo, I sat up! Next morning I was back in town talking it over with Livermere.

" 'Are you sure that Herman Schultze ever got out of this country?' I asked him.

" 'He was supposed to have,' said he.

" 'A man devilish like him was seen at Hull trying to ship

himself to Holland,' I told him. 'He was headed off, and after that all traces of him were lost.'

Livermere whistled.

" 'Then the milk has practically never been out of the coco-nut,' said he. 'And the one in a million chance has come off, Carrington.'

" 'I said it was a million to one against her being a *spy*,' I corrected. 'This is rather different. What would any devoted wife do?'

"He looked pretty thoughtful for a minute or two, and then he said—

" 'The point now is: What are we going to do? Searching the house would be a mere farce if we didn't search every corner of every one of those dashed hiding-holes.'

" 'Whatever we search, if we find nothing it will be a good deal worse than a farce,' I argued. 'We'll have given the whole show away, made fools of ourselves, and possibly raised Cain. For there are limits to the patience of the public if they hear of houses being watched for weeks, and then ransacked, with not a scrap of justification to show for it. We'll weaken our hands against the next time.'

" 'Do you know the run of these passages and things well enough to make sure of covering them all?'

"I shook my head very decidedly.

" 'I've gone into that, and I know a bit about them, but even that architect has only a sketchy idea of them. He says they are the most extraordinary rabbit-warren of that sort to be found in any house in England.'

" 'Then how are we to get at the fellow? We can't leave a Hun hiding in his own house within a couple of miles of the North Sea coast.'

"I had been wrestling with the problem pretty well all night, and I put my solution to him now, not as a very pretty one, or the kind of solution that either of us liked – especially myself, who had to do the dirty work – but simply as the only feasible solution I could think of. Its chief merits were that it wouldn't give our hand away if it didn't come off, and that nobody could be blamed but me.

"Well, we made our plans, and proceeded to set our trap, and first of all, I must ask you to believe that I never felt such a swine in my life, and never liked a job less. However, war is war.

"The next afternoon a motor rolled up to the door of the chateau Schultze, and a very smart and fashionable gentleman alighted. That was me. He was driven by a chauffeur whose face was shrouded by a cap with an immense peak. That was Livermere. The housekeeper alone was in the know, and had given us the tip as to the proper hour to call, so as to catch the lady as near napping as we could. I was shown straight into a very charming old-fashioned room used as a sort of boudoir, and as soon as I had disappeared, the chauffeur slipped into the hall and stood ready to do a sprint to my rescue if need be.

"I went slap into that room on the heels of the maid, and if ever a lady was flurried and found a guest unwelcome, it was the fascinating Mrs. Schultze. She was so flurried (though she carried it off marvellously) that she never noticed one little object lying on a small table till I had closed my hand over it and slipped it into my pocket. It was a half-smoked pipe, and by Jingo, it was *warm!* So was the scent, thought I.

"I had picked up enough of the run of the secret passages to feel perfectly certain that one of them opened into this room somehow and somewhere. Looking round it, I at once suspected either a certain old portrait or a section of the bookcase as being the door. Within a couple of minutes I had plumped for the bookcase. I had heard a sound, very faint and gentle, but still an unmistakable sound. And I could see that the lady had heard it too, and was trying to cover it up.

"There was no doubt I was in luck's way, and all seemed to depend on my having enough assurance and brutality to carry the thing through. Lord, how I would have liked to kick myself! However, instead, I went straight at it. I had taken a small nip of raw whisky just before I got out of the car, so as to give my breath a good alcoholic reek, and if I describe my manner as sprightly, I don't exaggerate in the least.

" 'My *dear* Mrs. Schultze!' I said, as I squeezed her hand, and breathed at her for all I was worth; 'I say, I hope you're all alone, and all the rest of it, eh? What? I simply couldn't resist the temptation of looking you up – literally couldn't keep away from you. I say, you know, you're even more beautiful than you were last time. You remember last time, eh? What?'

"She was deadly pale, poor creature, but her voice was very quiet, and her dignity perfect. If war hadn't been war, I'd have chucked it, and bolted. However, war being war, I didn't.

" 'I remember you, Mr. Carrington,' she said, 'and you were very kind and polite to me – last time.'

"It was a fair hit on the point, but I was prepared for it, and merely beamed the more affectionately.

" 'I say, sit down and tell me what you've been doing?' I said, and put out my hand to catch her arm.

"She whisked herself away, but still kept her composure.

" 'Will you come into the drawing-room?' she said, and tried to head for the door.

"I was expecting that move, and got in front of her.

" 'We're jolly quiet here – nobody to disturb us!' said I, and, of course, I was pitching my voice pretty high. On top of that she gave a smothered cry when she saw my arms opening amorously, and knocked over the small table in getting clear.

" 'If that husband was anything but a Hun, this would have brought him out already!' I said to myself, and the next instant I did hear a most distinct sound from the neighbourhood of the bookcase. But he still stayed in his burrow, and there was nothing for it but piling on more insults.

" 'I'm in love with you!' I cried, right out loud too.

" 'You are drunk!' she said, stinging and low.

"I pretended to get annoyed at this.

" 'Drunk!' said I. 'By George, I'll make you pay something for saying that! A kiss! Damn it, I'm going to have a kiss!'

"She made a dive at the bell, but I was ahead of her again, and did catch her by the arm this time. Mind you, I was acting the part of half-sprung ravisher for all I was worth, and though her nerve was good, it gave when I had actually caught hold of her. She gave one piercing cry, and that did the trick. The old bookcase flew open in the middle, and out leapt a most furiously indignant gentleman in khaki!

" 'In khaki!' we cried. 'Do you mean that Schultze was disguised as—'

"Unfortunately it wasn't the lady's husband at all," said Carrington.

"Yes," he added a few minutes later, when we had recovered from the shock of this *dénouement*, "as I said to Livermore driving home, 'If you really want to make sure of winning your money, Livermere, back a wounded officer against an absent Hun as often as you get the chance.'"

The Case of Mr
and Mrs Stetson

E. Phillips Oppenheim

I

M r. John T. Laxworthy, Mr. Forrest Anderson, and
Sydney Wing were standing together upon the platform
at Toulon. Mr. Laxworthy was in one of his most enigmatic
moods, and Sydney Wing, who acted always as courier to the
little party, was beginning to get a trifle irritable. As yet he had
received no precise instructions as to their destination.

"It is fate, beyond a doubt," he admitted, "which has caused
the train for Marseilles and Paris to break down at Nice, and
fate again which decrees that the Luxe, when it arrives, should
have to wait here for twenty minutes. But meanwhile, the porter
desires to know where we want our luggage registered to."

Mr. Laxworthy drew his shawl a little closer around his neck.

"This Toulon station," he declared testily, "is the draught-
iest place in Europe. Every time I spend a few minutes here I
am terrified of a chill. I am conscious already of a tickling in my
throat. Have you the formamint lozenges, Anderson?"

Mr. Forrest Anderson produced a small bottle from his
pocket. Mr. Laxworthy gravely thrust one of the lozenges into
his mouth.

"To London, Paris, or Monte Carlo?" Sydney Wing persisted.

It must be confessed that Mr. Laxworthy, considering the
reasonableness of the inquiry, treated it with indifference.

"What does it matter?" he asked. "There are adventures

everywhere, even, no doubt, in Toulon. Let us cross the line and see the train from Paris arrive. We may, perhaps, see some one who will tell us whether it is raining in London. Other things being equal, why should not climatic conditions influence our destination? Your porter shall receive his orders, Sydney, in a quarter of an hour."

Thereupon Sydney Wing explained to the official in question that Monsieur desired to speak with a gentleman travelling from London, and that after a conversation with him immediate instructions concerning the luggage should be given. This information being accompanied by a preliminary pourboire of a substantial nature was accepted as entirely satisfactory, and the three travellers crossed the line.

The train de luxe from Paris had just thundered in. Notwithstanding the early hour, a fair number of passengers had already descended. These, however, instead of occupying themselves in the usual manner, by buying coffee or flowers, were standing about talking to one another or to any uniformed official who would stop to answer a question. All the way down the train other passengers, in various stages of déshabillé, were to be seen peering curiously from behind cautiously raised blinds. Several of the attendants were talking together with the station-master and another official of the railway company. No less than four gendarmes, accompanied by an inspector, were drawn up opposite a certain compartment of the train.

"Something has happened," Mr. Forrest Anderson, with rare acumen, ventured to observe.

"A man has been killed – probably murdered," Mr. Laxworthy, who had been watching intently the inspector's lips, declared.

"I will go and get the tickets and our luggage registered to Monte Carlo," Sydney Wing decided promptly.

The inspector who was in charge of the gendarmes held a little informal court of inquiry upon the platform. Then he disappeared into the train. Presently his head was to be seen from a window. He beckoned to the four gendarmes who, with the air of men of consequence embarking upon a fateful errand, also mounted the train. Mr. Laxworthy a few moments later followed them. When he reappeared, he was looking a little annoyed. Mr. Anderson, who was drinking a cup of coffee, looked at him questioningly. The news had spread, and quite a surprising number of the blinds had been raised during the last few minutes. The station-master himself was examining the tickets of the two or three passengers who had descended.

"Raining hard in London," Mr. Laxworthy announced, gloomily. "Also a fog. Give me another formamint."

"Can't see that that makes any difference to us," Mr. Forrest Anderson remarked cheerfully, producing his little bottle. "It'll be all right at Monte, anyhow."

"It matters," Mr. Laxworthy declared, "because we happen to be going to London."

Mr. Anderson stared slightly, but he declined to be surprised. "Not interested in this little affair, after all then?"

"On the contrary," Mr. Laxworthy replied, "I am very much interested in it. Only it is my opinion that monsieur the inspector, with his corps of gendarmes, is making rather a mistake in going on. Back to London is my idea. We shall see."

"What happened, anyhow?" Mr. Anderson asked.

"Unpleasant affair," Mr. Laxworthy explained with some relish. "Elderly English gentleman, travelling alone, chloroformed and strangled in his sleeping berth. Not a sound heard. Attendants sleeping both ends of the car all night. Empty pocket-book discovered at foot of bed. Man's name Simonds. Presumptive evidence that he was a bookmaker and was going to Monte Carlo to shoot pigeons."

"Is it known how much money he had with him?"

"Not to any of us," Mr. Laxworthy answered dryly.

"What are the gendarmes doing?" Mr. Anderson inquired curiously.

"Guarding the attendants and the passengers in the adjoining compartments till the train arrives at Nice," Mr. Laxworthy announced. "There the authorities will take the matter over."

"What about the passengers who have descended here?"

"There were only two," Mr. Laxworthy replied. "You can see them over there – the young couple waiting for the Hyères train. The inspector has examined their tickets and asked them a few questions. He has, apparently, no further interest in them."

Mr. Anderson nodded. He rather prided himself on his powers of intuition.

"Honeymooners," he declared positively. "New clothes, new luggage, man looking like a self-conscious ass, girl wearing a thick veil. Look, he's buying her flowers. See him squeeze her hand then?"

"Just a trifle overdone," Mr. Laxworthy remarked critically. "Not bad, though. The telegram will be a good test."

"What telegram?"

"He has arranged to have a telegram calling him back to London, delivered within a few minutes." Mr. Laxworthy replied. "He is looking about for it much too anxiously."

"Do you mean to say that these two are concerned in the murder?" Mr. Forrest Anderson asked in sudden amazement.

"Of course they are!" Mr. Laxworthy answered a little irritably. "Why else should I have pointed them out to you? Let us walk up the platform a little distance – so. Now back again. Watch this man, my friend. Here is psychological interest for you, if you like. Such a chance may never occur to you again. You can study at close quarters the features and deportment of a man who, within the last few minutes, mind – certainly within the last hour – has committed a brutal murder. To the casual observer he seems callous and unconcerned, doesn't he? In reality he is nothing but a quivering mass of nerves and suspicions. Did you see his face twitch just then?"

They passed within a few feet of the couple. The man was young, of a little more than medium height, with broad shoulders, a brown moustache, and somewhat florid complexion. His companion was slim and small. Her figure was certainly girlish, but she wore a veil of the pattern affected by travelling Americans, and very little of her face could be seen. She seemed certainly either shy or nervous. Her hands were linked in her husband's arm, and she kept whispering in his ear. They were both well enough dressed, but their clothes were a little obvious in their newness. Their deportment, too, when one studied it closely, was suspicious.

The man's exuberant good spirits were overdone; the girl's timidity was perhaps real, but the reason for it seemed insufficient. Mr. Forrest Anderson was hugely interested. There was a new reverence in his tone as he addressed his wonderful master.

"Did you notice," he whispered, as they passed down the

platform, "how the man's hand was shaking? The cigarette, too, he was pretending to smoke, had been out for a long time."

Mr. Laxworthy nodded.

"An amateur criminal," he decided, "beyond a doubt. Certain to be caught in the long run. How long will it be, I wonder," he continued in a tone almost of annoyance, "before these people who decide upon a criminal career realise that it is absolutely necessary for them to learn the A B C of their craft if they wish for any permanent success in it. It isn't reasonable to suppose that an affair like that" – Mr. Laxworthy waved his hand toward the train – "can be successfully carried through by bunglers."

Sydney came hurrying up with the tickets, and met with a little surprise.

"You will keep one of these," Mr. Laxworthy told him, "and proceed as far as Nice. You can wire us the course of events to the cloakroom, Lyons, and to Charing Cross Station. Anderson and I are returning to London."

It was one of the precepts instilled by his instructor into Mr. Sydney Wing that surprise, however natural and reasonable it might be, was an emotion sedulously to be concealed. He handed the two tickets to Mr. Laxworthy.

"You will be able to recover on these, sir," he remarked. "Am I to wait at Nice?"

"Use your own discretion," Mr. Laxworthy replied. "I think that you will probably return."

Sydney hurried off to take his seat. In a moment or two the great train rolled slowly out of the station. From where Mr. Laxworthy and his companion stood, they caught a glimpse of the fateful compartment, with its blind carefully lowered, and at the adjoining windows an impression of the gendarmes. Mr. Forrest Anderson shivered a little.

"Poor fellow!" he muttered. "Off on a holiday, too. It's a brutal thing, this taking of life!"

"I can tell you one thing more sickening," Mr. Laxworthy said slowly, "and that is the intense, awful anxiety of the man who has committed a murder and who fears arrest. The deed seems simple enough when it is planned, the chances of arrest remote. The prize is great. The man, naturally enough, if he is of sporting proclivities, backs himself to take the chance. Then comes the afterwards. The very air seems full of whispers. New horrors are hatched in the brain. A new set of fears is born; a shivering, hideous doubt of every human being poisons life. I am sorry for the lump of clay they are taking on to Nice. If I were in the habit, however, of feeling compassion for anybody, I should be more sorry still for the young man whom they are taking on to London. There's his telegram, just on the point of being delivered. See his clumsy air of surprise. We will proceed to the other side."

"Are you not afraid," Mr. Anderson asked, as they retraced their steps, "that even if we get on the same train they will not leave it somewhere en route. Why should they go all the way to London?"

"Because London is the finest hiding-place for criminals in Europe," Mr. Laxworthy replied promptly. "Furthermore, I saw him tell her that they would be in London to-morrow night."

Mr. Laxworthy and his companion obtained seats in the train with some little difficulty. They found themselves, however, in an empty compartment vacated by some passengers descending for Costabelle.

"I wonder where our friends are," Mr. Anderson remarked, as they proceeded to settle themselves down for the journey.

Very soon they were to know. There was the sound of a somewhat heated discussion in the next compartment. Suddenly the young man himself appeared in the doorway.

"Are these two seats engaged, sir?" he asked Mr. Laxworthy.

"They are not," Mr. Laxworthy replied.

The young man disappeared and presently ushered in his wife and began to pile up the rack with small articles of luggage.

"Hope we're not disturbing you, sir," he said to Mr. Laxworthy, "but the next carriage was full up, and there was an old Frenchman near the window wouldn't have it moved. Couldn't stick it at any price," he added, taking off his cap and wiping his forehead.

"Foreigners are somewhat peculiar with regard to fresh air," Mr. Laxworthy admitted. "I am myself susceptible to draughts, but I am most opposed to anything in the nature of an overheated carriage. Would the young lady care for my seat near the window!"

"Oh, please not!" she exclaimed. "I am quite comfortable here. It's such a relief not to hear all those people chattering a language you don't understand."

The two young people settled down for the journey. They occupied opposite seats on the corridor side of the carriage, and with their heads close together talked a good deal on matters apparently of frivolous import. For some reason or other, the nervousness which they had certainly exhibited on the platform at Toulon had completely vanished. The young man showed no signs of being anything else than what he appeared to be – a commonplace, healthy, middle-class person, probably a manufacturer or professional man from the country. The girl, who looked prettier without her hat, was a veritable type of the suburban belle. In opening her handbag to search for a handkerchief, a little shower of rice fell upon the floor. Their confusion, the girl's giggle, and the man's half-conscious glance towards Mr. Laxworthy and his companion were perfectly done. Mr. Laxworthy smiled upon them genially and in a few moments all four were in conversation. Their name, it appeared, was Stetson, and they had been married four days. The girl's home had been at Balham, and the man's at Manchester. The names of relatives and friends were freely mentioned. By the time they had passed Marseilles, the quartette were on such terms that Mr. Laxworthy had ordered in a bottle of wine and some biscuits to drink the health of the newly-married couple.

"By the by," he remarked, "my friend and I thought we saw you waiting by the Hyères train."

It was the critical moment. Mr. Laxworthy had asked his question with apparently unconscious but subtle suddenness. The embarrassment of the two, however, was tempered with smiles. With a hearty laugh the young man explained.

"We were going to Hyères," he said, "but, to tell you the truth, I've got a mother-in-law who is rather a nuisance to us. It was all we could do to stop her from starting on the honeymoon with us, and just an hour or so ago I had a telegram to say that she had gone to Hyères and was waiting for us there. We couldn't either of us stick it. We are going to pretend we didn't get the telegram and we are going back to Paris to spend the rest of our time there."

"Poor mother!" the girl murmured. "She'll be fearfully disappointed, but she really is a nuisance."

Mr. Laxworthy commended their plan, and, the wine being finished, he dozed. The young couple went down for lunch early. They left their bags and small luggage scattered about the seats. Mr. Anderson looked at his chief doubtfully. The tragedy of a mistake was a thing which as yet they had never encountered.

"Clever young couple, that," he remarked tentatively.

"They are either," Mr. Laxworthy replied simply, "the cleverest young people I have ever met in my life, or" – his voice shook for a moment; he smothered his hesitation with a cough; it was not a pleasant thing, this, which he had to say – "or," he concluded at last, "I have made a mistake."

Mr. Anderson, who had made up his mind, said nothing. They lunched almost in silence, and on their return surprised their fellow-travellers sitting very close together indeed. The girl hid her face behind a magazine; the man grinned, unabashed. Mr. Laxworthy settled down into his corner with a premonition of disaster.

"At Lyons," Mr. Anderson whispered, "we shall receive a telegram."

Mr. Laxworthy nodded. He was remarkably sparing of speech for the remainder of that journey. He had even given up watching his fellow-passengers. At Lyons the telegram came. He opened it with firm fingers, but he felt beforehand a grim conviction as to its contents. It was dated from Nice a few hours back:

Attendant of train arrested. Portion of murdered man's property found upon him. Simple case – SYDNEY.

Mr. Anderson coughed as he handed it back to his chief. Mr. Laxworthy faced the situation boldly. The greatest men in the world had been famous for their mistakes.

"Better get off with us at Paris, sir," the young man suggested, as they drew near the end of the journey. "You and your friend, too. We are going to the Grand Hotel. Proud to entertain you there for a little supper. Our first guests you'd be, eh, Edith?"

The young lady smiled amiably.

"We'd be very glad indeed if you would," she declared. "Henry always likes company. Not that I blame him," she went on hastily. "I'm fond of it myself."

Mr. Laxworthy shook his head regretfully.

"I am sorry," he said. "My friend and I are travelling to London to keep a most important engagement."

"Bad luck!" the young man declared. "Anyway, here's my card," he added, producing one. "I've taken a little house up on Laking Heights, near Manchester. Healthy situation, and near a golf club. Look us up there if ever you come that way."

"I will do so with pleasure," Mr. Laxworthy assured him. "Permit me to offer you my own card," he added, drawing one from his case. "I am rather a bird of passage, but when I am in London I can always be heard of at my club."

"I am a member of the Junior Conservative myself," the young man remarked. "A club in town's always useful, even for a countryman."

His wife tossed her head.

"You gentlemen and your clubs!" she exclaimed. "Let me tell you, Henry, your club isn't going to be much use to you. When you come up to London, I'm coming. I made that bargain with him," she added, turning to Mr. Laxworthy, "before I consented to go and live at Manchester."

"Quite right," Mr. Laxworthy murmured. "I feel sure that your husband's visits to the Metropolis will be more acceptable to him than ever with your charming society."

The train was drawing in to the platform at Paris. They all shook hands. The young man put his head back after their final farewells had been spoken.

"What did you say the French for porter was, sir?" he asked Mr. Laxworthy.

Mr. Laxworthy stepped out on to the platform and played the part of kindly courier to the young people. He watched them drive off in a cab before he returned to his seat.

"My friend," he said to Anderson, "I am now going to sleep. In the morning let us settle down to forget this little incident. A few days in London will be good for us."

Mr. Anderson agreed, with enthusiasm.

"I shall turn in myself presently," he declared.

The remainder of the journey was uneventful. On the following morning, having collected their luggage, Mr. Anderson presented himself at the cloakroom at Charing Cross, in case there should be any further telegrams from Sydney. He came back to Mr. Laxworthy with two. The first which he opened was unexpectedly long.

"It's in our cipher!" Mr. Anderson exclaimed.

"I have the book here," Mr. Laxworthy remarked. "Let us go into the refreshment room and sit down."

They found a small table and Mr. Laxworthy ordered a glass of milk and an apple. With the book before him, he commenced to decode the message. Except for one startled exclamation from Mr. Anderson, they neither of them spoke till their task was completed. Mr. Laxworthy's fingers, however, trembled slightly as he traced out the last few words. This message, also, was from Nice:

A thousand congratulations and apologies. Attendant only accomplice. Has made full confession. Murder was committed by famous American criminal, Greenlaw, travelling with young woman, posing as honeymooners. Capture of Greenlaw a veritable triumph. Once more my humble congratulations – SYDNEY.

Mr. Laxworthy looked at his companion across the table. Mr. Anderson was speechless.

"I asked him once," Mr. Laxworthy said slowly, "whether he had travelled in America. I fancied I caught the suspicion of an accent. What is in the other telegram?"

Mr. Anderson, who had forgotten it, tore open the envelope. They read it together. It was dated from Paris in the early hours of the morning:

Have just drunk your health at a pleasant little supper party – MR. AND MRS. STETSON, OF MANCHESTER.

"I think," Mr. Laxworthy said, rising, "that we will go round to the hotel now. I shall lie down for an hour or so. I feel that I need rest."

II

Mr. Laxworthy spent the greater part of his time during the next few days in a state of curious absorption. He did not stir out from the small suite at the Milan which had been reserved for him. Mr. Anderson, who was used to his ways, went to his club for bridge in the afternoons and visited the theatres in the evening. On the third day, Sydney Wing arrived. Mr. Anderson met him at the station and explained the situation. They discussed it gloomily.

"Our chief," Mr. Forrest Anderson remarked, as they drove to the hotel, "is suffering from profound mortification. As you know, since our association with him, at any rate, this is his first failure."

"I would have given a good deal," Sydney Wing declared wistfully, "to have seen you four in the railway carriage."

Mr. Anderson smiled grimly.

"It was," he admitted, "the most superb piece of acting I have ever seen. Until all these particulars about the man came out in the newspapers during the last few days, I must admit that the whole affair was absolutely incomprehensible. Now we know that he, too, understands the lip language."

"And many other tricks as well," Sydney remarked. "They say that no one else in the world has been so skilful at disguises. There isn't a reliable description of the fellow in existence."

"I could give a pretty close one," Mr. Anderson grunted. "I sat within a couple of yards of the fellow for the best part of twelve hours."

Sydney shook his head.

"According to those detectives down there, his changes of appearance are almost miraculous."

"Is the identity of the girl known?" Mr. Anderson asked.

Sydney shook his head.

"It is through his penchant for women that they hope to catch him some day," he replied. "They say that this last enterprise must have brought him in over ten thousand pounds."

Their cab rolled into the courtyard at the Milan.

"I'm not at all sure," Mr. Forrest Anderson said doubtfully, "whether the chief will see you. However, we must let him know that you have arrived."

They ascended the stairs and knocked at the door of Mr. Laxworthy's sitting-room. Mr. Anderson barely repressed an exclamation of surprise. Mr. Laxworthy was sitting before a table covered with notes and newspapers. A visitor who had very much the air of a detective was just departing. Mr. Laxworthy welcomed his two friends briskly.

"Sit down, Sydney, if you please," he invited. "I have a list here of thirty questions to ask you. Afterwards I shall require to be alone for an hour or two. Kindly understand that I shall want every moment of your time for the next four days at least."

"Glad to hear it, sir," Sydney replied cheerfully.

Mr. Laxworthy seemed anxious to hear every incident which had happened at Nice, and every item of gossip, even the idlest, concerning the man Greenlaw. He made notes of some of Sydney's replies and dismissed him finally with a little wave of the hand.

"I have a little work to do privately," he announced. "At six o'clock I shall want you both. You, Anderson, had better be prepared for a journey. I may want you to go to Paris."

"You are going for Mr. Greenlaw, then?" Mr. Anderson asked briskly.

"We are going, without a doubt," Mr. Laxworthy declared, "to assist the police in the capture of a criminal of that name."

III

Mr. Forrest Anderson left for Paris by the night train, with a sealed letter of instructions in his pocket, not to be opened until he had actually arrived in the city. Sydney Wing was invited to call upon his chief at nine o'clock that same evening. He found Mr. Laxworthy with a letter spread out before him upon the table.

"Come in, Sydney, and close the door," the latter directed. "Anderson has gone, eh?"

"He left by the nine o'clock train, sir," Sydney replied.

Mr. Laxworthy cleared his throat.

"As you may have surmised," he began, "we are interested in the case of this man Greenlaw. My friend John Marlin has been giving me some interesting information. You have heard me speak of John Marlin? He is now deputy-inspector at Scotland Yard."

"I remember him perfectly, sir," Sydney agreed.

Mr. Laxworthy took up a few notes which lay by his side.

"It seems that Scotland Yard has been trying to arrest this man for the last three years, and for the last twelve months, at least, there has been a detective over here from New York, looking for no one else. The fellow has great gifts, without a doubt, but success has made him over-confident. What do you think of this for bravado? It is addressed to Detective Marlin and was delivered to him at Scotland Yard. He brought it to me here only a few hours ago."

Mr. Laxworthy read out the letter:

"MY DEAR FRIEND MARLIN,

"You fellows make me tired. There's no fun to be had over on this side, so I'm off home, and pretty quick, too. You've been after me for three years and I've never had even to hurry to get out of your way. You've seven jobs up against me, most of them 'lifers,' but you're just about as slow as that old dead-head from New York, who has been trapesing after me for the Lord knows how long! Now see here, I'm a bit of a sport, and I'm going to give you your last chance. There's some money of mine lying in London, and I'm coming over myself to fetch it on Tuesday, May 15. I shan't tell you by what train, or where I am going to stay, but it will probably be at one of your best hotels. Now do make one last effort. It would really give me a thrill to meet you face to face and read suspicion in your eye. Come, why should we not take a drink together? I will make an assignation with you. I am very fond of a glass of vermouth before my dinner. Between six and seven each evening I am in London, I shall call either at the bar of the Milan Hotel, the

Metropolitan Bar, or Fitzhenry's. Shall I say au revoir? –
Yours,

DAN GREENLAW."

"Do you believe that he means to come?" Sydney asked
eagerly.

Mr. Laxworthy did not reply for a moment. He appeared to
be deep in thought.

"Marlin himself," he said at last, "has not the slightest faith
in the letter. He believes it to be a complete hoax. That,
however, is not to be wondered at. Marlin's limitations are
almost too painfully obvious. He is entirely destitute of a sense
of humour. It is one of my theories that without a sense of
humour no man can succeed in any profession which brings him
in touch with his fellows."

"And you, sir, what do you believe?" Sydney persisted.

"I believe that he will come," Mr. Laxworthy declared. "I
have thought this matter out very carefully indeed. I have come to
a certain conclusion. I may be wrong. We shall see. On the other
hand, if I am right, it will, I must confess, afford me a peculiar
satisfaction. I shall not easily forget that journey from Toulon."

"What will there be for me to do?" Sydney asked.

"To-morrow," Mr. Laxworthy replied, "is Tuesday. Marlin, of course, is all for watching trains, and that sort of thing.
Quite useless, in my opinion. Greenlaw, if he comes, will
probably travel by motor-car from some insignificant port. I
have some idea of asking you to frequent the bar rooms which
he mentions, with the exception of the Milan. I will attend to
that myself."

"Are there any descriptions of the man?" Sydney asked. "I
know his height, which I suppose he cannot alter – six foot
exactly – and they say he is fairly broad, and his natural
complexion is florid."

Mr. Laxworthy touched a little pile of papers by his side.

"There are seventeen descriptions here from Scotland
Yard," he remarked. "They vary slightly in detail, but they
are all much about the same. They are, I imagine, the chief
reason for the wonderful confidence which this man Greenlaw
displays."

"You don't believe that they are accurate, then?" Sydney inquired. "Yet Anderson's description of the fellow coincided exactly with this."

Mr. Laxworthy nodded thoughtfully.

"Well," he said, "I have an idea of my own. I have mentioned it to Marlin, but he only laughs at me. Nothing remains but for me to test it myself."

"Are there no instructions for me, sir?" Sydney asked.

"None for this evening," Mr. Laxworthy replied. "To-morrow I shall require you to be my companion. We will go round to a few of these bars. To-night I shall retire early. I drank a little Chablis with my lunch which has not wholly agreed with me. I shall not dine this evening."

Mr. Laxworthy, on the following evening, drank vermouth at Fitzhenry's, mixed vermouth at the Metropolitan, and a cocktail at the Milan, without the slightest result. He dined alone, in a very bad temper, went to bed early, and received this letter next morning:

"MY DEAR OLD LADY,

"So you are in the game, too! It made my heart ache this evening to see you trotting round to those bars and peering into every strange face from behind those disfiguring spectacles of yours. Besides, at your time of life three apéritifs are extremely bad for the digestion. I can assure you that I felt quite guilty when I saw you struggling with your third.

Come now, to-morrow night I will have mercy. We will leave out the Metropolitan. I don't know how it struck you, but I didn't care for the place at all. A very mixed crowd, and I had my doubts of the vermouth. We will visit Fitzhenry's and the Milan only. Who knows but that we may have luck and drink our cocktail together?—

Ever yours,
D. G".

Mr. Laxworthy's eyes sparkled as he read.

"This is indeed worth while," he said to himself. "He has the real instincts, this man."

Mr. Laxworthy showed this letter to several mysterious personages from Scotland Yard, and to Sydney Wing. They all treated it in the same manner. Scotland Yard concentrated upon the Metropolitan, and from six till half-past seven every harmless stranger who drank his cocktail or sherry and bitters there was subjected to a very searching and inquisitive scrutiny. Mr. Laxworthy, on the other hand, obeyed strictly the invitation of his letter. He visited Fitzhenry's first, and after half an hour there drove to the Milan. From the small smoke-room it was possible to see into the American Bar through a glass swing-door. Mr. Laxworthy peered into the room and stood for an instant quite still. A very small and apparently a very young gentleman of Indian extraction was leaning against the counter with a cocktail before him. Mr. Laxworthy turned to Sydney, who accompanied him.

"Sydney," he said, "the thing is finished. You see those two men in the corner of the smoke-room?"

Mr. Laxworthy pointed out two harmless-looking individuals who were talking together upon a settee.

Sydney nodded. At that moment, one of them looked up cautiously. Mr. Laxworthy beckoned to them. They came over at once.

"You will hold this door," he directed in a low tone. "The man for whom we are seeking is inside."

"Let me go in with you, sir," Sydney begged.

Mr. Laxworthy assented. They approached the bar. The young man who was leaning against the counter was dressed in the height of fashion. His silk hat was exceedingly glossy, his shirt front immaculate. He was really very little darker than an ordinary olive-skinned Englishman. He eyed the new-comers a trifle insolently, and turned to his cocktail. Mr. Laxworthy stood by his side.

"Will you give me a cocktail – the same as you have mixed for this gentleman, if you please?" Mr. Laxworthy ordered.

The girl mixed it in silence. As they all three stood there, a somewhat curious change took place in the attitude of the young man. He slipped furtively back from the counter. Mr. Laxworthy turned suddenly towards him.

"My friend," he said, "Daniel Greenlaw, or Mrs. Stetson, or

whatever it pleases you to call yourself this evening, I have come to take my apéritif with you. Our friends outside can wait. There are so many questions it would interest me to ask you."

Mr. Laxworthy was absolutely prepared, and he was, without doubt, extraordinarily proficient in all the ordinary tricks of wrestling and jiu-jitsu. Nevertheless, he was lying two seconds later upon his back in the bar. The young man sprang for the door, saw the two figures waiting there for him and hesitated. The moment's hesitation was fatal. Sydney's arms were round him from behind. Even then he struggled like a wild cat, and it took the united efforts of the three men to secure him. Marlin arrived just as the struggle was over. He shook his head doubtfully as he saw their prisoner.

"This isn't Greenlaw," he exclaimed.

Mr. Laxworthy smiled.

"You take him along," he directed, "and I promise you that when he is brought up before the magistrates to-morrow morning I will prove that he is Greenlaw half a dozen times over." . . .

Mr. Laxworthy dined that night in the café with Mr. Forrest Anderson, who had returned from Paris, and Sydney Wing. He was in high good humour.

"I don't see, even now," Mr. Forrest Anderson remarked, "how you guessed the truth."

Mr. Laxworthy sipped his wine with the air of a connoisseur.

"You see," he explained, "the man has been wanted for three years. No one has ever laid their hands upon him. Every description of him is the same. Naturally I began to wonder whether something might not be wrong with that description. I read up all the notes about him that were collected by Scotland Yard, and I noticed that although he had the reputation of having endless women friends, he was invariably accompanied by a small dark woman, especially when any particularly startling outrage was on foot. It just occurred to me as both possible and ingenious that the man might have concealed his identity all these years and gone about as his own companion. His Mrs. Stetson was certainly wonderfully done, but there were one or two flaws, and when I came to put everything together I felt pretty certain that my guess was a true one. Marlin and his men were looking everywhere for a big man. I was looking for the real, unknown Greenlaw – a small, dark man in any plausible form of disguise. The fellow's last little piece of bravado will cost him his life."

A porter from outside came up and addressed Mr. Laxworthy.

"I beg your pardon, sir," he announced, "but there is an important telephone message for you from the Charing Cross Hospital."

Mr. Laxworthy rose deliberately from his place and followed the man out of the room. He stepped into the telephone box and held the receiver to his ear.

"Is that Mr. Laxworthy?" a voice inquired.

"Yes?"

"I am Dr. Wendell, of the Charing Cross Hospital," the voice continued. "I am requested to give you a message by a man named Marlin who has just been brought in, badly hurt."

"What is it?" Mr. Laxworthy asked.

"He wishes me to tell you," the doctor continued, "that Greenlaw is free. He has stabbed one policeman and hurt Marlin badly. He escaped from the cab, and so far they have not been able to recapture him. Marlin wants you to be exceedingly careful, as this man Greenlaw, whoever he may be, will probably feel that he has a grudge against you. Excuse me, if you please, I am in a hurry."

Mr. Laxworthy laid down the receiver and went back to his dinner.

The Episode of *Torment IV*

C. Daly King

We were driving straight towards horror. Though we didn't know it yet.

Valerie said, "Dar*ling*, I do hope Trevis' friend has a decent place. I want a big room, with blinds to make it dim and none of those awful New Hampshire spiders. And I want a nice, long bath."

"Oh, I guess his place is all right. Nothing much anyone can do about New Hampshire spiders, though; they're big and nasty. But there won't be any in our room. The fellow probably has a good enough shack. Why shouldn't he?"

"Ugh! . . . Spiders." Valerie grimaced. "Yes, I suppose it'll be a good house. Trevis is rather tasteful about places himself."

We were motoring down from Canada and had arranged to pick up Tarrant at Winnespequam Lake where he had been staying with a friend named Morgan White, whom neither Valerie nor I had met. Tarrant planned to come along with us to New York a couple of days later, for White had been good enough to write, asking us to break our trip at his place for a day or so. We had gotten well along now, had passed Lancaster and were scooting through the Crawford Notch as fast as we could. It was as hot as blazes.

I said, "Another hour and a half will get us there. Then a swim, before anything else. I feel like a strip of wilted cardboard."

"I want a nice, long bath," Valerie repeated.

Ahead of us a small truck and a touring car loaded with about eighteen sweating travellers in their shirt sleeves were creeping along the hot asphalt through the centre of the valley. I gave the horn some lusty digs and we swerved past them.

And that, though we didn't know it, either, was our introduction to the episode of *Torment IV*.

"The most intriguing problem I have ever heard of," said Tarrant, "is the mystery of the *Mary Celeste*. It is practically perfect."

As he spoke, he leaned back in the hammock chair and the moonlight glinted through dusk against the sharp lines of his lean, strong face. Across the water came the twinkle of little, twin lights, red and green, where a motor-boat, a mere shadow on the darkening lake, put out from the opposite shore.

Valerie and I had arrived, hot and tired, about five in the afternoon. And I had had a most refreshing swim. Winnespequam, as a good many people know, is a New Hampshire lake. It is typical. Surrounded by hills, it has gathered around itself an almost unbroken line of the estates of prosperous merchants and professional men whose winter homes are in New York and Philadelphia. Some of the natives, too, boast modest bungalows nestling near the water, to which they repair during the summer months from their more permanent quarters in the little town that runs down to the northern tip of the lake. Even the motor highway that circles the shore travels chiefly between forested slopes and does little to disfigure the scene. It is a pleasant and carefree resort.

White, a big man and a good host, grunted, "Don't know it. I'm sure you do. What's the *Mary Celeste*?"

"You don't know the *Mary Celeste*?" Tarrant was plainly surprised. "Why, it's the perfect problem of all time. Dozens of people have had a whack at it, including some fairly clever ones, but it remains to-day as unsolved and apparently insoluble as it was sixty years ago."

He paused; then, as we were all quiet, obviously waiting for further information, he went on again. "The *Mary Celeste*, sometimes wrongly called the *Marie Celeste*, was a 200-ton brig owned by an American called Winchester. She was picked up by the barque, *Dei Gratia*, one pleasant afternoon early in December, 1872, about three hundred miles west of Gibraltar.

This was what was wrong about her: there was not a soul on board and she was sailing derelict on the starboard tack against a north wind that was driving her off her course. Her chronometer, her manifest, bills of lading and register were missing. A further examination showed that a cutlass hanging in her cabin bore stains as if blood had been wiped from it; but a medical officer in Gibraltar, who subsequently analysed these stains, declared that they were not of blood. There was a deep cut in her rail, as if made by an axe; but no axe has been mentioned as having been found aboard. On both sides of the bows a small strip, a little more than an inch wide and six or seven feet long, had recently been cut from her outer planking a few feet above the water line; this strip was only about three-eighths of an inch deep and had no effect upon her seaworthiness. Her log had been written up to the evening of the twelfth day previous and the slate log carried to eight a.m. of the eleventh day before. In other words the log was not up-to-date.

"But what was right about her was more astonishing. In the galley were the remains of a burnt-out fire above which stood the victuals for the crew's breakfast. Some of their clothes were hanging upon a line to dry and their effects were in good order and undisturbed. In the master's cabin breakfast had been partly eaten; some porridge was left in a bowl and an egg had been cut open and left standing in its holder. A bottle of cough mixture had been left on the table, its cork beside it. An harmonium stood in one corner and in a sewing machine was a child's garment, partly sewed. None of these articles were in any way disturbed. In the first mate's quarters, moreover, was found a piece of paper with an unfinished sum upon it, just as he had put it aside when interrupted. For the eleven days during which the log had not been kept, the weather over the course from the point last noted in the log to the position where the *Mary Celeste* was found, had been mild. The cargo, some casks of alcohol for Genoa, was intact and securely stowed. The boat itself was staunch in all respects, hull, masts and rigging. There was no sign whatsoever of fire or other hazard. And last of all, the single small boat with which the brig was equipped, was upon its davits, untouched and properly secured.

"Those are the essential facts, as evidenced by many and reliable witnesses. They make a very pretty problem . . . Of course, a good many hypotheses have been advanced. But actually not one of them is even as easy to credit as the curious state of affairs that was discovered when the *Mary Celeste* was boarded that December afternoon . . . What could possibly have happened to make a competent crew, not to mention the captain's wife and small daughter, abandon a perfectly sound ship in fine weather, without so much as attempting to launch her boat?"

There was a little silence.

"Match your mystery," White grunted. "Right here."

Tarrant twisted round in his chair. "Yes? I think you would be put to it to find another enigma with such simple and such contradictory factors."

"Judge for yourself," said our host. "The Blacks. That big place just across the lake is theirs. Closed up now. They had the *Torment IV* and they were—"

Struck by his unusual expression, I interrupted. "What in heaven's name is a torment four?" I asked. "How do you mean they had it?"

"Oh, no mystery there," he assured us. "That is the name of their motor-boat. Blacks have been coming up here for years, and a good many years ago now they got their first boat. Just when steam launches were going out and gas engines coming in. Wasn't much of a boat; jerky and spasmodic, and among other essentials it lacked a self-starter. A fairly thorough nuisance, and they named it, quite properly, *Torment*.

"Presently they got another; though the second one had a self-starter it was just one more thing to be spasmodic and *Torment II* was a good name for that one also. The third was much better, really a proper boat, but by that time the name had become traditional. *Torment III* was turned in only a year ago and the new one, *Torment IV*, is a beauty; long, fast, polished up like a new dime. I was out in her early this summer; I remember at the time that *Torment* seemed a foolish title for such a beautiful piece of machinery, but now – well, I don't know."

He paused, and, "Yes, but what happened?" asked Valerie.

"All killed. Lester Black and his wife, Amelie, and their small daughter. Just like your captain and his family."

"I didn't say the captain had been killed." Tarrant's reservation came softly across from the railing.

"Touché," said White. "Wrong myself. They're dead; at least two of 'em are. Said they were killed, but I don't even know that. No one knows what actually happened to them."

The voice from the railing was plainly interested now. "Come on, Morgan, what did happen?"

"I tell you I don't know. It was really extraordinary . . . Well, here's the story. Blacks came up early this year and so did I. It occurred about the end of June; hot spell then, if you remember, and we got it here, too. It was a beautiful, bright day and very warm for that time of year. Middle of the afternoon, *Torment IV* ran ashore a little way up the lake from here; that was the first we knew anything was wrong.

"Let me take your method and tell you what was right about her first. To begin with, her keel was hardly scratched and that came from her grounding, which happened by good luck on a strip of sand. Later, when the affair turned into a tragedy, I went over her carefully with the sheriff and there wasn't another mark or dent of any kind on her. Engine, transmission, and so on, in perfect condition – ran her back to the Black's dock myself after we found her. Have to tell you the cushions and pillows on the after-deck are life preservers in themselves, filled with some kind of stuff that will keep you afloat if necessary. Not one of 'em had been disturbed in any way; all present and accounted for. Not a leak, not a single miss from the motor – nothing.

"In fact, only two items were wrong. First, one of the chairs on the after-deck was overturned; might have happened when she ran ashore. Second, no one was in her. I know, for I saw the boat a hundred yards or so off land and watched her bump . . . That's all."

Tarrant threw the remains of his cigar in a wide arc and, three seconds later, came a tiny *phizz* as it struck the water below.

"You mean these three people simply vanished?" he demanded. "How do you know they even went out in the boat, in the first place?"

"Found that out when I took the boat back. They had gone out after lunch, apparently for a joy ride. And they were drowned somewhere in the middle of the lake – two of the bodies were recovered later, Black's and his wife's, not the child's – but how or why is a complete mystery."

"But in the middle of a bright afternoon—" Tarrant began. "There were no witnesses at all? No one saw them?"

"Well, they went up to the town dock at the end of the lake and got some gas; that was established. Then they headed out again – Lester Black was running the boat – and that is the last anyone saw of them. Of course, end of June, not many people around the lake, still a bit early for the summer people. Just the same it *is* strange. Inquiries were made all around the lake, of course, but no one was found to throw even a glimmer on the thing."

"H'm," remarked Tarrant. "There was no obvious cause, I suppose? No trouble, financial or otherwise? An estrangement between husband and wife, something serious?"

"Not a chance," White grunted. "I wasn't an intimate friend but I've known them for years. Man had plenty of money, lived a leisurely life, great family man, as a matter of fact. Very fond of his wife and daughter and they of him. Last thing in the world he would do, kill them and drown himself, if you've anything like that in your head."

Tarrant, meantime, had lit a cigarette and now smoked silently for some minutes. Finally he spoke. "Still, something like that is all you leave, if your other facts are right, isn't it? People don't jump out of a perfectly good motor-boat in the middle of a lake for nothing. Could they swim?"

"They could all swim, though probably none of them would have been good for a mile or more. And I've told you about the life preservers, every one of them in the boat. We made a careful check of that, naturally."

"Well, there you are. The more you say, the more it appears to have been a purposeful performance . . . There are lots of things in people's lives that are kept pretty well hidden . . . What happened to the boat?"

"I don't believe there was a thing in Lester Black's life that would account for that kind of tragedy," our host insisted.

"Prosaic man, prosaic as hell. The boat was inherited by the Constables, cousins of the Blacks. Live next them up here, down the road a bit. They didn't use the boat for some time; didn't care to, I guess. Lately they've been taking her out once in a while. Boat's really too good to throw away."

Again there came a pause, but just as I was about to enter an opinion, Tarrant summed the matter up. "Let's see; here it is, then. Black took his wife and daughter out for a spin on a nice, clear day. First they went to the village dock and bought gas. Then they turned out into the lake once more. From the time when they left the village— By the way, when was that?"

"Between two and two-thirty."

"And when did the boat come ashore?"

"Just about four o'clock."

"Then some time during that hour and a half the man and his wife went overboard and doubtless the child too. There is no way, apparently, of fixing it closer than that?"

"No, none. Boat may have come ashore directly they were out of it or it may have cruised around for an hour or more. No one noticed it."

"The boat was entirely unharmed and, in any event, they would not have abandoned it ordinarily in the middle of the lake without the precaution of providing themselves with the life preservers so readily at hand. I'm sure there was no fire or you would have mentioned it."

"Absolutely not," White declared. "Not a trace of anything like fire. Anyhow, since it obviously didn't burn up, they would have had plenty of time to throw over *all* the preservers in that case."

I had a sudden thought. "How about some sort of fumes from the engine that might have affected all of them at once so that they were forced to jump without waiting for anything?"

White merely grunted and Tarrant's tone was quizzical. "Hardly, Jerry. In an open boat proceeding at a fair speed no fumes would get much of a chance to affect the passengers. And some mysterious poison fumes that would make them jump instantly are simply incredible. If the engine burned ordinary gas, as it did, carbon monoxide is all that could possibly come off. So that if we grant the impossible and assume that it came through the floor instead of going out the exhaust – and then stayed near the deck – the result would surely have been to asphyxiate the people, certainly not to throw them overboard . . . No, that's out.

"There remain, of course, several alternatives," he continued. "The first is that White threw his wife and daughter out and followed them as a suicide. That's the one you don't care for, Morgan."

"Can't see it at all. Silly."

"There are a number of reasons to account for such an action. A bitter quarrel is only one of them. There is temporary aberration, followed by remorse, for example."

"Nonsense. Still silly. You didn't know Black."

"All right, we'll reverse it. The wife hits the man over the head while he is running the boat, throws him out and then follows *him* with the child. The aberration theory fits a woman better than a man, anyhow; they are more highly strung. How about that?"

"Trevis, come off it." White seemed almost provoked by the last notion. "Aside from Amelie's being incapable of such a thing psychologically, I'll tell you why it's absurd. She was a little woman, much smaller than Black. She couldn't possibly have tossed him out *unless* she hit him first. And he hadn't been hit. The autopsies showed that neither of them had a single mark of violence on them."

Undoubtedly Tarrant was smiling in the darkness as he said, "Very well, we'll leave that theory entirely. I was only thinking abstractly, you know; no reflections intended . . . Then we are left with one more hypothesis, the accident one."

"Ugh."

"Perhaps it's the most reasonable of all, anyhow. The child falls overboard, the mother jumps to save it, the father, who is running the boat, is the last to act. He jumps to save them both, and they are all drowned, while the boat, which in the excitement he has failed to close off, speeds away."

White answered at once. "Won't do, either. Naturally, we've been over that possibility up here. There is not merely one, but three or four points, against it. Altogether too many. As I said, they all knew how to swim and the daughter was about ten, not helpless in the water by any means, even with her clothes on. In the second place, the Blacks have been aquaplaning for years, and aquaplaning behind a fast boat is no joke. Matter of fact, not even aquaplaning; they did it on water skis, much harder. The point is, if anyone had fallen over, they would naturally have followed what they have done so often when there was a spill off the skis; swung the boat about and come up to the swimmer. They were used to doing that; they could do it quickly; it was a habit. They were all used to the water, to being on it and in it; couldn't possibly have lost their heads completely over a mere tumble.

"But last and most impressive of all, I tell you that Black was a prosaic and methodical man, known for it. Supposing some real emergency – though what it could have been, God knows – supposing the wife did jump and he prepared to go after her. He would never have left his boat empty without shutting off the motor, it doesn't take an instant. Granting even that impossibility, however, it is simply beyond belief that he would have jumped to their rescue himself before throwing them at least a couple of preservers, which would reach them more quickly than he and be of as much use. You must remember that they weren't at all helpless in the water, either of them. He would surely have done that first. Then, I grant you, he *might* have gone in, just to make sure. But the theory you built won't do . . . No, it won't . . . Really."

"The objections are strong," Tarrant acknowledged. "Of course, I didn't know the people at all . . . Well, that's the end of the list, so far as I can see now. You discard them all; the first as being impossible on grounds of character, the second on physical grounds, the third on grounds of habit and familiarity with the water and its hazards. I—"

For the first time during the discussion Valerie interrupted. She had been sitting quietly beyond Tarrant and smoking while the talk went on. Now she said, "May I suggest something? Perhaps it's pretty wild . . . What about this? The parents had received some kind of threat, kidnapping or something. No, this is better. They were hailed from the shore while they were riding about and they landed. There the child actually *was* kidnapped. The parents were stricken with grief, they were quite out of their heads for a time. They went out on the lake again and presently made a suicide pact and both honoured it at once. That covers it all, doesn't it? The child's body, I understood, hasn't been found."

Tarrant's chair creaked as he turned towards her and a match, flaring in his hand, showed his surprised and interested expression. "Valerie," he said, "you have constructed the best theory yet. Really, that's very good. It covers all the facts of the case except one. So I'm afraid it won't work, but I can see that you and I are going to get on famously. It's too bad you have forgotten that one little point. Black was a well-to-do man. Kidnapping is done for ransom; and surely he would have paid a ranson as an alternative to his wife's and his own suicide. It is unreasonable to suppose that even a week's separation would cause him to choose so absurdly. The only possibility would be that the child was taken by some enemy for revenge and no return intended. That's too much like a bad shocker; I'm afraid it won't do . . . It was a good try, though."

He rose and stretched. "I'm going to take a stroll for a bit and then turn in early. I imagine Valerie and Jerry would like to, too, after their ride." He turned and wandered slowly down the verandah.

"So you give it up?" White called after him. "No answer?"

"No. All the first answers are washed out. I'll grant you this, though, Morgan. You have a very good replica of the *Mary Celeste;* all the essential items are there. It's a problem all right; I'm not through thinking about it yet."

The matter remained in this state of suspense while we were sitting about the following morning after breakfast. The day was bright and clear but gave promise of becoming even hotter than the previous one; I was distinctly glad that Valerie and I were not to be touring the roads again.

A half-hour or so later Morgan White made the suggestion that we try his tennis court, since if we delayed much longer it might well become too uncomfortable for playing. Every one was agreeable and we trouped down to the court, which turned out to be of clay in excellent condition. "Jim Duff, the Constables' hired man, rolls it for me every other morning before he goes up to their place," White confided.

We proceeded to enjoy the fruits of Duff's labours. After several sets it was getting considerably hotter and Valerie voted for doubles. We won, though I am not at all sure it was due entirely to our play; during the second and last set I, for one, was beginning to feel a touch weary.

Everyone agreed, at the conclusion of that set, that swimming was the form of exercise now indicated. All of us except Val were dripping. In fifteen minutes or less we had reassembled at White's boathouse in bathing suits and stood smoking a final cigarette along the little platform by the side of the boathouse proper that covers his *Grey Falcon*. I remarked upon the diving-board protruding over the water at the platform's end and White assured us all that the lake here was seven or eight feet deep, so that diving was feasible. The afternoon before I had simply jumped off the end of his dock.

"I think I'll be trying it," I informed the rest, just as White turned to Tarrant and pointed out over the water.

"There, see that boat?" he said. "About two-thirds across the lake, heading north. That's *Torment IV*, the one we were discussing last night. Wait till I get my glasses from the boat-house and you can have a good look at her, Trevis."

He unlocked the boathouse door and disappeared inside, returning at once with a pair of binoculars which he handed over. At the moment, however, I was more interested in getting wet than seeing a motor-boat. Valerie was already in the water, shouting that it was perfect and calling the rest of us Sissies. "You look," I told Tarrant. "I'm for a dive." White apparently felt the same way, for upon turning the glasses over to his friend, he immediately took a header into the lake.

Thus it happened that the first intimation of excitement reached me in mid-air. I had struck the end of the board hard and it threw me high. At the top of the spring I was just touching my feet for a jack-knife when Tarrant's shout came to me. "Morgan! Morgan, come here! Hurry! We must get your—" Swish into the water went my head and his words were cut off; but on the way I got an upside-down view of Tarrant holding the binoculars steadily to his eyes, his mouth suddenly grim as he called out.

Under the water I twisted back towards the dock and, reaching an arm over the platform above me, pulled myself partway up. "What ho?" I demanded.

White was already clambering up and Tarrant disappearing through the door. "The boat," he called after him. "Hurry up! How fast can we get her out?"

Tarrant's calm is proverbial, but when he wants to, he can certainly work quickly. By the time I got inside he had the slide-door at the end almost up and White, dropping into the driving seat of the *Grey Falcon*, was pushing the starter-button. "All clear," called Tarrant; the rat-tat-tat of the motor fell to a grind as the clutch went into reverse. Just as the boat began to back out, Valerie jumped down into the rear deck.

We came around in a wide circle and headed out into the lake, the motor coughing a little as it was opened full without any preliminary warning. Tarrant said, "They jumped. You'll have another tragedy unless we can get there in time."

"*What is* this about?" cried Valerie. "Who jumped where? Have you boys all gone crazy?" Valerie has noticed, I think, that men of Tarrant's age rather like to have her call them boys.

His voice was unpleasantly serious as he answered. "The people in that boat I was watching, this *Torment* of yours, Morgan. There were two people in her, a big man and a little one, or maybe a man and a boy—"

"Tom Constable and junior, his son, undoubtedly," White put in, without turning his head.

"Suddenly the man who was driving scrambled out of his seat and into the rear deck, where the boy was riding. He grabbed the boy's arm and immediately jumped overboard, pulling the boy with him . . . Here, Morgan, don't follow the boat! There's no one in it. The place where they went out is almost on a direct line between your boat and that big rock on the other shore."

All of us except White were on our feet looking helplessly across the water to where, a good two miles away now, *Torment IV* was still speeding up the lake with her bow waves curving high on both sides. It gave me a queer feeling, that boat which I could just see was empty (now that I had been told), driving along as if operated by an invisible pilot. The sun was burning down, making such a glare on the lake that it was impossible to discern any small object on the surface. Such as a man's head, for example. Tarrant had the binoculars (being Tarrant, of course, he had not failed to bring them) held to his eyes with one hand, attempting to shade their glasses with the other.

"Have you got her at top speed, Morgan?" he demanded. "Best part of a mile yet to go, as I judge it."

"Everything she's got," grunted White. "Full out. Check my direction if you see anything."

"Thought I saw them a minute ago. Right together. Lost them now."

"Not good swimmers. Nowhere nearly as good as the Blacks. Doubt if they can stay up long enough."

"Oh," said Valerie, and sat down abruptly, her rubber bathing trunks making a squdging sound on a cushion. "Hurry, Mr. White. Oh, hurry!"

White said, "Agh!"

"Lost 'em," Tarrant announced definitely. "Not a sign."

Nor was there a sign when, some minutes later, we came up to the spot where, as closely as Tarrant was able to guess, the thing had happened. For five or ten minutes we floated, with the motor cut off, peering over the sides and in all directions around the *Grey Falcon*. Nothing but the calm, bright water of Winnespequam, ruffled by the lightest of breezes, met our gaze. Valerie, too, searched with the rest of us, although I could see from her expression that she wasn't very anxious to discover anything. "Of course," Tarrant pointed out, "I can't be positive as to the spot. The line is right, but the exact distance from your boathouse, Morgan, is another thing."

We began to circle slowly, in wider and wider courses.

"Any use diving?" I asked, having some vague notion that these people could possibly be brought up and resuscitated.

"No good. Deep here; take a deep-sea diver to fetch bottom. Besides we don't know where they went down. Even if the line is right, they may have swum some distance in any direction before they gave out . . . Not to the shore, though. They never made that."

Our search went on. But though we circled over a large area

for more than two hours, not a trace did we find either of the man or of the boy. Finally, "Nothing more we can do," said White gloomily. "They sink in this lake. Didn't recover the others for three days . . . Might as well run up towards Winnespequam and see what happened to the boat." He turned the wheel and we headed north.

Scarcely had we gone a mile when on the shore off our starboard side we saw a knot of persons gathered at the edge of the lake; and a little distance from them, what was obviously the boat we sought. I wondered, as we approached, at the unmistakable signs of excitement evidenced by the small group, for surely *Torment IV* must have grounded here nearly two hours previously.

We landed a hundred yards to the south at a disused and ramshackle dock, and made our way to the scene. An old man passed us as we drew near; he was hobbling along, shaking his head, and his mumbling reached us clearly enough— " 'Tis bewitched, she be a devil's boat."

It took us some time to discover, from the excited replies of the people we came up with, that yet a further tragedy had occurred. They interrupted each other and told the story backwards rather than forwards, but at last we pieced together the following account.

Torment IV, after the affair that Tarrant had witnessed, had run ashore upon a small island so close to the town wharf that she had been seen by numerous loungers. Among these was Jim Duff, in the village on an errand, and he had at once procured another boat and been taken out to salvage that of the Constables. The latter seemed, at any rate, to possess her own luck, for neither in running afoul of the island nor in her present landing had she suffered much harm. Duff had put himself aboard and, finding all in good order, had set off towards the Constables' dock alone, after expressing his fears to his companions that some ill must have befallen his employers.

The story then passed to four fishermen who, having been almost where we now stood, had witnessed the sequel. Duff, they asserted, had been passing not far from shore on his way south when, without any evident cause, he leapt from the seat he occupied and dived overboard. No doubt he twisted the wheel as he jumped away, for *Torment IV* turned and headed in. Two of the fishermen, however, seeing their friend struggling in the water, had immediately put out in their row-boat and gone to his rescue. Duff was a strong swimmer, accustomed to the lake since boyhood, but to their astonishment, no sooner did he note their approach than he turned and, in place of coming ashore, swam out into the lake with every appearance of panic. They were still some distance away from him when this happened and, though they made all possible efforts to overtake the man, he had sunk three times before they reached him, and he had drowned. Nevertheless, after much exertion they had been able to recover his body.

For the first time we noticed a still form, covered by one of the fisherman's blankets, lying farther up the bank among the trees.

"Have you tried resuscitation?" asked Tarrant sharply.

"More'n an hour an' a half we tried," he was told. "He be dead, he be."

White and Tarrant walked over to the body and, after sending Valerie back to the *Grey Falcon*, I followed. When I arrived, they had drawn back the blanket and were looking at the corpse. It was not a pleasant sight. I have been led to believe that persons who have drowned wear a peaceful expression but this one assuredly did not. He was a man of about forty-eight or fifty, a native New Hampshireman, bony and obviously strong. But on his face there was stamped a hideous grimace, an expression so obviously of extreme horror that it would have been essentially identical on any cast of features.

With a grunt Morgan quietly replaced the blanket. "That's him, all right; that's Jim Duff."

When we returned to the shoreline, arrangements were being made to tow *Torment IV* back to the Constables' dock. No one seemed anxious to pilot her, and I noted a bit absently that our host did not volunteer his services this time, however willing he may have been on the first occasion he had told us about. Once more in the *Grey Falcon*, we backed out on the water and steered for home. A subdued party. It was Tarrant who broke the silence after it had continued for several minutes.

"No use trying to avoid the subject," he said. "We're all

thinking about it . . . If what I saw earlier, and what has just happened here, isn't due to some form of insanity arising with the utmost suddenness, God knows what it may be."

Silence again.

White spoke this time, gruffly. "How can a boat drive people insane? Certainly not a hard-boiled old-timer like Duff."

"Could it, could it be sunstroke?" Valerie asked in a small voice. "It's awfully hot."

Tarrant admitted, "There's no question it's hot. But I don't see a sunstroke theory. None of us feel any symptoms, do we? And we have been on the lake longer than any of them were."

"But what *can* have made them do it?"

"I don't know," said Tarrant in a low tone. "I confess I don't know . . . At first I felt that some deep cause for suicide must be operating in the Black-Constable family. What I saw surely looked like nothing so much as a determined suicide combined with murder, or perhaps a double suicide . . . But that's out now, definitely. This man Duff could hardly be involved in such a thing and, furthermore, I don't believe for a moment that he had the least idea of doing away with himself when he started that boat down the lake."

No one had even a conjecture to add. The rest of our return was only the purring of the engine and the slap-slither of the little waves against our boat. As for me, I was completely bewildered. Here were a succession of calamities; first three persons, then two, finally one, who for no reason at all had abruptly cast themselves into the lake to drown. The last two tragedies had been amply witnessed, one by Tarrant himself through the binoculars, the other by no less than four fishermen, friends of the unfortunate man, and this time at a reasonably short range.

One must suppose, at all events, that the first disaster had been similar to its successors, a finding that scarcely did much to account for any of them. The last victim's relations with the others had certainly not been of a nature so serious as to form a bond of death. What could possibly have caused such different types of people, in broad daylight, on this peaceful lake, and plainly menaced by no danger, to jump and die? Duff's reported actions, surely, appeared to indicate that, once out of the boat, he was determined to drown. Suicide seemed absurd; and yet his actions had comported with it. Both sight and sound – for his friends had shouted at him – had combined to assure him that help was close at hand. But he had renounced all aid. Involuntarily I shook my head. It just didn't make sense.

When we landed, Tarrant made an abrupt excuse and hurried off to the house in his bathing suit. Apparently he changed with some speed, for he was nowhere to be found when the rest of us climbed the path.

He was late for dinner. We were half-way through the main course when he came in and sat down at the table. "Glad you didn't wait for me," he said, a little absently. On his forehead there still lingered the trace of the frown that always accompanies his most strenuous thinking.

"Didn't know whether you'd show up or not," White remarked in explanation. "Where have you been?"

"Looking over that boat."

"Thought so. Find anything?"

"Not a thing," answered Tarrant frankly. "That is, if you mean, as I take it you do, anything that throws light on these strange deaths."

For a time he applied himself to his meal, but when he had caught up with us at its end, he pushed back his chair and addressed us. "I examined this *Torment IV* from stem to stern. She is a beautiful boat, Morgan, no doubt about it; and she has gotten out of these mishaps herself with no more than a few dents in the bows. And a long gash coming back from the bow on one side where she careened off a rock when grounding on the island. It's above the water-line and scarcely an eighth of an inch deep. No real harm; but just another item resembling the *Mary Celeste*. You remember *she* had strips in her, running back from the bows, too. It's a strange coincidence how these circumstances match, even down to the condition of the boat – so far as a motor-boat *can* exhibit the same conditions as a two hundred-ton brig. . . ."

In the short pause I queried, "Still, that doesn't get us anywhere, does it?"

He agreed. "As you say. Even if we had reason to believe that the same causes were operating – since several of the same symptoms have appeared – we have no further clue, since we don't know what could have brought about the situation on the *Mary Celeste*. And of course we have no right to assume even similar causes; a hundred to one this is merely a superficial resemblance."

Came one of White's grunts. "Nothing at all, eh? Nothing? What were you looking for?"

"To tell you the truth," Tarrant confessed with a smile, "I'm afraid I was looking for some sort of mechanical arrangement. I don't know exactly what. Something along the lines of Jerry's idea of a poison gas, possibly. Since it obviously couldn't come from the motor in the routine way, I considered the possibility of a small, hidden tank concealed somewhere on board. With a blower or insufflator arrangement, of course. Although I have some knowledge of gases and have never heard of one having the observed effects, it is still possible. That would at least indicate malice, murder, in fact; and we should have a reasonable background for these events. Pretty far-fetched, I admit. You see to what conjectures I have been reduced by the apparently inexplicable data . . . I have never cared much for supernatural explanations."

"Hmph. Why 'apparently' inexplicable? Looks actually inexplicable to me."

"Nothing," said Tarrant shortly, "is actually inexplicable. That is, if you credit Causation. I do. What is loosely called the 'inexplicable' is only the unexplained, certainly not the unexplainable. The term is quite literally a mere catchword for ignorance. That's our present relation to the deaths; we are still ignorant of their cause."

"Guess we'll have to remain so this time."

"Oh, no. After our experience to-day, it's a challenge I accept."

Something in his tone interested Valerie. She said, "I'm glad you won't give it up. But what else can you do now, if you have already examined the boat?"

"I've examined the boat. Thoroughly. I even had the floor-boards up; I couldn't take the engine out but I did everything else. Had a boy go under her in the dock and he reported everything ship-shape and just as it ought to be along the keel."

"Well, then," Val repeated, "what is left that you can do?"

Tarrant smiled. "Now I'm disappointed in you, Valerie. Surely that is obvious. There is something pretty drastic that happens to people in that boat. There is only one alternative left now. With Jerry's help I propose to find out to-morrow what it is that happens. When we know that, it may be possible for us to deal with it."

"Oh. Oh, I see. Of course. You're going out in the boat yourself." Val paused; and added suddenly, "Not with Jerry, you're not! No, I won't listen to it. I won't let Jerry go anywhere near the horrible thing!"

I expostulated. If Tarrant was willing to risk his neck, it seemed only fair that someone else should go with him. Morgan White offered to go immediately, but it appeared that Trevis preferred me for some reason.

"He won't have to go very near it, Valerie," Tarrant assured her. "I wouldn't myself permit him to come with me in the boat. I only want him to follow me, at a respectful distance in the *Grey Falcon*, so that, if I jump over, he can pick me up . . . There must be a reason why people jump."

In the end we persuaded her, though Tarrant did most of it. There are times when Valerie seems hardly to listen to *me*. He persuaded her not only to permit me to follow him but not to come along herself. As usual, he had his way.

We all went down to the boathouse after breakfast. White explained to me how to run his boat, which was simple enough; and Tarrant and I started off for the Constables' dock, leaving Valerie and our host behind. He agreed to run *Torment IV* up and down the lake opposite the boathouse, so that they could observe what happened, if anything.

On the way over, Tarrant produced the implements with which he had equipped the *Grey Falcon* earlier in the day – so as not to worry Valerie unnecessarily, he said. They made a curious collection. There was a shotgun and, somewhat redundantly, a rifle; an axe and a long rope with a lasso at its end completed his equipment.

Naturally my attention was caught by the fire-arms. "But what can we use those for?" I inquired curiously. "Is there someone to shoot at? But no, there wasn't anyone in the boat except the people who jumped out of it, each time. And this morning you are going alone, aren't you?"

"I don't know. I'm going alone, yes. On the other hand, there is certainly villainy of some kind here, and where there is villainy, it has been my experience that there is usually a villain . . . I'm glad it turned out a good hot day again."

More puzzled than ever, I said, "We threw out the sunstroke theory, didn't we? What in heaven's name has a hot day got to do with it?"

"I don't know, Jerry, honestly I don't," Tarrant grinned. "I have the haziest notion about this thing, but it is much too vague for me to tell you. So far as I know, there are only two conditions leading up to these deaths, a ride in *Torment IV* and a bright, warm day. Since I want to see duplicated whatever happens, I am glad that both conditions are fulfilled."

There was no time for more, as we had now reached the Constables' dock. Tarrant, who had taken the precaution of donning his bathing trunks, landed and was admitted to the boathouse by a man who evidently had been waiting for him. After a short delay – no doubt he was making another examination of *Torment IV* – I heard him start the motor and, a moment later, the ill-omened motor-boat slid slowly out of its shelter.

The events that succeeded constituted a series of complete surprises for me, culminating in sheer amazement. He turned and headed the boat out into the lake, opening her up fairly wide, and I brought the *Grey Falcon* along in his wake as closely as I dared, constantly alert for any change of direction or other sudden action on his part. *Torment IV* had a driving seat stretching entirely across the centre of the boat, and my first surprise was to observe Tarrant clamber up on this and crouch there in a most uncomfortable position, as he manipulated the controls. Nothing further happened, however, and while continuing to watch carefully, I could not avoid wondering again for what purpose he had provided the weapons in my own craft.

I realised that it was foolish and yet I could think of no other type of explanation of the tragedies than a supernatural one. A ghost or ghoul? In broad daylight, on a motor-boat? Even so, a shotgun isn't of much use against a ghost. But of course that was nonsense, anyhow. Even the strange coincidence of sudden, self-destructive madness on the part of these diverse people in similar circumstances, was better. And again, you can't shoot madness. The rope and the axe I abandoned hopelessly.

By now we had reached the centre of the lake and Tarrant motioned to me, without turning around, that he proposed to slow down. As I did so, too, I saw that he had produced a length of stout cord and was lashing *Torment IV*'s wheel in such a way that the boat would continue forward in a large circle.

When he had done so, he scrambled out of the driver's seat altogether and, passing right by the rear well-deck with its comfortable chairs, gained the upper decking of the hull itself as far astern as he could get, immediately over the propeller, in fact. There he stood upright, balancing easily on both feet and intently observing the entire boat ahead of him, almost all of which was visible from his position.

And nothing happened. *Torment IV* continued to circle at a reduced speed and Tarrant continued to watch as tensely as ever. It went on for so long that I am afraid I was beginning to get a little careless. I must have been all of seventy-five yards away when suddenly I saw him stiffen, start to turn away, take one more glance forward – and dive!

I strained my eyes, but I could see no change whatsoever in his boat, which was keeping placidly on her circular course. It certainly looked as if he had seen something, but if so, it remained invisible to me. Abruptly I came to and swung the *Grey Falcon* towards where he was swimming with more speed than I had thought him capable of. Even yet I was not much concerned. Tarrant was neither a Philadelphian merchant nor a backwoodsman. Furthermore, he was a good swimmer and in his bathing suit. Accordingly my astonishment all but took my breath away entirely when, as I came up towards him, he gave a horrified glance over his shoulder, and twisting abruptly away from the *Grey Falcon*, dug his arms into the water in a panic-stricken Australian crawl!

In that moment I realised we were up against something serious. I threw in the clutch and went after him. Fortunately I could always overtake him with the motor-boat I had; and I prepared to jump in for him if he showed signs of sinking. I was sure that, no matter how good a swimmer he was, he would sink before he reached Winnespequam, some eight miles away, for he was heading up the lake directly towards the town, although the nearest shore was well within a mile.

I was drawing up to him again, but this time, instead of slowing down, I sent the boat past him as closely as I dared. And as I went past, I yelled at the top of my voice, "Tarrant! For God's sake, what the hell has gotten into you!"

Evidently one of his ears was out of the water, for he hesitated and raised his head. For a moment he regarded my boat and myself without recognition, then he trod water and looked anxiously all about. I was coming about now, having been carried beyond him, and I heard his hoarse shout, "All right. I'm coming aboard."

He was literally shaking when I helped pull him over the side and for a minute or so he merely stood in the *Grey Falcon* and gasped. Then he said suddenly, "Where is that devil's boat?" I was struck by the same expression the old man had used the day before.

"There she is," he went on. "She's getting too close in to shore. She mustn't land again!" In the chase after Tarrant I had almost forgotten *Torment IV*, but now I saw that she was, in fact, circling closer and closer to the edge of the lake.

"We shall have to get near enough, Jerry, so that I can rope that little mast on her bow," he grated. "Don't get *any* closer than you have to, though." And he added under his breath, "God, I hate to do this." Well, I gave up; in view of these unbelievable happenings it didn't seem even worth while asking questions. No matter what occurred, I didn't think my friend had gone mad.

I settled down to the job and soon made a parallel course with *Torment IV*. "Not so close, for God's sake!" yelled Tarrant. I eased off a little; and he threw his coiled rope. The third time he succeeded; the noose settled accurately over the small mast and he jerked it tight. "Make for the centre of the lake now, Jerry. Give it all you've got; you'll have to pull the other boat out of her course. I didn't dare stop her completely for fear it wouldn't happen." As he spoke he was securing his end of the rope to a cleat, and immediately caught up the axe and took his stand above the taut line, looking anxiously along it. So that was why he had brought the axe! Apparently he foresaw the possibility of having to sever the rope even before it could be released. It was hard going, pulling against *Torment IV's* powerful engine, but finally we were well out in the lake again. With an audible sigh of relief Tarrant brought down the axe, the rope snapped.

"Now," he said, "the rifle," retrieving it from the floor and slipping in a cartridge. It was a regulation Winchester, a heavy weapon. "Go parallel again but at least twice as far away from her," he admonished me.

When this course had been taken up to his satisfaction and we were a good hundred yards and more from *Torment IV*, he commenced firing at the empty boat. The shots crashed out over the lake, a round dozen of them, and I saw that he was quite literally attacking the motor-boat itself. A little series of spurts appeared just along its waterline as the bullets punched a neat row of holes through the hull.

"Enough, I guess," he observed, putting down the rifle and catching up the shotgun, hastily loading both chambers. We waited then, still accompanying *Torment IV* at the same distance; and shortly she began to list on the side towards us. This had the effect of straightening her course somewhat but only for a few hundred yards, for she was filling rapidly now and beginning to plough down into the water. Deliberately she settled on her starboard side until the lake poured over her rail; then with a final swirl her stern lifted a little and she went under.

But, just as she did so, something climbed up on her port side and hopped away. At the distance I couldn't see what it was, except that I should have judged it to be about two feet or more in diameter. It made a dark spot against the bright water, and it did not sink. On the contrary it scrambled over the surface and it was making directly for our boat. "Easy, Jerry," Tarrant grated, as I instinctively put on speed; "we've got to get it."

Reluctantly I swung to port in order not to catch the thing in our wake. It seemed to be coming towards us with the speed of lightning; I doubt if we could have distanced it, anyhow. Tarrant's face was white and strained, and a tremor ran over his body as he raised his gun. For a few seconds he waited, then fired. Just behind the creature the water splattered where the shot struck the lake. He had one more shot; the thing was closer now and still coming rapidly. It was so close I could begin to see it clearly – the most repulsive animal I have ever looked at. Spiders always make me creepy, but this monstrous creature with its flashing legs, its horribly hairy bulb of a body, was nauseating and worse than nauseating. There was something so horrifying about it that I very nearly jumped before it reached us. I could see, or imagined that I could, a beady, malignant eye fixed definitely upon me. If Tarrant had missed his last shot I don't know what would have happened. It's one of those things I don't let myself think about.

He didn't miss. Simultaneously with the roar of the gun, the water about it churned and the monster disappeared, blown to bits.

For the next ten minutes we drifted aimlessly. I was being sick over the side of the *Grey Falcon*.

"I think," said Tarrant that evening, "that it was some member of the *Lycosidæ* or wolf-spider species. Or else one of the larger species of *Aviculariidæ*, some of which grow to great size. Even so, I have never heard of anything as large as this having been reported. And judging from the experiences here I judge it unlikely that many observers will live to report it. Although the poisonous effects of most spider bites are exaggerated, I have a feeling that this one's bite was fatal.

"Of course I had some inkling as to what to expect. Oh, not such a spider, I couldn't guess that. Although I should have done. When I was examining the motor yesterday, I did see some heavy cobwebbing way up under the bow, but at that time I didn't think that any sort of spider could be so terrifying; I am not greatly upset by spiders myself. Just the same, reason told me that something appeared on that boat which drove people overboard in a panic. And since the motor was the only portion of it that I was unable to examine thoroughly, it was from that direction that I looked for it. That is why, as soon as I could, I lashed the wheel and got as far away from the driving seat as was possible. The heat, I believe, brought it out; not only the heat of the motor but also that of the sun pouring down on the forward deck. How it got into the driver's cockpit I don't know; the first I saw of it was when it sprang up on the back of the seat.

"I can't express the horror and loathing its appearance inspired. It was sufficient to make Jerry pretty ill – and it never got within twenty yards of him. Sheer panic, that's what one felt in its presence. When I struck the water, I had no thought of where I was going, only a hopeless conviction that I would surely be overtaken. I forgot everything, all my own preparations; and the mere swish of Jerry's boat when he first came toward me only increased my terror. That is why Duff turned away from his rescuers; in his panic-stricken condition he may even have imagined that the rowboat with its oars was the beast itself . . . Well, thank God I recovered sufficiently to get into the *Grey Falcon* and finish the job."

"Suppose there'll be no trouble about the motor-boat?"

"Oh, no. I didn't see the widow, but she sent word that I could blow it up if I wished and good riddance. The loss of the boat was a small price, I think."

Valerie shuddered and reached for my hand. "Jerry," she said, "it's nice here, but take me home tomorrow, please?"

The Three Strangers

Thomas Hardy

Among the few features of agricultural England which
retain an appearance but little modified by the lapse of
centuries may be reckoned the high, grassy and furzy downs,
coombs, or ewe-leases, as they are indifferently called, that fill a
large area of certain counties in the south and south-west. If any
mark of human occupation is met with hereon, it usually takes
the form of the solitary cottage of some shepherd.

Fifty years ago such a lonely cottage stood on such a down, and
may possibly be standing there now. In spite of its loneliness,
however, the spot, by actual measurement, was not more than five
miles from a county-town. Yet that affected it little. Five miles of
irregular upland, during the long inimical seasons, with their
sleets, snows, rains and mists afford withdrawing space enough
to isolate a Timon or a Nebuchadnezzar; much less, in fair
weather, to please that less repellant tribe, the poets, philosophers,
artists, and others who "conceive and meditate of pleasant things".

Some old earthen camp or barrow, some clump of trees, at
least some starved fragment of ancient hedge is usually taken
advantage of in the erection of these forlorn dwellings. But, in
the present case, such a kind of shelter had been disregarded.
Higher Crowstairs, as the house was called, stood quite detached and undefended. The only reason for its precise situation
seemed to be the crossing of two footpaths at right angles hard
by, which may have crossed there and thus for a good five
hundred years. Hence the house was exposed to the elements on
all sides. But, though the wind up here blew unmistakably when
it did blow, and the rain hit hard whenever it fell, the various
weathers of the winter season were not quite so formidable on

the coomb as they were imagined to be by dwellers on low ground. The raw times were not so pernicious as in the hollows, and the frosts were scarcely so severe. When the shepherd and his family who tenanted the house were pitied for their sufferings from the exposure, they said that upon the whole they were less inconvenienced by "wuzzes and flames" (hoarses and phlegms) than when they had lived by the stream of a snug neighboring valley.

The night of March 28, 182 –, was precisely one of the nights that were wont to call forth these expressions of commiseration. The level rainstorm smote walls, slopes, and hedges like the clothyard shafts of Senlac and Crecy. Such sheep and outdoor animals as had not shelter stood with their buttocks to the winds; while the tails of little birds trying to roost on some scraggy thorn were blown inside-out like umbrellas. The gable-end of the cottage was stained with wet, and the eavesdroppings flapped against the wall. Yet never was commiseration for the shepherd more misplaced. For that cheerful rustic was entertaining a large party in glorification of the christening of his second girl.

The guests had arrived before the rain began to fall, and they were all now assembled in the chief or living room of the dwelling. A glance into the apartment at eight o'clock on this eventful evening would have resulted in the opinion that it was as cozy and comfortable a nook as could be wished for in boisterous weather. The calling of its inhabitant was proclaimed by a number of highly polished sheep crooks without stems that were hung ornamentally over the fireplace, the curl of each shining crook varying from the antiquated type engraved in the patriarchal pictures of old family Bibles to the most approved fashion of the last local sheep-fair. The room was lighted by half a dozen candles having wicks only a trifle smaller than the grease which enveloped them, in candlesticks that were never used but at high-days, holy-days and family feasts. The lights were scattered about the room, two of them standing on the chimneypiece. This position of candles was in itself significant. Candles on the chimneypiece always meant a party.

On the hearth, in front of a back-brand to give substance blazed a fire of thorns, that crackled "like the laughter of the fool."

Nineteen persons were gathered there. Of these, five women, wearing gowns of various bright hues, sat in chairs along the wall; girls shy and not shy filled the window-bench; four men, including Charley Jake the hedge-carpenter, Elijah New the parish-clerk, and John Pitcher, a neighboring dairy-man, the shepherd's father-in-law, lolled in the settle; a young man and maid, who were blushing over tentative *pourparlers* on a life companionship, sat beneath the cor-ner-cupboard; and an elderly engaged man of fifty or upward moved relentlessly about from spots where his betrothed was not to the spot where she was. Enjoyment was pretty general, and so much the more prevailed in being unhampered by conventional restrictions. Absolute confidence in each other's good opinion begat perfect ease, while the finishing stroke of manner, amounting to a truly princely serenity, was lent to the majority by the absence of any expression or trait denoting that they wished to get on in the world, enlarge their minds, or do any eclipsing thing whatever – which nowadays so generally nips the bloom and *bonhomie* of all except the two extremes of the social scale.

Shepherd Fennel had married well, his wife being a dairy-man's daughter from a vale at a distance, who brought fifty guineas in her pocket – and kept them there, till they should be required for ministering to the needs of a coming family. This frugal woman had been somewhat exercised as to the character that should be given to the gathering. A sit-still party had its advantages; but an undisturbed position of ease in chairs and settles was apt to lead on the men to such an unconscionable deal of toping that they would sometimes fairly drink the house dry. A dancing-party was the alternative; but this, while avoid-ing the foregoing objection on the score of good drink, had a counterbalancing disadvantage in the matter of good victuals, the ravenous appetites engendered by the exercise causing immense havoc in the buttery. Shepherdess Fennel fell back upon the intermediate plan of mingling short dances with short periods of talk and singing, so as to hinder any ungovernable rage in either. But this scheme was entirely confined to her own gentle mind: the shepherd himself was in the mood to exhibit the most reckless phases of hospitality.

The fiddler was a boy of those parts, about twelve years of age, who had a wonderful dexterity in jigs and reels, though his fingers were so small and short as to necessitate a constant shifting for the high notes, from which he scrambled back to the first position with sounds not of unmixed purity of tone. At seven the shrill tweedle-dee of this youngster had begun, accompanied by a booming ground-bass from Elijah New, the parish clerk, who had thoughtfully brought with him his favorite musical instrument, the serpent. Dancing was instantaneous, Mrs. Fennel privately enjoining the players on no account to let the dance exceed the length of a quarter of an hour.

But Elijah and the boy, in the excitement of their position, quite forgot the injunction. Moreover, Oliver Giles, a man of seventeen, one of the dancers, who was enamored of his partner, a fair girl of thirty-three rolling years, had recklessly handed a new crownpiece to the musicians, as a bribe to keep going as long as they had muscle and wind. Mrs. Fennel, seeing the steam begin to generate on the countenances of her guests, crossed over and touched the fiddler's elbow and put her hand on the serpent's mouth. But they took no notice, and fearing she might lose her character of genial hostess if she were to interfere too markedly, she retired and sat down helpless. And so the dance whizzed on with cumulative fury, the performers moving in their planet-like courses, direct and retrograde, from apogee to perigee, till the hand of the well-kicked clock at the bottom of the room had traveled over the circumference of an hour.

While these cheerful events were in course of enactment within Fennel's pastoral dwelling, an incident having considerable bearing on the party had occurred in the gloomy night without. Mrs. Fennel's concern about the growing fierceness of the dance corresponded in point of time with the ascent of a human figure to the solitary hill of Higher Crowstairs from the direction of the distant town. This personage strode on through the rain without a pause, following the little-worn path which, further on in its course, skirted the shepherd's cottage.

It was nearly the time of full moon, and on this account, though the sky was lined with a uniform sheet of dripping cloud, ordinary objects out of doors were readily visible. The sad, wan light revealed the lonely pedestrian to be a man of supple frame; his gait suggested that he had somewhat passed the period of perfect and instinctive agility, though not so far as to be otherwise than rapid of motion when occasion required. At a rough guess, he might have been about forty years of age. He appeared tall, but a recruiting sergeant, or other person accustomed to the judging of men's heights by the eye, would have discerned that this was chiefly owing to his gauntness, and that he was not more than five-feet-eight or nine.

Notwithstanding the regularity of his tread, there was caution in it, as in that of one who mentally feels his way; and despite the fact that it was not a black coat nor a dark garment of any sort that he wore, there was something about him which suggested that he naturally belonged to the black-coated tribes of men. His clothes were of fustian, and his boots hobnailed, yet in his progress he showed not the mud-accustomed bearing of hobnailed and fustianed peasantry.

By the time that he had arrived abreast of the shepherd's premises the rain came down, or rather came along, with yet more determined violence. The outskirts of the little settlement partially broke the force of wind and rain, and this induced him to stand still. The most salient of the shepherd's domestic erections was an empty sty at the forward corner of his hedgeless garden, for in these latitudes the principle of masking the homelier features of your establishment by a conventional frontage was unknown. The traveler's eye was attracted to this small building by the pallid shine of the wet slates that covered it. He turned aside, and, finding it empty, stood under the pent-roof for shelter.

While he stood, the boom of the serpent within the adjacent house, and the lesser strains of the fiddler, reached the spot as an accompaniment to the surging hiss of the flying rain on the sod, its louder beating on the cabbage leaves of the garden, on the eight or ten beehives just discernible by the path, and its dripping from the eaves into a row of buckets and pans that had been placed under the walls of the cottage. For at Higher Crowstairs, as at all such elevated domiciles, the grand difficulty of housekeeping was an insufficiency of water; and a casual rainfall was utilized by turning out, as catchers, every utensil that the house contained. Some queer stories might be told of the contrivances for economy in suds and dishwaters that are absolutely necessitated in upland habitations during the droughts of summer. But at this season there were no such exigencies; a mere acceptance of what the skies bestowed was sufficient for an abundant store.

At last the notes of the serpent ceased and the house was silent. This cessation of activity aroused the solitary pedestrian from the reverie into which he had lapsed, and, emerging from the shed, with an apparently new intention, he walked up the path to the house-door. Arrived here, his first act was to kneel down on a large stone beside the row of vessels, and to drink a copious draught from one of them. Having quenched his thirst, he rose and lifted his hand to knock, but paused with his eye upon the panel. Since the dark surface of the wood revealed absolutely nothing, it was evident that he must be mentally looking through the door, as if he wished to measure thereby all the possibilities that a house of this sort might include, and how they might bear upon the question of his entry.

In his indecision he turned and surveyed the scene around. Not a soul was anywhere visible. The garden path stretched downward from his feet, gleaming like the track of a snail; the roof of the little well (mostly dry), the well-cover, the top rail of the garden gate, were varnished with the same dull liquid glaze; while, far away in the vale, a faint whiteness of more than usual extent showed that the rivers were high in the meads. Beyond all this winked a few bleared lamplights through the beating drops – lights that denoted the situation of the country town from which he had appeared to come. The absence of all notes of life in that direction seemed to clinch his intentions, and he knocked at the door.

Within, a desultory chat had taken the place of movement and musical sound. The hedge carpenter was suggesting a song to the company, which nobody just then was inclined to undertake, so that the knock afforded a not unwelcome diversion.

"Walk in!" said the shepherd promptly.

The latch clicked upward, and out of the night our pedestrian appeared upon the door-mat. The shepherd arose, snuffed two of the nearest candles, and turned to look at him.

Their light disclosed that the stranger was dark in complexion and not unprepossessing as to feature. His hat, which for a moment he did not remove, hung low over his eyes, without concealing that they were large, open, and determined, moving with a flash rather than a glance round the room. He seemed pleased with his survey, and, baring his shaggy head, said, in a rich deep voice, "The rain is so heavy, friends, that I ask leave to come in and rest awhile."

"To be sure, stranger," said the shepherd. "And faith, you've been lucky in choosing your time, for we are having a bit of a fling for a glad cause – though, to be sure, a man could hardly wish that glad cause to happen more than once a year."

"Nor less", spoke up a woman. "For 'tis best to get your family over and done with, as soon as you can, so as to be all the earlier out of the fag o't."

"And what may be this glad cause?" asked the stranger.

"A birth and christening," said the shepherd.

The stranger hoped his host might not be made unhappy either by too many or too few of such episodes, and being invited by a gesture to a pull at the mug, he readily acquiesced. His manner, which, before entering, had been so dubious, was now altogether that of a careless and candid man.

"Late to be traipsing athwart this coomb – hey?" said the engaged man of fifty.

"Late it is, master, as you say – I'll take a seat in the chimney-corner, if you have nothing to urge against it, ma'am; for I am a little moist on the side that was next the rain."

Mrs. Shepherd Fennel assented, and made room for the self-invited comer, who, having got completely inside the chimney-corner, stretched out his legs and his arms with the expansiveness of a person quite at home.

"Yes, I am rather cracked in the vamp," he said freely, seeing that the eyes of the shepherd's wife fell upon his boots, "and I am not well fitted either. I have had some rough times lately, and have been forced to pick up what I can get in the way of wearing, but I must find a suit better fit for working-days when I reach home."

"One of hereabouts?" she inquired.

"Not quite that – further up the county."

"I thought so. And so be I; and by your tongue you come from my neighborhood."

"But you would hardly have heard of me," he said quickly. "My time would be long before yours, ma'am, you see."

This testimony to the youthfulness of his hostess had the effect of stopping her cross-examination.

"There is only one thing more wanted to make me happy," continued the new-comer, "and that is a little baccy, which I am sorry to say I am out of."

"I'll fill your pipe," said the shepherd.

"I must ask you to lend me a pipe likewise."

"A smoker, and no pipe about 'ee?"

"I have dropped it somewhere on the road."

The shepherd filled and handed him a new clay pipe, saying, as he did so, "Hand me your baccy-box – I'll fill that too, now I am about it."

The man went through the movement of searching his pockets.

"Lost that too?" said his entertainer, with some surprise.

"I am afraid so," said the man with some confusion. "Give it to me in a screw of paper." Lighting his pipe at the candle with a suction that drew the whole flame into the bowl, he resettled himself in the corner and bent his looks upon the faint steam from his damp legs, as if he wished to say no more.

Meanwhile the general body of guests had been taking little notice of this visitor by reason of an absorbing discussion in which they were engaged with the band about a tune for the next dance. The matter being settled, they were about to stand up when an interruption came in the shape of another knock at the door.

At sound of the same the man in the chimney-corner took up the poker and began stirring the brands as if doing it thoroughly were the one aim of his existence; and a second time the shepherd said, "Walk in!" In a moment another man stood upon the straw-woven door-mat. He too was a stranger.

This individual was one of a type radically different from the first. There was more of the commonplace in his manner, and a certain jovial cosmopolitanism sat upon his features. He was several years older than the first arrival, his hair being slightly frosted, his eyebrows bristly, and his whiskers cut back from his cheeks. His face was rather full and flabby, and yet it was not altogether a face without power. A few grog-blossoms marked the neighborhood of his nose. He flung back his long drab greatcoat, revealing that beneath it he wore a suit of cinder-gray shade throughout, large heavy seals, of some metal or other that would take a polish, dangling from his fob as his only personal ornament. Shaking the water-drops from his low-crowned glazed hat, he said, "I must ask for a few minutes' shelter, comrades, or I shall be wetted to my skin before I get to Casterbridge."

"Make yourself at home, master," said the shepherd, perhaps a trifle less heartily than on the first occasion. Not that Fennel had the least tinge of niggardliness in his composition; but the room was far from large, spare chairs were not numerous, and damp companions were not altogether desirable at close quarters for the women and girls in their bright-colored gowns.

However, the second comer, after taking off his greatcoat, and hanging his hat on a nail in one of the ceiling-beams as if he had been specially invited to put it there, advanced and sat down at the table. This had been pushed so closely into the chimney-corner, to give all available room to the dancers, that its inner edge grazed the elbow of the man who had ensconced himself by the fire; and thus the two strangers were brought into close companionship. They nodded to each other by way of breaking the ice of unacquaintance, and the first stranger handed his neighbor the family mug – a huge vessel of brown ware, having its upper edge worn away like a threshold by the rub of whole generations of thirsty lips that had gone the way of all flesh, and bearing the following inscription burnt upon its rotund side in yellow letters:

THERE IS NO FUN
UNTIL I CUM

The other man, nothing loath, raised the mug to his lips, and drank on, and on, and on – till a curious blueness overspread the countenance of the shepherd's wife, who had regarded with no little surprise the first stranger's free offer to the second of what did not belong to him to dispense.

"I knew it!" said the toper to the shepherd with much satisfaction. "When I walked up your garden before coming in, and saw the hives all of a row, I said to myself, 'Where there's bees there's honey, and where there's honey there's mead.' But mead of such a truly comfortable sort as this I really didn't expect to meet in my older days." He took yet another pull at the mug, till it assumed an ominous elevation.

"Glad you enjoy it!" said the shepherd warmly.

"It is goodish mead," assented Mrs. Fennel, with an absence of enthusiasm which seemed to say that it was possible to buy praise for one's cellar at too heavy a price. "It is trouble enough to make – and really I hardly think we shall make any more. For honey sells well, and we ourselves can make shift with a drop o' small mead and metheglin for common use from the comb-washings."

"Oh, but you'll never have the heart!" reproachfully cried the stranger in cinder-gray, after taking up the mug a third time and setting it down empty. "I love mead, when 'tis old like this, and I love to go to church o' Sundays, or to relieve the needy any day of the week."

"Ha, ha, ha!" said the man in the chimney corner, who, in spite of the taciturnity induced by the pipe of tobacco, could not or would not refrain from this slight testimony to his comrade's humor.

Now the old mead of those days, brewed of the purest first-year or maiden honey, four pounds to the gallon – with its due complement of white eggs, cinnamon, ginger, cloves, mace, rosemary, yeast, and processes of working, bottling, and cellaring – tasted remarkably strong; but it did not taste so strong as it actually was. Hence, presently, the stranger in cinder-gray at the table, moved by its creeping influence, unbuttoned his waistcoat, threw himself back in his chair, spread his legs, and made his presence felt in various ways.

"Well, well, as I say," he resumed, "I am going to Caster-bridge, and to Casterbridge I must go. I should have been almost there by this time; but the rain drove me into your dwelling, and I'm not sorry for it."

"You don't live in Casterbridge?" said the shepherd.

"Not as yet; though I shortly mean to move there."

"Going to set up in trade, perhaps?"

"No, no," said the shepherd's wife. "It is easy to see that the the gentleman is rich, and don't want to work at anything."

The cinder-gray stranger paused, as if to consider whether he would accept that definition of himself. He presently rejected it by answering, "Rich is not quite the word for me, Dame. I do work, and I must work. And even if I only get to Casterbridge by midnight I must begin work there at eight tomorrow morning. Yes, het or wet, blow or snow, famine or sword, my day's work tomorrow must be done."

"Poor man! Then, in spit o' seeming, you be worse off than we," replied the shepherd's wife.

"'Tis the nature of my trade, men and maidens. 'Tis the nature of my trade more than my poverty . . . But really and truly I must up and off, or I shan't get a lodging in the town." However, the speaker did not move, and directly added, "there's time for one more draught of friendship before I go; and I'd perform it at once if the mug were not dry."

"Here's a mug o'small," said Mrs. Fennel. "Small, we call it, though to be sure 'tis only the first wash o' the combs."

"No," said the stranger disdainfully. "I won't spoil your first kindness by partaking o'your second."

"Certainly not," broke in Fennel. "We don't increase and multiply every day, and I'll fill the mug again." He went away to the dark place under the stairs where the barrel stood. The shepherdess followed him.

"Why should you do this?" she said reproachfully, as soon as they were alone. "He's emptied it once, though it held enough for ten people; and now he's not contented wi' the small, but must needs call for more o' the strong! And a stranger unbeknown to any of us. For my part, I don't like the look o' the man at all."

"But he's in the house, my honey; and 'tis a wet night, and a christening. Daze it, what's a cup of mead more or less? There'll be plenty more next bee-burning."

"Very well – this time then," she answered, looking wistfully at the barrel. "But what is the man's calling, and where is he one of, that he should come in and join us like this?"

"I don't know. I'll ask him again."

The catastrophe of having the mug drained dry at one pull by the stranger in cinder-gray was effectually guarded against this time by Mrs. Fennel. She poured out his allowance in a small cup, keeping the large one at a discreet distance from him. When he had tossed off his portion the shepherd renewed his inquiry about the stranger's occupation.

The latter did not immediately reply, and the man in the chimney-corner, with sudden demonstrativeness, said, "Anybody may know my trade – I'm a wheelwright."

"A very good trade for these parts," said the shepherd.

"And anybody may know mine – if they've the sense to find it out," said the stranger in cinder-gray.

"You may generally tell what a man is by his claws," observed the hedge-carpenter, looking at his own hands. "My fingers be as full of thorns as an old pincushion is of pins."

The hands of the man in the chimney-corner instinctively sought the shade, and he gazed into the fire as he resumed his pipe. The man at the table took up the hedge-carpenter's remark, and added smartly, "True; but the oddity of my trade is that, instead of setting a mark upon me, it sets a mark upon my customers."

No observation being offered by anybody in elucidation of this enigma, the shepherd's wife once more called for a song. The same obstacles presented themselves as at the former time – one had no voice, another had forgotten the first verse. The stranger at the table, whose soul had now risen to a good working temperature, relieved the difficulty by exclaiming that, to start the company, he would sing himself. Thrusting one thumb into the arm-hole of his waistcoat, he waved the other hand in the air, and, with an extemporizing gaze at the shining sheep-crooks above the mantelpiece, began:

> "O my trade it is the rarest one,
> Simple shepherds all –
> My trade is a sight to see;
> For my customers I tie, and take them up on high,
> And waft 'em to a far countree!"

The room was silent when he had finished the verse – with one exception, that of the man in the chimney-corner, who, at the singer's word "Chorus!" joined him in a deep bass voice of musical relish—

"And waft 'em to a far countree!"

Oliver Giles, John Pitcher the dairyman, the parish clerk, the engaged man of fifty, the row of young women against the wall, seemed lost in thought not of the gayest kind. The shepherd looked meditatively on the ground, the shepherdess gazed keenly at the singer, and with some suspicion; she was doubting whether this stranger were merely singing an old song from recollection, or was composing one there and then for the occasion.

All were as perplexed at the obscure revelation as the guests at Belshazzar's Feast, except the man in the chimney-corner, who quietly said, "Second verse, stranger," and smoked on.

The singer thoroughly moistened himself from his lips inwards, and went on with the next stanza as requested:

"My tools are but common ones,
Simple shepherds all–
My tools are no sight to see:
A little hempen string, and a post whereon to swing,
Are implements enough for me!"

Shepherd Fennel glanced round. There was no longer any doubt that the stranger was answering his question rhythmically. The guests one and all started back with suppressed exclamations. The young woman engaged to the man of fifty fainted half-way, and would have proceeded, but finding him wanting in alacrity for catching her, she sat down trembling.

"Oh, he's the –!" whispered the people in the background, mentioning the name of an ominous public officer. "He's come to do it! 'Tis to be at Casterbridge jail tomorrow – the man for sheep-stealing – the poor clockmaker we heard of, who used to live away at Shottsford and had no work to do – Timothy Summers, whose family were a-starving, and so he went out of Shottsford by the high road, and took a sheep in open daylight defying the farmer and the farmer's wife and the farmer's lad, and every man jack among 'em. He" (and they nodded towards the stranger of the deadly trade) "is come from up the country to do it because there's not enough to do in his own county-town, and he's got the place here now our own county man's dead; he's going to live in the same cottage under the prison wall."

The stranger in cinder-gray took no notice of this whispered string of observations, but again wetted his lips. Seeing that his friend in the chimney-corner was the only one who reciprocated his joviality in any way, he held out his cup towards that appreciative comrade, who also held out his own. They clinked together, the eyes of the rest of the room hanging upon the singer's actions. He parted his lips for the third verse; but at that moment another knock was audible upon the door. This time the knock was faint and hesitating.

The door was gently opened, and another man stood upon the mat. He, like those who had preceded him, was a stranger. This time it was a short, small personage, of fair complexion, and dressed in a decent suit of dark clothes.

"Can you tell me the way to—" he began: when, gazing round the room to observe the nature of the company among whom he had fallen, his eyes lighted on the stranger in cinder-gray. It was just at the instant when the latter, who had thrown his mind into his song with such a will that he scarcely heeded the interruption, silenced all whispers and inquiries by bursting into his third verse:

> "Tomorrow is my working day,
>   Simple shepherds all—
> Tomorrow is a working day for me:
> For the farmer's sheep is slain, and the lad who did it ta'en,
>   And on his soul may God ha' merc-y!"

The stranger in the chimney corner, waving cups with the singer so heartily that his mead splashed over on the hearth, repeated in his bass voice as before:

> "And on his soul may God ha'mercy!"

All this time the third stranger had been standing in the doorway. Finding now that he did not come forward or go on speaking, the guests particularly regarded him. They noticed to their surprise that he stood before them the picture of abject terror – his knees trembling, his hand shaking so violently that the door-latch by which he supported himself rattled audibly: his white lips were parted, and his eyes fixed on the merry officer of justice in the middle of the room. A moment more and he had turned, closed the door, and fled.

"What a man can it be?" said the shepherd.

The rest, between the awfulness of their late discovery and the odd conduct of this third visitor, looked as if they knew not what to think, and said nothing. Instinctively they withdrew further and further from the grim gentleman in their midst, whom some of them seemed to take for the Prince of Darkness himself, till they formed a remote circle, an empty space of floor being left between them and him—

. . . circulas, cujus centrum diabolus

The room was so silent – though there were more than twenty people in it – that nothing could be heard but the patter of the rain against the window-shutters, accompanied by the occasional hiss of a stray drop that fell down the chimney into the fire, and the steady puffing of the man in the corner, who had now resumed his long pipe of clay.

The stillness was unexpectedly broken. The distant sound of a gun reverberated through the air – apparently from the direction of the county-town.

"Be jiggered!" cried the stranger who had sung the song, jumping up.

"What does that mean?" asked several.

"A prisoner escaped from the jail – that's what it means."

All listened. The sound was repeated, and none of them spoke but the man in the chimney-corner, who said quietly, "I've often been told that in this county they fire a gun at such times; but I never heard it till now."

"I wonder if it is *my* man?" murmured the personage in cinder-gray.

"Surely it is!" said the shepherd involuntarily. "And surely we've zeed him! That little man who looked in at the door by now, and quivered like a leaf when he zeed ye and heard your song!"

"His teeth chattered, and the breath went out of his body." said the dairyman.

"And his heart seemed to sink within him like a stone," said Oliver Giles.

"And he bolted as if he'd been shot at," said the hedge-carpenter.

"True – his teeth chattered, and his heart seemed to sink; and he bolted as if he'd been shot at," slowly summed up the man in the chimneycorner.

"I didn't notice it", remarked the hangman.

"We were all a-wondering what made him run off in such a fright," faltered one of the women against the wall, "and now 'tis explained."

The firing of the alarm-gun went on at intervals, low and sullenly, and their suspicions became a certainty. The sinister gentleman in cinder-gray roused himself. "Is there a constable here?" he asked, in thick tones. "If so, let him step forward."

The engaged man of fifty stepped quavering out from the wall, his betrothed beginning to sob on the back of the chair.

"You are a sworn constable?"

"I be, sir."

"Then pursue the criminal at once, with assistance, and bring him back here. He can't have gone far."

"I will, sir, I will – when I've got my staff. I'll go home and get it, and come sharp here, and start in a body."

"Staff! – never mind your staff; the man'll be gone!"

"But I can't do nothing without my staff – can I, William, and John, and Charles Jake? No; for there's the king's royal crown a-painted on in yaller and gold , and the lion and the unicorn, so as when I raise en up and hit my prisoner, 'tis a man without my staff – no, not I. If I hadn't the law to gie me courage, why, instead o' my taking up him he might take up me!"

"Now, I'm a king's man myself, and can give you authority enough for this," said the formidable officer in gray. "Now then, all of ye, be ready. Have ye any lanterns?"

"Yes – have ye any lanterns? – I demand it!" said the constable.

"And the rest of you able-bodied—"

"Able-bodied men – yes – the rest of ye!" said the constable.

"Have you some good stout staves and pitchforks—"

"Staves and pitchforks – in the name o' the law! And take 'em in yer hands and go in quest, and do as we in authority tell ye!"

Thus aroused, the men prepared to give chase. The evidence was, indeed, though circumstantial, so convincing, that but little argument was needed to show the shepherd's guests that after what they had seen it would look very much like connivance if they did not instantly pursue the unhappy third stranger, who could not as yet have gone more than a few hundred yards over such uneven country.

A shepherd is always well provided with lanterns; and, lighting these hastily, and with hurdle-staves in their hands, they poured out of the door, taking a direction along the crest of the hill, away from the town, the rain having fortunately a little abated.

Disturbed by the noise, or possibly by unpleasant dreams of her baptism, the child who had been christened began to cry heart-brokenly in the room overhead. These notes of grief came down through the chinks of the floor to the ears of the women below, who jumped up one by one, and seemed glad of the excuse to ascend and comfort the baby, for the incidents of the last half-hour greatly oppressed them. Thus in the space of two or three minutes the room on the ground-floor was deserted quite.

But it was not for long. Hardly had the sound of footsteps died away when a man returned round the corner of the house from the direction the pursuers had taken. Peeping in at the door, and seeing nobody there, he entered leisurely. It was the stranger of the chimney-corner, who had gone out with the rest. The motive of his return was shown by his helping himself to a cut piece of skimmer-cake that lay on a ledge beside where he had sat, and which he had apparently forgotten to take with him. He also poured out half a cup more mead from the quantity that remained, ravenously eating and drinking these as he stood. He had not finished when another figure came in just as quietly – his friend in cinder-gray.

"Oh – you here?" said the latter, smiling. "I thought you had gone to help in the capture." And this speaker also revealed the object of his return by looking solicitously round for the fascinating mug of old mead.

"And I thought you had gone," said the other, continuing his skimmer-cake with some effort.

"Well, on second thoughts, I felt there were enough without me," said the first confidentially, "and such a night as it is, too. Besides, 'tis the business o' the Government to take care of its criminals – not mine."

"True; so it is. And I felt as you did, that there were enough without me."

"I don't want to break my limbs running over the humps and hollows of this wild country."

"Nor I neither, between you and me."

"These shepherd-people are used to it – simple-minded souls, you know, stirred up to anything at a moment. They'll have him ready for me before the morning, and no trouble to me at all."

"They'll have him, and we shall have saved ourselves all labor in the matter."

"True, true. Well, my way is to Casterbridge; and 'tis as much as my legs will do to take me that far. Going the same way?"

"No, I am sorry to say! I have to get home over there" (he nodded indefinitely to the right), "and I feel as you do, that it is quite enough for my legs to do before bedtime."

The other had by this time finished the mead in the mug, after which, shaking hands heartily at the door, and wishing each other well, they went their several ways.

In the meantime the company of pursuers had reached the end of the hog's-back elevation which dominated this part of the down. They had decided on no particular plan of action; and, finding that the man of the baleful trade was no longer in their company, they seemed quite unable to form any such plan now. They descended in all directions down the hill, and straight-away several of the party fell into this snare set by Nature for all misguided midnight ramblers over this part of the cretaceous formation. The "lanchets", or flint slopes, which belted the escarpment at intervals of a dozen yards, took the less cautious ones unawares, and losing their footing on the rubbly steep they slid downward, the lanterns rolling from their hands to the bottom, and there lying on their sides till the horn was scorched through.

When they had again gathered themselves together, the shepherd, as the man who knew the country best, took the lead, and guided them round these treacherous inclines. The lanterns, which seemed rather to dazzle their eyes and warn the fugitive than to assist them in the exploration, were extinguished, due silence was observed; and in this more rational order they plunged into the vale. It was a grassy, briery, moist defile, affording some shelter to any person who had sought it; but the party perambulated it in vain, and ascended on the other side.

Here they wandered apart, and after an interval closed together again to report progress. At the second time of closing in they found themselves near a lonely ash, the single tree on this part of the coomb, probably sown there by a passing bird some fifty years before. And here, standing a little to one side of the trunk, as motionless as the trunk itself, appeared the man they were in quest of, his outline being well defined against the sky beyond. The band noiselessly drew up and faced him.

"Your money or your life!" said the constable sternly to the still figure.

"No, no," whispered John Pitcher. "'Tisn't our side ought to say that. That's the doctrine of vagabonds like him, and we be on the side of the law."

"Well, well," replied the constable, impatiently; "I must say something, mustn't I? And if you had all the weight o' this undertaking upon your mind, perhaps you'd say the wrong thing, too! Prisoner at the bar, surrender in the name of the Father – the Crown, I mane!"

The man under the tree seemed now to notice them for the first time, and, giving them no opportunity whatever for exhibiting their courage, he strolled slowly towards them. He was, indeed, the little man, the third stranger; but his trepidation had in great measure gone.

"Well, travelers," he said, "did I hear ye speak to me?"

"You did: you've got to come and be our prisoner at once!" said the constable. "We arrest 'ee on the charge of not biding in Casterbridge jail in a decent proper manner to be hung tomorrow morning. Neighbors, do your duty, and seize the culpet!"

On hearing the charge, the man seemed enlightened, and, saying not another word, resigned himself with preternatural civility to the search party, who, with their staves in their hands, surrounded him on all sides, and marched him back towards the shepherd's cottage.

It was eleven o'clock by the time they arrived. The light shining from the open door and a sound of men's voices within, proclaimed to them as they approached the house that some new events had arisen in their absence. On entering they discovered the shepherd's living room to be invaded by two officers from Casterbridge jail, and a well-known magistrate who lived at the nearest county-seat, intelligence of the escape having become generally circulated.

"Gentlemen," said the constable, "I have brought back your man – not without risk and danger; but everyone must do his duty! He is inside this circle of able-bodied persons, who have lent me useful aid, considering their ignorance of Crown work. Men, bring forward your prisoner!" And the third stranger was led to the light.

"Who is this?" said one of the officials.

"The man," said the constable.

"Certainly not," said the turnkey; and the first corroborated his statement.

"But how can it be otherwise?" asked the constable. "Or why was he so terrified at sight o' the singing instrument of the law who sat there?" Here he related the strange behavior of the third stranger on entering the house during the hangman's song.

"Can't understand it," said the officer coolly. "All I know is that it is not the condemned man. He's quite a different character from this one; a gauntish fellow, with dark hair and eyes, rather good-looking, and with a musical bass voice that if you heard it once you'd never mistake as long as you lived."

"Why, souls – 'twas the man in the chimney-corner!"

"Hey – what?" said the magistrate, coming forward after inquiring particulars from the shepherd in the background. "Haven't you got the man after all?"

"Well, sir," said the constable, "he's the man we were in search of, that's true; and yet he's not the man we were in search of. For the man we were in search of was not the man we wanted, sir, if you understand my everyday way; for 'twas the man in the chimney-corner!"

"A pretty kettle of fish altogether!" said the magistrate. "You had better start for the other man at once."

The prisoner now spoke for the first time. The mention of the man in the chimney-corner seemed to have moved him as nothing else could do. "Sir," he said, stepping forward to the magistrate, "take no more trouble about me. The time is come when I may as well speak. I have done nothing; my crime is that the condemned man is my brother. Early this afternoon I left home at Shottsford to tramp it all the way to Casterbridge jail to bid him farewell. I was benighted, and called here to rest and ask the way. When I opened the door I saw before me the very man, my brother, that I thought to see in the condemned cell at Casterbridge. He was in this chimney-corner; and jammed close to him, so that he could not have got out if he had tried, was the executioner who'd come to take his life, singing a song about it and not knowing that it was his victim who was close by, joining in to save appearances. My brother looked a glance of agony at me, and I knew he meant, 'Don't reveal what you see; my life depends on it.' I was so terror-struck that I could hardly stand, and, not knowing what I did, I turned and hurried away."

The narrator's manner and tone had the stamp of truth, and his story made a great impression on all around. "And do you know where your brother is at the present time?" asked the magistrate.

"I do not. I have never seen him since I closed this door."

"I can testify to that, for we've been between ye ever since," said the constable.

"Where does he think to fly to? What is his occupation?"

"He's a watch-and-clock-maker, sir."

"'A said 'a was a wheelwright – a wicked rogue," said the constable.

"The wheels of clocks and watches he meant, no doubt," said Shepherd Fennel. "I thought his hands were palish for's trade."

"Well, it appears to me that nothing can be gained by retaining this poor man in custody," said the magistrate; "your business lies with the other, unquestionably."

And so the little man was released off-hand; but he looked nothing the less sad on that account, it being beyond the power of magistrate or constable to raze out the written troubles in his brain, for they concerned another whom he regarded with more solicitude than himself. When this was done, and the man had gone his way, the night was found to be so far advanced that it was deemed useless to renew the search before the next morning.

Next day, accordingly, the quest for the clever sheep-stealer became general and keen, to all appearance at least. But the intended punishment was cruelly disproportioned to the transgression, and the sympathy of a great many country-folk in that district was strongly on the side of the fugitive. Moreover, his marvellous coolness and daring in hob-and-nobbing with the hangman, under the unprecedented circumstances of the shepherd's party, won their admiration. So that it may be questioned if all those who ostensibly made themselves so busy in exploring woods and fields and lanes were quite so thorough when it came to the private examination of their own lofts and outhouses. Stories were afloat of a mysterious figure being occasionally seen in some old overgrown trackway or other, remote from turnpike roads, but when a search was instituted in any of these suspected quarters nobody was found. Thus the days and weeks passed without tidings.

In brief, the bass-voiced man of the chimney-corner was never recaptured. Some said that he went across the sea, others that he did not, but buried himself in the depths of a populous city. At any rate, the gentleman in cinder-gray never did his morning's work at Casterbridge, nor met anywhere at all, for business purposes, the genial comrade with whom he had passed an hour of relaxation in the lonely house on the coomb.

The grass has long been green on the graves of shepherd Fennel and his frugal wife; the guests who made up the christening party have mainly followed their entertainers to the tomb; the baby in whose honor they all had met is a matron in the sere and yellow leaf. But the arrival of the three strangers at the shepherd's that night, and the details connected therewith, is a story as well-known as ever in the country about Higher Crowstairs.

The Dublin Mystery

Baroness Orczy

"I always thought that the history of that forged will was about as interesting as any I had read," said the man in the corner that day. He had been silent for some time, and was meditatively sorting and looking through a packet of small photographs in his pocket book. Polly guessed that some of these would presently be placed before her for inspection – and she had not long to wait.

"That is old Brooks," he said, pointing to one of the photographs, "Millionaire Brooks, as he was called, and these are his two sons, Percival and Murray. It was a curious case, wasn't it? Personally I don't wonder that the police were completely at sea. If a member of that highly estimable force happened to be as clever as the clever author of that forged will, we should have very few undetected crimes in this country."

"That is why I always try to persuade you to give our poor ignorant police the benefit of your great insight and wisdom," said Polly, with a smile.

"I know," he said blandly, "you have been most kind in that way, but I am only an amateur. Crime interests me only when it resembles a clever game of chess, with many intricate moves which all tend to one solution, the checkmating of the antagonist – the detective forces of the country. Now, confess that, in the Dublin mystery, the clever police there were absolutely checkmated."

"Absolutely."

"Just as the public was. There were actually two crimes committed in one city which have completely baffled detection: the murder of Patrick Wethered the lawyer, and the forged will of Millionaire Brooks. There are not many millionaires in Ireland; no wonder old Brooks was a notability in his way, since his business – bacon curing, I believe it was – is said to be worth over £2,000,000 of solid money.

"His younger son, Murray, was a refined, highly educated man, and was, moreover, the apple of his father's eye, as he was the spoilt darling of Dublin society; good-looking, a splendid dancer, and a perfect rider, he was the acknowledged 'catch' of the matrimonial market of Ireland, and many a very aristocratic house was opened hospitably to the favorite son of the millionaire.

"Of course, Percival Brooks, the eldest son, would inherit the bulk of the old man's property and also probably the larger share in the business; he, too, was good-looking, more so than his brother; he, too, rode, danced, and talked well, but it was many years ago that mammas with marriageable daughters had given up all hopes of Percival Brooks as a probable son-in-law. That young man's infatuation for Maisie Fortescue, a lady of undoubted charm but very doubtful antecedents, who had astonished the London and Dublin music halls with her extravagant dances, was too well known and too old-established to encourage any hopes in other quarters.

"Whether Percival Brooks would ever marry Maisie Fortescue was thought to be very doubtful. Old Brooks had the full disposal of all his wealth, and it would have fared ill with Percival if he introduced an undesirable wife into the magnificent Fitzwilliam Place establishment.

"That is how matters stood," continued the man in the corner, "when Dublin society one morning learnt, with deep regret and dismay, that old Brooks had died very suddenly at his residence after only a few hours' illness. At first it was generally understood that he had had an apoplectic stroke; anyway, he had been at business hale and hearty as ever the day before his death, which occurred late on the evening of February 1st.

"It was the morning papers of February 2nd which told the sad news to their readers, and it was those selfsame papers which on that eventful morning contained another even more startling piece of news, that proved the prelude to a series of sensations such as tranquil, placid Dublin had not experienced for many years. This was, that on that very afternoon which saw the death of Dublin's greatest millionaire, Mr. Patrick Wethered, his solicitor, was murdered in Phoenix Park at five o'clock in the afternoon while actually walking to his own house from his visit to his client in Fitzwilliam Place.

"Patrick Wethered was as well known as the proverbial town pump; his mysterious and tragic death filled all Dublin with dismay. The lawyer, who was a man sixty years of age, had been struck on the back of the head by a heavy stick, garrotted, and subsequently robbed, for neither money, watch, or pocket book were found upon his person, whilst the police soon gathered from Patrick Wethered's household that he had left home at two o'clock that afternoon, carrying both watch and pocket book, and undoubtedly money as well.

"An inquest was held, and a verdict of willful murder was found against some person or persons unknown.

"But Dublin had not exhausted its stock of sensations yet. Millionaire Brooks had been buried with due pomp and magnificence, and his will had been proved (his business and personalty being estimated at £2,500,000) by Percival Gordon Brooks, his eldest son and sole executor. The younger son, Murray, who had devoted the best years of his life to being a friend and companion to his father, while Percival ran after ballet dancers and music hall stars – Murray, who had avowedly been the apple of his father's eye in consequence – was left with a miserly pittance of £300 a year, and no share whatever in the gigantic business of Brooks & Sons, bacon curers, of Dublin.

"Something had evidently happened within the precincts of the Brooks's town mansion, which the public and Dublin society tried in vain to fathom. Elderly mammas and blushing *débutantes* were already thinking of the best means whereby next season they might more easily show the cold shoulder to young Murray Brooks, who had so suddenly become a hopeless 'detrimental' in the marriage market, when all these sensations terminated in one gigantic, overwhelming bit of scandal, which for the next three months furnished food for gossip in every drawing-room in Dublin.

"Mr. Murray Brooks, namely, had entered a claim for probate of a will, made by his father in 1891, declaring that the later will, made the very day of his father's death and proved by his brother as sole executor, was null and void, that will being a forgery.

"The facts that transpired in connection with this extraordinary case were sufficiently mysterious to puzzle everybody. As I told you before, all Mr. Brooks's friends never quite grasped the idea that the old man should so completely have cut off his favorite son with the proverbial shilling.

"You see, Percival had always been a thorn in the old man's flesh. Horse racing, gambling, theaters, and music halls were, in the old pork butcher's eyes, so many deadly sins which his son committed every day of his life, and all the Fitzwilliam Place household could testify to the many and bitter quarrels which had arisen between father and son over the latter's gambling or racing debts. Many people asserted that Brooks would sooner have left his money to charitable institutions than seen it squandered upon the brightest stars that adorned the music hall stage.

"The case came up for hearing early in the autumn. In the meanwhile Percival Brooks had given up his race-course associates, settled down in the Fitzwilliam Place mansion, and conducted his father's business, without a manager, but with all the energy and forethought which he had previously devoted to more unworthy causes.

"Murray had elected not to stay on in the old house; no doubt associations were of too painful and recent a nature; he was boarding with the family of a Mr. Wilson Hibbert, who was the late Patrick Wethered's, the murdered lawyer's, partner. They were quiet, homely people, who lived in a very pokey little house in Kilkenny Street, and poor Murray must, in spite of his grief, have felt very bitterly the change from his luxurious quarters in his father's mansion to his present tiny room and homely meals.

"Percival Brooks, who was now drawing an income of over a hundred thousand a year, was very severely criticized for adhering so strictly to the letter of his father's will, and only paying his brother that paltry £300 a year, which was very literally but the crumbs off his own magnificent dinner table.

"The issue of that contested will case was therefore awaited with eager interest. In the meanwhile the police, who had at first seemed fairly loquacious on the subject of the murder of Mr. Patrick Wethered, suddenly became strangely reticent, and by their very reticence aroused a certain amount of uneasiness in the public mind, until one day the *Irish Times* published the following extraordinary, enigmatic paragraph:

> We hear, on authority which cannot be questioned, that certain extraordinary developments are expected in connection with the brutal murder of our distinguished townsman Mr. Wethered; the police, in fact, are vainly trying to keep it secret that they hold a clew which is as important as it is sensational, and that they only await the impending issue of a well-known litigation in the probate court to effect an arrest.

"The Dublin public flocked to the court to hear the arguments in the great will case. There were Percival Brooks and Murray his brother, the two litigants, both good-looking and well-dressed, and both striving, by keeping up a running conversation with their lawyers, to appear unconcerned and confident of the issue. With Percival Brooks was Henry Oranmore, the eminent Irish K.C., whilst Walter Hibbert, a rising young barrister, the son of Wilson Hibbert, appeared for Murray.

"The will of which the latter claimed probate was one dated 1891, and had been made by Mr. Brooks during a severe illness which threatened to end his days. This will had been deposited in the hands of Messrs. Wethered and Hibbert, solicitors to the deceased, and by it Mr. Brooks left his personalty equally divided between his two sons, but had left his business entirely to his youngest son, with a charge of £2000 a year upon it, payable to Percival. You see that Murray Brooks therefore had a very deep interest in that second will being found null and void.

"Old Mr. Hibbert had very ably instructed his son, and Walter Hibbert's opening speech was exceedingly clever. He would show, he said, on behalf of his client, that the will dated February 1st, 1908, could never have been made by the late Mr. Brooks, as it was absolutely contrary to his avowed intentions, and that if the late Mr. Brooks did on the day in question make any fresh will at all, it certainly was *not* the one proved by Mr. Percival Brooks, for that was absolutely a forgery from beginning to end. Mr. Walter Hibbert proposed to call several witnesses in support of both these points.

"On the other hand, Mr. Henry Oranmore, K.C., very ably and courteously replied that he too had several witnesses to prove that Mr. Brooks certainly did make a will on the day in question, and that, whatever his intentions may have been in the past, he must have modified them on the day of his death, for the will proved by Mr. Percival Brooks was found after his death under his pillow, duly signed and witnessed and in every way legal.

"Then the battle began in sober earnest. There were a great many witnesses to be called on both sides, their evidence being of more or less importance – chiefly less. But the interest centered round the prosaic figure of John O'Neill, the butler of Fitzwilliam Place, who had been in Mr. Brooks's family for thirty years.

"'I was clearing away my breakfast things,' said John, 'when I heard the master's voice in the study close by. Oh, my, he was that angry! I could hear the words "disgrace," and "villain," and "liar" and "ballet dancer," and one or two other ugly words as applied to some female lady, which I would not like to repeat. At first I did not take much notice, as I was quite used to hearing my poor dear master having words with Mr. Percival. So I went downstairs carrying my breakfast things; but I had just started cleaning my silver when the study bell goes ringing violently, and I hear Mr. Percival's voice shouting in the hall: "John! quick! Send for Dr. Mulligan at once. Your master is not well! Send one of the men, and you come up and help me to get Mr. Brooks to bed."

"'I sent one of the grooms for the doctor,' continued John, who seemed still affected at the recollection of his poor master, to whom he had evidently been very much attached, 'and I went up to see Mr. Brooks. I found him lying on the study floor, his head supported in Mr. Percival's arms, "My father has fallen in a faint," said the young master; "help me to get him up to his room before Dr. Mulligan comes."

"'Mr. Percival looked very white and upset, which was only

natural; and when we had got my poor master to bed, I asked if I should not go and break the news to Mr. Murray, who had gone to business an hour ago. However, before Mr. Percival had time to give me an order the doctor came. I thought I had seen death plainly writ in my master's face, and when I showed the doctor out an hour later, and he told me that he would be back directly, I knew that the end was near.

"'Mr. Brooks rang for me a minute or two later. He told me to send at once for Mr. Wethered, or else for Mr. Hibbert, if Mr. Wethered could not come. "I haven't many hours to live, John," he says to me – "my heart is broke, the doctor says my heart is broke. A man shouldn't marry and have children, John, for they will sooner or later break his heart." I was so upset I couldn't speak; but I sent round at once for Mr. Wethered, who came himself just about three o'clock that afternoon.

"'After he had been with my master about an hour I was called in, and Mr. Wethered said to me that Mr. Brooks wished me and one other of us servants to witness that he had signed a paper which was on a table by his bedside. I called Pat Mooney, the head footman, and before us both Mr. Brooks put his name at the bottom of that paper. Then Mr. Wethered give me the pen and told me to write my name as a witness, and that Pat Mooney was to do the same. After that we were both told that we could go.'

"The old butler went on to explain that he was present in his late master's room on the following day when the undertakers, who had come to lay the dead man out, found a paper underneath his pillow. John O'Neill, who recognized the paper as the one to which he had appended his signature the day before, took it to Mr. Percival, and gave it into his hands.

"In answer to Mr. Walter Hibbert, John asserted positively that he took the paper from the undertaker's hand and went straight with it to Mr. Percival's room.

"'He was alone,' said John; 'I gave him the paper. He just glanced at it, and I thought he looked rather astonished, but he said nothing, and I at once left the room.'

"'When you say that you recognized the paper as the one which you had seen your master sign the day before, how did you actually recognize that it was the same paper?' asked Mr. Hibbert amidst breathless interest on the part of the spectators.

" 'It looked exactly the same paper to me, sir,' replied John, somewhat vaguely.

" 'Did you look at the contents, then?'

" 'No, sir; certainly not.'

" 'Had you done so the day before?'

" 'No, sir, only at my master's signature.'

" 'Then you only thought by the *outside* look of the paper that it was the same?'

" 'It looked the same thing, sir,' persisted John obstinately.

"You see," continued the man in the corner, leaning eagerly forward across the narrow marble table, "the contention of Murray Brooks's adviser was that Mr. Brooks, having made a will and hidden it – for some reason or other under his pillow – that will had fallen, through the means related by John O'Neill, into the hands of Mr. Percival Brooks, who had destroyed it and substituted a forged one in its place, which adjudged the whole of Mr. Brooks's millions to himself. It was a terrible and daring accusation directed against a gentleman who, in spite of his many wild oats sowed in early youth, was a prominent and important figure in Irish high life.

"But John O'Neill had not finished his evidence, and Mr. Walter Hibbert had a bit of sensation still up his sleeve. He had, namely, produced a paper, the will proved by Mr. Percival Brooks, and had asked John O'Neill if once again he recognized the paper.

" 'Certainly, sir,' said John unhesitatingly, 'that is the one the undertaker found under my poor dead master's pillow, and which I took to Mr. Percival's room immediately.'

"Then the paper was unfolded and placed before the witness.

" 'Now, Mr. O'Neill, will you tell me if that is your signature?'

"John looked at it for a moment; then he said: 'Excuse me, sir,' and produced a pair of spectacles which he carefully adjusted before he again examined the paper. Then he thoughtfully shook his head.

" 'It don't look much like my writing, sir,' he said at last. 'That is to say,' he added, by way of elucidating the matter, 'it does look like my writing, but then I don't think it is.'

"The learned counsel," continued the old man in the corner, "went on arguing, speechifying, cross-examining for nearly a week, until they arrived at the one conclusion which was inevitable from the very first, namely, that the will *was* a forgery – a gross, clumsy, idiotic forgery, since both John O'Neill and Pat Mooney, the two witnesses, absolutely repudiated the signatures as their own. The only successful bit of calligraphy the forger had done was the signature of old Mr. Brooks.

"It was a very curious fact, and one which had undoubtedly aided the forger in accomplishing his work quickly, that Mr. Wethered the lawyer, having, no doubt, realized that Mr. Brooks had not many moments in life to spare, had not drawn up the usual engrossed, magnificent document dear to the lawyer's heart, but had used for his client's will one of those regular printed forms which can be purchased at any stationer's.

"Mr. Percival Brooks, of course, flatly denied the serious allegation brought against him. He admitted that the butler had brought him the document the morning after his father's death, and that he certainly, on glancing at it, had been very much astonished to see that that document was his father's will. Against that he declared that its contents did not astonish him in the slightest degree, that he himself knew of the testator's intentions, but that he certainly thought his father had entrusted the will to the care of Mr. Wethered, who did all his business for him.

"'I only very cursorily glanced at the signature,' he concluded, speaking in a perfectly calm, clear voice; 'you must understand that the thought of forgery was very far from my mind, and that my father's signature is exceedingly well imitated, if, indeed, it is not his own, which I am not at all prepared to believe. As for the two witnesses' signatures, I don't think I had ever seen them before. I took the document to Messrs. Barkston and Maud, who had often done business for me before, and they assured me that the will was in perfect form and order.'

"Asked why he had not entrusted the will to his father's solicitors, he replied:

"'For the very simple reason that exactly half an hour before the will was placed in my hands, I had read that Mr. Patrick Wethered had been murdered the night before. Mr. Hibbert, the junior partner, was not personally known to me.'

"After that, for form's sake, a good deal of expert evidence was heard on the subject of the dead man's signature. But that was quite unanimous, and merely went to corroborate what had already been established beyond a doubt, namely, that the will dated February 1st, 1908, was a forgery, and probate of the will dated 1891 was therefore granted to Mr. Murray Brooks, the sole executor mentioned therein.

"Two days later the police applied for a warrant for the arrest of Mr. Percival Brooks on a charge of forgery.

"The Crown prosecuted, and Mr. Brooks had again the support of Mr. Oranmore, the eminent K.C. Perfectly calm, like a man conscious of his own innocence and unable to grasp the idea that justice does sometimes miscarry, Mr. Brooks, the son of the millionaire, himself still the possessor of a very large fortune under the former will, stood up in the dock on that memorable day in October, 1908, which still no doubt lives in the memory of his many friends.

"All the evidence with regard to Mr. Brooks's last moments and the forged will was gone through over again. That will, it was the contention of the Crown, had been forged so entirely in favor of the accused, cutting out everyone else, that obviously no one but the beneficiary under that false will would have had any motive in forging it.

"Very pale, and with a frown between his deep-set, handsome Irish eyes, Percival Brooks listened to this large volume of evidence piled up against him by the Crown.

"At times he held brief consultations with Mr. Oranmore, who seemed as cool as a cucumber. Have you ever seen Oranmore in court? He is a character worthy of Dickens. His pronounced brogue, his fat, podgy, clean-shaven face, his not always immaculately clean large hands, have often delighted the caricaturist. As it very soon transpired during that memorable magisterial inquiry, he relied for a verdict in favor of his client upon two main points, and he had concentrated all his skill upon making these two points as telling as he possibly could.

"The first point was the question of time. John O'Neill,

cross-examined by Oranmore, stated without hesitation that he had given the will to Mr. Percival at eleven o'clock in the morning. And now the eminent K.C. brought forward and placed in the witness box the very lawyers into whose hands the accused had then immediately placed the will. Now, Mr. Barkston, a very well-known solicitor of King Street, declared positively that Mr. Percival Brooks was in his office at a quarter before twelve; two of his clerks testified to the same time exactly, and it was *impossible*, contended Mr. Oranmore, that within three-quarters of an hour Mr. Brooks could have gone to a stationer's, bought a will form, copied Mr. Wethered's writing, his father's signature, and that of John O'Neill and Pat Mooney.

"Such a thing might have been planned, arranged, practiced, and ultimately, after a great deal of trouble, successfully carried out, but human intelligence could not grasp the other as a possibility.

"Still the judge wavered. The eminent K.C. had shaken but not shattered his belief in the prisoner's guilt. But there was one point more, and this Oranmore, with the skill of a dramatist, had reserved for the fall of the curtain.

"He noted every sign in the judge's face, he guessed that his client was not yet absolutely safe, then only did he produce his last two witnesses.

"One of them was Mary Sullivan, one of the housemaids in the Fitzwilliam mansion. She had been sent up by the cook at a quarter past four o'clock on the afternoon of February 1st with some hot water, which the nurse had ordered, for the master's room. Just as she was about to knock at the door Mr. Wethered was coming out of the room. Mary stopped with the tray in her hand, and at the door Mr. Wethered turned and said quite loudly: 'Now, don't fret, don't be anxious; do try and be calm. Your will is safe in my pocket, nothing can change it or alter one word of it but yourself.'

"It was, of course, a very ticklish point in law whether the housemaid's evidence could be accepted. You see, she was quoting the words of a man since dead, spoken to another man also dead. There is no doubt that had there been very strong evidence on the other side against Percival Brooks, Mary

Sullivan's would have counted for nothing; but, as I told you before, the judge's belief in the prisoner's guilt was already very seriously shaken, and now the final blow aimed at it by Mr. Oranmore shattered his last lingering doubts.

"Dr. Mulligan, namely, had been placed by Mr. Oranmore into the witness box. He was a medical man of unimpeachable authority, in fact, absolutely at the head of his profession in Dublin. What he said practically corroborated Mary Sullivan's testimony. He had gone in to see Mr. Brooks at half-past four, and understood from him that his lawyer had just left him.

"Mr. Brooks certainly, though terribly weak, was calm and more composed. He was dying from a sudden heart attack, and Dr. Mulligan foresaw the almost immediate end. But he was still conscious and managed to murmur feebly: 'I feel much easier in my mind now, doctor – I have made my will – Wethered has been – he's got it in his pocket – it is safe there – safe from that—' But the words died on his lips, and after that he spoke but little. He saw his two sons before he died, but hardly knew them or even looked at them.

"You see," concluded the man in the corner, "you see that the prosecution was bound to collapse. Oranmore did not give it a leg to stand on. The will was forged, it is true, forged in the favor of Percival Brooks and of no one else, forged for him and for his benefit. Whether he knew and connived at the forgery was never proved or, as far as I know, even hinted, but it was impossible to go against all the evidence, which pointed that, as far as the act itself was concerned, he at least was innocent. You see, Dr. Mulligan's evidence was not to be shaken. Mary Sullivan's was equally strong.

"There were two witnesses swearing positively that old Brooks's will was in Mr. Wethered's keeping when that gentleman left the Fitzwilliam mansion at a quarter past four. At five o'clock in the afternoon the lawyer was found dead in Phoenix Park. Between a quarter past four and eight o'clock in the evening Percival Brooks never left the house – that was subsequently proved by Oranmore up to the hilt and beyond a doubt. Since the will found under old Brooks's pillow was a forged will, where then was the will he did make, and which Wethered carried away with him in his pocket?"

"Stolen, of course," said Polly, "by those who murdered and robbed him; it may have been of no value to them, but they naturally would destroy it, lest it might prove a clew against them."

"Then you think it was mere coincidence?" he asked excitedly.

"What?"

"That Wethered was murdered and robbed at the very moment that he carried the will in his pocket, whilst another was being forged in its place?"

"It certainly would be very curious, if it *were* a coincidence," she said musingly.

"Very," he repeated with biting sarcasm, whilst nervously his bony fingers played with the inevitable bit of string. "Very curious indeed. Just think of the whole thing. There was the old man with all his wealth, and two sons, one to whom he is devoted, and the other with whom he does nothing but quarrel. One day there is another of these quarrels, but more violent, more terrible than any that have previously occurred, with the result that the father, heartbroken by it all, has an attack of apoplexy and practically dies of a broken heart. After that he alters his will, and subsequently a will is proved which turns out to be a forgery.

"Now everybody – police, press, and public alike – at once jump to the conclusion that, as Percival Brooks benefits by that forged will, Percival Brooks must be the forger."

"Seek for him whom the crime benefits, is your own axiom," argued the girl.

"I beg your pardon?"

"Percival Brooks benefited to the tune of £2,000,000."

"I beg your pardon. He did nothing of the sort. He was left with less than half the share that his younger brother inherited."

"Now, yes; but that was a former will and—"

"And that forged will was so clumsily executed, the signature so carelessly imitated, that the forgery was bound to come to light. Did *that* never strike you?"

"Yes, but—"

"There is no but," he interrupted. "It was all as clear as

daylight to me from the very first. The quarrel with the old
man, which broke his heart, was not with his eldest son, with
whom he was used to quarreling, but with the second son whom
he idolized, in whom he believed. Don't you remember how
John O'Neill heard the words 'liar' and 'deceit'? Percival
Brooks had never deceived his father. His sins were all on
the surface. Murray had led a quiet life, had pandered to his
father, and fawned upon him, until, like most hypocrites, he at
last got found out. Who knows what ugly gambling debt or debt
of honor, suddenly revealed to old Brooks, was the cause of that
last and deadly quarrel?

"You remember that it was Percival who remained beside his
father and carried him up to his room. Where was Murray
throughout that long and painful day, when his father lay dying
– he, the idolized son, the apple of the old man's eye? You never
hear his name mentioned as being present there all that day. But
he knew that he had offended his father mortally, and that his
father meant to cut him off with a shilling. He knew that Mr.
Wethered had been sent for, that Wethered left the house soon
after four o'clock.

"And here the cleverness of the man comes in. Having lain in
wait for Wethered and knocked him on the back of the head
with a stick, he could not very well make that will disappear
altogether. There remained the faint chance of some other
witnesses knowing that Mr. Brooks had made a fresh will,
Mr. Wethered's partner, his clerk, or one of the confidential
servants in the house. Therefore a will must be discovered after
the old man's death.

"Now, Murray Brooks was not an expert forger; it takes years
of training to become that. A forged will executed by himself
would be sure to be found out – yes, that's it, sure to be found
out. The forgery will be palpable – let it be palpable, and then it
will be found out, branded as such, and the original will of 1891,
so favorable to the young blackguard's interests, would be held
as valid. Was it devilry or merely additional caution which
prompted Murray to pen that forged will so glaringly in
Percival's favor? It is impossible to say.

"Anyhow, it was the cleverest touch in that marvelously
devised crime. To plan that evil deed was great, to execute it

was easy enough. He had several hours' leisure in which to do it. Then at night it was simplicity itself to slip the document under the dead man's pillow. Sacrilege causes no shudder to such natures as Murray Brooks's. The rest of the drama you know already—"

"But Percival Brooks?"

"The jury returned a verdict of 'Not guilty.' There was no evidence against him."

"But the money? Surely the scoundrel does not have the enjoyment of it still?"

"No; he enjoyed it for a time, but he died about three months ago, and forgot to take the precaution of making a will, so his brother Percival has got the business after all. If you ever go to Dublin, I should order some of Brooks's bacon if I were you. It is very good."

The Biter Bit

Wilkie Collins

FROM CHIEF INSPECTOR THEAKSTONE, OF THE DETECTIVE
POLICE, TO SERGEANT BULMER OF THE SAME FORCE.

LONDON, 4th *July*, 18–.

SERGEANT BULMER, – This is to inform you that you are wanted
to assist in looking up a case of importance, which will require
all the attention of an experienced member of the force. The
matter of the robbery on which you are now engaged, you will
please to shift over to the young man who brings you this letter.
You will tell him all the circumstances of the case, just as they
stand; you will put him up to the progress you have made (if
any) towards detecting the person or persons by whom the
money has been stolen; and you will leave him to make the best
he can of the matter now in your hands. He is to have the whole
responsibility of the case, and the whole credit of his success, if
he brings it to a proper issue.

So much for the orders that I am desired to communicate to
you.

A word in your ear, next, about this new man who is to take
your place. His name is Matthew Sharpin; and he is to have the
chance given him of dashing into our office at a jump –
supposing he turns out strong enough to take it. You will
naturally ask me how he comes by this privilege. I can only
tell you that he has some uncommonly strong interest to back
him in certain high quarters which you and I had better not
mention except under our breaths. He has been a lawyer's clerk;
and he is wonderfully conceited in his opinion of himself, as

well as mean and underhand to look at. According to his own account, he leaves his old trade, and joins ours of his own free will and preference. You will no more believe that than I do. My notion is, that he has managed to ferret out some private information in connection with the affairs of one of his master's clients, which makes him rather an awkward customer to keep in the office for the future, and which, at the same time, gives him hold enough over his employer to make it dangerous to drive him into a corner by turning him away. I think the giving him this unheard-of chance among us, is, in plain words, pretty much like giving him hush-money to keep him quiet. However that may be, Mr. Matthew Sharpin is to have the case now in your hands; and if he succeeds with it, he pokes his ugly nose into our office, as sure as fate. I put you up to this, Sergeant, so that you may not stand in your own light by giving the new man any cause to complain of you at headquarters, and remain yours,

FRANCIS THEAKSTONE.

FROM MR. MATTHEW SHARPIN TO CHIEF INSPECTOR THEAKSTONE

LONDON, *July 5th*, 18–.

DEAR SIR, – Having now been favoured with the necessary instructions from Sergeant Bulmer, I beg to remind you of certain directions which I have received, relating to the report of my future proceedings which I am to prepare for examination at headquarters.

The object of my writing, and of your examining what I have written, before you send it in to the higher authorities, is, I am informed, to give me, as an untried hand, the benefit of your advice, in case I want it (which I venture to think I shall not) at any stage of my proceedings. As the extraordinary circumstances of the case on which I am now engaged, make it impossible for me to absent myself from the place where the robbery was committed, until I have made some progress towards discovering the thief, I am necessarily precluded from consulting you personally. Hence the necessity of my writing down the various details, which might, perhaps, be better communicated by word of mouth. This, if I am not mistaken, is the position in which we are now placed. I state my own impressions on the subject, in writing, in order that we may clearly understand each other at the outset; and have the honour to remain, your obedient servant,

MATTHEW SHARPIN.

FROM CHIEF INSPECTOR THEAKSTONE TO MR. MATTHEW SHARPIN

LONDON, 5th *July*, 18–.

SIR, – You have begun by wasting time, ink, and paper. We both of us perfectly well knew the position we stood in towards each other, when I sent you with my letter to Sergeant Bulmer. There was not the least need to repeat it in writing. Be so good as to employ your pen, in future, on the business actually in hand.

You have now three separate matters on which to write to me. First, you have to draw up a statement of your instructions received from Sergeant Bulmer, in order to show us that nothing has escaped your memory, and that you are thoroughly acquainted with all the circumstances of the case which has been entrusted to you. Secondly, you are to inform me what it is you propose to do. Thirdly, you are to report every inch of your progress (if you make any) from day to day, and, if need be, from hour to hour as well. This is *your* duty. As to what *my* duty may be, when I want you to remind me of it, I will write and tell you so. In the meantime, I remain, yours,

FRANCIS THEAKSTONE

FROM MR. MATTHEW SHARPIN TO CHIEF INSPECTOR THEAKSTONE

LONDON, 6th *July*, 18–.

SIR, – You are rather an elderly person, and, as such, naturally inclined to be a little jealous of men like me, who are in the prime of their lives and their faculties. Under these circumstances, it is my duty to be considerate towards you, and not to bear too hardly on your small failings. I decline, there- fore, altogether, to take offence at the tone of your letter; I give you the full benefit of the natural generosity of my nature; I sponge the very existence of your surly communication out of my memory – in short, Chief Inspector Theakstone, I forgive you, and proceed to business.

My first duty is to draw up a full statement of the instructions I have received from Sergeant Bulmer. Here they are at your service, according to my version of them.

At number 13, Rutherford Street, Soho, there is a stationer's shop. It is kept by one Mr. Yatman. He is a married man, but has no family. Besides Mr. and Mrs. Yatman, the other inmates in the house are a young single man named Jay, who lodges in the front room on the second floor – a shopman, who sleeps in one of the attics, – and a servant-of-all-work, whose bed is in the back-kitchen. Once a week a charwoman comes for a few hours in the morning only, to help this servant. These are all the persons who, on ordinary occasions, have means of access to the interior of the house, placed, as a matter of course, at their disposal.

Mr. Yatman has been in business for many years, carrying on his affairs prosperously enough to realise a handsome independence for a person in his position. Unfortunately for himself he endeavoured to increase the amount of his property by speculating. He ventured boldly in his investments, luck went against him, and rather less than two years ago he found himself a poor man again. All that was saved out of the wreck of his property was the sum of two hundred pounds.

Although Mr. Yatman did his best to meet his altered circumstances, by giving up many of the luxuries and comforts to which he and his wife had been accustomed, he found it impossible to retrench so far as to allow of putting by any money from the income produced by the shop. The business has been declining of late years – the cheap advertising stationers having done it injury with the public. Consequently, up to the last week the only surplus property possessed by Mr. Yatman consisted of the two hundred pounds which had been recovered from the wreck of his fortune. This sum was placed as a deposit in a joint-stock bank of the highest possible character.

Eight days ago, Mr. Yatman and his lodger, Mr. Jay, held a

conversation on the subject of the commercial difficulties which are hampering trade in all directions at the present time. Mr. Jay (who lives by supplying the newspapers with short paragraphs relating to incidents, offences, and brief records of remarkable occurrences in general – who is, in short, what they call a penny-a-liner) told his landlord that he had been in the city that day, and had heard unfavourable rumours on the subject of the joint-stock banks. The rumours to which he alluded had already reached the ears of Mr. Yatman from other quarters; and the confirmation of them by his lodger had such an effect on his mind – predisposed as it was to alarm by the experience of his former losses – that he resolved to go at once to the bank and withdraw his deposit.

It was then getting on towards the end of the afternoon; and he arrived just in time to receive his money before the bank closed.

He received the deposit in bank-notes of the following amounts: one fifty-pound note, three twenty-pound notes, six ten-pound notes, and six five-pound notes. His object in drawing the money in this form was to have it ready to lay out immediately in trifling loans, on good security, among the small tradespeople of his district, some of whom are sorely pressed for the very means of existence at the present time. Investments of this kind seemed to Mr. Yatman to be the most safe and the most profitable on which he could now venture.

He brought the money back in an envelope placed in his breast-pocket; and asked his shopman, on getting home, to look for a small flat tin cash-box, which had not been used for years, and which, as Mr. Yatman remembered it, was exactly the right size to hold the bank-notes. For some time the cash-box was searched for in vain. Mr. Yatman called to his wife to know if she had any idea where it was. The question was overheard by the servant-of-all-work, who was taking up the tea-tray at the time, and by Mr. Jay, who was coming downstairs on his way out to the theatre. Ultimately the cash-box was found by the shopman. Mr. Yatman placed the bank-notes in it, secured them by a padlock, and put the box in his coat-pocket. It stuck out of the coat-pocket a very little, but enough to be seen. Mr. Yatman remained at home, upstairs, all the evening. No visitors called. At eleven o'clock he went to bed, and put the cash-box along with his clothes, on a chair by the bed-side.

When he and his wife woke the next morning, the box was gone. Payment of the notes was immediately stopped at the Bank of England; but no news of the money has been heard of since that time.

So far, the circumstances of the case are perfectly clear. They point unmistakably to the conclusion that the robbery must have been committed by some person living in the house. Suspicion falls, therefore, upon the servant-of-all-work, upon the shopman, and upon Mr. Jay. The two first knew that the cash-box was being inquired for by their master, but did not know what it was he wanted to put into it. They would assume, of course, that it was money. They both had opportunities (the servant, when she took away the tea – and the shopman, when he came, after shutting up, to give the keys of the till to his master) of seeing the cash-box in Mr. Yatman's pocket, and of inferring naturally, from its position there, that he intended to take it into his bedroom with him at night.

Mr. Jay, on the other hand, had been told, during the afternoon's conversation on the subject of joint-stock banks, that his landlord had a deposit of two hundred pounds in one of them. He also knew that Mr. Yatman left him with the intention of drawing that money out; and he heard the inquiry for the cash-box, afterwards, when he was coming downstairs. He must, therefore, have inferred that the money was in the house, and that the cash-box was the receptacle intended to contain it. That he could have had any idea, however, of the place in which Mr. Yatman intended to keep it for the night, is impossible, seeing that he went out before the box was found, and did not return till his landlord was in bed. Consequently, if he committed the robbery, he must have gone into the bedroom purely on speculation.

Speaking of the bedroom reminds me of the necessity of noticing the situation of it in the house, and the means that exist of gaining easy access to it at any hour of the night.

The room in question is the back-room on the first-floor. In consequence of Mrs. Yatman's constitutional nervousness on the subject of fire (which makes her apprehend being burnt alive in her room, in case of accident, by the hampering of the lock if the key is turned in it) her husband has never been accustomed to lock the bedroom door. Both he and his wife are, by their own admission, heavy sleepers. Consequently, the risk to be run by any evil-disposed persons wishing to plunder the bedroom, was of the most trifling kind. They could enter the room by merely turning the handle of the door; and if they moved with ordinary caution, there was no fear of their waking the sleepers inside. This fact is of importance. It strengthens our conviction that the money must have been taken by one of the inmates of the house, because it tends to show that the robbery, in this case, might have been committed by persons not possessed of the superior vigilance and cunning of the experienced thief.

Such are the circumstances, as they were related to Sergeant Bulmer, when he was first called in to discover the guilty parties, and, if possible, to recover the lost bank-notes. The strictest inquiry which he could institute, failed of producing the smallest fragment of evidence against any of the persons on whom suspicion naturally fell. Their language and behaviour, on being informed of the robbery, was perfectly consistent with the language and behaviour of innocent people. Sergeant Bulmer felt from the first that this was a case for private inquiry and secret observation. He began by recommending Mr. and Mrs. Yatman to affect a feeling of perfect confidence in the innocence of the persons living under their roof; and he then opened the campaign by employing himself in following the goings and comings, and in discovering the friends, the habits, and the secrets of the maid-of-all-work.

Three days and nights of exertions on his own part, and on that of others who were competent to assist his investigations, were enough to satisfy him that there was no sound cause for suspicion against the girl.

He next practised the same precaution in relation to the shopman. There was more difficulty and uncertainty in privately clearing up this person's character without his knowledge, but the obstacles were at last smoothed away with tolerable success; and though there is not the same amount of certainty, in this case, which there was in that of the girl, there is still fair reason for supposing that the shopman has had nothing to do with the robbery of the cash-box.

As a necessary consequence of these proceedings, the range of suspicion now becomes limited to the lodger, Mr. Jay.

When I presented your letter of introduction to Sergeant Bulmer, he had already made some inquiries on the subject of this young man. The result, so far, has not been at all favourable. Mr. Jay's habits are irregular; he frequents public-houses, and seems to be familiarly acquainted with a great many dissolute characters; he is in debt to most of the tradespeople whom he employs; he has not paid his rent to Mr. Yatman for the last month; yesterday evening he came home excited by liquor, and last week he was seen talking to a prizefighter. In short, though Mr. Jay does call himself a journalist, in virtue of his penny-a-line contributions to the newspapers, he is a young man of low tastes, vulgar manners, and bad habits. Nothing has yet been discovered in relation to him, which redounds to his credit in the smallest degree.

I have now reported, down to the very last details, all the particulars communicated to me by Sergeant Bulmer. I believe you will not find an omission anywhere; and I think you will admit, though you are prejudiced against me, that a clearer statement of facts was never laid before you than the statement I have now made. My next duty is to tell you what I propose to do, now that the case is confided to my hands.

In the first place, it is clearly my business to take up the case at the point where Sergeant Bulmer has left it. On his authority, I am justified in assuming that I have no need to trouble myself about the maid-of-all-work and the shopman. Their characters are now to be considered as cleared up. What remains to be privately investigated is the question of the guilt or innocence of Mr. Jay. Before we give up the notes for lost, we must make sure, if we can, that he knows nothing about them.

This is the plan that I have adopted, with the full approval of Mr. and Mrs. Yatman, for discovering whether Mr. Jay is or is not the person who has stolen the cash-box:

I propose to-day, to present myself at the house in the character of a young man who is looking for lodgings. The back-room on the second-floor will be shown to me as the room to let; and I shall establish myself there to-night, as a person from the country who has come to London to look for a situation in a respectable shop or office.

By this means I shall be living next to the room occupied by Mr. Jay. The partition between us is mere lath and plaster. I shall make a small hole in it, near the cornice, through which I can see what Mr. Jay does in his room, and hear every word that is said when any friend happens to call on him. Whenever he is at home, I shall be at my post of observation. Whenever he goes out, I shall be after him. By employing these means of watching him, I believe I may look forward to the discovery of his secret – if he knows anything about the lost bank-notes – as to a dead certainty.

What you may think of my plan of observation I cannot undertake to say. It appears to me to unite the invaluable merits of boldness and simplicity. Fortified by this conviction, I close the present communication with feelings of the most sanguine description in regard to the future, and remain your obedient servant,

MATTHEW SHARPIN.

FROM THE SAME TO THE SAME

7th July.

SIR, – As you have not honoured me with any answer to my last communication, I assume that, in spite of your prejudices against me, it has produced the favourable impression on your mind which I ventured to anticipate. Gratified beyond measure by the token of approval which your eloquent silence conveys to me, I proceed to report the progress that has been made in the course of the last twenty-four hours.

I am now comfortably established next door to Mr. Jay; and I am delighted to say that I have two holes in the partition, instead of one. My natural sense of humour has led me into the pardonable extravagance of giving them appropriate names. One I call my peep-hole, and the other my pipe-hole. The name of the first explains itself; the name of the second refers to a small tin pipe, or tube, inserted in the hole, and twisted so that the mouth of it comes close to my ear, while I am standing at my post of observation. Thus, while I am looking at Mr. Jay through my peep-hole, I can hear every word that may be spoken in his room through my pipe-hole.

Perfect candour – a virtue which I have possessed from my childhood – compels me to acknowledge, before I go any further, that the ingenious notion of adding a pipe-hole to my proposed peep-hole originated with Mrs. Yatman. This lady – a most intelligent and accomplished person, simple, and yet distinguished, in her manners – has entered into all my little plans with an enthusiasm and intelligence which I cannot too highly praise. Mr. Yatman is so cast down by his loss, that he is quite incapable of affording me any assistance. Mrs. Yatman, who is evidently most tenderly attached to him, feels her husband's sad condition of mind even more acutely than she feels the loss of the money; and is mainly stimulated to exertion by her desire to assist in raising him from the miserable state of prostration into which he has now fallen.

"The money, Mr. Sharpin," she said to me yesterday evening, with tears in her eyes, "the money may be regained by rigid economy and strict attention to business. It is my husband's wretched state of mind that makes me so anxious for the discovery of the thief. I may be wrong, but I felt hopeful of success as soon as you entered the house; and I believe, if the wretch who has robbed us is to be found, you are the man to discover him." I accepted this gratifying compliment in the spirit in which it was offered – firmly believing that I shall be found, sooner or later, to have thoroughly deserved it.

Let me now return to business; that is to say, to my peep-hole and my pipe-hole.

I have enjoyed some hours of calm observation of Mr. Jay. Though rarely at home, as I understand from Mrs. Yatman, on ordinary occasions, he has been indoors the whole of this day. That is suspicious, to begin with. I have to report, further, that he rose at a late hour this morning (always a bad sign in a young man), and that he lost a great deal of time, after he was up, in yawning and complaining to himself of headache. Like other debauched characters, he ate little or nothing for breakfast. His next proceeding was to smoke a pipe – a dirty clay pipe, which a gentleman would have been ashamed to put between his lips. When he had done smoking, he took out pen, ink, and paper, and sat down to write with a groan – whether of remorse for having taken the bank-notes, or of disgust at the task before him, I am unable to say. After writing a few lines (too far away from my peep-hole to give me a chance of reading over his shoulder), he leaned back in his chair, and amused himself by humming the tunes of certain popular songs. Whether these do, or do not, represent secret signals by which he communicates with his accomplices remains to be seen. After he had amused himself for some time by humming, he got up and began to walk about the room, occasionally stopping to add a sentence to the paper on his desk. Before long, he went to a locked cupboard and opened it. I strained my eyes eagerly, in expectation of making a discovery. I saw him take something carefully out of the cupboard – he turned round – and it was only a pint bottle of brandy! Having drunk some of the liquor, this extremely indolent reprobate lay down on his bed again, and in five minutes was fast asleep.

After hearing him snoring for at least two hours, I was recalled to my peep-hole by a knock at his door. He jumped up and opened it with suspicious activity.

A very small boy, with a very dirty face, walked in, said, "Please, sir, they're waiting for you," sat down on a chair, with his legs a long way from the ground, and instantly fell asleep! Mr. Jay swore an oath, tied a wet towel round his head, and going back to his paper, began to cover it with writing as fast as his fingers could move the pen. Occasionally getting up to dip the towel in water and tie it on again, he continued at this employment for nearly three hours; then folded up the leaves of writing, woke the boy, and gave them to him, with this remarkable expression : "Now then, young sleepy-head, quick – march! If you see the governor, tell him to have the money ready when I call for it." The boy grinned, and disappeared. I was sorely tempted to follow "sleepy-head," but, on reflection, considered it safest still to keep my eye on the proceedings of Mr. Jay.

In half an hour's time, he put on his hat and walked out. Of course, I put on my hat and walked out also. As I went downstairs, I passed Mrs. Yatman going up. The lady has been kind enough to undertake, by previous arrangement between us to search Mr. Jay's room, while he is out of the way, and while I am necessarily engaged in the pleasing duty of following him wherever he goes. On the occasion to which I now refer, he walked straight to the nearest tavern, and ordered a couple of mutton chops for his dinner. I placed myself in the next box to him, and ordered a couple of mutton chops for my dinner. Before I had been in the room a minute, a young man of highly suspicious manners and appearance, sitting at a table opposite, took his glass of porter in his hand and joined Mr. Jay. I pretended to be reading the newspaper, and listened, as in duty bound, with all my might.

"Jack has been here inquiring after you," says the young man.

"Did he leave any message?" asks Mr. Jay.

"Yes," says the other. "He told me, if I met with you, to say that he wished very particularly to see you to-night; and that he would give you a look in, at Rutherford Street, at seven o'clock."

"All right," says Mr. Jay. "I'll get back in time to see him."

Upon this, the suspicious-looking young man finished his porter, and saying that he was rather in a hurry, took leave of his friend (perhaps I should not be wrong if I said his accomplice) and left the room.

At twenty-five minutes and a half past six – in these serious cases it is important to be particular about time – Mr. Jay finished his chops and paid his bill. At twenty-six minutes and three-quarters I finished my chops and paid mine. In ten minutes more I was inside the house in Rutherford Street, and was received by Mrs. Yatman in the passage. That charming woman's face exhibited an expression of melancholy and disappointment which it quite grieved me to see.

"I am afraid, Ma'am," says I, "that you have not hit on any little criminating discovery in the lodger's room?"

She shook her head and sighed. It was a soft, languid, fluttering sigh; – and, upon my life, it quite upset me. For the moment I forgot business, and burned with envy of Mr. Yatman.

"Don't despair, Ma'am," I said, with an insinuating mildness which seemed to touch her. "I have heard a mysterious conversation – I know of a guilty appointment – and I expect great things from my peep-hole and my pipe-hole to-night. Pray, don't be alarmed, but I think we are on the brink of a discovery."

Here my enthusiastic devotion to business got the better of my tender feelings. I looked – winked – nodded – left her.

When I got back to my observatory, I found Mr. Jay digesting his mutton chops in an arm-chair, with his pipe in his mouth. On his table were two tumblers, a jug of water, and the pint bottle of brandy. It was then close upon seven o'clock. As the hour struck, the person described as "Jack" walked in.

He looked agitated – I am happy to say he looked violently agitated. The cheerful glow of anticipated success diffused itself (to use a strong expression) all over me, from head to foot. With breathless interest I looked through my peep-hole, and saw the visitor – the "Jack" of this delightful case – sit down, facing me, at the opposite side of the table to Mr. Jay. Making allowance for the difference in expression which their countenances just now happened to exhibit, these two abandoned villains were so much alike in other respects as to lead at once to the conclusion that they were brothers. Jack was the cleaner man and the better dressed of the two. I admit that, at the outset. It is, perhaps, one of my failings to push justice and impartiality to their utmost limits. I am no Pharisee; and where Vice has its redeeming point, I say, let Vice have its due – yes, yes, by all manner of means, let Vice have its due.

"What's the matter now, Jack?" says Mr. Jay.

"Can't you see it in my face?" says Jack. "My dear fellow, delays are dangerous. Let us have done with suspense, and risk it the day after to-morrow."

"So soon as that?" cried Mr. Jay, looking very much astonished. "Well, I'm ready, if you are. But, I say, Jack, is Somebody Else ready too? Are you quite sure of that?"

He smiled as he spoke – a frightful smile – and laid a very strong emphasis on those two words, "Somebody Else." There is evidently a third ruffian, a nameless desperado, concerned in the business.

"Meet us to-morrow," says Jack, "and judge for yourself. Be in the Regent's Park at eleven in the morning, and look out for us at the turning that leads to the Avenue Road."

"I'll be there," says Mr. Jay. "Have a drop of brandy and water? What are you getting up for? You're not going already?"

"Yes, I am," says Jack. "The fact is, I'm so excited and agitated that I can't sit still anywhere for five minutes together. Ridiculous as it may appear to you, I'm in a perpetual state of nervous flutter. I can't, for the life of me, help fearing that we shall be found out. I fancy that every man who looks twice at me in the street is a spy—"

At those words, I thought my legs would have given way under me. Nothing but strength of mind kept me at my peep-hole – nothing else, I give you my word of honour.

"Stuff and nonsense!" cried Mr. Jay, with all the effrontery of a veteran in crime. "We have kept the secret up to this time, and we will manage cleverly to the end. Have a drop of brandy and water, and you will feel as certain about it as I do."

Jack steadily refused the brandy and water, and steadily persisted in taking his leave.

"I must try if I can't walk it off," he said. "Remember to-morrow morning – eleven o'clock, Avenue Road side of the Regent's Park."

With those words he went out. His hardened relative laughed desperately, and resumed the dirty clay pipe.

I sat down on the side of my bed, actually quivering with excitement.

It is clear to me that no attempt has yet been made to change the stolen bank-notes; and I may add that Sergeant Bulmer was of that opinion also, when he left the case in my hands. What is the natural conclusion to draw from the conversation which I have just set down? Evidently, that the confederates meet to-morrow to take their respective shares in the stolen money, and to decide on the safest means of getting the notes changed the day after. Mr. Jay is, beyond a doubt, the leading criminal in this business, and he will probably run the chief risk – that of changing the fifty-pound note. I shall, therefore, still make it my business to follow him – attending at the Regent's Park to-morrow, and doing my best to hear what is said there. If another appointment is made the day after, I shall, of course, go to it. In the meantime, I shall want the immediate assistance of two competent persons (supposing the rascals separate after their meeting) to follow the two minor criminals. It is only fair to add, that, if the rogues all retire together, I shall probably keep my subordinates in reserve. Being naturally ambitious, I desire, if possible, to have the whole credit of discovering this robbery to myself.

8th July.

I have to acknowledge, with thanks, the speedy arrival of my two subordinates – men of very average abilities, I am afraid; but, fortunately, I shall always be on the spot to direct them.

My first business this morning was, necessarily, to prevent mistakes by accounting to Mr. and Mrs. Yatman for the presence of two strangers on the scene. Mr. Yatman (between ourselves, a poor feeble man) only shook his head and groaned. Mrs. Yatman (that superior woman) favoured me with a charming look of intelligence.

"Oh, Mr. Sharpin!" she said, "I am so sorry to see those two men! Your sending for their assistance looks as if you were beginning to be doubtful of success."

I privately winked at her (she is very good in allowing me to do so without taking offence), and told her, in my facetious way, that she laboured under a slight mistake.

"It is because I am sure of success, Ma'am, that I send for them. I am determined to recover the money, not for my own sake only, but for Mr. Yatman's sake – and for yours."

I laid a considerable amount of stress on those last three words. She said, "Oh, Mr. Sharpin!" again – and blushed of a heavenly red – and looked down at her work. I could go to the world's end with that woman, if Mr. Yatman would only die.

I sent off the two subordinates to wait, until I wanted them, at the Avenue Road gate of the Regent's Park. Half an hour afterwards I was following in the same direction myself, at the heels of Mr. Jay.

The two confederates were punctual to the appointed time, I blush to record it, but it is nevertheless necessary to state, that the third rogue – the nameless desperado of my report, or if you prefer it, the mysterious "Somebody Else" of the conversation between the two brothers – is a Woman! and, what is worse, a young woman! and what is more lamentable still, a nice-looking woman! I have long resisted a growing conviction, that, wherever there is mischief in this world, an individual of the fair sex is inevitably certain to be mixed up in it. After the experience of this morning, I can struggle against that sad conclusion no longer. I give up the sex – excepting Mrs. Yatman, I give up the sex.

The man named "Jack" offered the woman his arm. Mr. Jay placed himself on the other side of her. The three then walked away slowly among the trees. I followed them at a respectful distance. My two subordinates, at a respectful distance also, followed me.

It was, I deeply regret to say, impossible to get near enough to them to overhear their conversation, without running too great a risk of being discovered. I could only infer from their gestures and actions that they were all three talking with extraordinary earnestness on some subject which deeply interested them. After having been engaged in this way a full quarter of an hour, they suddenly turned round to retrace their steps. My presence of mind did not forsake me in this emergency. I signed to the two subordinates to walk on carelessly and pass them, while I myself slipped dexterously behind a tree. As they came by me, I heard "Jack" address these words to Mr. Jay:

"Let us say half-past ten to-morrow morning. And mind you come in a cab. We had better not risk taking one in this neighbourhood."

Mr. Jay made some brief reply, which I could not overhear. They walked back to the place at which they had met, shaking hands there with an audacious cordiality which it quite sickened me to see. They then separated. I followed Mr. Jay. My subordinates paid the same delicate attention to the other two.

Instead of taking me back to Rutherford Street, Mr. Jay led me to the Strand. He stopped at a dingy, disreputable-looking house, which, according to the inscription over the door, was a newspaper office, but which, in my judgment, had all the external appearance of a place devoted to the reception of stolen goods.

After remaining inside for a few minutes, he came out, whistling, with his finger and thumb in his waistcoat pocket. A less discreet man than myself would have arrested him on the spot. I remembered the necessity of catching the two confederates, and the importance of not interfering with the appointment that had been made for the next morning. Such coolness as this, under trying circumstances, is rarely to be found, I should imagine, in a young beginner, whose reputation as a detective policeman is still to make.

From the house of suspicious appearance, Mr. Jay betook himself to a cigar-divan, and read the magazines over a cheroot. I sat at a table near him, and read the magazines likewise over a cheroot. From the divan he strolled to the tavern and had his chops. I strolled to the tavern and had my chops. When he had done, he went back to his lodging. When I had done, I went back to mine. He was overcome with drowsiness early in the evening, and went to bed. As soon as I heard him snoring, I was overcome with drowsiness, and went to bed also.

Early in the morning my two subordinates came to make their report.

They had seen the man named "Jack" leave the woman near the gate of an apparently respectable villa-residence, not far from the Regent's Park. Left to himself, he took a turning to the right, which led to a sort of suburban street, principally inhabited by shopkeepers. He stopped at the private door of one of the houses, and let himself in with his own key – looking about him as he opened the door, and staring suspiciously at my men as they lounged along on the opposite side of the way. These were all the particulars which the subordinates had to communicate. I kept them in my room to attend on me, if needful, and mounted to my peep-hole to have a look at Mr. Jay.

He was occupied in dressing himself, and was taking extraordinary pains to destroy all traces of the natural sloven-liness of his appearance. This was precisely what I expected. A vagabond like Mr. Jay knows the importance of giving himself a respectable look when he is going to run the risk of changing a stolen bank-note. At five minutes past ten o'clock, he had given the last brush to his shabby hat and the last scouring with bread-crumb to his dirty gloves. At ten minutes past ten he was in the street, on his way to the nearest cab-stand, and I and my subordinates were close on his heels.

He took a cab, and we took a cab. I had not overheard them appoint a place of meeting, when following them in the Park on the previous day; but I soon found that we were proceeding in the old direction of the Avenue Road gate.

The cab in which Mr. Jay was riding turned into the Park slowly. We stopped outside, to avoid exciting suspicion. I got out to follow the cab on foot. Just as I did so, I saw it stop, and detected the two confederates approaching it from among the trees. They got in, and the cab was turned about directly. I ran back to my own cab, and told the driver to let them pass him, and then to follow as before.

The man obeyed my directions, but so clumsily as to excite their suspicions. We had been driving after them about three minutes (returning along the road by which we had advanced) when I looked out of the window to see how far they might be ahead of us. As I did this, I saw two hats popped out of the windows of their cab, and two faces looking back at me. I sank into my place in a cold sweat; the expression is coarse, but no other form of words can describe my condition at that trying moment.

"We are found out!" I said faintly to my two subordinates. They stared at me in astonishment. My feelings changed instantly from the depth of despair to the height of indignation.

"It is the cabman's fault. Get out, one of you," I said, with dignity – "get out and punch his head."

Instead of following my directions (I should wish this act of disobedience to be reported at headquarters) they both looked out of the window. Before I could pull them back, they both sat down again. Before I could express my just indignation, they both grinned, and said to me, "Please to look out, sir!"

I did look out. The thieves' cab had stopped.

Where?

At a church door!!!

What effect this discovery might have had upon the ordinary run of men, I don't know. Being of a strong religious turn myself, it filled me with horror. I have often read of the unprincipled cunning of criminal persons; but I never before heard of three thieves attempting to double on their pursuers by entering a church! The sacrilegious audacity of that proceeding is, I should think, unparalleled in the annals of crime.

I checked my grinning subordinates by a frown. It was easy to see what was passing in their superficial minds. If I had not been able to look below the surface, I might, on observing two nicely-dressed men and one nicely-dressed woman enter a church before eleven in the morning on a weekday, have come to the same hasty conclusion at which my inferiors had evidently arrived. As it was, appearances had no power to impose on *me*. I got out, and, followed by one of my men, entered the church. The other man I sent round to watch the vestry door. You may catch a weasel asleep – but not your humble servant, Matthew Sharpin!

We stole up the gallery stairs, diverged to the organ loft and peered through the curtains in front. There they were all three, sitting in a pew below – yes, incredible as it may appear, sitting in a pew below!

Before I could determine what to do, a clergyman made his appearance in full canonicals, from the vestry door, followed by a clerk. My brain whirled, and my eyesight grew dim. Dark remembrances of robberies committed in vestries floated through my mind. I trembled for the excellent man in full canonicals – I even trembled for the clerk.

The clergyman placed himself inside the altar rails. The three desperadoes approached him. He opened his book, and began to read. What? – you will ask.

I answer, without the slightest hesitation, the first lines of the Marriage Service.

My subordinate had the audacity to look at me, and then to stuff his pocket-handkerchief into his mouth. I scorned to pay any attention to him. After I had discovered that the man "Jack" was the bridegroom, and that the man Jay acted the part of father, and gave away the bride, I left the church, followed by my man, and joined the other subordinate outside the vestry door. Some people in my position would now have felt rather crestfallen, and would have begun to think that they had made a very foolish mistake. Not the faintest misgiving of any kind troubled me. I did not feel in the slightest degree depreciated in my own estimation. And even now, after a lapse of three hours, my mind remains, I am happy to say, in the same calm and hopeful condition.

As soon as I and my subordinates were assembled together outside the church, I intimated my intention of still following the other cab, in spite of what had occurred. My reason for deciding on this course will appear presently. The two subordinates were astonished at my resolution. One of them had the impertinence to say to me:

"If you please, sir, who is it that we are after? A man who has stolen money, or a man who has stolen a wife?"

The other low person encouraged him by laughing. Both have deserved an official reprimand; and both, I sincerely trust, will be sure to get it.

When the marriage ceremony was over, the three got into their cab; and once more our vehicle (neatly hidden round the corner of the church, so that they could not suspect it to be near them) started to follow theirs.

We traced them to the terminus of the South-Western Railway. The newly-married couple took tickets for Richmond – paying their fare with a half-sovereign, and so depriving me of the pleasure of arresting them, which I should certainly have done, if they had offered a bank-note. They parted from Mr. Jay, saying, "Remember the address, – 14, Babylon Terrace. You dine with us to-morrow week." Mr. Jay accepted the invitation, and added, jocosely, that he was going home at once to get off his clean clothes, and to be comfortable and dirty again for the rest of the day. I have to report that I saw him home safely, and that he is comfortable and dirty again (to use his own disgraceful language) at the present moment.

Here the affair rests, having by this time reached what I may call its first stage.

I know very well what persons of hasty judgment will be inclined to say of my proceedings thus far. They will assert that I have been deceiving myself all through, in the most absurd way; they will declare that the suspicious conversations which I have reported, referred solely to the difficulties and dangers of successfully carrying out a runaway match; and they will appeal to the scene in the church, as offering undeniable proof of the correctness of their assertions. So let it be. I dispute nothing up to this point. But I ask a question, out of the depths of my own sagacity as a man of the world, which the bitterest of my enemies will not, I think, find it particularly easy to answer.

Granted the fact of the marriage, what proof does it afford me of the innocence of the three persons concerned in that clandestine transaction? It gives me none. On the contrary, it strengthens my suspicions against Mr. Jay and his confederates, because it suggests a distinct motive for their stealing the money. A gentleman who is going to spend his honeymoon at Richmond wants money; and a gentleman who is in debt to all his tradespeople wants money. Is this an unjustifiable imputation of bad motives? In the name of outraged morality, I deny it. These men have combined together, and have stolen a woman. Why should they not combine together, and steal a cash-box? I take my stand on the logic of rigid virtue; and I defy all the sophistry of vice to move me an inch out of my position.

Speaking of virtue, I may add that I have put this view of the case to Mr. and Mrs. Yatman. That accomplished and charming woman found it difficult, at first, to follow the close chain of my reasoning. I am free to confess that she shook her head, and shed tears, and joined her husband in premature lamentation over the loss of the two hundred pounds. But a little careful explanation on my part, and a little attentive listening on hers, ultimately changed her opinion. She now agrees with me, that there is nothing in this unexpected circumstance of the clandestine marriage which absolutely tends to divert suspicion from Mr. Jay, or Mr. "Jack," or the runaway lady. "Audacious hussy" was the term my fair friend used in speaking of her, but let that pass. It is more to the purpose to record that Mrs. Yatman has not lost confidence in me and that Mr. Yatman promises to follow her example, and do his best to look hopefully for future results.

I have now, in the new turn that circumstances have taken, to await advice from your office. I pause for fresh orders with all the composure of a man who had got two strings to his bow. When I traced the three confederates from the church door to the railway terminus, I had two motives for doing so. First, I followed them as a matter of official business, believing them still to have been guilty of the robbery. Secondly, I followed them as a matter of private speculation, with a view of discovering the place of refuge to which the runaway couple intended to retreat, and of making my information a marketable commodity to offer to the young lady's family and friends. Thus, whatever happens, I may congratulate myself beforehand on not having wasted my time. If the office approves of my conduct, I have my plan ready for further proceedings. If the office blames me, I shall take myself off, with my marketable information, to the genteel villa-residence in the neighbourhood of the Regent's Park. Anyway, the affair puts money into my pocket, and does credit to my penetration as an uncommonly sharp man.

I have only one word more to add, and it is this:—If any individual ventures to assert that Mr. Jay and his confederates are innocent of all share in the stealing of the cash-box, I, in return, defy that individual – though he may even be Chief Inspector Theakstone himself – to tell me who has committed the robbery at Rutherford Street, Soho.

I have the honour to be,

Your very obedient servant,

MATTHEW SHARPIN.

FROM CHIEF INSPECTOR THEAKSTONE TO SERGEANT BULMER

BIRMINGHAM, *July 9th.*

SERGEANT BULMER, – That empty-headed puppy, Mr. Matthew Sharpin, has made a mess of the case at Rutherford Street, exactly as I expected he would. Business keeps me in this town; so I write to you to set the matter straight. I enclose, with this, the pages of feeble scribble-scrabble which the creature, Sharpin, calls a report. Look them over; and when you have made your way through all the gabble, I think you will agree with me that the conceited booby has looked for the thief in every direction but the right one. You can lay your hand on the guilty person in five minutes, now. Settle the case at once;

forward your report to me at this place; and tell Mr. Sharpin that he is suspended till further notice.

Yours,
FRANCIS THEAKSTONE.

FROM SERGEANT BULMER TO CHIEF INSPECTOR THEAKSTONE

LONDON, *July* 10*th*.

INSPECTOR THEAKSTONE, – Your letter and enclosure came safe to hand. Wise men, they say, may always learn something, even from a fool. By the time I had got through Sharpin's maundering report of his own folly, I saw my way clear enough to the end of the Rutherford Street case, just as you thought I should. In half an hour's time I was at the house. The first person I saw there was Mr. Sharpin himself.

"Have you come to help me?" says he.

"Not exactly," says I. "I've come to tell you that you are suspended till further notice."

"Very good," says he, not taken down, by so much as a single peg, in his own estimation. "I thought you would be jealous of me. It's very natural; and I don't blame you. Walk in, pray, and make yourself at home. I'm off to do a little detective business on my own account, in the neighbourhood of the Regent's Park. Ta-ta, sergeant, ta-ta!"

With those words he took himself out of the way – which was exactly what I wanted him to do.

As soon as the maid-servant had shut the door, I told her to inform her master that I wanted to say a word to him in private. She showed me into the parlour behind the shop; and there was Mr. Yatman, all alone, reading the newspaper.

"About this matter of the robbery, sir," says I.

He cut me short, peevishly enough – being naturally a poor, weak, womanish sort of man. "Yes, yes, I know," says he. "You have come to tell me that your wonderfully clever man, who has bored holes in my second-floor partition, has made a mistake, and is off the scent of the scoundrel who has stolen my money"

"Yes, sir," says I. "That *is* one of the things I came to tell you. But I have got something else to say, besides that."

"Can you tell me who the thief is?" says he, more pettish than ever.

"Yes, sir," says I, "I think I can."

He put down the newspaper, and began to look rather anxious and frightened.

"Not my shopman?" says he. "I hope, for the man's own sake, it's not my shopman."

"Guess again, sir," says I.

"That idle slut, the maid?" says he.

"She is idle, sir," says I, "and she is also a slut; my first inquiries about her proved as much as that. But she's not the thief."

"Then in the name of heaven, who is?" says he.

"Will you please to prepare yourself for a very disagreeable surprise, sir?" says I. "And in case you lose your temper, will you excuse my remarking that I am the stronger man of the two, and that, if you allow yourself to lay hands on me, I may unintentionally hurt you, in pure self-defence?"

He turned as pale as ashes, and pushed his chair two or three feet away from me.

"You have asked me to tell you, sir, who has taken your money," I went on. "If you insist on my giving you an answer—"

"I do insist," he said, faintly. "Who has taken it?"

"Your wife has taken it," I said very quietly, and very positively at the same time.

He jumped out of the chair as if I had put a knife into him, and struck his fist on the table, so heavily that the wood cracked again.

"Steady, sir," says I. "Flying into a passion won't help you to the truth."

"It's a lie!" says he, with another smack of his fist on the table—"a base, vile, infamous lie! How dare you—"

He stopped, and fell back into the chair again, looked about him in a bewildered way, and ended by bursting out crying.

"When your better sense comes back to you, sir," says I, "I am sure you will be gentleman enough to make an apology for the language you have just used. In the meantime, please to listen, if you can, to a word of explanation. Mr. Sharpin has sent in a report to our inspector, of the most irregular and ridiculous kind; setting down, not only all his own foolish doings and sayings, but the doings and sayings of Mrs. Yatman as well. In most cases, such a document would have been fit for the waste-paper basket; but, in this particular case, it so happens that Mr. Sharpin's budget of nonsense leads to a certain conclusion, which the simpleton of a writer has been quite innocent of suspecting from the beginning to the end. Of that conclusion I am so sure, that I will forfeit my place, if it does not turn out that Mrs. Yatman has been practising upon the folly and conceit of this young man, and that she has tried to shield herself from discovery by purposely encouraging him to suspect the wrong persons. I tell you that confidently; and I will even go further. I will undertake to give a decided opinion as to why Mrs. Yatman took the money, and what she has done with it, or with a part of it. Nobody can look at that lady, sir, without being struck by the great taste and beauty of her dress—''

As I said those last words, the poor man seemed to find his powers of speech again. He cut me short directly, as haughtily as if he had been a duke instead of a stationer.

"Try some other means of justifying your vile calumny against my wife," says he. "Her milliner's bill for the past year, is on my file of receipted accounts at this moment."

"Excuse me, sir," says I, "but that proves nothing. Milliners, I must tell you, have a certain rascally custom which comes within the daily experience of our office. A married lady who wishes it, can keep two accounts at her dressmaker's; one is the account which her husband sees and pays; the other is the private account, which contains all the extravagant items, and which the wife pays secretly, by instalments, whenever she can. According to our usual experience, these instalments are mostly squeezed out of the housekeeping money. In your case, I suspect no instalments have been paid; proceedings have been threatened; Mrs. Yatman, knowing your altered circumstances, has felt herself driven into a corner; and she has paid her private account out of your cash-box."

"I won't believe it," says he. "Every word you speak is an abominable insult to me and to my wife."

"Are you man enough, sir," says I, taking him up short, in

order to save time and words, "to get that receipted bill you spoke of just now off the file, and come with me at once to the milliner's shop where Mrs. Yatman deals?"

He turned red in the face at that, got the bill directly, and put on his hat. I took out of my pocket-book the list containing the numbers of the lost notes, and we left the house together immediately.

Arrived at the milliner's (one of the expensive West-end houses, as I expected), I asked for a private interview, on important business, with the mistress of the concern. It was not the first time that she and I had met over the same delicate investigation. The moment she set eyes on me, she sent for her husband. I mentioned who Mr. Yatman was, and what we wanted.

"This is strictly private?" inquires her husband. I nodded my head.

"And confidential?" says the wife. I nodded again.

"Do you see any objection, dear, to obliging the sergeant with a sight of the books?" says the husband.

"None in the world, love, if you approve of it," says the wife.

All this while poor Mr. Yatman sat looking the picture of astonishment and distress, quite out of place at our polite conference. The books were brought – and one minute's look at the pages in which Mrs. Yatman's name figured was enough, and more than enough, to prove the truth of every word I had spoken.

There, in one book, was the husband's account, which Mr. Yatman had settled. And there, in the other, was the private account, crossed off also; the date of settlement being the very day after the loss of the cash-box. This said private account amounted to the sum of a hundred and seventy-five pounds, odd shillings; and it extended over a period of three years. Not a single instalment had been paid on it. Under the last line was an entry to this effect: "Written to for the third time, June 23rd." I pointed to it, and asked the milliner if that meant "last June." Yes, it did mean last June; and she now deeply regretted to say that it had been accompanied by a threat of legal proceedings.

"I thought you gave good customers more than three years credit?" says I.

The milliner looks at Mr. Yatman, and whispers to me –
"Not when a lady's husband gets into difficulties."

She pointed to the account as she spoke. The entries after the
time when Mr. Yatman's circumstances became involved were
just as extravagant, for a person in his wife's situation, as the
entries for the year before that period. If the lady had economised in other things, she had certainly not economised in the
matter of dress.

There was nothing left now but to examine the cash-book, for
form's sake. The money had been paid in notes, the amounts
and numbers of which exactly tallied with the figures set down
in my list.

After that, I thought it best to get Mr. Yatman out of the
house immediately. He was in such a pitiable condition, that
I called a cab and accompanied him home in it. At first he
cried and raved like a child: but I soon quieted him – and I
must add, to his credit, that he made me a most handsome
apology for his language, as the cab drew up at his house
door. In return, I tried to give him some advice about how
to set matters right, for the future, with his wife. He paid
very little attention to me, and went upstairs muttering to
himself about a separation. Whether Mrs. Yatman will come
cleverly out of the scrape or not, seems doubtful. I should
say, myself, that she will go into screeching hysterics, and
so frighten the poor man into forgiving her. But this is no
business of ours. So far as we are concerned, the case is now
at an end; and the present report may come to a conclusion
along with it.

I remain, accordingly, yours to command,

THOMAS BULMER.

P.S. – I have to add, that, on leaving Rutherford Street, I met
Mr. Matthew Sharpin coming to pack up his things.

"Only think!" says he, rubbing his hands in great spirits,
"I've been to the genteel villa-residence; and the moment I
mentioned my business, they kicked me out directly. There
were two witnesses of the assault; and it's worth a hundred
pounds to me, if it's worth a farthing."

"I wish you joy of your luck," says I.

"Thank you," says he. "When may I pay you the same compliment on finding the thief?"

"Whenever you like," says I, "for the thief is found."

"Just what I expected," says he. "I've done all the work; and now you cut in, and claim all the credit – Mr. Jay of course?"

"No," says I.

"Who is it then?" says he.

"Ask Mrs. Yatman," says I. "She's waiting to tell you."

"All right! I'd much rather hear it from that charming woman than from you," says he, and goes into the house in a mighty hurry.

What do you think of that. Inspector Theakstone? Would you like to stand in Mr. Sharpin's shoes? I shouldn't, I can promise you!

FROM CHIEF INSPECTOR THEAKSTONE TO MR. MATTHEW SHARPIN

July 12*th.*

SIR, – Sergeant Bulmer has already told you to consider yourself suspended until further notice. I have now authority to add, that your services as a member of the Detective Police are positively declined. You will please to take this letter as notifying officially your dismissal from the force.

I may inform you, privately, that your rejection is not intended to cast any reflection on your character. It merely implies that you are not quite sharp enough for our purpose. If we *are* to have a new recruit among us, we should infinitely prefer Mrs. Yatman.

Your obedient servant,
FRANCIS THEAKSTONE.

NOTE ON THE PRECEDING CORRESPONDENCE, ADDED BY MR. THEAKSTONE

The Inspector is not in a position to append any explanations of importance to the last of the letters. It has been discovered that Mr. Matthew Sharpin left the house in Rutherford Street five minutes after his interview outside of it with Sergeant Bulmer – his manner expressing the liveliest emotions of terror and astonishment, and his left cheek displaying a bright patch of red, which might have been the result of a slap on the face from a female hand. He was also heard, by the shopman at Rutherford

Street, to use a very shocking expression in reference to Mrs. Yatman; and was seen to clench his fist vindictively, as he ran round the corner of the street. Nothing more has been heard of him; and it is conjectured that he has left London with the intention of offering his valuable services to the provincial police.

On the interesting domestic subject of Mr. and Mrs. Yatman still less is known. It has, however, been positively ascertained that the medical attendant of the family was sent for in a great hurry, on the day when Mr. Yatman returned from the milliner's shop. The neighbouring chemist received, soon afterwards, a prescription of a soothing nature to make up for Mrs. Yatman. The day after, Mr. Yatman purchased some smelling-salts at the shop, and afterwards appeared at the circulating library to ask for a novel, descriptive of high life, that would amuse an invalid lady. It has been inferred from these circumstances, that he has not thought it desirable to carry out his threat of separating himself from his wife – at least in the present (presumed) condition of that lady's sensitive nervous system.